THE BEST OF

THRILLING ADVENTURES

THRIL
ADVEI

THE BEST OF

LING TURES

THRILLING PUBLICATIONS

2017

Introduction

BY WILL MURRAY

ONE OF THE most neglected of the straight adventure pulp magazines of the 1930s was Standard Magazines' *Thrilling Adventures*. It ran a dozen years, from 1931 to 1943, the year when the increasing shortages of pulp paper created by America's entry into World War II caused most surviving magazine houses to drastically curtail their roster of titles.

During that decade, Leo J. Margulies was editorial director under publisher Ned Pines. Margulies oversaw a team of assistant or sub-editors whose shifting responsibilities meant that they might edit *Thrilling Love* one day and *Sky Fighters* another. Between 1934 and 1939, Jack Schiff was senior among them. Around Schiff were gathered a largely anonymous group who came and went, including Donald Bayne Hobart, Bernard Breslauer, Charles Greenberg, Charles S. Strong and many others.

The editor of record for this new entry was J.S. Williams—a house name. Possibly Archibald Bittner, formerly with *Argosy* and *The Frontier,* performed the main chores. He had been senior copyeditor under editorial director Margulies when Schiff joined the staff in 1934 and was going by the name of Wayne Rogers, in print and in real life. He was said to have run off with a Munsey secretary and some loose office cash, temporarily ending his editorial career just scant years before. But either the money ran out, or the lure of pulp was too strong in his blood. In 1931 he did a short stint at Dell, editing *War Stories* and *Western Romances* as A.H. Bittner. In his reform period, Bittner became Wayne Rogers and joined the Thrilling team, debuting in print under his new name in the May 1932 *Thrilling Adventures* with "Yellow Treasure." He soon married a *Thrilling Love* editor, Charlotte Lane by name. By 1935 or before, he had moved on to freelance for Popular Publications, specializing in the new boom in weird menace horror fiction and ghosting both *The Spider* and *Operator #5* before again relocating to Florida in 1940 to manage a chain of movie theaters.

It's unlikely that the editor of the superpulp *Adventure* magazine quivered very much when the Thrilling chain announced the arrival of *Thrilling Adventures* in 1931.

Certainly no one should fear that *Adventure's* star contributors would start submitting to *Thrilling Adventures* in preference. But from the start, *TA* was essentially a closed market.

In its October, 1932 issue, *The Author & Journalist* reported that:

> *Thrilling Adventures, Thrilling Detective,* and *Thrilling Love Magazine,* 570 7th Ave., New York, are purchasing only from a selected list of writers at present, according to word from the editors.

The first issue boasted a lead novel by Lt. John Hopper as well as stories by such pulp luminaries as Edgar L. Cooper and Victor Rousseau, so they evidently commenced with a few recognizable names, but subsequent issues were a mixture of the known, the unknown, and the hopelessly obscure.

This situation continued into early 1933 when reports of *Thrilling Adventures'* imminent cancelation were being reported in the trade, apparently to make way for a new title, *Thrilling Ranch Stories.* In its March issue, *The Author & Journalist* scuttled all such talk but noted that "The bulk of material for this group is written by a limited group of staff writers. For free-lance material found acceptable, rates are understood to be 3/4 cent a word or less, on acceptance."

For *Thrilling Adventures* was a "dump" market. It took the castoffs and leavings that the better titles refused.

Adventure contributor W. Ryerson Johnson explained the authorial point of view this way: "If you were writing for the two-cent pulps and had an occasional 'down-river' sale to the cent or less markets, you'd sometimes use a pen name on the cheap story, because if a two-cent editor happened to see your story in a cent-a-word magazine, he'd wonder why he was paying you two cents. And maybe after that he wouldn't!"

All that changed by the Autumn of 1933. As *The Author & Journalist* reported in November:

> Standard Magazines, Inc., 570 7th Ave., New York, are now in the open market for material. Leo J. Margulies, editorial director, writes: "Here's a strident call to the free-lance fiction writer of America, be he well known or unknown. Standard Magazines, Inc., is decidedly in the market for all kinds of material. The contributor must only know how to turn out a good story with something suitable to our wants. And allow me to correct a fallacy that we have for a long time chosen to ignore—but it has become a canard and no longer can be overlooked. That is, that our magazines are a closed market—that a favored few write most of our stuff, and a New York bunch at that. We purchase as much, if not more, material from outside sources as any publishing house in the country. We are very much in the market for stuff for all of our books."

Regarding *Thrilling Adventures*, Margulies is quoted as wanting:

> "Fast-moving, exciting, all-action stories with foreign locales, but American heroes. Bring out the atmosphere and characterization in terms of action. Occasional pseudo-scientific stories. Strong, virile plots required; woman interest almost nil...."

No doubt this is when the rejects started flooding in.

Mort Weisinger, who began interning on *Thrilling Adventures* several months before he joined the editorial staff early in 1936 to run *Thrilling Wonder Stories,* used to tell writers that the best manuscripts went to Munsey first, then Street & Smith, and then on down the line, usually landing at Thrilling sooner than later, because they all paid promptly.

Margulies also bought out-and-out substandard manuscripts for less than the going rate of one cent a word, leaving it to his editorial staff of "trained seals" to whip it into printable shape.

Writer's Digest explained the editorial trained seal this way:

> In the back room of Standard Publications are three men who wash most of Mr. Margulies' dirty linen. Jack Schiff, Mort Weisinger, and Bernie Breslauer are Leo's trio of lyrical treats; rewrite men take scripts that most other houses would reject and distill them into passable fiction. Once in a while, they turn the crank and a year later Edward J. O'Brien tells them that a masterpiece came out.
>
> Such editorial workers are called "trained seals" by the trade. Their names never appear in print, no magazine reader knows they exist. But trained seals are the greatest literary insurance any freelance writer has. The trained seal takes the "almost" story and whips it in shape.

As added insurance, the author was given the option to have his name left off the story, Thrilling having a bullpen of house names they employed to protect authorial reputations. More than any other pulp house, the Thrilling Group relied upon house names to populate their contents pages. Some of their more significant authors were, in fact, imaginary.

Lieutenant Scott Morgan was an early contributor to *Thrilling Adventures*. His story, debut, "Pirates and Gentlemen," appeared in the June 1932 issue. No one knows who Morgan really was, but the assumption remains that he was not any individual contributor. No doubt there were several Scott Morgans—if not in the beginning, once his "career" took off. For in 1933 the Thrilling Group launched *The Lone Eagle*, built around the adventures of John Masters, a World War I fighter pilot who starred in the magazine built around his adventures. The series author was Lieutenant Scott Morgan.

Once the byline began appearing every month in *The Lone Eagle* magazine, his presence in *Thrilling Adventures* dropped significantly—yet the house name continued well into the 1940s on another series, most notably the Captain Danger stories in *Air War,* as well as sporadic appearances in *Thrilling Wonder Stories* and *Thrilling Baseball* into 1950.

The star writer for *Thrilling Adventures* began his career with "Legion of the Frontier," in the February 1933 issue. That was the same month that *The Lone Eagle* was launched. It wasn't long before new author Captain Kerry McRoberts was appearing regularly.

It's generally assumed that McRoberts was entirely a house name but, as always, it's not impossible that it began as an individual author's personal pseudonym, and was appropriated by the Thrilling editors for wider use.

One popular scribe, Oscar Schisgall, often used the pen name Jackson Cole on his Western stories. Somehow, he abandoned all claim to the the alias and it became a Thrilling house name, calling into question any Jackson Cole story that cannot be traced back to Oscar Schisgall. "Pearls of Peril," May 1933, was his *TA* debut. In *Thrilling Western's* February 1934 debut issue, Schisgall penned the lead novel, while a short bylined Cole was lodged deeper in the issue. When Thrilling launched *Texas Rangers* in 1936, Jackson Cole became the author of record for the Jim Hatfield lead novels. With that, the house name was reserved exclusively for Western stories—and any last vestiges of Schisgall's proprietary interest peeled away. Legend has it the byline was a twist on Jackson Hole, Wyoming.

Kerry McRoberts remained a *Thrilling Adventures* property almost to the end, although in 1940 the house name also appeared upon the lead novelettes in *Thrilling Spy Stories* featuring Jeff Shannon, the undercover U.S. operative also known as the Eagle. Norman A. Daniels wrote most of those, but Daniels was definitely not Kerry McRoberts in his earlier incarnations.

The writers behind both the Morgan and McRoberts house names were likely Thrilling staff writers—at least in the beginning.

One early contributor to the magazine was Edward Vernon Burkholder, who most often wrote under the personal pen name of George Allen Moffatt. In the late 1920s Burkholder had been Leo Margulies' landlord and when he discovered how much loot was to be made in writing pulp fiction, decided to give it a shot, no doubt under Margulies' able tutelage.

In his early career, Burkholder specialized in writing for the gangster pulps, along with others who drifted over to Thrilling, Jack D'Arcy, George A. McDonald and Anatole France Feldman. He comes onto the scene around 1928. By 1932, Burkholder switched over to the more stable detective field and began contributing to *Thrilling Detective* under his Moffatt byline. He seems to have a knack for writing adventure fiction set all over the world because *Thrilling Adventures* soon became his playground. His *Thrilling Adventures* debut was "The Devil from Devil's Island" in 1932. He is said to have ghosted some of the *Phantom Detective* novels and later became known for writing the Hook McGuire "bowling detective" stories in the back of *The Shadow Magazine.* For *Doc Savage,* he penned many stories of the type that he ground out for *Thrilling Adventures.* Certain pseudonymous stories in this volume may be Burkholder's work, specifically the Larry Weston yarns and "The Web of the Green Spider."

Other contributors include more mature professionals such as Victor Rousseau Emanuel, Johnston McCulley, creator of Zorro, Major Malcolm Wheeler-Nicholson and Major George Fielding Eliot. Adventure authors who had military titles are obviously highly prized, which would explain why the fictitious Kerry McRoberts was promoted to captain and why Scott Morgan was styled a lieutenant.

Some contributors appeared to be prominent pulpsters whose careers were winding down. As case in point was Perley Poore Sheehan who wrote the Captain Trouble yarns, while his alter ego, Paul Regard, penned the Kwa of the Jungle series.

Starting in 1935, *Thrilling Adventures* began sprinkling science fiction into their pages. Two veteran writers, Paul Ernst and Ray Cummings, contributed tales in that vein.

Westerns appeared occasionally, but they never overwhelmed it as they did similar titles such as Fiction House's *Action Stories.* A. Leslie's "Curse of the Shining God" is one example. The author was really Alexander Leslie Scott, who sometimes wrote as Bradford Scott. He's not to be confused with Lieutenant Scott Morgan, although it's possible he wrote under that name from time to time. Nor is Scott to be confused with another frequent *Thrilling Adventures* contributor, John Scott Douglas, who was an actual author using his semi-honest byline. (Douglas' middle name was actually Francis.)

Thrilling Adventures was probably an easy magazine to maintain, given that authors' trunks were full of mss. rejected in turn by *Adventure, Argosy,* etc. No doubt said trunks flew open at the first announcement that *TA* was now open to submissions, and the eight-by-twelve envelopes arrived a manila flood.

Not that all of these castoffs were out-and-out rejects. It was common for editors to discover manuscripts with very similar themes landing on their desks at the same time, many inspired by current events or a popular book or movie. An editor couldn't purchase them all. Often he took the best story, but he might select the one whose byline was most likely to sell magazines when splashed on the cover. The others were shipped home.

Since manuscript inventories were kept lean during the Depression, and most pulps ran to 128 pages, a lot of perfectly good yarns were bounced with a note along the lines of: "We almost bought this story, old man, but one came along we liked better. Try us again."

True, pure adventure pulps were uncommon. *Adventure* dominated the field, with *Blue Book* not far behind. *Argosy* had a high adventure quotient, but it was really an all-fiction title mixing genres ranging from romance to SF. Fiction House published

Action Stories, but it traded in its world-wide theme for cowboy stories after 1933. Street & Smith had *The Popular Magazine, Complete Stories* and *Top-Notch*. All succumbed at various point during the Great Depression.

Meanwhile, Thrilling flourished. Early in 1935, Leo Margulies sent out a bulletin: "It is with pleasure that I am able to announce that from now on, the Thrilling Group will pay 1 cent a word and up on all material for all its magazines. As usual, this means, too, that we will continue to give our quick decisions and prompt payment on acceptance."

Along the way, the editors may have purchased the unprinted inventory of Dell's defunct *All Fiction Stories* which expired in 1931. The final issue had announced Lester Dent's "Under the Ice" and Dex Volney's "Silver Reds."

Under the house name of Jackson Cole, "Valley of Giants" may have been a heavy rewrite of the Dent novel. Both were written in response to news stories about Sir Hubert Wilkins's daring but doomed attempt to travel under the North Pole in his specially-outfitted submarine, *Nautilus*. If so, Dent was revised almost to unrecognizability. The failed 1930 venture was old news by 1934.

Was "Red Silver" Volney's "Silver Reds?" Not if the story descriptions are accurate.

Malcolm Wheeler-Nicholson's *All-Fiction* series character, Alan de Beaufort, also made a lone appearance in *Thrilling Adventures*. That might signify a rejected story—or another part of that lost Dell inventory.

This volume collects many of the most prominent yarns of the magazine's formative period. All five of Scott Morgan's Larry Weston stories are included, as are tales by pulp masters Arthur J. Burks and Johnson McCulley. Be advised that although those gentlemen are represented by only one story each, either or both may be under house names as well.

Make no mistake: This is not *Adventure*-quality material for the most part. It sure ain't *Blue Book*. Some of these yarns might have found their way into the pages of *Argosy*, but the great portion are gloriously pulpy to the extreme. Which is why you should get cracking and start reading!

Riley of the Bengal Lancers

BY **LIEUT. SCOTT MORGAN**

A Thrill-Packed Novel of Native Fighting Men in Wild Charges, With Plunging Steeds and Zipping Bullets!

CHAPTER I

BORROWING TROUBLE

CAPTAIN RILEY OF the Bengal Lancers lounged easily against the table and calmly flicked the ashes from the tip of his cigarette.

But, despite his casual manner, there was a stubborn set to his determined jaw, and his voice was dangerously cool when he spoke.

"We are hardly well enough acquainted," he drawled, "to allow me the privilege of calling you—a liar. But I *did* hear a woman crying in that room which you have just left."

The tall, swarthy individual to whom the remark had been addressed, glared at the indolent, red-haired officer who blocked his path. Fierce black eyes bored into bold ones of remarkable blue. The dark visage scowled.

"I told you—you are mistaken," he grated.

"Not when a woman is in question," replied Riley, with an irritating smile. "My friend, I advise you to learn the wisdom of the gurus. Permit me to

quote from the Holy Scriptures: 'A lie, when it is uncalled for, is a double-edged sword.' There is a white girl in that room, and she is crying. We heard her. We thought, my friend and I—" he indicated the uniformed figure at the table beside him—"we thought that perhaps we could be of some assistance."

Riley's voice was too suave, too polite. There was a biting lash to his honeyed words and glinting devils of anger darted from his eyes. The other, however, refused to back water. He appraised Riley, coolly, from head to foot, then his lips curled in scorn.

"I fling the lesson back in your teeth, sir," he said insolently. "Surely the excellent captain also knows the proverb that 'he who borrows trouble shall receive more than he can repay.' "

Riley smiled and bowed. "The point is well taken, sir. But temperamentally, trouble is meat and drink to me. I die without it."

　　　THE BEST OF THRILLING ADVENTURES

The swarthy man looked at him for a long moment without answering. His eyes narrowed to venomous slits. "Did you ever stop to consider that some day you might die *of* it, my friend? I advise you not to interfere with me or with any of my doings!"

"Ah, you warn!"

Riley bowed ironically, reached inside his tunic and extracted a card. He presented it to the other with a flourish,

"Captain Francis X. Riley, 17th Cavalry, Bengal Lancers, at your service."

THE DARK-VISAGED MAN snapped himself erect to sharp military attention.

"Honored! Alexis Petroff will not forget the name or the captain. We shall meet again."

Though they had met and spoken but a scant two minutes, a burning animosity already existed between the men. There in the cloistered interior of the tavern run by that Prince of Thieves, Jamadar Hazrat Gul, they faced each other, arrogant and proud.

An electric tension strained the

silence of the room; a silence broken only by the raucous buzz of a fly as it battered its wings against the *jalousie* that hung at the window and the faint swish of a *punkah* that essayed to dissipate the enervating heat of Bannu. Then the two men bowed stiffly to each other.

With a sharp click of his heels, Petroff turned and marched for the door. Riley gazed after his retreating back till it was lost in the bustle of the inn's courtyard. Then he seated himself once more beside his companion in arms.

"Nice fellow," he said easily.

"Nice like a snake," answered Lieutenant Jeffery Moore. He scowled thoughtfully at the tall frosted glass before him. "You've made yourself an enemy who won't forget."

"An enemy," mused Riley. "Do you know, Jeff, I love them almost as well as my friends. They make life interesting, Jeff. If it weren't for a few enemies, a few raids, and a little blood-letting, this country would get the best of us."

MOORE SHOOK HIS head sadly as he surveyed his companion. The sunlight sifting through the *jalousie* glinted on a thatch of flaming red hair. Riley's large and aggressive nose, now buried in a tinkling glass, was set above a wide and humorous mouth.

Temperamentally, he was endowed with all the volatile qualities of his Irish ancestors. He loved a fight almost as well as a friend, and next to those a bottle of good Irish whiskey stood high in his estimation.

Moore surveyed his rugged, fighting face and shook his head again.

"The Scriptures say something about loving one's enemies, I'll admit," he stated, "but they say nothing about trusting them. Beware the Russian!"

Riley grinned broadly and with an airy gesture waved the counsel aside. For the next few minutes they discussed the Russian in animated tones, speculated vainly on the identity of the white girl and the reason for her crying.

Jamadar Hazrat Gul replenished their glasses, and as he was leaving, Riley flung a rupee at him.

"Yes, *Hazoor?*"

"The Russian, Jamadar—and the girl. Why does she cry?"

Jamadar Hazrat Gul shrugged expressive shoulders. "Why ask a low-caste Indian to explain why a white girl cries?" he replied evasively.

"Where are they bound for?"

"Peshawar and beyond that?"

"And from where do they come?"

Jamadar tried to hide the smirk on his face. "*Hazoor,* it is not fitting that an innkeeper know too much about the comings and goings of his guests. The Russian has honored my house several times in the past six months. He pays well, and I see nothing and hear nothing."

"And does he always bring the woman with him?" persisted Riley.

"And does she always cry?" put in Moore.

"A woman travels with him—yes," replied Jamadar with an oily smile. "Only Allah knows whether it is the same one. Even now my boys are preparing the *tonga.* The Russian sahib leaves in a few minutes."

FURTHER CONVERSATION WAS made impossible by a din and commotion in the courtyard. Jamadar Hazrat Gul shuffled over to the door, looked out, and an evil curse rolled off his lips. Riley and Moore pushed back their chairs and followed after him.

A sudden wave of hot color mantled Riley's cheeks. The breath whistled sharply from his nostrils, and his teeth clicked together, accenting the hard outline of his jaw.

There, in the center of the courtyard, surrounded by a group of sullen Afghans stood the Russian, Petroff. He was holding a racy-looking Kathiawari mare by the halter, while he beat her unmercifully across her velvety muzzle with a heavy leather quirt.

The mare reared and plunged. Her eyes rolled back wildly in her head. Her dainty forelegs struck out viciously in a mad attempt to strike down her tormentor. But the more she struggled, the heavier became the hand on the stinging lash.

Riley stiffened. "A man who would beat a horse like that would beat a woman," he spat out.

Moore laid a restraining hand on his arm, but Riley shook it off impatiently. The lazy inertia of a few minutes before was gone. He leaped through the inn door and in three long strides crossed the courtyard.

Just in time he caught the upraised arm of Petroff as it was about to descend in another blow. He wrenched it down, yanked the Russian about to face him.

"Stop beating that horse, you swine," he grated.

Riley's face was red with anger. In turn, Petroff's turned a livid white. Riley's fists were clenched into hard knots at his side; the Russian's hands trembled slightly. But not from fear. He was struggling violently to keep control of his voice and nerves. He succeeded at last.

"So you interfere again, eh?"

"Hit that mare again, and I won't borrow trouble—I'll make it!" shot back Riley.

THE HORSE CEASED its frantic plunging. All activity in the courtyard stopped as the two men faced each other. There was a long silence, ominous, pregnant with explosive danger. Twin devils looked out of Petroff's eyes and bored into Riley. Thin flecks of foam collected at the corners of his thin lips.

Suddenly the iron restraint he had willed upon himself was shattered. He tore his whip hand free from Riley's clutch, flung it back and lashed out viciously with the quirt for Riley's head.

Riley ducked, side-stepped and caught the stinging lash across his shoulder. With a bellow, he closed in, rushed Petroff, grabbed the lash and tore it from the Russian's hand. With one convulsive movement of his fingers, he snapped it to bits and flung it from him.

The Russian was on him. They closed in a clinch, fought savagely out of it. Riley bore in again. All his explosive anger of a moment before was dissipated. He was cool, calm, efficient—a perfect fighting machine.

The light of battle was in his eye and a happy smile on his lips as he blocked the

Russian's blows. His own were short, swift, traveling no more than six inches. But so perfectly timed were they, so perfectly coordinated with the bulging muscles of his back that they carried dynamite.

He feinted with his left, got inside Petroff's guard, and then crossed his right. An iron fist collided with an iron jaw. Petroff staggered back on his heels, clawed wildly at the empty air for support, then his knees buckled, and he pitched headlong to the offal-littered dirt of the courtyard.

Back at his table in the tavern, Riley had many tall Rickeys before he succeeded in drowning the lust for battle within him. Lieutenant Moore, with wisdom beyond his years, called a halt at last.

"For," said he, "if ever a man had the look of a killer in his eye, it was Petroff. And it's a much more simple matter to kill a drunken man than a sober one."

CHAPTER II

THE AMBUSH

THE SUN WAS setting at last behind the Kush Mountains. A half hour after the departure of Petroff, with his handful of armed Sikhs surrounding the closed *tonga,* Moore convinced Riley that it was time to start for quarters—if they intended to get there in time for mess.

The regiment was quartered some half mile from the walled city on a grassy upland and after giving their mounts a quart of barley water, they mounted and cantered slowly out of the inn's courtyard.

Few words were said between them as they threaded their way through the narrow streets of Bannu. But each knew of what the other was thinking, Petroff and the crying girl!

"WHAT COULD HE be doing with the girl?" said Riley abruptly, when the city's walls were behind him.

Moore had heard that eager note in his companion's voice before, and he knew what it usually portended. Trouble, nine times out of ten. It wasn't anything new for Riley to be overcome by a Quixotic urge and go on a one-man crusade for the rescue of a fair damsel in distress.

So he answered soberly, "His wife, probably."

"No," replied Riley with conviction. "I don't know why, but I'd swear it wasn't his wife. Something in the way she cried. Did you notice, Jeff—a weary, helpless, despairing cry. I wonder—"

The statement was never finished. Riley's horse suddenly snorted, shied to one side on four mincing feet, then reared up. A split second behind this action the staccato crack of a rifle rent the still air.

Something whined venomously past Riley's ear. He clapped spurs to his mount, gave him free rein, urged him off the trail up a short embankment. Moore came charging after him.

The embankment was topped by a lush growth of wild sugar cane. It afforded perfect cover for an ambush.

And such being the case, Riley preferred by far to charge into death than to sit supinely and wait for it.

There was no question in his mind but that the bullet had been intended for him. If it hadn't been for the keen instincts of his horse, it would have drilled him.

Riley patted his charger affectionately and drove him through the rank tangle and came out onto the grassy plateau beyond.

A horse's hooves thundered to his left, Riley wheeled, spurred again and took up the pursuit of the cloud of dust that marked the escape of his attacker.

His revolver was out, and he rode high on his horse's neck, urging him on to greater and even greater speed. The imminent death of a moment before was gone clean from his mind. It was a game now—a match—his horse against the other's.

Little did it matter to him that if his gallant four-legs closed up the intervening distance, the death of himself or his quarry would end the chase.

He whooped joyously, flung a hasty glance back over his shoulder and grinned appreciatively as he saw Moore cut off at right angles to prevent their quarry from taking the trail again.

He was charging now in the dust cloud of his foe. Twin explosions rent the air above the thunder of the horses' hooves. Lead whined over his head. Riley only grinned and saved his fire.

"Keep it up, laddie," he urged in his horse's ears. "The more lead he wastes, the more time he loses."

A HUNDRED YARDS, eighty, seventy! The earth leaped back into the distance in great lunging strides. The distance between the two riders narrowed but mighty four-legs never once shortened his stride.

A frantic burst of fire from ahead! Riley crouched low in his saddle, leveled his revolver, took careful aim and squeezed the trigger once.

The figure ahead lurched in the saddle, the hand loosened on the reins. The horse faltered, stumbled. Riley's finger constricted on the trigger twice and suddenly the horse was free, its rider a limp and still figure in the dust.

RILEY PULLED UP his mount, descended. With the revolver thrust before him, ready for instant action, he warily approached the crumpled figure in the dirt. Moore reigned up a moment later and together they rolled the body over.

Death had been sudden, swift and sure. Both men had seen it many times before, in many guises, and it left them unmoved. From his dress and his features, the man was a Sikh. Riley stared for a long moment at the bloodless face, and a faint memory stirred in the back of his brain.

"I've seen our friend before," he said to Moore.

"Yes," replied the other dryly, "an hour ago in the courtyard of Jamadar's Inn. He's one of the Russian's men."

A low whistle escaped Riley's lips. "Petroff, eh? So he means business. I'm sorry I didn't use the whip on him."

Riley stooped down and went through the Sikh's pockets. In one he found a little chamois bag, heavy and full. He shook it—and it clinked.

"The price of my murder," he grinned up at Moore. Then he turned back to the dead man. "Never mind, old fellow. I'll repay the money to Petroff with interest." He went through the other pockets. There was the usual miscellany of articles, a few prayer papers, an odd coin or two, a cracked mirror.

Riley was about to give up the search when a bit of feminine lace attracted his attention. He pulled it out from the Sikh's darkest pocket, shook it and held it up for the inspection of Lieutenant Moore.

It was a woman's handkerchief, a fragile bit of flimsy lace. And both Riley and Moore knew that Indian women had no use for such finery.

"Now what in the devil was he doing with this?" demanded Riley of the world in general.

He examined the handkerchief carefully. In one corner twin initials were neatly embroidered. He studied them for a moment.

"C.W.," he said to Moore. "That explodes your wife theory, Jeff."

"You mean it belongs to the girl with Petroff?"

"I do that," answered Riley solemnly. He sniffed the delicate perfume emanating from the lace, then stowed it away carefully in his *cummerbund.* "And I mean more than that," he went on. "Unless I miss my guess our lady fair gave her kerchief to the Sikh on purpose."

"On purpose of what."

"So it would fall into our hands. It's a cry for help!"

"Rot!" snorted Lieutenant Moore. RILEY WAS NOT perturbed by this blunt statement. He grinned at his companion. "Where's your sentiment, your romance?" he demanded. "C.W.," he mused. "Cathleen, maybe, or Carmen or Carroll—"

"Forget it," broke in Moore. "Before you know it, you'll be saying that Petroff kidnapped her with the intention of selling her into bondage to one of the Mad Mullahs of the Powindahs."

"That's just what I do believe," answered Riley soberly, and there was no smile to his words, no laughter in his voice when he said them.

For the next two days Riley thought of little else but three things: namely, Petroff the Russian, the mysterious crying girl and the scented handkerchief bearing the initials, C.W.

Amidst the litter and offal of stable inspection, the delicate scent tickled his nostrils. At Company Inspection on parade, the sound of that low and persistent weeping he had heard at the inn drowned out the bellowed orders of his colonel. At night in his cot, beneath a faintly stirring *punkah,* the wind breathed the twin initials over and over again.

Riley became a man of destiny; a man with an obsession. He felt that he had received the call, that the mantle had fallen upon him to rescue the unknown owner of the kerchief from whatever dire peril hung over her.

In his romantic soul he knew that

THE BEST OF THRILLING ADVENTURES

she was fair; knew that she looked to him for succor and salvage. And Riley was Irish, if nothing else. He couldn't resist the call.

By the time a weary dawn had arrived on the third day, he had made up his mind. He would apply to the colonel for leave. Any reason but the real one would do. Then he would go on a little private free-booting expedition of his own. And if he didn't find Petroff and the girl at the end of the trail, he wasn't the man he thought he was.

He rolled out of bed, kicked into slippers, clapped his hands and called: *"Quai Hai."*

As if he had been awaiting the order, Amin Khan, his orderly, appeared.

"A bucket of hot water," said Riley. *"Pushtu!"*

"Yez, *Hazoor,*" replied Amin Khan, bowing low.

FIVE MINUTES LATER, when Riley had his face nicely lathered and was in the midst of his shave, Amin Khan brought word that the colonel wished to speak to him at the earliest possible moment.

Riley damned the C.O. and his windy speeches. Undoubtedly the Old Man wanted to detail him on some tour of sanitary inspection within the walls of Bannu. And that meant the leave he was going to ask for would be out.

He shaved the last of his stubble from his chin, had Amin Khan douse a bucket of cold water over him, then dressed swiftly. He selected his blue and gold regimental dress with the chainmail epaulettes, and with the assistance of his orderly twirled himself into a resplendent *cummerbund* and cocked a blue and gold turban jauntily over one ear.

THE C.O.'S OFFICE was in a dilapidated mud hut at the north end of the parade grounds. A fierce looking Indian with a bright red beard stood on guard at the door. He saluted smartly on Riley's approach, stepped aside, and the Irishman stepped into the dim interior.

Colonel Clayborne was deeply immersed in a letter on Riley's entrance. Without looking up, he indicated a chair.

"Sit down, captain," he said tersely.

Riley took the proffered chair. From the crisp tone of the Old Man's voice he knew that something more serious than a sanitary inspection was on foot. He waited with ill-concealed patience for orders.

Colonel Clayborne finished the letter at last and tossed it across the table to Riley.

"Read that."

Riley picked up the missive and read:

Colonel Grayson P. Clayborne,
Commanding 17th Cavalry,
Bannu, Northwest Frontier Province.
Sir:
I wish to inform you of a series of disturbances that have done much to hinder the progress of our work here in the past week.

The trouble began with the murder of two of my drillers. With that beginning, the men became sullen, restless, insubordinate. I tried to ferret out the seat of the trouble, but did not succeed. I increased rations, posted guards and tried to continue with our work.

The men did not respond. A dozen have

disappeared—deserted—for they have taken rifles and ammunition with them.

Pronounced trouble is breeding. Who or what is stirring up the men, I cannot ascertain.

Since you realize the importance of our work and the conditions under which we are handicaped, I respectfully request your assistance to the extent of a detachment of men.

Respectfully yours,

ROY T. GATES, *Engineer,*

Anglo-Indian Oil Concession.

The letter was dated three days before from Naushara. Riley took in the pungent statement of facts and passed the letter back to the colonel. Though he didn't understand the reference made by Gates, as to the conditions by which he was handicaped, he knew that the engineer was in charge of drilling operations for the Anglo-Indian Oil Company, under a concession granted by the Asmar Rukan Din Khan.

He asked no questions, however, and waited for the colonel to continue.

"Gates' work is important. It has to go on. It's our job to give him adequate protection."

"My especial job," put in Riley with a grin.

"Yes," replied the colonel. "Probably nothing to it; more than likely some Afridi has a bellyache, and wants to go home."

He was lying, and deceiving nobody, not even himself. Both Riley and the colonel knew that when murder begins to stalk and a band of Afridis get moody and sullen, all hell is apt to pop loose at any minute.

"A platoon and a lieutenant ought to be sufficient," continued the C.O.

"Yes, sir," replied Riley. "Lieutenant Moore would be fine."

"Suit yourself. Start at once. I'll have your papers ready by the time mess is over."

Riley rose from his chair, saluted casually and started for the door. The colonel looked quizzically after his retreating back.

"And remember, Riley, this is a serious business. No hell raising on the way."

CHAPTER III

THE RAID

UNDER FORCED MARCH, Riley, Moore and a hand-picked platoon of fighting Pathans made Peshawar in the early forenoon of the following day. Riley had spared neither his men nor their horses, but now he called a much-needed halt. Naushara lay some eight hours' march to the eastward and if they started in the cool of the evening, after a well deserved rest, they would arrive fit and fresh for any emergency.

The horses were stabled and quartered. Riley saw that they were rubbed well down and given sparingly of barley water and clean hay. Then, after a bath in a couple of buckets of tepid water, he ate sparingly, pitched his tent under the walls of the city and tried for an hour's sleep.

His slumber was troubled by dreams

of marauding Afridis, crying maidens and the scowling face of Petroff. He awoke with a start and his hand slipped down to the revolver strapped to his belt.

Then he threw his feet over the edge of the cot and grinned up into Moore's face.

"Why so jumpy?" asked the lieutenant.

"Sorry, old man," replied Riley. "I was dreaming. Thought you were Petroff." He threw back the flap of the tent, saw that the sun was descending in a long arc in the west. "Better rouse the men. Light rations, and then we'll be off."

THEY WERE OFF again with the first blessed breath of air that stirred with the sinking of the sun behind the Karakorum Range. Decked in all his finery, Riley rode at the head of his slender column, a gay whistle on his lips.

They jostled their way through the crooked streets of Peshawar, and created quite a stir in the bazaars and market places. But for once Riley had no eyes for the alluring nautch girls behind their veils; he didn't respond to the bangles, the colors, the lilting note of the reeds in the market places.

It was with a grunt of relief that they sallied forth from the Eastern Gate and picked up the rocky trail that led to Naushara.

Riley issued a terse order to Amin Khan, who promptly relayed it to the platoon. The ranks closed up, moved forward at a fast trot.

An hour passed. The trail wound slowly upward, became rock-strewn, barren. The lush fields of flowering bamboo in the *baghs* surrounding Peshawar, gave place to an arid upland, as barren of life as of vegetation.

It was wild country, the traditional battle ground for raiding expeditions from the north. But though it had been well watered with blood—the blood of Englishmen as well as of Pathan, Afridi and Afghan, nothing grew there.

Riley gave the order for double time, turned his horse and circled his men, offering them a word or two of encouragement. He loosened the revolver hanging from his *cummerbund* and his dark eyes searched in the dark shadows by the side of the trail.

AN HOUR OUT from their destination a thin, sickly moon showed above the ridge towards which they were advancing. A pale, unearthly light flooded the stark uplands. Though the visibility had been increased a hundred percent, lessening the chance of an ambushed attack, Riley didn't relax his vigilance.

There was an uncanny presentiment stirring in his heart, a feeling of hovering menace and danger. A league further on he suddenly drew rein, held up his hand, and brought the platoon to a halt. He listened sharply, but heard nothing. No sound save the muffled thud of the horses' hooves and the clank of a bit broke the unnatural silence of the night.

"What's up?" questioned Moore sharply, reining up beside him.

"Hear anything?" asked Riley.

"No—what?"

"Listen!"

They listened. Standing in their

stirrups, they strained their ears to catch some alien sound in the awful void of silence about them. A faint wind stirred from dead ahead. And then carried on that slightest stirring of air they heard.

It was faint with distance, but clear, distinct, unmistakable, nonetheless. Gun fire! Rifle fire! Both Riley and Moore had heard that sound before.

Riley wheeled his charger about; shouted the order of advance to the platoon, then roweled his spurs deep into his horse's flanks. The horse leaped ahead and under free rein lunged powerfully up the rocky trail.

The platoon charged up after him. A half a mile on, they thundered single file through a narrow pass. On the other side of the cut lay the plains of Naushara.

The sounds of the firing came to them clearly, now, distinctly. They could even see the lurid streaks of flame in the night.

A mile below him in the valley, under the ghostly light of the moon, three trellised derricks pointed their shafts heavenward. A few squat buildings loomed up vaguely in the foreground. Riley knew the site for the base of operations of the Anglo-Indian Oil Company.

It was his destination. And as the fates would have it, he and his platoon had arrived just in time! Or had he?

He spurred the foam-flecked flanks of his horse, brandished his revolver in the air and with a lusty cry on his lips led the charge into battle.

FROM THE ROCKY pass the ground swept sharply downward to the level stretch of terrain occupied by the oil camp. Under heel and spur the platoon swept forward. The thunder of their juggernaut charge echoed and re-echoed between the hills that hemmed in the tiny valley.

For their part, the men of the 17th Cavalry held their fire. But as they swept down into battle like an irresistible tidal wave, their coming was heralded by a sudden furious outburst of firing.

Two hundred yards away from the actual scene of conflict, a tall column of flame shot skyward. One of the raiders had applied the torch to one of the derricks. In the lurid glow that painted the sky a crimson red, Riley made out the attacking force. They were mounted, and from the way they rode they were native Afridis.

All but one! He sat his horse in true military fashion. And it was this individual who led the attack. Riley had but a moment to consider this strange fact. Ten yards in advance of his men, he was the first to close with the enemy.

A black stallion bore down suddenly on his left. A glinting sword circled his head. Riley wheeled his charger back on two legs, felt the crimson steel lift the turban from his head, then as the two horses plunged together fired his revolver at point blank range.

THE AFRIDI CRUMPLED in the saddle, and the heavy sword clattered to the dust. The black stallion reared, wheeled, and with the roaring flames striking terror to his heart, plunged madly for the open fields, dragging his dead master by the stirrup.

Riley was suddenly engulfed in a

swirl of swearing, fighting, blood-hungry men. Steel flashed before his eyes; guns exploded in his ears; venomous lead sang a song of death over his head. He steadied his horse with his knees, took careful aim and made every bullet count.

Moore and the platoon swept on. The fighting rose to a fierce crescendo. Then Riley saw that he was free, no longer hemmed relentlessly in by a half dozen fanatical madmen.

He shouted to Moore to follow him, but the words were lost in the din of battle. Riley pressed forward. The horseman who rode like a white army officer was still leading the attack on one of the buildings.

Unquestionably, Gates and his faithful followers had managed to barricade themselves in the administration building. It was the focal point of the battle.

Men fell before the lethal death that belched from Riley's gun. When it was empty he snatched a double-bladed sword from one of the conquered foe, and, swinging it in a savage arc before him, spurred his steed through the milling press.

His hungry blade made a feast of bone and blood. He cleared a path before him and at his foolhardy example his men rallied and closed in.

Though the rescuing party was outnumbered two to one by the raiders, slowly the tide of battle went in their favor. Riley alone did the work of five men. In a veritable frenzy he fought his way forward.

The bullet that clipped his arm was but the sting of a bee. The saber cut across his cheek that sent the blood coursing to his mouth was but tonic wine.

The raiders were retreating! Riley swore viciously. He had to drive through! He had a mad desire to come to grips with that tall, lean figure who led the attack astride the Kathiawari mare.

Both rider and horse were familiar. He had seen them both a few days ago at Bannu in the courtyard of the inn owned by the rascally Jamadar Hazrat Gul.

CHAOS! CONFUSION! THE night was rent asunder by the staccato crack of rifles and the clash of steel. Battling forward, foot by foot through a seething wall of horses and men, Riley ever kept one eye on his particular quarry.

Suddenly he saw him lurch forward in his saddle, saw the smoking revolver drop from his limp fingers. Riley cursed. A bullet had reached the foe, and he would have much preferred to have ended the matter with steel.

But the mysterious white rider was not down. Wounded and with the tide of battle going against him, he shouted the signal for retreat. His men fell back in wild confusion, spurred their horses and charged for the rocky uplands.

Lieutenant Moore, bespattered with blood and with the fanatical light of battle in his eye, galloped up beside Riley.

"Shall we give chase?" he shouted.

But for once the Irishman refused to continue a battle.

"Not now," he called back. "Later, when we know what this is all about."

CHAPTER IV

THE STING OF
THE LASH

DEATH HAD CLAIMED seven of Riley's men in the engagement, but there was not one man there who had not tasted blood. Of the workers at the oil field, some twenty had been wounded and a half dozen killed.

When the dead had been buried and the wounded made comfortable, Riley and Moore went into secret conference with Gates, the engineer in charge of the operations.

In swift detail he elaborated on the meager details he had given in his letter to Colonel Clayborne, culminating with the story of the raid that night.

Riley heard the story through in silence, then asked the question uppermost in his mind.

"The man who led the attack—do you know him?"

Gates shook his head. "No. The fighting was so thick and fast I didn't have much opportunity to observe him closely. But this I know: He was a European."

"You saw that, too, eh?"

Gates nodded.

"Any reason for the trouble you've been having; any reason you know of for this raid?" asked Moore.

"There can be only one reason," replied Gates. "My company is operating under a concession granted by the Asmar Rukan Din Khan. Under the terms of the agreement we must produce oil by the twentieth of this month. If we fail, the concession is retracted; it reverts back to the Asmar."

Riley nodded his head. "Then you think someone is trying to prevent you from fulfilling the agreement."

"Exactly!"

"It's a valuable concession, eh?"

"To England it is very valuable," answered Gates simply.

"And you don't know who is back of the trouble, eh?"

"No; I haven't the slightest idea."

Riley growled something deep down in his throat. "Well, I have," he muttered. Moore and the engineer plied him with questions, tried to get him to elaborate on his suspicions, but Riley turned a deaf ear to all their pleas.

He paced up and down the room for a few minutes in deep thought. A heavy frown furrowed his usually placid brow and the laughter had died out of his eyes.

HE TURNED AT last to face Lieutenant Moore. There was a crisp note of decision in his voice.

"Jeffery," he began, "I'm leaving you here in command of the platoon. The safety of Mr. Gates and his men is in your hands. It's up to you to see that nothing further delays operations here."

Lieutenant Moore snapped to attention. He would have given a month's pay to have known what Riley intended to do, but he was too good a soldier to ask.

"Yes, sir," he said tersely, and started for the door.

Riley gazed after him with a fond eye, then called him back. He extended his fist with a smile and the two men shook hands with a fervid clasp.

"Good luck," said Lieutenant Moore simply.

"Thanks. Same to you, Jeff. I'm going to trail back to Peshawar. I think I can pick up some valuable information there."

His gaudy uniform of a Bengal Lancer discarded, and disguised as an Afghan horse trader, Riley lost himself in the welter of humanity that swarmed in the streets of Peshawar. He spoke Pushtu like a native, and it was easy to lose his identity in the bazaars and streets that were crowded with the men of a score of different tribes, different races, different religions.

THERE WERE BRAHMINS, Mohammedans, Animists. There were warlike Sikhs, savage Afridis, bearded Pathans.

Riley drifted slowly through the streets from canteen to bazaar, to public house. His eyes were ever alert for a certain tall figure with glowing eyes over a hawked nose. His ears were ever attuned to catch the slightest whisper of a word that would put him on the trail of his quarry.

It was late on the evening of his second day that success crowned his efforts. Entering the bar of the Oriental House, a tavern frequented by Europeans, his eye immediately focused on the tall figure of Alexis Petroff, seated at a table at the far end of the room.

The Russian was in whispered consultation with a small and withered Kahar. The heads of the two men were bowed close together. Petroff was speaking now, rapidly into the Kahar's ear. The native's lips pulled back in an avaricious grin, revealing a row of broken, yellow teeth.

Riley watched the two men from the corner of his eye as he sidled up to the bar. He ordered a drink, but instead of drinking it at the mahogany, turned and started for the table adjoining the one at which sat the Russian.

Riley was full of suspicions, but he had no definite proof that Petroff was the leader of the raid on the oil field. Before he proceeded further, he had to know definitely. There was one sure way of finding out. And he decided to put his theory to the test immediately.

The Russian and the Kahar were too engrossed in their secret conversation to notice his approach. Riley grinned to himself with anticipation under his false beard.

Just as he was passing Petroff's table, he conveniently stumbled. The glass tumbled from his hand, his arm shot out and innocently, as if he were trying to regain his balance, his fingers grasped the Russian's shoulders. They dug in, biting deep.

Petroff bellowed with pain, wrenched his shoulder free and glared fiercely at the bowing figure of Riley. A lurid string of profanity rolled off his working lips.

"A thousand pardons, Sahib," murmured Riley in Pushtu, still bowing low so that his face was concealed.

"Go, clumsy dog!" snarled Petroff.
BUT RILEY DIDN'T go.

"Did the Sahib Petroff by any chance receive the wound while leading the raid on the oil works?"

The breath whistled sharply from between Petroff's teeth. His eyes narrowed dangerously. His right shot out and imprisoned Riley by the wrist. Riley straightened up and confronted him squarely across the table.

Swift recognition dawned in Petroff's eyes. They turned a smoky red with hate. His lips twitched convulsively and his long fingers clenched and reclenched at his sides.

"So it's the interfering Captain Riley again, eh?" said Petroff in a strained voice.

"And as ever at your service," replied Riley with irony.

Without waiting for an invitation he kicked out a chair and sat down.

PETROFF FOUGHT HARD to control his mounting anger. He became hot under the collar, and tiny beads of sweat stood out on his forehead. The eyes of the two men clashed audibly.

"I warn you again—" began Petroff.

"Save your warnings!" snapped Riley. "And listen to this one. There was a raid on the Anglo-Indian oil field two nights ago. It was led by a European"—Riley surveyed the Russian from head to foot—"a man just about your build, Petroff."

The Russian snarled. "Are you accusing me of—"

"I'm not accusing you of anything. I'm just wondering how you got that bullet hole in your left shoulder."

The blow was a telling one. Petroff chewed at his under lip, tried to think of some excuse to make, but words failed him. Riley followed up his advantage.

"Next time, Petroff, let us hope that we come to grips personally. Cold steel, hand to hand, is much more satisfying than bullets at a hundred yards."

The Russian bowed mockingly across the table, but said no word. Riley kicked back his chair and rose slowly to his feet.

"Just one more thing, Petroff," he said easily. "How is C.W.?"

The question broke like a bombshell on the Russian's ears. His lips pulled back in a savage snarl and the devils of murder leaped out of his eyes.

"I see," said Riley with a contemptuous sneer. "She still resists your tender advances. Take good care of her, Petroff. I'm going to claim her from you one of these days. And if one hair of her head is harmed—"

He left the threat unfinished, turned on his heel, and stalked out of the room.

But Riley wasn't finished with Alexis Petroff so soon that night. On leaving the Oriental House he crossed the street and lost himself in the dark shadows of a sheltered doorway. Secluded in the heavy gloom, he kept his eyes fastened on the hostlery across the way.

He hadn't long to wait. Ten minutes after taking up his vigil, Riley stiffened and crowded back against the stone archway that concealed him.

Petroff and the Kahar had emerged from the bar of the Oriental. Riley saw the Russian cast a hurried glance up and down the street, then urge the wizened Indian on by his side.

RILEY PERMITTED THEM to take a lead of a hundred feet before he came out of his place of concealment. Keeping close to the grimy walls of the buildings, he followed them.

Petroff's movements were swift and sure. Though he followed an erratic course, turned many corners and doubled back on his trail, he seemed to know exactly where he was going. Though Riley managed to evade detection, he had great difficulty in following the trail.

Petroff and the Kahar suddenly made a right-handed turn and disappeared down the mouth of a dark alley, Riley increased his stride, but when he in turn made the corner, the alley was deserted. The Russian and the Indian had disappeared into thin air.

Riley stood irresolute for a moment cursing his luck. Then from between the chinks of the shutters of a house half way down the alley, a faint light seeped out. That light had just been made. It hadn't been there a moment before when Riley had turned the corner.

There could be only one answer. Petroff and the Indian had entered the house.

RILEY CAME TO a quick decision. One glance assured him that the alley was deserted. Swiftly he stalked down the street, crouched low at the door of the house from which the faint light glowed.

No sound came to his ears. He was stumped for a moment. What if he were wrong? What if Petroff had not entered here and he broke in, only to be caught as a thief? A wry grimace twitched at his lips as he thought of the consequences.

There were cruel deaths for white thieves in the northwest frontier.

But after a moment's indecision Riley knew he had to risk it. Nine chances out of ten he had run his quarry down and it would have been ridiculous to let him escape.

Another hurried glance up and down the alley told him it was still empty of all life. Riley withdrew a long, keen-bladed knife from his sash and tried the door. It was latched from the inside.

Fortunately, the battered door was warped with age. It sagged an inch or two away from the jamb, and, inserting the blade of his knife in this opening, Riley slowly lifted up the latch.

As silently he dropped it and then with cautious fingers pushed the portal inward. The grate of the rusted hinges screamed in his ears. He froze to immobility, and his fingers tightened around the haft of the knife.

Riley expected the noise of his entrance to bring the Russian and the Indian down on him at any minute. He crouched there in the gloom of the doorway, tense, waiting, expectant. But no sound came to him. Only the steady pounding of his heart throbbed in his ears.

He closed the door behind him, latched it again. It took a few moments for his eyes to accustom themselves to the stygian gloom. Riley found himself in a vile and smelly hallway. Feeling his way along the greasy wall, he moved stealthily forward.

He negotiated a right-angled turn on tiptoe, then his pulses raced with elation. At the far end of the passageway, a thin sliver of light shone out from beneath a door. He advanced cautiously forward.

The low indistinct murmur of voices came to him. Pressing his ear to the jamb, he recognized them as belonging to Petroff and the Kahar. The Russian was speaking,

"So the rifles have gone forward, eh, Hamzullah Khan?"

"YES, *HAZOOR.* TWO cases and a third case of ammunition. And the gun that speaks with a thousand tongues of death, I entrusted especially to Ahmed Abdullah."

Riley's eyes narrowed dangerously as he listened. Hamzullah Khan could be referring to but one thing—a machine gun. The Russian, after all, was a man to be reckoned with.

Petroff was speaking again. "Have your men in readiness. Give them liberally of gold and drink, but breathe no word of their mission. When my plans are ripe I will give you the word for action."

"Yes, *hazoor.*"

There was an oily, obsequious note in the voice of Hamzullah Khan. Listening at the door, Riley could almost see him rub his dirty hands together at the mention of gold.

"And the whip, Hamzullah Khan— you have secured one for me?"

RILEY'S BROW DREW down in a frown. What did the Russian want with a whip? He was soon to find out.

"Yes, *hazoor,*" came the voice of the Indian. "A light and supple one as you directed. See for yourself."

Riley heard the faint swish of a lash from behind the locked door.

"Perhaps for an unruly horse. Sahib?" whined Hamzullah's voice.

"No, not for a horse," replied the Russian. "It's for a little white bird in a cage who eats not, sings not, but only cries."

The hot blood pounded in Riley's veins. He realized full well the subtle meaning behind the cryptic words. Petroff had secured the whip to use on his captive—the mysterious girl whom he knew only by the initials C.W.

Riley's jaws shut. His muscles tensed. His fingers constricted around the haft of his knife. He was just on the point of barging through the door, when something sharp and cold pricked him in the throat.

Without turning around, without a word having been said, Riley knew that a blade of steel was pricking at his jugular.

A soft voice whispered in his ear.

"The Sahib could hear much better if he stepped inside the door."

Riley was trapped. So intent had he been on hearing the words of the Russian that he had failed entirely to hear the opening of the outer door, had been altogether unaware of the approach of the man who now held the point of an evil knife against his throat.

He had been in tight spots before, but never one quite as ticklish as this. He cursed himself bitterly for a fool. He had to escape somehow, some way, and preferably before his captor discovered his real identity.

Half the advantage he had gained from his spying maneuvers on the Russian would be lost if it was known that he had eavesdropped.

Riley's nerves and muscles tensed preparatory to going into action. His captor, however, evidently read his thoughts. The knife pricked a little deeper into his throat, and the low voice continued with significant inflection:

"It would be foolish for the Sahib to struggle. The knife is sharp and my fingers steady."

There was a dire threat in the soft words. Riley knew that it was suicide to disregard them.

"The trick is yours, friend. Take the knife away from my throat. Maybe we can discuss this over a bottle of *ghiz*."

THE CAPTAIN TAKES me for a fool," replied the other with scorn. Riley started at the words. So his identity was known after all!

At the risk of feeling the blade slit his gullet, he squirmed about and faced his captor. Unfortunately, however, he didn't recognize the tall Afridi who confronted him. With a swift movement the Indian snatched the blade from his fingers, then with a mocking smile playing about his thin lips, he hammered on the door with the butt of the knife.

The summons was answered by a sudden tramp of heavy feet behind the barrier. Riley shrugged his shoulders helplessly. There was no other way out of the situation but to face the music.

The door was yanked open in his face. Petroff stood glaring on the threshold, an automatic clutched in his hand, ready for instant use. His eyes narrowed sharply, then opened wide with gloating triumph.

SWIFTLY HE TOOK in the little tableau, understood its grim significance.

"We meet once again, Petroff," purred Riley.

"And sooner than I had any right to hope for," smirked the Russian. "Very obliging of you, Captain. Your looking me up this way has saved me a lot of trouble and inconvenience. Very thoughtful of you."

His honeyed words dripped with a deadly venom. Riley knew that he could expect no mercy at the hands of the Russian.

His captor explained rapidly in Pushtu, how he had caught Riley listening at the door. Petroff grinned evilly at the recitation, barked out an order, and the knife was lowered from Riley's throat.

Under the prodding impulse of the automatic in the Russian's hand, Riley was marched into the room. The door was immediately closed and bolted behind him.

"*Quai Hai!*" snapped Petroff to Hamzullah. "A rope to tie this dog!"

Petroff ground the nozzle of the automatic into his spine while the Indian rummaged in a corner for the necessary twine. Riley took advantage of the momentary respite and swiftly surveyed his surroundings.

There was only one window to the room, but the first glance told him that it was heavily barred. No escape that way. The door behind him was locked and bolted. Odd pieces of furniture cluttered up the floor, but none of them offered a likely weapon.

To his right a dusty curtain hung in an arched opening, which probably led to a bedroom. It stirred faintly, persistently. Riley was about to dismiss the swaying drapery when he suddenly realized that there was no breath of moving air in the room.

Someone was behind that curtain. Someone was moving it purposely to attract his attention. If there was any escape for him from the trap into which he had fallen, it lay that way.

The Kahar bustled up with a long length of rope. Grinning evilly, he lashed Riley's hands behind him under the direction of the Russian. When the process had been completed, Petroff stuffed the automatic into his belt, jutted his chin aggressively to within an inch of Riley's and spit into his face.

Riley felt the blood in his veins turn to molten acid at the insult. All he asked then of the Fates was twenty seconds alone with Petroff, free and unhampered. He would make the Russian pig pay for that insult.

PETROFF READ THE thought as it marked itself indelibly on his face. "You'll never get the chance, my Captain," he gloated.

"I only need half a chance," replied Riley defiantly.

Petroff sneered.

"A braggard! A boaster!"

"Anything but a renegade," shot back Riley.

A tide of crimson slowly mantled the Russian's face.

"You will eat your words before you die, my Captain."

"I may die," answered Riley coolly, "but when I do I'll curse you with my dying breath."

Petroff's face was convulsed with fury. From the table he snatched up the whip that Hamzullah had secured for him. He shook it wrathfully under Riley's nose.

"A few days ago you were pleased to break one of my whips. Now it is my turn to break one. Only I'll break it over your head."

SUITING ACTION TO the word, he threw back his arm, snapped it forward and sent the long, rawhide coil snaking across Riley's face. The lash ate at the flesh like a tongue of fire. Blood spurted from Riley's cheek, ran crazily down into his mouth.

After the first instinctive cringing of the flesh, he did not move. He stood there, silent, motionless.

His stoic calm under the lash of the whip drove Petroff to a frenzy. He drew back his arm. Again and again he sent the rawhide writhing across the prisoner's face.

Riley's left eye was closed. Long livid welts stood out in ridges on his throat. With each stroke of the lash ribbons of flesh were gouged from his face.

His heart was pounding against his ribs like a sledge hammer. Twin pulses vibrated crazily in his throat. The muscles of his shoulders, arms and hands constricted violently. But he had been cunningly tied. His bonds held.

A living, searing hate surged through Riley's veins and concentrated in his eyes. With the terrible eyes of the killer he confronted the Russian. Petroff

   THE BEST OF THRILLING ADVENTURES

quailed beneath that baleful glare, his whip arm stayed in mid-air.

Then a new paroxysm seized him. He flung the lash from him, stepped close to Riley and drove his fist flush into the bloody face. Riley staggered back under the blow, stumbled against a chair and went crashing to the floor. His head and shoulders came to rest with a sickening thud against the wall by the hanging draperies.

Riley was out. How long he remained in that condition he never knew. Slowly he crawled back to consciousness out of a deep abyss. A brass gong was beating violently inside his skull. Mad devils of light danced before his eyes.

He could not see at first. But the vague, indistinct murmur of voices came faintly to his ears as if from a great distance. He puzzled over them. Then came recognition. It was the Russian's voice. Slowly, grisly detail after grisly detail, he recalled the terrible beating he had taken and the incidents leading up to it.

Then a peculiar scratching on his hands, which were still tied behind him, occupied all of his still puzzled wits. He relaxed. Something soft touched his fingers, traveled to his wrists. The contact filled Riley with a strange elation. New blood pounded through his veins; new strength tensed his shattered nerves and muscles.

SLOWLY WITH RETURNING strength his brain cleared. The Russian was still speaking. His voice was louder now. Riley kept his eyes closed and listened. The soft thing was about his wrists again. Suddenly the bonds that held him relaxed, gave a notch.

And then with a sudden burst of inspiration he understood. Someone was untying the rope that held his hands! He didn't stop to question who or why. It was sufficient that with each passing second his bonds became looser.

And with this new hope came new strength. A savage flame of hatred coursed through Riley's body. The last rope was off. His hands were free.

He lay there, still, inert, eyes closed, waiting for further developments. If only he had a weapon now! And then, as if in answer to the unspoken prayer, he felt something hard and smooth pressed into his hand. His fingers wrapped around it lovingly. Instinctively he knew it for the haft of a knife.

Riley asked for no more. Free again and armed he was perfectly willing to go up against the Russian and his two native allies. Once more the unseen fingers touched his own and a crumpled ball of paper was pressed into the palm of his left hand.

There was nothing else. The faint stirring of the air told of the furtive departure of his benefactor.

For a brief minute Riley puzzled over the identity of the mysterious unknown who had come to his aid in his hour of direst need. Then he put the thought from his mind. Time for that later. He had more important work to do.

Moving inch by inch he slowly worked his arms from behind his back. The knife was gripped in his hand, concealed under the folds of his robe. After stuffing the wad of paper in his belt, he opened his eyes a slit and surveyed the room.

PETROFF WAS SEATED at the table in the center of the floor. He was issuing orders to the man who had captured Riley. The Kahar was busy in the far corner over a large brass-bound case.

From the last of the Russian's words, it was evident to Riley that Hamzullah was about to leave the room. When that moment arrived, he determined to strike.

With a fighting chance for freedom in the offing, his strength returned to him in pulsating waves. From the corner of his half-closed eyes he watched the Kahar. Hamzullah finished with the brass-bound case at last, straightened and crossed the room to the door.

Riley's nerves became as tight as steel wires; his muscles tensed. Slowly he gathered his body together, drew his legs up under him.

Hamzullah's hand was on the latch of the door. The portal swung inward. In that instant, Riley catapulted to his feet. With the bellowing roar of a Bashan bull he charged across the floor straight for Petroff.

He caught the Russian with a jolting left as the latter spun around in his chair. Table, chair and Russian collapsed with a crescendo roar to the floor.

Riley cleared the barrier of splintered wood and kicking legs in full stride. A gun exploded on his left and a streak of acid fire pierced his shoulder. It was the Pathan going into action.

RILEY IGNORED THE wound. For once discretion was the better part of valor. If he tarried to battle it out to the finish, all was lost. He grunted, crouched low and zigzagged towards the door.

A fusilade of shots behind him marked Petroff's entrance into the fray. And before him in the doorway, blocking his way to freedom, crouched Hamzullah, a ten-inch blade of steel swinging before him.

There was no getting past that blade this side of hell. Riley knew that he could never cover the intervening few feet between him and liberty, without feeling steel in his heart. He had less than a second to act.

In a single swift movement he swung his right arm forward. His tense fingers released the knife in his hand and at the same time he threw himself forward at Hamzullah's feet.

A gun exploded violently behind him. Bullets whined angrily over his head. But the Kahar no longer blocked the doorway. Riley's knife had caught him clean in the throat.

Without waiting to say a last prayer over the dear departed, Riley rocketed down the narrow passageway, lurched around the corner and without checking his speed, assaulted the outer door in a flying charge.

His shoulders connected with the rotting wood with the force of a battering ram. Hinges ripped from their screws, the rusted lock shattered to bits. In full stride Riley cleared the wreckage to the accompaniment of a final fusilade from Petroff's automatic.

On the other side of the city, in the

native quarter, he found peace and surcease from his wounds. Here for the first time he extracted the crumpled ball of paper thrust into his hand by the good Samaritan who had untied his bonds.

He unrolled it carefully, smoothed it out, focused his eyes on the few words written there in a delicate, feminine hand.

Tonight. The Palace of Abdel Khan. Help.

Riley read the terse message twice over, but his eyes were not on the words. A faint elusive perfume arose from the scrap of paper—the same perfume that had clung to the handkerchief bearing the initials C.W.

CHAPTER V

THE PALACE OF ABDEL KHAN

SO IT WAS the girl who had saved him! With an oath Riley staggered to his feet. A fine man, a fine officer he had proved himself. The girl had unquestionably saved his life and like a coward he had fled, leaving her to her fate.

He read the note again. *Tonight. The Palace of Abdel Khan. Help.*

It was a piteous appeal in its stark simplicity. Riley determined on immediate action.

Showering a handful of gold on his host, he negotiated for the loan of a keen ten-inch blade of steel, an automatic and a Kathiawari charger.

Then leaping into the high saddle, he thundered off into the night. A short half hour ago he had fled from the rendezvous of the Russian. Now, the spurs roweling the flanks of his horse, he retraced the distance.

HIS HEART WAS heavy within him. Somehow, he felt that a stain was on the bright shield of his honor as a gentleman and an officer. There was little chance of his finding the girl and Petroff, still in the house from which he had escaped. But he had to make sure.

He thundered up to the door through which he had barged a short half hour before. He leaped from his horse, and with gun advanced threateningly before him, plunged through the shattered portal.

But no burst of lead stayed his progress. No warning cry announced his precipitous arrival. It was but the work of a minute to verify his suspicions. The place was deserted. Petroff had flown, taking the girl with him.

Riley leaped into the saddle again, clapped spurs to his mount. Like a shadow of avenging doom he thundered through the cobbled streets of Peshawar.

He cleared the city's walls, set his horse into a long, loping gallop. The Palace of Abdel Khan was some twenty miles distant, secluded in the rugged hills of the border. He should reach there a little before dawn. He *had* to reach there before dawn!

His thoughts were bitter and dark. He gave little consideration to how he would accomplish the rescue when he arrived. He was armed with a knife and a gun. He would use them both if need be. No one was going to stop him that night.

The horse's hooves pounded hollowly in his ears. The weary miles seemed never ending. Riley winced and groaned in his saddle. But it was not his wounds that wrung the anguish from his heart. He thought of the Russian and his whip. *For a little white bird in a cage!*

A savage oath spewed off his lips and his spurs dug deep into the heaving flanks of his horse.

Riley reined his sweating mount to a halt on the crest of a small, rocky knoll. Below him loomed the vague, shadowy outlines of the stronghold of Abdel Khan. He slid from his horse, tied the reins around an outcropping boulder. THE MOON WAS sinking fast behind the ridge of the Kahalan Mountains. A blanket of dark shadow moved slowly across the valley. He grunted to himself with satisfaction, thrust the automatic into his belt and, with the knife clutched in his hand, began a stealthy advance toward the stronghold.

It was surrounded by a wall, he knew. There would be a guard at the gate. His first and immediate problem was to get past that guard without raising an alarm.

Creeping warily along from boulder and gully to outcropping ledge of rock, he managed to make the high wall unobserved. The darker shadow in the night, some twenty feet to his left marked the gate. Slowly on tiptoe he crept toward it.

He paused, tense, breathless, listening, The rhythmic beat of feet behind the wall marked the progress of the sentry before the portal. How to get that massive, iron-ribbed gate to open. That was the question. Riley considered the proposition a moment, then stooped down and scooped up a handful of pebbles.

He tossed one into the night, heard it rattle against the ponderous door. Another and another followed in quick succession. There came a pause in the steady tread of the guard.

Riley slithered up close to the portal, flattened himself against the wall. The keen point of his knife was thrust forward ready for the lunge.

He threw another pebble. And then, with pounding heart he heard the rusty creak of a bolt. His muscles tensed; his fingers ached around the haft of the knife. His narrowed eyes strained into the darkness ahead. The black oblong that marked the gate was slowly limned out by a narrow strip of light as the portal swung inward.

Still Riley did not move. The breath died in his nostrils. A head appeared in the opening, shoulders. Then Riley lunged forward.

With a massive left arm he smothered the cry that sprang to the guard's lips. The knife in his right described a short, vicious arc through the air. Blood spurted from the Indian's throat. The body leaped once convulsively in Riley's arms, then lay still.

It was all over. Death had come suddenly, swiftly, silently.

RILEY LOWERED THE body silently to the ground, stepped through the half-opened gate, closed and bolted it behind him. Before him stretched the cobbled courtyard of the palace. To his right the ornate entrance of the palace itself loomed up.

He had succeeded so far, but only in the most simple feature of the venture he proposed. How was he to locate the girl? In which of the hundred rooms of the palace was she being held prisoner?

Like a darker shadow in the dark night, Riley streaked across the courtyard and darted down the side of the building. A dim light shone out into the darkness from a trellised window on the floor above.

He watched it intently for a moment. Then his pulses leaped as he saw a shadow pass across the latticed *jalousies*. Riley came to a swift decision. Someone was in that room. Either the girl, the Russian, or one of his men, as they had but lately arrived some half hour before him.

No matter who it was, it was the only starting point he had in his search for the girl. Whoever it was, with the point of his knife at his throat, he would talk. **GRIPPING THE KNIFE** between his teeth, he began to climb toward the balcony above him. The rough joints of the stones gave him treacherous footholds, but he persisted. Two minutes later he threw a leg over the ledge of the balcony and crawled to momentary safety.

He lay still and quiet in the shadows for a long moment. Then the thought that the dead guard might be discovered at any minute spurred him to action. He whipped the automatic from his belt and crept stealthily toward the long window.

It was locked from the inside. He could not see through the drawn blinds. Yet the light still burned from within.

He was on the point of attacking the lock of the window and a peculiar sound froze him to immobility. He listened, tense, rigid. It came from the room beyond.

Then in a burst of illumination he understood. It was the sound of weeping. The fickle fates had favored him at last, had led him straight to the girl.

With the haft of his knife he knocked discreetly on the window. The crying stopped instantly. He knocked again. Light footsteps hurried across the floor of the room beyond the barrier. For some inexplicable reason Riley felt his heart pounding against his ribs. **THE SHADE WAS** pulled back a crack and in the narrow opening Riley made out a pair of startled, tear-stained eyes. Then swiftly a bolt was thrown, and the long window opened silently.

Riley stepped across the threshold. The girl tried to stifle the inarticulate cry of thankfulness that leaped to her throat. Her hands went out instinctively to the big Irishman.

"Thank God! Thank God!" she murmured fervently.

Riley gripped her tiny hands in his two massive ones, and for the first time in his life felt foolish. No words came to his lips. With eager, hungry eyes he devoured the slim form of the girl, trembling in his arms.

A strange elation was in his heart.

He felt strong, mighty, the equal of fifty men. He had come to rescue this girl from the hands of the Russian, from a fate worse than death and rescue her he would, though the heavens fell.

"S-h-h! Don't cry. Stop trembling, child," he urged.

"You've come," she said with tears in her voice. "Oh, I knew you would!"

Riley smiled at such faith.

"And how did you know?"

"Because I saw you in Bannu and in that house in Peshawar—and then I prayed."

"Good girl," encouraged Riley. "How did you fall into the hands of Petroff?"

THE GIRL COVERED her eyes with her hands. "He tricked me. I'm a nurse, you see. Said he had a patient for me—his wife—" Her voice broke off in a sob. "I don't know what I would have done if you hadn't come. I would have killed myself."

Riley comforted her with awkward words.

"What's your name?"

"Coleen."

"Sure, and I should have known it," grinned Riley. Then he was all seriousness again. "Listen, Coleen. We must get away from here. It will be dangerous. Men may be killed—but we will escape for all that. You must be brave and you must trust me."

"I do," answered the girl simply.

"Fine," whispered Riley. "Where does the Russian sleep?"

"At the end of the corridor."

"And the guards?"

"I heard Petroff station the men at their posts after he put me in here," answered the girl. "There's one at the head of the stairs. Another at the gate to the palace."

Riley swore under his breath. Two men to get past and at any moment the body of the sentry he had killed might be discovered. The girl noted the look of concern on his face, and her hands went out to him appealingly.

"Can—can we do it?" she pleaded tearfully.

Riley forced a smile to his lips and lied cheerfully.

"Sure, my child."

But despite the arrogant confidence in his voice and words he knew that it would not be as easy as all that. He glanced back at the balcony and considered the way he had entered the room. No, that was out. The girl would never be able to negotiate the descent down that steep wall.

They had to risk getting by the guards. After all, he was armed and the factor of surprise was in his favor. Speed was essential.

He slid back the safety on the automatic and thrust it into the girl's hand. He was pleasantly surprised to find her fingers cool and steady. The knife he kept for himself.

"Follow me. Keep close behind me," he whispered, as he started for the door. He opened it a crack and peered up and down the dimly-lit corridor outside. It was deserted. He turned back to the girl.

"If there is to be any fighting, let me do it," he warned. He indicated the knife in his hand. "This is more quiet than

                THE BEST OF THRILLING ADVENTURES

the gun. Use it only if you have to. Understand?"

The girl nodded her head silently. Twin spots of color leaped to her pale cheeks, and her eyes were bright with excitement. She showed her pluck, however, for when Riley pushed open the door and crept out into the corridor, she followed hard on his heels.

Silently they crept down the passageway. The palace was as still as the tomb. No one stayed their progress, and inch by inch they crept up on the broad flight of marble stairs that led to the floor below.

Riley was prepared for a swift, silent struggle to be terminated by the flash of his knife. But to his utter surprise no guard stood at the head of the stairs. COLEEN'S HAND GRIPPED his in a swift, impulsive movement, Riley returned the pressure of her fingers, but there was a doubt in his heart. Why wasn't the guard on post where he had been placed? A sharp, tingling sensation that raced down his spine warned him of danger.

However, he had no recourse now but to press on. Swiftly and silently they negotiated the broad flight of stairs. Fifty feet before them across the large, marble hallway, was the doorway to freedom.

They paused and crouched low by the balustrade. No sound in the corridors of the palace but the faint tramp of the sentry by the door.

Riley nudged Coleen and gave her the signal for the advance. He descended the last step, came out from behind the protection of the marble balustrade, the girl behind him.

A sudden, shrill scream from over his shoulder whirled him about in his tracks. But Riley's movement was too late. He came up short on the points of two long sabers held in the hands of a pair of natives. A third had just succeeded in wrenching the automatic from Coleen's hand.

AND THERE, FIVE feet away, watching the scene with sardonic humor, grinning evilly like a demon from hell, stood Petroff.

Riley raged at himself, though he said not a word. He was a fool, a colossal ass. He should have expected a trap when he had missed the guard on the floor above. He turned to the white-faced girl, and tried to reassure her with a smile.

Petroff stalked over to him with an arrogant swagger. With the two natives still digging the points of their sabers into Riley's ribs, the Russian raised his hand, and with a vicious swipe snapped his open palm across Riley's face.

"Fool! Swine!" he spat out.

"Anything but a beater of women," grated Riley.

A cruel leer came to the Russian's face. His lips bared back from yellowed teeth. "And you, by your meddling, my Captain, have made her hell just a little bit hotter."

Riley lurched forward instinctively, only to feel the sabers cut into his flesh. He looked at the girl and anguish wreathed at his heart. But the smile on her face was proud, disdainful.

"I die first," she said simply.

Though he knew before he started that it was a forlorn hope, Riley decided to appeal to the Russian's sense of honor.

"Why not let the girl go, Petroff?" he asked. "You have me. Do what you want with me, but let the girl go."

The Russian smiled evilly. "A gallant offer, Captain, but I must refuse it. I fail to see I gain anything by the bargain. You seem to forget that I have you both in my power. Why should I release the little bird before I have heard her sing?"

"Because I will kill you if you lay your filthy hands on her."

"Forever warning, eh, Captain Riley. You seem never to learn. You seem determined to throw your life away foolishly. You have been lucky so far—"

"My luck hasn't changed yet," replied Riley. "It's in the cards that there's at least one more thing I do before I go to the happy hunting grounds."

"Yes?" mocked Petroff, pulling at the lobe of his left ear, "And pray, what is that?"

"To beat you with a horse whip before I kill you."

THE COLOR DRAINED from the Russian's face; his nostrils dilated and his hands trembled.

"You will regret those words, Riley," he said with an ominous quiet in his voice. "Yes, my friend, you will regret those words."

Twin devils leaped out of his eyes and seared Riley's face. Then he turned to the girl, still standing on the stairs. He stepped close to her, placed his arm around her cringing shoulders in a lecherous caress.

She shrank from the foul embrace. Petroff placed one heavy hand beneath her chin and tilted her face up to his.

"You and I, my pretty one," he gloated. "We shall see him die, eh. A slow death, and a long one."

Coleen's eyes blazed anger and scorn. Her lips found the torrent of words that welled to her lips but only two words came.

"You beast!"

Petroff laughed.

"I like my women to have spirit. And while your gallant captain dies inch by inch, maybe you will sing for him, eh. Sing for him from your cage."

"Never!"

"Or maybe the captain would prefer to hear you wail under the sting of the little present I bought for you?"

FOR ANSWER, COLEEN'S dainty hand swung sharply forward and caught the Russian across his mocking lips. Petroff was taken back by the sudden blow, snarled viciously, then his thin lips parted in a cruel laugh.

He stepped in close to the girl, placed his two hands on either side of her face and turned her lips up to his. Ruthlessly he kissed her full on the lips, then flung her from him.

"For every blow a kiss, my dear," he taunted. "Bear that in mind. Just my way of showing you that I am equally as gallant as the captain."

Riley could stand no more. Something exploded inside him. Despite the sabers pressing into his ribs he lunged forward. An automatic sprouted suddenly in Petroff's hand.

"One step more and I fire."

If there had been no one but himself to have considered, Riley would have risked it. But he had the girl to think of. Snarling his defiance, he pulled up short.

Petroff whipped a small silver whistle from his tunic and blew three sharp blasts upon it. Instantly there was a stir throughout the palace. Guards appeared as if by magic from the dark corridors and with sullen eyes surrounded the two captives.

A moment later, preceded by two tall Indians, Abdel Khan appeared at the head of the marble stairs. He was dressed in a long, flowing robe of purple, and in his jeweled right hand a shining knife was clutched.

From the head of the stairs he took in the grim tableau below him, then with regal tread began to descend.

Riley had never met the Khan before, but he knew him by reputation as a prince both arrogant and cruel. The mere fact alone that he had formed an allegiance with the Russians, spoke volumes against him. He and the girl could hope for little mercy at his hands.

"What is the meaning of this, Alexis?" he asked in perfect English.

Petroff bowed ironically. "Let me present to your Excellency Captain Riley of the Lancers. You have already made the acquaintance of the lady."

Watching his face closely, Riley saw a dark shadow of hate spread over the Khan's sharp features.

"And when did I extend an invitation to the captain?" he demanded frigidly.

"That's just the point, Excellency," replied Petroff. "You didn't. The fool has delivered himself into our hands." Abruptly the suave cruelty left the Russian's voice. His accent became frigid, sharp with death.

"Captain Riley took it upon himself to effect the rescue of our esteemed lady guest. In attempting to do so he murdered the guard at the outer gate. Justice is justice, Abdel Khan, and the blood of one of your followers cries out for vengeance."

"And he shall have vengeance," replied the Khan.

Petroff bowed low.

"There is just one favor I would ask of you, Abdel Khan," he said in an ingratiating voice.

"And what is that?"

"It was I who discovered the murdered body of the guard. It was I who captured the captain and the lady as they were making their escape. Turn him over to me to devise the manner of his death."

A cruel light sprang up in the Khan's eyes.

"Your wish is granted, just so long as his death shall be slow and long."

"Never fear," grated Petroff. "He should die hard, Your Excellency. He should give us good sport before the ants eat out his eyes."

PETROFF TURNED AND issued a series of sharp orders to the native soldiers. Coleen was roughly grabbed and dragged up the marble stairs to some new prison. A half dozen men surrounded Riley and, prodding him forward, forced him across the broad hallway and through a narrow door at the far end.

Through tortuous narrow passages, down, ever down, Riley was pushed along at the points of the sabers. The walls became damp, fetid. Rats squealed and scurried underfoot. At last the little party stopped before a heavy, impenetrable stone door.

Petroff himself lifted back the heavy iron bar that sealed it and swung the portal open, A dozen eager hands propelled Riley violently forward into the stygian gloom of the dungeon.

"Just a temporary precaution, Captain," taunted Petroff, as he slammed the door shut. "By sunup my cunning brain will have devised the manner of your death."

CHAPTER VI

THE IRON CAGE

WITH HEAVY FEET and bitter heart, Riley tramped up and down the length of his narrow cell. He never doubted for a moment but that the Russian would devise some particularly cruel death for him. But it was not the anticipation of this that brought the lines of anguish to his face.

He had faced death before unafraid. It held no terrors for him. But the girl—the girl with the lilting Irish name! He had to do something! He had to save her! The barren walls flung back his impotent curses in hollow mockery. How? How?

There was no answer. Slow, never ending minutes dragged by into hours that brought the weight of centuries. Riley paced his cell relentlessly. He was not aware that his limbs ached, that his throat was parched and dry.

The iron bar that held him in was lifted at last. A squad of men marshaled him out of the dungeon and led him up to the broad hallway of the palace. But they did not tarry there. As he was roughly jostled out of the building, Riley tried in vain to catch a glimpse of the girl. To see, by some sign at least, in which room she was being held prisoner.

Out in the courtyard, Petroff was awaiting his arrival. He saluted mockingly and then led the little procession down the front façade of the palace, turned the corner in the full face of the sun.

With keen eyes, Riley quickly perceived the trap that had been made ready for him. Against the whitewashed walls of the palace stood an iron cage. It was some ten feet square by twenty high. The bars were thick and strong; a heavy lock guarded the narrow iron door.

There was no roof to the cage. The top was open to the sun. The sun! That was it! That devil of a sun! Riley knew it of old. A half hour's exposure to it in the heart of the day and demons crawled in one's brain.

That was the hellish death Petroff had devised for him!

The door to the iron cage was flung open. Roughly he was thrown into the interior and the lock snapped shut behind him. A hoot of derision swelled from the throats of the onlookers.

Riley knew the hellish torture he would go through. His first impulse was to fling himself at the iron bars in a mad effort to break the confining cage. Then came sanity. If he would survive, he must keep his head, keep cool at all costs.

HE KNEW WITHOUT trying that there was no escape through those iron bars by mere brute strength alone. His only salvation lay in matching his wits with the Russian's.

Slowly, calmly, as if he hadn't a care in the world he strolled to the far end of the cage and lay himself down against the walk

The sun rose, beat down unmercifully like a ball of molten fire. No matter where he lay, where he turned, it discovered Riley, filtered insidiously into his fevered brain.

His mouth was dry as dust. His tongue became swollen and puffed. It was an agony of pain to swallow.

And this was only the beginning. There were hours yet—long, never ending hours, till the sun went down.

And then there was the morrow! How long could he hold out? He had to hold out for the girl!

In a window high up in a wing of the palace that projected at right angles to Riley's cage, something white attracted his attention. He stared at it a moment, uncomprehendingly. Then he understood. It was the girl standing there in the enclosure, looking down on him.

Riley couldn't face the unseen anguish in her face. He turned away. Another fevered hour passed. He had to think. Had to think despite the brass gong beating in his brain.

Late in the afternoon Petroff and the Khan strolled by. An awning was raised for them and there seated under the shade, sipping nectar from tall, frosted glasses, they watched the fevered anguish of their victim.

Riley lay stretched full length in the sun. He didn't stir. No muscle moved. He was fighting the tongues of flame leaping in his brain. And he was thinking, thinking, thinking, torturing his already over-wracked brain in a vain search for a solution to a problem to which there was no answer.

And so passed the first day.

THE COOLNESS OF the night gave Riley a respite. He still suffered the agony of the damned from thirst, the licking fires that had consumed his brain during the day subsided.

He rarely moved, save for an occasional turn of his head toward the barred window where Coleen stood. He knew that the only hope he had—and it was so slender that it cast no shadow—was in conserving his fast ebbing strength to the last degree.

The cage was strong. There was no breaking through it. No help could he expect from the outside. He had to match his wits against the Russian's and he had to win, despite the overwhelming odds he fought against.

The sun rose the following day and with the first burning rays of the fiery orb, Petroff sallied forth from the palace. He was freshly bathed, dressed in cool white linens.

A comfortable breakfast beneath his belt, a cigarette dangling from his thin lips, he took his place under the canopy and amused himself watching the faint, convulsive jerkings of Riley's seared body.

BUT HOLDING ON to his sanity with the last of his strength, Riley determined to rob him of half his pleasure. He made no outcry. No word of prayer or plea was wrung from his tortured lips. If the Russian thought he would grovel in the dust, he would show him how an officer of the Bengal Lancers met his death.

Petroff taunted him with vile curses and epithets, Riley received them in stony silence. The Russian swallowed tremendous beakers of cool, fresh water. Riley refused to hear, And then as a final thrust, the Russian emptied a tall demijohn of water on the dusty ground.

The cool liquid laughed and gurgled as it spilled from the neck of the bottle. The bubbling sound insinuated itself into Riley's smoldering brain until he thought he would go mad.

God alone knew what effort and will power it took to keep from crying out for just one drop of water—just one drop!

Petroff gave up the futile game at last. With a cruel leer on his face he stepped up close to the bars. Riley wasn't dying as hard as he had anticipated. Too bad; half his amusement was gone. He had expected the Irishman to survive for at least three days and now it appeared he would die on the second.

"Dog!" snarled Petroff. "There is less fight in you than I thought. Before the ants claim you, and I throw you to the dogs, you might be interested in hearing the little plan I have arranged for your men."

Riley was very interested, but by the movement of no muscle did he show it. He lay full length on his back in the broiling sun, eyes closed, apparently insensible. But his ears were keen and sharp and he listened avidly to Petroff's words.

"Tomorrow," continued the Russian, "tomorrow early I lead forth a hundred of Abdel Khan's men. We shall proceed swiftly to the Lybia Pass and from there sweep down in a surprise attack on your men at the oil field. We shall wipe them out, exterminate them to the last man. But the gallant captain will have been dead before then, and he will not care."

Every devilish word of the Russian sank into Riley's fevered brain. However, he made no sign that he had heard. Petroff glared at him savagely for a moment, then with a bitter curse turned away in disgust.

"HE DIES LIKE a jackal," he muttered to himself. "No fight in him despite his boasting words. No spirit!"

Lybia Pass! Lybia Pass! Lybia Pass! The words echoed and reechoed in Riley's tortured brain. Something stirred in his failing consciousness. Those words had a pregnant significance for him, besides the geographical name, if he could only put his finger on it.

Lybia Pass... surprise attack... his men wiped out!

   THE BEST OF THRILLING ADVENTURES

And then something clicked in Riley's brain. He saw it all now, vividly, clearly! For just such an emergency, the Bengal Lancers had secretly cached in every pass on the frontier arms and munitions.

Marshaling the faculties of his throbbing brain he mentally visualized the physical characteristics of the Lybia Pass. He saw it all in his mind's eye. There was a machine gun hidden there—with a hundred rounds of ammunition.

If he could escape—if he could beat Petroff to the pass—he could hold him off till reinforcements came up. He had to escape!

The blazing sun rose high in the heavens. Riley's flesh became scorched and livid. But the torment of his body was nothing compared to the anguish of his brain as he forced it on, ever, ever, seeking to discover some way of escape.

High noon. Early afternoon and the sun slowly arched across the dome of heaven to settle in the west, Riley was an inert heap of livid flesh in the far corner of his cage. But in his brain a strange fire burned. And the flames that consumed his spirit were not caused by the scorching sun.

CHAPTER VII

DEATH AT LYBIA PASS

THE INDIAN NIGHT fled across the snow-capped hills in the distance. From the east, a live flaming thing, the red sun thrust itself over the horizon and hurled its merciless rays down upon the arid earth. The jungle sighed as the coolness of the night left it, and once again the terrific heat of the day descended furiously upon the country.

Alexis Petroff, having breakfasted well, strode into the palace courtyard and barked a crisp order at the waiting Hamzoolah. The latter saluted, disappeared, and a few moments later in response to the relayed orders, the men of Petroff and Abdel Khan lined themselves up before their chief, armed and ready for whatever expedition he might order.

PETROFF SURVEYED THEM with a keen all-seeing eye. Then satisfied that his little army was prepared for the mission upon which he was sending them, he turned again to Hamzoolah.

"March them off to the Lybia Pass, Before you have covered much distance I shall have joined you. In the meantime I have a duty to perform."

Hamzoolah saluted, shouted three brisk commands to his men. Smartly the group left-turned and started off on their journey. Petroff stood watching their lithe brown figures disappear in a cloud of dust on the road, then with a smile of satisfaction, he strode from the courtyard toward the spot where his enemy was dying.

As he approached the cage, he was aware of a sense of misgiving tugging at his heart. For in the distance he could see a prone, motionless figure lying inert on the bottom of the iron prison. Was it possible that Riley was dead? Petroff frowned, as he realized that perhaps he had been deprived of the sadistic pleasure of watching his enemy die. He increased his pace slightly.

A moment later he stood before the hot iron of the cage peering in through the bars. Some few feet from the rear wall lay Riley. He was not a pleasant sight. His head was thrown back. His mouth was open, and his tongue lolled out like that of a thirsting animal. His eyes were closed. And beneath the filth and sweat of his tunic, his muscles were inert.

Petroff grunted. He then thrust his stick through the steel bars and prodded the helpless man within. Again he rammed the stick forcefully into the prone figure. There was no movement. Again Petroff grunted. And for the moment the fact that Riley was dead compensated for the fact that Petroff had not seen him die.

Then as the Russian raised his eyes from his victim, his brows lowered. A puzzled expression crossed his face. Then it was gone and furious rage replaced it. He swore under his breath in his native tongue. Then for the second time he read the words that were written in crimson upon the wall at the back of the cage.

Abdel:

Petroff feeds his men cow flesh. Is THIS, then, your ally?

PETROFF GLANCED ABOUT hastily. No one was in sight, and for that fact he breathed a sigh of relief. Even in his dying moment this dog, Riley, had attempted to thrust trouble into Petroff's life.

Of course, the statement written in Riley's blood upon the wall, was untrue. But the Russian was well aware of the sensitivity of the Mohammedan prince on religious ritual. If he even suspected that Petroff rationed his men with the flesh of the sacred animals—kine—it would certainly do the Russian no good.

Grudgingly, Petroff admitted to himself, the resourcefulness of his enemy. Impotent and dying, Riley had yet evolved and executed a plan which would nettle his adversary, writing in his own blood a message calculated to cause bad feeling between Petroff and his Indian ally.

Well, the Russian reflected, it was fortunate for him that no one else had read the message first. Now that the Irishman was dead, Petroff could safely enter the cage and erase those damning words ere the prince himself could read them.

He took a bunch of keys from his pocket, selected one and twisted it in the padlock which held the cage door fast. Then he entered.

He paused for a moment as he came close to the corpse, and a triumphant, exultant gleam came into his eyes as he regarded the inert heap that lay at his feet. Then, with a smile on his lips, he stepped across the body to the wall. He took a handkerchief from his pocket and commenced to obliterate the offending words from the whitewashed stone.

Exactly what occurred in the ensuing twenty seconds, Alexis Petroff never quite knew. He was dimly aware of a sudden movement behind him. The corpse of Francis Riley beat all existing records for swift resurrection. It sprang to sudden and vivid life. A grimy hand snatched the stick from Petroff's hand.

The Russian whirled on his heel, stark amazement stamped in his eyes. He caught a secondary glimpse of his own stick hurtling through the air above his head. A shooting pain bit into his temple. A red and yellow cyclorama flashed before his eyes. Then an infinite blackness transcended all sight, all sensation. His knees buckled and he fell.

Riley permitted himself to enjoy a moment of triumph. He gazed down at the fallen Russian, smiled grimly and muttered softly:

"So, my friend, virtue again overpowers the machinations of evil."

THEN HE TURNED and fled through the open door of the cage a free man once more—free to frustrate the deep-laid plans of Petroff and his Mohammedan ally, the prince.

He paused for a moment just outside the palace courtyard and strained his eyes peering up the arid road that ran out toward the hills. There in the distance he saw a faint cloud of dust. It seemed to be moving away from him. He nodded his head in satisfaction. Apparently Petroff's men had already left for the pass. That should simplify matters for him.

Just across the threshold of the courtyard he saw a single sentry. In a holster at his side he wore a heavy .45. Riley approached on stealthy feet.

When he was less than five feet away from the Indian, when he was preparing the spring, the man suddenly turned.

His mouth opened to cry out. His right hand fell to the black butt of the revolver at his side. But neither of these things was ever executed. Again that flailing stick of Petroff's was lifted high in the air. Again it descended viciously upon a man's skull, and for the second time within as many minutes, again it claimed a victim.

SILENTLY THE INDIAN fell to the flagstones of the courtyard. His revolver clattered out of his holster to the ground.

Riley stooped swiftly and retrieved it. He thrust the stick through his belt, and boldly entered the palace, his weapon held steadily before him, ready to mow down anyone who should offer resistance.

He raced up a broad flight of marble stairs without encountering anyone. Then as he sped down the hall toward the door which held Coleen prisoner, he came suddenly face to face with two servants of Abdel's household. They were unarmed, and apparently scared out of their wits at the sight of this berserk apparition who appeared from nowhere and pointed a sinister black .45 at their fluttering hearts.

"Come with me," he snapped in native dialect. "Do as I tell you and you shall not be harmed."

Docilely, not daring to parley with this madman, the pair obeyed. Riley halted before the door. Then he took a chance. He turned to one of the trembling servants before him. The muzzle of the .45 was brandished ominously.

"Unlock that door," he commanded.

The pair of them exchanged glances. The .45 dug into the nearest man's heart.

"Unlock that door," said Riley again, and in his tone was an unspoken hint of death.

One of the Indians hastily concluded that the wrath of their master, the prince, was a more merciful thing than the sudden death which this white man had offered them.

With trembling fingers he took a bunch of keys from his robe, and inserted it into the door. Riley drove the pair of them into the room before him.

He slammed the door shut behind him, and turned to confront Coleen. Her blue eyes were lighted up with fresh hope. Her lips wore a smile of gratitude.

"I saw what you did in the cage," she said. "Thank God, you're alive. I, as well as Petroff, thought it was all over."

"Hush," he said. "There is little time for words. We must be off at once. God, what's that?"

HIS EYES HAD suddenly perceived an earthen pitcher of water standing on a small table. Water! The element that every fiber in his parched being was crying out for. Hastily he approached the table and held the pitcher to his lips. But despite his terrible thirst he dared not drink too much. Carefully he rinsed out his mouth, sipped a little of the precious fluid and then turned again to the girl.

"Come," he said. "We need horses. Good fresh horses, and even yet we may outwit these cutthroats."

He walked to the door, paused upon the threshold and addressed the two Indians in Pushtu.

"You two shall remain here locked in. You will make no outcry for at least five minutes. If you do, I shall return and slay you."

He scowled ferociously. The two utterly cowed natives bowed in acquiescence. Riley slammed the door, locked it, and, with Coleen holding his hand tightly, beat a hasty retreat down the stairway from which he had come.

This time he did not leave the courtyard. Instead he led the way through a small door to the left. Twenty feet to the rear of a large enclosure were the prince's stables. It was in that direction that he headed.

THE BRUTAL SWINGING muzzle of his gun disposed of the pair of startled grooms who attempted to bar his way at the entrance to the stables. Then in an instant he had untethered two of the best looking pieces of horseflesh in the place. A moment later he and Coleen were riding hell bent for leather over the flagstones of the courtyard.

But the getaway was not to be as easy as he had anticipated. Someone, evidently, had discovered the unconscious form of the sentry at the entrance to the court. As they emerged, urging their horses, half a dozen of the prince's retainers bore down upon them shrieking imprecations.

A pair of brown arms clutched at the neck of Coleen's horse. Riley's gun spoke once. The brown arms ran wet with crimson. A hoarse scream ripped through the air. Riley's horse shied violently, sprung in the air, and landed with heavy hoofs upon a writhing piece of humanity below.

A Gurkha knife whizzed through the air, neatly detaching a piece of cloth from the Irishman's tunic, and drawing blood from a flesh wound.

With one hand steadily gripping the bridle of the girl's horse, Riley urged the mounts on, through the wall of human flesh that barred their way. The metal-shod hoofs of the horses struck heavily against the brown skins of the Indians. Riley's .45 took the toll of half the enemy.

Then, at last, they were clear.

Down the dusty road, through the terrible heat the two horses galloped like Bucephalus and Pegasus off to keep a tryst with the gods. On and on they went.

No word was spoken between them as they rode madly on their way. Riley knew that in order to put his plans into execution he must conserve every ounce of strength that he possessed. His body ached with a weary, maddening pain. His lungs breathed with difficulty and every nerve of his being thirsted for water.

Then he pulled back on the reins, and waved a signal to the girl to halt. For a moment they took a brief respite at the side of the road.

"We'll cut off the trail here," he said. "It's our only chance. We can save twenty minutes, and with luck we should reach Lybia Pass before Petroff's men. There's a Lewis gun cached there. I can hold them off while you go down and get reinforcements from the oil settlement."

SHE NODDED AND flashed him a smile. Then she turned her steed's head toward the rocky uplands.

"Then," she said courageously, "come on."

His own mount swerved and the pair of them set off through an arid waste of boulders. Some few feet in from the road they picked up the broken trail that Riley had estimated was at this point. Then at a steady lope, the girl riding behind, they pressed forward, silent and grim, driven onward through peril and pain by a terrible resolution, by an all-consuming desire to foil the machinations of the Russian.

It was high noon when their spent horses came wearily into Lybia Pass. High up on the plateau the pass was a jagged cut through the mountain which looked down on the flat plain beneath. Some miles to the rear lay the oil fields. While before them down on the plain, Riley saw Petroff's little army marching through the terrible heat toward Lybia, little aware that the enemy already held that vantage point.

Riley climbed down from his horse. He walked over to Coleen and took her hand in his.

"You go down to the oil fields," he said. "Tell the men not to come here, but to flank the enemy and attack them from the rear. In that way we'll have them between two fires which should compensate for their superior numbers. Fast now, and good luck."

For a moment their eyes met, and Riley felt an alien sensation of warmth flood his heart. The pressure of their hands grew stronger. Then the girl said: "And good luck to you, Francis Riley. You'll need it more than I will."

She stooped suddenly in the saddle and before he could divine her motive, kissed him full on the lips. Then she whirled her mount about, and galloped at express train speed down the other side of the mountain.

For a long moment Riley gazed after her, a strange, unaccustomed tenderness in his eyes.

"My dear," he muttered to himself. "I've got to be lucky now. Never before has Francis Riley had such an excellent reason for escaping with his life."

Then as he turned his head and gazed at the marching troops below, he brought his sentimental interlude to an abrupt conclusion. The brown marching men were bearing down, concentrating at the bottom of the hill. He saw them fall out, recline at the side of the road and pull their water bottles.

Then as he gazed beyond them he saw the figure of a lone horseman approaching in the distance. Without distinguishing the rider's features, Riley knew who it was. Petroff, having recovered from his blow on the head, was now hastening to the pass to lead his men on to victory.

Riley turned away from his contemplation of the scene below and prepared to get down to the grim business of war. At the side of the jagged rocky cut in which he found himself was a small cave. Into this he wormed himself.

HE REAPPEARED A moment later dragging a Lewis gun with him. Three drums of ammunition were hung around his neck. He set the gun at the mouth of the pass, lay comfortably on his stomach behind it, and resumed his contemplation of the enemy's movements below.

The horseman had come up with his men by now. Apparently he had no idea that his escaped prisoner had gained the pass before him. For now his troops resumed marching order again and slowly filed up the narrow path that crawled up the side of the mountain.

Riley shut one eye, and with the other stared through the sights of the Lewis gun. He was in no hurry. There was plenty of time, and he had no desire to waste ammunition. He was going to have enough trouble holding out until aid arrived.

Then when the toiling troop was plainly silhouetted against his sights, Francis X. Riley sighed wearily and pressed his finger against the trigger.

The sun dipped in the west. The molten copper ball had run its torturous journey through the heavens spreading a day of arid heat in its wake. Now wearily it made for the haven of the horizon. A purple haze fell over the baked plain.

RILEY WEARILY PLACED his last magazine on the post of the Lewis and stared over his sights down on to the plain, regarding the havoc he had wrought.

Blurred and indistinct in the distance he saw prone turbaned figures lying on the ground, mute testimonials to the accuracy of his aim. Riding back and forth shrieking orders from his twisted

THE BEST OF THRILLING ADVENTURES

mouth was Petroff, rallying his men to another charge against the single man who had held the pass for four long, weary hours.

Petroff's force had been decimated by the chattering Lewis gun, but yet enough men remained to outnumber the small platoon from the oil fields. Riley cast an anxious eye at the sun, and another at the single magazine which remained between him and destruction.

Below, he saw the Russian's force preparing for another foray against him. This time instead of storming en masse up the trail on the mountainside, they spread out and clambered over the craggy rocks in open order.

At once Riley's military mind divined their intention. While part of the force attacked him from the front, the other would climb the rocky crags and drop down on him in the pass from above.

He had feared that Petroff would think of this device, and now he could only thank the Fates that it had taken four long hours to do it.

Half a dozen steel messengers of death pinged against the rocks at his side as the fresh offensive began. Riley drew back the cocking handle with a click and pressed the trigger. The return spring leaped forward, the magazine rotated on its posts and a streaking thread of doom hurtled through the air into the approaching men.

Three of them fell, but under the lash of Petroff's tongue the others struggled forward. It was their last desperate attempt. The Russian was staking all on this final frantic throw of the dice. Riley realized that by now his magazine was half empty.

Well, he reflected grimly, it was all over now. In a moment Petroff's men would spring on him from above and that would be the end. He was aware of a terrible desire to live within his breast.

True, the Reaper himself held no terrors for Riley, but now just when he had achieved something for which to live, life itself was to be snatched away from him. He grinned at the irony of it. **THEN HIS HEART** picked up a beat. His keen eyes peering through the sights of the Lewis suddenly perceived a drab khaki figure in the distance. His gaze swept the landscape in a semicircle. Advancing fanwise on the plain below were the Bengal Lancers. Now he could make out the forms of their purebred horses.

Swiftly the figures became larger as they galloped to the charge. The clear lucid notes of a bugle ripped through the air. A wild yell was heard. They charged!

The air was suddenly alive with steel. The men of Petroff's troop surprised by this attack in the rear, paused a moment in their tracks and stared stupidly behind them. Riley's finger again crooked about the trigger of the machine gun. A stinging hail of lead ate its way into the human targets before him.

Up the slope, firing as they came, raced the Lancers of Bengal to the rescue. Riley sighed. He stood up over his empty gun stretching his weary muscles for a moment. Then abruptly he became aware of something above him.

He sidestepped swiftly, and not a second too soon. A shadowy figure dropped into the pass from the rocks above, stumbled, then came to its feet to be revealed as Petroff, an ugly snarl on his lips, and a .38 in his hand.

"All right," he said bitterly. "You win again, Riley. But death shall beat us both."

The revolver's muzzle was bearing directly on Riley's heart.

Even as the Russian's finger tightened on the trigger, Riley sprang. Something ate into his shoulder and a thousand devils of agony crawled through his muscles. His ears rang with the reverberations of the Russian's pistol.

Yet when his hands met around Petroff's knees and brought him down, the Irishman was still alive.

Desperately they struggled there for possession of the weapon. Riley's hands were taut over Petroff's, on the butt of the gun. Sweating and swearing they fought, fought to the death in the lonely Lybia Pass.

Suddenly, a deafening explosion burst in Riley's ears. Cordite stung his eyes. The body with which he grappled became inert in his grasp—supine. Blood was on his hands. But it was not his own blood.

He stood up and regarded the dead figure of Petroff at his feet. In the struggle the revolver had been somehow discharged and the steel death that lurked in its chamber had sped swift and true into the Russian's brain.

Below him, the enemy was in full flight, pursued whole-heartedly by the wild riding Lancers. Francis X. Riley placed his hands on his hips and sighed. He turned suddenly as he heard a horse's hoofs behind him.

Coleen Wright smiled at him from her saddle, then hastily she dismounted, put her arm around him and placed a canteen of water at his lips. He gulped the fluid thirstily. He was aware of a terrible weariness assailing him.

"Thank God, you got through," he said. "I couldn't have held out much longer."

"I'm glad," she said simply, "glad that we got here in time." Then she regarded him anxiously. His face was pale and wan. Blood stained his tunic. "Oh, Francis," she said, concern marring her pretty features, "you're all right, aren't you? You're not going to die."

Francis X. Riley gazed squarely in her eyes. "Die?" he said, uttering what he meant to be a laugh, but what emerged from his lips a horrible parched gasp. "Die? Why, I've only just started to live."

Tenderly she helped him toward the horse, who with an equine discretion had turned his face from them and moodily contemplated the sinking Indian sun.

Valley of Giants

BY JACKSON COLE

Amazing, Astonishing Adventures on a Daring Expedition that Finds a Lost Valley Inhabited by Mighty Giants and Prehistoric Monsters

CHAPTER I

THE LAKE OF FIRE

THERE'D COME A crash, then such a shriek of metal and ice in conflict that you would have said the ship was being torn apart. The ship was a submarine. They called her the *Golden Harpoon*. Then she'd fallen, twisting—end over end, it seemed—like a barrel going over Niagara. But a Niagara at the bottom of the sea—three hundred feet below the surface she'd been when the trouble started; and the sunken ceiling above her a world of ice.

It had been that transition from ice to fire that had knocked the crew unconscious. There'd come the crash and the grinding shriek and the *Golden Harpoon* had been as if hurled into a roaring furnace.

The roaring was there as Captain Shale Dixon struggled into consciousness.

He remembered.

For two days the *Golden Harpoon* had been groping her way under the South Polar ice. He'd found the submerged sea cave he'd been looking for.

Captain Dixon was in a wedge of men and steel. The ship was whirling. It had become as a gyroscope of flame, it seemed. But he wouldn't give up. He had ship and crew to think about. It wasn't the first time that a Dixon had battled with death in the South Polar ice.

One of his whaling ancestors had once fought a strange whale in these waters and had found a still stranger harpoon in the blubber of the great beast.

It was a harpoon of solid gold, hence—the *Golden Harpoon,* the name of this submarine.

It was another Dixon who'd found the warm current flowing from under the thousand-foot ice cliffs of the South Polar continent. It was this submerged river of mystery that the *Golden Harpoon* and her crew of fourteen—adventurers all—lunatics, the world had considered them—had come to explore.

Lunatics like as not, Captain Dixon's reeling thought admitted. And now in a crazy submarine!

He struggled up and hauled himself to the steering column.

It was as if the *Golden Harpoon* were now standing on her tail—flaming like a torch. There was dynamite aboard. When would she blow? All but Dixon, her captain, were still unconscious. Or dead already, maybe!

Not everything was lost. The ship was still alive. So was he. At any rate, the *Golden Harpoon* was no longer plunging deeper. He could tell that—even before he brushed the blood from his eyes and studied the depth gauge. She was rushing now for the surface.

But headed for what port?

JUST A MATTER of split seconds all this was. But seconds shattered like atoms and enough energy released to blow the whole world to pieces.

While Dixon still clung to his post—testing his ship for response to her wheel, trying to read the riddle of her whirling action—the *Golden Harpoon* slewed and lifted, then fell. She'd found the surface again.

Where?

The periscopes were out of commission. He'd have to risk the hatch of the conning tower.

Then, as he unlocked the hatch—hot to his touch—and pushed it back, he was met by such a gust of flaming gas that he jerked the hatch shut again and dropped below.

His senses cleared still more.

He knew about where his position was—three hundred miles south and west of Little America—Byrd's old camp—somewhere near the heart of the South Polar continent.

He had a flash of an idea, now, as to what had happened.

While feeling her blind way through that submerged sea cave, the *Golden Harpoon* had found herself in the drag of another current—a current feeding one of the geysers or volcanoes that made of this frozen continent a land of fire as well as of ice.

All this passing with the speed of a dream.

THE ELECTRIC MOTORS were beginning to die. In a last desperate effort, Dixon sparked the surface engines. They responded. Rudder almost out of commission and propellers twisted; but the *Golden Harpoon* welcomed the chance to run for her life.

When Dixon next risked the conning tower, there was no more fire. He'd come into a world of roaring steam—then into a zone of mist.

The *Golden Harpoon*, riding high, was running across a strange sea—misty hot—yet almost under the shadow of the distant plateau, eternally frozen, that marked the South Pole.

Once through the drift of warm fog, Dixon glimpsed those frozen mountains—then again—far away, what he took to be the mirage of a tropic shore.

A faint shiver ran through the strained body of the submarine. It was as if she had scraped bottom, then was clear again.

And yet, in that contact, there was something that filled Dixon with a foreboding he couldn't explain.

Again the ship struck—lightly enough, it seemed; yet again a shiver passed through her. It was like the shiver of a living thing.

In a sudden panic, Dixon dropped below and reduced the speed of his engines almost to a stop. Even as he did this he was listening. The noises of the outer world were reduced to the single organ-like drone of the distant fountain of steam still roaring up from the depths—and this growing fainter.

Then, through this thinning curtain of sound, Dixon heard another note. It was one that pierced him through with a shiver of cold—then of wonder. He would have sworn that he'd heard the siren of a steamer—the long, mournful hooting wail that vessels unloose when feeling their way through a fog.

His heart stood still as he listened. He heard it again—then again.

With his foot on the ladder there came down now from the open hatch an answering hoot that might have come from the *Golden Harpoon* herself.

This was sheer craziness! But had he run into a fog-bound fleet?

Again at the hatch of the conning tower Captain Dixon surveyed the world around him. The *Golden Harpoon* was riding strangely high—when he remembered the amount of water ballast she carried. The surface of the sea was like melted glass—colored glass that had been melted. A mist was closing in—hiding sea and mountains. The mist gave the sky itself the look of a dome of colored glass.

THERE WAS A sun somewhere—due north, behind that great veil of steam which was now off a mile or so over the port stern.

So much he saw—then a vision of terror.

Before his eyes a strange monster was rising from the sea. It had the head and forepart of a mammoth serpent.

For seconds, it seemed, Captain Dixon was riveted where he was—staring into eyes that were like copper plates, and then into a fanged and gaping mouth.

CHAPTER II

STRANGE BATTLE

ALMOST AT THE same instant the reptile had flashed down its head. It missed Dixon by a matter of inches and caught the edge of the hatchway. The blow brought with it a gust of hot breath that was like a wave of poisonous gas.

Dixon dropped.

For a moment he was on the floor-deck of the submarine looking up—still half-stunned but his mind racing. He'd heard a thousand tales of sea serpents and other monsters of the less traveled oceans. He'd been convinced of it before—not all of the men who'd told such tales had lied; not all of them had been victims of their own imaginations.

A head the size of a barrel, armored with a skin that looked like a mosaic of giant oyster shells. There was no intelligence in those saucer eyes. The barbed mouth—split to the capacity of seizing the girth of a man—was now grinding at the steel combing of the conning tower.

Even while Dixon watched, in the swift interval that it was taking him to get his senses back, he saw a clawed foot—it was like a slimy, colossal hand—seize the rim of the hatchway.

The *Golden Harpoon* heeled and trembled.

A little more and the huge reptile would be hauling the vessel over on her side—perhaps rolling her over completely. That would be death for all on board.

Even with his other preoccupations, Dixon didn't forget his stricken crew. His hands and brain worked with the automatic precision of some of his own instruments as he started the air compressors and released oxygen to revivify the stifling atmosphere in the submarine's hull.

Some of the other men were already stirring—Hawley among them, the engineer.

The *Golden Harpoon* carried no heavy ordnance. But there were weapons enough aboard. Dixon seized a magazine rifle of heavy caliber that had been kept ready in case the submarine was attacked by killer whales.

From the open hatch of the conning tower he fired up twice at that nightmarish head. The monster merely winced, repeated its attack—clawing, gnashing.

Dixon understood. For that huge beast of terror up there—whatever it was—the *Golden Harpoon* was itself some sort of a living thing, a rival in these waters that the creature of mystery now wanted to slay. Slain the submarine would be—with all hands—if the monster succeeded in canting the vessel over much further while that hatch was open. To get the hatch closed, that was the vital necessity; and no time to lose.

THE CAPTAIN PUT aside his gun and took an ax—short-handled and heavy, such as the divers sometimes carried in their undersea work.

The *Golden Harpoon* was heeling—she was about ready to turn turtle—as Dixon thrust head and shoulders through the hatch. One of those great feet—like clawed hands with a twenty-inch span—still clutched the combing of the hatch.

It was at this that Captain Dixon struck.

It was like striking into the gnarled roots of some abnormally tough creeper. He'd struck through skin of plated bone—then into bone itself that turned the edge of the tempered steel.

There was a snorting roar as the clawed horror quivered and jerked up with a clutching movement.

Dixon—in what seemed like a moment of absolute nightmare—saw the arm, or front leg, of the creature. It was stringy and slack like the arm of an alligator, yet as big as the hind leg of a horse.

SOME FIGHTING INSTINCT must have told him what was coming. Back of him somewhere was the twin to this clawed foot he'd struck. He'd half-turned to defend himself. As he did so, he was clutched by the shoulder and snatched into the air.

He swung there suspended—shot through with what seemed like currents of electric fire. And strangely, in that first second or two his only terror was to see that the *Golden Harpoon* was moving away without him—he could see the deck sliding away at what was like a great distance beneath him.

Then some shift of the clawed hand that had taken him by the shoulder twisted the *Golden Harpoon* out of sight altogether and he was gazing again at the head of the reptile. This swung over him and came close. At the same time up came the hand or foot he'd struck with the ax and held him by one of his legs.

Dixon had his ax. He still held it with both hands.

As the head of the monster leered close he struck at it. He may have struck a number of times. All he could remember was an impact as if he'd started to chop down a tree.

Then he was flung into the water.

Even as he fell he heard again that familiar sound—one that struck him as familiar. It was like the fog siren of an ocean liner and it wasn't until seconds afterward that he knew that this was the voice of the thing he'd been fighting—the voice of a dinosaur, the great sea lizard.

On dropping him, the reptile must have turned its attack once more against the *Golden Harpoon*. It slewed the submarine around, clawing at its steel hull.

All that saved Dixon at all just then was that the patent bowsprit of the *Golden Harpoon* came his way. He grappled with this and succeeded in pulling himself out of the steaming water.

He'd been badly mauled. In his throat there was a taste of a strong mineral unlike the taste of any seawater he'd ever known before. The water here about the *Golden Harpoon* was warm but no longer hot. The submarine had continued to travel.

Her wake was crooked—crooked like that of a hooked and all but exhausted fish as the great sea lizard fought her and brought her this way and that.

Captain Dixon lay there on the forward deck of his vessel doing his best to get back reason and sense into a world from which these things had fled. He was looking now at something that no human eyes had ever seen before—a prehistoric monster battling with a submarine.

This was a submarine that had originally been built for the United States Navy, then condemned under some international treaty or other; then rebuilt for this cruise under the Antarctic ice.

Was she to end like this?

Dixon sought other normal details. This day was Christmas—mid-summer in these far southern latitudes. Somewhere the sun shone—far to the north behind that sky-high curtain of steam and fog. Daylight would last for another three months.

He heard the far hoot of another sea lizard, then another and another. And as he looked away across the misty surface of this lake of fire he could see them. There were maybe a score of them, swimming with their heads and necks reared up like the periscopes of super submarines.

Then he saw something else—something that struck him at first as an optical illusion. Behind the fog screen, dimly, yet unmistakably for a dozen seconds, he'd seen a flash of paddles or oars—a movement of boats.

He forgot all this in a pang of horror as he uttered a cry of warning.

CHAPTER III

BARBED WITH GOLD

THE CRY WAS for Hawley, the engineer.

Coming to himself down there in the compression hull, it had been but a matter of seconds for Hawley to realize that something was wrong. This rocking and veering of the vessel, that open hatch—and his captain missing!

Still half-dazed, Hawley had climbed up and thrust himself part way from the conning tower. It was at a moment when the dinosaur was lashing about the tail of the vessel, looking for some vulnerable part to attack. It was while Captain Dixon still lay sprawled on the prow of the submarine.

But suddenly, swiftly, the monster lizard had caught that movement as Hawley showed himself and it was writhing in his direction with the speed of a swimming seal.

DIXON HIMSELF WAS now trying to reach Hawley to warn him of his danger. But it was like running along the deck of a small boat tossed in a hurricane. As Dixon ran, he drew out his knife—the only weapon he had; but a knife with a spring blade, all of four inches of razor-edged steel with a dagger point.

Before Dixon had covered a third of the distance, the great lizard had reared its huge neck and head above Hawley, twisting and staring down at him. Then it had seized him and lifted him bodily from the hatch.

Meantime, Dixon had flung himself forward. In a breathless second, Dixon found himself in contact with a breast of white leather that rose and fell in time to the beat of a colossal heart.

Dixon struck—then struck again.

Then he himself was hurled away.

It had been a blind stroke by the brute that knocked him over. The great lizard was spouting blood and lashing about. In the midst of the turmoil, Dixon found Hawley, dazed and broken, and eased him toward the *Golden Harpoon.*

Others must have awakened down in the hull of the vessel. The boat had stopped. Her propellers were still.

Just as Dixon brought Hawley to the side of the ship, Ben Wiley, Hawley's second, bobbed up from the hatch. He gave a comprehensive look about him. In a flash he was gone. But in a flash, it seemed, he was back again, bringing along a line and a gun.

Hawley and Dixon came over the side.

"Get him below," Dixon command-ed, and took the gun. "Stand by the engines—"

Ben broke in.

"Back of you—for God's sake!"

Dixon swung around.

Undulating across the surface of the sea—close up now—were half a dozen other giant reptiles. Then, true to some nearer surface sign Ben Wiley had seen, there was a heave alongside and another head shot up on a neck that might have belonged to a Chinese dragon.

DIXON HELD HIS fire—held it as the fierce head lifted and the slimy column of a neck slid higher. Just when that pulsing expanse of white leather ap-peared—there where the throat and body met—Dixon let out three shots in quick succession.

It was as if a derrick had fallen on the *Golden Harpoon.*

Dixon was felled as if he'd been caught beneath that derrick. He came out of it stunned to find Hawley strug-gling at his side. But Ben Wiley had disappeared.

Hawley pointed.

Dixon saw the monster he'd just shot tossing its head about and in its jaws the body of his second engineer.

He was over the side and swimming, calling encouragement.

There was a mass of horn and hide, shapeless like a slab of tidal rock, where the first giant reptile tossed and slowly coiled, dead or dying. On this as if for support—or because the two had been mates—the second dinosaur new rested one of its mighty feet as it held aloft the squirming human shape.

But the second monster also was pulsing its life away.

Just as Dixon came close it dropped Ben Wiley and went into a flurry like that of a stricken cachalot.

Through a whirlpool of bloody froth, Dixon found his man and started to swim away.

The mist was thickening again. Even

Suddenly, Dixon hurled himself into action.

the mist had a crimson tinge. It was as if this whole Satanic world was tinged with blood. There was a taste of blood in the heavy brine.

Out of the thickening fog there came the bellowing of other monsters.

Over there on the flat sled deck of the *Golden Harpoon* man after man now appeared. They were excited—armed. Dixon, swimming with the wounded Wiley at his side, was stricken with horror as he saw two of the dinosaur herd bearing down on the submarine with swinging heads and necks.

Just then there was a heaving lift of the bloody froth about him and the head of another monster came up—lifting higher and higher.

While Dixon stared, momentarily helpless, there was a flash and a stabbing impact. A heavy arrow, big as a broom handle, had struck into the throat of the brute.

The beast at once forgot its attack and began to fight this weapon that had struck it.

ANOTHER ARROW CAME—THEN another and another.

One struck the armored head of the monster and flew off and back as if it had taken impact with elastic steel.

Dixon seized the arrow as it fell. It would serve him as some sort of a weapon.

And then—here and now, in the midst of the swirling excitement—he felt the thrust of an excitement keener still. The barbed head of the arrow was like no other arrow he had ever seen, but one, and that was the head of the historic golden harpoon that had given his submarine her name.

Gold also—gold hardened with an alloy of platinum.

The giant reptile was still tearing at the arrow in its throat with its weird ungainly forefeet—fingered like the hands of some primitive giant.

Other monsters were attacking the submarine over there. There was a riot of shots in the air—of screams—of hooting wails that were like a dirge of suffering giants. Yet Dixon felt a breath of triumph. In his hand he had a replica of the golden harpoon that an ancestor of his had found more than a century ago in the body of that strange whale.

Through the red fog that was drawing closer about the field of battle, Dixon again saw something that made him forget during the flash of a new wonder even these wonders that had already stunned him and brought him so close to death.

Emerging now from all directions— there they were—a ring of queer yellow barges—flat and broad but riding light.

The boats were each driven, it seemed, by a hundred paddles.

And in the bow of each boat he saw a colossal human shape—bearded men incredibly big, armed with incredible bows.

And the barges in which these giant huntsmen stood and peered ahead shone with the same yellow metallic luster as that of the golden harpoon.

CHAPTER IV

THE ARCHERS

DIXON WAS IN for a closer acquaintance with those giant huntsmen than he might have wished on such short notice.

He'd started to swim back to the submarine taking both the big arrow and Ben Wiley with him—a floundering swim in that thick water—when some gust of a special shout came through the din and confusion. He turned his head and discovered that two of the barges were bearing down in his direction with a quick flash of paddles.

He was ready for a rescue, but he didn't like the looks of it. There was something in the expression of those giant and bearded archers that gave him a creep of suspicion. But there was no escape.

HE'D NEVER SEEN man-propelled craft better handled. The boats were shallow, with a depth of not more than a couple of feet, he guessed; with a seven-foot beam and a length that couldn't have been much less than eighty feet.

All he could make out regarding the paddlers in that first wild moment was that they were naked savages—white, almost dazzling in their whiteness, yellow haired, heavy about the shoulders, but, if anything, smaller than the average man.

It was the contrast of these with the big men in the front ends of the barges that concentrated about the giants a sort of special atmosphere of terror. The archers must have been ten feet tall, or twelve; even more perhaps; black bearded and black haired, thick lipped and cruel-eyed. They brought to Dixon a memory of the bearded men represented in the carvings of ancient Babylon.

He had just time to see that the archers in the other barges—there must have been fifty of them—were still making sport of the dinosaur herd when the two that were headed for him were on him.

One of the barges had headed the other by a few feet and the big Goliath in the bow uttered a harsh cry. He was on his knees. He'd tossed his bow aside. In an instant he'd seized Dixon and the still unconscious Wiley in his two hands and scooped them up.

It was a savage snatch—fascinated but a little fearful.

As Dixon looked into the huge face he wasn't sure but that he'd rather have taken his chances with the dinosaurs. This face was cruel—cruder than any face he'd ever seen; brazen and malicious—leering, sneering, the facial front for a cunning and ferocious mind.

Dixon controlled himself. He gave the giant a look that was cold and challenging, then spoke. There was no possibility that the Goliath would understand his words, but there was a power in the human voice that could reach the brain even of animals.

"That man's wounded," he said—and there was command in his voice. He put out a shielding hand over Wiley.

Dixon was one of those men who'd never cursed in his life. He'd never had to. He could see that the words had had some effect on the giant. The big archer had lost something of his leer; but there was a lurking menace in its place.

DIXON KNELT OVER Ben Wiley who lay on his back where the giant had dropped him. He'd been terribly clawed. Some of his ribs may have been staved in. But he was breathing. His eyes fluttered open.

Suddenly Ben had jerked around and sat up.

"What the hell!" he exclaimed.

"Steady, old man!" Dixon told him.

Dixon gave another quick look at the yellow-haired paddlers. They had the squat faces of Esquimaux—but of a lower order of Esquimaux than any he had ever seen.

Each wore about his neck what looked like a solid gold collar as of a half-inch wire and suspended from this was a tag of the same metal—big as a man's palm—on which some sort of a seal was stamped. They were naked except for shorts that seemed to be made of a cloth woven from gold.

The giant master himself was naked half way to the waist where there was a broad band of leather that might have been cut from the white throat of a dinosaur. From this there hung a sort of long kilt of similar material on which weird primitive pictures had been painted.

THE PADDLERS HAD been staring absorbed at Dixon and Wiley. But as Dixon looked at them every face became like an ivory mask—fixed and changeless. He didn't have to be told that they were slaves—with a fear of sudden death stamped into their very souls—and that the giant was their commander.

The archers in the other boats had by this time about slaughtered the big sea lizards or driven them off. There were carcasses and writhing blood fountains in every direction. Most of the barges were closing in about the submarine and the two barges that had raced for Dixon and Wiley.

The barge alongside the one where Dixon was had nosed up so that the giant commander of this second boat could have a look at the strangers his rival had caught.

The two giants exchanged speech in a curious rolling bleat. Then he who was in charge of the boat that had taken in Dixon and Wiley picked up Wiley and passed him over to his mate of the second barge before Dixon could intervene.

There came a hail from the *Golden Harpoon*. It was Doc Harris calling. Doc was the *Golden Harpoon's* second in command.

"Captain, shall we open fire?"

"Only on command! How are your engines?"

"All right, sir; but the rudder and propellers are out of commission."

The crew of the *Golden Harpoon* were huddled on the sled deck—some down, some crouched, some standing. But Dixon made a quick count—twelve. No one missing; and he was thanking God for that; even if some of them had been badly mauled. He'd been mauled himself.

Dixon called again to Doc Harris.

"Watch close! They may try to board you! Get your wounded men below and leave a deck watch of not more than two men to be stationed at the hatch. In case of trouble duck under and defend the ship."

Even while he was speaking, one of the big arrows was shot from a barge—evidently just an experimental shot. For these men were marksmen with their big bows. There'd been plenty of evidence of that. And the arrow just fired had hit the *Golden Harpoon* well forward—evidently to test the quality of this strange craft. The arrow glanced and skipped into the sea.

From the barges there came a chorus of exclamations—of surprise, of admiration.

FROM JUST BACK of him, Dixon heard a groan and a grunting curse. It came from Ben Wiley as the men who handled him thrust him to the bottom of the boat and there held him down with a foot like a shovel.

The gesture was so swift—all of this was of such swift development, that words lag in the telling of it—that Dixon had sprung to Ben's defense with no thought at all of what the consequences might be. Landing in the other barge he'd stumbled for a moment among the stolid paddlers. From one he'd snatched a paddle—of metal, sure enough, balanced to his hand and with a blade as sharp as that of a whaler's blubber spade.

CHAPTER V

HOSTAGE

FAST AS DIXON'S reaction had been his brain had been faster yet. A battle with the giants just now was the last thing on earth he wanted. Yet neither could he allow one of his men to be mistreated here before his eyes. Ben Wiley was on the floor of the boat. The giant's foot was on Ben's chest.

Dixon came around with the metal paddle ready to deliver a blow. He met the startled eyes of the giant—deep-set and black under brows that formed a single hairy ridge over the root of a hooked and dilated nose. It was the scowling, awakened glance of a mammoth black-eyed hawk rather than anything human.

"Get back!" Dixon gritted.

The giant's bearded lips parted over clamped teeth but he gave no sound. Then swift as the stroke of a cat that spears at a rat the giant made a grab at Dixon with one of his hairy hands.

At the same moment Dixon struck. Even then he didn't strike to kill! His idea had been to send the giant into the water. It would be a gain of seconds, anyway, and every second gained would be of value at least for the men on the deck of the *Golden Harpoon.*

The blade of the paddle should have caught the big brute flat side on. But as the giant now ducked, his face came in contact with the sharp edge of the blade. It was as if he'd been slashed by a razor—from temple to chin, narrowly escaping an eye.

He let out a howl, but his foot was off Wiley.

In the confusion that followed, Dixon struck again; but took the blow of a fist that would have crushed his skull if he hadn't dropped.

For a moment he was on one knee and what looked like a mountain of hairy flesh coming down to crush him. Into this mass he now thrust his spade with all his strength. The man-mountain over him sagged lower—bringing his own death if he wasn't dead already—as his weight forced the golden blade deeper and deeper into his colossal body.

The handle of the paddle was propped against the floor. Its blade was buried in that floundering body just over the girth. Fate alone could have guided that broad blade between the stricken Goliath's ribs.

Dixon strained. The paddle aiding him, he tilted the burden sideways. The giant slanted over. It was a spasm of his own that brought him to his back with his head hanging down over the side of the boat.

Dixon staggered to his feet—panting, bathed in blood.

HE HAD A swift impression of the yellow-haired slaves back of him transfixed with some emotion that was more like awe than anger—anyway there was nothing to fear from them. Not just now. He retreated a little way, to seize another paddle.

"Wiley," he panted softly, yet without panic, "are you able to get over the side?"

Wiley caught a slow breath. "Don't mind me!"

"Okay, son; but I won't leave you!"

Other things happening all at once. Other impressions coming all at once.

"Steady, over there," Dixon sang out to the *Golden Harpoon.*

What he feared just now was that the battle should spread—become a free-for-all. In that event not one of the sub's crew would escape alive. Yes, for a while, perhaps. But later. What would be the line of escape?

In the same second of time he'd glanced at the other barges. Then he faced the giant who'd seized him first.

"Listen, you," said Dixon. "You're dead, too, if you try to get rough!" He raised his voice and sang out: "Give us a hull shot!"

IT WAS MORRIS who fired—the best shot in the crew. A soft-nosed bullet tore a hole through the gunwale a few inches from where the giant captain of the barge was standing.

It had been a shot at fifty yards— close enough for the detonation and the smash of the bullet to be practically instantaneous. Morris had been a big-game hunter in Africa. Just as instantly he could have sent the bullet crashing through the Goliath's skull.

It was a fact that Dixon conveyed to the giant with a swift gesture of pantomime.

The giant got the idea all right. He also was capable of swift reactions of a sort. The death of his comrade had caught him by surprise. He'd given a start of amazement, then rage, then a return to amazement.

The bullet that had smashed through the gunwale had flattened against the other side and dropped to the floor of the barge at the giant's feet. He looked at the missile for a moment as if it had been some poisonous insect.

Without moving he raised a throaty cry—not very loud but rolling. It sounded like:

"Hoa! Hoa! Hoa! Ola-lo! Hoa! Hoa!"

Dixon stepped over the fallen giant and knelt at the side of Ben Wiley. Ben had tried to rise and had dropped back.

"How's she makin'?" Dixon asked, easing Wiley to a much better position.

"Fine!" said Wiley, and he tried to grin but he closed his eyes.

Dixon looked up.

So had the giant brought his attention to a fallen comrade—the Goliath whom Dixon had speared. The victim may not have been dead. Or his movement now may have been due to a mere post-mortem reflex of twisted muscles. But his mighty body had lurched. Seeing which, the Goliath of the first boat leaned over and grappled the head of the victim with both hands, then jerked him free of the barge and thrust him under the turgid red and purple water.

As he did this once more he raised his bearded face and let out that curious cry of his:

"Hoa! Hoa! Ola-lo!"

     THE BEST OF THRILLING ADVENTURES

If it meant "Retreat!" it was an order or a suggestion that must have met with the approval of the other members of this strange hunting party.

But Dixon, held by a dread fascination, watched the giant making sure that his comrade was dead before releasing his body into the bloody waters of the place. Then, sharply, he was aware that the paddlers had reversed their position and were smoothly bringing the two barges into speed.

HE CAST A look at the *Golden Harpoon.*

Doc Harris and others were still occupied there in getting the wounded down the hatch of the conning tower.

A hail came across from Doc Harris:

"Shall we stop them?"

"No! Await orders—forty-eight hours—then—"

Across the widening space of stained water Dixon could feel a breath of comradeship to strengthen the heart of any man. He completed what he had to say with a voice that stirred those who heard him like a bugle call—

"Affirmation sealed instructions!"

Sealed instructions were for survivors, in case of catastrophe, to rendezvous at Little America where a relief ship might be expected before the South Polar winter set in.

All the barges were drawing away— melting with smooth speed into a red fog. The red fog dropped like a fateful curtain to a weird chant:

"Hoa! Hoa! Ola-lo!"

CHAPTER VI

"HOA-HOA!"

CAPTAIN SHALE DIXON, aged twenty-nine, white, unmarried—"

There could have been other descriptive details on his papers if such details had been in fashion—five feet eleven, one hundred and fifty-odd pounds of animated whalebone; a jaw and a steel-gray eye that meant command; and yet that something about him that made him as careful of Ben Wiley's comfort as Ben's own mother would have been—if Ben had happened to have a mother.

"You're off watch, Ben," Captain Dixon said. "Better snatch a snooze."

Ben snoozed. The captain of the *Golden Harpoon* crouched beside him. The metal barge—shallow draught and broad, almost like one of those coaster boats at a picnic resort, but ten times as long—slid across the oily surface of this sea like a phantom—a phantom unit in a phantom fleet.

It wasn't the first time that a Dixon had sailed a sea uncharted and unnamed. The fact that it might be the last time such a thing should come to pass wasn't bothering this Captain Dixon at all.

His keen eyes searched the horizon, searched the surface of the sea, speculated on the presence here of dinosaurs—monsters that were being called prehistoric in the outside world.

The red fog lifted, drifted, opened up unending vistas. And gradually the nature of this sea revealed itself—the brimming crater of what was probably the world's greatest geyser. Up through the central bore of this geyser the *Golden Harpoon* had found her way.

An inland sea land-locked and mountain-locked—too wide to see across; but wide, he judged, not only because of the lay of the surrounding peaks but because—well, you wouldn't find a herd of dinosaurs in a bathtub.

He gathered at least a part of what must have happened this day besides the arrival of the *Golden Harpoon* in these uncharted waters.

The *Golden Harpoon* had come plunging up from the unknown into the midst of a hunting party. The sea monsters must have been more or less in flight from the hunters when the submarine broke from the depths.

THESE GIANT HUNTSMEN had already been in pursuit. Dinosaurs were, after all, not so different in their general habits, most likely, from their cousins, the whales.

Where were the hunters headed for now? Some ship that lay veiled behind the haze? Or to some camp of theirs on the shore?

Of one thing Dixon became increasingly certain; and that was that there'd be no open-sea outlet from this fiery lake into which the *Golden Harpoon* had found her way. In that case, never again would the *Golden Harpoon* retrace her course. Tempered steel even couldn't again take the punishment of that passage under the ice and earth and through that hell of fire. It would be suicide for human beings to try it again.

CAPTAIN DIXON TURNED and took a last glance at the blurred low hull in the distance that was all he could now see of his vessel. Still on her deck he could see a couple of diminishing figures moving about. Was he ever to see them again?

He checked the thought.

At any rate, they had those sealed instructions—instructions they'd severally sworn to follow before the cruise began. In three months now, if all went well, the relief ship would be waiting at Little America. Would the survivors be there in time—after having scaled the ice mountains that shut in this lost valley? Would he—and Wiley—be among those survivors?

All hands still lived; and that was something.

There'd been no move to offer violence to either Dixon or Wiley since this run back from the field of slaughter had begun. Dixon had signaled for food and water and had received both—at once and both together in the shape of a sweetish melon.

Dixon himself had been without sleep for upward of forty-eight hours so far as he could remember. But perhaps he had slept in stretches of a minute—two minutes at a time.

He slept a little now—as whaling captains used to sleep in times of stress—with a brain that was at rest but with senses alert. He wasn't missing anything, overlooking anything.

He was as alert as ever when a slight change of speed told him that something was about to happen.

The fleet of barges, sticking pretty close together and moving without a sound, had cut across a twenty or thirty mile arc of shore The shore was close. It looked like solid yellow rock—glistening in places where the wash had polished it.

The captain felt an inner lurch.

This shore was gold! This whole sea was a solution of gold. The shore was a gold deposit. There was gold enough in sight to upset the monetary standards of the world.

A gold cup—a saucer, at any rate—perhaps a hundred miles round. He saw that the rim of the sea was considerably higher than the surrounding land. As he stood up in the barge and looked away, what he saw beyond the shore was like a tropic valley lush with a tangle of green jungle.

Then a shift of the barge opened up a long straight avenue through the jungle. At the end of the avenue he saw another shine of yellow—a high-stepped pyramid surmounted by a sort of portico.

There was some delay at the landing-place where Dixon commanded help—and got it—to carry Ben Wiley ashore without further injury.

THE YELLOW-HAIRED SLAVES did the work—in a way that put into Dixon's head the thought of using them later—and serving them too—as allies.

Then the slaves disappeared and the tall giants milled around. They showed a fierce curiosity, yet with a tinge of admiration in it. They held hands off. They talked to each other in hooting, warbling undertones like a talk of owls. Huge men. Not one but reared to twice the height of Dixon. And well-shaped, heavily muscled. With here and there among them a face that was almost comprehending.

It was to the owner of such a face that Captain Dixon spoke. He spoke in English, as was his custom when among strange natives, at the same time backing up what he said with signs.

He pointed now to the pyramidal building at the end of the long avenue and asked what the place was called.

The giant replied:

"Hoa-hoa."

That was good enough. The place was Hoa-hoa. In future geographies there would be a region somewhere on the map of the South Polar continent marked Valley of Giants and the capitol of it would be put down as Hoa-hoa.

Hoa-hoa wasn't more than a mile away. But evidently these giants were lords who must go in state.

Dixon, with one of those barbed arrowheads hidden under his shirt, stood and watched a strange procession of elephants now coming out of the jungle. The elephants were as shaggy as buffalo and carried pads on their heads and shoulders held in place with heavy gold harness.

It was to these pads that the giant lords mounted as the march toward Hoa-hoa was about to begin.

For Dixon and Wiley a litter had been provided—big enough to have carried a dozen ordinary men and swung between two of the shaggy elephants.

"Cheer up!" Dixon encouraged Wiley. "We'll beat them yet."

CHAPTER VII

DEATH IN THE WOODS

"AT YOUR ORDERS," said Wiley, as the yellow-headed slaves who were carrying him shifted him, gently enough, to the couch of the litter. "But was I a sap to let them put me out!"

"You're not out yet," said Dixon.

"But I'm no good. Captain, sir, if you see the chance, beat it! Don't mind me."

Dixon laughed. "I may beat it, Wiley. But not for long. I've got to get word back to the ship."

"Swim?"

Dixon shook his head. And he explained what he had in his mind.

At least there was no call to whisper. Even if there had been anyone else there to understand, their voices would have been drowned out by a booming as of gongs that now arose about them.

A THOUSAND GONGS, it seemed—with a tone as soft as that of great bells heard at a distance.

On either side of the procession of elephants the boatmen from the barges were now lining up. As they struck their paddles together there was the same smooth rhythm as when they were propelling the boats. But now the paddles were drumming out a sort of monotonous marching chime, and it was to a music like this that the soft-footed, curly-hided elephants swung into movement.

Dixon peered through the curtains of the litter.

A few of the giants, he speculated, were riding ahead. More of them were riding to the rear. All were in single column. But there was no real effort to guard the prisoners in the litter. Escape, it must have seemed to these assembled Goliaths, was out of the question for these pygmy strangers, whatever their power of magic might be.

The jungle that hedged in the avenue through which they were now passing was, Dixon noted, a close-grown and luxuriant garden, heavy with fruit and flowers, deserted in stretches but generally alive with a swift and furtive movement of animals and people.

All of these people were of the yellow-haired, ivory-colored slave class, he judged. He saw them hunchbacked but nimble. Except for their color they were suggestive of the missing link.

How far could he trust them? How far could their understanding respond to his own?

Further than one might suspect, perhaps; as it often is with the minds of children and animals. And he had noticed that peculiar expression that had swept over the faces of some of these slaves when he'd killed the giant in the boat. The expression of one of these men he'd noticed especially—the look of the yellow-haired boatman from whom he'd seized the paddle.

He recognized this man now marching at the side of the litter.

Dixon reached out and touched him.

The man responded with a quick, animal-like look. The look was as glinting as that of a monkey, but, even so, there'd been a flash of understanding in it.

Dixon touched the man again. There was another glance, and this time Dixon made a swift gesture to indicate the jungle and that he intended to jump and run.

WHEN THE MAN glanced at him again, Dixon completed his communication. He of the yellow hair was to come along.

There swept across the beast-like face at this suggestion a sudden spasm of swift yearning, then something that was unmistakably a look of assent.

"I won't be long," Dixon told Wiley.

"Boss, keep going!" Wiley's lips formed the words. But his voice was inaudible in the boom of the metallic blades.

Dixon smiled and shook his head.

In another moment he was on his way. He had his arrowhead poniard in his hand. That was in case he should meet immediate interference. Even as he jumped, with his free hand he poked the Yellowhead at his side and motioned him to follow.

IT WAS AS if he'd touched a tame tiger or gorilla, the reflex was so quick. In an instant, the two of them had disappeared like shadows into the dense green of the immediate jungle. It was doubtful even if their leap had been noticed except by the other Yellowheads there. And it wasn't for them to break ranks—or break the rhythm of that strange music they were making.

They came to a sort of glade before they'd covered a hundred yards—it was like a dense green arbor there in the midst of the crowded growth—and it was here Dixon halted.

The Yellowhead was looking at him now with the same expression of mingled dread and hope that Dixon had seen on the squat face after the killing of the archer in the barge.

Dixon smiled at him and lightly touched his head.

"You and I are friends," he said. "And you're going to take a message to the *Golden Harpoon*."

There is an eloquence in sign language that can't be put into words. The Yellowhead was helping matters considerably. Whatever he lacked in other respects, he had an animal's sense of direction.

"Over there," said Dixon—and so did he have a sense of direction. "Men like me!"

He was still explaining, when the Yellowhead himself broke in with a sudden gesture. It was a gesture of warning.

Suddenly, the Yellowhead had stooped and glided toward the edge of the little clearing. Dixon followed.

It was from an unexpected quarter that a giant shape rushed into the clearing—whether one of the archers from the dinosaur hunt or a Goliath whom he'd never seen before, Dixon would never know.

There had come one of those swift moments of tragedy such as might have passed in any primitive jungle—when the tiger springs, or the snake strikes. But this was like neither of these. And in a flash of revelation, Dixon had seen the real nature of it.

This Yellowhead had seen a paddle used this day to slay one of the giant masters of this lost world. The Yellow-head had a paddle in his hand. It had become an instrument of death.

In an instant—swift as any striking snake—the Yellowhead had made a beastlike spring and plunged the blade of the paddle up and under the ribs of the colossus.

THE GIANT LURCHED. His knees buckled.

He was dead before he hit the ground.

He lay there face down, and from his side there spread a broadening pool of blood.

Dixon for a moment stood as trans-fixed as was the Yellowhead himself. He knew that he'd started something here in this Valley of Giants that wasn't apt to end so soon. What one slave had learned others would learn.

"Well done!" Dixon said.

From the dead giant's kilt he cut a broad square. It was as white and soft as parchment. He picked up a stick. On the parchment he wrote a message in red and gave it to the messenger.

It was a desperate chance, but every chance was desperate now.

The Yellowhead disappeared into the green shadows. He'd taken the direction of the Lake of Fire.

Dixon himself was torn between two impulses just then. One was to join his comrades on the submarine. The other was to keep his promise to his wounded comrade who was still a prisoner—or dead.

It was with a feeling that he was con-demning himself to death that he set off, running, in the direction of the avenue leading to Hoa-hoa, that strange capitol of the Goliaths and their king.

CHAPTER VIII

BEFORE THE THRONE

FROM THE MOMENT that Captain Dixon looked into the murderous dark eyes of Ola-lo, king of these giant people who, he learned, called themselves the Hokay, the Great Ones, he knew that only by more killing would this adventure end.

And—who would be the slayer, who the slain?

He'd caught up with the procession of elephants and their riders just as his absence had become known. There'd been a brief period of tumult which in itself had resulted in blood-letting enough.

A dozen of the Yellowheads lay in a tumbled heap at the side of the jungle highway with their heads battered in. But Wiley was safe.

There may have been a look about Dixon now that caused the bearded archers to keep their hands off both Dixon himself and this comrade of his. Anyway, messengers must have already gone ahead to notify the head of the clan in Hoa-hoa that a wonder was on its way—two wonders: two creatures no bigger than Yellowheads, but who'd come up out of the Lake of Fire in the belly of a metal fish and who could kill nearby or at a distance.

"Gold!" said Dixon. "Gold and blood!"

There was no mistaking the one than there was the other.

This avenue was paved with gold. It was a golden city that loomed ahead—a city of many pyramids with a great royal pyramid in the center.

It was on a broad terrace, big as a city block, at the top of this pyramid that Wiley and Captain Dixon were brought into the presence of King Ola-lo.

A curious name; and no less subhuman than that great brute of a man who bore it. In fact, it was impossible almost to think of Ola-lo as a human being.

There was too much about him to suggest again those old wall carvings of Babylon or Egypt—one of those primitive half-gods, or a half-human; a man thewed like a bull with the head of a harpy eagle on his massive shoulders.

Swart and low-browed, with deep-set eyes glowering from under shaggy eyebrows that made a hedge across the bridge of the nose.

THERE WAS NO sense of humor in that brutal face. Nothing but a sort of sullen mockery. But his interest manifestly grew as the other giants told him what was obviously the story of what had happened on their dinosaur hunt.

Dixon guessed that their idea of the submarine was that it was some sort of fish. It had swallowed these human maggots in some distant place and had been poisoned by them. Or—Dixon and his crew had managed to kill the monster, once they were in its maw.

The woolly elephants had carried all hands to this upper terrace of the pyramid. Here the royal residence was a vast portico.

The portico was a place of columns—gold like the pyramid itself; but with figures painted on the polished surface and on the gold rafters overhead that supported a ceiling of golden tile. In the midst of this portico was an open space in which there was a black tent, and this tent was the canopy of a couch on which King Ola-lo had apparently been taking his nap.

THERE WASN'T MUCH formality. Everything was free and easy within certain limits—except for the yellow-haired slaves. Twenty of these had carried in the litter on which Dixon and Ben Wiley had been brought from the sea. The moment they'd set the litter down before the royal bed the slaves crawfished out of sight.

But the crowd had grown. As Dixon looked about him he judged that there must have been five or six hundred of the giants—none of them less than ten feet tall, dark and hairy, muscled like wrestlers but swift and silent on their big bare feet.

The crowd formed a packed crescent—the royal couch between the horns of the crescent and Dixon and Wiley, still on their litter, in the middle, the curtains drawn back.

Wiley was all in—Dixon was afraid Wiley was going to die—but Wiley lay still and made no complaint.

Seeing which, Ola-lo, having heard the story, finally pulled himself up from his bed, where he'd been sitting, and got to his feet. Towering high. Scornful. Cruel as a hawk. He put out his right foot and tried to stir Wiley to a sign of life.

So far, Dixon had remained at a crouch on the litter. He'd been fearing some such move as this. He'd seen what they did to one of their own who was wounded.

"Stop it!" he said to the king, and he'd come up to his feet with his hand in his shirt.

He stood there bloody and ragged with his feet apart looking up at this king of the Great Ones. The two of them looked at each other, Wiley on the litter between them.

Wiley made a sharp effort and came to his elbow.

"And not even a gun!" he gasped.

"Okay, Wiley," said Dixon gently.

But the king never winced. He'd lost interest in Wiley. He was keeping his black eyes on Dixon.

Neither did Dixon wince. Nor make a move. He was set for an attack, and his hand still on that weapon of his under his ragged and dirty shirt. But he spoke.

"Hold on! Hold on!"—slowly, not very loud, as if he'd been speaking to a tiger that had him cornered.

He was cornered, all right—with Wiley helpless at his feet, his ship and his crew back there somewhere on that unholy lake, and no telling how many murderous brutes—human and subhuman—ready to blot out his expedition. BACK HOME THE newspapers had called him crazy. Was he? He must have been. But so far as that was concerned it had always been crazy, too, for men even to put out in flimsy boats to kill a whale.

The thought was still riding him when Ola-lo put out a big hand with his fingers crooked.

Dixon drew the weapon from his shirt. The arrow head made an ugly poniard—a foot-long blade, barbed on one side and on the other side a cutting edge. The ringed socket into which the shaft had been fitted was long enough for a hilt.

Now Dixon backed around a little. He didn't want Wiley to be trampled. But Wiley was already dragging himself out of it. Wiley somehow shuffled to his feet and staggered toward the royal couch.

It was just as Dixon caught a finger of that outstretched hand and jerked it to his side with a pressure that almost threw the giant chief off his balance. At the same moment Dixon had brought the point of his poniard against the bare breast of the colossus.

All these events were slipping by in a haze of speed. But here was one of those poised seconds when the whole world hangs in the balance—so it seemed; the measureless interval between life and death.

CHAPTER IX

FREE FOR ALL

"EASE UP OR I'll kill you," Dixon said. His words came swift and soft.

You would have said that Ola-lo got his meaning. In any case, he got the meaning of that grip on his finger and the touch of the point against his breast. He gave a sort of cough and jerked back—all of him—as if he'd been stung. Then he let out a grunting, rolling call, laughing a little as if what had just happened was a joke—but with a whine of poison in that laugh that told Dixon that his troubles were but fairly started.

At the call of the big chief there was a hustling and a shuffling somewhere back in the mob, and one of the giants who'd been standing in the background pushed through. Or was pushed.

He was as big as the others, but there was something more human in his face. He looked puzzled, baffled. He rolled his eyes and almost smiled. He seemed slow to understand what was wanted of him. He brought his eyes at last to Dixon.

There'd been no delay in Dixon's understanding. The meaning of it all struck Dixon's brain as clear as a command in the navy—in code, perhaps, but unmistakable.

The king was ordering this newcomer to kill or get himself killed. Dixon had seen the same look in the eyes of a bull—the first and last time he'd ever watched a bull fight.

This fighting bull of a giant wasn't afraid. He simply didn't want to kill—or be killed. His preoccupation was somewhere else.

There came a guarded jeering then a more open jeering note, from the huddle of giants. The mocking commands of Ola-lo grew louder.

Suddenly, as if by a flash of blinding light, Dixon himself hurled himself into action. But it wasn't at the newcomer he directed his attack. He'd sprung at the king himself.

His move was so unexpected, so tigerish in its concentrated speed and purpose, that he'd caught the king of the giants a jagged gash in the side almost before anyone else but Ola-lo himself knew what was meant.

BUT OLA-LO HIMSELF had seen what was coming all right. He'd flailed a parrying blow at Dixon that was like the swing of an elephant's trunk. And the fight would have ended right there—with the king the winner—if Dixon hadn't dodged even as he lunged.

The impetus of his attack had brought him close in. The swing of that bludgeon of an arm caught him into a strangling embrace. While he was still hugged like that—panting out his own life with every glinting second lost—he kept on stabbing, cutting.

In the midst of it all he could feel a blind hand groping for his eyes—the fingers of the hands like the claws of a cave bear.

Dixon went into a momentary eclipse of darkness. This was death. It was almost the peace of death. There was an escape from pain—from memory. THEN SUDDENLY, HE was fighting again. His throat and his face were free. He still had his dagger in his hand. It was such a thing as his own people had called "the golden harpoon." Back in America! It had become the symbol of his race.

A fresh tide of strength surged through him. He'd thrust his left hand under the shaggy chin and plunged the dagger into Ola-lo's throat.

Even as he did this he knew he was under the shadow of instant death.

Nothing had stopped. Everything was happening at once.

At the moment of Dixon's attack, Ola-lo had bawled a roaring scream. The echo of it still filled the air—stirring up other turmoil—setting loose an avalanche of clamor.

One giant quicker than another had plunged over to help his chief. As he did so, Ben Wiley was suddenly alive and on his knees. He'd found on the royal couch a sword like a scimitar—a yard of curving blade and razor-edged. With the last ounce of strength that remained to him he swung this with a two-handed blow.

It was as if the blade had gone through everything as it caught the charging giant under an arm. Together they rolled—Ben Wiley and the giant together.

Another giant was there—too late to save his king but as full of murder as a falling wall.

Dixon jerked back, bringing out his dagger from the king's throat. He was so drowned in blood that the enemy must have taken him, Dixon, for the corpse—killed by the king. It was a mistake—swift as light—that caused his loss. Dixon stabbed again, then went to the floor and brought the edge of his weapon across the straining tendon of a giant heel. He stabbed this second Moloch as he fell.

Three Hokay killed—including the king of them all; but this wasn't going to save the two lone Americans. It might mean the death of all hands even now. Dixon knew the temper of Doc Harris and those others on the *Golden Harpoon*. They'd be out searching—or fighting— sticking it out in any case, until none of them lived.

Dixon was at the bottom of a slaughter pen, it seemed. Ben Wiley was there with him. Under Ben lay that two-handed scimitar. As Dixon reached for it another hand reached down—a hand as wide as two of his together, yet nervous and shapely.

Dixon was about to stab at it when some strange intuition stayed him. Had he found a friend?

THAT PRIMITIVE WHITE savage with the yellow hair and the ivory-colored skin who this day had learned from a stranger—a man no bigger than himself— how to kill a giant, had kept running for a time after he'd left Shale Dixon in the jungle. With him he'd brought that strange message that Dixon had written with the victim's own blood on the square of dinosaur parchment.

There in the depths of the greenery the Yellowhead paused. There was a terror upon him. But it was no ordinary fright. This was the terror of man or beast in the presence of a miracle.

He'd understood, all right, what he was intended to do. The stranger had meant that he was to take this magic inscription of his to that strange huge fish in the Lake of Fire—the metallic fish that had brought the visitors up from the underworld.

Would he dare to do it? Not alone.

After a time, the Yellowhead uttered a curious call. The call was a flutelike note, not very loud, but long sustained. It was a note that would carry far—that would mean much to those who heard it.

The messenger waited. Not for long. There were answering notes. They came from all directions. Then swiftly enough the other Yellowheads who'd heard and answered his call began to appear. They came singly and in couples through the jungle, making no sound as they came.

They squatted on their haunches. The latecomers climbed into trees. They were patient. They stared with their curious, monkey-bright eyes at the thing their comrade held up in his hands. Then, finally, the messenger began to address them.

"Ho!" he began.

And he started to tell how even a Yellowhead could kill a giant.

CHAPTER X

SEALED INSTRUCTIONS

THE SUBMARINE *GOLDEN HARPOON* crawled on across the Lake of Fire—as the name of this sea had been entered in her log. But she was no longer the brave craft that had left New York Harbor to a salute of flags and whistles the better part of a year ago. Her rudder was gone. Her twin propellers were twisted and bent. Her frame was sprung because of the terrific racking she'd undergone.

But she'd kept her fighting spirit.

As she reeled and tacked—trying to find her way in the right direction with nothing but her broken propellers to steer her—she spat fire at those who would complete her wreck and kill the faithful few who'd brought her to this unnamed port.

Scattered about her at various distances was a darting horde of yellow barges. From these barges came an intermittent rain of arrows.

Those surly giants had been quick to learn in some respects.

The forward ends of the barges were now protected with metallic hoods that could turn even a steel-jacketed bullet except at close range. And the archers thus protected had taken to a plunging flight for their heavy arrows.

The hull of the *Golden Harpoon* was beginning to take on the appearance of a porcupine. So far, none of her crew had been struck, but the submarine was doomed.

The sealed instructions had been opened by Doc Harris and read and discussed with the assembled crew. With the passage of the first forty-eight hours since the disappearance of Captain Shale Dixon, it was "Captain" Harris now—Doc was in command.

The sealed instructions had been direct and simple.

They had been prepared for some such emergency as this.

At no time should the general purpose of the expedition be put in danger out of consideration for the welfare of an individual member.

The rule should always be—first the success of the expedition itself, then the safety of the greatest number.

THERE WAS MORE in the same style—all of which, anyway, had been written into their papers as the members of the crew signed on. This wasn't to have been, in any case, a pleasure cruise. It had been a fighting adventure from the start.

The crew of the *Golden Harpoon*

fought on with heavy hearts. But dogged—dogged as the pioneering ancestors of America in covered-wagon days.

Those archers in the yellow barges were like raiding Apaches. The *Golden Harpoon* limped and staggered like a covered wagon.

Word had come up to economize ammunition. There was plenty for ordinary purposes; but the *Golden Harpoon* hadn't been outfitted as a war boat.

Packed away in her compression hull—where every inch of space was priceless—there was ample retreat equipment—if the retreat didn't last too long.

Four hundred miles by ruler to Little America, Byrd's old camp. But the distance might be doubled when it came to climbing mountains, hunting passes, dodging blizzards. And there'd be no supply bases on the way. All they'd have would be what they could carry—on their backs and on two skeleton sledges: tents, guns, Primus lamps, food, extra clothing.

CAPTAIN HARRIS—"DOC" STILL to his comrades—worked through the forty-eight hours mending the hurts that various members of the crew had received in the battle with the dinosaurs.

Now on the upper deck Doc Harris spoke softly to Morris, his second in command. "Jay—for God's sake!—have you thought of a reason for disobeying those sealed instructions?"

Jay Morris shook his head and avoided the chief's eyes.

"Neither have I. There's not a chance in a thousand that Dixon is left alive. If he'd been able to make a truce with these killers they wouldn't have come back at us so quick—"

"Unless he gave them the slip."

"He couldn't have given them the slip with Ben Wiley on his hands."

"Ben may have died."

"If Ben died, Dixon was there when he did pass out—unless he was already dead himself or disabled."

"Doc—Captain, sir—"

"I'm Doc—with half the crew in the sick bay—"

"Let me go out on the scout alone—try to find out what happened."

"I can't afford to lose you. You'd be going out to get yourself murdered. You can't fight a nation of giants—on foot and alone. They'd have you smoked before you were ashore an hour."

MORRIS WAS SILENT. He knew that Doc Harris was right. He also knew what Doc's feelings were about trying to get away—in accordance with those sealed instructions—without some special effort to find and rescue the missing captain and his man.

"I'm with you," Morris said at last, as he turned and faced his superior in command. Neither of them was much beyond college days in the matter of years, but experience had aged them. "What are the final plans?"

"We'll get the vessel to the north shore of the lake and there abandon ship. I'll need you for the landing party. On the shore we'll throw up cover for our wounded—then move on as we can."

It was going to be a fighting retreat at the best—all the way—and in this war there'd be no truce.

Even without the presence of those murderous Goliaths the chances would be that cold and starvation would finish the story once the Valley of Giants was left behind. There was no telling what the Valley of Giants itself would become, once the sun went down and the six months of Polar night began.

The natives of this valley were no ordinary human beings. No ordinary human beings were apt to survive in conditions that permitted these bearded giants and their yellow-headed slaves to survive.

Hour after hour—one twenty-four hour span after another—and forever the sun was there somewhere behind the high curtain of steam that hung and shivered over the center of the Lake of Fire. It was a curtain that stretched away for miles. It was a curtain that merged with the clouds.

Under the fringe of that curtain was the *Golden Harpoon's* only hope for a hiding place—for a little respite from that circling, dashing menace of killer fanatics.

Lying on the sled deck of the *Golden Harpoon,* under an improvised shelter of steel plate, Jay Morris periodically fired and watched. Both his rifle and his binoculars were powerful.

Killer fanatics, all right—those towering, bearded, kilted nightmares of men. They kept themselves under cover but they drove their yellow slaves on under fire.

From the first, Morris had spared the slaves. It was only at the giant archers he shot and made good practice. He'd started to keep score but had stopped at twenty.

Merely twenty made no difference.

Suddenly Morris saw one of the yellow-headed slaves rise and strike the giant archer of his boat a stabbing blow with his metal paddle.

Morris laid his rifle aside and snatched up his binoculars. He wasn't mistaken. There had been some sort of mutiny in one of the barges. One of the yellow-haired crew of slaves had stabbed his giant master.

But Morris wasn't prepared for the revelation that followed.

The leaderless barge was now racing in the direction of the submarine. In the prow stood one of the slaves waving what looked like a flag of truce.

CHAPTER XI

WRIT IN BLOOD

MORRIS HAD SENT a hail down the hatch of the conning tower and Doc Harris was up from below at the double-quick. Quick as he'd been, he was hardly on deck before the barge hauled near with a flash of paddles. Then, suddenly, the barge had stopped and he who held what had looked like a flag of truce was holding up the message that Captain Dixon had written.

"Written in blood!" Doc exclaimed.

"But written! A message from Dixon!"

The barge crept a little closer. Others of the *Golden Harpoon's* crew had come up on deck. There was something like a cheer.

Dixon safe. A word of hope. All of those on deck were now able to read that message scrawled large in red-black letters on the strange square of parchment.

GH CR E 30 M WAIT SIG 48 H AD BEF RET D

The abbreviated message flashed its meaning as clearly as the lights of a semaphore to those on the submarine.

This was the way it ran:

Golden Harpoon: Cruise East thirty miles and there await signal forty-eight hours additional before retreat.

(Signed) Dixon.

Now there was a cheer from the crew of the *Golden Harpoon.*

At the shout, the barge with the messenger in it wavered and was ready to bolt like a frightened walrus. Even that moment of doubt was costly.

Just as the messenger himself—with some quiver of understanding keener than that of his fellows, turned to reassure them—a plunging arrow from a war barge struck him through the shoulder and knocked him overboard.

Morris was into the water and after the wounded native at once. The man was dying when Morris brought him back to the submarine. His companions of the barge had made no effort to save him. But now they watched—with a sort of fascination and an indifference to the danger they themselves were in—as the crew of the submarine assisted rescued and rescuer from the water.

Dying, but the messenger raised a hand. He let out a strangled cry. It was to his fellows he was talking—some dying message of his own. And even to the watching Americans there came some hint of that speech the dying savage made:

"Strike! Strike! Even as I struck! Until no tyrant remains alive!"

They on the submarine who listened and watched could see some change going on behind the ivory masks of the yellow-headed men in the barge. They would be slaves no longer. Better even to die—die as a fighting man—one who had fought for freedom—than to live a slave.

IT HAD BEEN a hint of something of this same thing that had come to Shale Dixon there in the midst of battle on the terrace of the great pyramid in the golden city of Hoa-hoa.

First the revolt of that giant who'd refused to become his executioner—or, at any rate, to obey the orders of the king. And the king now dead of that savage thrust that Dixon had delivered.

It was a further hint that had come to Dixon in the midst of the fighting. Here with red death settling about him and the devoted Wiley at his side, he had found an ally in this self-same giant rebel.

It was the hand of the rebel Goliath who'd reached for the scimitar with

　　THE BEST OF THRILLING ADVENTURES

which Wiley had struck a death blow. And, after that, Dixon had been fighting blindly—blindly as most battles are fought once the words for death and life, fear and courage, have lost their meaning.

It was as if there'd been a sunset after all—a blood-red sunset that would mean the going down of the sun of life. THEN, A SPEEDY night—a fall of darkness—darkness coming down with a roar of thunder as Dixon took a blow on the head that knocked the sight from his eyes and—for all he knew—the life from his brain and heart.

He awoke to a movement of fighting, and the first words he uttered were a call for Wiley.

Wiley's voice came from far away: *"Here!"*

Dixon kept on fighting—or thought he did. He came up to a sitting position, blinking and still wild. And then for more seconds of concentrated struggle, knew that he was down and out. But Wiley was still alive—and so was he.

Dixon found himself in a jungle glade. He couldn't understand what had happened at all. But, gradually, swiftly enough, he was getting his reason back. Sheer will power was helping him to that.

Wiley's voice again. Wiley telling someone to give him water. And on top of that a splash of water across his head and naked shoulders.

Dixon was wide awake. He saw the jungle. In the jungle he saw a half-concealed haze of faces. The faces of Yellowheads, these were, and no unfriendliness in them. Nor friendliness, either, at first glance—the blank stare of animals.

Then, another face. Not Wiley's—the face of a giant.

After his first spasm of fighting reaction, Dixon recognized this face. It was the face of the giant who had taken sides with him after the killing of Ola-lo, the king.

The giant now sat there at a little distance from him. In the giant's hand there was a shell the size of an ordinary washbasin, and the shell was still half-filled with crystal water.

In the giant's face, in any case, there was some recognizable look of friendship.

The giant offered his shell, and Dixon drank.

WILEY WAS THERE, propped up on a sort of makeshift bed a little to one side of the giant.

"The Big Boy's all right, chief," Wiley said. "He brought us here."

"What happened?"

"You were knocked out in the mix-up. Big Boy fought off the mob and got us both away—the three of us on an elephant."

Dixon studied the face of the giant. It was a wild and massive mask—something from the first pages of the Book of Creation about it. So ran Dixon's mind. But in it, just the same, some hint of the later chapters of that book—chapters that would tell of such strange developments in the human animal as friendship, understanding.

A murmur of warning came from the watchful Yellowheads.

CHAPTER XII

THUNDER OF THE GODS

DIXON PULLED HIMSELF together. He was still shaken. But he was on his feet again.

"Where's that elephant?" he asked. It was as if the animal had answered itself—a squeal of pain or rage off in the jungle somewhere, less than a hundred yards away.

So was the friendly giant on his feet, crouched and listening. In his hand he still held that murderous long scimitar that had come from the pyramid home of the king. Some of the Yellowheads now came to the giant and murmured excitedly as they looked away. The giant answered them. Most of the slave people, though, were gone—melting away into the dense green like so many phantoms.

Other elephant notes now sounded through the hothouse thickness of the jungle. The trumpeting came from a dozen directions, as if on command. And then, over this coarser web of sound, an unmistakable blur of rolling, hooting calls in the thick, soft voices of the Goliaths.

"They're hunting us," said Dixon. "They've got us almost surrounded." There was confirmation in the unceasing shifting glance of the bearded giant who had brought them here. The giant was shifting his scimitar, undecided to fight or run, but ready to fight if he had to. And crowded near to the giant now were a number of the Yellowheads, their bright blue eyes showing a gleam of excitement. It was an excitement in which there was both fear and frenzy.

So would these people fight—it flashed on Dixon—if they were properly led.

Dixon thought fast in that crowded moment. The only hope, after all, for any of them, would be to establish contact once more with the submarine.

Meantime, the *Golden Harpoon* herself was in danger. So were all those on board of her.

Through the jungle green, Dixon caught a slant of misty sunlight. It was good as a compass, so far as he was concerned.

He clapped a hand lightly on the shoulder of the crouching giant and gestured for him to pick up Wiley. It was only in the half-second of hesitation that followed on the huge fellow's part that Dixon dared take the scimitar from him.

Maybe this thing called intelligence is a sort of liquid—like water, taking on unexpected power under pressure. And there's no pressure like a sudden danger of death—a pressure that will either paralyze or, just the contrary, step up the hydraulics of an ordinary mental outfit to a power like that of genius.

In any case, those beastlike Yellowheads were suddenly aware that they were men. So it seemed. The giant let Dixon take the scimitar, then, in arms that themselves were like the twin trunks of trained elephants, he lightly lifted Wiley up and swung him as if in a hammock.

"This way!" said Dixon.

That slant of light had given him the direction of the Lake of Fire. Over there, somewhere, they'd find the *Golden Harpoon.*

SO HAD THE *Golden Harpoon* found allies—a growing swarm, as she slowly, crazily kicked her way across the Lake of Fire, fighting every mile and every hour of the way.

That original hunting fleet of the giant archers was back again, and multiplied, so far as anyone could tell in the drift of fog, a hundred times.

The dying harangue of the Yellowhead who'd brought that message from Dixon had had its effect. The crew of the barge had stuck close to the submarine—men like missing links, who still kept all the keenness of perception they'd inherited from their animal ancestors, yet now with a quickening of all that was purely human about them. It was as if these yellow-haired slaves of the giant people had suddenly cast off some hampering bondage on soul as well as body.

THEY WERE FREE. They'd become the associates of what they themselves recognized as free men—men without fear.

These were the first of the allies.

Now, with their peculiar whistling cries, the Yellowheads called in three other masterless barges from the rolling, blood-colored clouds of mist that drifted across the surface of the colored water.

Doc Harris spoke to Morris.

"They'll help us," he said. "They've learned how to strike back."

"We'll need them then," said Morris. "The big brutes know how to use these shifting fog banks like the boys of the Navy use a smoke-screen. That's how they surprised that herd of big lizards—"

"And us!"

"God send dark! I never knew before how I'd miss the night. The sun's hung there in the same place ever since we got here. It'll be hanging there still for the next three months."

"We'll need those three months," said Doc. "We're going to have a long walk ahead of us."

"That's right. We can't take the sub back the way we came."

"And there's no other way to get her out. What's that?"

And Doc had snatched up the binoculars, staring away through the veils of mist. Morris lay ready with his rifle.

"They're massing," said Doc. "They'll try to rush."

"If the fog lifts enough—"

Morris fired. But he was like a man half-blinded by the curling mist. Even as he fired, a flight of arrows came from the invisible archers. A dozen of the Yellowheads in the neighboring barges were struck. They were like animals also in this respect—they could take their pain in silence, meet death without a protest.

"I'll send you help," Dec told Morris. "Hurry them. I've got a plan—to break them up and let Dixon know we're on our way."

Among the retreat equipment of the *Golden Harpoon* was the smashed wreckage of an eighteen-foot boat still lashed to the sled deck of the submarine. But the outboard motor designed for the boat was still intact, stowed below.

There was a shifting of crews in the nearby yellow barges until one of these was free, then to the stern of this Hawley, the engineer, shipped the motor. In the hull of the barge was a long steel box that was heavy and had to be handled with care. From this box there came a strand of insulated wire and this paid out as the barge—with no one in her but her motor churning—finally started off in the direction of the massed fleet of enemy craft.

WHAT HAD HAPPENED? What was going to happen?

The insulated wire spooled off from the *Golden Harpoon* for a hundred fathoms—then half a hundred fathoms more. And by this time the barge which traveled with no one in her was almost lost to view.

Just as the drifting fog was swallowing her from sight, Doc Harris, straining and concentrated at his binoculars, caught a movement of enemy barges closing in about the barge that went alone.

Doc pressed a switch.

There was a gust of thunder.

CHAPTER XIII

THE FIGHTING CHANCE

DIXON HEARD THAT explosion. He recognized something of the nature of it. And it answered a question that was in his mind.

He'd brought his little band—Wiley, giant and Yellowheads—to the gold shore of the Lake of Fire. Gold, all right.

And gold the barge that some of his Yellowheads brought from a hollow that was up the shore a piece.

They were just getting ready to put out when a party of three other giants came running along the misty bank to head them off.

A fight seemed hopeless. Sudden flight was impossible with a delay like this.

But at the sound of that explosion less than a mile away, Dixon was suddenly inflamed as if he himself had received some injection of dynamite.

"Get into the barge," he commanded. And his signs made his meaning clear. Neither was there any questioning of his authority just then.

What was this authority? Ask a den of half-tamed tigers how about it when the animal trainer cracks his whip.

The giant and Wiley were in the barge. The Yellowheads were making ready as if this were one of their regular masters who was commanding them.

Back through the jungle could be heard the crash and squeal of a troop of elephants as the pursuers from the royal city came this way. The chase had never been far off the trail. Not since the pursuit began.

And Dixon held the boat—and held himself—as the three giants stormed close, laughing in their beards, eager to take him alive.

There'd been a triple question in Dixon's mind—to run? to fight? to parley? It was always there, the knowledge that it wasn't of himself alone that he had to think.

But at that muffled shot of thunder from the sea he'd run forward to meet the enemy. He'd taken them by surprise. A thousand times more than Dixon was himself, they'd been surprised by that awesome sound of explosion. The explosion itself had been expanded by a sort of hooting, shrieking chorus from the Lake of Fire that only they could understand.

Wholesale murder was what that hooting must have meant to them— more devil's work by this spawn of the fire pit.

Dixon had swung his scimitar twice before the giants—slow-witted at the best—knew what was coming. They also hooted. They ran.

Dixon was back and into the barge— more captain than ever now. The whole thing had been so quick that the barge was well away from the shore just as a strange rain began to fall—bits of debris—some of which had been boats and gear, some of which had been men.

NO WHITE MAN ever had a stranger crew.

Nor, for that matter, a more willing one. Through a rift of mist and acrid smoke—there'd been five hundred pounds of dynamite on that barge Doc Harris had sent against the enemy— Dixon saw the familiar whaleback of the *Golden Harpoon.*

Almost thirty days had passed—with the *Golden Harpoon* nosed in against the northern shore of the Lake of Fire, and on the shore itself a fortified camp where the sick and injured were getting into shape for more battle and the long trek out of the Valley of Giants.

Waiting too long meant death. Too early a start meant death. The ordeal that lay ahead was going to be one to test the strength of every man.

But a fighting chance. Here there would be no chance at all.

From all parts of the valley—it was circular, with a diameter of two hundred miles—the giants had assembled. The Hokay, the Mighty Ones, as they called themselves. There must have been two or three thousand of them in all. And they were bent on the extermination of the strangers and all those who'd become their friends.

First, the giant who'd taken Dixon's part.

BOLO WAS HIS name. And a haphazard language—half signs, half words—had grown up between him and the crew of the *Golden Harpoon*—particularly with Wiley. Then such Yellowheads as had thrown in their lot with the Americans. These also were slated for destruction.

If—never was there a more gripping "if" in the history of the planet perhaps— the fighting Yellowheads didn't succeed in killing off the Hokay first.

But there was a turn to events that even Wiley—who'd become the interpreter of the expedition—hadn't foreseen.

It was a development that began with a gradual assemblage of strange yellow-headed tribesmen about the camp of the expedition. Thousands of them—all of them armed in their different ways.

Wiley had learned that most of the arms came from some huge grotto that ran off through the mountains to the north. It had been the arsenal—that grotto, it seemed—of a race of higher culture than either the Yellowheads or the Hokay, an ancient race now long extinct. Knives and scimitars, maces and battleaxes, all the thousands and the tens of thousands of arrows or harpoons that had become the Hokay's chief munitions of war and sport.

THE NEWLY ASSEMBLED Yellowheads were peaceful at first. Everyone thought that they'd assembled there for the sole purpose of protecting the crew of the *Golden Harpoon* from the giants.

Then the Yellowheads got to fighting among themselves.

And the truth came out. More than half of that wild army had determined to keep the strangers here among them and to make Dixon their king.

Dixon promulgated an order— whether it was understood or not no one would ever know—that Bolo should be their king. In any case, this merely made matters worse. Bolo now had his followers. So did Dixon. And the curious thing about it was that neither of them wanted the job.

Bolo himself came to Dixon and made this clear. Bolo—all of twelve feet tall when he straightened up—and with an arm and a fist on him that could have knocked out a curly-haired elephant with a single punch, sat crosslegged in front of Dixon and almost wept.

He wanted Dixon to take him along to that country—"beyond the sun and the moon," he called it—from which Dixon and his companions came.

And, after all, why not?

All set for the retreat to begin, and there was a haze of murder in the air like a drift of red fog. The friendly Yellowheads had collected a herd of fifty elephants for the first stages of the retreat.

The *Golden Harpoon* had found her last port. She would have to be abandoned. But the gallant vessel would still serve those she'd already served so well.

Just before the zero hour, the submarine, her engines running, her hatches closed and the Stars and Stripes afloat— but not a soul on board—left the shore and headed away across the Lake of Fire.

Just as she disappeared in the mist, a Hokay float of war barges closed in about her. Then, once more, the Valley of Giants was shaken by a terrific explosion.

"Now!" said Dixon, and the fighting retreat began.

CHAPTER XIV

DEATH GROTTO

FIFTY ELEPHANTS THAT looked like animals from before the flood. Fourteen Americans, some of them with the scratches of dinosaurs down their backs. A drifting horde of naked people with shaggy yellow hair who were probably as much like the early "cave men" of Europe as ever again would be seen alive. And then, in the offing somewhere, under cover of earth steam and a jungle garden in which weird birds screamed and croaked, a race of bearded giants—"tall as trees"—engaged in the ancient miracle play of murder.

The pity of it was, as Doc Harris said, that none of this could be carried out under cover of the night. Barker Smith, the cameraman, gave Doc the laugh.

Barker's only kick was that there was so much fog—that and the fact that he didn't have about forty miles of extra film. Ever since he'd recovered from a head wound he'd got when the *Golden Harpoon* sprang her first leak, Barker had been grinding—giants and golden pyramids, Yellowheads and curly elephants.

Twenty of those elephants in the strange caravan, each with a small pack on its back—a small pack but weighing five hundred pounds; five hundred pounds of gold. The United States of America needed gold. Here went five tons of gold—and, at that, like hauling away so many pebbles from any riverbed.

Gold, all right—gold and platinum. Doc Harris had made sure of that, testing the metal in various ways. And it was on his recommendation that the comrades made a compact to keep the secret of this valley from the world, except from the President himself at Washington.

Otherwise, what would happen to the money standards of the world?

But even gold evaporated as a subject of speculation in the mounting tide of death.

THE TIDE WAS almost a physical thing— like a rising flood from which none could escape—this tide of a feeling that death was in the offing somewhere, gaining strength, ready to splash over and blot out this thing called life.

The fifty elephants smelled it or felt it—as cattle in some countries are said to know in advance when an earthquake's coming. The elephants—shaped like mammoth buffalo except for their trunks and their twisted tusks—would stop every now and then and show a desire to turn back. Or suddenly one of them would raise a trunk and scream like a banshee.

Then, just as they were breaking camp for the second march, and the snow-mountains still six marches away, the party who wanted to keep the strangers among them kidnaped Dixon and tried to carry him off.

Dixon had gone up to an outlying rock pinnacle for an observation, and before he could guess what was doing—there were a thousand strange Yellowheads churning around him, men he'd never seen before. They were silent as ghosts. But as strong as gorillas. It must have been a selected regiment—willing to die, if they had to—willing and able to take it without a cheep.

In a minute, Dixon was fighting again for his life—mauling and kicking. He was as helpless as a fly in a spiderweb— the way they handled him was that soft and overpowering.

He let out a shout.

In a moment there was a squalling battle. He thought at first that it was the giant Bolo who'd come to his aid. Then—it was coming to him in snatches—he saw that the giant who'd loomed among the Yellowheads wasn't Bolo at all, but the big Hokay archer who'd captured him on the day of the fight with the dinosaurs.

The giant must have been out on scout duty and been taken by surprise.

In any case he was armed—with a two-handed sword that must have been fashioned in the days of Adam.

He cut a swath about him—taking cuts and knocks of his own. Then he saw Dixon and rushed him with a bellow. But this time Dixon had something better than an arrowhead. He jerked an automatic. He had time to fire just once—and he wasn't taking a chance on a head shot, either. This was a heart shot. THE RACKET WAS such that Dixon didn't even hear the bark of his own gun. Neither did anyone else. And the bullet made no more of a surface wound than a bramble might have made. Yet a thousand eyes had seen the play—Dixon standing braced but ready to jump and the big Hokay tumbling there in front of him.

It was something else that Dixon saw—confirmation of something he'd glimpsed from the hummock of rock; and that was a cloud of Hokay mounted on elephants bearing down on the battleground from behind a ridge less than a quarter of a mile away.

DIXON SHOUTED A warning to those about him and was on the run. His own fifty elephants were packed and ready. The expedition was on its way again.

Hour after hour—while the sun stood still, or seemed to—the chase and the fighting kept up. This polar day without a sunset except every six months could become a thing of horror. But once more a friendly fog was rolling over the valley from the Lake of Fire.

There was a halt and a council, when the fog got thick enough to serve as cover.

And still under cover of the fog, with Bolo as the guide, the elephant train of the *Golden Harpoon's* expedition ghosted off on another tack. Bolo explained.

But most of his explaining was by means of maps and pictures that he traced on the ground with one of his big fingers.

There was a pass, he said, that led up through the mountains to the north. The Hokay called these mountains the Mountains of the Sun, for the sun was north. And everyone knew now that north was the way that the expedition was headed and there'd be an effort to cut them off at the pass.

It would be better, therefore, Bolo said, to make for—he used a curious phrase that Wiley worked out as meaning either Sleeping Cave or Dead Man's Cave—marked now on the charts (charts that have never been made public) as Death Grotto.

Death Grotto was as good a name as any. With an outer gate of basaltic rock as black as jet; twin columns that went up to about the height and the size of the Empire State Building, New York's (and the world's) champion skyscraper.

Scraped or scarred into these twin funeral peaks was a steep and winding trail. This looked from any distance like a goat track but when you got to it, it proved to be wide enough for the elephants to follow—if they didn't slip.

As Dixon looked at this trail he was glad to think that no enemy had got here first. He could guess what might happen if a stampede should happen on a road like this—broad enough, perhaps, except in places; but steep, slippery as glass, no guard rail or rampart of any kind and as full of twists as a ravelled yarn. Not all imagination. At the bottom of the chasm below this skyscraper trail was a bone-pile that formed a fair-sized hill in itself. Bleached white—dead white against the contrast of the jet black cliffs; the bones of men and beasts who'd fallen or been cast down from that dizzy path.

They were up perhaps to what would have been the fortieth or fiftieth story of any man-made skyscraper when the elephants went into a panic; and Bolo, who was leading, let out a warning scream.

CHAPTER XV

DARK SLAUGHTER

THERE WAS NOTHING to do but go ahead. If a retreat ever got started down that roller coaster of a trail it would have gone out of control like an auto with broken brakes before it had traveled a dozen yards.

Under Dixon's orders they fought the elephants to comparative quiet before any catastrophe happened and started to hobble them against stampede. They began with the equipment carriers. It was just as well they did.

BEFORE THEY'D GOT very far with the task there was a hail of rock and projectiles from above—more as a warning, Dixon guessed, than an actual bombardment, for no one was hit. The enemy up there, whoever he was, meant to turn them back.

That meant Yellowheads, Dixon guessed—they that had wanted him to become their king.

He gave instructions to follow in half an hour—even if he didn't show up—and started on alone.

There was sufficient reason for the order. From the time they'd left the lower levels they'd been in sight of practically the entire valley. And these people—both the Yellowheads and the Hokay—had eyes like condors. There was no use overlooking that. They'd be already closing in for the kill.

There was confirmation of this as Dixon made the next steep turn on an overhanging shelf where the trail made a hairpin loop. It was here like walking the cornice of a skyscraper. And there, looking down to the valley floor he saw what looked like a war of ants and beetles.

The beetles were Hokay and the ants were Yellowheads. And even while he looked, the locked columns, whether battling or in flight, swarmed up the road below and were out of sight.

As Dixon lost sight of the enemy below, he had merely to turn his head to see the enemy above. And right then was when his heart "froze"—like an overheated bearing—and lost a beat or two. It was seconds before he was all right again—playing his wits on the situation.

Those weren't Yellowheads at all who'd come up there first—who were up there now above him, in a position to send him and his elephants and friends to that bleached bone pile down below.

Behind one point of rock he'd seen a bearded face—then another—almost merged with those black cliffs—human scabs deadly to the touch.

He had half an hour's delay to think—to act. But no time to lose. He walked on as if he'd seen nothing. His hand was on his automatic. He'd always been quick on the draw. Any man who isn't, as a matter of fact, had better leave such tools alone.

Eyes alert, he paced along until he knew that for the moment he was out of sight of the watchers above. Then he slipped back, flattened down. He sent over and up one shot, then another, and there were two Hokay tumbling down the cliff—like airmen bailing out without their parachutes.

THEY LOOKED LIKE rags of tar paper as they fell.

But he didn't watch them long. He'd run, hard as he could, until he knew that he was again leaving cover. And there once more he strolled and lingered, pretending to look down—but really looking up.

He sent another brace of the giants to the boneyard. And by that time he'd guessed at least a part of what had happened. These were sentinels that had been set to watch. Ten or a score would have been enough to hold this pass—all other things being equal.

But all other things hadn't been equal. The brains of these giants were perhaps as much as a thousand centuries behind the times. They'd never yet been able to figure out the significance of firearms.

Dixon returned swiftly to the place where he'd left his caravan.

There wasn't a second to spare. Whoever they were—Hokay or Yellowheads, or the two together—that rush of pursuers from below, their presence meant confusion and death.

He'd got a pretty good idea from Bolo as to what lay above. Here, at the head of the trail, the giant cliffs leaned together and formed a sort of inverted crotch—it was a place that would have housed a cathedral, yet with a narrow entrance, there where the trail came in, and another narrow tent-like opening, there where the trail came out on the other side.

But dark.

With his train on the move, Dixon again went on ahead.

Where the cliffs came together it was like the entrance to some tremendous cavern, sure enough—dark and foreboding. Yet, far ahead in the darkness he could see a star of light—looking due north and shining with the sun.

It was like a lighthouse on an unfriendly shore—one that would give him his course.

INTO THE GREAT crevice the trail wound away into the dark.

Just as Dixon entered this place of shadows, he heard a hooting voice. Then, before he could retreat or discover what lay ahead or about him, there was a riot of shouting. And the shouting magnified by a thousand echoes.

A giant form loomed above him in the dusk.

Dixon fired.

As the detonation of that shot joined the racket of shouting, the air itself became a riot as a cloud of huge bats came tumbling and circling about.

In a moment the place was a screaming madhouse.

Dixon himself sang out in a voice that was like a scream:

"All hands!"

And all hands responded.

"Doc Harris!"

"Here!"

"You and Hawley with your heavy rifles block the entrance—"

And he told them how.

Two others were told off to watch the exit. The balance of the crew were sent in support.

DIXON HIMSELF, KEEPING close to the side walls, as he'd ordered the others to do, ran back along the road down through the pass—on and on, until he'd found that place that had reminded him of the cornice of a skyscraper, and there he took up his stand. He hated to do it, but he was adding to the bone pile—under the black cliffs, a thousand feet down; adding to the bone pile—and praying for night, when there wouldn't be any night—not for two months yet.

The next three hours seemed like two months.

For the Yellowheads and the Hokay were jammed together—down shore— and shoving each other over into the abyss—singly, at times, again in squads of twenty and thirty.

All Dixon could do—and that was plenty—was to shoot close and, so far as possible, see that those yellow-haired slaves who'd wanted to make him their king didn't get the worst of it because of their size.

And the Yellowheads would never have guessed, at that, what he'd done for them, except for the fact that about five hundred of them, who'd made their way up and around the cliffs by a way of their own, took him from the rear.

They must have mistaken what he was doing for them. It must have been that way, for they tried to kill him.

CHAPTER XVI

OUT OF THE UNKNOWN

IT WAS THE rush of the last of the Hokay from the covered pass that brought the danger to a head.

While the Yellowheads and the giants were having it out, Dixon threaded his way through the battle. It was like getting caught in a log jam at the moment of a spring freshet.

Only by the grace of God he got through at all. There are moments like that in the life of any man.

Once more he was back in the covered pass—they call it Cathedral Pass now on the secret maps.

In there also there'd been slaughter. But thanks to the orders none of the Americans had been killed. Nor Bolo, the Hokay friend. Although all of them had been in the shadow of death—and taking chances—while the fight was on.

But some of the elephants had fallen.

Dixon had the other elephants haul those monstrous hulks to the opening where the high pass entered the covered way and used them to seal the entrance.

Then, with his diminished caravan he was on his way again—out into that high tangle of peaks and chasms that was the side of the Mountains of the Sun that lay away from the Valley of Giants.

One last look at the valley was granted them—the members of the expedition. It was through a gap in the hills—hills that glistened white in the sun, frozen since a million years. But down there lay that tropic valley—in which the life of a million years ago had been conserved—where a boiling sea was a vast retort for the fabrication of unheeded gold. Would they ever see it again?

Would they ever see their own country again?

The sun was getting low. In a few weeks the long Antarctic night would be closing down upon them. Even now, as they turned their eyes to the north and west—over there where, beyond other unmapped mountains, lay Little America—they could see a sky-filling shiver of black and white where a blizzard raged.

Then, from back of them somewhere, echoed among the hills, there came again that howl they'd come to know and dread—wolflike, but as of wolves like men, men like giants.

The giants, the Hokay, had again taken up the chase. That was their following cry.

Down through the passes from the first great rise of the Mountains of the Sun, Bolo—he of the giants who had been their friend—guided them to that other great hole in the world that may some day become known to the outside world as Death Grotto.

IT WAS, AS Bolo himself had already described it in his dumb and fumbling yet graphic way, the sleeping place of prehistoric generations, the storehouse from which both Hokay and Yellowheads drew their supplies of tools and weapons.

All of gold—gold tempered hard with some alloy of platinum.

It was here that the expedition pulled itself together and prepared for what was to be an even greater battle than any that it had thus far been up against.

That far glimpse they'd had of the world of blizzards would have been reminder enough, had they needed one.

In any case, it had started Bolo on another line of thought.

"Not for me!" he finally made his meaning clear. "Me, Bolo!"—and he waved one of his huge hands to the south—back there where lay the Valley of Giants. That was where he belonged. There he would return. He'd had a vision. He'd had a glimpse of another civilization. He'd go back and try to hammer this into the lives of those about him—Hokay and Yellowhead alike.

Hard to explain how he did it; but he got it over.

So it was here that Bolo turned back, taking most of the curly elephants with him.

The other elephants would still be used a little longer. Then they'd also be sent back. And as no better place was likely to offer, it was here that Dixon decided to cache such gold as they'd brought thus far.

It had been a foolish dream from the start—trying to carry tons of gold along when you're starting on a race for life.

And this was what the next few weeks were going to be—down through those unknown mountains, then up again over other barrier ranges. Held up by blizzards—while strength and provisions declined—when every hour's delay meant less of a chance to reach Little America before the relief ship came and went.

The race was on.

STRAIGHT ON DOWN into blizzard country—while each day the sun withdrew—sinking like a foundered boat—and taking the warmth of life along.

There was one camp where—just in case anything happened—they planted a flag on a spare staff and at the foot of this put down a brief record of some of the things that they'd seen and done.

But they struggled on—against wind and ice—down through a frozen hell.

FOR TWO WEEKS now, the relief ship *Spirit of Columbia* had been fighting gales and increasing ice floes in the Bay of Whales.

There was still no trace of those she'd come to find. There was little hope of finding them anyway.

As the ship worked her way back and forth under the thousand-foot cliffs of ice that here come down to the sea— with other ice threatening from hour to hour to crush her—she'd picked up two melancholy relics of the expedition of the *Golden Harpoon*.

One was a bit of charred wreckage— part of a boat that the lost submarine had carried lashed to her sled deck. The other was a bottle with a message in it telling of a battle with dinosaurs in some boiling nameless sea.

Just as the *Spirit of Columbia* was about to shape her sad course for the long beat back to less savage seas, there was an almost frantic hail from her lookout.

The hail became a complicated cheering. It was a note of jubilation in which the stout ship herself seemed to join as she let out one long blast after another.

Over a high snowcrest fourteen crawling specks had come into view. Fourteen! Not a man lost!

Six hours later the gaunt and hairy specters who were Captain Dixon and his men—fed, warmed, tasting tobacco, feeling again the heartbeat of a world they'd almost lost—began to tell the story of the Valley of Giants.

Brother of the Tong

BY **LIEUT. SCOTT MORGAN**

*Introducing Larry Weston—
American Adventurer in
the Orient—in the First of
a New and Colorful Series
of Fast Action Stories*

THE COLD DAWN which presaged the terrific heat of the day abruptly put the night to flight; and once more in the inevitable cycle of time, the vastnesses of Thibet lay barren and exposed in the light of the morning.

Larry Weston opened his eyes, stretched his aching muscles and glanced around at the bare unclean room where he lay uncomfortably upon a pallet of straw.

He rose and dressed swiftly. Then, crossing the room, he pulled back the hanging skin that covered an aperture in the wall, and stared through the makeshift window toward the rocky mountain that lay to his left.

His gaze traversed its granite heights, and came to rest upon a huge edifice constructed of the same grim rock as the mountain itself, which perched itself precariously upon its rocky heights. Larry Weston sighed.

The slither of slippered feet behind caused him to turn and behold the Cantonese guide who had led him to this remote village in the fastness of the Thibetan mountain country.

"Ah Lee bids good morning," intoned

the Chinese in a sing-song voice. "He brings food."

He set a steaming bowl of rice down upon the floor, and by its side he placed a fragrant jug of tea. Then, with a low salaam, he bowed and was gone.

Larry Weston sighed again as he squatted down native fashion to partake of the food. As he ate, his mind was occupied with the rock-hewn structure at the top of the hill. His single consuming ambition in life was to enter that monastery. For that purpose he had traveled thousands of miles, only to be told by the sentry at its gates that no one save a brother of the Lo Chang Tong was permitted to cross its threshold. So, it was, heartsick and weary, he had descended the hill to this village, where he had remained the night, hoping against hope that something might occur which would gain him entrance into the granite sanctuary at the top of the mountain.

Suddenly his hand held a chunk of fleshy rice poised in midair. For an instant it seemed that his whole body was petrified.

He froze to immobility, essaying a diagnosis of the noise which had just intruded itself into his consciousness.

Then it came again, and now there was no mistaking its source. It was the shrill high scream of a helpless human being in dire distress.

Larry Weston did not hesitate, A moment later, one hundred and eighty pounds of fighting American youth was tearing like a maniac through the scattered village in the direction of the thatched shack from which the scream had come.

Even as he approached the dilapidated building, another cry split the air and rang horribly in his ears. His right hand descended to his hip, and his .38 was in his hand as he jerked aside the dried skins which hung over the doorway and stood, covering the occupants of the room.

As a matter of cold hard fact, the men inside the shack were certainly no less surprised than was Larry Weston at the sight he beheld.

First, here in the mountain regions of Thibet where not two white men passed in a decade, he found himself staring at a group of grim-visaged Caucasians who in turn glared back belligerently.

At the rear of the room, two natives were tied. Obviously they were the rightful occupants of the hut. While in the centre of the room, surrounded by the white men, lay an old Chinese clad in a scanty gray robe. He was tied to a rude bench. And stark horror was reflected in his countenance as he tried to shrink back from a red hot poker which was held in the hands of one of the white men.

Larry frowned. His hand tightened slightly on the butt of his weapon.

"What's this?" he said. "What's going on here?"

A heavy-bearded man detached himself from the group. Anger shone in his eyes but the dominant emotion which gripped him seemed rather amazement at this interruption.

"Who the devil are you?" he demanded. "What are you doing here?"

Larry regarded him imperturbably. "I'll be glad to answer those questions in a minute," he said. "I'd prefer that you answer mine first."

For a moment their eyes met. They stood silent. A low murmur went up from the comrades of the bearded man. At last the latter spoke:

"Mind your own darned business," he said. Then, with deliberate recklessness, he turned his back on Larry's gun, and spoke to his men. "Go ahead, boys, give him the works. We'll get him to open up."

The man with the poker bent forward. The old Chinese priest unleashed another cry that sprang from the heart of a human being undergoing unendurable torture. Larry's voice was hard and metallic as he spoke.

"The first man who touches him dies," he said. "Now stand back all of you."

Despite the bearded man's apparent contempt for Larry, there was something in his tone now that caused them to pause. Then, as they looked at the intruder, they saw a glint in his eyes which somehow compelled them to obey his words. Silently, reluctantly, they backed away from their victim.

Larry spoke again.

"One of you—just one, mind, come forward and untie his bonds. Fast now."

SLOWLY ONE OF them advanced. He took a knife from his belt and slashed the old man free. The Chinese rose from the bench, stretched his cramped muscles and came toward Larry, who became unutterably astounded as the old man spoke in excellent English.

"I thank you, my son," he said. "I was in dire peril."

"Who are you?" said Larry, not removing his gaze from the white men who stood within range of his weapon.

"I am the head priest of Lo Chang. The monastery on the hill that you visited yesterday is my home. With your permission I shall return there. Come to me when you are able, and in my humble way I shall attempt to reward you for the service you have done me here this morning."

The old man made his way slowly from the shack, leaving Larry standing there rather bewilderedly. In the manner of his race, who are laconic to the point of dumbness, the Chinaman had left without even explaining to his rescuer what this mess was all about. Larry realized that his lack of knowledge was a disadvantage. Perhaps, after all, the old man had stolen or in some other way outraged these white men. Though it was hardly logical, he told himself as he looked at the hard faces before him. THE BEARDED MAN stepped forward and spoke again, This time rage and anger distorted his features.

"You dog," he said, "See what your butting in has cost us. But you can't get away with it. You can't hold off the three of us. Come on, boys. Let's get him."

Whatever the vices of the bearded man, cowardice was certainly not among them. Disregarding Larry's weapon, he hurled himself upon his captor. Larry's finger constricted on the trigger. But even as he sprang, the bearded man threw his head down low, and a brace

  THE BEST OF THRILLING ADVENTURES

of steel slugs whistled harmlessly over his head.

Then, in an instant it seemed that the three of them had flung themselves at him. Larry Weston found himself at the bottom of a struggling mass of humanity. Half a dozen hands clutched at the wrist of the hand which held the gun. He felt hot breathing on his face. Grunts and shouts sounded through the shack.

He well realized that his life hung in the balance, that the outcome of this battle would probably decide whether or not he was to see another sunrise. Perhaps it was this thought that suddenly gave to him the superhuman strength momentarily to fling off the bodies that squirmed above him. He rose through the fighting mass, and jerked his whole body spasmodically. For a moment he was free. But yet one set of fingers held his wrist.

He swung his left with all his strength. It landed flush on the point of a squint-eyed individual's jaw. The man dropped. From somewhere a shot rang out, and Larry heard the whining song of a bullet as it sped past his head. The bearded man picked himself up and charged at him.

IT WAS AT this point that Larry Weston decided that, perhaps after all, discretion is the better part of valor. He turned tail and ran like a madman through the doorway.

After came men and bullets. He steered a zigzag course up the road in order to render himself a more difficult target.

He thanked the Fates as he ran that he had been a ten-second man at college. He thanked them that the winding path up the mountain held few straight runs. It weaved and wound, and the intervening rocks granted him effective cover, as the others plowed panting up the mountainside behind him.

Why he had selected this particular route along which to flee, he could not have told. However to return to the shack where he had slept was impossible. His pursuers would have as little scruple about invading that as they had had about taking over the other hut.

Up, up, he went. His lungs were bursting, yet he realized with a certain amount of assurance that the condition of the men behind was no better than his own.

THEN, SUDDENLY, AS he came within a scant half mile of the tremendous rocky temple at the crest of the hill, he saw a sparse gray robed figure scrambling over the rocks with a speed and agility which was remarkable in a man of his age. He came up to the priest to recognize the man whom he had saved below.

The Chinese saw him and regarded him with a bland imperturbability.

"So they follow, my son. Very well, you shall have sanctuary in the temple—come."

Together they made their way toward the tremendous building. From behind two shots clanged into the rocks at their side. They increased their pace. Larry emptied his revolver at a dark object which bobbed up from behind a rock at the rear.

The old priest cried out as they approached, and slowly the gate to the temple swung open. Panting and exhausted the pair of them staggered into the courtyard of the monastery. Slowly the ancient gate closed behind them, barring the murderous march of the men who were on their trail.

The priest waved Larry to a bamboo bench.

"Sit here, my son," he said, "until I send for you."

Larry bowed and threw himself down to a grateful rest as the old man disappeared within the building.

Less than fifteen minutes later, a wizened Chinaman appeared and beckoned Larry within. He followed his guide with a beating heart, and a quickened pulse, down a long stone corridor into a tremendous room whose ceiling was so high that it seemed infinite.

Gathered there were a host of gray robed priests. The man he had saved from the knife came forward. He spoke gravely.

"My son," he said. "I have been told that you desire to see the great Buddha and the pearls of Lo Chang which will last until the world ends. No man who is not of Lo Chang has ever gazed upon them. Yet they tell me that your desire, your purpose is a noble one. You are preparing a tome which will give knowledge to the world. Very well. I, the chief priest of Lo Chang, owe my life to you. I have discussed it with the brothers and we are of a single mind. You shall enter the holy chamber."

LARRY BOWED HIS head reverently. He was so excited that he dared not trust his voice. The old priest continued speaking.

"But," he said, "ere you enter you must swear an oath on your own life. While you are in the Holy Chamber, anything that may happen we shall hold you directly responsible for. No matter what it is. No matter whether or not you control the event, we shall hold you responsible on your life. Do you swear?"

"I swear," said Larry Weston.

The old priest beckoned to a henchman who approached bearing a tremendous book with silver hasps. Larry noticed with a start that it was the Bible.

"You shall swear on the book of your own religion," said the priest.

Larry raised his hand, kissed the book and swore that, on his own life, no harm should come to the holy chamber or its contents while he was in the room.

"Then go," said the old priest. "And go alone. It is not meet and fitting that one of us should enter the holy chamber in the company of one who is not of the faith or the brotherhood. It is the third entrance to the right of the corridor."

Larry bowed again and, with an ill-concealed excitement, walked from the room to the door which the old priest had indicated.

A filmy curtain hung over the doorway. With a trembling hand Larry thrust it aside and peered into a huge gloomy room beyond.

NOW, AT THE age of twenty-six, Larry Weston found himself in possession of something slightly in excess of two million dollars. In addition, he found himself without living relations, without ties and sans those onerous responsibilities which civilization inflicts upon the average man.

Having little taste for dissipation, and no desire at all for those fleshpots of the world at which most young millionaires gather to drink deeply of what they consider life, he was confronted with but one alternative to save him from an existence of sheer and utter boredom.

He must acquire a hobby.

Now, that in itself was not particularly difficult. Because, for the better part of his life—ever since the day he had seen the ancient Buddha in his uncle's library—Larry Weston had evinced an intense interest in the mystic religions of the Orient.

So now that the uncle had died and left to Larry his vast fortune, it was that glamorous subject to which he had turned.

For twelve months he had wandered up and down the plains and hills of Asia; through the mosques and monasteries of the East, drinking deep of the font of knowledge which is almost as old as the world itself.

In his portmanteaus there reposed copious notes which, when collated and set down in order, would furnish a startled scientific world with facts regarding Larry's hobby, which hitherto had been hidden from the civilized world.

Thus is was that for the first twenty-six years of his life Larry Weston had led a quiet sedentary career—a career that in no wise taxed his muscular frame, that in no wise called forth all the resourcefulness within him, that

had asked but little from his brains, his courage, or his morale.

In short, he was a clean-living, well-built normal American youth, who had never been compelled to ask much of himself, who, as a matter of fact, had as little knowledge of what was contained within him as the rest of the world.

He would have been exceedingly jolted and disconcerted no little had he seen what the next year of his life was about to bring forth; had he seen the flaming live or die existence which was in store for him.

AND NOW HE was here. Here in the very chamber where reposed the three pearls of Lo Chang. When the old Brahmin in Benares had at first told him of this, he had considered it one of the innumerable religious legends of the world. But apparently it was true. And his brow clouded for a moment when he realized that those white men who had pursued him must also believe it true. That explained why they had tortured the priest—in order to gain entrance to this very room where Larry now stood. Although for a very different purpose.

With a sense of exultation and triumph, Larry entered the dim chamber. At last he had achieved that which had led him to this barren country. He peered into the room. As his eyes became used to the dusk which pervaded the holy chamber, he made out the figure of a tremendous fat Buddha at the far end of the room. Slowly he made his way toward it.

The ugly god's head towered into the rafters of the room. The thickness of his legs was almost five feet. Larry glanced straight ahead and saw that the left hand of the god was extended, palm upward, and in the centre of the palm, lay three white marbles, whose radiant iridescence glittered even in the murkiness of the chamber.

He could hardly suppress a gasp as he looked at them. Here, then, were the three pearls of Lo Chang—the three pearls whose brilliance could only be impaired when the Gabriel of a totally different religion blew his golden trumpet.

FASCINATED, LARRY STARED at the jewels. The three pearls were almost an inch in diameter. They were absolutely matched. Individually, each was worth a fortune, but the three matched pearls together could never be bought for a king's ransom. Here was the like of which the civilized world had never, and for that matter, *would* never see.

He took a small pad and a pencil from his pockets and made some notes. Carefully he scrutinized the massive, bejeweled idol, his pencil flying over the paper as each detail registered itself upon his eager brain.

So intent was he on his work, that he became totally immersed in it. Time flew by and he was oblivious to it. This was his own discovery. For this, the god of Lo Chang, and its three pearls, scientists and archeologists would praise his name. So intent was he upon his labors that he failed to hear the heavy tread of booted feet nearby he failed to hear an inarticulate scream of alarm from the courtyard.

But when the heavy footfalls sounded loud on the flagging of the holy chamber, he could not help hearing it. He looked up, notebook still in hand, and what he saw caused a cloud of utter bewilderment to mask any trepidation he may have felt.

Charging down upon him, led by the ruffian who had struck the priest, the day before, were a band of white men. Revolvers were in their hands, and a flaming blood lust shone from their eyes. Greed and gluttonous avidity were stamped indelibly on their countenaces.

Larry still stared at these intruders in amazement as they came closer. He had not the slightest idea how these white men had invaded the temple. They ignored him. The leader rushing toward the idol suddenly pointed a grimy finger at the pearls.

"There," he yelled, his voice vibrant with excitement. "There they are!"
THEN IN A flash, understanding came to Larry. How these crooks had gained entrance to the monastery he did not know. But their motive was now quite clear. They were here to steal the pearls—the pearls which he had sworn to be responsible for.

He waited no longer.

With a shout of rage he flung himself at their leader, even as that worthy bent forward to scoop the jewels into his big hands. His right fist crashed against the man's jaw. The man staggered backward.

Furious with rage and disappointment that now perhaps his mission had failed, Larry threw himself upon a second man. Again his right fist shot forward like a piston and found its mark on the other's chin. Then, suddenly he was aware of an upraised revolver butt above his head.

Too late he saw it descending viciously upon his skull. He attempted to duck. Desperately he threw out his hands, essaying to grasp his adversary's coat, to pull him off balance. His fingers just touched the other's clothing above the breast pocket. For a fleeting second his hand came in contact with a small piece of yellow paper which protruded from his assailant's pocket.

ALMOST INSTINCTIVELY HIS fingers closed around it at precisely the same moment that the steel butt of the other man's weapon completed its journey through the air and found its vulnerable human destination.

The last thing of which he was conscious was a small moon-shaped scar on the hand that swung the weapon on him.

Larry heard the dull thud it made as it crashed against his head, heard it objectively as if it was thunder from some distant place. A streak of zigzag lightning ripped before his eyes. His knees crumpled beneath him. And the dimness of the holy chamber suddenly evolved to a blackness darker than a tropic night.

Consciousness returned slowly to the body and mind of Larry Weston. He stirred, then opened his eyes. He blinked in bewilderment as he found himself gazing into the sober, grave faces of half a dozen priests gathered around a rough couch.

They stared at him in utter silence as he gradually oriented himself. Clearness came back to his brain. He raised himself on one elbow.

"What happened?" he asked.

His answer was a bitter flow of Chinese invective from menacing lips bent over him. Then suddenly the speaker stopped talking. His hand appeared above Larry's heart, and held in it was a wicked looking knife with a curved blade.

Then, from the back of the group, a sharp staccato voice spoke a single syllable. The knife became suspended in midair. The group parted, and the sparse gray-robed figure of the priest whom Larry had saved from the bearded man made his way slowly through the group. As he spoke to the white man there was a resigned sadness in his voice.

"My son," he said. "You have failed. The pearls of Lo Chang have been stolen. The brothers hold you to your oath. I, whose life you once saved, regret it. But there is only death left for you."

Now, for the first time, since he had regained consciousness, the full purport of the situation came to Larry's mind. Now he recalled with perfect clarity everything that had happened. His oath, the foray of the crooks, the pearls. He swung himself off the couch and came to his feet.

"Tell me," he said excitedly, "what happened? How did those men get in here?"

"At the gate one of them sent in word that he was your servant, that he must speak to you right away. The sentry came to tell me. He left the gate unguarded. By means of a ladder they swarmed in. They bore firearms. Already three of the brothers are dead. They raided the holy chamber and took the pearls. That is all. But the brothers demand you must die. You vowed it. The brothers are right."

AT THAT PARTICULAR moment the emotions of Larry Weston were inextricably mixed things. But most overwhelming of all was a terrible hatred for the band of crooks who had perpetrated this outrage. He was not afraid of death. It was certainly not fear that held his mind in thrall. Instead he was aware of a terrible desire to revenge himself upon those who had violated the holy chamber for their own predatory purposes, and in so doing had signed his own death warrant.

"Yes," the old priest was saying. "You must die, my son. You must die as we all must die. We are dishonored and death is our only salvation. Prepare yourself, I must strike you down with my own hand."

HE EXTENDED HIS hand, and another priest thrust a knife into his palm. His eyes met Larry's and in that single instant Larry Weston was struck by a flashing, illuminating thought.

"Stay!" he said. "Stay your impatient hand, oh, father. Let me ask the Lo Chang this. Which is more important? Our deaths or the recovery of the pearls of Lo Chang?"

The old man's eyes lit up with a sudden hope, then the momentary gleam died down again and his gaze was dull.

"The recovery of the pearls, of course," he said. "But how can that be done?"

"Listen," said Larry, and the sincerity in his voice flooded the words. "Listen to me. The arm of Lo Chang is long. The tong lives in all the world. They can always strike me down. To leave here is not to escape. If I betray my trust, the Lo Chang may kill me no matter where I am. But let me try. I shall recover the pearls. I shall do it. Give me some time and a chance. Give me three months—a month for each pearl. Then may we all live and the tong be not dishonored."

Hope once again glinted in the old man's eyes. He turned to his comrades and translated rapidly.

A low murmur ran through their ranks as he finished. Then one of the younger priests stepped forward and handed a piece of yellow paper to the chief priest. He spoke a few words. The old priest turned to Larry.

"This was found in your fingers when we found you."

Larry took it. He suddenly remembered the fragment of paper which had protruded from the breast pocket of the man who had knocked him out. Eagerly he opened it. His eyes scanned the writing, and his heart leaped as he read it.

FINAL INSTRUCTIONS FROM
NUMBER ONE:

When the pearls are taken, each of us shall take one. We have more chance for a getaway if we are separated. All China will be on guard to prevent the jewels from leaving the country. Each man shall take whatever means he considers best to get clear. One year from date we shall meet in the Wright Hotel at San Francisco. There we shall divide the spoils. That is all and good luck to us all.

It was then that the whole amazing scheme leaped to Larry's brain. Three men, plus some hired thugs, had come for the pearls of Lo Chang in order that each of the three might take one and escape from a country who would maintain the most stringent guard when the alarm was given.

Further, the three crooks ran no chance of being double-crossed by their comrades. The value of the matched pearls so enhanced the value of each single one, that to run out would cost more money than it would to be on the level.

IN ADDITION THIS knowledge helped Larry tremendously. Here at last was a clue to work on. Rapidly he made known this new development to the old priest, who in turn translated to the brothers of Lo Chang.

When the head priest concluded there was a sudden hum of excited conversation among the gray robed figures. Larry stood still and silent—tense as his life hung in the balance. Finally the head priest turned to him.

"It is well, my son," he said. "You shall have your chance. But first you must be made one of the brothers in order that the great Buddha may help you in your search, without his aid your mission is impossible of fulfillment. Will you become our blood brother? Blood brother to the tong?"

Larry nodded gravely.

"I will," he said, "I shall be your blood brother. I swear allegiance to Lo Chang." THE OLD PRIEST rolled up his voluminous sleeves. With the knife which he still held, he gashed a cut in his arm. He took Larry's hand. Again the knife bit deep, this time into the white man's flesh. Then the priest held the two arms together, yellow and white. Their blood flowed in unison, intermingled.

"Now," said the priest, "you are a Lo Chang. Go and return when you have recovered our pearls. Three months we grant. Go, But first take this."

He thrust a yellow jade ring on Larry's finger.

"That is the summons to the tong. No matter where you are. No matter what far lands you traverse in your search, the sight of this ring will bring to you the Lo Changs anywhere. Now go, my brother, and may the great Buddha crown your efforts with glory and success."

Larry bowed and walked slowly from the room. The gates of the monastery opened and closed behind him. He had entered the temple free and untrammeled—a white man. He had left, bound by his most solemn oath to fulfill a mission, his Caucasian birthright behind him. For now he owed his allegiance to Lo Chang.

He was brother to the tong!

THE LONGEST BAR in the world at Hongkong was crowded with humanity representing every nationality on the face of the globe. Groups chattered volubly over their drinks, but at the far end of the bar a lone, silent figure stood meditatively regarding a glass of beer.

At last Larry Weston took another sip of his drink and muttered a silent prayer to the fates to grant him a modicum of luck. He had come to Hongkong as the town offering him the best chance to catch up one of the looters of the temple treasure.

For some hours now he had stood in the bar. It was more of fact than legend that if one waited here long enough every white man in China was bound to pass sooner or later.

But tonight that axiom seemed due to fail. He sighed wearily, and had made up his mind to return to his hotel when his roving eyes fell on something which galvanized his whole being into alertness.

That something was nothing more than a man's hand with a moon-shaped scar on the wrist.

But Larry Weston had seen that scar before.

He had seen it in the holy chamber of the Lo Chang monastery. And the wrist that bore it had been descending rapidly in the general direction of his own skull. It was the hand of the man who had knocked him out with the revolver butt.

He glanced across the room at the man's face. He was short, swarthy and stocky. Beneath his khaki coat and breeches he appeared a man of tremendous strength.

He was alone, and before him were four empty whisky glasses. He picked up a fifth, tossed it down his gullet, paid his reckoning and turned from the bar. A few moments later a rickshaw was bearing him through the narrow streets of Hongkong—and less than fifty feet away a second rickshaw carried Larry Weston fast on the trail of the first pearl which belonged to the Lo Chang.

The first rickshaw came to a stop before a cheap bungalow-type hotel on the outskirts of the city. The stocky man descended and disappeared into the building. Larry clambered down from his vehicle, tipped the runner liberally and made his way slowly toward the one-story building.

He did not enter the lobby, however. Instead he stealthily made his way around the building. His keen eyes peered carefully through the latticed blinds of the lighted rooms. Then as he gained the rear of the building, he found what he was looking for.

The stocky man stood in the center of the room drinking from a bottle. In a moment he replaced the bottle on a table, and with a cunning glance about him, he withdrew a wallet from his inner pocket. HE THRUST HIS forefinger and thumb within and withdrew a marblelike object which he held up to the light, admiring its pristine, gleaming beauty. Even Larry could not refrain from giving vent to a gasp of admiration as he saw the iridescent glittering of the gorgeous pearl of Lo Chang in the light of the room.

However, he reflected, there was little time now for meditating over the beauty of the jewel. This was the time for action.

His right hand sought and found the automatic at his hip. Holding it firmly, he raised the lattice with his left hand so silently that the man inside the room did not hear him. His little beady eyes remained intent on the pearl, avidly

Larry's right fist crashed against the bearded man's jaw.

drinking in its lustre. "Put up your hands," said Larry Weston.

The stocky man's face turned white. His head swerved around quickly. He essayed to conceal the pearl in the palm of his hand.

"Don't bother trying to hide it," said Larry. "I know it's there. In fact, it's what I came for."

The other snarled.

"You dog! How did you find me? How did—?"

Larry smiled grimly and vaulted over the window sill.

"In the same manner that I intend to find the remainder of your cutthroat crew," he replied. "Now hand over that pearl, friend."

"The hell I will."

Larry moved the muzzle of the automatic a trifle so that it pointed directly at the man's heart.

I'VE COME FOR that pearl," he said, and his voice was jagged ice, "It matters little to me whether you give it to me or whether I take it from the lifeless hand of your corpse. Now what's the answer?"

With a trembling hand the stocky man extended the priceless white marble toward his captor.

"All right," he said. "You win this time. But I'll get that back if I have to track you all over Hongkong. And you'll pay for this in blood."

Larry took the pearl.

"I can stand your threats," he said, "And if you do find me, I assure you that I'll be ready for you."

Hastily he backed to the window, dropped over the sill and raced to the street looking for a rickshaw.

He had no fear of the other, but he realized that if he was followed there would probably be trouble and he had no desire to let the native police in on the little deal concerning the pearls of La Chang.

He sprang into a rickshaw at the corner and realized as they sped down the street that a stocky man had emerged from the hotel and was screaming in bad Chinese for a similar conveyance.

LARRY WESTON'S BAGS were packed in his room. He sat in the dining room of his hotel sipping a cup of breakfast coffee preparatory to his departure. His heart was light and he was elated at his initial success in his venture. In his vest pocket there reposed the first of the pearls that he had dedicated his life to recovering. He ordered a second cup of coffee. His hand had just stretched forth toward the sugar bowl when he became aware of a disheveled, panting figure opposite him. The man's hand was in his coat pocket.

"Well," said a harsh voice. "I've found you. Don't move. You're covered. The slightest piece of funny business on your part and that's the end."

Larry stared into the eyes of the stocky man from whom he had recovered the pearl the night before. He assumed a jaunty nonchalance which he was far from feeling.

"So," he said, "you really did find me. A pretty tribute to your persistency."

"No funny business," snarled the other. "I've been to every hotel in Hongkong looking for you. Now I've got you."

"And what," inquired Larry mildly, "are you going to do with me?"

"I'm going to get that pearl back."

"But I haven't got it."

"You're lying. You've had no chance to dispose of it. The banks haven't opened yet, so it's not in a safe deposit box. You certainly wouldn't trust a thing like that to the Chinese mails. No, Mr. Wise Guy. It's either on your person or in your baggage and you're coming with me while I find out. Come on now, we're going to your room."

The silhouette of the muzzle of a .38 appeared from his coat pocket. Larry rose slowly to his feet.

"All right," he said. "You leave me little choice." He turned to a waiter who hovered nearby. "Oh, by the way, I must go with my friend for a moment. Leave my coffee there. I'll be back soon, and I like it better if it's cooled off."

IN LARRY'S ROOM the stocky man ripped his luggage apart with a dexterous left hand while he kept Larry covered with the right. At last with clothes and papers strewing the floor, he gave up that angle of the search. "Well, it's not there. Now let's go through your pockets."

His fingers ran through Larry's clothes, but still the gleaming pearl was not forthcoming. Finally he stood back and regarded his captive with smoldering eyes. "You rat," he said. "Now come clean or I'll drill you. Where is it?"

"I told you I haven't got it. Isn't that enough?"

"No," snapped the other. "It isn't.

Now, I'll tell you what I'm going to do. I'll count three, if you haven't talked by then I'll plug you. I owe you that anyway, whether I find the pearl or not. Now get ready."

Larry surveyed him calmly enough, though his heart was pounding madly within him. His eyes were glued to the muzzle of the automatic as he calculated his chances. The stocky man's voice sounded dully in his ears. "One. Two. Thr—"

Well, it was now or never.

With a swinging side motion of his body Larry ducked low. As he moved, his right hand fell to his hip pocket. Even as the weapon of the stocky man barked twice, Larry's own gun belched forth its message. The stocky man reeled and fell to the floor.

Larry thrust his gun in his pocket and swiftly bent over the figure of the dead man.

Deftly his fingers ran through the luckless man's papers. Then at last he smiled, and selecting a large sheet of foolscap, replaced the others in the man's coat.

Carefully he read the typewritten words on the sheet. On it were the names and addresses of a number of men. And Larry Weston felt full well that among these were the names of the men that he must see in order to recover at first hand the pearls of Lo Chang.

JAUNTILY LARRY WALKED back to the restaurant. He noticed that his coffee still remained on the table. He seated himself and drank the now cool beverage down.

Then with a quiet smile, he dipped his spoon into the cup and scooped up something from the bottom. His smile grew broader as he regarded the contents of the spoon.

For there, coated with wet sugar was the pearl of Lo Chang, exhumed from its hiding place at the bottom of a cup of coffee where he had dropped it with the sugar as his enemy sat across the table from him.

It was one of Fate's simple ironies that the thing to which he had pledged his life should have been saved by a child's trick of palmistry.

But as he replaced the invaluable jewel in his pocket, he realized that this was not the end. Somewhere, scattered over the face of the globe were two more of these pearls, two more that he must retrieve ere he could fulfill his oath—and he realized full well that the recovery of the others might not be as easy as this.

Guerrilla Brand

BY JACKSON COLE

Moments Packed With Peril in an Exciting Struggle Against Desperate Mexican Bandits

"COLD HANDS FROM a cold deck—but they're hot tamales, eh?" cried Rory McCrory, his blazing hazel eyes boring into the smoldering black-opal eyes in the mahogany face across the table. "Let me corral all the cockeyed chips till I get excited, and then you call 'em all back to Poppa! Cold decks in the sleeves, in the pants, in the boots! Reckon that half-bushel hat o' yours is full of 'em! But you can't kid a red-headed McCrory—not all the time!"

The swart face of the Mexican, three-quarters Indian, had scarcely changed, but its deep-set eyes glowed like coals. He shifted the gaudy serape that was draped over his right shoulder, and uncovered the hilt of the bowie knife which rested handily in the folds of the rainbow sash about his ample waist.

He could chuck that knife, Rory knew, right into a man's heart or neck, as swift and sure as an arrow. Or he could stick or slash with it, right across the narrow table, with the deft hand of a butcher.

With calm, cool insolence the Mexican lifted the bottle of *tequila* and poured a drink for himself. Rory had sampled and rejected the liquor, saying that it would be better in the gas tank of his car.

"Pick up your cards!" Rory said sharply. "You got what you wanted, didn't you? What is it this time, a royal flush?"

"I AM—WHAT YOU call—a gentleman!" the Mexican bandit announced haughtily. "I am a general of the Revolution! And you would say, then, that I cheat, *Señor?*"

He leaned back from the table as he spoke, and hooked the thumb of his right hand into a fold of the sash, close to the hilt of the knife.

Rory's right hand was itching to reach for the .45 Bisley Colt in the holster on his right hip, but he knew Mexicans—especially when they were dark red with Indian blood.

The bandit was a big fellow, getting fat from heavy eating and drinking, but his kind had inherited the craft and cunning, and the lightning quickness of motion of the Plumed Serpent.

Rory had no chance to work his holster into position for a jerk that would fetch the gun out blazing; he might even fumble the draw in a fatal split second; but that gleaming knife was ready, resting loosely in the sash, and it would flash out like the fangs of the rattler.

So Rory yawned and shrugged his shoulders.

"Oh, no, you don't cheat, General," he sighed wearily. "You just pick 'em out and hand 'em to yourself—and you don't care who sees you do it. No, that isn't cheating!"

"Yankee pig!" cried the bandit, "you insult General José Maria Bustamante!"

His eyes blazing, he lurched forward across the table in his fury, and the tense hand glided like a snake's head toward the hilt of the knife.

Rory lurched forward, too, and the hand which could not travel fast enough to that holstered gun, traveled in another direction. His clenched fist shot up and out, with muscle and brawn behind it, and hooked the burly Mexican on his jutting lower jaw.

Back he went, as if hit by a sledge hammer—back into his chair. And the chair was hurled back against the wall with a crash. General José Maria Bustamante's hand groped uncertainly for the knife, and his eyes rolled in his head like a dying man's as he tried dazedly to see his assailant and recover his equilibrium.

But now the .45 Bisley Colt was yanked from its holster, with its muzzle trained to blast the heart out of the bandit.

"Grab some air—'way up high!" Rory commanded fiercely. "Make one more move for that pig sticker and I'll blow you higher than Popocatepetl!"

The Mexican's brown hand was on the knife, and he was gathering his scattered senses together by sheer will power, but the Colt was so big and so close that courage flopped, and the hands shot into the air.

RORY REACHED ACROSS the table and plucked the knife from the sash with his left hand, then frisked his captive and took a seven-inch barreled .38, all nickel and ivory, from a shoulder holster under the velveteen bolero jacket.

"Yankee coyote!" muttered José. "Always the double-cross. You come to this inn for eat and drink—you make friends with me—and then the double-cross!

"But you make for yourself suicide!" he added with a cunning gleam in his eye. "All alone, you pull the seex-gun on the general of the Revolution. You attack the ar-r-r-rmy of the Revolution!"

"Yes, I know you're a big shot, José," Rory chuckled. "General Bustamante, horse thief and field marshal of guerrillas! But your army is a long way off, José, and we're stopping here in this nice, quiet little village. You start anything now, and I'll be making you just a historical guy for folks to read about.

"I'm arresting you as a plain, lowdown horse thief, and I'm going to take you down to Durango, to the police. I trailed you from Nazas this morning, and I didn't see anything of your army or your Revolution. This is the first news broadcast I've heard about your cock-eyed revolution."

"YOU WILL HEAR plenty!" growled the general, with ominous dignity. "All Durango—all Chihauhua!—the people will rise—they *are* rising! I shall be president!"

He heaved a sigh of weariness and eased his strained arms by letting them sag at the shoulders.

"Keep 'em up!" snapped the American. "The presidential candidate is charged with horse stealing, so the revolution is off. Forty-four yearling polo ponies, run off William McCrory's hacienda!"

"It is war!" José declared proudly. "Ponies are needed for the cavalry of the Revolution. I am the general, so I requisition the ponies for my ar-r-rmy. Be careful, *Señor,* how you speak of horse stealing to one who shall be the president!"

"I've got the general and the horse thief!" said Rory, "and I'm perfectly satisfied. And you—you old fox!—reported in Sonora this morning, traveling north!"

"*Quien sabe?* Perhaps I *am* in Sonora," said José, with a grin of savage humor.

"Perhaps you are," said Rory; "I've heard about your black magic—or yellow magic! All you 'breeds look alike, anyhow. They say Pancho Villa had half a dozen ringers. He could be in Mexico City, and lead a border raid up north the same day. My brother, *Señor* William McCrory, didn't fall for the Sonora alibi, however, and he's looking for you right now with a troop of *rurales.* I was headed for his hacienda when I spotted you riding out of Nazas."

"And you came all the way to this inn to play the treacherous trick upon me—to take me by surprise!"

"I don't like to make mistakes," said Rory. "I didn't want to drag you to the police at Durango, and then find that I had nabbed some poor village *caballero.* I knew you would crow, like any gamecock if I gave you a little time. And you did, José! Already you've crowed about stealing the ponies, and you've built up the whole case for the prosecution."

"You do not like to make mistakes, *Señor,* but you have made one!"

Bustamante remarked portentously. "You think I am your prisoner? You think I have fear of you and your se-ex-gun?

"Ha, ha! I laugh at you! Two guns and my knife you have—yet you are *my* prisoner! To escape from the dungeon of San de Ulloa, that would be more easy, *Señor,* than for you to escape from me here."

ALL RIGHT, I can laugh, too, José," said Rory. "You are a funny guy! Do you get all your dreams from mescal and *tequila,* or do you hit the poppy pipe? You are all alone with me in this peaceful little pueblo, yet you're still seeing armies an' things—and I reckon you get a kick out of it. Trouble is, the rural guard is just as hard boiled with a *hombre* for dreaming he has an army as they would be if he had one."

José laughed, and the grin that was left on his face was wolfish.

"Wait and see, amigo! You are the brother of *Señor* William McCrory. He is rich. I shall take the big ransom, if I permit you to live. But I shall put my brand upon you, you Yankee maverick!—*the brand of the guerrilla,* General José Maria Bustamante y Robredo!"

He clapped his hands, and a Mexican peon of doubtful age came to the door of the room, and halted with a nervous start as he saw Rory's gun. His face was wrinkled and weatherbeaten, but his blue-black Indian hair, bobbed at the neck, was without a trace of gray.

RORY OBSERVED HIM alertly, watching for signs of hostility, and discovered that he had no ears. The straight, coarse hair hung close to the head, over scars where the ears had been.

"Excellencia!" muttered the man, bobbing his head in a salute to José, then continued to regard Rory with a dull, but apprehensive eye, as a dog might watch a man with a whip.

"Pedro, attend me!" the bandit said grandly. "I will give orders to the men of the pueblo. You shall take them for me."

"Si, Señor—Excellencia!"

"You observe, *Señor* McCrory," José murmured suavely, "that my faithful Pedro is branded. He committed a crime, and he is branded that all men may know of his crime. He disobeyed my orders, and he was branded. Now he is a faithful servant, and he will never disobey another command.

"My brand, you will see, *Señor,* is not easy to change. It is better than the brand of the hot iron, for it cannot be changed by a double-cross, like the brand on a maverick's hide. You can only change my brand by cutting off the head, *Señor* McCrory. A man's ears are not easy to put back."

Pedro stood waiting.

"Go!" said Bustamante. "Give orders to all the pueblo, that men and horses shall be ready for my command when the moon rises. We ride tonight to the fine hacienda, where there are more good horses—and much meat and wine also."

"Come, José!" Rory said impatiently, "we've got to be shoving off. The only hacienda you are riding to is the calaboose at Nazas, and then the court at Durango. You've got a fine imagination, and you're pretty well hopped up on *tequila;* but you can't bluff me with your tales about cropping ears and commanding armies and things."

"Wait and see!" muttered Bustamante ominously. "The Revolution, it has commenced. There will be no rich men, no more big haciendas. Your brother comes to Mexico to have a great range for his horses and cattle, and the *vaquero* of Durango gets not so much pay as the cowboy of Texas. Your brother is *caballero,* an oppressor of the poor; I shall divide his hacienda among the peons, also his horses and his money.

"Your brother, then, and you also, I shall brand with the guerrilla's brand!"

THE PUEBLO WAS little more than a single street of stone and adobe houses with palm-thatched roofs. As in nearly all Mexican villages of that class, there was little activity around the houses in the heat of the day. Children and goats were in the street, but the men and women were resting and keeping cool.

Now, all at once, however, Rory looked out the window, and saw with surprise that men were crowding into the street.

"Get up, José!" Rory said sharply. "It's time for us to start along. I'm not afraid that any one will stop me, but I don't want to be bothered with any public meetings, and I don't want to hear you make any more speeches."

Heavy boots grated on the adobe floor of the inn, and José's dark face expanded in a grin of savage delight and triumph.

"To me! *compañeros!*" he cried fiercely, starting up. "Seize this gringo!"

Rory sprang back to the wall, facing the door, and kept his gun leveled upon his prisoner.

THERE WAS NO rush in answer to the bandit's call for help, but five men came into the room adjoining the small dining room.

They peered furtively at Rory through the doorway, muttering together sullenly.

Rory's sharp eyes caught a sudden movement in the group and the flash of metal.

He whipped his gun around and fired, and there was a wild yell in the other room, and a helter-skelter retreat from the doorway.

At the same instant José Bustamante lunged forward recklessly, and the table between the two men crashed against Rory's legs.

Rory fired as he fell, but the plunge forward spoiled his aim. He saw José reaching for him, and, at close grips, he crashed the gun down upon the bandit's head.

The weight of the Bisley Colt and the force of the blow crumpled the steeple crown of the Mexican sombrero, and José's two hundred pounds went down with a thud of dead weight upon the adobe floor.

A gun flashed and popped in the other room, and the bullet flicked Rory's thick hair and singed his scalp.

He was on his feet, and he vaulted the overturned table, gained the doorway and emptied the Colt at the men who were jammed in the outer vestibule of the inn. All of them shrieked, and one slumped down, the others trampling on the body as they fought to escape.

The American drew back and got José's ivory-handled .38 where it had fallen from the table, and the knife with it, then filled the cylinder of the Bisley with cartridges. All was quiet at the moment, and he had twelve cartridges ready for business, and cold steel if the battle were brought to close quarters.

The bandit leader lay huddled by the table, breathing stertorously now, puffing out his thick lips at every snort. A man who has had a heavy Colt bent over his head, as they put it in Texas, is likely to remain "out" for some time, and Rory gave all his attention to his immediate situation. He turned the oblong table on end, with the top toward the door, to serve as a fortification. The top was formed of a one-inch oak plank, and would resist any sort of ordnance likely to be found in the village.

The small dining room had two other tables similar in design, and he turned them over and ranged them, with the first, making an effective breastwork.

As he stepped back to consider the setup, a gun roared like a cannon in the other room, and buckshot peppered the tables and the whitewashed wall.

HE SPRANG FORWARD and let go with the Colt, and dropped another man as there was another stampede of foes through the vestibule.

For a moment he considered tying José up with his rawhide boot laces, but the gaudy rainbow-striped serape and sash presented themselves, and he tore the serape into strips and bound its owner securely hand and foot.

José was groaning now, showing more signs of returning consciousness, but Rory rolled him along the floor and arranged his bulky form in front of the table tops.

"Hey! you *hombres* out there!" he shouted at the unseen enemy outside. "Here's a target for you. You can't miss it! Give us another load of buckshot, and you'll bag a general—*Excellencia* General José Maria Bustamante y Robredo. Now, blaze away, you yellow-livered coyotes!"

DARKNESS HAD FALLEN on the inn of the pueblo in the valley, and Rory McCrory sat on a chair back of his barricade with the Colt in his hand, listening to the guttural swearing of José Bustamante.

Pale light came in through the one unglazed window of the room from a first-quarter moon, and the same light faintly illuminated the adjoining room. There was a dirty oil lamp within Rory's reach, but he did not light it, as it would be of greater benefit to the enemy than to him.

José had been fully conscious for two hours, and now Rory had serious thoughts of gagging him. The bandit chief raved continually. He appealed piously to his favorite saint in one breath, for life and liberty, then filled his lungs to pour forth blasphemous curses upon all mankind.

At intervals he complained, whimpering plaintively, that his skull was fractured and he was dying, but there was strength and vigor in his voice, and Rory mocked him contemptuously.

"Dog of a gringo!" he howled in fury, "turn me loose, and you too shall be free! I swear you shall be free!

"You have the word of honor of José Bustamante. Come! Let me loose, before I am paralyzed!

"Ah, my poor legs are dead to the hips! Set me free, *Señor* McCrory, and—I take my oath!—we shall part as good friends. Believe me, I am magnanimous! I have a soft heart! Better for any man, that I should be his friend. You will never regret the truce!

"But refuse to liberate me!" he thundered, dropping his voice an octave, "and you shall curse the day of your nativity! Listen to me, gringo! That is my oath! You cannot escape, whatever happens. Here we have you, treacherous coyote! caught like a *javelino* in a pit. Fool that you are, you are only prolonging your agony and making the fate that awaits you a thousand times worse for every minute of delay.

"Listen well, Yankee booby! pig! toad!" he yelled, the voice soaring again to shrill treble, "you shall be made to surrender, and then—then! A-h-h-h! the brand of the guerrilla! It shall be a double brand, a triple brand! With my own knife I shall carve your face as the sculptor carves his clay. The ears—I shall slice them with my knife!—as one carves the wings from the roasted turkey.

"The nose!—yes, that impudent nose of yours shall be next. A fine sight you shall be, for all to behold. To kill you, you reptile!—No! that would be tender mercy. I shall turn you loose, when the carving is done. That will be justice!

"Women will faint at the sight of you! Little children will shriek and run away! Men will turn pale, but they will mock you and spit upon you! 'He was the vile and treacherous enemy of the great José Bustamante,' they will say, 'and justice has been done!' "

"Hooey! Boloney!" Rory chuckled softly. "Viva Bustamante!"

José shrieked in his wild fury and floundered helplessly on the floor, groaning and straining to break his bonds.

All about the inn his henchmen whispered and chattered furtively, but none came into the adjoining room within range of Rory's gun.

The bar of moonlight left the white wall and streaked along the floor. Soon the moon would pass over the inn, and the room would be left in darkness.

Rory considered the situation, and decided that darkness would afford the foe too much advantage. He would light the lamp and place it so that it would cast some light across the other room. HE WAS TIRED and hungry, and his throat was parched, but he planned to hold the fort against all odds till morning. His hope of escape was based upon the probable movements of his brother and the posse of the rural guard, and the likelihood of their return to Nazas through the little pueblo. Failing to find Bustamante in western Durango, they would scarcely prolong the search and cross the Sinaloa border; and the road to Nazas would be the logical route for their return.

If they did not come—well, that would be another problem for another day. He had plenty of ammunition for the sort of skirmishing he had done,

and he felt no great respect for the intelligence of the enemy or the rough tactics of guerrilla warfare.

Suddenly the room was thrown into darkness. Something had been thrust into the deep embrasure of the window to shut out the light.

Rory held his gun ready, aimed at the doorway, and looked anxiously about. The moonlight was gone from the other room, too. The enemy had blocked both windows, evidently in preparation for an attack.

"There's going to be a battle now, General," he said to José, "and believe me, you are in a tough spot!"

José struggled and yelled, threatening his friends with his wrath, then begging them to be careful.

Meanwhile Rory lighted the oil lamp and placed it at one end of the barricade, where its rays would reach the outer room.

The men outside the house were still at work on the windows, and by the light of the lamp Rory saw that a large pad of palm matting had been stuffed into the opening. They were poking it, jamming it farther through the embrasure, and as an experiment he fired one shot from José's .38 into the wad of matting.

Jeers answered the shot, and the poking was continued. Apparently the men were using poles, and their actions were vaguely mystifying. The light was effectually cut off, if that were their object, but they seemed intent on making a thorough job of blocking the opening substantially, and Rory could not guess at a reasonable explanation.

"What are they doing, General?" he inquired of his prisoner.

"You shall see!" hissed the helpless captive, unwilling to admit ignorance. "You are not dealing with fools, gringo!"

I'M TELLING YOU, General, we're both in a tough spot! I'm no tenderfoot in Mexico, you know; I know your country and your people from Sonora to Yucatan. Give me three guesses, and I'll guess three times that *you* are out, José. Down and out! Your Mexicans love a change, and want it every few minutes. They're sick of your raving and yelling, and they've elected a new leader. Does that make sense?"

The bandit cursed him for the suggestion.

"All right! *You* wait and see!" chuckled Rory, driving the captive to fresh raving.

José took a breath after a series of spasms, and issued orders in a shrill, cracked voice. He commanded his men to come in boldly and rescue him. He ordered a charge, over Rory's fortifications, and a swift termination of the siege. If men must die, he intimated, they would die in a noble cause. His immediate rescue was imperative, he declared, whatever the cost might be.

THE RESPONSE WAS silence—an eloquent silence, heavy with significance.

Rory laughed aloud, and his ridicule drove the bandit to the verge of madness, and made the night hideous with his outcries.

All at once Rory snapped to attention with a gun in each hand.

"Listen!" he snapped sharply to José. "Damn you! will you shut up and be quiet?"

The howls ceased abruptly, for José was quick to take fresh alarm.

A low grating noise came from the other room. It sounded as if something were being pushed along the sanded floor.

Rory thrust the .38 into his belt, and with his left hand picked up the lamp and raised it above the edge of the barricade.

At first he could see nothing unusual, but the grating rasp on the adobe continued; then something moved into his field of vision.

In a moment he made out the form of the object, and knew instantly its significance. It was a copper brazier as large as a sugar boiler, mounted on a massive iron standard—the primitive heating equipment of the Spanish colonials, and still in use in many Mexican houses.

Pale blue wisps of smoke rose from the brazier, and he knew that a damper had been fitted over the charcoal embers, and that the dangerous gas was already being generated in the room.

Long poles were used to push the brazier to a position in the center of that room, and presently the poles were withdrawn, and a door slammed and was fastened from outside with a bar.

Rory advanced from his stronghold and reconnoitered with caution. Peering around the door casing, he viewed the closed door, and was not surprised to discover a hole in the upper panel at least two inches in diameter.

He advanced a foot and scraped it on the rough floor, as if he were walking into the room, and instantly there was movement outside. He drew back swiftly, and a gun roared through the peephole and showered the room and the brazier with buckshot.

He was not surprised at that. The besiegers were using the tactics of simple common sense, anticipating his logical actions.

The smell of the gas was already strong in the inner room, and Bustamante coughed, and began to whine and rave.

Rory cast about him for ways of meeting the danger, but there was no water in the room, and nothing with which he could reach the brazier.

TO TEST THE enemy's alertness, he moved a chair across the threshold, and another burst of buckshot rained upon it. Then he picked up the chair and hurled it at the brazier with all his strength.

The heavy iron standard tipped at the shock, then righted itself, but the lighter copper bowl was dislodged, and it crashed on the floor, scattering charcoal embers and ashes all around.

Near the iron base, however, was lodged a mass of glowing coals, and spirals of opal vapor wound upward and spread out on the still air in thin veils.

José suffered a violent paroxysm of coughing. He wheezed and choked, gasping for breath, and suddenly he relaxed and seemed to lose consciousness.

Rory tried to think, but he felt dizzy. The light seemed to be growing dim, or else it was obscured by the thickening vapor.

HE TOOK A step forward but felt himself sway drunkenly. Then, desperate, he charged into the other room, blundered against the door, and fired three shots from the Colt through the peephole.

He heard startled cries, then the shuffling of feet; and then he heard nothing more.

Some time during a prolonged period of mental darkness, Rory McCrory either dreamed in feverish delirium or actually sensed that he was being held by strong hands and bound with rough cords. In the dream, or in actual fact, he resisted and struggled against his captors, straining his muscles to break the harsh bonds and escape.

When he returned to full consciousness he was still in the room in the tavern; it was broad daylight and the matting had been withdrawn from the windows, having served its purpose in the process of asphyxiation.

And, in sequence with the dimly remembered delirium, he was bound fast to a chair; his ankles lashed to the front legs of it, and his cut and bleeding wrists bound by cords which passed under the seat.

He was very ill, feverish, nauseated and giddy, but he pulled himself together for a fresh ordeal, and grew interested as he saw José Bustamante before him, not exactly hale and hearty, but on his feet and still able to talk and harangue the multitude.

"Behold! He lives again!" cried the general to a dozen peons that were in the room. "It was not for nothing, then, that I was spared, in spite of your treacherous attempt on my life—pigs and vipers! It was written that I should live to meet this man again!"

"My general, we must leave the pueblo, and now!" said a sober, anxious villager. "The *rurales* were quartered last night at a hacienda three hours' ride from here. They may come!"

Bustamante silenced him with a regal gesture, and rushed suddenly upon Rory.

His eyes were filled with hate.

"Ha! Little rat!" he cried, "do you know, then, that I saved your worthless life last night? More dead than alive, I fought valiantly against these fools who would have butchered you like a pig.

"And why?" he thundered dramatically. "Why should I lift one finger to spare such a wretch? It was because my word was spoken. Whatever I promise, whatever I declare to be my will—that thing must be fulfilled, if I live."

RORY SET HIS teeth and steeled himself against a shudder as the bandit slowly drew from his belt the knife which had figured in their encounter of the day before.

"Think twice, general," he said huskily, his eyes never wavering as he looked the man in the eye. "The Mexican law is hard on a half-breed bandit, and international relations are involved."

"Bah!" exclaimed José, drunk with the sense of power and vengeance, "if I were to die in the next moment, I would do this duty! The maverick is to be branded, and the branding iron is mine!"

Grinning grotesquely, he flashed the bright blade in front of Rory's eyes, then with a tip of a finger he lightly touched the top of his right ear.

"The right one first," he chortled fiendishly.

Rory's heart was pounding, and he felt dazed. He saw the grinning face and the bright knife in a lurid haze, and then he saw his own prized Bisley Colt sticking in the torturer's belt.

HE STRAINED AT his bonds desperately, but quietly, and he made no outcry. The cords cut into his scarified flesh, but he was able to turn his wrists. In that dream, or in fact, he had strained against his captors' efforts to bind him, and in doing so he had expanded his muscles. Now the muscles were relaxed, and the cords did not bind so tightly.

Through the film over his burning eye he saw the knife flash, and then he tore his right wrist loose, stripping the skin from it.

In the space of a lightning flash, he jerked the Colt from Bustamante's belt and pressed the trigger with his almost senseless forefinger. In the flash and the explosion Bustamante seemed to fade out of his vision, but blindly he pressed the trigger again and again, and the faces of yelling, wild-eyed men swam in the mist before him.

He heard, in the general delirium, a new sound, outside the house, on the road, and then someone shrieked:

"The *rurales!* The police! They are here!"

He settled back then, relaxing, striving to clear his mind and readjust himself to the maze of events.

Then men stormed into the room

with heavy boots and clinking spurs, and he saw them; but they were not *rurales*—they were *vaqueros* of the plains, and a villainous lot by every sign.

Suddenly the face of Bustamante rose again before him.

"What's this?" cried Bustamante sharply, "and *who* are you?"

"*You* should ask!" said Rory faintly. "For that matter, who are *you?*"

"I am José Bustamante!" said the other proudly, and Rory then noticed with amazement that he wore a Stetson hat and modern well-sprung riding breeches.

"Oh, yes," murmured Rory. "All right, I suppose you *are* José Bustamante, but—how many of him are there? Are you twins?—or are there more than that?—triplets—quadruplets—"

"There is but one," said the man with dignity. "It is my misfortune that there are reptiles who resemble me. Even Pancho Villa was impersonated by treacherous jackals who betrayed his confidence. Now, I have been betrayed by a locoed 'breed, and I am humiliated and disgraced.

"I have heard a report of the man's treachery," he went on, "and now you shall see how I deal with vermin who take my name in vain."

HE MADE A sign to his men, and drew a gleaming Cuban *machete* from a scabbard at his side.

"You shall see, Americano," he said, "how elegantly the keen *machete* can administer the guerrilla brand to one who fails in his loyalty to me!"

The man who had been Rory's captive and captor was dragged forward, struggling and shrieking, and he was bleeding from a wound in the side made by Rory's gun.

A vaquero had cut Rory's bonds, and he suddenly staggered to his feet.

"No, no, *Señor* Bustamante!" he said to the new leader. "This man is my prisoner. I have my duty, you see, to turn him over to the authorities at Durango. I protest, as an American citizen, against any outrage like the guerrilla brand, and I demand the custody of this fellow."

"The saints will bless you, noble young man!" cried the bogus Bustamante.

"General! The *rurales!*—they are upon us!" shouted a frantic *vaquero;* and José Maria Bustamante, the bandit general, turned with tragic dignity and listened to the thunder of iron-shod hoofs on the highway.

"Well, then, so be it!" he said coldly. "I am not a woman to turn pale at the sound of hoofbeats. Present my compliments to the captain of the *rurales.*"

Soldiers of the rural guard came clanking into the inn, and William McCrory, ranchman and polo player, rushed upon the dazed Rory with yells of relief and joy.

"Thank God we were in time, old boy!" he cried.

"Sure, it's fine!" Rory exclaimed, "but I'm a little groggy with all this excitement. It seems—well, I've been saved so many times, I can't get the whole thing straight."

"You've been the means of capturing

José Bustamante," said his brother, "and now I may get my ponies back."

"Yes, I know," said Rory, "but this new José Bustamante never took your ponies. I have the confession of the other one, who has been prancing around the State of Durango in the guise of José Bustamante, and we'll be finding the ponies pretty close to this village.

"The real Bustamante may be wanted by the police, but he saved me before you did, Bill, and I'll have to do all I can for him in court. He's not the sort of a guy that would cut off a white man's ears!"

The Devil Fish

BY **CAPT. KERRY McROBERTS**

Treachery, Peril and Breathless Adventure Stalk the Decks of the Schooner Spindrift in the Region of Dead Man's Isle

FROM WHERE HE leaned against the lee rail of the little auxiliary schooner, *Spindrift,* Lane Yancey studied the rugged line of the distant islands to the north. He watched that far-flung shore-line, strangely fascinated. Like a sleeping snake it lay outstretched along the edge of the horizon, deadly and still. A sleek, fat snake, gorged with cankerous, gangrened blood of lost and forgotten men. The terrible penal settlement of New Caledonia—to which only the most desperate of French criminals are banished!

He pictured the sweltering plantations where condemned murderers and degenerate felons worked out their endless sentences, the unfathomable forests where stark, watchful natives lurked in the shadows of the trackless jungles, the barrier of shark-infested reefs that barred escape by way of the open sea—

Suddenly his eyes tensed, narrowed against the blinding glare of the calm, still waters.

"What do you make of that, skipper?" he called to the bronzed, broad-shouldered man at the wheel on the little bridge just above him. He pointed to the northwest where the gray land mass merged into haze at the edge of the Coral Sea.

"Looks like a piece of wreckage!" he added.

Jerry Desmond—Captain Jerry to the members of his little crew—turned quickly, peered in the direction indicated. Glass in hand, he intently surveyed the distant object lying low in the water. "Huh!" he grunted. Swung the wheel hard over.

"What do you make of it?" Yancey repeated.

THE SKIPPER SHOOK his head gravely. "Dead men, looks like to me," he announced. "They're generally dead, Yance—when we pick 'em up in the sea like this."

Yancey was on the bridge by now. He took the telescope from the skipper's hand, glued it to his eye. He saw the object was a raft, very small —across which two almost naked men lay sprawled.

"Two poor devils who've tried to escape from the convict settlements," Desmond surmised. "They often put out to sea without sufficient food and water—and die like this."

He rang for half speed ahead, then for the engines to be stopped. Shortly they drew alongside the raft with its lifeless burden.

The crew of Tahitian boys clustered at the starboard rail. Pete Randall, the second officer, threw a rope over the side. One of the crew slipped down, stepped gingerly onto the raft. He grabbed one of the men, shook him,

knelt closer, shouted out something in his native tongue.

"They're still alive" the skipper exclaimed.

He called down to Randall: "Get 'em on board—quick as you can. We'll try savin' the poor devils."

Yancey stared hard at the pitiful bundles that lay stretched out on deck a few minutes later under the shade of a deck awning tended by Jack Duval, the half-caste bo'swain.

Contrasting types they were. One strong-muscled, hulking, massive— built like a gorilla. The thick black beard he wore, and the hair on every part of his visible body, made him look more like an ape than a man. The other was obviously of a better breed—tall, slim, firm-muscled.

The beast-like one recovered first. He drank greedily of the water offered him. Glazed eyes cleared as he looked about him, saw the deck of the schooner. He said nothing—only stared dumbly at the limp form of his companion still lying unconscious beside him.

"Where do you two hail from?" the skipper snapped sharply.

The man only grunted. Jack Duval asked him the same question in French. Even then he gave no answer.

THE OTHER WAS coming round now. He moved slightly, lifted his head. Smiled feebly as his eyes met those of Yancey.

"Bonjour, m'sieurs!" he said slowly, thanking the men about him—"Je vous remercie!" The words edged out through dry, swollen lips.

"That's all right," Yancey said cheerily.

He pointed to the ape-like man at the other's side. "Can't your partner speak?" he asked.

"Ah, Anglais!" the man exclaimed. Then he broke into almost perfect English. "I must make my thanks for your so timely arrival. Water, it is finish. We almost finish, too. I—" he glanced up into the bronzed features of Captain Desmond. "Where are we, M'sieur Capitan?"

"If you came from the convict settlement," the skipper replied sternly, "you haven't come far. There's the island over there."

The man raised himself on one elbow, gazed at the distant shore.

"But we are not escaped convicts," he smiled grimly. "You mistake, M'sieur Capitan. We are from the schooner *Rapanui*—got away from the wreck three days ago, after that so terrible storm. This"—he pointed to the hairy man at his side—"is by name Pierre Gaspard, one of our seamen. I myself was first officer of the *Rapanui*. My name is Antoine Latouche. You must not think we are escaped convicts. Eh, Pierre?"

THE OTHER NODDED. "Oui," he growled, watching his companion's lips.

The skipper grunted. "H'm!" he observed. He had noticed the marks of the leg irons on their ankles and knew they were lying. "However, I'll give you the benefit of the doubt," he said. "There's a reward offered for the return of escaped convicts—but I want no such blood money."

Latouche's face lighted up. He staggered to his feet. "You are a ver' kind man, M'sieur Capitan," he bowed. "Merci!—we thank you greatly."

"The bo'swain will give you some clothing," the skipper concluded. He had not the heart to send these poor brutes back to the misery of their island prison. "You will lend a hand with the crew when needed, When we arrive at Brisbane, if you two get ashore without my seeing you, well and good. If not— well, I'll have to report you. Understand?"

Latouche nodded. "I understand," he said. *"Oui,"* agreed the other. Duval took the two new arrivals down below as the captain ordered. They were to be under his care for the rest of the trip. Desmond put the bows of the *Spindrift* back on to her course. It had been just another incident in the day's work.

As the little schooner headed across the changeless ocean, Yancey stood at the rail and watched the distant islands fade into the murk of the tropic twilight. The island of the dead—of the dead-alive!

Since the day six weeks before, when he had accepted the invitation of his old friend Captain Jerry to accompany him on one of his periodical tours of the trade stations in the Fijis and New Hebrides, never had Yancey experienced such a feeling of awe and dread as now surged through him. Until today the South Seas had held only glamor and beauty, the charm and mystery of perfumed isles, exotic and alluring. Now, there was a new note in the air, a discordant harmony.

Somehow—since the two fugitive criminals had been brought aboard—the ship seemed different. That horrible, beastly grin on the face of the animal-like man below. The crafty, smile-masked eyes of Antoine Latouche. The ghastly prison's deadening hand had seared them both with its loathsome mark, poor wretches!

CHAPTER II

FOR TWO DAYS the *Spindrift* plowed her way across the Southern sea. Gaspard and Latouche had settled down to the routine life of the schooner. The third night, Yancey had relieved the skipper for a spell at the wheel, as had been his custom. It was a moonless night, but the sky was ablaze with stars.

He heard voices and looked back to see a tall, slim shadow in conversation with Randall, the first officer, who stood on the bridge behind him, silhouetted against the rail at the head of the companionway. It was not one of the Tahitians. The skipper was below in his bunk. It could only be Antoine Latouche.

What was he doing on deck?

When he looked again, Latouche had gone. Randall was alone. Yancey gave no further thought to the incident.

An hour went past. The first officer was not now in sight. A short, squat figure suddenly loomed up beside Yancey. It was Jack Duval.

"I'm takin' over now," the half-caste announced abruptly.

"You're what?" Yancey snapped. "What's the big idea? The skipper takes over after me. Who told you to take this trick?"

THE TONE IN the bo'swain's voice was firm. "Orders," he said simply. "I'm takin' over—that's enough." As he spoke he glanced quickly over Yancey's shoulder. Yancey turned quickly. But he was not quick enough. Two great hands flashed out of the shadow of the binnacle, jerked him suddenly away from the wheel. Duval shouldered in, grasped the wheel firmly, swung the schooner sharply about on her course.

Taken by surprise by the sudden maneuver, it was some seconds before Yancey could recover his balance. He had recognized his assailant as Pierre Gaspard, the silent, brooding convict with the ape-like build. With all his available strength behind the blow he struck out straight into the brutish face before him.

But the powerful blow provoked nothing but a grunt. Hairy, steel-muscled arms reached forward, circled Yancey's body. He was powerless in their crushing embrace. Slowly he was being lifted high into the air—was being rushed to the side of the rail. His breath was leaving him. He could not struggle free from the monster's death-grip.

Why?—What?—His brain was swirling madly—

He felt himself being held poised in the air above the rail—had the vague impression that the powerful muscles were tensing for that final effort to heave him far out over the side of the vessel,

like a useless burden, into the dark depths beyond—

A sharp, commanding voice stayed the mad rush of the murderous beast.

"None o' that! No killing! I said no killing, you—!"

Yancey recognized the voice—Pete Randall's. The first officer held an ugly revolver in his hand. His eyes gleaming like pinpoints, he had bounded to Yancey's side. The beast-man uttered no sound—but slowly he set down his burden, obedient to the imperative voice and the threat of the menacing revolver.

As Yancey felt his feet on the firm deck again, he did his utmost to wriggle free. A great hairy hand took him around the throat, almost choked the life from him. With his last despairing breath he called out to the first officer:

"Good God, Randall—make him—let me go! I'm—"

But Randall seemed not to have heard. He was calling loudly for Latouche. Gun in hand Latouche quickly appeared— yelled to his brutish companion:

"No killing! You hear! Take him down below, as I told you—throw him in with the skipper."

BREATHLESS, FAINT, YANCEY was carried forcibly below by the husky giant. The door slammed, was bolted shut from the outside. He turned to see the skipper wriggling to free himself from the ropes that bound him.

"What's all this about?" Yancey inquired, still breathless.

"It's mutiny—rank mutiny! Quick! get these ropes untied."

"But—Randall; why Randall? He's sailed with you for years."

"I can't understand what's come over him. Something those two murderous devils 've cooked up, I reckon. Every man-jack aboard's against us, Lane. They're at the bottom of everything—the damned wretches."

Things had happened suddenly, he explained. He was dozing in his bunk—had awakened, startled—someone was in the cabin—it was Latouche, the revolver in his hand pointing dead at his heart. Before he realized what was happening, the muscular ape-man pounced on him, held him tight while Latouche bound him fast to his bunk. Then they looted the arms from the gun rack, went out, bolted the door. They were determined, these men. Why? What was afoot? Why had the vessel's course been changed?

THEY WERE NOT to know that night. Early the next morning, the door was unbolted and the two ex-convicts, Pete Randall at their side, came resolutely in, revolvers in hand. The doorway behind them was blocked with members of the Tahitian crew. Randall spoke:

"You're wonderin' what this is all about, Cap'n," he said, haltingly.

"I certainly am," the skipper roared. "I'll see you lose your ticket for this, you mutinous dog! I'll see you in prison, you whelp!"

"Keep your shirt on, Cap'n," Randall said coolly. "I saved your hides last night, both of you. My friends here wanted to heave you over the side—but I prevented 'em. I felt sure you'd listen to reason, Cap'n—an' come in with us on this thing and—"

"What thing?" Desmond barked. "What are you talking about?"

"We're on our way to make our fortunes, Cap'n—an' I rather think you'll want to come in with us. We didn't ask you out'n'out last night because some of us had the idea you wouldn't agree—an' they wouldn't give me the location of the treasure until I'd first captured the ship and turned her about. So—"

"Treasure! What do you mean—treasure?"

"THESE TWO MEN"—RANDALL indicated Gaspard and Latouche—"spent some years in the convict settlements. From time to time men try to escape from there. Most of 'em die at sea—some of 'em get away, picked up by ships like ours; but others neither get picked up nor die.

"They just drift—drift with the tides—to an island they call *Homme Mort,* to the north—one of the rocks in the group marked Huon on the maps. The winds and currents finally carry all floating things, boats and rafts, up there.

"Gaspard here escaped on a raft with two other convicts, about a year ago. The others died. But Gaspard had the good fortune to reach shore—found the men on Dead Man's Island—and the treasure they had discovered there. There are eleven escaped convicts on the island.

"They're waiting for a ship to get away. Gaspard got away—hailed a trade ship one day when he was out fishin'—was picked up. But the captain was after the reward—took him back to the settlements. That was how Latouche got to know about—"

"You mean to say you mutinied just to get a ship to rescue these eleven murderous castaways?" Yancey exclaimed.

"No—not for that," Randall explained. "The treasure, man!" His eyes glistened. "Wedged in a cave, where it was driven by the storms, the convicts found a big sailing vessel—the *Esperance,* about eighty years old. Its hold is packed with bar—gold and bullion—probably a treasure ship returning from the East when it was wrecked. That's the treasure we're after. Pierre says there's enough wealth there to make us rich for life. An' I mean to get mine, no matter if—"

So that was the bait that had been dangled before the officers and crew of the *Spindrift*—that had tempted them to mutiny.

"And your intention is—?" the skipper interrupted, calmly.

"To go to the island, rescue the men, land 'em in some faraway spot—Australia, perhaps. We'll make our own conditions for aiding 'em to escape—a half share of all the treasure, divided between us."

LATOUCHE AGREED. "THAT is the proposition, m'sieur. I was for killing you and your friend here—but Randall he say no! He say you are good skipper—we talk business with you. You come in with us—captain the schooner for us—an' one-fifth of the gold we salvage shall be your own share, personal."

Desmond's voice was thick with rage. "You thought I'd lend myself to a scheme that's going to return eleven blood-thirsty criminals to the world—for the sake of a pile of dirty gold."

To Randall:

"You'll have to take the ship alone. I'll have nothing to do with this. I'll—"

"It's the only chance you'll get," Randall threatened, fingering his revolver. "We're playing fair with you, skipper. We mean to get that gold—whether you come in with us or not."

Latouche snarled impatiently:

"Pah! I told you this cochon was pigheaded. These two will not see sense. Better get them out of the way. There is a quick way to end this talk—once and for all!"

Randall suddenly stepped forward. The fact that Duval and he were the only men aboard who could navigate the *Spindrift* gave them some degree of power over the murderous pair.

"No killing!" he roared. "There's to be no killing!"

Latouche snarled. "You want we let them live—make trouble?"

"They'll make no trouble," Randall said. "That island—it's a mighty lonely place," he leered. "There's men there haven't sighted a ship in more'n ten years, you say. Once you're marooned there, you're stuck for a good long stretch. Well, now—here's an idea, Antoine. When we've taken these friends of yours off—and the gold—we'll dump this pair ashore. Let 'em have the damned island all to themselves. No killing! —an' we'll be easily rid of 'em."

A gleam came in Latouche's eyes. He clapped Randall on the back.

"Bon!" he agreed. "That is ver' good idea." He backed to the door. "Come, mes amis—let us leave." The door was slammed tight, bolted. Yancey and Desmond were left alone once more.

CHAPTER III

DEAD MAN'S ISLE! The two prisoners viewed it through the open porthole. They had been penned in for three days and nights, fed liberally, but never once permitted on deck. It was a rugged-looking island, high in the centre above the frowning cliffs, covered with dense jungle. The vessel lay a half-mile or so outside the reef, her steam siren tooting frantically. One of the ship's boats was threading its way through the reef. It contained Latouche, Duval and four of the Tahitian crew.

The afternoon passed. The evening twilight deepened. Then the ship's boat returned—accompanied by two other boats from shore. That night there was great activity aboard the *Spindrift,* strange voices, quarreling.

Early the next morning, Randall and Latouche opened the cabin door.

"You're a damn fool not to come in on this, skipper," Randall said. He was in high spirits. "The gold's there—they've got some of it out of the wreck. Going to change your mind?"

"No," snapped Desmond. "You yellow-bellied hound!"

Randall laughed. "Then you two'll stay in the cabin till we're ready to leave here—that'll be about two weeks, maybe."

Latouche swaggered up with two pistols in his belt. "They'll be of use to us, mon ami," he grinned. "We'll send them ashore—to help us move the gold down to the boats. We need all the men we can get." Randall nodded approval. "Right. They'll come ashore with us now."

AS THE LONGBOAT neared the inhospitable beach, Yancey and the skipper hunched in the bows, Latouche, Duval and Randall facing them, Gaspard and two of the Tahitians pulling at the oars, Yancey surveyed the strange group at the water's edge waiting their approach. They appeared to be more like beasts than men. They howled and gibbered in several languages as they rushed out and dragged the boat up on the sand.

They were almost naked, with leathery, sun-scorched skins, heavy-bearded jowls, eyes that glared out wildly from beneath tangled, matted hair that hung down over their foreheads. Marooned here for years—many of them. Dead men! Yancey shuddered at the thought that such beings might be free again to roam the civilized world! Beasts; Animals!

Latouche and Gaspard climbed ashore ahead of the others. Tools from the ship were being heaved onto the beach. Yancey felt that every eye was that of a foe as he climbed down from the boat, mingled with the strange horde that had circled Desmond and himself. Pete Randall stood to one side, revolver in hand, looking rather bewildered.

"Let's get to work," Randall called out sharply to Latouche. "Let's get some of that gold stowed on board, right away. We're wasting—"

Latouche turned on him with a lightning gesture. He was smiling a twisted smile. "Sorry, mon ami," he sneered. "You'll never see that gold!"

"I'll never— What!" gasped Randall. Stark fear was in his eyes.

The answer came in a flash from Antoine Latouche's hip, Randall reeled backwards, one hand clutching his breast where the bullet had drilled through, the other vainly trying to pull the trigger with his last despairing flash of energy. He fell forward, sagged to the ground.

Latouche was still smiling. "Your work is finish', M'sieur Randall. Now we have navigators of our own. We need not divide with white-livered scum like you." He wheeled sharply, turned to Yancey and Desmond.

"Your turn now!" he snarled.

The revolver rose level with Captain Desmond's eyes. In a split second the bullet would have stabbed through into the man's brain. But quicker even than the trigger finger of the killer was Lane Yancey. He flashed in under the outstretched arm—caught Latouche about the knees—hurled him backwards. The bullet went high. Instantly, the howling horde rushed forward to their leader's assistance.

YANCEY WAS UP in an instant—just in time to meet a rush from the apeman. He ducked aside like a dancing phantom, drove his fist with all his strength into the centre of the brute's stomach. He glanced toward his companion. Three of the murderous horde were hanging on to the flailing arms of the muscular captain. These human tigers would tear them to pieces.

As Gaspard doubled from the impact of Yancey's stomach punch, Yancey darted to one side—and the third bullet, the bullet which Latouche had meant for him, took one of the others in the chest, dropped him.

A chunk of driftwood lay at Yancey's feet. He seized it, darted between the clawing, clutching beast-men like an elusive halfback, reached the skipper's side just as one of the horde fastened a death-grip around Desmond's neck, from behind. Crash! The man's skull was shattered under the impact of the blow from Yancey's club. The stranglehold was broken. Two lightning blows from Desmond's great fists drove the others back.

"The jungle," Desmond gasped. "It's our only chance!"

Latouche was maneuvering for a position to fire again. Gaspard was up, growling like a maddened beast. A bullet seared Yancey's ear. He turned—poised just long enough to take aim—drove the chunk of driftwood with all his might at Latouche's snarling face.

"That'll stop him shooting for awhile," he said as, followed by the half-naked fiends in human form, screaming like savage beasts, they raced to reach the cover of the tangled, protecting jungle.

CHAPTER IV

BREATHLESS, THEY STUMBLED among the trees. The creepers caught at their feet. Spiny spikes clutched at their clothes. But they did not slacken. The wild beasts behind wanted their blood. Latouche, with bleeding mouth, was driving them on.

The interior of the island sloped sharply upward. That very fact saved their lives. One by one their half-starved pursuers dropped back out of sight. They were out of range of Latouche's questing bullets. The cries died away. Desmond leaned against a palm and panted. Yancey peered back, down into the death-still jungle.

"They'll waste no more time searching for us," he observed. "They'll be too eager to get that gold aboard, I rather imagine. That fiend Latouche! The way he shot Randall down—in cold blood!"

"Pete Randall was a fool to think they'd play him fair," Desmond said. "They only wanted him as navigator. When Latouche found capable seamen among these brutes, it was taps for that yellow traitor."

Yancey said suddenly: "We've got to find that wreck. We may find a way to delay 'em from getting away with the gold—and we'll have more time to do things. Maybe we can get back to the *Spindrift*—get guns and ammunition, and get out of this mess. The old treasure hulk is in a cave somewhere on the north side—where the cliffs are high enough for caves."

THE TWO RESUMED their tramp through the rising jungle. It was the middle of the afternoon before they emerged on the cliffs on the far side, above the water's edge. Yancey pointed down to the sea below. One of the boats from the schooner, with four convicts aboard, was making for the foot of the cliff almost below them. Soon it pulled in, out of sight, When it reappeared two hours later the boat was low in the water. There was a weight amidships.

"The old ship's under the lee of the cliff here," Yancey said. "They're getting the bars out. I'm going to have a look at her."

Desmond gazed down the sheer wall of the cliff. "It's a tough climb, Lane!"

"I'll make it, Jerry—don't worry." He threw off his coat, tightened his belt. "I'll be back before dark," he said, as he swung over the edge.

The first part of the downward climb was easy. But the last sixty feet was almost perpendicular. He clung on by fingers and toes, picked out crevices that gave him a firm foothold, worked his way from projecting rock to scrubby bush—and finally reached the rock-strewn beach below.

It was an isolated beach, cut off by projecting rocks on either side. The only approach was by way of the sea or cliff. Where the beach bent in beneath the cliff, he found the deep, high cave he sought. A dark, shapeless mass dimly showed, wedged beneath the rocky walls. It was the treasure ship. At high tide the cave might be half full of water. But just now the water was not more than a foot or so deep.

 THE BEST OF THRILLING ADVENTURES

YANCEY WORKED HIS way into the cave, found a rusty ladder that gave access to the crumbling deck. The rotting hulk was covered with slimy seaweed. Everything smelled of the sea. Many men had been there before him. Hatchways were ripped up; rotting cargo lay strewn over the foredeck.

Down one of the gloomy hatchways he climbed by way of the rusty iron ladder that still existed. He found himself in a long corridor which had once joined the forepart of the old windjammer with the officers' quarters in the stern. It was getting dark outside, under the cliff.

He took from his shirt pocket a precious box of matches, lighted one, felt his way back along the corridor, struck more matches. Finally he reached what had been the ship's strong room. Under masses of fallen woodwork he saw crumbling boxes wedged in behind the rubbish. A week's work at least, before the convicts could saw through this mass of wreckage. A chance for Desmond and himself, after all.

For some time he rummaged around inside the old hulk. Time to get back up that cliff, now. He fumbled his way along the corridor to the open hatch, was about to mount the ladder—when there came a heavy creaking sound on the deck overhead. It was as though some heavy weight was being hauled across the deck. Had the convicts returned?

The lapping of the waves told him that the water had risen higher about the old hulk since he had come aboard. He would have to swim for it, to reach the foot of the cliff. Even though men were working above, he must risk it. They might not see him, if he took advantage of the darkness.

Stealthily he mounted the ladder, peered over the rim of the hatchway. No one was on deck. The cave was in deep shadow—but Yancey could see that the water was half way up the vessel's side. He edged cautiously toward the crumbling rail of the old hulk—stumbled over something! A thick rope that lay across the slimy planks! Impatiently he kicked if—to move it out of his way. The rope squirmed! Rose in the air!

SHEER HORROR HELD Yancey spellbound. Then a gasp of fear escaped him as he sprang back to escape the loathsome thing that reared quivering before his eyes. A tentacle! Alive!

Swish! Something lashed in from the other side—closed tight about his waist! Thick as a hawser—covered with mouth-like suckers! Yancey strained back with all his might—tore at the thing—was free before it could tighten. The waving tentacles stroked the air—feeling for him.

He sprang back, made for the hatchway. A great squat head with two huge, glowing eyes and a beaklike face appeared over the side of the hulk. Squirming, waving tentacles advanced before it. A giant devil-fish! This cave was the lair of this menacing sea monster.

Hastily he slid down the ladder. Above him the ominous creaking of the crumbling deck gave notice that the slimy monster was now on board the hulk—crouching, feeling, waiting for its prey to come within reach.

There was no escape for him that night. It would be too dark to climb the cliff. He must remain in that creepy old hulk all night, hoping the sea monster would go away with the next ebb tide. He made his way into the treasure room in the stern. It was like spending a night in a grave!

CHAPTER V

THE ENDLESS NIGHT had passed. The lapping of the sea against the side told Yancey the tide had gone down again. Cautiously he crept along the gangway, mounted the ladder, peered over the edge of the hatchway. There was no sign of those loathsome tentacles. The way was clear.

He was about to slip into the shallow water, when a burst of ribald singing crashed in from the sea at the mouth of the cave. One of the boats from the schooner was rounding the jutting rocks. He counted six among the motley crew. He ducked down quickly, crawled backwards to the open hatch. His retreat was again cut off. He must find a hiding place.

The noisy crew boarded the wreck, yelling lustily. Yancey recognized Latouche's voice. Heavy feet clumped down the ladder. Soon the whole gang was at work below, only one remaining on deck to take the heavy bars which the others passed up to him. Yancey concluded that the one above was Gaspard.

An hour passed. Then the boat pulled away from the schooner. Yancey heard Latouche order Gaspard to remain behind—until they returned later. Now to get away. Only the ape-man stood between him and safety.

SLOWLY YANCEY CRAWLED up the ladder. His searching eyes picked out the hulking bulk of the hairy beast-man standing by the crumbling rail far astern, gazing out toward the sea. He edged to the vessel's side, slid down into the shallow water. So far—good! He was halfway to the rocky beach before Gaspard spied him.

The beast-man let out a savage bellow of rage, hurled himself over the side, plowed through to the rocks where his quarry madly scrambled up the first few feet of the almost sheer wall, reached out his ape-like hand.

The clutching fingers closed about Yancey's ankle. With a crash he fell back. The great arms seized him, held him in their steel embrace, dashed him violently to the ground. Claw-like hands were at Yancey's throat—his senses were swaying—his breath was being shut off by those steel fingers! The scene turned red! Lights flashed across his brain! The horrible pressure continued. Then—

He felt the hand being snatched away from his throat—felt the air rush back into his lungs. Through a film he saw Gaspard's face, contorted in horror. The snarling beast was being slowly dragged back—too terrified to struggle against the resistless force which held him!

Yancey's brain cleared. He felt limp with horror! For the ally which had saved him was the hideous sea monster—the giant devil fish!

From the deeper water, twelve feet away, it reared its slimy, bulging body from the sea, supporting itself on unseen legs upon the mud! Two of its tentacles had caught Gaspard around the body from behind. As Yancey watched, a terrible change came over Gaspard's face. Limp as a corpse, he had been dragged halfway towards the parrot-like beak. Now—suddenly awake to his fearful doom—the beast-man went stark, raving mad!

He screamed wildly, braced his feet in the mud, clawed at the scaly tentacles which had him. But he could not squirm free. Other slimy, cup-covered tentacles reached up from beneath the water, coiled about him, held him in their death grip. Yelling like a maddened beast, he was drawn back slowly, far from the shore.

Like a spider entrapping a fly, the horrible monster enmeshed the struggling, raging brute, binding his powerful legs, his steel-muscled arms. Slowly, relentlessly, the hideous creature mastered the writhing man. Then it sank slowly beneath the water, dragging its victim with it.

THE SEA SHUT out the rest of the nightmarish sight. But the thrashing, foaming waves gave evidence of the losing fight the beast-man was making—until the merciful waters drowned him, clutched tight between those dread, crushing tentacles.

Yancey's legs felt weak. To escape! Could he make the grade? It needed all his reserve energy, nerve and resource before he finally reached the top of the cliff. He threw himself on the ground to rest.

From his elevated perch he could see some distance beyond the headland. Suddenly he tensed. There was the boat with Latouche and his crew—pulling madly for the outer reef. Latouche stood in the bow, waving his arms wildly. His companions bent hard at the oars. There was the *Spindrift* where it had been anchored since their arrival.

IT WAS SLOWLY putting out to sea! No sails were set. The auxiliary engines must be in use. Could it be? Had the resourceful skipper regained command of her? He watched the men in the longboat. They seemed as greatly surprised as he. Was he to be marooned here with these human tigers?

The schooner tacked, veered into the wind, stopped with such perfect precision that Yancey knew it could only be Captain Jerry at the wheel. About a mile out she lay, placidly rocking in the slight swells.

Latouche and the men in the boat redoubled their efforts at the oars. The longboat was about four hundred yards from the vessel—when a puff of smoke showed from the deck. The report of the rifle told the convict horde that they were not to be tolerated aboard. Latouche waved his men on, grabbed an oar. One of them had been hit.

Something was fluttering from the mizzen-mast. The recall signal! Yancey strained his eyes. That signal was meant for him! In some way the crafty skipper had regained his ship, was lying off there in the hope that he was watching from the cliff.

He ripped off his shirt, waved it in the breeze. For several minutes he did this. Then one of the crew in Latouche's boat spied him. Shots followed—wild shots. But they had served a purpose. The recall signal dipped in acknowledgment.

He must reach the beach, negotiate that mile swim to the side of the schooner! He put on his shirt, drew back into the jungle. He had seen Latouche signalling to the shore. The longboat was coming in. They would soon be searching for him. Now was his chance or maybe never.

Food and drink were his first problem. A cocoanut palm provided him with both.

Then he began to worm his way down to the shore.

Torn and ragged, he at last emerged on the beach, some distance from the spot where Latouche's boat had landed. It was a longer swim from here, but he could make it. If he was spotted, he would have to trust to luck and his muscles. Captain Jerry and his rifle would take care of his pursuers, once he got under way.

He threw off his shirt and shoes, raced down to the water's edge, was about to dive in—when something struck him flat in the back! He staggered forward, fell to his face. Before he could regain his feet, someone jumped upon him.

Strong hands gripped the back of his neck—drove his face deep into the sand.

"So! Caught you neat and pretty, *mon ami!* Now it won't be long before we get the schooner once again. *Allons!*" he called out gruffly.

IT WAS ANTOINE Latouche. The murderous, half-savage mob swarmed down to join him from the bushes where they had been waiting. But for their leader's interference, they might have torn the prostrate, struggling Yancey to shreds. Latouche screamed wildly at them, his face contorted with rage:

"Back, pig-dogs! Have you the brains of cockroaches? Tie his hands!

"Into the boat with him. We must have that schooner!"

CHAPTER VI

HIS ARMS TIED in front of him, Yancey was pressed down in the bottom of the longboat when they reached it some distance down the beach. Immediately the boat was launched. The men at the oars pulled straight for the silent schooner.

Evidently Captain Desmond had not witnessed the struggle at the water's edge. No doubt he believed Latouche and his crew were going to make another attack. About five hundred yards distant from the vessel the men at the oars stopped rowing. Latouche stood boldly in the bow of the boat, cupped his hands to his mouth. "Ahoy there, M'sieur Captain!" he shouted.

"What do you want, you damned scoundrel?" the skipper roared.

"We want your ship."

"Like hell you do. I'll fill your damned carcasses with lead."

"Mais non! M'sieur Capitan." Two of the men lifted Yancey into sight. "Here—you see?—we have your ver' good friend. You see him alive! Shall I tell you what we do to him—before he dies?" He held his revolver at Yancey's head. "He will not die prettily, *mon capitan!* You will watch us shoot him to little pieces? *Oui?* It is for you to make the choice. His life—or your ship! First will I shoot off one ear—then the nose—then the other ear. You will hear him shriek. *Oui?*"

Yancey gritted his teeth. "Don't give in to him," he yelled.

Latouche smiled. "See—I will make him one ear less."

Searing flame tore close against Yancey's head. He felt a stinging pain in his ear. Warm blood flowed down his face. The lobe of his left ear would always be missing. Captain Desmond reeled back in horror. What must he do? If he gave up the ship, they would both be murdered. As he hesitated, Latouche called out savagely: "Make up your mind—before I shoot off the other ear." He turned to carry out his threat.

AS LATOUCHE TURNED, Yancey—who had been bracing himself between the two human tigers who held him—swerved suddenly to one side. The quick jerk tumbled one of the men overboard into the sea. The gunwale dipped. The next moment they were all in the water. A triangular fin appeared less than a hundred yards away! Shrieks of terror arose from the fear-stricken convicts.

"Sharks! Sharks!" they screamed.

Yancey was as conscious of his peril as anyone. Bound though he was, he still had his legs free. He kicked out—managed to keep above water. Mad yells arose beside him. The swimmers were endeavoring to reach the *Spindrift.* Aboard the vessel there were signs of activity.

A boat was being lowered. Captain Desmond, revolver in hand, stood in the bow, urging the Tahitian rowers on to greater speed. He was risking the loss of his vessel in an endeavor to save the life of his friend. Hands clutched at the boat from all sides. All was mad confusion. A shriek! One of the struggling men disappeared beneath the water, leaving a blood-stained trail behind. A pair of human arms encircled Yancey, dragging him under! It was Latouche who had clutched him, in a last desperate effort to bargain with the skipper.

"Save both of us—or neither!" he screamed to Desmond.

Yancey butted him under the chin, freed himself and burst to the surface. Strong arms seized him, dragged him aboard the lifeboat. Through a forest of waving arms, the fighting skipper pressed back to the schooner's side. He cut Yancey's arms free. Carried him up the ladderway to the deck. Bandaged his ear.

"Now let the murderous devils come aboard—one at a time," he said to the Tahitians, who had finally recovered from their mutinous mood. The terrified convicts were dragged on deck. One by one they were locked in the cabin, the strong door bolted tight. "How many?" he asked, when no more were in sight.

"Five," Yancey reported. "Latouche and one other are missing."

The skipper stared over the side. There was no sign of the convict leader. But there was a disturbance in the water on the portside—as though a struggle was going on below the surface of the water.

"Some shark is making a meal out of the most poisonous criminal I've ever met," he said to Yancey.

HE STROKED HIS chin thoughtfully. "The others—the best place for them is the island. They might as well stay dead—out of harm's way, poor devils. The world will be well rid of 'em, when they finally die off." He warped his vessel in as close to the reef as he dared, drove the five men over the side, watched them swim ashore and rejoin their remaining companions on the beach.

Not until they were far out at sea, bound for Brisbane, were they reminded of the gold bars which Latouche and his crew had already shipped aboard the *Spindrift*—enough, they found, to make them secure for life.

Some day—when the motley, half-starved crew had died away—they might return and salvage the rest of the gold. Until then, the island of dead men could retain its secret. The *Esperance* could continue to rot—watched over by its slimy guardian sea monster and the beast-like horde that had once been men.

Red Silver

BY JACKSON COLE

*An American Mixes It
With Spanish Desperadoes
and Raiding North African
Moors in the Black Sierra*

CHAPTER I

ENEMIES ALL

BUCK CARNEY WAS suddenly wide awake. For ten electric seconds, on raised elbow, he listened intently. His other hand snaked along the floor toward his ready gun.

His keen eyes bored into the ebon night, piercing the shadows of the room. Body tense, he tried to catch again that whisper of sound that had awakened him.

Once again came that hint of stealthy movement. It quivered alert every sense of the straining man who lay in the upper room of the queer inn in the most out-of-the-way spot in all Southern Spain—of Buck Carney to whom peril and danger were the very breath of life.

Buck Carney knew what it was to ride with Death as a stalking companion, but nowhere had he felt its eerie presence more greatly than since his foot had touched Spanish soil. Was its dread presence touching again, with chill fingers, all the hopes that had brought him across mountains and across miles of sea, with a high heart, toward treasure?

There it was again!—that whisper of a sound! A mere tremolo of movement! Ears less well-trained to warn of danger than Carney's would have heard no sound at all.

He softly moved his blanket aside, came up on his knees to a crouch, with gun clasped grimly. The uncurtained window behind him was open to the night. Through it there came a silvery radiance that filled the room with a dim illumination. Slithering across the room, like a shadow, Carney moved out of the moon glow.

He had been sleeping on the floor beneath that window, following the admonition of a soldier of fortune's invaluable sixth sense, that warned him not to occupy the massive bed in the room. Except for hat and boots, he was fully clad.

A faint gleam of another light flickered out of the darkness to meet his eye. It came from below, through a crack in the floor. Carney dropped down, noiselessly, and brought an eye to the crack. Men were in that room below—silent, waiting, ominously black-browed men.

Carney's whisper of recognition of one of them came in a raspingly indrawn breath. *El Lobo!*

The Wolf of the Sierra Morena again! How came he here? And why?

The dread El Lobo, mountain of human sinew, whose very name was spoken in frightened whispers! The man who had honored Buck Carney with his obviously murderous intentions ever since Buck had arrived from America a month ago! The man whose vigilance had made for Buck Carney a death threat around each street corner of Cadiz!

And as suddenly changed. For some reason, as unaccountable as his desire for Carney's death, the Wolf had shown indications of wanting Carney to live. WHY? DID EL Lobo also know of the treasure of Montecristo! Or had he decided that the American adventurer, held captive, would be worth a pretty penny. Even an American without a cent could bring heavy ransom if properly advertised.

It was evident that El Lobo had caught up with him again. Buck hadn't expected successfully to evade the Wolf for any length of time. And he hadn't—for here he—El Lobo—was now at this *Tavern of the Three Snakes* with his band of guerrillas.

Carney knew that he was looking down into the main room of the tavern—without having to recognize his one-eyed host, Don Pancho, who was silently passing around glasses of wine. All the men below were quiet— strangely silent. They must have arrived in silence, or he would have heard them sooner.

CARNEY SAW EL Lobo, with mountain cat litheness, move across the floor and out of sight.

Carney's glance came back to the room and centered of a sudden on the big old cupboard against the wall. *It was swinging noiselessly open!*

From within, a shadowy face appeared—a face Buck Carney would have known anywhere in the world, in shadow or sunshine. El Lobo!

Carney's gun came up and forward, square in the man's, face. He hissed a command for silence. Thank God for his years in Mexico, and his ability to speak Spanish like a native!

Carney caught a glimpse of the cupboard that showed him an open trapdoor.

"Hands up!" his whisper rasped. "And come out of that!"

Just one second too late. El Lobo's hands came up, but at the moment of the raising of one of them a knife whirled and gleamed through the dim moonlight straight at Carney's gun wrist.

Carney's gun roared. His bullet sent El Lobo reeling to a fall. But the handle of the thrown knife—loaded with lead to balance the heavy, five inch blade—caught Carney's wrist. His pistol spun from his hand. The knife sped on and sunk itself into the soft wood of the floor.

For one blind moment, Carney was stunned with pain. But he headed in, dodged and plunged, then he and the murderous El Lobo were locked and rolling in fierce embrace.

It was gouge and strangle while it lasted, but Buck knew what part of the room he meant to reach—or was trying to reach. His gun was lost, under the bed somewhere. But there was the knife that had whizzed by him and stuck into the floor!

In a few minutes' tense struggling, he had jerked and jolted the battle to where he could reach the weapon. With the point of the blade he plucked his antagonist under the chin.

EL LOBO LET out an agonized gurgle and relaxed. And then Carney himself let out a shout, in raucous, blasphemous Spanish.

"Quick!" he howled. "You, below! El Americano jumped out of the window! Catch him! He's wounded!"

The ruse succeeded. There was an answering bellow and stampede below. The bandits were off in hot pursuit.

"Amigo," Carney gritted to El Lobo, "shall I cut your throat? Or will you do as I say?"

El Lobo nodded his answer.

"Bueno!"

Carney let him up. He felt the mesh of mystery surrounding him that he had felt ever since reaching Spain. He did not know its reason but he would let no bandit alive kill or capture him for an unknown reason.

"El Lobo," he gritted, "you know the way to Montecristo and to the Don Bartolo Valdez you have not wanted me to see?"

The man wavered for a moment, but Carney's knife was at his throat.

"Sí—!"

"You'll be my guide there—if you want to live!"

The hullabaloo still roared from below, and there was instant danger of more bandits—followers of El Lobo—coming up through the trap door.

But Carney, safe for a moment after he had stuffed El Lobo's own dirty neckerchief into his mouth as a gag, recovered his gun, and reached for his hat.

He prodded the bandit chief in the back with his gun as a signal to advance. On the double-quick they went toward the main door of the room and out into the stygian darkness.

At the foot of the steps, Carney gave one sibilant order:

"March!"

El Lobo "marched," with Carney guiding with prodding gun, straight to the stable doors. Not for one second did the American relax vigilance. He meant to shoot on sight if he was seen or interfered with.

Eyes straight ahead, Carney did not see the one witness to his getaway with the Wolf of the Morenas. From an embrasure in a window outside in the patio, Pancho, the one-eyed proprietor of the inn, looked and gloated. He gave

   THE BEST OF THRILLING ADVENTURES

no hand to help El Lobo. He raised no outcry.

Crooked and sidewise, he slid from his shadowed retreat as the yells of hunting men grew more muted in the distance, and made his way back into the inn. The shadows swallowed him as he muttered:

"I shall go to the Moors!"

CHAPTER II

THE BANDIT GUIDE

WHILE THE NOISE of the search reached them in echoing, yelled reverberations, Buck Carney ordered his captive to saddle and bridle two horses—his own and another. El Lobo demurred for only one second.

"You'd like to live, maybe?" Carney

menaced. "You might, for a while longer, if you do as I say! But you'll have a bullet bored through you as sure as you're a foot high, if you don't lead me to the *Castillo de Montecristo* before sunup!"

"*Sí!*" El Lobo growled and cast one helpless look for aid into the shadows where his own men had disappeared.

A gesture from Carney ordered him onto a horse, and his eyes narrowed with hope. A bandit on a horse! What might not come—even with a man with weapons back of him! The next moment his hopes were hurled to the earth. The Americano was busy—busy with data. Over the bandit's heavy shoulders, the American tossed a rope. A running noose. It tightened, held the man's arms to his sides.

"Ride!" said Buck Carney, and they were off, El Lobo in the lead, the rope that bound, him held in the unrelenting hand of the man who followed him on horseback.

The reason for El Lobo's sudden renewed activities deviled Buck Carney's mind every second during the time it took him and his captive, riding steadily, to leave the *Posada de las Tres Serpientes* behind.

What if it *were* known he had come to Spain bent on a treasure hunt? Spain had been in existence for some centuries, and others had searched for troves. Why should he be, from the moment of his landing, a special focal point on which bandits set their gaze—and their pointed knives?

A GLEAM CAME to Buck Carney's eyes as he thought of Don Bartolo! The grandest pal a man ever had, though a dreamer. The Spaniard he had run across three years ago in Sonora, Old Mexico—Don Bartolo Valdez, to give him his whole name, who had turned out to be one regular guy when it came to standing by a man when there was trouble—

And back there in Mexico, under the moon one night, sharing the same saddle for a pillow, Bart had spilled the wild yarn—Buck had not really believed that Bart was one of the Spanish grandees until about a month or so ago when Bart had been called back to Spain. Bart's story had sounded like a romance—all about his home back in Spain, and the mine that went all the way through the mountain under the castle—"Full of gold, a king's ransom in gleaming pearls and rubies and sapphires—" Buck could see Bart's eyes gleam as he had said that. And Bart had said:

"It's there! It's there! It's been there a thousand years—just waiting for somebody to get the clue to where the treasure chamber is—The Moors sealed it up with all that wealth when they were forced out of Spain—They never came back—"

And all Buck said was:

"Well, let me know any time Mr. Aladdin comes around and drops a lamp or a key or something—"

THAT WAS WHAT a fellow *would* say, Buck thought. Peril-seeker, adventurer, gambler in life as he was, he could not yet quite account for the impulse that had made him drop everything and head for Spain when, something more than

THE BEST OF THRILLING ADVENTURES

a month ago, a cablegram had come to him from Don Bartolo.

A cablegram exactly like Bart. Buck would have known it was from Valdez even if it had not held their code words—"Red Silver." He and Bart had agreed upon them when they had talked about the abandoned mine under the Valdez castle. The mine, Bart said, had once been noted for its production of sulphide of mercury, Red Silver. That was to be the code when, and if, Bart ever got a line on where all that treasure was.

Such a legend! But Spaniards—they always dreamed—Cortez and Balboa, and—Bartolo Valdez wasn't such a bad dreamer himself— Anyway, Buck meant to give him a whirl. He took the next steamer after he got the message:

"Looks like hot stuff Stop Meet me in Cadiz 13 Calle San Stefano Stop The silver is red—"

The *Calle San Stefano* was there all right, but no Don Bartolo. No one who knew anything about him. But there had been an El Lobo quite, quite prominent, as Buck knew after dodging knives plenty of times. Why? It didn't make sense. But it made him stubborn. Even a week of careful questioning in the neighborhood proved fruitless. No one seemed to know *Señor* Bartolo Valdez, or cared who he was!

Then one night—that old man on the street who had whispered:

"If you want to see certain friends, you can find them in Montecristo—"

That was all. The old man had faded into the street shadows. Buck was nonplused, for the moment, but soon guessed why. He had already learned of El Lobo—and the interest El Lobo had in activities around this place. And this old man, surely a friend of Don Bartolo, couldn't be seen talking to anyone looking for *Señor* Valdez, of the treasure trove.

There was nothing left for him to do but find a place named Montecristo, and to avoid a few cutthroats in so doing. Where in time was Montecristo? No one seemed to have heard of it. A lot of blind trails had been followed before Buck Carney at last reached the country that sheltered it and—*The Tavern of the Three Snakes.*

CARNEY SPOKE ONLY once or twice during the first of the ride, and then only to assure El Lobo, in unmistakable terms, that he meant what he said about shooting him if the *castillo* was not sighted by sunup.

Buck Carney did mean it. He had no illusions about the outlaw who was serving him as an involuntary guide. El Lobo would dump him if he could. He would circle around and bring him to the cutthroat inn if he dared—on the chance that one of his comrades back there would get a chance for a pot shot.

But Buck kept his eyes front and trusted to his ears to keep a look out on the back-trail.

There was little chance of a flank attack, even if they were followed. The trail followed mostly side hills and ridges, where any shooting would have to be done from a risky distance, especially in the dim moonlight.

The moon was still fairly high. But it was in the last quarter. And much of the trail led through the heavy shadows of a forest that had never been cut.

The riata around El Lobo, though, was like a live nerve. Carney kept it taut in the dark places along the trail. Even where enough light strained through the branches of the trees to give him a silhouette of the huge man on the leading horse.

A half mile further on, after a stretch of hard going, Carney brought the horses to a stand for a breather on a level bit of ground. El Lobo took the opportunity for a parley.

"*Señor,*" El Lobo said, "will your grace permit me the favor of a word?"

"Yes," said Carney, "if you make it short enough and keep your voice down."

"*Señor,* we meant you no ill tonight."

"I'm not interested in lies!" growled Carney.

"*Señor,* pardon! It is no lie. Will you hear me? It was only information we wanted—"

"By cutting my throat!"

"No, *Señor!* If you would only have been willing that your belongings be searched—"

"Silence!" commanded Carney.

THROUGH THE MOUNTAIN stillness he thought he heard the click of a horse's hoof against a stone. But even in his tenseness, his mind was asking: "What could it possibly be that he was supposed to have that El Lobo wanted?" Carney could think of nothing. But he meant to play the game through, force his way to Don Bartolo and the precious treasure.

"We're moving on!" Carney warned his bandit captive as he flicked the horse ahead with the end of his rope.

Somebody else was out in that dark forest now! This game was getting interesting.

His thoughts were incompleted.

Suddenly the riata with which El Lobo was noosed fell slack! In spite of all Carney's watchfulness, the bandit must have been cutting at the rope in the darkness all along, most likely with his teeth. He could reach it by lowering his head.

Before Carney could move in his one moment of astonishment, El Lobo was disappearing from his sight as the bandit dived from his horse into the brush!

Carney fired once, and shot out a curse as he knew that he had missed in the darkness. The bullet whizzed by El Lobo's shoulder as the bandit lurched to one side to escape it. Carney saw the man stumble and fall as his gun hand once again jerked to position.

EL LOBO'S HORSE, freed of the weight, jumped, squealed at the sound of the pistol shot and bounded ahead. Carney's horse gave a leap to follow, but Carney checked him with one hand as he swung the muzzle of his gun down on El Lobo.

"Don't move!" snapped Carney. "I've got you this time!" El Lobo's life was worth no more to Buck Carney at that moment than a gnat's.

"*Señor!*" El Lobo began. He was squirming and panting.

"Shut up and lie still!" gritted Carney.

El Lobo's eyes narrowed as he heard the other horsemen. There was a thread of hope. They might be his own men! But the hope was gone almost as quickly as it came. He breathed out a frightened whisper: *"Los Moros!"*

Moors! But Carney was wasting no time. At that moment, Moors meant nothing to him. In a single lithe movement he slid from his horse and crouched under the cover of the rocks and bushes near where El Lobo was sprawled, The huge bandit was shivering with fright.

"Free me!" he begged.

But there was no pity in either Carney's heart or voice. His gun covered El Lobo.

"Turn over and put back your hands!" he ordered.

El Lobo tried pleading. Carney put an end to that with a slap from the flat of his gun. Rapidly he was binding the man. But he had thrown only the first few hitches around El Lobo's arm when a hail came out of the darkness.

"Ola! Americano!"

"What?"

"We are friends of yours!" came the shouted reply. "We will do you no harm—All we want is the bandit, El Lobo! Our scouts saw you take him from the *posada, Tres Serpientes!"*

"No! No!" El Lobo pleaded in a hoarse whisper. "Amigo! Save me! I have not that which they seek! *El Americano* himself knows that well!"

CHAPTER III

UP FROM AFRICA

"LOS MOROS!" MOORS! How much that name was to mean to the seriousness of Buck Carney's adventure! How much of an attempted frustration of the plan to carry out triumphantly that scheme for wealth at which Bart had hinted, and that to the American was appealing, if nebulous! Gold! Treasure! Wealth! Moors? Of course—Carney had expected them. In the offing, but—

Now they were here! Moors! And at his feet a pulling, pleading giant of a bandit begging to be saved from them. Why?

Buck Carney laughed. But curiously that appeal of El Lobo's to be saved from a black Nemesis, so far as Carney was concerned, found support from an unexpected quarter. He had given his word to this bandit that he should live if *he,* Carney, saw a certain place by sunrise. He would have to make good his promise.

For now, he threw up his head to meet—the sunrise! Even on the lower levels of the Sierra Morena a certain glory of the morning was promised. It was the hour when Buck Carney had promised death to El Lobo unless the *castillo* was sighted, and—

The upper peaks were already flaming red and gold. Carney, raising his eyes in the direction of the unknown voice that was addressing him, gave a start of surprise. For, just emerging from the mist, in the middle distance, was a ruined castle. He knew on the instant that it was the one for which he had been looking. Montecristo!

There could not be two castles like that—not in the Sierra Morena; probably not in all Andalusia. It was as Bartolo had described it to him: The two great towers that stood out, joined by a battlemented wall—all of it so massive and so old and overgrown that if might have been a part of the mountain itself.

The castle by sunrise! Well, this dog of a bandit, El Lobo, had made good on one thing! There it was—less than a mile away, crowning a flat-topped mountain spur on the opposite side of a narrow, thickly wooded valley.

Montecristo! Bart was there—Don Bartolo!—his partner! It was almost like going home.

THERE WAS NO time for more than a glance. A longer look would have been sheer recklessness.

"Show yourself!" Carney commanded the unseen spokesman. "I won't shoot."

"Is El Lobo there?"

"Yes."

"Armed?"

"No. Tied. And I have him covered."

Suddenly from the rocky, wooded ridge just ahead a tall figure rose up, no more than fifty yards away—one of the strangest figures Carney had seen in Spain. In spite of his strangeness, he was instantly recognizable as a fighting man by the way he carried himself.

"Me," he announced, "I am Abd-el-Kerim."

His face was jet black. No white showed, even in his eyes. As if to contrast it, he was dressed almost entirely in white. A high white turban was on his head, bound tight and set low, and a long white cloak fell from his shoulders almost to his heels. Under it he wore some sort of khaki uniform of regulation European cut, with a holster belted to his hip. And spurred boots!

He stood for a second or so as if to let the power of his name sink in. Then he strolled forward.

Carney stood where he was. El Lobo was insufficiently tied. He would need watching. But he had a quick, instinctive feeling that the advancing, armed Moor would bear watching, too.

"You're near enough to talk!" he snapped. "Stay where you are!"

A SWIFT BLAZE of anger flared into the jet eyes of Abd-el-Kerim. But he stopped.

"I want this man!" he said arrogantly, and flicked his black eyes at El Lobo.

The bandit was crouched almost at Carney's feet—a fact that the American could not overlook. It was as if a dog were crouched there, seeking protection.

"What is this?" Carney snorted. "A request, or a demand?"

"I want him. That's all."

"Maybe it's not enough."

"You go. You're all right. My men won't shoot you. You leave him here."

Carney shook his head.

"Are you his friend?" the Moor demanded with sudden intensity. "In league with him to defraud the sons of the prophet?"

"He's my prisoner," said Carney laconically. "I don't know any sons of prophets."

   THE BEST OF THRILLING ADVENTURES

Abd-el-Kerim stood for a moment thinking. Then he nodded.

"Prove it," he said. "If you wish, if you have nothing to do with what he would carry out, with the theft of which he is guilty, you go ahead and kill him."

"Listen!" Carney told him. "When I do a little job of killing, it's because I have to—not because some guy orders me to!"

The Moor shifted his hot black eyes to El Lobo.

"He would torture for what he wants," he said. "So I would torture to get it back. If you have it, he would torture you for its possession. Prove to me your innocence by at least picking out one of his eyes—cutting off his nose—"

"For what?" snapped Carney. "What's worth all of that?"

Abd-el-Kerim shrugged. "You know," he said shortly. "You have been watched since you arrived in Spain—you are harmless, Americano, unless—"

"Adios!" snapped Carney. "The parley is ended."

Abd-el-Kerim moved a hand toward that holster belted under his cloak.

"Don't draw that gun!" snarled Carney.

"Why not?"

"You might try to use it."

THE MOOR HELD his hand, but his jetty eyes were blazing a threat into Carney's gray ones.

"This man is to be tortured for information he possesses," he announced calmly. "To the death! You try to stop it, you die, too!"

Carney shrugged. "Maybe you'll join us."

"I've got you both covered with a dozen guns."

"I've got *you* covered," said Carney softly, "with one gun."

Black men rose up on every side, more ebon-hued sons of the blazing sun than Carney had ever seen before in his life. Each one with a carbine held in a steady hand. It was goodnight! Or farewell to the bright new day!

Just when there appeared no way out, just when it seemed that a crash of gunfire was already the matter of a split second, El Lobo made his dash for freedom.

His life in this spot could by no possibility last more than a short time longer. The Moors wanted him—in deadly, venomous earnest. Why, Carney could have no idea. But he recognized a death threat when he saw it. With a moment to think, he could not have blamed El Lobo for his sudden action.

But he was busy himself—looking into that black sheik's eyes. And in the moment of the American and the man from Africa taking one another's measure—El Lobo leaped! His movement was so unexpected that action from any man, black or white, was for the moment suspended.

ONLY ABD-EL-KERIM, THE Moor, moved. He had to.

For it was at the Moor that El Lobo sprung. Behind his leap was all the feral savageness of the wolf for which he was named.

Carney risked one shot as El Lobo rushed toward the Moor. It nicked the bandit along a shoulder, but did not halt him. He dared not shoot again because of the Moor. Even now there would be some among Abd-el-Kerim's followers who would be certain that Carney's one shot was for their chief.

He got a plain view of black faces peering at him from behind screening carbines. He leaped forward! A roar followed him as bullets sang past his hurtling body.

He plunged for cover.

Where he was headed, Carney had no idea. But he knew he must not pause for an instant. He must keep going— downhill as he was headed! He had no choice. He had still less when he reached the slope's bottom. It suddenly stiffened there until it was a precipice— not bare rock, fortunately—but shaggy with broken rock and brush.

Above him they were still firing. Fusillades rang out and reverberated as he scrambled, slid, and dropped.

He found a sloping shelf that would hold him for a time, protected from the pursuing riflemen by a rocky needle that tilted outward toward the valley. He rested there, waiting, catching his breath, looking out toward the mountain shoulder above which reared the ruined towers and ramparts of Montecristo.

A rustling, scrambling sound beyond the rock whirled him to a quick alertness. But before he could balance himself for defense or attack, he was once more facing—El Lobo!

NEITHER OF THEM was armed. Carney had lost his gun in his headlong plunge. But that did not stay them. With snarls of animal rage they hurled themselves on one another, fighting like primitive men. They fought to the edge of the precipice, hung there for minutes, swaying, struggling on the sloping, crumbling shelf. Then they were falling!

They whirled and clutched as they fell. Rocks came up to meet them, bushes, the tops of trees. The valley mist was thickening about them.

Carney had no idea how long afterward it was before he came to himself. His first hazy idea was that he had been put out by a bullet. But he was not forgetting El Lobo. He, too, had fallen. He must be somewhere around. Cautiously Buck pulled himself together, crawling over rocks and low growth.

It must have been a quarter of an hour later when he suddenly raised his eyes from the edge of a little pool to which he had crawled, and saw—a girl!

CHAPTER IV

LAURA

SHE STOOD ON the other side of the gulch, up a little way, in full view, but obviously ready to take quick cover in the rock and brush that surrounded her.

Carney gave her the chance to disappear. He looked about him. El Lobo was nowhere in sight. Smashed in the rocks, maybe, or gone if he could still drag himself.

He raised his eyes. The girl was still there. She was dressed in some unstriking way that a man would never

Carney's rock caught El Lobo in the chest.

remember or be able to describe. But her face and her figure!

Dark-eyed, she was—eyes that seemed almost too big for her delicate heart-shaped, ivory colored face. She was bare-headed, and her wavy black hair cascaded about her shoulders.

A delicate, feminine girl. Yet she carried a rifle in her hands, a high-powered tool. The way she held it was sufficient proof that she knew how to use it.

Carney pulled himself up, first to his knees, then to his feet. He faced her, holding out his wet empty hands.

"Buenas dias!"

"Are you hurt?" she called to him.

"Not particularly. But perhaps you can help me. I'm an American—"

Before he could say more, she uttered a sharp, glad cry. A flash of vivid expectation came into her eyes.

"Not—not *Señor* Carney!"

"The same! How did you guess?"

The girl took eager steps forward.

"You are my brother's friend!" she cried. "Don Bartolo! Oh, his joy, his relief, when he knows!"

IT WAS EVIDENT it was a joy and relief she shared. She flashed on flying feet down to the rocky bottom of the gorge—a torrent when it rained.

"No greater than mine to know that I've dug up his hiding place," Buck assured her, hurrying to meet her. "Where is he?"

"At the *castillo*." She tossed her head toward where the ruined castle was somewhere up above them, but out of sight.

"He hasn't met up with any trouble, I hope?" Buck asked quickly, and saw her face grow serious.

"He—he's had an accident," she admitted. She was still a little breathless from her run, but her eyes were shining with excitement. "Oh, but I'm sure he will be all right now! Your coming will make such a difference!" She rounded the pool, cradling the rifle against her breast as she put out her hand in the welcome a man might have given. "I'm Bartolo's sister," she said.

"Doña Laura?"

"Laura!"

A second Buck hesitated. "Aren't you afraid to go about like this in a bandit-infested land?"

She nodded slowly, in confession.

"Barto and I have both been afraid for me—for both of us," she said. "But what must be, must." She added, with a brightening, unmistakable smile: "But part of our fear is gone now." Her voice was soft and thrilling.

Their tones were casual enough, but in the manner of each was that of two pioneers who had happened to meet in a hostile country. Laura Valdez was as alert to danger as a young doe. Carney, too, was on his guard—with a swift thought for those black ruffians who had sent him on the run down the mountain; remembering, too, El Lobo and his men.

"What's all the trouble around here?" Carney asked soberly.

"Too much to tell in a day—or a week," Laura said, with a brave attempt at a laugh that was more of a sob. "Come with me—if you're sure you're not hurt—I heard shots up there. I saw you coming down the mountain—"

"That's past," assured Buck, and he reached over for her rifle. "I'm still able to carry arms, you see," he added cheerfully.

AS THEY MADE their way up through the rocks and heavy forest, Laura Valdez was able to tell Carney at least a little of what he wanted to know. Her information was more or less vague.

Since the revolution she and her brother, her father and a few other Royalists had come to the *castillo* as the safest refuge. And Bartolo, it appeared, since his experiences in America, had stepped into a mess of trouble. It was not a dream—all he had told Buck in

America about treasure under the castle. The trouble was that others knew, too, and the family had discovered that to their sorrow since they had fled to the *castillo* when the revolution had taken away all that was worthwhile financially in their lives. They had been more than willing to call the *Castillo de Montecristo* a sanctuary merely—for them and their friends—until Bartolo had returned from America with a New World idea of making Old World wealth come to their aid.

It was true. There was treasure—in abundance—somewhere beneath the *castillo.* Their real trouble now was that those others knew it. The bandit, El Lobo, for one. And the Moors who had recently come over from Africa to claim the wealth as theirs by right! Life, said Laura, had come for the Valdez family to be just one bit of dodging one death after another.

And, she added informatively—the big thing that showed Buck Carney why he had been of especial interest— nobody knew just where was the map that would show the exact location of the "treasure chamber" in the vast maze of mines under the *castillo.* It had been stolen from the Moors who had held it for a thousand years since their exile from Spain. The Moors were deadly in earnest about getting it back. *They* thought—and others thought, that El Lobo, the bandit, had stolen it. He showed too great interest in the mines and in The Cave that Talks which was at the mines' entrance, and where the remaining Moors were now camping and trying to ferret out, without the chart, the treasure chamber entrance. OTHERS STILL, AND of recent date, apparently, the bandit, El Lobo, believed that Bartolo Valdez was the man who was custodian of the valued map—and that he had taken it with him to America, possibly given it to a trusted friend for safekeeping. So—

"So," said Laura Valdez to the man she was not the only one to know was "closer-than-a-brother" to Don Bartolo Valdez, "we've all been working at deadly cross purposes—no one knows what step to take next except to kill whoever really has the map. You can perhaps realize its seriousness since you have been honored by their espionage since your arrival. My brother could not meet you as planned. He was hurt, painfully, as you will learn. He will tell you how and why— Oh, please, please don't ask me everything! You have come! You have come! It is enough!"

"Not quite enough," said Carney. "The Moors—what have they got to do with all the mess?"

"Bartolo will tell, you—"

"Bart!" said Buck Carney grimly. "Bart! What happened to him?"

"Hurt," said Laura, slowly. "I told you. He came—when I sent for him. Father was gone—missing—he went down in the mines—alone—*his* mines—he came upon a party of Moors—" She stopped, looked away from Carney. "Barto went after him—the Moors—they almost killed him! Wild Moors from Africa. And our father is missing yet!"

She stopped suddenly, startled,

looking off into the forest. She laid an arresting hand on Carney's arm.

"Listen!"

CHAPTER V

DON BARTOLO

DOÑA LAURA, POISED for flight or quick action, spoke tensely. Buck Carney nodded. He had already caught that flutter of movement that had brought the girl to attention. On the other side of the wooded ravine—they had been following its steep up-slope—someone was on the move. A figure came into sight. "Pancho!" Carney breathed. "That one-eyed innkeeper!"

The host of the cutthroat *posada* was not more than a quarter of a mile away, headed down the ravine straight toward them, but it was plain he had not seen them yet. He plodded along, the lead rope of a loaded burro in his hand.

"You know him?" Laura whispered.

"I ought to!" Carney's mirthless laugh rumbled under his breath. "I spent last night in his assassin's den—as El Lobo's prey."

"El Lobo!" Laura whispered awedly. "The bandit! Oh, *he* is the one to be reckoned with—*I* know it now as well as the Moors!"

Carney did not question her further, then, looking down into her distressed eyes.

"How far are we from the *castillo?*" he asked.

"Not far—just around the next shoulder—"

"Here! Take the carbine! You're not afraid to go alone. You've shown that. Just tell Don Bartolo I've stopped to pick up a little information. It's about time somebody found out just *who* has that map!"

The girl's eyes were startled.

"Not unarmed!"

"I'll not be unarmed long!" Carney promised. "Hurry—but be careful! There's no time to lose!"

For one moment their eyes met. It was as if they had known each other always.

And there was no doubt where the authority lay. Without a word, Doña Laura took the carbine as Buck turned and disappeared into the brush.

FOR A FULL minute after he left her, Laura Valdez stood watching. With this new friend gone, so, too, was some of her confidence. She was in the grip of a terror that left her motionless. She, who had believed she had become so familiar with terror that nothing could shake her any more.

With a sharp start of recollection, she turned and her eyes swept the secretive forest. Slowly she made the sign of the cross. Then she was running up the trail towards the castle like a frightened deer—to the *Castillo de Montecristo.*

The Castle of Montecristo, to the Moors, in the days long gone, before they had been expelled from Spain, had been more than a castle. It had been their *Cazba K'vair,* the greatest of all their strongholds— The descendants of those ravaged blacks had never forgotten—!

WATCHFUL, WITH HER rifle held ready, Laura Valdez panted up the trail toward the castle. Not even here could she relax vigilance. With all speed she found her way through a ruined and overgrown labyrinth of walls and brush to one of the monumental towers. She entered and sped through narrow and twisting passageways until at last she was climbing two narrow flights of stairs. At the head of the top one, she came to a small door and knocked. She went in when a voice was raised to bid her enter.

The small door gave admittance to a room as big as a church. It looked like a church, with its groined roof of stone arches supported by massive stone columns.

In a far corner, by a tall mullioned window, were two men. One of them was old, dressed in black, a professional man. The other, younger, more distinguished in appearance, lay before the window on a rough cot—a cot that had been made by stretching a green cowhide over a wooden frame and letting it dry.

He wore pajamas and an old dressing gown. His head was swathed in bandages.

"You are better, Don Bartolo," the doctor was saying.

"But you need at least another week of quiet—"

"Quiet?" Don Bartolo shot out. "When hell's to pay around here!"

Both men rose as Laura Valdez came into the room and hurried toward them. Bartolo reached her side in a moment.

"Thank God!" he breathed, when he felt the warmth of her presence, "you *are* here! You got back! When we heard that gunfire down in the valley—"

"I've seen him!" Laura cried breathlessly. "He's come! *Señor* Carney!"

"Buck? Where is he?"

"Careful!" warned Dr. Alfredo, once of the Spanish court, now exiled.

He was thinking only of his patient. But sister and brother ignored him. Laura went on excitedly:

"He's gone to find out *why* El Lobo wants him, Barto!" Laura cried eagerly. "He thinks he may be on the trail of the map that's made us all look death in the face!" Suddenly she broke down, sobbing. "But oh, they'll kill him! They'll kill him!"

No one knew better than Don Bartolo the menace that Buck Carney now faced. His face was drawn and white as he dropped down onto the cot, the sudden weakness overcoming him. It was the first time Bartolo had been on his feet since his accident, or his premeditated fight, rather, with the Moors in the subterranean depths of the Montecristo mines.

THEN, AS SUDDENLY, Don Bartolo was on his feet again. He leaped toward a pile of leather packs and mule harness that lay in an embrasure in another window. He tore at them feverishly.

"Don Bartolo!" Dr. Alfredo cried out. "For the love of Heaven!"

Don Bartolo turned, a rifle in his hands, standing proudly erect.

"Sorry, Doctor," he said, "but it's my friend! Out there alone—with fiends!"

With firm, determined stride, he walked to the door.

CHAPTER VI

THE SNAKE AND THE WOLF

BUCK CARNEY FELL upon bigger game than he had started out after when he left Doña Laura.

He was willing enough to see the one-eyed innkeeper alone. Some instinct told him that from Pancho he would find out much that was puzzling, and an innate sense of character reading had already told him that Pancho knew more of the business that was disturbing the Sierra Moreno than he had let on. His business out here right now, for instance, was not altogether the peaceful one of taking supplies to the Moors who had encamped themselves in the Cave that Talks. As if they had a right and leave to it that no man could challenge!

For almost an hour Carney stalked the one-eyed man, watching his every movement, with the patience and skill of an Indian. At last he circled to head him off in what appeared to be a likely place and was laying in wait for his one-eyed erstwhile host when be made the startling discovery that he was not the only one who had spotted Pancho and his burro on that secret mountain trail.

Around a shoulder Pancho came in sight. So, too, did someone else—El Lobo!

The two were walking slowly along, side by side, with the burro trailing along behind. They were at the bottom of a wide arroyo, or "wash" when Carney first saw them. Both men were uneasy. El Lobo, undoubtedly, because he was still on the scout. Pancho, for reasons of his own.

With all the precaution of his Indian-trained woodcraft, Carney edged himself from cover and crawled out, inch by inch, on the rock ledge just above them. Now, luck being with him, he would discover why they had tried to kill him in the inn! *Now* he would learn why, day after day, night after night, ever since he had come to Spain, Death had been at his right hand!

He waited, crouched, as still as the stones about him. His reward was swift enough. The hoarse voice of El Lobo rose to him as the bandit growled:

"I've a good mind to slit your gizzard right now, One Eye!"

"Why, El Lobo?" Pancho softly whined. "When I've always been your friend!"

"*My* friend! Death of a rat, you sewerage-saving cook for friends of hell! Do you think that I don't know that you are now on this trail for a chance to take from the Americano the map that has been stolen from the blackamoors!"

CARNEY FROZE. PANCHO was whining in a conciliating tone:

"But what if I were coming to you, Chief? What if I knew that the Americano had not the map, that I knew where it was taken, and had come to tell you where to look—"

El Lobo's hand was suddenly at the innkeeper's throat.

"I'll throttle you, spawn of hell! Where is it?"

Pancho pulled away from the bandit, grinned evilly, as one who recognizes he has the upper hand.

"I fear not death," he said, "while I hold information—The damned Americano—he does not know—" With El Lobo's hand still at his throat, he boasted: "For pesos, there is much I could tell El Lobo of what it is the blackamoor have talked since they came not so long ago to the posada, *Tres Serpientes*," Pancho cackled: "Gypsies, Spanish gypsies, like Pancho, know the language of the blacks of Morocco as they know their tongue of Spain— Ha! Ha! El Lobo would know? El Lobo would spend hours and many pesos on the Americano who never saw the map of the Moors that tells of the secret treasure chamber in the deep mines of Montecristo!"

BUCK SAW THE giant hand of the bandit shoot out, grasp the throat of the inn-keeper. Pancho's one good eye popped from its socket. El Lobo was gritting, with the positiveness of his election to the right of power:

"By all the unholy fiends of hell that have made me the lord of the bandits of the Sierra Morena, where then, is that map that would lead to world treasure? If not in the keeping of the Americano, where then—fool!"

The one-eyed innkeeper's laugh came in echoing cachinnation:

"Find out, oh, lord of all the robbers!"

"If you—if you—"

Carney heard the scream and the bang of Pancho's head against a rock. And El Lobo's gutturals—

"No! Spawn of the gutters! You but make mirth! You would play with your lords and masters! I will not believe that a dog of a filthy cook could ever get near enough the secrets of the Moors to look at, much less possess, the map that would lead to fortune!" Carney could see with what viciousness and contempt he hurled aside the owner of the *posada*. "You would make game of me! The Americano has that map! Don Bartolo took it to him! I shall kill the Americano!"

El Lobo dismissed the subject as swiftly as he had entered it.

"Basta!" he said. "What have you in your pack?"

Pancho, hoarse from the release of his choking, whimpered:

"Cheese, bread, oranges—"

"Sausages?"

"The *Moros,* to whom I take rations, will not eat Christian sausages."

"The swine! Anything to drink?"

"The *Moros* won't drink our wine."

"I'll make them drink their own blood before I'm through with them!" El Lobo promised. "Go and bring me some bread and cheese. Then on your way! And the Lord on High save you, One Eye, if ever I find that you *do* know where is that which I seek!"

BUCK CARNEY HEARD Pancho cursing his burro. Presently he was back with what he had to offer. El Lobo, in turn, cursed him, but notwithstanding, began to eat—

No further word was spoken as Pancho and his burro moved on. Buck Carney flattened closer against the rock. After his feed, would El Lobo sleep?

It was the obvious thing to do in that land of siestas—wait. But Carney had no time to wait. He must have his showdown with this bandit here and now—If one of them should die, then at least Buck should have learned something of this map of mystery that so clearly concerned his friend, Bartolo, and for the possession of which the most desperate bandit in all Spain was willing to risk his life and liberty—to kill anyone who stood in the way of his possessing it.

Carney had but one uncomfortable moment realizing that he was the objective of the merciless "Wolf's" present seeking.

Now!—*Now* was the time for that showdown!

No man can listen well when his jaws are working. El Lobo was totally unconscious of any immediate danger threatening as he worked at satisfying his hunger. That was an added inventive to the husky American. For hours no morsel of food had passed Buck Carney's lips.

El Lobo, with what workings in his distorted mind no man knew, had his eyes fixed on a mountain vista horizon as Buck Carney worked his way back on the rock ledge above the bandit's outdoor dining room. Noiseless as a cat, Carney dropped from the ledge and slipped around in a careful detour to one side of where the bandit sat.

In Carney's hand was a long, sharp rock splinter he had found—a weapon almost as good for swift work as a knife.

But on rounding the rock, coming upon El Lobo in the clear, Carney realized on the instant that he was up against odds that might well mean disaster—for him! The first thing he saw was a long-barreled revolver glinting in the sun as it lay on the ground at El Lobo's side. The bandit must have borrowed or taken it from one-eyed Pancho! QUICK AS THE human hand could travel, El Lobo snatched at the weapon. But he was at a disadvantage, too—half choked with food, in an unfavorable position, caught wholly by surprise.

With his hand on the ground, two swift finger moves jerked the trigger twice. Both shots missed! And before the bandit could raise his hand for a truer shot, Buck flung his rock. It caught El Lobo in the chest and kicked him over against the rock.

Head down, Buck dove for him. They came together in a snarl so swift and so compact that they might have been hammered from a single piece.

El Lobo's gripping fingers had not loosened on the gun. Buck Carney's whole effort—all he had, and then some—was also centered on that gun. He got the barrel of it in his left hand! The barrel was hot. It was hotter—in the tenth of a hundredth of a second—for he had barely touched it before it let out another blast of fire and a stifling breath!

Carney felt a smear of flame across his forehead; then blood. His hold on the revolver barrel was slipping when he smashed his right hand over to clutch El Lobo's pistol hand.

He was fighting for his life. So, too, was El Lobo. The bandit must have outweighed Carney by all of fifty pounds.

With a snarl of rage, El Lobo lowered his bull head and set his teeth into Carney's shoulder! It was the very pain of this unexpected, savage new attack, perhaps that gave Buck Carney the strength he needed. In one last supreme effort he wrested the smoking gun from the murderer's hand. Two more shots rang out, spitefully reverberating along the ravine!

Two shots—only! But those two spattered El Lobo's life away.

CHAPTER VII

THE WOLF PACK

CARNEY CAST ONE flaming glance at the man who lay on the ground. He recoiled at the thought of touching him. El Lobo—dead! No doubt of that! But he must touch him—

The map of mystery—the map that meant much to Barto, to Laura, to *him,* Buck! He must search for it wherever it might be found. This dead bandit may have been lying, like his kind.

His hand went swiftly through El Lobo's pockets. No map—nothing—one relief!

Buck's hand felt cleaner when it came out from a pocket jingling with the robber's gold. Well, that was that! Now, any moment, he might be discovered.

With a gesture of repugnance, he flung down the bandit's empty gun and ran across the arroyo in the direction the one-eyed Pancho had taken. HE WATCHED HIS trail carefully, however.

No use leaving a trail another enemy might follow—not in such a crisis.

On the far side of the arroyo he picked out a leaning oak that offered cover in its crotch and at the same time would give him a view both of the trail taken by the inn-=keeper and his burro, and the water hole where El Lobo lay. He crouched into the tree's hiding. His jaws clamped shut on a thought.

Just a little while longer—and he was going to take a map from Don Pancho!

Right now he would wait—he did not have long to wait. As he had foreseen, Pancho had heard those shots— He was coming back—coming on a sliding run, exactly like a snake when it knows there is danger in the wind. He had left his burro up the trail for the sake of better speed. But speed was nothing to the man's caution.

He came to a pause for reconnaissance on the rim of the arroyo in a clump of brush, watching, so close to Buck's hiding place that the American could have jumped him. Which the American was tempted to do, but which was not in his plan.

There would be no benefit in seizing the little crook and demanding that he turn over "the map." He would simply lie—say he didn't have it. There was only one course to be taken with the one-eyed innkeeper for the present—follow him. Watch for a chance!

Seeing nothing, hearing nothing that was out of the way, Pancho, snake-like, slitheringly, slid down the side of the wash and started across. He was halfway to the water hole before he saw El

Lobo lying there. Dead. There could be no mistake about that!

Torn between curiosity and fear, still the snake, Pancho lingered. Then he was slinking forward again. Suddenly he stopped with a jerk, stooped and turned and took it on the run in the direction from which he had come.

The next moment Carney knew the reason. A gun banged and a haze of smoke lifted off to the left! Another off to the right! Both bullets whistled close to Pancho's head! As suddenly as he had started to run, Pancho dropped in his tracks and crouched.

A couple of riders were jumping their horses into the arroyo. Others followed. All of them white—a dozen or so—El Lobo's men, Buck knew on the minute. They must have been scouting for him all along, following his trail.

One of the horsemen let out a shout as he located Pancho. He roused the fugitive out of his hiding place with the flick of a quirt. Pancho was talking with voice and hands, protesting, trying to explain. But he was driven on the run back to where El Lobo lay.

SOME OF THE horsemen had dismounted by the water hole to look at their fallen chief. Others still sat their horses and were milling about with their carbines, ready for an attack or a chase.

In his hiding place, Buck Carney grinned wryly. Small chance of his tracks being discovered now, with all that stamping about.

A roar of shouts broke out when his captors brought Pancho in, and a fresh burst of excitement. Men on foot and riders crowded in menacingly. There were signs enough that El Lobo had died with food in his mouth. And beyond doubts it was Pancho's own gun that lay beside the fallen robber chief.

They were accusing Pancho of El Lobo's murder!

Little time was going to be lost there by the water hole. That was certain. Buck knew how such things went. He had not spent the years he had on the western plains of America without knowing lynchings. But this was different again. He *couldn't* let them lynch Pancho without a word of protest. In the first place, it was not Pancho's murder, but his, Buck's. Not that that made a great deal of difference. El Lobo's number had been up a long time. The principal thing now was—

HE WANTED PANCHO himself! He wanted what that wily innkeeper had hidden some place—probably to sell to the highest bidder—and he wanted nobody else to find it. None of the attackers, so far, could suspect. They were followers of El Lobo, but the Wolf kept his own secrets.

These men thought only of swift vengeance— They were getting ready—

Buck Carney slid out of the crotch of his tree as he saw the men by the water hole make their first movements.

Without any great excitement, one of the horsemen uncoiled his rope and tossed it over a tree branch. He sat there ready to ride away as others noosed the rope around Pancho's neck.

Across the arroyo echoed Pancho's

final scream of protest. And the laugh from his captors as he moved back.

Buck Carney started across the arroyo on the run, keeping to cover as much as possible. He was not taking any chances he did not have to take. But he did not let caution hinder his speed. One good jerk on that rope and Pancho would be beyond saving!

He was almost on the fringe of the mob when he uttered his shrill cry of warning:

"Quida'o! Los Moros!"

Look out! The Moors!

It was as if he had hurled a firebrand into a pack of wolves. Panic struck El Lobo's men—a moment of circling, quick movement.

BUCK SPOTTED A horse with a carbine swung at the saddle. With the excitement at its height, he ran to the horse. He had vaulted into the saddle and jerked the carbine free almost before he was seen. Only the owner of the horse was vigilant. He was one of the men who had been preparing Pancho for his execution. Now he was after Buck Carney on the run.

Even now it was not a mere getaway that was uppermost in Buck's mind. He was here to get Pancho out of his mess; and to get Pancho's secret.

The bandit on the ground made a leap for the reins as Buck pivoted the horse. *"Quién—"*

The butt of the carbine ramming at his head broke off his sentence. It was a glancing blow, but the Spaniard, never so much at home on his feet as in the saddle, spilled over as he bawled and cursed.

It had all happened in a few moments. But they were big seconds, stuffed not only with events, but with perceptions; things that all hands, with the possible exception of Pancho, had been trained to notice.

That false alarm was not going to last forever. These men were outlaws. They were fighters. They lived on the scout.

With a yell, Buck jumped his horse through the flurry of men and horses, rock and brush, sand and water.

In this part of the world they did not tie their ropes to the horn of the saddle. That was lucky—for Pancho. Otherwise, he would have already been jerked to the tree branch—and over it—as the horseman who had noosed him jumped his mount twenty or thirty yards away.

All the horsemen were scattering. It was part of their system in a fight, and Buck's one hope of making a getaway—with Pancho!

Still dazed, Pancho stood with the rope about his neck. At that moment he had no more recognition for Buck than for the man in the moon. As Buck swung down to collar him and lift him up, Pancho dodged, dragging his rope like a frightened dog. In his panic he jumped right under the neck of the horse Buck rode.

Buck called to him. Pancho was deaf. He scrambled. The rope he was dragging snarled a root, came taut.

Buck's mount struck it. It stumbled. It fell.

CHAPTER VIII

THE CAPTIVE

BEFORE BUCK COULD struggle to his feet, gun muzzles were drilled on him. Commands were barked for him to raise his hands. The guns backed the orders up. He raised his hands—and kept them raised—as he came up from the ground.

Other horsemen were circling in. The horse which had tossed Carney scrambled to its feet and shook itself. Pancho sat on the ground, the rope still about his neck. His one eye was squinting, beginning to gleam.

It was Pancho who was first to recognize Buck. His tone told that in the recognition he read some happy omen to himself.

"Por Dios!" he cackled. "The Americano!"

"Quién?"

"Que—"

"It's the Americano, I say!" Pancho shrilled. "It was he who killed El Lobo! For the map!"

That appeared to be language they could all understand. The map! Apparently every bandit in Southern Spain knew what "the map" meant, for eyes gleamed suddenly; some of the riders began to show signs of recognition of Buck. Some of the glances were more curious than fierce. In the faces of some was even something approaching admiration. This Americano, then, did know more about the map than had been told; it was possible, too, from what Pancho said, that he had battled El Lobo for it, to the death. And El Lobo had made them all believe that he still sought it! What was the truth! Where was the map now? Search would soon show. There were men there who would make good use of it, even with El Lobo gone! But groans of disappointment went up as grimy hands sought quickly through Buck's clothing—through every possible hiding place—no map was on him! But he would know where it was. There were ways of finding out.

They crowded around again.

"El Americano!"

"Que guapo!"

But there was no admiration on the face of one Spaniard on foot who rushed in. He choked out an epithet as he flourished a knife in his hand. It did not take the smear of blood and black on his face to warn Buck that this was the man whose horse he had borrowed.

The spot was warm. But after all, as Buck figured it, he might as well die of a couple of bullets—and swiftly—as to be cut to ribbons with a knife. And it would all be in the same cause—the cause of adventure! Too bad, though, if he had to die now, that he would never get near that treasure.

Here went, then—the chance!

As the Spaniard plunged, Buck fell back on one hand and shot out a kick. It was one of the first tricks he had ever learned as to the proper guard of an unarmed man against an attacker with a knife. The kick caught the Spaniard squarely in the middle. The horsemen roared with laughter. They liked brutality in any form, those men, so long as

     THE BEST OF THRILLING ADVENTURES

it did not touch them. No man's hand lifted a gun for a shot. Buck's hand on the ground found a rock. He came up with it, shouting to the man with the knife to hold off, but ready to make him if it came to that.

Others were calling to the knife wielder to hold off. Still others were mocking him, urging him on. The voices were guttural, and not too loud.

All the horsemen were dancing around, head in. These riders were horsemen—none better in the world. And it was not so strange—Buck having always been a horseman himself—that he could sympathize with the man who menaced him with the knife.

"Brother," Buck said, "permit me to explain—"

HE WAS STALLING, playing for time. Murder was in the air, and there seemed no way out. His words were broken short as another horseman scrambled in—a man who had been off on the scout. His horse was smoking.

"Basta!"

He spat out the word—"Enough of this!"

Steady as a rock, he sat his nimble-footed horse—a dark man with cold and level eyes—staring at Buck. Carney took quick note of the respect with which the others regarded the man. With El Lobo dead, here was the new leader—right now, at any rate. There could be no mistake about that. And a man who would never give in as long as he thought Carney might know of that damned map! Carney knew he was facing an even worse struggle than

when El Lobo had haunted him from pillar to post, from street corner to forest and to the inn of the three serpents.

"Pedro!" the new leader snapped. "Put up your knife. A dead man can tell no secrets! I want this man! And you, Americano, drop that rock!"

HE SPAT OUT a couple of names, ordering their owners to tie this *cimarron* before he could play any more tricks.

Cimarron! An outlaw of the animal world. The epithet burned!

Buck was tied. No easy way of getting out of those ropes, without plenty of time! He could tell that by the expert way in which the job was done. How was he to get hold of the innkeeper now! Hell, here he was, as excited as every bandit in Spain over that map they were all raving about—and he thought he knew at this minute where it was! And couldn't lift a hand to get it! Pancho must be laughing in his sleeve—if he was not scared to death about dying.

The new leader told off scouts. The men sent on outpost did not want to go, but they went. There was a slight diversion—and Buck Carney's heart was higher with hope than any of those outlaws imagined—when Pancho was picked up in the brush while he was trying to slip away, and brought back with his hands tied behind his back. A little later Pancho's burro was also found and sent in. That was not so bad! Still a chance!

Sitting in the gravel with his back against a rock, most of Buck's attention was taken up in watching men scoop out a hollow in the arroyo bottom. Most of it was done with hands and knives. Presently, without any ceremony, but with a certain solemnity, the body of El Lobo was laid in the hole and the hole filled. At the new chief's orders, one of the men cut a couple of sticks and tied them together with a withe in the form of a cross. It was stuck into the turned earth.

Buck remembered— There was a scattering of such crosses along all the trails of the Sierra Morena.

The simple ceremony over, Buck, tied hand and foot, was hoisted onto the burro—Pancho behind, an added burden to the already over-packed little animal. The whole party moved on up the arroyo a mile or so and into a gulley that tightened into a gorge between high cliffs. Pancho, the American noted, did not have his hands tied. Probably these bandits who held him and the innkeeper captive, held their Spanish confrere in more or less contempt. They had no fear of his trying another escape—as the Americano might, given the opportunity. But then, they knew nothing of how much Pancho knew of what was their life interest, as Buck Carney did. PANCHO, BEFORE THE battle, had believed El Lobo alone guessed that he might know something about the map. El Lobo was dead now—Pancho would have to depend on Buck Carney if he meant to cash in on any knowledge he might possess— Or if he really had the map, his only customer was Buck. Once let these bandits know that he had it, and they would take it from the one-eyed man, and toss his body aside for the jackals.

Buck recognized the strategy of the bandits' move up the gorge the instant he saw the spot. It was a place that one man could have held against a hundred, for in one place the gorge was no more than four or five feet across—room enough only for the passage of a pack animal.

Beyond, it widened to a basin where there was grass and shade, water, and a long tilt of smooth rock. It was time for food and a smoke when they reached the place, and the long afternoon siesta. It was a spot fitted by Nature herself for outlaws!

Pancho's whisper came to Carney from where the innkeeper sat on the burro's back, behind the American.

"Hist, *Americano!*"

Carney growled: "Well? What have you got to say?"

Then Pancho's whisper: "You would have the map? You heard me talk to El Lobo! I did not lie! He was too sure— Last month I, Pancho, the reviled, took from the Moor, Abd-el-Kerim, the bit of old paper that means a king's ransom—"

Carney growled again. "And now you would sell it to me?" But it was well for his bargain that the Spanish gypsy on the back of the burro could not see the gleam of elation in his eyes!

Pancho spoke for a moment, eagerly, swiftly.

"*El Americano!*" he said then. "I will place within your pocket the map! We will bargain later!"

BUCK CARNEY FELT the rustle of a paper— Pancho's hand in his pocket. He laughed aloud. He had that damned map that had meant death and destruction! *What was he to do with it now? How use it?*

Pancho's move was not a moment to soon. As soon as the bandits arrived at their camping place, he was moved on to a spot away from Buck Carney. Carney was never to see the man again—though at the moment such an idea never occurred to him.

A bandit they called El Gaucho—because, as the outlaw himself told Buck, he had spent a number of years in the Argentine—took care of Carney. When it came time to eat, he fed the American from the point of a knife. Now a hunk of sausage or cheese from Pancho's pack. Now a hunk of bread. None of them felt it safe to allow the American the use of his hands.

El Gaucho made a game of the feeding, and laughed heartily, poking the morsels too far to the left or to the right.

Buck flattered El Gaucho for his wit. There was hope to be derived from this clown—not much, perhaps, and that little forlorn, but it was something. EL GAUCHO CAPPED the game by giving Buck water from a gourd, pouring it over his face and down his neck.

The sinister successor of El Lobo came over to see the sport, but there was no smile on his face, nor laugh on his evil lips.

"Amuse yourself, Americano," he said tonelessly. "Later, I'm going to hang you—barefoot—over a little fire. You shall tell, then, of the map."

But he was going to have his siesta first. From the position of the sun, it was already about noon.

"Gaucho, *amigo*," said Buck softly, as the unsmiling chief turned away, "he will never hang me."

"Why?"

"Because I'm buying that knife of yours—for one hundred dollars gold!" Buck's words came in a voice no louder than a breath.

El Gaucho stretched and loudly yawned. Others were beginning to turn in, but there were still plenty of eyes shifting in their direction.

"Ho!" said El Gaucho. "I will stake the hands and feet of this damned *cimarron!*" More softly than Buck had spoken, he whispered, "Where?"

"At the *castillo.*"

"When?"

"Moonrise—this night."

"Bueno!" El Gaucho now roared aloud, as he hammered home a stake with a rock between Buck's hobbled feet.

CHAPTER IX

THE HOT TRAIL

EVEN AS EL Gaucho drove home the stake, it was not clear, even in his own mind, just what he would do. He wanted that hundred dollars oro the Americano offered. The prospect of a trip to the *castillo* and being smiled on by Royalists tickled his clownish heart. At the same time he hated to think of the fun he would miss seeing this *cimarron* dance at the end of a rope over a little fire.

Anyway, while he was making up his mind, he might as well have a little more fun of his own. El Gaucho was a humorist.

Having staked Buck's feet, he pulled out his knife and began to play with it—a five-inch blade as sharp as a razor, yet heavy enough to slit the throat of a steer; needle-pointed.

"Ava!"

He tossed the knife into the air whirling. It came down so close to Buck's face that the point of it almost reached an eye before El Gaucho, quick as a cat, caught it by the handle.

El Gaucho laughed and performed the trick again.

"Que bonita!"

He said that the knife was his little sweetheart. Nobody could buy a knife like that. It was sacred. He would as soon think of selling his honor. And he laughed again. Time after time he repeated his trick, but as Buck neither laughed nor winced, nor paid any apparent attention, El Gaucho tired of that sport and proceeded to stake down Buck's hands as he had his feet. He paused now and again during the process to jerk back Buck's head and playfully pass the blade around his throat.

Buck said nothing. He could tell. El Gaucho was simply trying to make up his mind.

Most of the other bandits were asleep—stretched out on the ground, with their heads wrapped up in their blankets. They were scattered, each near his own picketed horse. The sentinels were too far away to see or overhear.

The way El Gaucho had him fixed now, Buck could neither lie down nor sit up straight. He was only half-seated, his legs stretched out in front of him, the weight of his shoulders supported by his arms staked and bound behind him. If he were forced to hold this position long, he would be too paralyzed for swift action even if his bonds were cut.

IT LOOKED HOPELESS. There seemed no way out for him this time. Buck tried to face the matter philosophically, realizing that there was no possibility of aid coming to him. Which was because he had no long-lensed eyesight that could look through rocks and mountains and see what was happening not so far away.

For down the trail from the *Castillo* of Montecristo a figure was riding a plodding donkey—what looked like the figure of an old woman. To all appearances, Don Bartolo Valdez was an old woman. He was shrouded in a huge hooded cape. His head was doubly concealed in a big cotton muffler, and a broken sombrero flapped about his shoulders. The flea-bitten donkey on which he was perched was only about two sizes larger than the average burro.

Buck Carney's friend was not trying to fool himself about how strong he felt, but he was going to the aid of his friend!

There was little chance, Don Bartolo believed, of his being attacked by the bandits who infested the region, or questioned.

He looked too much like a native. But then it was no time for taking chances.

It was not too likely the bandits would

       THE BEST OF THRILLING ADVENTURES

give him more than a passing glance. Scattered native families were here in the Sierra Morena—charcoal burners, goatherds, poachers, even a few small farmers. They could be useful to outlaws on occasion. They might, at times, go in for a little outlawry on their own. In any case the regulars never bothered them.

VALDEZ FOUND THE trail for which he was looking. Following it, however, was slower than he had counted on—

He was in a "draw" between two brushy slopes and a steep forest of black pine when suddenly he cut the trail of a party of horsemen going at a gallop.

He picked up a fresh cork and smelled it. *Aguardiente!* El Lobo's men!

He gave his donkey the heel and let the little animal hit its high along the trail after the galloping horsemen.

Back in the bandit camp, El Gaucho lit a cigarette and sat down crosslegged at Buck Carney's feet.

"Two hundred gold?" he murmured through the smoke. "And how do I know I'll get it? You may get shot in the getaway."

"Bueno!"

"Three hundred!" said El Gaucho. "You see, I may get hung myself."

Buck held still, looking at the man. El Gaucho evaded his eyes.

"That," said Buck, "is quite true. This new chief you've got doesn't like you, anyway."

El Gaucho scowled. He drew out his knife and contemplated it.

"Five hundred!" he muttered. "Five hundred gold!"

He jerked the knife into the air and

this time—either willfully or by accident—missed his catch. Buck jerked with a half-groan, half-curse, as the blade nicked the raw flesh where the bullet had grazed him earlier in the day.

"Leave the knife where it is," he said, panting a little.

But he saw El Gaucho suddenly start and stare. Then the bandit leaned over and picked up the knife. He made a pass with it before Buck's eyes.

For some reason, El Gaucho was tremulous with fear. That was plain to Buck. Had he been spied on? As yet Carney knew nothing of the stranger El Gaucho had caught sight of, staring at him. Who was he? El Gaucho went on with his bluff.

"Goat!" he growled. "Sewer-filth! For a little, I'd—"

A cold voice cut in:

"Death—if you make another move!"

CHAPTER X

THE LONG CHANCE

THE VOICE, SCARCELY more than a whisper, yet as edged and deadly as El Gaucho's knife, stopped Buck's heart for the space of a beat. The words were such as might have been uttered by the sinister successor of El Lobo. They might have been aimed at El Gaucho or at Buck himself. Still— A memory! Something in that voice! A thrill started Buck's heart beating to make up lost time.

"Bart!" He whispered it sibilantly—in English.

"Me! Don't turn your head— There's a sentinel looking."

Then Don Bartolo, dragging his step a little, came around where Buck could see him! He had put aside most of the outer wrappings he had worn when he left the *castillo*. But a blanket was now muffling his head and shoulders, and on his head was one of the bandits' hats— big enough to stay on in the wind—and pulled low.

"Stuck up a sentinel in the middle of the gorge," he said. "He's tied—"

Don Bartolo went to work with all speed. In a pair of seconds he had wrenched the knife from the gaping El Gaucho and cut the rope on Buck's feet and arms. He kept El Gaucho covered every minute, never relaxing, but speaking to him only by looks and signs.

"Ease yourself, Buck," Valdez told Buck. "But keep your general position. Take this gun. I've got two more."

FOR THE FIRST time since his original threat, Valdez spoke to El Gaucho.

"Turn round, you! Sit as the Americano sits—unless you want your throat cut!"

And the speed with which El Gaucho was tied would have won for Don Bartolo a prize in any rodeo.

The stake that had held Buck's feet now held El Gaucho's hands—behind his back, his bound arms propping the weight of his heavy shoulders.

"We're right here back of you," Valdez menaced El Gaucho softly. "Move—or bawl—and I'll cut your heart out!"

El Gaucho quivered as to the touch of a branding iron as Valdez lifted off his hat and passed it over to Buck.

"Okay?"

"Set!"

"Get up and stretch yourself. Have a look. We'll need a pair of broncs."

Valdez did not move as Buck got up— with El Gaucho's hat on his head. Buck's own movements were measured—the juice squeezed from every second, though, and no time wasted.

His first glance, veiled and casual, was for the sentinel Valdez had mentioned. The man was on a bald spot of the high ridge that helped shut in the basin. Unquestionably he was looking this way. But of what were his thoughts or his suspicions there was no sign. He was motionless, squatted on his heels. THERE WERE A couple of likely looking horses picketed not far apart down in the general direction of the gorge. That would have to be the way they would make their getaway. The head of the basin was choked with brush and timber. The sides could have been ridden under ordinary conditions. But this condition was not ordinary. Speed was going to be needed when the shooting began, and a chance for cover.

"Those two horses over there!" jerked Buck. "Ready? Go!"

Both men leaped forward. At their second bound, the sentinel on the hillside shrilled a whistle. He was on his feet. He banged out a signal shot!

The two comrades put on speed. They separated a little, each headed for the horse he had selected.

For precious seconds, Buck was occupied with his animal and the bandit who claimed it—while hell was beginning to pop in the little valley behind him. But his bandit was down. He had forked his horse and built a hackamore—no saddle, no bridle. He was ready to go!

He jerked his head around to see how Bart was making it. Bart was not making it. He was on the ground—propped up on one arm. His gun was drawn, but he was not shooting!

BUCK JUMPED HIS horse to where Bart lay and slid from his back. The horse tried to go somewhere else, but he was no kicker. Buck held him.

"For the love of God, ride!" Don Bartolo pleaded.

"To hell with you!" Buck roared.

He put down a hand. Valdez took it.

They were not wasting time in arguments. Buck hoisted him.

"I've only got one good leg," Valdez panted. "The other flopped."

He put his two hands to the horse's mane. Buck mounted. He had Valdez across the withers of the animal before it could rear and they were off at the gallop!

All that saved them in those first few seconds—and every second sweating blood—was the confusion in camp. Blankets must come off before heads could pop up. Wide awake on the instant, the bandits were running then for their mounts, saddling and bridling. From where he sat tied and staked, El Gaucho was bawling his head off.

"Qué hay!"

Some one must have put a bullet into the substitute prisoner by mistake.

It took more seconds before El Gaucho could make the world understand that he was El Gaucho.

But Carney knew what was coming—and when it did come it would be fast. That neck of the gorge where it was only a few feet across! He must reach it! His horse thundered on, and he took one deep breath of relief when he passed the place in safety. As soon as there was room enough, he turned his horse to one side.

The first of the pursuers to reach the spot was the black-browed successor to El Lobo.

Carney's bullet went through his heart.

"Uno!"

He passed the information to Don Bartolo.

Bart, sagging down onto the horse's mane, braced as if he had received a stimulant.

"Dos!"

Carney fired again.

There was no missing in this rocky bottleneck, even shooting from the back of a dancing horse.

"Y tres!"

THREE RIDERLESS HORSES—PANIC-STRICK-EN horses—rearing, kicking, striking, as wild to get out of the line of fire as humans, wheeled and thundered back the way they had come.

They left their riders sprawled on the rocky trail.

Pursuit was blocked. Not for long, as Carney well knew, but long enough for any man in such a tight squeeze to make the most of it.

Which Carney did—

The bandits left behind were still cursing and trying to get through the pass when the horse carrying their late prisoner and Don Bartolo Valdez was panting up the trail toward the *castillo.*

Don Bartolo was all in—he would be in no physical condition to enter any frays for some time more to come. But he was still able to tell Buck Carney, before they reached the castle, something of what the romantic story which had urged him to send for his American friend was all about.

CHAPTER XI

INTO THE DEPTHS

IT WAS A story of which Carney already knew considerable, but Don Bartolo expatiated, telling some of the things he shrewdly guessed, more that he knew from the history of his Spain.

It had much to do with the Moors being back in Spain—and why. They had come for treasure—treasure of which they believed they alone knew.

When the Moorish chieftain, said Bart, was preparing for his treasure raid into Spain, the only obstacle in his path, or so he believed, was the presence at the castle of Montecristo of the Valdez family, who now had owned the *castillo* for hundreds of years.

The Slave-of-the-Merciful and certain of his followers had had an eye on the ruined castle in the depths of the Sierra Morena for a long, long time. They had already done quite considerable preliminary exploring about Montecristo, which for years had lain there as wild and empty before the new revolution as most of the country around it. The Moors had been able to camp there for weeks at a time, unobserved.

There had never been any difficulty connected with their secret visits. Moors had always been able to come and go as they pleased in Spain, even after they had been expelled.

It was only a short run from Morocco to Spain—one that any kind of a boat could make between sundown and dawn. Or they could come over in the daytime—to sell dates and coral. Many of them were smugglers. As for that, there were Moors in Spain who had never left, but who lived on—generation after generation—in some hole in the mountains where it would have been unhealthy for Spanish troopers to have found them.

But of all the Moors who had come to Spain, or who had continued to live there, Abd-el-Kerim and his band were the only ones who remembered the history of Montecristo or who now took an interest in it.

When the Moors had ruled Spain it was not as Montecristo that the castle was known. It was the *Cazba K'vair*— the Stronghold Supreme.

It was a place that could never be captured. It was as safe to the followers of the Prophet as Mecca. The Moors thought so.

WHEN THE SPANIARDS began to drive the Moors out of other parts of Spain, a curious change took place. For a thousand years treasure had flowed out of the *Cazba K'vair* and the mountain under it; now treasure of other sorts began to flow back to it. The followers of the Prophet, on the run, were bringing their treasures here for safekeeping.

There were tons of it—silver, gold, gems and ivory, works of art—

An earlier Abd-el-Kerim had been the custodian of all that wealth. When it began to look as though the Stronghold Supreme itself was likely to fall into the hands of the Christians, that earlier Slave-of-the-Merciful got busy. For a hundred days and nights his slaves were busy carrying wealth down into the depths of the mountain. There was a natural cave down there—two thousand feet below the subcellars of the castle; a cave as big as any mosque in Bagdad. When all the treasure had been transferred to it, the custodian had sealed it up.

No Dog-of-an-Unbeliever would ever get it. The only known entrance to the cave was closed with upward of two hundred feet of rock and cement.

But—just in case of accident to himself or any successor of his before the Moors again came back as masters— the earlier Abd-el-Kerim made a map. It was a secret map, showing just where the treasure lay, and where the bore would have to be made to get at it again.

The map had gone to Morocco.

It had been there for five centuries, until the present Abd-el-Kerim found it. And now it had been stolen! Blood was flowing over all Southern Spain in an effort to get it back!

Don Bartolo's own father, *Señor* Valerio Valdez, once a prince, had been kidnaped because the Moors thought he might know of its whereabouts. They suspected him almost equally with El Lobo. And at all events they would hold Don Valerio prisoner to keep him from interfering with them.

Where his father was now, Barto had no idea— But Barto was now in this present condition of physical disability because he had gone down into the mines to try to find him.

Bartolo said solemnly:

"So you see that I did need you, Buck—even above and beyond treasure! That was what I thought about first when I sent for you. Now my sister and I need the only man in the world who can help us. My father *must* be found!"

Carney's laugh was not mirthful.

"I have the map," he said simply. "How I got it will be for a story another day. The thing now is your father. Where do you believe he is?"

"Somewhere in the mines," said Bartolo. "And I—"

"I go into the mines—today," said Buck.

They had hardly realized that they had reached the castle or that Laura Valdez was there, with her eyes full of heartfelt thanks for their safety as she came to meet them.

"And I," she said to Buck Carney, "will go to guide you."

Buck looked at her a long minute, then back at Don Bartolo. Bart was reeling, his eyes already closing with his weakness. Buck said to Laura Valdez: "Yes—we go today!"

CHAPTER XII

THE CAVE-THAT-TALKS

THEIR PREPARATIONS WERE swift and simple. Doña Laura prepared a haversack with what they might most need—rope, candles, matches. And both of them were armed.

Even while the shaking Don Bartolo was being put to bed after his faint—he held up till the last minute—Doña Laura and Buck Carney were hastening to a disused wing of the ruins and making their way through the tangle. Through jungly gardens and broken walls, they reached a breach in the ancient ramparts. They found themselves on the rim of a steep drop covered with black oak and laurel.

Through that dense thicket they went on, straight down, until they came to a ruined *"templete"* or pavilion. The little marble building disguised the entrance to one of the ancient Montecristo mines. They stopped to light their candles.

For a shadowy interval they paused before plunging into the dark that lay ahead.

"Go back!" urged Buck.

Laura looked at him levelly.

"Do you want to go back?"

With one accord they moved ahead.

Nothing more was said, except an occasional whisper—or warning, or explanation.

But Buck could see that the girl was right in more ways than one. He would never have been able to thread this strange underworld alone—not, at any rate, without taking weeks about it. He could see, however, that Laura was following a steady course that took them down and down—always down to lower levels—and always in the same general direction. He could tell the direction, in a general way, by the drift of the strata.

This was a mine all right. And it was a mine where Moors worked, making their way toward treasure, regardless of human life if it interfered. It might still be one of the richest in the world. But before it could begin to produce new fortunes, another fortune would have to be put into it—for modern equipment, for drainage.

That bugbear of all deep mines—water!—was here in plenty. Hardly ever were they out of hearing of water. It was drip and ripple, and now and then they would be following a swift flow of dark water; again there would come to their ears the drone of some far-off cataract—SUDDENLY, BOTH OF them stopped in their tracks as if at a sharp signal!

From down below somewhere, there came to their ears the sound of a steady thudding—muted and still far down: the sound of heavy hammers. As suddenly as they had heard—the sound, the hammers stopped.

Still Buck and Doña Laura stood still, holding their breath, their candles tilting in the breeze. A sharper sound rumbled through the old mine—louder, louder! Shouts came! Yells! And the muffled shock of gunfire!

Buck Carney grasped the girl's arm tightly.

"El Lobo's men!" he exclaimed. "And the Moors!"

It was a wild guess, but one that was instinctively correct. Too far away to see any man of those who at the moment were hurling themselves into a battle to the death, his reasoning power told him that there could be no other reason for the gunfire ahead.

He was right! El Lobo's men had come! They *had* come to the Cave-that-Talks, to kill off the blacks and seize the treasure for themselves! If Moors could do it, so could they—map or no map!

The chain of caverns running back to Abd-el-Kerim's treasure-chamber was a roaring hell of sound. El Lobo's men— all that were left—had worked their way into the Cave-that-Talks through one of El Lobo's old hideouts. They had taken the Moors by surprise.

And the Cave-that-Talks was justifying its name!

CHAPTER XIII

DON VALERIO

THE CAVE-THAT-TALKS HAD always been not so much a whispering gallery as a thunder gallery, a natural and colossal loudspeaker, picking up every sound and multiplying it, then sending the multiplied sound up and around and back again, often after long intervals, in rolling echoes.

Such sounds as reverberated from it now made it thunderous. No living soul within the depths of the mine could keep from hearing what was happening. It came thus to the ears of one man, a prisoner.

Back in the hollow of the cave not far from where the Moors had worked at their business of trying to open a way into that long sealed-up chamber of theirs, Don Valerio Valdez—former grandee, Knight of the Golden Fleece, once millionaire—had lain for almost a month as a prisoner of Abd-el-Kerim.

Don Valerio had no doubt that the Moor would eventually kill him. He had a perfect conception, by this time, of what the Moor was trying to do.

The place where he lay had been used as a prison before. It was a place—as he could see each time a light came in—that had a hundred chains and links fastened to floor and walls. One such chain was fastened to one of his ankles. It was heavy enough to have held an elephant, let alone a man.

But now, as Don Valerio heard that mounting thunder from the outer caverns, there flashed through his mind thoughts of the plan that had been growing there. But it had formed more as a dream than as something he could carry out.

"Ali!" he called out suddenly and sharply.

A tall Moor, carrying a torch and a knife, ran into the place.

"Those are not brigands, but troops!" Don Valerio shouted.

Ali, already touched with panic, drew nearer and bent his head to listen. Don Valerio was ready for him. Using his last ounce of remaining strength, he lifted his hand and struck the tall Moor over the ear with an iron link. Ali staggered. He stood there swaying. Would he fall? Would he recover himself?

Already, with flying fingers, Don Valerio was picking at the cement that held his chain to the prison's damp wall. He had not failed to note that dampness, nor that the cement had crumbled.

Ali fell.

With a wrest of his body, Don Valerio wrenched the long spike free from its hole in the wall! Except for the chain and the link on his leg, he was free— Free to die! But his enemies would die with him. He knew how the Moors had been working with dynamite that they hoped would open up the still lost treasure chamber!

All the time he had been lying there in his echoing prison, Don Valerio had been hearing things—shouts and laughter, queer songs; screams. Now shots! But, through it all, he had always heard the sound of water.

Once, long ago, he had studied mining at the royal university in Salamanca. Forgotten things were now returning to his mind.

Dragging his chain, he picked up the torch and knife that Ali had let fall. He hauled himself in the direction of the dynamite blast the Moors had prepared!, and which his keen ears had told him about as though he had seen it.

Yes, there was the fuse. There were the caps— Searching rapidly, he found a stick of dynamite in a cache. He fastened a cap onto the end of a length of fuse, then kneaded the cap into the oily, soft dynamite—

THIS WAS GOING to be the end! It would be the end of many things. It would be just as well. If things went on as they were, why, he would be killed, which did not matter so much now. But Don Bartolo would be killed! And Laura—

The length of fuse ran out. With a steady hand, he touched the end of it to the flame of the torch. Like a red eye, the lighted fuse began to retreat in the direction from which he had just come.

A burst of echoing shouts came nearer! Don Valerio lifted his eyes. Abd-el-Kerim was coming on the run along the gallery where he stood.

Abd-el-Kerim, at sight of the Spaniard, stopped. His face was like a jet of black flame. He held a torch in one hand, but his pistol was in the other.

There could have been only one thing that made the Moor hold his shot just then. The thing was a mystery. And the mystery was—that Don Valerio raised a hand and smiled—

From that first outbreak of shouts and shooting, Carney and Doña Laura made a desperate attempt at speed. And this was no trail for a race. It was a maze of traps and pitfalls. Yet they rushed on.

The thunder of the place, growing instantly louder, held them mute. A growing dismay descended on them, freezing their hearts. Not on their own account—but for the sake of him they had come to save.

It was as if they were speeding into a battle of underground devils; as if they were already in the midst of it. Through a twisted cleft and down a long, jagged descent they made their way until they reached the first of a series of great natural hollows in the earth. Laura gasped:

"The Cave-that-Talks!"

CARNEY RAN, CROUCHING, but with his candle held high and his pistol ready. Suddenly he fired!

The shot came so swiftly it was as if it had not been a premeditated shot at all, with no thought of direction. Yet the shot went true.

There had been a Moor standing over there on the other side of a pool of darkness, and beyond the Moor was a white man—

The Moor slumped over sideways, groping for support. From his limp hand dropped gun and torch. Laura Valdez' cry rang out: *"Padre!"*

By the flickering light of the torch, Don Valerio looked as if he had been challenged by a ghost. He shot one glance at that running eye of red at the end of the fuse, then he labored forward. His drawn white lips were shouting:

"Run! Run! For God's sake! To the higher level! Don't wait for me!"

It was at that moment that Buck Carney did what he had already done once before that day—lifted a member of the ancient Valdez family in his arms. He ran, shouting to Laura. Laura ran. She led, holding the flickering torch.

Breathlessly they were just climbing back into that steep and ragged cleft when the explosion came!

IT ROCKED MONTECRISTO! It was to shake it from depths to dome, change the entire inner map of the mountain— wipe from Southern Spain the menace of brigands, black and white!

For, even before the multiple roar of the dynamite rose to its full volume, there sounded from the bowels of the earth an even greater roar—the roar of pent-up waters!

Abd-el-Kerim's treasure chamber was at last open. There no longer was a need of any map. But in the course of centuries it had become a stupendous reservoir!

It took hours for the waters to pour out of the mine and clear a way to see what was in the chamber.

The glory of sunset was pouring down once more as Dona Laura, holding to her rescued father's arm, stood with Buck Carney on the mine's rim.

It was true! All that Don Bartolo had said! Layer on layer, gold, silver, gems lay flashing in the sunset! Rubies, emeralds, silver encrusted by the centuries, but still shining! The wealth of Montecristo! The Valdez family had come at last into their own! And Buck Carney?

Looking down at treasure so great that it would take months even to pile up, his glance went once to Laura Valdez. She was looking at him—shyly. All the treasure in the world was not in gold and silver!

The Avenger of Lo Chang

BY LIEUT. SCOTT MORGAN

*The Further Perilous Adventures
of an Intrepid American
on the Exciting Trail of the
Three Pearls of Death*

GEORGE DANE, BROKER in investments and securities, sat at his broad desk in his London office and beamed professionally upon the visitor who reposed languidly in a chair at his side. Dane, despite his immaculate dress, hardly reflected the picture that popular opinion carries of a broker.

He was a strong, sturdy man with the air of the outdoors about him, and he appeared rather out of place in this luxurious office behind his gleaming mahogany desk. This fact also applied to his visitor.

Younger than Dane was this prospective buyer of Mr. Dane's securities, younger and apparently he had lived a cleaner life. He sat quietly while Dane unburdened himself of the same sales talk which had already unloaded half a million pounds' worth of the very securities that this young man was interested in.

Then, even as he was speaking, George Dane became aware of a vague sensation of apprehension. Something—indefinite it is true—some part of that intricate mental mechanism in the back of his memory, clicked for a moment. It seemed to him that he had seen this young man before. A faint fear pervaded him, a remote uncharted section of his emotions told him that his previous meeting had been under unpleasant circumstances.

HOWEVER, HE DISMISSED the peculiar sensation almost immediately, for George Dane was a practical man who refused to pay attention to the inexplicable quirks of his own psychology.

The office door opened and a trim young girl entered. Silently she laid a handful of mail on her employer's desk, then left the room again. Mr. Dane paused in his rhetorical flight between two adjectives and said: "You'll excuse me a moment while I glance at these?"

The young man assured Mr. Dane that he would.

Dane picked up two letters. The first, a circular, he tossed into the waste basket. The second he glanced at with a frown. Then, with a slightly trembling finger he ripped open the envelope.

He ran bulging eyes over its contents—contents which seemed to be as ominous as he had expected when he opened the envelope.

In a state of high excitement he threw the letter down on the desk and picked up the telephone with trembling fingers. His visitor craned his neck slightly and read the typewritten paper that had so disconcerted the broker. These words leaped to his black eyes:

This is the last warning. I shall call for the pearl today. Have it ready for me or you die.

Brother to the Tong!

Hastily, Dane barked orders through the mouthpiece to an unseen underling.

"See that my bags are packed. Get me a ticket on the international express. Yes, I'm leaving this afternoon. Hurry."

He turned a pale excited face to his visitor.

"I'm sorry, Mr. Lines," he said. "But I've just had some urgent news. You can speak to my assistant about these bonds. I'm leaving London immediately."

The man he had addressed as Lines rose to his feet. His air of careless detachment suddenly vanished. His eyes which a few seconds ago had been lifeless and sleepy became alert and hard. His hand dropped to his coat pocket.

It reappeared again holding a revolver.

"You're not leaving London today, Mr. Dane," he said in a voice of jagged ice. "You're staying right here until I get that pearl."

Dane lost what little composure remained to him. He gasped audibly.

"You—" he said in a thick, dry voiced "You! I thought I'd seen you before."

"You did," said the grim-faced man before him. "You saw me once before in a remote temple on the border of Tibet. Now I'm here to recover the pearl that you took from there. Do I get it or do you die?"

DESPITE THE THREAT of the gun, Dane was so overcome that he sank back into his swivel chair. Perspiration stood out on his pallid brow. His breath came short and fast, and if there was a faint, crafty gleam in his eyes, the man with the revolver failed to see it.

Dane licked his lips nervously.

"You—you are the brother to the tong? What does that mean?"

His visitor regarded him with cold, relentless eyes.

"It means that on that day when you stole the pearls of Lo Chang, I became a blood brother to the tong. A brother whose life was dedicated to the recovery of the jewels you stole. I've tracked you down here to your own office, George Dane, and I am waiting for that pearl."

"And if I refuse to hand it over?"

"You die."

FOR A MOMENT the eyes of the two men met and held. In the gaze of one there was grim, deadly purpose; in the other stark fear, tempered by a gleam of hope.

Beneath the desk the right foot of George Dane moved imperceptibly. The other failed to notice the movement. Instead he watched the broker's face intently, his fingers never loosening the grip on the gun.

"Come," he said at last. "Stop stalling. You haven't got a chance. Get me the pearl. If it isn't here I will accompany you to its hiding place. On the way I shall have you covered with this gun in my pocket. One false move and you're a dead man. Come on. Let's start, unless you prefer to die in that chair."

George Dane stared at the speaker.

He stared beyond him, and a faint smile of relief crawled across his frozen features. A hard voice spoke from the doorway.

"If anyone's dying, partner, it's you. Don't turn your head, and drop the gun on the desk."

For a single second Larry Weston's heart stood still. A terrible futile despair deluged his whole being. He had failed in his mission! Worse than that, he had been trapped by the enemy.

With a clatter the automatic dropped from his nerveless fingers upon the desk. Two men came up, one on each side of him. He felt the muzzle of a .38 press into his side. On the other side of the desk, George Dane rose, flooded with the return of his old confidence.

"Ah," he said, vast satisfaction beaming from his features. "So you don't win after all, my friend. I, as you probably have surmised, live a somewhat precarious existence. That fact accounts for my bodyguard and the button beneath my desk which I pressed a moment ago."

He turned to the two armed men.

"Take him out. Up along the Thames. Some lonely spot. Get rid of him. He's dangerous."

Larry stared dully at the man who uttered his death sentence. So this was the end. This was the end of the great adventure to which he had pledged himself and his life.

"Yes," continued Dane. "You, who style yourself *Brother to the Tong*, are a dangerous person. If I don't kill you, you'll probably hound me to my death. It's better to make an end of things now. Good-by, my friend. I enjoyed your little notes immensely. I regret that I shall read no more of them."

Then the mocking affability vanished.

He turned again to his henchmen, and on his face was an expression of bitter vindictiveness.

     THE BEST OF THRILLING ADVENTURES

"Gorbes, Radner," he said, "I'm depending on you. Get rid of him. It means a lot to me. I'm holding you both directly responsible."

"All right, boss," said one of the men. "Leave him to us."

AGAIN LARRY WESTON felt the barrel of a .38 press against his side.

"Now, march," continued the bodyguard. "And remember that as we drive through the streets, there's a gun covering you, even if you don't see it. Hop to it, now."

Between the two men, Larry Weston was marched ignominiously through Dane's offices into the street. There parked at the curb was a blue coupe. Into that the two men climbed, Larry between them. One sat at the wheel. He stepped on the starter and a few moments later the three of them were running on the smooth London streets toward Kingston-on-Thames.

NOW, IT IS a far cry from the remote mountain fastnesses of Tibet to the busy hubbub of a London street at high noon. Yet at that moment to Larry Weston there was a very direct and pertinent connection.

For it was in the Lo Chang monastery on the far-flung outposts of Tibet that the occurrences which were now apparently leading to his death had taken place. It was from that temple that the three magnificent pearls of the Lo Chang had been stolen. Stolen while he was responsible for their safe-keeping.

To save his own life and the honor of the Chinese that had befriended him, he had vowed that he would recover the jewels. Three men had stolen them. And at this moment only two of those men retrained possession of one pearl each. They were to meet at an arranged date to put their loot together and thus obtain a far greater price for the matched pearls than any one of them could have done for each pearl sold singly.

It was to recover these pearls ere that meeting had taken place that Larry Weston had sworn a great oath by everything which he held holy. Already one of those three pearls was in his possession. And a month ago in Shanghai an unidentified man had been buried, a man who had been the first victim to Larry's revenge. The pearl which he had carried was now safely put away in a London deposit box in Larry's name.

He had discovered on the dead man's person a paper which had contained the names of the other miscreants who had robbed the temple. George Dane was the second person to whom Larry had come in order to retrieve the jewels.

He had sent him two warning letters, signed *Brother to the Tong*. The signature was genuine enough. Because the Lo Changs had made him a blood brother before he had departed from the temple on his mission of revenge and recovery.

And now after one success it seemed that not only his venture but his very life must end.

The coupe passed through the business section, and soon was making its way through London's ubiquitous slums. The three men within the car rode in a grim silence. The two thugs were intent on getting a routine job done quickly, while Larry's brow was knitted as his brain clicked on all six, desperately trying to evolve some scheme to extricate himself from the precarious position into which he had been plunged.

THE SMELL OF the sea floated to them from the river. The slums gave way to the great warehouses of the East India Company. These in turn yielded to the ramshackle houses of that great oriental settlement of London's Chinese colony—Limehouse.

A gray fog was borne on the river. It floated wraith-like over the sprawled city. The buildings became gray and damp, and Larry Weston, recognizing the section through which the car was passing, found his heart give a sudden bound of hope. He glanced down surreptitiously at the ring finger of his left hand. Reposing there was a splendid jade ring, with an intricately carved silver setting.

It was the means of identification to Lo Changs the world over. The bauble which had been given him by the head priest in order that he might identify himself to his tong brothers no matter where he found himself.

AND NOW FATE had brought him to Limehouse. Brought him to the one place in the world where, perhaps, outside of China, the largest number of Lo Changs resided. Larry realized that if he put into execution the plan that had flicked across his brain he must take a long desperate chance.

But when one's life hangs in the balance, long odds look the same as short ones.

Silently, quietly, yet with every nerve in his body tingling, he awaited his chance. The coupe slowed down as the fog grew thicker. Then hard by a crossing, it stopped, entirely surrounded by two huge trucks that momentarily blocked the traffic.

Larry glanced swiftly through the window of the car. There on the sidewalk strolled a number of long-gowned Chinamen. Larry wondered if any of them owed allegiance to the same tong that he had sworn to avenge. Then, as he peered more carefully into the fog, he saw something which sent hope beating hard and fast through his veins.

On a dirty shop window about half way down the block he saw a weird Chinese dragon that breathed smoke through but one nostril. It was the symbol of the men of Lo Chang—the dragon of the tong to which he was a blood brother. A sudden idea flashed through his mind. It was a long and desperate chance, but it was all that stood between him and ignominious death.

They were stopped on the street corner by the cross traffic. The smoke-breathing dragon was now right at the side of the car. Larry peered through the fog. Chinamen hurried hither and thither through the gray haze that blanketed the metropolis.

Then, in that single second, he gathered himself for his literal leap for life. Every muscle in his body tensed. Every nerve was alert.

With a sudden movement he swung his right hand to the point of the jaw of Gorbes. The astounded gunman fell back in the seat, momentarily stunned. Larry swiftly climbed over his knees, opened the door and jumped to the street.

Even as his feet hit the pavement he heard the shout of alarm from Radner. The latter emerged hastily from the door on the other side of the car. He rushed around the still vehicle, and even in the opaque gray haze that covered everything, Larry saw the black outlines of an automatic in his right hand.

"Stop, you fool, or I'll shoot!"

RADNER'S VOICE CAME to Larry's ears as he raced across the street to the sanctuary offered by that dingy painting of the dragon on the even dingier glass of the window.

A staccato crack ripped through the sodden air. Larry heard a bullet sing its ominous threnody over his head. There was a sudden crashing of glass as the steel slug ate its way into the plate glass window. From within a startled oriental screamed. Larry knocked aside an indignant pedestrian and raced into the building.

As he opened the door he found himself on the threshold of a large hall, apparently the meeting room of the Lo Chang tong. Toward him there rushed a score of Chinese; knives and hatchets gleamed in their hands as they came to avenge this outrage of a white man in their conference hall.

THEN, BEFORE LARRY could speak, before the Orientals could close upon him, the door opened again. Radner entered the room, and close behind him, panting and glassy-eyed, came Gorbes, now recovered from the first shock of Larry's unexpected blow.

The charging Chinese halted temporarily as they saw the two white men standing in the doorway, drawn pistols in their hands. Between them stood Larry, glancing swiftly from the ominous muzzles of the white men's guns to the glinting steel weapons of the Chinamen. It was Radner who broke the tension.

"We're police officers," he said. "This man is our prisoner. He escaped. We're sorry for the intrusion. We'll just take him along and go."

A man clad in a long flowing robe moved out from the group of yellow men. He flung a staccato command over his shoulder to the Lo Changs. At his word, they replaced their weapons in their belts and stood quietly behind their leader.

He turned to the white men and bowed.

"It is well," he said. "I apologize for the unseemly conduct of my brothers. But they were taken by surprise. They resented the intrusion. But it is done now. Take your man and go."

He indicated Larry. With a smile of triumph, Radner advanced, gun still in hand. On his other side the Chinese stared implacably at Larry, hostility in their gaze despite the sudden armistice. Radner jammed his gun in Larry's ribs.

"Come, on," he said. "The game's up."

Larry met his gaze squarely. A faint smile was on his lips as he replied.

"Perhaps, Radner," he said quietly. "Perhaps."

He thrust out his arm. His hand, palm downward, stretched forth before the tong leader's eyes. The Oriental in the flowing robe looked down. He raised his head again and though his countenance was still the expressionless bland face of his race, there was a peculiar gleam in his eyes.

"Come on," said Radner again. "We can't wait here all day."

"Wait." It was the Chinese who spoke. Then he turned to Larry. "Is it help you desire, brother?"

Larry nodded.

"Deliver me from my captors, oh, brother," he said. "Then set upon them and make them prisoners."

Radner stared in astonishment. Behind him Gorbes frowned.

"Come on," he said. "What's all this parleying? Let's get out of here. You, Weston, march."

"Wait!"

THIS TIME IT was the Chinaman who spoke again, but in his tone was a terrible command. He turned to his yellow cohorts and spoke rapidly in Cantonese.

A shrill scream rent the air behind them. The Chinese suddenly broke their ranks and charged. Half a dozen staccato shots, from the two white men's weapons, ripped the air, but they were soon overwhelmed by the superior numbers of the Chinese.

Larry stood calmly to one side as the battle raged. Then, a moment later, Radner and Gorbes, badly battered and lacerated, were dragged before him. The tong leader bowed politely to Larry.

"Here my brother," he intoned. "We have obeyed your orders. We have made your captors prisoners because of the ring which you wear, because the ring declares that you are brother to the tong. Am I correct?"

"I am, indeed, brother to the tong of Lo Chang," said Larry gravely. "I am on a mission now for the brotherhood. That is how I happened to run into danger here." The Oriental bowed again. "It is well," he said. "Your orders have been obeyed. Is there anything else that we can do for our brother?"

LARRY'S BROW WRINKLED in thought for a moment. True, he had, for the time being, outwitted Dane, but that fact had put him no nearer the second pearl of the Lo Chang. At last, however, he shook his head.

"No," he said. "Merely keep these two white men prisoners until you hear from me. That is all."

"Say," said Radner, speaking for the first time. "You can't leave us here. You can't—"

Larry turned on him.

"You're lucky that I'm leaving you alive, Radner," he said. "It's more than you were going to do to me."

With that Weston turned and strode from the building, assured in the knowledge that as long as he possessed the jade ring which had been given him in the temple, he would know allies all over the world, everywhere that Cathay had her living representatives.

Yet he still had a task before him.

He had escaped death, true, but his mission was not advanced save in the negative way of his still being alive. He walked slowly through the fog, his mind working swiftly, and gradually there trickled into his brain an idea to ascertain the location of the second pearl of Lo Chang, which was in the unrightful possession of George Dane.

WITH A SLEEK Corona between his lips, Dane slid into the swivel chair before his desk with a grunt of satisfaction. The unpleasant incident of the preceding day was no more than an exhilarating memory now. He felt smug, completely satisfied with his ability to take care of himself and the pearl of Lo Chang as well.

He picked up the neat stack of letters piled up before him on his desk and with a casual eye scanned them over. Then for the second time within the past twenty-four hours, he received a swift and sudden shock.

The dozen or so envelopes fluttered from his nerveless fingers to the table top—all save one. The color drained slowly from Dane's face, then returned with a wave of hot crimson, as he studied the bold address.

George Dane, Esquire.

It wasn't three words that riveted his attention; it was the hand in which they were written. He recognized it instantly. That warning letter he had received the day before had been written by the same hand.

With a savage oath and a swift, impetuous movement, he inserted a broad thumb under the flap of the envelope and jerked out the sheet of paper within. With fingers suddenly clumsy, he unfolded it, focused his narrowed eyes on the brief message.

You will require more than gunmen to dispose of the avenger of Lo Chang. This is my last warning! Within the next twelve hours after you receive this letter, I will again call on you.

Be prepared, either to deliver the pearl to me—or die!

Brother to the Tong.

Dane read the message through twice, at first unable to believe the stunning import of the words. He was suddenly aware that his mouth was hot and dry. Beads of sweat stood out on his forehead. He ran a pudgy finger around the rim of his collar. All his smug self-assurance and placidity of a minute before were gone—destroyed completely by the ominous words of the warning.

With a physical effort, Dane threw off the paralysis of fear that crept about his heart. There must be some mistake, he tried to assure himself. Some ghastly joke. Radner and Gorbes had never before failed him on such a simple matter as disposing of a man, once he had been turned over to their tender mercies.

He snapped out of his momentary funk, leaped to the telephone. Violently he pumped the hook up and down, tersely snapped a number into the mouthpiece. His fingers beat an impatient tattoo on the table top for the connection to go through. He waited tense—ten, twenty, thirty seconds. The buzz in the receiver told him that the phone was ringing at the other end.

But no one came to answer the summons!

DANE SWORE SAVAGELY under his breath. He had given Radner and Gorbes orders to stay there in the house until he called them. They would have obeyed—unless something had gone wrong. And with each passing second, Dane was more firmly convinced that something had.

That grim warning clutched in his hand was no joke or jest. It meant business—the business of death!

He pumped the receiver again, called a half-dozen numbers in quick succession. But nowhere was he able to get any word of his two henchmen. As far as Dane was concerned, they had disappeared off the face of the earth.

If nothing else, George Dane was a man of quick decisions and just as quick action. And he was wise enough to realize that at times discretion was the better part of valor.

He yanked open a drawer of his desk, extracted a briefcase and hastily jammed it with a varied assortment of papers.

He called his secretary into the office and issued a series of brief, terse orders to her.

"Now tell Jarsen I want to see him," he concluded. "At once."

JARSEN, A TALL brute of a man, entered the private office a moment later.

The word killer was written clearly in the low brow, the small colorless eyes.

"Look to your gun," snapped Dane without any preliminaries.

Jarsen's eyes narrowed to glinting slits at the order. He smelled action— trigger action. With a swift movement, he unlimbered a glinting automatic from a holster concealed beneath his left arm pit. He examined it thoroughly, expertly, patted it once affectionately and returned it to its leather.

"It's ready and hungry," he said laconically.

"Good," grunted Dane. "I have several calls to make this morning and I want you to be at my elbow all the time, understand? There may be trouble. If there is, I want you to shoot first and ask questions after. Get that?"

"Sure, I get it," grinned Jarsen. "But after I shoot, there'll be no need to ask questions. You won't get any answer."

Dane reached for his hat and picked up the briefcase. He nodded for Jarsen to lead the way.

"Right! You go first!"

Leaning against the grimy bricks of Holbrook Court, his bearded face buried in the advertising section of the *London Times,* was a man. By him the hurrying throngs of Fleet Street drifted in swirling eddies of pedestrian traffic. The man with the beard was unnoticed, or if he did warrant a casual glance he was put down for one of the countless number of the unemployed looking for a job.

But why should a man looking for a day's labor pack an automatic on his hip? Why should a man supposedly reading the want ads cast such a furtive, wary eye at the entrance to Holbrook Court? There was only one answer. He was not a day laborer and neither was he looking for a job.

In fact, he was looking for a specific individual—one George Dane.

LARRY WESTON WAS thankful enough at having escaped from Dane's men with the aid of the Lo Chang brotherhood, but now that adventure was over, he realized that he was no closer to the possession of the second pearl than when he had started his quest.

He felt reasonably sure that Dane would not be so easily trapped again in his office, and just as sure that if he were, the pearl would not be on his person.

Though he had sworn a personal vengeance on the violators of the Monastery, the death of Dane would achieve him little unless he thereby secured the priceless gem held by that individual.

His first problem was to locate the hiding place of the jewel. Larry had devoted a number of hours of hard concentration to the matter and finally evolved a plan he hoped might work. He figured that if he could frighten Dane sufficiently to make him run to cover, Dane would take the pearl with him. This would not only reveal the hiding place of the jewel, but put it on the person or in the personal effects of the broker.

And Larry felt every confidence that he would be able to lift it from Dane with bloodshed or without, by fair means or foul.

WITH ALL THIS in mind, he had sent his second letter of warning to the broker, and now in his unkempt beard and ragged clothes he leaned against the grimy wall of Holbrook Court, awaiting developments.

They were not long in coming. Larry suddenly stiffened to sharp attention behind the concealing pages of his newspaper. From the corner of his eye he caught sight of the familiar figure of Dane as the latter emerged from the door of the building. Larry noted with a grim smile the gorilla-like man by his side and correctly appraised him as a bodyguard.

As he watched, he saw Dane cast a swift glance up and down the crowded street, then speak to his man. The other nodded, and together they breasted the traffic of Fleet Street toward the bank on the far corner.

Larry's heart lifted as he saw their destination. Undoubtedly his letter had had the proper effect and Dane was going to hide out for a while. The trip to the bank probably meant that he was going to take the pearl with him.

This assumption was strengthened as he followed the broker and his body-guard into the bank and saw them repair immediately to the safety vaults.

Weston wasted a few minutes at one of the counters making out a mythical check. Two minutes later, when Dane and his man reappeared, he casually drifted out of the bank after them into the turmoil of Fleet Street.

For the next hour Larry clung to the trail of the two men like a leech. He was consumed with a feverish impatience to come at once to grips with his adversary. But fear of a second failure imposed caution on his impatient spirit.

It would have been a dangerous gamble to have tackled Dane and his bodyguard in the streets, with a million people about. No, common sense dictated that he wait till he got them in more secluded surroundings, or, better still, alone.

But that desire was not to be fulfilled. He trailed the two to a steamship ticket office, saw Dane stuff a cardboard into his pocket. But what his destination was, Larry had no way of finding out just then.

He was tying his shoelace at the curb when the two men emerged to the street again. They talked for a few minutes in low tones together, then Dane hailed a cruising cab.

Before Larry was quite aware what had happened, Dane had leaped into the still moving vehicle, snapped an order at the driver and was lost almost immediately in a tangle of traffic.

For a split second, Weston was tempted to charge after the cab, but he realized instantly the futility of the chase. Instead, he turned, glanced swiftly up the street just in time to see the broad shoulders of the bodyguard rounding the far corner.

With pounding pulses he took up the chase. Bitterly he cursed himself for a rank amateur, for having let Dane get away from right under his very nose. If he should lose the bodyguard, too—

But he didn't. He came swiftly upon his quarry. His automatic was transferred to the side pocket of his coat. Now, without any preliminaries, he stepped close to Jarsen, jammed the gun savagely into that individual's side.

"Keep walking ahead as if nothing was the matter!" he snapped tersely.

There was latent death in the tone of his voice. Jarsen had heard that tone of voice before and he was wise enough to obey.

"Edge over to the curb and hail the first cab!" ordered Larry.

JARSEN OBEYED, BUT not without some verbal protest.

"What's the idea, guv'nor?"

"You'll find out soon enough. Flag that cab!"

Jarsen obeyed reluctantly and with Weston's gun still prodding him from behind, climbed into the vehicle. Larry sank to the seat beside him, his gun ready for instant action. To the driver he snapped the address of the Lo Chang tong room.

"Where you taking me?" demanded Jarsen sullenly. "Why throw a gun on me?"

"I'll take you no place if you want to talk," shot back Weston.

"Talk about what?"

"About your employer, Dane."

Jarsen's eyes narrowed at the challenge. "Well, what about him?" he said truculently.

"He just bought a steamship ticket. Where's his destination?"

"How should I know, mister?"

"Too bad for you if you don't," smiled Weston, but there was no humor in his voice.

"Say, who are you anyway?"

"I'm the man Dane is running from."

"Well, what's that got to do with me?"

"Plenty. If you tell me where Dane is going—what boat—nothing happens to you. If you don't—" Their cab had pulled up before the building of the Lo Changs. "Chinamen here, you see. They're friends of mine. They have lots of cunning ways to torture information out of a white man. Unless you tell me what I want to know, you'll get what Radner and Gorbes got—only worse."

"Radner and Gorbes!" exploded Jarsen.

"Right. Unless I'm mistaken, their bodies are floating in the Thames now."

"Bluff!" snorted Jarsen. "You can't get nothing out of me I don't want to tell."

"No?" purred Weston in an icy voice. "We'll see!" He prodded his gun into the other. "Get out. There are ten Chinamen watching you now. One move and it's all over with you."

SULLENLY JARSEN OBEYED. Close behind him as they crossed the sidewalk, Larry called back to the taxi driver.

"Wait for me," he said confidently. "I'll be out in a few minutes."

But the few minutes stretched to a grim twenty. Jarsen proved to be a much tougher nut to crack than Weston had anticipated. Larry sweated him at first with words and dire threats, a grinning crew of the Lo Chang brotherhood making an effective background to the scene.

From threats he switched his attack to

cajolerie with little better results. Larry began to lose patience. He tried a little manhandling of his victim. He had no taste for the work. He had nothing personally against Jarsen.

But he had to find out George Dane's destination. He threw away his easy sympathy, stripped off his coat and got down to the serious business of choking the truth out of his quarry. A scarce half inch from death, glinting, relentless eyes drilling their dire purpose into his, Jarsen broke down at last.

"The—Channel Boat," he sobbed. "Sailing—at—two!"

Weston flung the limp figure from him with a violent gesture. He glanced at his watch swiftly. Eighteen minutes to two! Could he make it? He had to make it, he swore to himself, as he ran pell-mell out of the room.

It was a mad, breakneck chase through London's congested traffic to the waterfront, but under the stimulation of a pound reward if he arrived at the pier before sailing time, the cabbie rose to the emergency.

He came to a skidding halt at the pier head just as the last line was being taken in. Larry knew that his game would be up if Dane saw his precipitous arrival, but he had to risk it and gamble that the broker would be in his cabin.

He scrambled aboard just as the packet pulled into the stream, repaired immediately to the purser's office. While the assistant purser was allotting him a cabin, he looked over the passenger list.

A thrill of exhilaration coursed through his veins as he noted Dane's name beside Cabin 26.

"Something up on A deck," suggested Weston. "Twenty-seven or eight—are they vacant?"

"I can give you twenty-seven."

"Fine."

LARRY MADE HIMSELF comfortable in his stateroom, lit a cigarette and concentrated on his next move. Indistinct sounds drifted to him from behind the bulkhead from Dane's compartment. Larry listened, arose himself a few minutes later when the door of the adjoining cabin slammed shut. Larry followed Dane onto the deck, strolled after him to the bar.

Dane ordered a whisky and soda and downed it as if he needed it badly. He called for a second, and gambling that a third and fourth would follow, Larry went out on deck again.

It was but a minute's work to gain Dane's cabin unobserved. Larry knew that he had to work swiftly and surely if he were to find the pearl. True, it might not have been concealed in the cabin, but if possible he had to make sure.

He went over the small cabin with swift precision. Nothing escaped his attention. Bed first, washstand, traveling bags, under the carpet, behind pictures. No slightest crevice escaped his attention, but no pearl was forthcoming.

Larry was about to give up his search, convinced that Dane carried the gem on his person. If that were the case, his problem was considerably more difficult. Then an idea occurred to him, and with a grim smile, he decided on a bold bluff.

Calmly and coolly, as if he were in his own cabin, he sank into a chair. He had not long to wait.

The knob of the door turned; the portal was flung wide.

Only half way across the threshold, Dane saw him and immediately whipped out a gun from his hip. An ugly snarl fought with the smile of triumph on his face as he closed the door behind him and leveled the gun at the intruder.

"Oh, so it's you," he grated from between clenched teeth. "You threatened murder, but you turn out to be nothing but a cheap housebreaker after all. You'll have a hard time explaining this intrusion to the ship's captain."

The gun was steady and menacing in his hand. It pointed unwaveringly at Larry's heart. And Weston knew that Dane would be only too glad for an excuse to use it. However, he never flinched. If anything, he smiled brazenly up at Dane's infuriated face and insolently cocked one knee over the other.

"You know, Dane," he said suavely, "you wouldn't have the nerve to turn me over to the captain. I know too much."

A mask of hate descended over Dane's ugly face. He stepped to within a foot of Weston, jutted forth his jaw aggressively and rammed the point of the gun into Larry's stomach. His lips worked convulsively, but it was a full ten seconds before he could speak.

"You're right, you know too much!" he snarled. "Maybe I won't turn you over to the captain. Maybe I'll just shoot you. A simple little story with no aftermath. I surprised you looting my cabin. You

attacked me. I shot you in self-defense. What have you to say to that?"

"Only that you'd be a fool to do it. What about your pearl?"

"Well, what about it?"

"Killing me would never get your pearl back for you."

A startled expression fell over Dane's face at the words, but he recovered almost immediately. The snarl returned to his lips.

"A pretty bluff, but it doesn't go with George Dane," he taunted. "You haven't got the pearl!"

Larry still hadn't moved from his easy position in the chair. His confidence and self-assurance was getting under the other's skin. He felt sure that if he could keep up the pose another minute he would succeed.

"What makes you so sure?" he mocked.

"Because you couldn't find it!"

"No? What does this look like?"

KEEPING HIS EYE ever on the gun in Dane's hand, Larry fished into the pocket of his vest and extracted a shimmering bauble of glittering light. It lay taunting, bewitching, compelling in the palm of his hand. Larry twisted Dane's wrist with his free hand and the gun went off harmlessly in the air. Dane whirled, sped swiftly for the small dressing table at the far side of the cabin.

With eagle eyes Larry followed his every movement, watched him snatch the powder box from the top of the dresser.

Then he sprang into action! In two swift strides he was across the cabin.

The nozzle of his gun ground deep into Dane's back. With his free hand he snatched the gun from Dane.

Some instinct must have told the broker that he had fallen into a trap. He whirled, lips bared back from snarling teeth, but there was no denying the menace in Weston's leveled gun, the cold glitter in his eye that belied the smile on his lips.

"Step away from that dresser!" ordered Larry. "March!"

Dane backed slowly away.

"Thanks for showing me the hiding place of your pearl," laughed Larry, picking up the powder can. As Dane watched him with fascinated eyes, he snapped off the lid, fished inside and extracted a gleaming twin to the jewel that now reposed securely in his vest pocket. He held it before the other's baleful eyes. "A beauty, eh? I looked all over the cabin for it, but couldn't locate it."

"But the one you had—"

"Fool. You fell right into my trap as I had planned. The pearl I showed you was the first of the three pearls of Lo Chang, which I took from my vault yesterday. I retrieved it in Shanghai. A dead man points the tale. This is the second."

With an inarticulate bellow of rage, Dane risked all on a foolhardy move. He lunged suddenly forward, made a desperate attempt to grasp Weston's gun arm. He half succeeded. There was a fierce struggle in the room for a swift two minutes. But it was terminated just as desperately by the dull explosion of a gun.

Dane staggered back. A look of bewilderment spread over his face, then slowly vanished. His knees buckled and he plunged headlong to the floor. Weston stooped down to the grotesque figure on the floor for a moment, saw that Dane was only wounded.

IN HIS POCKET reposed another of the pearls of Lo Chang, and in his heart was a strange mixture of triumph and wistfulness. He, whose life had been such a quiet, uneventful thing, was now a flaming adventurer who stalked the byways of the world, his life dedicated to a task of revenge and blood.

He sighed wearily.

Then his brain put an end to his emotional imaginings. He must get off this boat somehow. It would never do to be aboard when Dane was discovered. He would be accused of being a thief. He left Dane's room and strode on deck.

There, twinkling to the southeast, were the lights of Calais. He walked to the stern. He glanced around carefully. There was no one in sight. For a moment he stood poised on the stern rail, then he dived.

And as the channel boat continued to her destination with her cargo of death below, the *Brother to the Tong* swam silently through the night to a safety which would only last until he caught up to Lo Chang's third matchless pearl.

Danger Trails

BY **CAPT. KERRY McROBERTS**

Charging Arabs and Fighting Legionnaires in an Exciting, Thrill-Packed Novel of the African Desert

CHAPTER I

LEGIONNAIRE BILL STIVERS saw the menacing, gleaming knife leave the hand of the dark-faced Mohammedan sitting three tables away from him!

He saw the knife coming through the filthy-laden air toward him.

Then, before Stivers could duck or dodge the weapon, he saw a drunken Algerian stagger across his view and crumple to the floor with a dull groan as the knife buried itself in his flesh. And then when the dull groan of the stricken man died away, a silence—oppressive, dangerous and sinister—settled over the filthy and stuffy room that housed Har Monken's dive.

The sweating, colorful jam of unholy humanity—Arabs, Mohammedans, Riffs, Moors, and every nationality that infested such places in Northern Africa—seemed to tense and rise slowly from their seats. The heat was stifling under the hot and gaseous haze of smoke that clung to the low ceiling.

The clamoring and clinking of glasses ceased: the roar of subdued conversation stopped, and the tenuous nasal whine of the flutists, chanting in a sing-song voice to the accompaniment of the squirming dance girls, died away weirdly.

Stivers was on his feet, his hands gripping the edges of the table. There was no doubt in his mind that the knife had been intended for him, and there was little doubt in his mind but that his body would be cut to ribbons before he got out of the dive.

The dark-faced Mohammedan that had hurled the knife through the air was gone, but three tall, powerfully-built Riffs had risen from their chairs and were moving slowly, in a half circle, toward Stivers' table.

Bill Stivers silently and mercilessly cursed himself for his stupidity in entering Har Monken's den alone. His eyes searched the crowd for the kepi of some brother Legionnaire, but there was none. He was alone in this hole of murder and death.

Hands gripping the table, Stivers watched the three powerful Riffs closing in on him in a narrowing half-circle. It flashed through his mind that the whole scene was grotesque and crazy, this tableau of death. Why would anyone want to murder him? He was a stranger, an unknown recruit in the Legion. He only had two sous left in his pocket—two days' pay given him by the French Republic for the hell and the suffering he had to go through. It couldn't be robbery, but what could it be?

ANOTHER KNIFE GLEAMED and flashed in the hazy light of the room, but this time Bill Stivers ducked. The knife grazed the edge of his neck. Blood spurted out from the flesh wound and dropped down on his newly laundered canvas whites. The blood dripped on the black *cummerbund* around his waist.

Stivers was down on his hands and knees behind the table. The narrowing circle had closed in on him. On his right and on his left was a crouching Riff; in front of him was the Riff that had hurled the knife. The muscles in Stivers' face contracted in thin ridges around his mouth: his steel gray eyes darted swiftly over the room.

The eerie, deadly silence of death continued to pervade the place. The crowd had risen from their seats and had backed away, watching the murder drama with a savage interest. The dancing girls had fled, and through the smoke-filled air Stivers caught a glance of the fat, slinking form of Har Monken standing near the door.

But Stivers wasted no time looking at the motley mob. One against three was odds he couldn't hope to overcome, especially since the three against him were armed with knives and, because of the regulations of the Legion, he had to enter the dive unarmed. Legionnaires when they went foraging in the night were not permitted to carry pistols or knives, a regulation that had long been followed at Sidi-bel-Abbes.

But Stivers, though he could not understand the insane desire to murder him, grimly vowed that he would sell his life as dearly as possible. The man in front of him took two steps nearer. With a mighty heave Stivers brought the table up and hurled it at the man. He wasted no time to see if his aim had been good. He swerved with the swiftness of a tiger and was on the Riff at his right.

And in that moment bedlam broke loose. He was not only fighting the three Riffs now. He was fighting a sea of black faces, black arms, black legs. Knives flew and men yelled in twenty different languages.

AIMING HIS BLOWS carefully, from his crouching position on the floor, Stivers shot out right and left. Dark faces bobbed up in front of him and then went down to the floor with sickening groans. Backward Stivers moved, still in the crouching position. He came to the wall. His face was set and hard. A grim smile played on his lips. He knew it all would be over in a few brief seconds. It would have been over sooner if the fight had been left to the three Riffs encircling him. A knife thrust would have ended it.

But the surging mob bearing down on him in their insane fury against a white man had spoiled the cleverly planned attack of the three Riffs. It threw Stivers into a melee of human forms and bodies and a well-aimed knife thrust was out of the question in that snarling mass of human flesh. Sheer weight of bodies, though, would soon overwhelm Stivers, crush him to the floor where a knife would end it all.

But until then—

Smack! Smack! Stivers threw his right and left out with a deadly, paralyzing precision. His blows connected with the grimy, greasy black faces in front of him. But the surging mob came on relentlessly, and with a fury that had been aroused to an insane pitch by the sight of blood and the hope of murder.

STIVERS KNEW THAT the three Riffs had approached him with a clearly defined plan of murder. The knife hurled by the Mohammedan had been the first part of this plan. There was nothing frenzied or hurried. It had been coldly calculated.

But the attack of the surging mob was different. They knew nothing behind any plan to kill this lone white man. They were driven on by their lust for blood and murderous hatred for the white heathen that had come and conquered them. In front of them was a white man, alone and unarmed. Someone had started the attack and they would finish it.

On and on the surging men pressed against Stivers. His arms ached. The smell and the stifling heat, made a hundred times worse by the bodies that closed around him, caused a feeling of sickness to come over him. But his right and left continued to drive out.

In a minute—perhaps, in the matter of a few seconds, it would be over. There was no chance for him to escape. His arms were heavy and tired now. His blows had lost their sting.

A glorious end to his career in the Legion! Murdered in a cheap dive by a sinister hand that moved in the dark, a hand that had sought him out among the thousands of Legionnaires—

His thoughts began to reel. What was it all about? His arms went dead. The snarling hiss of savage faces near him closed in relentlessly. Something hit him alongside the head. He felt himself falling forward to the floor. He heard a wild yell. Someone was pulling at his arm and his body was being dragged across the floor.

Slowly darkness—the stygian overwhelming darkness of unconsciousness—closed down upon him. He tried to raise his arms. He couldn't.

Then he fell forward on his face and remembered nothing more.

CHAPTER II

THE GODDESS OF ILL LUCK

STIVERS CAME TO with a jerk of the body and a feeling that a thousand tons of rock had suddenly descended on his head. Every muscle and bone in his body ached and his head was filled with sharp shooting pains. He opened his eyes, but all he could see was jet black darkness.

For a moment his mind seemed numbed. He tried to think, to remember what had happened and where he was. But his mind was a windmill of jumbled thoughts—crazy, bewildering thoughts that raced through his brain wildly. He had left the barracks that evening. He had come to Har Monken's dive.

And then suddenly the memory of the fight in the dive flashed back to him. He tried to struggle to his feet. There were the black bodies that had descended over him like a cloud. The last thing he had remembered was the sickening blow on the side of his head and the feeling that his body was being pulled across a floor. But where was he now?

HE TRIED TO sit up, but the muscles in his body didn't respond to his attempt to rise. He laid back again and closed his eyes. Was he dead? The thought struck him as silly—childish. He wasn't dead, but what had happened?

"Vite, fool of an American," he heard a voice close to him, a voice that spoke pure French. *"Mon Dieu,* I saved you from those black dogs, but if we don't get out of here in a hurry, they'll cut us to ribbons. Move! Get up and move!"

Dazed and stunned by the sudden sound of a human voice, a voice that was that of a white man. Stivers struggled to get on his feet. Two strong arms helped him and the arms continued to assist him as he staggered through the wall of darkness in front of him. He could not see the man at his side; he could see nothing in that dungeon-like blackness.

"We are in a rear room of Monken's dive," the man at his side said. "Don't ask me how I got you in here. There is a door to our right that leads out into an alley. If we get there safely—"

The words were drowned out by the roar of voices behind them. Savage fists were pounding frantically on the wall. The roar increased.

"Saint Suplice," the man whispered. "If they knock the wall down—"

There was a crash of wood behind them. Stivers was running now, with his new-found friend's arms around his waist, giving him support. He was running blindly in the darkness. Suddenly they crashed against a wall. Men were yelling a few feet behind them.

"*Vite, mon ami,*" his friend cried. "Here is a door."

Stivers stumbled and staggered after the man. His senses reeled again, but he kept on. How he ever got out of the door and into the night air was something he never remembered. But he got there. The night air cleared his brain in a flash and brought strength to his body. Ahead of him he saw the familiar kepi, the white canvas trousers, and black *cummerbund* of the Legion.

His newly-found friend was a Legionnaire! Stivers dashed after the Legionnaire, down the narrow half-darkened alley. Behind them he heard shouts, savage and wild, but as they raced through the night the shouts died away. Suddenly Stivers turned sharply to the right and the man ahead of him stopped running and leaned against the mud wall of a building, breathing hard, and looked at Stivers with a grin on his sharply featured face.

"THE LITTLE PIG of a recruit," the man said with a laugh. "The little recruit goes into Har Monken's place for the great honor of being murdered. But name of a name, *mon enfant,* look at the rent in your elbow. Five nights in the *salle de police* for that. But ordinary arrests are nothing. *Sacré mon nom,* it will be better than death at the hands of those dogs."

Stivers looked at the Legionnaire addressing him. His mind was still a little dazed and befuddled, He was still wondering how the Legionnaire saved him from the wall of knives that had flashed over his head just before unconsciousness had come over him.

He recognized the face of the man before him. It was a face that once seen would never completely be forgotten. The man had come to the company that day. There had been a buzz of excitement when he appeared. He was no recruit. Everything about him—his bearing, his face, his calloused hands, told the story of years spent in the Legion.

But Stivers had been unable to learn the cause of the subdued excitement that had spread among the men when this man arrived.

The man's face was striking and a little ghastly. A shock of jet black hair stuck out from underneath the jaunty kepi, sweeping a high, intelligent forehead covered with white scars, The face was gaunt and grim, with the same white scars of the forehead running down his leather bronzed cheeks. The features of the face were strongly chiseled—the features of a man who had suffered much, of a man of steel courage and a will that defied death and misery with a jaunty laugh.

But it was the eyes that caught Stivers' attention. Even in the shadowy darkness of the narrow alley-like street, he could see that they were blue—a bright, liquid blue, flashing a gleam that was startling and piercing. The man's body was tall and thin, with not an ounce of surplus flesh on it, the body of a man whom the merciless sun of Africa and the cruel, bitter punishment the desert meted out to human beings had molded into fibers of cold, hard steel.

STIVERS GRINNED BACK at him and extended his hand. The other man took it with a grip that was powerful and friendly.

"You saved my life," Stivers said quietly. "I don't know how you did it. I really don't know just what happened back in that dive. I wandered in there to get a drink and a Mohammedan tried to kill me and when he failed three Riffs tried it, and before they got through the whole dump was after me. I passed out, thinking that I was starting for the pearly gates, but when I opened my eyes I was in that rear room and you were near me."

"La Tour is my name," the man said quietly. "That is, it is my name in the Legion, and other names don't count much here. I am in your company, but you had no occasion to meet me. You were pointed out as the new recruit, the first one in several weeks, but recruits are usually weak-kneed fools, who haven't been molded into men yet by the Legion. *Mon Dieu,* I say they usually are. But you! Name of names! Such courage! Such blows you struck in there! Superb—wonderful, and when I saw that—I decided to save you."

Stivers shook his head slowly.

"You saved me," he said, "and I'll never forget it, but how did you come to save me and how did you get me out of that cursed room? The whole damn thing is a mystery to me."

La Tour laughed easily. There was something contagious, reckless and daring in that clear laugh. Stivers felt this and liked the man fully and completely, regardless of who he was or what was the mystery about his return to the company.

"You have not heard about me?" La Tour said with a laugh. "You have not heard about the *enfant terrible;* the Legionnaire La Tour? Only this morning I returned from Oujda, the Legionnaire's hell. *Saint Marie,* what a living hell, those penal stone quarries. Two years, *mon ami,* in those stone quarries. Few men live one month. But *l'enfant terrible* lived there for two years."

La Tour laughed carelessly, recklessly. Stivers had heard enough about the hell of Oujda to gasp in wonderment at the face of La Tour. Two years in that hell hole! There was only one hell the members of the French Foreign Legion feared, That was Oujda.

"Yes," La Tour added, laughing. "It was for planning desertion that I was sent there. A friend betrayed me, but that is another story. What concerns you is this: There will be a rumpus about that dead Algerian in Har Monken's dive. You can rest assured that the treacherous-handed Mohammedan will not suffer for it. Because I have a very interesting story to tell you. It was planned to murder *you* there and because a certain person failed once, is no reason why it will not be tried again—with a little greater success."

"TO MURDER ME?" Stivers gasped.

"*Mon ami,*" La Tour replied, "was it for a little exercise that that knife was hurled at you? You Americans have the brains of fools. Name of a name. A man tries to kill you and you gasp in wonder that such a thing is possible. I do not know why a certain man, or men, wish to kill you, but I know they do. I heard it with my own ears. That is why I followed you to Har Monken's place and pulled you through that rear door, out of reach of the dogs. Oh, yes, I know Har Monken's place very well.

BUT MARK THIS: Today I returned to the regiment and tonight I was strolling near the concert square. It is getting dark. I saw an officer of the Legion and a tall, dark-faced man talking together. Their backs were to me as they were standing on the other side of the tree. I could hear their voices. They were saying that it would be well for them if a certain American was murdered. If the tall, dark man could locate this soldier and see that he was killed, the officer would see that the matter was hushed up and the murderer would receive money to pay those that helped him and a good price for himself.

"I must tell you that I have found it dull back here and I was looking for excitement. A murder is usually interesting—and exciting. So I follow him around the town for a little while and then a Riff native comes running up to the man and talks to him, and pretty soon two more Riffs come and the four go to Har Monken's place, and I follow. I knew if I appeared on the floor, it might interfere with the fun, so I hide in a doorway, wondering how our little recruit will act when he sees a knife.

"And name of a thousand pigs, how he fought! Once I could have fought that way—with my fists and like a gentleman. And so, *mon ami,* because you are not a dog and because I do not love the man that sent the Riff against you, I butted in to spoil his little game. You backed up to the wall, near a doorway. You didn't notice that in the fight. It was nothing. I rushed to the room behind you and opened the door and pulled you out of reach of those cowardly dogs. But aunt of the devil, you were saved this time, but the next—"

Stivers grabbed La Tour's arm.

"La Tour," he said quickly, "was the officer tall and heavy, and did he have a red scar down the right cheek? Black hair and a reddish, waxed mustache, thick lips and a hooked nose?"

La Tour smiled and nodded.

"You have described the fiend of the Foreign Legion," he said. "Captain Pierre Forteau. If he is your enemy, my little recruit, you had best start running now. He came to the company late this afternoon, and tomorrow or next day he is to lead us into the desert to Fort Deron, dubbed by the Legion—Hell's Mouth."

Bill Stivers smiled grimly and kicked the dirt at his feet.

"There is, La Tour," he said hoarsely, "a nice woman called the Goddess of Ill Luck. This dame has been following me for several years, and it looks like she is still on my heels. My life story and the reason why I landed in the Legion won't interest you, but I'll give you a few details. For a number of years I have lived in France, interested in aviation. My ability to speak French has likely told you I am not a stranger to your country.

"I had a good job in Paris, but one night there was a murder in the Palais Blanc Hotel. It was a nasty affair, and I was mixed up in it. A woman was killed. I didn't murder her, but I know who did, and because I knew my life wasn't safe in France, there were a lot of family complications back in the States that caused me to want to disappear until the whole thing was forgotten.

"I could have remained in France, but if I had, I would either have been killed or have had to kill someone. So I came to the Legion to escape being forced to talk and get myself all mixed up in the affair. The man that committed the murder was an officer in the French army, an officer called Pierre Forteau."

La Tour looked at Stivers and shook his head sadly.

"I am afraid, *mon ami,*" he said dryly, "that all my efforts to drag you through that door were wasted. It would have been far better that you died by the knives of those dogs than to be taken by Forteau to Fort Deron. He is brutal and cruel. The death he plans for you there will be a death that will be as certain as the rising sun and as terrible as the inquisition of old Spain."

CHAPTER III

DEATH IN THE DESERT

BILL STIVERS STAGGERED blindly along the desert trail. To his right and left and in front of him men staggered and plodded on. For three days the column of Legionnaires had marched, sullen, blinded, choked and miserable, like scourged cattle, over the trail.

Before that there had been a train ride into the desert, with the company crammed in a stifling, suffocating old box car. After that came this forced march through the terrifying heat, with the sun blinding them and the sand filling their throats and choking back the breath that came painfully through parched and swollen throats.

Stivers, even before the train ride, had spent two days in ordinary arrest for tearing his uniform the night before in Har Monken's place. This had exhausted him and left him weak. The train ride had given him no rest or strength. And now the forced march under the savage sun that peeled the skin from the cheeks; shoulder straps that moved back and forth over the shoulders, tearing the raw blisters deeper and deeper with every step. The torturing thirst at times seemed to drive him mad. When he tried to talk only a rattling chuckle stirred his swollen tongue.

La Tour marched alongside him, but this seasoned Legionnaire marched as if he were out for an evening's stroll. He was caked with dust and his eyes were red-rimmed and his face covered with the perspiration that poured out of every pore; but his two years of slavery in the stone quarry had made his muscles like steel fiber and a mere three days' forced march across the desert a playful jaunt. His body did not drag nor bend back like the others; he walked easily, leaning forward a little.

"They make you tough, like leather, in the stone quarries," he said with a laugh, patting Stivers on the shoulder. "But you are a good Legionnaire yourself, *mon ami.* Not many little pigs of recruits could be going even as you are now. But look, your friend is coming back to take a look at his little victim again. He can very easily have you killed at Fort Deron and no one will know the difference."

STIVERS LOOKED UP and through the blinding light that came off the desert, through the flood of perspiration that covered his eyes, he saw a tall, heavy-set officer on horseback coming to the rear of the column.

Captain Forteau, his face hard and brutal, was lashing the men in the column on with a bitter, abusive tongue. He passed La Tour and Stivers and his face leered greedily as he saw Stivers, but he said nothing and rode on; but Stivers caught the look in his red eyes and saw the heavy lips curl in hatred. Forteau was playing a waiting game—a safe game now.

On and on the column moved. Even the non-coms felt the pace and sagged under their loads. They took their feelings out on the men and the men took it out on each other. But Stivers took no part in the brawling that went on around him. His mind was working rapidly, trying to figure out some escape from the death hole he had fallen into. THE FACT THAT Captain Forteau, who had been out of the Legion for years, should have been sent back to command the very company Stivers was in, seemed like a trick of fate that made any effort against it foolish and futile.

The events of that night in the Palais Blanc Hotel, when the strange exotic woman was murdered, came back to him. It had been foolish—stupid of him to get mixed up in it. It had been one of those questionable parties, organized in the questionable night clubs on a night when all cares are forgotten. Stivers was young and reckless. The woman was with Forteau, an army officer. She was young and beautiful and it was obvious from the first that she was looking at him pleadingly—as if she wanted him to help her.

The party ended in the hotel. Stivers never knew exactly what had happened there before the murder. He was slightly intoxicated or he would not, even then, have interfered, but he had staggered into Forteau's room just as the captain stabbed the woman. Stivers had sense enough to get out of the place and the hotel, knowing the mess that would follow.

But he knew that Forteau had seen him. The murder stirred Paris. Stivers, sober the next morning, realized the position he was in. Family connections at home made it impossible for him to get mixed up in the sordid scandal. So he kept silent.

But that night an attempt was made on his life.

He wasn't a coward and he did not fear death. He knew that the power behind Forteau was great, greater than would be behind the ordinary army captain. And there was something sinister and mysterious about this power, just as there had been something strange and mysterious about the exotic murdered woman.

Rather than be hauled in on the scandal, Stivers took the route of complete disappearance and joined the Foreign Legion. And now a month later, he was hiking across the desert, blinded by heat and choked with thirst, and riding alongside the column was the man he had seen commit a murder, the man that had tried twice to have him killed.

AND HE WAS going into the mouth of hell with this man as his captain—into that hell hole of Fort Deron where Stivers knew there would be far less than one chance in a thousand that he would come out alive.

The question of desertion had come to him, but back at Sidi-bel-Abbes that was out of the question, and out here on the desert, escape would mean nothing more than a terrifying death from thirst and starvation on the great sea of white sand that spread in every direction.

He staggered on blindly, the raw blisters on his shoulders sending pain to every part of his body. The men at his side growled and cursed at each other like crazed men. The piercing, sharp tongue of Captain Forteau lashed the men on and on. Non-coms staggering along at the side of the column cursed the men savagely.

"Plenty of trouble ahead," La Tour said, coughing sand from his throat. "Maybe your friend Forteau will not have to kill you after all. There will be plenty of bullets to kill us all. Last month the entire garrison of Fort Deron was killed, their eyelids cut off, and the men buried in the sand. A nice little burial these cursed Arabs have for white heathen. They think that pleases Allah or something like that."

STIVERS SAID NOTHING. His throat was too parched and his tongue too swollen for conversation.

"We are going into the district of a devil called Said-el-Trijia. This chap is a shrewd old warrior and he hates the white heathens and has killed more than his share. But the brain behind his dogs is a chap named Tun Hammond. Name of pigs. This Tun Hammond has brains and is a fighter. Rumor has it that he was once in the Greek army. Anyway, his men have made Deron a hell hole. Something of a mystery, this Tun Hammond. No one has ever seen him, but everyone knows about him."

Captain Forteau came riding up on his horse and La Tour stopped talking. Stivers looked up into the heavy face of the captain—at the red scar down his cheek, at the heavy lips, at the cold and brutal eyes. The captain had not changed since that night in Paris.

It suddenly occurred to Stivers that Captain Forteau, hearing that he had joined the Foreign Legion, had pulled strings to get transferred to the Legion and in command of his company. It was possible—but now it didn't make much difference how it all happened. It had happened and that was that to Stivers.

"You American cochon," the captain cried shrilly. "Move faster and don't let the men behind you walk on your heels. Move on or you'll get a whip across your back."

Stivers staggered on a little faster, every part of his body boiling with rage.

"A fine pair of *lezards* you two make," he continued in his biting, shrill voice, looking at La Tour. "One a deserter that I know too well and the other a pig of an American that landed in arrest the first two weeks in the Legion. *Alors,* you two troublesome *cochons,* out here we have ways of taking care of you and they aren't pleasant."

The captain rode on, swearing and cursing at the men. Stivers plunged on blindly.

"Your friend," La Tour laughed, "doesn't like either you or me, and when we get to Fort Deron, things are going to be interesting. But before we get there, we'll taste some of Tun Hammond's bullets. He has a way of striking when you don't expect it."

THE MEN MOVED on slowly and painfully, stopping every fifty minutes to rest ten and to wash their dry throats with the dirty, vile water in their canteens. The sun continued to beat down relentlessly. All around them, like a great sea of gray, spread the unfathomable desert, dazzling bright in the sun—elusive and deathlike. Noon came and then three o'clock. The curses of the men had died down. They were too weak, too utterly exhausted now to curse each other. They were stumbling and staggering forward.

The broad endless sea of sand dunes gave way to a rocky, hilly country, where the sand and the winds had polished the rocks to a glistening white. Deep gorges and endless ravines ran off the narrow trail the Legion column was following, and over them loomed the steep desert hills, bare of any vegetation or grass or life.

"I passed this same place once before," La Tour said to Stivers. "It was on my first trip to Fort Deron, and—" LA TOUR NEVER had a chance to finish his sentence. The shiny hills suddenly burst forth with life and death. Bullets rained down on the helpless column of staggering Legionnaires. Captain Forteau had blundered his column into an Arab ambush.

Only the well-known bad marksmanship of the Arabs prevented the whole column from being wiped out before the men could dive face forward to the shelter of the rocks along the trail, As it was, ten of the Legionnaires lay wounded and dead along the trail when the column, not waiting for any orders from the captain, had plunged for cover.

Captain Forteau's horse was shot out from under him, but he was on his feet, yelling orders to his men. Cruel and brutal and a murderer, Captain Forteau was, in a pinch, every inch a soldier— cool and brave and in full command of the situation, even though his men had been so suddenly ambushed.

With machine gun bullets raining down from the hills, he managed to deploy his men, after the first headlong plunge they took for the rocks, in positions where they could return the fire of the Arabs with a remarkably small loss of men, considering the death trap they had walked into.

But with the men deployed in ravines and behind rocks, it was soon obvious to all that the column had fallen into a death trap that no deploying, no fighting, could hope to get them out of. The hills swarmed with the white-cloaked Arabs. The rifles of the Legionnaires brought many of them down, but for every one brought down, five others appeared.

Stivers and La Tour lay in a deep ravine, protected from the bullets by jagged rocks. With them was Sandow, the big Russian Legionnaire, and Schmidt, the German.

"Tun Hammond," La Tour remarked dryly, "isn't taking any chances of this column getting to Fort Deron. I know this damned death hole too well. I was in it once before and only five of us got out alive."

Stivers lay with his heavy pack thrown off his shoulders and the muscles of his body stretched and at ease. He had washed his throat with a good drink of water. His tongue was no longer swollen. The heat of the sun burned down on him unmercifully, but it no longer bothered him.

THE SUDDEN ATTACK had brought a strange relief to his mind. Here was action, action against a legitimate enemy, an enemy that he had a chance against, and for the time being it caused him to forget the sinister presence of Captain Forteau and his leering, brutal eyes and his heavy lips and red waxed mustache.

The knowledge that the column had walked into a death trap brought no terror to him. Since that night at Har Monken's he had been staring at a death trap, a death trap far more sinister and terrifying than the bullets of Arabs, and this present situation came as a relief to him.

The bullets continued to rake the rocks and cut down into the deep ravines that hid the men. There was something deadly—nerve-racking in the monotony of the bullets. The Legionnaires were seasoned veterans—hard and used to death. But the exhaustion of the forced march and the heat and the thirst of those three days had weakened them. They were fighters, all of them, but lying behind the rocks and waiting—with no chance to fight out of the trap, produced a sense of utter futility among them.

"This is the terror of fighting these Arabs," La Tour growled. "Always squatting behind a rock or a sand dune and waiting—and never a chance to get out and fight in the open."

SANDOW, THE BIG Russian, growled: "The dogs! They are afraid to fight."

The muttering among the men increased as the weary minutes dragged on. There was no chance to make a break for it. The trail ran up to the top of the hill and wound through a narrow pass, and behind the column the trail entered the valley through a similar pass. Stationed at both ends of the basin were Arabs, with machine guns, and scattered among the rocks above the Legionnaires other Arabs poured a deadly fire into them with rifles. Night might bring hope, but it was hours off and in those hours only a few of the Legion column would be left.

A bullet cracked against the rock Stivers was hiding behind. La Tour raised up a little and his rifle spat fire. Far above them the grotesque form of an Arab, clothed in the long, white robe, lurched forward and came rolling down the hill. A cheer went up from the Legionnaires, Their nerves were on edge and they were ready to cheer anything.

Slowly the minutes dragged on. Stivers lay behind the rock, taking such pot shots as he could at the white forms above him. Behind them Captain Forteau lay in a deep ravine, with two of his non-corns with him. He was talking excitedly to them, pointing to the narrow pass at the top of the trail, where the Arabs had a machine gun hidden.

Suddenly he crawled forward, his automatic in his right hand and his face covered with a leering, brutal smile. He came up behind Stivers and La Tour.

"You pig of an American!" he shouted at Stivers. "You and your deserting friend are going to clear that pass up there. You are going to crawl up and take that machine gun. We'll see how brave you are now. Forward, or I'll shoot."

Stivers turned slowly. He had forgotten all about Forteau. He saw the cruel face of the captain, distorted with a hatred that made him look insane. Then Stivers looked up at the head of the trail, far up in the rocks. He might get three feet or he might get ten feet up that trail, but no further. A weary smile came to his lips.

THE CAPTAIN WAS making sure that he and La Tour would die in the death trap. It was his best chance and if he and the remains of the column got out safely when night came, he would be rid of the one enemy in the world that knew the truth about the murder of the beautiful girl in that Paris hotel room.

"Name of a name," La Tour muttered. "He wants us to die as heroes."

"Move," the captain bellowed. "Move, you dogs, or I shoot."

Stivers looked at La Tour and smiled grimly. La Tour shook his heavy head of black hair and grinned back.

"Come on, my little recruit," he laughed. "The Legion never retreats, they say, and I prefer a bullet from the Arabs than from the cur behind us."

The big Russian, Sandow, and the German, Schmidt, stared at Stivers and La Tour with amazement in their faces. This was deliberately sending men to their deaths and not knowing what was behind it, they were puzzled and startled as if they believed the captain had gone *cafard* all of a sudden.

La Tour raised his body up a little and went over the side of the rock with a leap, landing flat on his stomach out on the narrow trail. Stivers, grim-faced and tense, followed after him, hitting the ground a little to La Tour's right.

A hail of bullets greeted them. The bullets cut the ground around their bodies and two cut through Stivers' clothes.

"Come on, you fool of an American," La Tour shouted with a reckless laugh. "We're going to die great heroes."

La Tour squirmed a little forward and Stivers followed after him.

But he didn't get far. There was a stinging, piercing pain on the side of his head and darkness descended over him like a huge cloud of black vapor.

CHAPTER IV

A LOSING BATTLE

THE GREAT VAPOR of blackness that descended over Stivers lifted slowly and in its place came a hazy light of yellow gray. For a moment this haze played in front of his eyes. He could hear the roar of the guns around him and over him; he could hear the snapping crack of bullets as they cut the ground near him. Then suddenly he heard a great cheer around him.

He opened his eyes wider, and as he did the gray haze that clung to him lifted and he could see some feet ahead of him the crawling, squirming form of La Tour, moving like an eel behind jagged rocks toward the top of the pass where the Arabs waited with a machine gun.

THE LEGIONNAIRES SUDDENLY realized what was transpiring; that two of their members were out there risking their lives to open the pass. Cheer after cheer went up. The Arabs on the hill saw what was happening and they redoubled their fire.

For a moment Stivers lay flat on his stomach. He could feel the warm blood trickling down the side of his head. He knew now what had happened. A bullet had creased his temple. The fire of the Arabs, however, was not directed at him now. Their bullets were clipping the rocks where La Tour, his shaggy head of black hair waving in the sun and his lithe body moving with a surprising swiftness, was crawling up toward the top of the pass.

With a spring Stivers was on his hands and knees and making for the row of jagged rocks along the trail, rocks that stuck up from the ground like teeth and gave protection from the bullets coming from both sides. He got behind them before the Arab rifles were directed at him. La Tour stopped in a deep gully between two large rocks and was lying on his side, watching Stivers. With a plunge and a shout Stivers landed in the gully alongside him.

"Alors, little recruit," La Tour said with his usual reckless laugh, "we are still alive, but we are not up at the pass and we haven't captured the machine gun."

Stivers looked up the long narrow trail. They were hardly halfway up. They had passed the last of the Legionnaires hiding behind the rocks. The rest of the way was a steep incline and there would be few Arabs shooting at them from the sides, but the rocking fire of the machine gun made any possibility of getting up there alive seem almost absurd.

"We have disappointed Forteau this far," Stivers said grimly. "It would be a joke on him if we didn't get killed."

"Name of a name," La Tour retorted, "it would be a joke on the whole world if we didn't get killed, but we better start moving or we'll be getting a bullet from the rear. It's a bullet any way we turn. Behind us is Captain Forteau and in front of us is a machine gun."

"I prefer the machine gun," Stivers said.

LA TOUR PATTED him on the shoulder and raised his body up slowly. Bullets were cutting around the edge of the small crater-like gully. Beyond the gully the side of the hill was pock-marked with deep ravines and white rocks that glistened with a dazzling brightness in the sun.

With a leap, disregarding bullets, La Tour was out in the open, dashing madly for the side of the hill. He made a headlong dive for the rocks when he got within a few feet of them and lay on the ground so still that Stivers thought, for a moment, that he had been hit. But then he saw La Tour turn and motion for him to follow.

Cheer after cheer came from the Legionnaires behind them. No longer were the Arab bullets nipping the rocks about the Legionnaires. The death trap had suddenly turned into a two-man show for the Legionnaires and the Arabs. The Arabs, unable to grasp the meaning of the insane rush of the two men up the hill, were bewildered and dazed, but they kept firing, a steady flood of bullets. DARTING AND CROUCHING and zigzagging, Stivers made a dash for La Tour. He landed at the side of his friend as a bullet clipped through his coat under his shoulder and got a shooting pain up over his neck. He moved his arm and found that there were no bones broken and then he forgot about the stinging pain.

"We are going to be heroes," La Tour said to him. "There are only four Arabs manning the machine gun and the rest of the Arabs are scattered along the hills far away from these men. If we can get that machine gun, we can take their flanks and give the column a covering fire while they follow after us out of that death-trap."

Stivers wet his lips and looked up at the machine gunners squatting behind the gun at the top of the trail now only thirty yards away. The machine gun was spitting fire and the bullets were breaking the rocks around La Tour and Stivers, but doing no harm.

La Tour's long rifle went out from the rocks. It belched fire. One of the machine gunners plunged down the hill. Stiver's gun roared three times. Another white-clothed Arab crumpled to the earth. The other two dropped on their stomachs, their bodies hidden by the rocks. The machine gun still belched fire, but the bullets were going wild now.

With a loud yell that sounded like an Indian war whoop, La Tour started up to the gun. The bullets from the Arab rifles to the rear cut the earth around him, but he moved on. Stivers followed. Slowly they made their way up the hill to the narrow pass the trail passed through. The bullets from the Arabs in the rear stopped.

The machine gun was spitting fire, but the bullets snapped above their heads harmlessly.

"They're coming to help the machine gunners," La Tour yelled. "Quick, or we will be surrounded."

Stivers saw what was happening. White-robed Arabs were racing across the top of the hill toward the machine gun, but now the Legionnaires, seeing what was really happening, had opened fire on the running Arabs and the white-robed figures crumpled and fell to the ground from the blistering fire of the Legionnaires. The spirit of victory suddenly came over the column far below among the rocks. With yells, they were on their feet, dashing up toward Stivers and La Tour.

THE ARABS, TAKEN by surprise and unable to stand the blistering fire the Legionnaires were pouring into them, fell down among the rocks and tried to mow down the charging Legionnaires.

Stivers and La Tour came to the top of the trail at the same time. La Tour's bayonet took care of one of the machine gunners and a bullet from Stivers' rifle sent the last one to the dust. On behind them came the charging Legionnaires, darting in and around the rocks. A few of them fell from Arab bullets, but La Tour and Stivers had the machine gun working in a moment and its bullets were raking the tops of the two hills that loomed over the basinlike valley that had proved such a death trap to the Legion column.

And then suddenly, like all the battles with the Arabs, it was over as abruptly as it had started. Arabs were fleeing down the side of the hills away from the death trap. They were fleeing in safety because the hill protected them from the withering fire of the machine gun manned by Stivers and La Tour.

Stivers and La Tour sent several bursts of fire after them and then stood up to receive the Legionnaires as they piled over the rocks with cheers for the two men who had gone through a wall of lead to save them from the slow, brutal death that was inevitable in the trap. CAPTAIN FORTEAU WAS leading the men. His eyes blazed an anger that he could not express in the presence of his men. He was smart enough to know that what Stivers and La Tour had done made them heroes in the eyes of his men, and that any show of his true feelings would react against him.

A cunning, treacherous look came into his eyes as he looked at Stivers and La Tour.

"Here is the machine gun, Captain," Stivers said dryly, "that you ordered us to take."

"Excellent work, my men," Captain Forteau said loudly. "It is worthy of as fine a citation as can be secured for you, and you can be assured that I will do all I can to get it."

Stivers smiled thin-lipped at the captain and said nothing. Captain Forteau flushed a little and a look flashed in his eyes that was murderous, but he kept control of himself and turned his attention to getting the column together and attending to the wounded.

Two hours later they were moving on toward Fort Deron.

"It will be different tactics when we get to the fort," Stivers said to La Tour.

"When we get to that hell hole," La Tour replied, "anything can happen. A knife in the back or a bullet from a wall. There are too many ways to kill a man there for comfort."

CHAPTER V

FORTEAU STRIKES AGAIN

SITTING ON THE top of a little ridge that jutted out over a long, narrow gully was perched the little adobe outpost called in official records of the French Republic, Fort Deron, but in the parlance of the Legion it was known as Hell's Mouth. All day long it baked in the torrid Sahara sun, its roof giving little protection from the penetrating rays that seared human flesh and sent men insane with the dreaded *cafard,* the desert insanity.

It was a small fort, capable of housing a detachment of several hundred Legionnaires and black Colonial troops. Located in the center of a hotbed of fanatic Islams, the fort was subject to almost daily attacks—sniping, dilatory attacks that wore the nerves of the men to the breaking point.

It was devastating to the morale of the troops and few remained there long until the dreaded *cafard* got them and sent them raving mad out on the desert, to die from thirst and heat and starvation.

Near the fort was the ancient city of Islam, Barkai. From time beyond the records of any historian this quaint old city had sat in that wild, desolate waste of sand and heat, a mecca for the followers of the Prophet from every corner of the Mohammedan world. Few Christians had ever entered the walls of the old city and the few who did rarely got out alive.

The ruler of the city was the Caid, Tirisi-el-Lizai. Old and fat and shrewd, Tirisi-el-Lizai recognized the rule of the French but never fully accepted it as far as the city itself was concerned. And because the city was a tribal stronghold that commanded the Arabs and Mohammedans for hundreds of miles around, the French were very careful never to bother the city of Barkai.

The troops of Tirisi-el-Lizai were in command of a brilliant military leader, Tun Hammond, and this gentleman, having learned the art of warfare from the Europeans and in the Balkan States, made life miserable and very uncertain for the garrison of the little fort of Deron.

TUN HAMMOND ADOPTED the wearing policy of sniping attacks, taking a chunk out of the fort one day and another chunk the next day and by doing so, kept the Legion pretty much within the walls of the fort and of no bother to the Caid, Tirisi-el-Lizai.

The column of Legionnaires commanded by Captain Forteau reached the little fort late in the afternoon of the day following the attack in the hills. They relieved a detachment of Legionnaires that had been in the fort two months and in that time had suffered the loss of half their men through the sniping tactics of Tun Hammond and through the *cafard* that hit the men. A detachment of black Colonials remained at the fort.

All during the march from the hills, where Stivers and La Tour had captured the machine gun, these two were conscious that the eyes of Forteau were constantly on Bill Stivers. The captain said nothing to him, but suddenly Bill Stivers had changed from a raw recruit to a hero of the Legion. Sandow, the big Russian, beamed on him with envious eyes and Schmidt jabbered loudly of the courage of the American. In the face of these words and this condition, Captain Forteau kept silent.

When the column was safely quartered in the fort, and Stivers was alone with La Tour, he said: "I may have peace for a few days, but after that anything is liable to happen."

La Tour smiled grimly and shook his head.

"It isn't hard to put a man on the firing step and have a bullet get him in the head," he answered. "Name of a dog, you can't fight him long out here. There isn't such a thing as murder in this fort and I see that Sergeant Dufont, an old friend of his, is staying on at the fort, which looks queer to me, because no one would ever want to stay here."

STIVERS SHRUGGED AND shook his head slowly and said nothing. There was nothing for him to say, nothing for him to do but to keep his silence and watch the next move Captain Forteau made.

The following morning this move was obvious. Sergeant Dufont, a huge, overbearing, dark-faced man, with little pig eyes and a brutality that was noted through the Legion, took over the work of Forteau in a way that brought things to a head in short order.

Stivers was never able to account for his actions on that following morning, actions that caused him to play so completely into the hands of Captain Forteau. La Tour said it was a touch of *cafard;* Stivers said it was a feeling of getting in one good blow before some form of hidden death struck him. The reaction of the three-day march and the fight in the death trap left him nervous and unstrung after he had had a chance to relax and rest.

His nerves were taut and strained the next morning. The sense of utter futility, the feeling that the few days that were to come before Forteau struck successfully would be days of utter misery—these two elements played a great factor in his actions toward Sergeant Dufont.

The reputation Sergeant Dufont had in the Legion for brutality and cruelty was a reputation well earned. Big and powerful, with a dark face creased with lines of hate, he drove the men on relentlessly, looking on them as so many cattle. His tongue was bitter and cutting and no man ever heard of the big sergeant saying a kind word to any Legionnaire.

From the start he signaled out Legionnaire Bill Stivers to vent his hate upon. La Tour informed Stivers that Dufont was close to Captain Forteau, his henchman in the Legion. So when Dufont approached Stivers, it was taken for granted by Stivers that Dufont was following out special orders from the captain. In view of the work of Stivers in capturing the machine gun and the feeling of the men toward him, Captain Forteau could hardly start his tongue lashing on the hero.

BUT DUFONT TOOK over the job lustily and with malicious pleasure. At the morning formation Dufont let go his bitterest tongue on Stivers.

"The pig of an American," he sneered. "The great big hero and you think you're running this company. *Sacré Bleu,* a pig of an American trying to stir up the men against the non-coms. We have a way to handle such dogs out here. One step forward."

Bill Stivers' face went a deathly pale. Blood came from his lower lip where he had bitten it to hold back the wave of anger that surged over him. The brutal face of Sergeant Dufont was only a few inches from his as he stepped forward. The little eyes in that big brutal face gleamed a hot red mixed with a gleam of triumphancy.

The company looked on in awe. Such outbursts from Sergeant Dufont were daily occurrences and the men took them with the best grace possible.

But suddenly something seemed to snap in Bill Stivers' mind. He was too new to the Legion to have developed that mental discipline that makes members of that fighting unit mere machine-like atoms, atoms that jumped when they were spoken to, that walked into battle and faced death because they had been trained to move when ordered; human beings whose minds had long ceased to function for themselves and who lived and fought and ate under the hypnotism of the world's greatest discipline.

A veteran would have listened to that harangue without a word, but Bill Stivers, every nerve in his body at the breaking point, did what a normal human being would have done.

HIS RIGHT HAND shot out like the piston of a steam engine, in a short, vicious uppercut to the chin of Sergeant Dufont, driving behind that blow every ounce of strength and weight there was in his body. The blow landed with a dull smack, a smack that could be heard by every man in the company. Sergeant Dufont stared, for one passing second, with glassy eyes at Stivers, and then his huge form plunged headfirst to the ground and lay there inert and still.

A muffled cry rose from the ranks of the Legionnaires. They looked at Bill Stivers and gasped again. The man had struck a non-com, had struck Sergeant Dufont and knocked him down. Never in the history of the Legion had such a thing been done. It was unbelievable— impossible. A touch of *cafard,* the men muttered to themselves.

But Bill Stivers neither gasped nor looked startled at what he had done. He knew he was not suffering from *cafard;* he knew at that moment he was perfectly sane, sane enough to do what a normal, healthy man would do. He had struck back at his enemy: no longer was he fighting helplessly in the dark. And because of that a great wave of relief passed over him.

"Fool," he heard La Tour mutter at his side. "Step back in the ranks and keep your head. Forteau could have wished for nothing better than this."

ACROSS THE LITTLE square came Captain Forteau, strutting with his head back and his dark eyes flashing anger. But Stivers knew that behind those flashing eyes was a feeling of joy in the mind of the captain, a feeling that Stivers had forced his hand and now it would be only a matter of a few days until he would be stark crazy.

First would come the *crapouillaude,* the world-famed Foreign Legion form of torture to rebellious soldiers and after that would come the *pas gymnastic* and then the lashes across the naked back until the skin was raw and the back mutilated, for the flies and the insects and the sand to play their havoc of pain and misery.

"*Cochon,*" the captain said with a snarl to Stivers as he walked up to him. "Dog of an American. So you are greater than the Legion. Bah, we can break such pigs as you."

And with that Captain Forteau's hand went out and cut Stivers across the eyes, a blinding, vicious slap. Stivers' body doubled up. With a howl of rage, he flung himself at the captain, but the powerful arms of his friend La Tour were around him, holding him back.

Captain Forteau backed away several

steps, his right hand falling to his automatic. A leering, cold smile of murder spread over the cruel features of his face.

"Let him go," he shouted to La Tour. "Let him strike me and I'll blow his dirty brains all over the fort. Let him go and let him strike me. I should kill him now, but I want him for an example to all other pigs that think they can strike a sergeant of the Legion."

Stivers struggled to free himself from La Tour's arms. Captain Forteau drew his automatic and his fingers played on the trigger. But Stivers never got loose from La Tour. Other non-coms came running up and grabbed Stivers and threw him to the ground in front of the captain and held him down.

"For this act," Captain Forteau spoke slowly, as if enjoying every word that fell from his mouth, "the pig of an American will receive a sentence of five hours *crapouillaude* for striking a non-commissioned officer. And for threatening to strike an officer, he will receive seventy lashes across a bare back and tied to a pole for the sun to heal his lashes."

CAPTAIN FORTEAU STOPPED and let his tongue play over his heavy lips lazily. His eyes indicated the feeling that lay back of them.

"And this punishment," he continued, "will be administered every day for two weeks. Fourteen days. Seventy hours of *crapouillaude,* and nine hundred and eighty lashes across the bare back. By that time, let us hope this American will know something of the discipline of the Legion."

The venomous gleam in his eyes turned slowly to La Tour. "And the person," Forteau continued, "who will administer these nine hundred and eighty lashes across the bare back will be his tall, pig-faced friend, with scars down his face, scars from punishment for desertion himself. Seventy lashes a day for fourteen days. That should make this beautiful friendship a lasting one."

CHAPTER VI

THE ATTACK

HIS BACK BENT double, his hands strapped to his ankles, Bill Stivers lay in the sand and groveled and writhed and struggled against the pains that shot through every part of his body.

His first hour of *crapouillaude!* Stivers moaned, pushing every ounce of his strength against the ropes that cramped his muscles and set his brain reeling. His fingers clawed helplessly and scooped up handfuls of the hot sand. Sweat made a plaster of caked dust on his face. His lips were dry and cracked and flies crawled slowly, torturingly over them.

His first hour of that soul breaking punishment! And there were four more hours ahead for this day and fourteen days after that.

As his brain reeled and his senses verged on *cafard,* he wondered if he could stand even the five hours of the first day. Captain Forteau would soon be rid of him, rid of him in a way that would leave his record absolutely clear.

Stivers had struck a non-com. Even the men who had cheered him when he captured a machine gun with La Tour, shook their heads sadly. Striking a sergeant was a crime inexcusable in the Legion. Only a man touched with *cafard* would do such a thing. The punishment Forteau had prescribed for Stivers was harsh and brutal, but the offense merited even that harsh punishment and he got no sympathy from the men.

Slowly he turned his body a little. Standing over him was Sergeant Dufont, his face wreathed in a smile that bespoke the utter cruelty of the man. Stivers blinked helplessly through the fog of sweat that ran down his face. The sergeant was holding a canteen of water in his hand.

"God!" Stivers gasped. "Water. Some water—for God's sake, water."

DUFONT SMILED AND waved the canteen in front of the tortured man's face, letting a few drops fall on the parched, cracked lips.

"So, you are thirsty," the sergeant sneered. "I was wondering when you would get thirsty. So you want water to trickle down your throat. *Sacré nom.* The American strikes a sergeant and then wants water. Here is a drop. Feel it on your lips. Fourteen days of this. Fourteen days. Tomorrow you will go *cafard* and we will turn you loose to run out on the desert. We will take your clothes off so the sun will bake you quickly. You might find water out there on the desert. Yes, water. Fool. You will be a raving maniac and you will scream and yell and try to run from the sun that will roast your body and you will reach to the skies for the water. And then in a little while you will die. So you would strike a non-com."

Dufont's words died away in a guttural laugh. He let another drop of water fall on the fevered lips of the tortured man and suddenly he turned and walked away. The touch of water on his lips drove Stivers into a frenzy of madness. He screamed and pulled at the ropes, but his screams remained unanswered and after a while he stopped tugging at his ropes and lay in the sun, gasping for breath.

And only one hour of that dread punishment had passed!

The sand bit into his eyes, caking itself into hot baked mud from the sweat and he could no longer see. He tried to raise his head from the sand, but by now every muscle in his body cried out in a pain that was fast setting him mad. He tried to open his mouth. Caked sand had formed there. He squirmed a little and then lay still.

How long he lay in the stupor of pain he did not know. Somewhere in the darkness his half-crazed mind recorded the sound of a shot. It sounded vague and far away, but suddenly other shots came. The air above him was filled with the rattle of machine gun bullets. Men were yelling some distance away from him. And then suddenly the ropes which tied him were released and he was pulled to his feet and the caked sand over his eyes wiped away with a rough hand.

"*Vite,*" he heard La Tour say. "It is an

attack. The Arabs are attacking in great numbers. Here, take this water and get your mind working."

A CANTEEN WAS pressed to Stivers' lips and water—cool, delicious water cooled his swollen tongue and caressed his burning throat. A wet rag was wiping off his face.

"Now you look more like a man," La Tour announced. *"Vite,* the Arabs are over us like fleas and it will be a real battle because they are well armed. Here, take this gun. Already several of our men have been killed and the fat one who owned this rifle has a bullet through his head and he is sitting on the firing step looking like a fat old fool."

Stivers looked at his friend and grinned weakly. He moved his arms and kicked his legs to get circulation back. La Tour had turned and was going toward the wall near the gate. Stivers followed, his brain still dazed and his body weak. Quietly and without attracting any attention, they took their places on the firing steps. Around them lay a group of wounded men and on the firing step below three bodies, with bullets in their heads, squatted in grotesque positions. Bullets rained against the mud fort and above the sounds of the bullets could be heard the wailings and groans of the wounded.

"Keep your head down," La Tour cautioned Stivers. "The Arabs are holding high ground and they can pick us off too easily."

Carefully Stivers raised his head up and looked over the parapet. Against the gray-white sea of sand beyond the fort, a wraith-like line of Arabs could be seen creeping down the slope of the dune. The sun, now setting in the west, played a red, glimmering light on the steel in the Arabs' hands. Smoke rose up in front of their exploding guns and through this haze flashing bursts of red fire danced and waved.

CLAD IN THE gray woolen *djeellabas* that seemed to be a part of the gray sea of sand, the Arabs made a difficult target: only the red bursts of flame that danced in the haze of smoke afforded a mark for the Legion to shoot at. There was something phantom-like—ghostly, in that slowly advancing line of gray. It seemed to be a part of the great desert that was rolling up and onward to engulf the little fort.

Stivers stared at it fascinated, but a bullet clipped the parapet close to his head and the fascination fled and he ducked quickly.

"Fool," La Tour laughed. "But listen! The Arabs have machine guns. Hear that tat-tat-tat. These guns cost the Arabs a small fortune for each of them and the French would pay a bigger fortune to find out who is selling these guns to the Caid, Tirisi-el-Lizai. That fat old pig sits in the city of Barkai and spends his time planning how he can capture and torture the white heathen. But these machine guns. Never before have they appeared so far south. The Berbers were able to buy them from Spanish smugglers, but down here they have been unknown."

The blistering fire from the machine guns in that gray line increased and

   THE BEST OF THRILLING ADVENTURES

hammered against the gates of the fort. Wood and splinters flew in all directions and it seemed that it was only a matter of minutes until the gate would be blasted to little splinters.

Loading and firing with the frenzy of doomed men, the Legionnaires kept a rifle fire pouring into that line of gray creeping forward, that came on with a weird, inhuman, relentless movement. It seemed that the moving forms were there by the thousands and the little fort of Deron, with its small detachment of Legionnaires, seemed but a mere dot in the gray sea of sand, a dot that would be passed over and totally destroyed by the ghost-like gray lines that came on, unmindful of the stream of lead poured into them from the parapets of the little fort.

STIVERS' RIFLE HAD gotten into action. With the gun butt pounding his shoulder, his rifle poured out a continuous stream of lead across the sand. The heat from the gun barrel scorched his fingers and his face was covered with sweat that ran from his chin and nose. At his elbow La Tour kept up a steady fire, his gun jumping and barking with a rapidity that was amazing.

Far up in the officers' observation tower Captain Forteau was watching the on-moving lines of Arabs. At his side was Sergeant Dufont. Stivers gave no thought as to whether the captain saw him or not. There was no time now to waste giving a member of the Legion punishment. It was a matter of life or death for the little fort and every man was needed. After the battle! Stivers smiled grimly as he thought of that time.

The pounding of the rifle against his shoulder continued. His arms ached and his legs felt weak and dead. He had to lean against the parapet to keep his knees from wabbling. The stench of blood and powder was overwhelming in the heat. It sickened him, but he kept his stream of lead going out into that line of gray ghosts, the line that was now close to the fort.

Slowly, relentlessly, the lines closed in. There was no hurry to the movement of those lines. Only certainty—deathly certainty that in a little while they would pass over the fort and it would be no more.

SUDDENLY DOWN IN the square a man was shouting orders. It was a thin-faced sergeant, his face black from gunpowder and his right arm hanging limply at his side and covered with blood. He came running from the officers' observation post.

A charge! Captain Forteau had ordered a charge into those advancing lines. The Legionnaires cheered. It was a desperate, last minute attempt to stave off destruction. There was little hope of its succeeding, but charging out there would be an easier death than waiting on the firing step for a death that was certain—a death that would mean inhuman torture if taken alive.

The gates of the little fort were thrown wide open. A squad of black Colonial troops clashed out, while with wild yells the Legionnaires dropped over the ramparts and rushed over the sand toward

The drunken Algerian crumpled with a dull groan.

the advancing lines, with their guns spouting white flames.

It seemed that the very daring of the attack caused the gray lines to waver and then to fall back a little. The Legionnaires, shouting like wild Indians, dashed on, their guns taking a terrible toll of the Arabs. The lines fell back before the mad rush. The machine guns sputtered, stuttered, and then went silent.

Stivers and La Tour were well in the lead of the dashing Legionnaires. All the aches and pains had left Stivers' body; the frenzied excitement of the mad charge gave him a renewed strength that

　　THE BEST OF THRILLING ADVENTURES

carried him on wildly. Bullets snapped over his head as he rushed, with La Tour at his side, up the slope of gray sand toward the wavering lines.

Then suddenly a miracle happened, a miracle to the charging Legionnaires. The Arab lines broke and retreated. Like phantoms in the haze of coming night, the gray-cloaked enemy fell behind the ridge of sand, and melted into the mist of the coming evening like ghosts.

THE LEGIONNAIRES RUSHED on to the top of the ridge.

"Sacré nom de nom!" La Tour gasped. "This is a weird battle. The tribesmen flee in front of us, but no order comes from Forteau to give chase. The whole thing seems crazy to me."

"They ran out of ammunition for the guns," he said. "That is why these guns sputtered and stopped. Queer, isn't it, that just as we charged their ammunition gave out!"

Suddenly Stivers and La Tour were alone on the edge of the ridge. The other Legionnaires had left. The sun had sank beneath the horizon and the shades of night were falling rapidly, cloaking the gray sands with a bewitching light.

Stivers grabbed La Tour's arm and his voice was husky.

"I know it's death," he said, "but I'm not going back to that damned *crapouillaude*. That means even a worse death for me. Forteau will get me. I can't fight against him. I'm going to run for it, and—"

"And run out on the desert to die," La Tour interrupted with a dry laugh. "Little nut of a recruit, you will die of thirst or the devils of Tun Hammond will get you and toast your head over a slow fire. But you are brave, *mon ami.* Brave and foolish."

"It will be death on the desert anyway," Stivers replied. "I can fall over this ridge and melt away into the night like the Arabs did. I will die tomorrow or next day, but I prefer that death than to go back to a living hell."

"Name of a name," La Tour said with a reckless laugh. "If you go, I go with you. Never would that whipping take place if I had to lay those lashes across your back, and I think Forteau won't be satisfied until I am also killed or sent out on the desert raving mad. Come, we can disappear over this ridge. Tomorrow we die in the sun—unless the Arabs catch us before that time. Come!"

CHAPTER VII

DESERT JUSTICE

NIGHT—COLD AND BLACK and impenetrable, dropped over the gray sand of the desert like a shroud of death. The thin sliver of a crescent moon rode down the sky, shedding a shaft of light that broke feebly through the darkness.

A star clung to the crescent tip of the moon, making that thin silver curve resemble an evil knife hanging from the star in the sky that was jet black.

There were stars overhead—little dots of light that bobbed and waved and danced grotesquely in and out of the great haze of black that tried vainly to hide them from the baked, merciless sands below. And far to the right and left, lonely and ominous and sinister, spread the black desert. Great sand dunes and sloping hills of white pulverized sand that, from the beginning of time, had moved and changed, loomed up in the darkness in faint outlines of black.

SILENCE—THE INEFFABLE SILENCE of that great waste of shifting sands clothed the night with that gloom, that unutterable sombreness of death. And in that silence no form moved, no sound came to break its deadly stillness.

For hours Bill Stivers had staggered on, following La Tour through the series of dunes outlined faintly in the darkness. Cold, penetrating and paralyzing, chilled every bone of his body. On the desert there is no respite in the implacable fight against life! In the daytime the sun beats down with a heat that roasts and bakes human flesh, and at night, as if tired of that form of punishment, the desert sends out a cold that is as deadly as the heat.

Stivers had no idea where La Tour was going, but the Frenchman, guided by his knowledge of the region, seemed to be following a straight line, guiding his steps by the star that hung at the point of the knife-shaped silver moon. The two Legionnaires hurried along as fast as they could to keep their bodies moving in their fight against the deadly chill. The pace had tired their exhausted frames and Stivers could only stumble blindly forward.

Suddenly before them appeared a flickering light, coming from the base of a great sand dune that loomed up ahead of them like some ogre of old. The fire gleamed and flickered feebly in the darkness. La Tour stopped and Stivers stumbled against him and stood swaying on his feet. His muscles cried out in pain against the punishment they had received in the last terrifying hour; cramps tortured his neck and back, and every breath he took seemed that it would be the last to come from the lungs that were a mass of stabbing pains.

He dropped slowly to the ground, gasping painfully and loudly. The sand was cold, colder than the night itself, but he didn't notice the chill that stung his body. He was gasping for breath. La Tour squatted beside him and for the first time in hours, he spoke.

"That fire can either come from the camp of a lone man," he said, "or it may come from a camp of fifty Arabs. *Saint Marie.* If we only had automatics instead of these long rifles, we might do something at close quarters. But there is food and water at that fire and that is what we want, so we will have to risk it."

I'M READY TO risk anything for food and water," Stivers said with a weak, hollow laugh. "Without food and water we can't keep going long."

"We are safe from pursuit from the fort," La Tour replied. "They will never be able to follow us and Forteau wouldn't bother. He knows there is about one chance in a million of our reaching Morocco. It never has been done and it has been tried a hundred times. Thirst usually gets the poor devils, but often the Arabs get to them first."

 THE BEST OF THRILLING ADVENTURES

Stivers bit his lip and pulled his body to a sitting position. The memory of those pictures in the barracks back at Sidi-bel-Abbes came to him, pictures of the mutilated bodies of deserting Legionnaires found on the desert after the Arabs had cut their eyes out and buried the bloody bodies, minus the head, in the sand.

"If it is the camp of a holy man, we are safe," La Tour said. "Only the holy man is safe on the desert. The Arabs are afraid to kill them. But holy man or a camp of Ali Baba and his Forty Thieves, we will have to find out. Come on."

CRAWLING ON THEIR stomachs, they wormed their way down the slope of sand toward the little flame of fire that cut through the darkness. They came to the shelter of a wash and stopped and got to their feet, their long rifles in position for ready use. Slowly they advanced toward the fire.

Suddenly La Tour stopped and whispered: "Fine! It is a *hadji* making his pilgrimage, and he is cooking something over the fire. He is a saint of Islam and he carries no weapons."

Stivers peered through the darkness. He could see the queer figure of an old man squatting near the fire, his long robes spread out from his body, making him look like a funny balloon in the darkness which was broken a little by the fire.

They walked up to the fire boldly. The old man sprang to his feet with a startled cry. He was a withered old creature, with taut brown skin stretched tightly over the bones of his face. His face looked like a human skull, from which all the flesh had not rotted away and which had an after-death growth of beard sticking out from the brown, lifeless skin. His legs were stiff, stick-like bones under the dirty white robe of a holy man, his arms were shriveled skin and bones.

Shaking the bony fist at his visitors, he hurled a flow of language at them that indicated they were not welcome. Stivers looked at the shriveled old body with distaste. La Tour jabbered back at the holy man and pointed down at the mess of food that was cooking in a clay pit over the fire.

The *hadji* spat oaths at La Tour and continued to shake his fists. La Tour silenced him by bringing his rifle up quickly. The old *hadji* screamed and then grew meek, drawing away from the fire, and squatted beside a bunch of rags in the sand. Stivers wondered if that bunch of dirty rags and the food were the only possessions the wretched creature owned.

"He says," La Tour explained, "that he used his last water to make this stew. He plans on reaching Barkai in the morning. That is fine. We will eat some of his food and take his white robe. A holy man's robe sometimes is invaluable in the desert."

The two Legionnaires dipped their fingers in the stew, but when it reached Stivers' mouth, he spit it out with disgust. In all his life he had never tasted anything quite so terrible as that stew. The meat was vile, like the meat of an aged goat, and it had been cooked in an olive oil that was rancid and foul. But he managed to get a little of it down his throat. La Tour managed to eat his share, but cursed like a fiend as he did.

THEN THE LEGIONNAIRES walked over to the old *hadji* and took his *djeellaba* from his back. The holy man cursed and screamed, calling on Allah, as La Tour afterwards explained, to rot the souls of these infidels in Gehenna for the millions of years to come. They left the old man, hurling his vile curses into the night, and plunged on into the desert, glad to be away from the holy presence and out into the night again.

"The mountains in the south of Morocco are many miles to the north," La Tour explained. "Name of a pig, we might fool the world and reach them, but we must hurry. We are not far from the fort and we must be fifteen kilometers away when dawn comes. There will be searching parties, but these parties will not wander far looking for us. We must push on until daylight and then find a place to hide, and then tomorrow night we can push on again."

"Okay," Stivers said with a dry laugh. "We will start again tomorrow night if we find food and water in that hiding place. But what the hell? We'll have to trust in Allah."

THEY STUMBLED ON. The hours passed slowly—like centuries to Stivers. It seemed to him by this time that he had been stumbling over that sand since the beginning of Eve. All memory of any other life was blotted out of his mind. Sand. Sand. Sand. That was all he had ever known or seen. His senses reeled. His feet burned. His throat seemed to be a hard knot somewhere far up in his neck. But he stumbled on, offering no complaint and somehow keeping to his feet.

Dawn came with a reddening glow that burst like a great fire through the blackness of the night. It came suddenly to Stivers as he stumbled along. He knew that there had been darkness— cold and black and silent: then came a red glow dancing in that blackness and then slowly, as if mocking his misery and his fate, the great expanse of gray rolling sands that seemed to stretch into eternity in all directions, appeared before his eyes—a vast, impenetrable stretch of death and utter desolation, shifting slowly with the winds and rolling back and forth in the restless blanket of gray death.

La Tour climbed to the crest of a crescent-shaped dune that lay at the base of a low line of sand hills. He stood, silhouetted against the gray of the desert like a phantom being, his body moving slowly as his eyes stretched out across the desolate waste in all directions.

Suddenly he pointed to a tumble of polished white boulders that stuck out of the sand beyond the dune and faced a smooth fan of level, barren ground.

"Look," he cried. "There is a mouth of a cave. I remember now there is a cave fifteen kilometers from the fort and that is what I want to find."

HE RAN DOWN off the dune and Stivers started after him. Yawning and black, the mouth of the cave, hidden in the center of the jagged white boulders, appeared to them. They slowed down to a walk as they neared the entrance.

THE BEST OF THRILLING ADVENTURES

La Tour suddenly stopped. His eyes were riveted on the ground. On the fan of level ground he saw were numberless footprints. At a point where the footprints came out of the desert a dirty old rag was tied to a pole in a little mound of pebbles.

"Uncle of Satan!" La Tour cried. "Someone has been coming to this cave."

Stivers had dropped to his knees, his eyes searching the ground. Brown blots were spread over the sand. The brown blots were made from machine oil.

"Oil," Stivers gasped. "See that rag on the pole. See those long tracks leading past the pole. Listen, a plane has landed here and landed within the last few days, for the oil is still fresh. See that track. It was scratched by the tail skid."

But La Tour had no time to look at the tracks or answer. He made a headlong dive behind a boulder and Stivers followed him as fast as his weary body would permit.

For coming over a dune to their right, was a large detachment of Arabs, headed directly for the cave.

CHAPTER VIII

THE MYSTERY OF THE CAVE

THE LINE OF gray-robed Arabs swept down over the slope of the dune rapidly. Stivers' long rifle darted out from behind the rock, but La Tour's arm shot out and pulled Stivers' arm back.

"Fool!" he whispered. "One shot and we are having our eyelids cut off and our heads taken back to Barkai. We must lie here and hide, hoping they may pass us."

But the line came straight for the mouth of the cave, and as it approached Stivers counted ten white-robed figures. They came forward silently, ghostlike. Stivers and La Tour crouched low behind the rock, their bodies hugging the sand.

Then suddenly Stivers felt a shudder pass through his body. Leading the Arabs was a tall, dark-faced Mohammedan, with a face that was brutal and intelligent.

It was the Mohammedan that had thrown the knife at him in Har Monken's dive.

The Arabs came to the mouth of the cave. They were moving silently and quickly. Five of the Arabs disappeared in the cave with the Mohammedan. The others stood at the entrance of the cave, their long rifles gleaming ominously in the sun.

The Mohammed and the five Arabs that entered the cave came out in a minute. They were lugging three machine guns. Quickly the other five Arabs grabbed the machine guns and silently, without a word, eight of the white-robed figures started up the sand slope with the guns. In a few minutes their gray *djeellabas* had melted away in the glimmering brilliancy of the desert sun.

Remaining at the mouth of the cave was the dark-faced Mohammedan and one Arab.

"That is the man," Stivers whispered to La Tour, "that threw the knife at me in Har Monken's place."

"And the man I saw talking to Captain Forteau," La Tour answered in a low whisper. "But name of a name. What is that? What interests me are those machine guns. They could only come from the Legion commissary depot."

"THOSE MEN," STIVERS said, "have water and I have a grudge against that cutthroat, and it's only two against two. Let's get them."

"We'll wait here," La Tour whispered. "Something very interesting is going to happen and the mystery might be cleared up."

"God, look!" Stivers gasped, turning his head around in the direction of the fort. "A Legion detachment."

Bobbing up and down in the shimmering light of the desert could be seen the red kepis of the Legionnaires, coming directly for the cave. The red kepis approached, and as they neared, Stivers could see that there were only three men in the detachment.

"Searching for us," he said to La Tour.

La Tour shook his head.

"Look a little closer," he said. *"Mon Dieu,* it is Captain Forteau and Sergeant Dufont and a black Colonial. Keep still. We are going to find out something."

Captain Forteau and his two companions walked quickly up to the mouth of the cave and the Mohammedan greeted them in short, nervous sentences.

"I HAVE BROUGHT the gold," he said. "My men have already taken the guns. But we must be careful, for Caid, Tirisi-el-Lizai does not like to pay so much gold for machine guns. And what about the American? The Caid is having that murder investigated."

Forteau laughed dryly.

"His bones are somewhere on the desert now," he said. "After the attack he deserted with another Legionnaire. Fear not, *mon ami,* that he will ever talk. He was near death from exhaustion when he escaped. We have nothing to worry from that source, Tun Hammond."

Tun Hammond! That name caused Stivers to gasp in surprise. Tun Hammond, the leader of the Caid's soldiers, the famous general of the Arabs. Forteau was selling Tun Hammond machine guns and the Mohammedan was extorting a huge price out of the Caid.

"Tomorrow at noon," he heard Forteau say to Tun Hammond. "The plane will come again and will bring more machine guns. We will sell the Caid six tomorrow."

"Vite," Tun Hammond cried. "My men are coming. I do not know the reason, but hurry before they see you."

The crest of a sand dune far away was suddenly dotted with white moving figures. From the distance they looked like specks of white in the sea of the shimmering light. Forteau and Dufont and the black Colonial grabbed the bags of gold handed them by Tun Hammond and disappeared around the wash of the dune behind the pile of boulders that surrounded the mouth of the cave. AS THE WHITE dots became larger, Stivers could see that the Arabs were mounted on horses, and in less than a minute the horsemen came charging down to the mouth of the cave. The leader dismounted and bowed in front of Tun Hammond and then jabbered something to the general.

"Name of the devil," La Tour gasped. "Our old friend the holy man is after us. That Arab just told Tun Hammond of our theft of the holy robe and our treatment of him. The Caid has ordered the desert searched for us, and if they catch us—well, if you touch a holy man you are honored with a trip to Barkai for a public torture and death."

While the leader of the Arabs was talking to Tun Hammond, the other Arabs dismounted and spread fan-shape over the boulders.

And in the next minute five of them gave loud yells and were on Stivers and La Tour, who had little chance to get their rifles in action. The yells brought the other Arabs to the spot.

Fighting madly, hopelessly, Stivers struck out with his right and left. The viciousness of his attack caused the Arabs to back away slowly, but no attempt was made to use their guns. Stivers saw that they were to be taken alive. Grimly he set himself. It was the end now, but he would go out with a blaze of fighting and if they took him alive, it would be when he was unconscious.

La Tour had scrambled to his feet, grabbed his rifle, and dodged back behind a rock. Three times his rifle roared and three Arabs plunged forward on their faces. Stivers had grabbed his gun and was behind another rock. His gun jumped in his hands as it roared. Two Arabs crumpled to the ground.

But it was a hopeless struggle, this struggle of two men against a hundred. Tun Hammond took command of the situation at once. The Arabs scattered among the rocks, surrounding the two Legionnaires. Desperately Stivers and La Tour sent out a stream of lead toward the Arabs, but suddenly Stivers' gun clicked ominously. He had run out of ammunition. La Tour's gun roared twice more and then was silent.

The Arabs, sensing what had happened, came over the rocks like flies and crushed the two men to the sand.

Stivers kicked against his attackers, but after a while he ceased resisting. His hands and feet were tied and he was being carried to a horse.

CHAPTER IX

THE CITY OF THE DEAD

THE CITY OF Barkai sprawled across a shallow desert gully and ran up the ridges of the two low hills that formed the gully. It baked wearily and lazily in the torrid sun, as it had baked for thousands of years, even on the day when Mohammed dashed to Medina; and in those thousands of years nothing about the city had changed. The odorous, stifling narrow streets, the flat-roofed houses, the noisy bazaars, the squalid courts and the vermin-infested costumes—all these passed on through the years as they were in the beginning. Even the minds of the citizens—a motley gathering of brown and black and yellow faces—thought and acted as their ancestors had acted the day Mohammed took flight to Medina.

Long before that day a desert tribe of Farikitas, a powerful, cruel tribe, had come somewhere out of the east and captured the city. They accepted the prophet Mohammed and their city was the stronghold of that religion from then on. The Farikitas were not famed for tolerance or good fellowship, even among the races of their own belief; and to the infidel whites they had carried through the centuries a hatred that never relented.

High walls enclosed the city, walls that had protected it for centuries. A few white men had entered those walls, but they never came out; and at the end of a long narrow street, near the mosque, their heads rotted away in the blistering sun, always with the eyebrows cut off.

IN THE LITTLE square near the mosque a great crowd had gathered some hours after the capture of Stivers and La Tour. In the narrow and filthy streets, white-robed men dashed eagerly toward the square and the bazaars were empty, and somewhere inside the great mosque a bell was ringing.

Two infidels had been captured, two white infidels that had defiled a Holy man of Islam. The walls of the city were closed and no one was allowed to enter. The eyes of the infidels would have to be plucked of their eyebrows and other forms of torture would have to take place before the heads would be cut off and stuck on the poles, alongside the bleached bones of other infidels.

Bill Stivers lay on his back on the dirty, sun-baked ground of the square, his arms lashed behind him and his ankles securely tied. La Tour lay close to him, bound in the same manner. Around them milled hundreds of fanatical Arabs, murmuring strange and weird prayers.

An old man, short and fat, with a greasy face, came out of the mosque. He wabbled up to them, guards on both sides of him. He spoke a few sharp words and out of the crowd came the wizened-faced holy man the two Legionnaires had met on the desert. The old man was cursing and screaming, and when he looked at the two men on the ground, his screams rose to an insane pitch.

"Grandpa seems to be angry," Stivers said grimly to La Tour. "That was a bright idea of yours to steal his holy robe."

La Tour grinned weakly.

"The fat man is the Caid, Tirisi-el-Lizai," he whispered. "We'll be thrown in dungeon cells to wait for evening, when the act of cutting our eyebrows off takes place."

The Caid barked out sharp orders to the guards and the two men were pulled to their feet and carried inside the dark, mosque-like building to the right of the square. They were borne down wet and worn stairs far underground and thrown in a damp cell, where a wall of darkness enshrouded them.

THE DOOR OF the cell closed with a creaking sound and the rusty old lock turned, and then silence, eerie and black and oppressive, settled over the dungeon. Stivers twisted and squirmed against the ropes around his ankles and wrists, but they did not give.

"Take it easy," La Tour said. "We have several hours and in that time something may happen."

Stivers laughed dryly. In that ancient city of Barkai, where no Christian was allowed to set foot and the fanaticism of Islam rose to insane heights, there was little chance for anything to happen in those few hours before the evening prayers, after which the ceremony of torture would take place.

"The pig of Forteau," La Tour growled, "will have all his wishes carried out. We will be dead and he will have plenty of gold. The traitor! The beast! To send the Legion—"

"He hasn't won yet," Stivers said bitterly, "but he will win if we lie here and wait for the Arabs to cut our eyebrows off."

He lurched forward with his body and then rolled over. He hit a cold rock wall. Hunching his knees up under him, he threw his body forward, landing full en his face on a sharp rock. A sharp pain shot through his forehead, but with a cry he squirmed and twisted and crawled until his body was close to the sharp rock.

THEN THROUGH ENDLESS minutes of pain he twisted his body over the sharp rock. Back and forth he moved his tied wrists, the rocks cutting gashes in the flesh. His breathing came heavy and labored. La Tour called out to him, but he didn't hear.

Again and again his wrists moved over that rock, with muffled cries of pain coming from his mouth as the rook cut deeper into his flesh. Then suddenly he fell on his side and lay still.

His arms were free!

He rested several moments and then he was sitting up, tugging away at the ropes around his ankles. With a cry he was on his feet, calling to La Tour.

La Tour answered him, and it took Stivers only a few moments to unloosen the ropes around the Frenchman's ankles and wrists.

"We're free," Stivers said grimly, "though we are still in a cell in a city filled with fanatical Mohammedans, but at least we can now die fighting."

La Tour stretched his arms and legs. Stivers was feeling for the door with his hands out in front of him. He found the door, tugged on the rusty old iron, but his tugging brought no results.

"We can wait until someone opens the door," he said. "Then we can get into action. I don't know how far underground we are, but that doesn't make much difference."

"If we could get to Caid, Tirisi-el-Lizai," La Tour suggested, "and tell him about Forteau and Tun Hammond—"

"We'd get our heads cut off just the same," Stivers broke in. "Squealing on that beast Forteau isn't going to save our lives now. We can take care of him—if and when we get out of this city alive."

"The girl that was murdered in Paris," La Tour answered. "She is connected with the Caid in some way and Tun

Hammond was very anxious to know whether you were dead or not."

"That won't save us, either," Stivers answered. "The only way we can save ourselves is by fighting. Tirisi-el-Liz-ai can take care of his enemies as he wishes."

"We'll have to wait until they come for us," La Tour said. "And we might as well sit down."

They sat down on the cold, damp floor and waited. Stivers rubbed the blood off his mutilated wrists. His arms and hands felt numb from pain, but his body and his mind were alert. It seemed that a second reserve of nervous energy had come to him and every nerve was tense and ready for action.

BUT THE MINUTES passed slowly in that deadly silence of the dungeon. They stretched wearily into hours. Stivers and La Tour sat on the floor and said little. Their ears were strained for the sound of a footstep outside the cell.

Another hour passed and it seemed to Stivers that he had been in that dark dungeon, with its dank and ill-smelling air, for days and weeks. La Tour got up and walked nervously around in the darkness, but Stivers remained on the floor, his face grim and set.

He knew there was little hope of getting out of the city alive. All he hoped was for death while fighting. They must not take him alive. The thought passed through his mind grimly and monoto-nously. They must not take him alive!

Suddenly Stivers' body stiffened and with a leap he was on his feet. A key was being turned in the rusty old lock of the door. In that tense moment, Stivers had no plan of action, no idea what he was going to do, other than to overcome whoever came in and try to get out of the dungeon hole.

AND WHEN THE door creaked and opened, and two white-robed Arabs carrying burning torches entered the cell he still had no plan of action.

But he wasted no time trying to figure one out. With the spring of a tiger, his body hurled itself against the leading Arab. Taken utterly by surprise, the Arab went to the ground in a white heap, his torch falling to the floor, the flame dying out in a haze of smoke.

La Tour was on the other Arab in the same manner. Stivers brought his right down with a smashing blow to the Arab's face under him and the man quivered a little and lay still.

La Tour was having a little difficulty with his man. This Arab, in the matter of a split second, had seen the hurtling body of Stivers and he had started to yell.

But the sound never left his mouth. La Tour's hand was over it and his free arm was trying to grapple with the Arab. But it took Stivers only the matter of a moment to hurl the man to the ground and gag him. Then he tied his wrists and ankles with the ropes taken from La Tour's body. The Arab that had been knocked cold by Stivers was tied and gagged.

"And now," La Tour said with a laugh, "we are free men, and where are we going. *Sacré Nom de Pitié.* While there is life there is hope—but we should have a plan."

"Our plan is simple," Stivers said. "We are going to be Arabs. It's a shame you didn't hide that robe of the holy man on you."

"There is no shame to that," La Tour said. "Here it is under my *cummerbund.* I told you the holy robe is a good thing to have on the desert."

Stivers had picked up one of the torches and was holding it above his head.

La Tour was unwinding his black *cummerbund,* the waist sash worn by the Legion, and wrapped under this was the dirty holy robe taken from the *hadji* on the desert.

"You will be the holy man," Stivers said. "I will take the robe of one of these Arabs and a holy man and his follower will try to walk out under the nose of these religious maniacs."

"And about the time we get upstairs," La Tour said with a laugh, "we'll meet someone coming down the stairs to find out why the infidels haven't been brought up to the mob."

"And then," Stivers said grimly, "you and I are going to have to do some tough fighting."

LA TOUR DONNED the robe of the holy man and Stivers stripped one of the Arabs of his white robe. A minute later, with the torch high over his head, Stivers led the way out of the dungeon cell to a flight of ancient stone steps that wound upward, each step worn thin by the treading footsteps of countless generations.

Slowly they wound their way upward, the white robes around them making them look weird and ghostlike in the flickering light of the burning torch. Up and up they went slowly, with every nerve tense and every muscle bunched for quick action.

They came to the top of the stairs, came out in a wide hallway, the stone floor of which was worn deep by the thousands of feet that had walked over it. They found more winding stairs, and up these they went on.

They got near the top, when suddenly there was a yell behind them. The darkened underground passageway suddenly seemed to spring to life. White-robed figures darted ahead of them. There was more yelling.

LETTING THE TORCH drop to the stone stairs, Stivers went up them two at a time, with La Tour following close behind. The yelling below them increased.

"*Nom de Pitié,*" La Tour yelled. "They have discovered the Arabs in the cell."

Stivers did not stop to listen to La Tour. He was at the top of the stairs, dashing toward a door that opened out on the square, where the crowd was assembled for the torture of the two infidels. Evening had fallen. It was not yet dark, but the first shades of twilight were filtering through the narrow, winding streets.

Stivers stopped suddenly.

In the doorway before him were five Arabs, armed with rifles and kris knives.

CHAPTER X

THE ROBE OF ISLAM

STIVERS' BODY LUNGED forward and a little to the left. A kris knife came hurtling through the air and hit the rock wall far behind, the twang of the fine steel blade echoing throughout the dark hallway.

And in the next second Stivers had dived forward, grabbed one of the Arabs around the legs and pulled him to the floor, throwing the Arab's body over his to act as a shield. La Tour had caught another Arab around the waist and had thrown him to the floor.

Rising to his feet, with the body of the kicking Arab in his arms, Stivers heaved the body at the other Arabs, and they crashed against the wall in a sprawling heap. With a leap Stivers was out of the door and dashing around the corner of the building. He heard someone running behind him, but he did not stop or look around.

As he dashed out of the mosquelike building, he saw, from the corners of his eyes, the crowd milling around the square, waiting for the infidels to be brought out for the torture. Other Arabs were rushing for the door, but because Stivers was clothed in the long white robe, none of them paid any attention to him.

The shouting around the door of the mosque building increased, but Stivers turned a corner and dashed down a side street. The running behind him increased and the next moment a white-robed figure was racing alongside him.

Stivers saw that it was La Tour.

"In this building," Stivers yelled to La Tour. "They are coming after us."

The two Legionnaires dodged into a low, squatty building. The building was dark and deserted. Their feet hit a dirt floor and they raced through the darkness to the rear of the house.

The door was suddenly filled with Arabs and they scattered over the dark room in a fan-like formation, but Stivers and La Tour had darted out a back door into a dark alley. Down the alley they raced madly, their robes flying behind them, making them look like grotesque figures in the darkness.

By this time the whole city was in an uproar. The din seemed to come from every part of it. The two Legionnaires stopped and hid in the shadows of an old building, standing against the mud walls, gasping for breath.

"WE ARE OUT but we're in," La Tour said with a weak laugh. "We're out of the dungeon, but we're still in the town, and there are high walls around it and ten thousand Mohammedans inside those walls wanting to cut our heads off."

"Walls can be scaled," Stivers said grimly.

The alley was suddenly filled with yelling white-robed Arabs. Stivers and La Tour walked out from their place of hiding quietly and joined the milling, angry mob that surged down the alley. The two Legionnaires, clothed in the white robes, were not recognized by the Arabs.

On up the alley they went with the mob, keeping close together. They came to the far end of the city and over them loomed the wall. The wall was about eight feet high, a wall of mud and baked sand bricks. Time had played havoc with its structure and everywhere the mud and bricks had fallen out and great yawning gaps appeared.

"Back in the shadows," Stivers whispered to La Tour.

The two Legionnaires darted back in the darkness of a building and the angry mob milled on. To the right of them was another mob, milling and yelling. This second mob passed Stivers and La Tour.

"Over the wall," Stivers said. "You first. I'll boost you up."

He and La Tour rushed to the wall and Stivers took La Tour by the foot and heaved him high in the air.

The Frenchman grasped at the top of the wall, got a hold, and pulled himself up.

Stivers started up the wall, putting his feet in one of the great yawning holes. La Tour lay flat on the top of the wall, which was several feet thick, and reached down to grab the hand of his friend. Slowly Stivers worked his way up. He was near the top when out of the darkness below burst a large number of Arabs.

Shots filled the air. Bullets clipped the mud near Stivers, but the far-famed poor marksmanship of the Arabs came as a life saver to the two Legionnaires. Stivers pulled himself to the top of the wall with one final supreme effort and then he and La Tour threw themselves over the wall and let their bodies drop to the ground.

THE FORCE OF the fall caused them to sprawl awkwardly on the ground, but they jumped to their feet; and as they did, they heard the gates of the city open and the next moment a swarm of Arabs were bearing down on them.

Stivers and La Tour turned and dashed down the wall, came to a turn and swung around this turn, their legs swinging like the fast pistons of an engine. The army of fanatical Arabs now realized that the two figures in white were the infidels, and came charging around the turn like insane fiends.

Flat on the ground, the two Legionnaires hugged the wall and the madly running Arabs swept past them, unseeing. Back toward the gate of the city the Legionnaires dashed.

There were a few Arabs near the gate, but these apparently did not recognize the two white-robed Legionnaires as the infidels that had escaped. Men on horseback were coming out of the gate to give chase.

With a wild yell to La Tour, Stivers made a spring for one of the horses. Behind him the first army of Arabs, the army that had plunged past them when they flattened themselves against the wall, was coming back.

Stivers' leap at the horseman landed him near the neck of the racing pony. With a terrific right to the jaw aimed from the crouching position Stivers was in, holding on to the horse; he knocked the rider off and was in the saddle, giving the pony all the rein it would take.

 horse raced madly out into the night. Other horsemen were following and in the next second a fleet Arab pony passed him and swung into the lead. In the darkness he could only see the white robe of the rider, but he heard the wild shout of La Tour.

On through the desert night, for by this time darkness had fallen, Stivers and La Tour raced the horses. Close behind came the Arabs, mounted on horses. Down through gullies and up over huge sand dunes Stivers and La Tour sent the fleet little ponies. They had a head start of a hundred yards on the Arabs behind them, and as they raced on through the night, they managed to keep this lead. Rifles roared behind them, but the bullets cut the air far over their heads.

Mile after mile passed by them. The horses picked their way with uncanny skill over the treacherous sand dunes; but always, several hundred yards behind, came the Arabs, driving their horses on at top speed.

A huge sand dune loomed up in front of the Legionnaires. La Tour turned his horse to the right and Stivers' mount followed; and then with a quick jerk of the rein Stivers pulled his pony to a stop, throwing it against the dune. La Tour turned his horse into a little gully that ran out of the dune.

Hoofs beating like hammers on the sand, the Arabs raced by, unable, because of the turn around the dune, to see the maneuver of the two Legionnaires. La Tour and Stivers swerved their horses around and sent them at top speed on into the desert night in the opposite direction.

They heard the Arabs yelling far behind them. They heard the beat of the hoofs of the Arab ponies, but as they raced on, the darkness of the desert night engulfed them and the sound of the pursuing horses died away completely.

A half hour later the two Legionnaires reined their mounts and jumped to the ground. On each of the horses was the Arab soldier's canteen and supply of food. The two Legionnaires washed their parched mouths with water and ate the goat cheese and Arab bread greedily.

"On horseback we can make Morocco," La Tour said, "but we will have to hurry, for horses can't go long without water."

WITHOUT MANY WORDS they got on their horses and started through the night, La Tour leading the way, picking his directions from the stars that dotted the dark sky.

They rode on until midnight and then rested. Exhausted from their race, their nerves still taut and racked from the experience in the city of Barkai, they talked little. After an hour's rest they mounted their horses again and continued on.

When dawn came they were surrounded by the endless desert—grim and silent and deathlike. They were following a narrow trail that led through a deep gully.

"But Forteau," Stivers said. "He'll hear about our escape."

"And he'll have half the Legion following us," La Tour said.

They turned a sharp corner, following the gully path and came out on a fan of level ground.

They halted their horses helplessly, and gaped at what they saw in front of them, gaped helplessly, with all color leaving their faces and their bodies sagging forward.

On the great stretch of level ground was camped a regiment of the Foreign Legion!

A MAN CAME riding up to them, saw their faces underneath the white hoods, and twisted his face in a half smile.

"Son of a swine," he growled. "We have two Arabs with the faces of white men."

Other men of the Legion had surrounded them. Stivers and La Tour got down, threw their Arab hoods away in disgust, and stood looking at the man on horseback.

The man, a captain, grinned unpleasantly, and shook his head.

"Deserters," he said. "Deserters dressed like Arabs."

La Tour looked at Stivers and Stivers looked at him, and they both shrugged.

Stivers laughed weakly, and said: "Forteau wins."

They were taken to Colonel Falltau, a tall, bronzed soldier of the Legion, with a face that was hard and cold, but with a reputation of being a fair and stern and just officer. He looked at the two men and said: "Deserters?"

La Tour nodded and said nothing.

"But name of a name," the colonel growled, "where did you get those horses and those robes?"

"We were captured by the Arabs, Colonel," Stivers said. "We escaped from Barkai."

TWO DAYS LATER Colonel Falltau's regiment was at the gates of Barkai. Word had been sent to Tirisi-el-Lizai that Colonel Falltau wished to have an audience with him, and the colonel, having a grim sense of humor, added that it was his desire to inform the Caid about a proper and just price for machine guns.

The Caid, being a fat man, shrewd in the ways of the world, and a man that knew, from experience, something of the power of the French armies, acceded to the wishes of the colonel for an audience.

And for the first time in the history of the ancient city, the gates were thrown open and the feet of Christians beat upon the streets.

The conference concerning the matter of military peace was a great success; but concerning the price of machine guns, the fat old Caid smiled and handed Falltau the blouse of a captain of the Foreign Legion and thanked him for his desire to speak of the price of machine guns. The Caid then told the colonel a story and the steel gray eyes of the colonel gleamed a little, and he said no more about machine guns.

Outside the gates of the ancient city Bill Stivers and La Tour lay on the hot sand and stared at the walls that several nights before had loomed up as symbols of certain death.

They spoke few words; both were wondering what would be their fate as deserters of the Legion.

The colonel came out of the gate and walked up to them.

"Pigs," he growled, "salute this coat. In the Legion we salute the coat of an officer who has died."

Stivers and La Tour were on their feet, staring grimly at the Legionnaire blouse in the colonel's hand.

It was the blouse of Captain Forteau. Quickly their hands went to salute, but their eyes remained on the coat, caked with blood and torn by bullets. The colonel dropped the garment on the ground.

"At ease," he said. "You have saluted the captain for the last time."

Colonel Falltau looked at the two men and grinned.

"The only Christians to enter that city and to escape," he said. "The only men in the world that could do it would be Legionnaires. But from where did you escape and what have you been doing?"

Briefly Stivers and La Tour told their story. They told it simply and directly, with no attempt to color any part of it. The steel gray eyes of the colonel flashed as he heard the story. He pulled at his mustache angrily.

"Here, you swine," he called out to his men. "Bring these men food and water. So Tun Hammond was tricking Caid, Tirisi-el-Lizai. That fat old swine will listen to me now. Tomorrow we are entering the city of Barkai. The French Government is sick of the sniping attacks from that city, and when the report of the attack on Fort Deron went over the air by wireless yesterday, I was detailed to attack Barkai. There is another regiment approaching the city from another direction. We will put a stop to that fat Caid's fighting tactics. But this story! Quick, bring these men food. Death wipes out all sins in the Legion and what you told me, which was confirmed by the Caid, has been buried in death. Keep your lips sealed."

Stivers was staring at the coat. He knew beyond doubt that Forteau was dead. A wave of relief came over him, but the sight of the bloody coat made him feel sick all over.

Then Colonel Falltau did several things decidedly unbecoming for a colonel in the Legion to do.

"For deserting," he said, "I could hardly give you a citation, but for capturing that machine gun in the death trap—well, that merits the highest citation in the Legion. And, by the way, it was a touch of cafard that caused you to go to that cave, wasn't it?"

The colonel smiled and winked at the two startled Legionnaires.

"A touch of cafard, *Mon Colonel*," La Tour laughed. "A bad touch."

Stivers stared at the bloody coat at his feet. A strange feeling came over him as he looked at the coat, and then he said: "But—Forteau?"

"Thieves often fight over gold," Colonel Falltau said grimly, "Tun Hammond killed Forteau and Dufont and took the gold paid by the old Caid for himself, but the Caid confronted him with certain facts and Tun Hammond fled, leaving the gold behind. Tirisi-el-Lizai, the fat old toad, got the machine guns and the gold, and kept the coat of Forteau, which he found near the cave, to give to me."

A bugle, blowing formation, broke shrilly on the desert air. La Tour said to Stivers: "Come on, *Ma Petit Cochon,* you're a real Legionnaire now."

Stivers grinned at him.

"Okay," he shouted. "I'm a Legionnaire now."

Pyramid of Gold

BY GEORGE ALLAN MOFFATT

*Exciting, Glamorous Adventure
and Breath-Taking Peril
in the Unexplored Depths
of the Mayan Jungle*

CHAPTER I

TREACHERY!

GORDON LEYBREN AWOKE as the dark form hovered over him, knife gleaming in the black hand. In the vast, desolate silence of the jungle night there had been no sound; yet deep in his brain that ever watching sixth sense, the sense that warns man of dangers he cannot hear or see, had telegraphed the alarm to his sleeping mind. His eyes snapped open. With lightning speed his right hand shot down to his knee. Then, as his fingers closed around the automatic, he hurled himself sideways out of the hammock.

And even as his body went plunging through the darkness to the ground, he heard the ripping of the hammock cords as the knife cut through them. He landed on his back. Two black legs, spread far apart—the legs of the man wielding the knife, were near him. He fired upward, the bullet hitting the groin of his assailant and plowing up through the body. With a yell—the sharp, piercing yell of sudden death—the man crumpled to the ground.

Leybren was on his feet, his cold, blue eyes searching the darkness. Another black form loomed in front of him. There was another whish of a knife. Leybren fired point blank into the black body, and it doubled up like a jackknife, then fell forward, hitting the ground at his feet—a writhing, groveling, gasping mass of human flesh.

Leybren swerved and faced the jungle river, a dark, velvet strip in the night, not more than ten yards from him. And as he swerved he saw from the corners of his eyes that the hammock next to his was empty.

A bitter, grim smile crossed his face. Von Schlossman's hammock empty! This discovery startled him but did not surprise him. For two weeks he had expected this. And now it had happened!

With body tense and nerves on edge, Leybren stood straddling his fallen hammock, his right hand gripping the automatic. No other forms moved in front of him, but from the dark river there came the splash of a paddle dipping into water. With a muffled curse, Leybren dashed forward.

As he did so, a long, darting flash of red came from the river, leaping through the night at him.

A bullet crashed through the *platanillo* leaves behind him. The echoes from the gun filled the forest, but before it had died away, the night was cut with sharp, stabbing flashes of red from his own gun. A man screamed out on the river. Then came the oppressive silence, broken only by the recurring splash of water.

Leybren turned and started down the river bank, after the fleeing canoe; but he crashed against the matted jungle growth that threw him back as if he were a mere atom against it. Far down the river now, the sound of the paddles was dying away; the splash in the water was indistinct and vague, and came at long intervals.

TO ATTEMPT TO follow the canoe along the bank in the dense undergrowth was futile, and Leybren turned and walked, grim-faced, back to his camp. A thin, pale moonlight filtered down through the trees in long, narrow shafts, dotting the ground here and there in splotches of light, outlining the trees and the brush and the giant *platanillo* leaves like phantoms of the night.

At the hammock Leybren's icy gaze clung to the two stark bodies, but at length he raised his eyes slowly and stared at the breathless jungle that seemed to engulf him, to press down on him mockingly and relentlessly.

HE WAS ALONE! This thought pierced his mind slowly. An hour before there had been six of them, six men who eternally watched each other's every move and knew that death hovered near when night fell. Yet to Leybren it had meant human companionship, a thing man craved in the jungle more than life itself. Now two of those six lay dead at his feet and the other three—Von Schlossman and the two remaining *mestizos*—were gone forever. He had won life in the furious fight, but he was alone in a breathless stillness that seemed to taunt and to laugh at his utter helplessness.

He shook his head violently and wet his dry lips. Then he faced the jungle with an unwinking gaze, mouth tight, jaws set, as if he were trying to chase away this new danger, this new fear, that had come to him. His body leaned forward a little, the muscles tense and alert. His sharply-featured face, with the muscles contracting in thin ridges around his mouth and jaws, remained immovable and cold. In his face showed the cold determination, the unbending tenacity with which he had faced danger and death before.

Beside him Schlossman's empty hammock was stretched taut between the trees. In front of him the ebony water of the river gleamed in its utter blackness. Overhead, the spreading *platanillo* leaves blocked out the moonlight. At his feet lay the two bodies.

That was all; all but the dense, gloomy

A leaping flame shot through the air. The knife of the first priest fell to the floor.

forest, spotted feebly by the shafts of pale yellow moonlight. And over it all lay utter silence, unbroken by the call of a bird or the rustle of a beast through the undergrowth. All nature seemed to be watching him breathlessly, waiting to see what move, what action this human prisoner in their midst would take.

What he did was simple. He reached up to a limb that hung over his hammock, took his cartridge belt down and reloaded his gun. Then he removed the holster from his leg and strapped it around his waist. And after that he walked away from the hammock, into the darkness under the trees, and kicked among the bushes with his foot. His foot hit something hard. He kneeled down and pulled some canned goods from the dark brush.

When the job of sorting out the necessary supplies from the meager store was over, he stood up. A grim, bitter smile crept over his face as he reached for the money belt around his waist.

The paper was there on which was scrawled the vague and indistinct directions that had sent him into the unexplored jungles that lay to the south of Yucatan and to the west of Belize—that desolate wilderness where many white men had gone and few had ever returned alive.

Von Schlossman, he was now convinced, had a copy of those crude instructions. He had gotten them before they had left Campeche and he had sent the Indians to murder Leybren simply to get him out of the way.

LEYBREN BACKED TO a tree, his automatic resting on his thigh, his body relaxed and at ease. Slowly the moonlight was fading away. It would be four hours between moonset and dawn.

And with the dawn? Leybren had four hours to make his decision—to go forward or to retrace his steps. It didn't make much difference now which way he went. Backward or forward, death lurked in his footsteps, grimly and hungrily.

The moonlight that filtered through the trees died away. Night—the ebony darkness of the jungle night fell over everything. Leybren welcomed this blinding darkness. It hid from his view the stark bodies at his feet; it left him alone with his thoughts.

He wanted to think, to reason all things out coldly, rationally, before he made his next move.

CHAPTER II

LAND OF SLEEPLESS DEAD

THE SERIES OF unbelievable events—all strange and furtive in themselves—that had sent him into this unexplored region of the world came back now like an ugly dream, a nightmare of gnawing fear and oppressiveness, during which he had waited for Von Schlossman to strike.

Six weeks before he had been in a hotel in New York City, without a job, wondering what he was going to do next. Then had come the strange gray-haired lady, dressed in black, with a face which was even yet beautiful and bewitching. The story she had told Leybren had sounded impossible and absurd, but he had checked up on some of it and found that the woman was telling the truth.

Twenty years before, she explained to him in a soft, well-modulated voice, she had been married to Thorton Hillright, who at that time was a professor at Harvard. Their life, she insisted, had been happy and complete together. There were children—two of them, and Hillright had been a model and affectionate husband.

Then one night he started for the university library, and that had been the last time she ever saw him alive. A search by the police of two continents disclosed no clue, no remote trace of what might have happened to her husband. The years went by and he became only a memory to her.

BUT SUDDENLY, TWO weeks before her visit to Leybren, coming as if from the grave, came the voice of Thorton Hillright, out of the air, through a thousand miles of space.

A wireless operator on a ship coming from South America heard a strange, sputtering message come over his set. At first the waves were so feeble and unintelligible that he could make nothing of it. Then it came again, each letter spelled out awkwardly, as if the hand behind them was feeble and little accustomed to the sending of messages.

"Martha Hillright—husband dying—Usumacinta River—West Belize."

Then the words died away abruptly, as if the set sending them had broken down or the finger operating it had stiffened in death. When the ship got to New York, the operator excitedly told the ship reporters about the message.

It was brought to the attention of Mrs. Hillright. She had heard of Leybren, and had come to him with the proposal that he go into that jungle and find her husband. In her hand was a draft for five thousand dollars and Leybren was promised ten thousand more, deposited to his credit in a New York bank, if he would return with Thorton Hillright or specific knowledge of his death.

Mrs. Hillright took from her pocketbook a paper. What was on this paper, she had explained to Leybren, was the only remote clue she could muster concerning the strange mystery of her husband's voice coming out of the void which had claimed him. She remembered very well a certain night on which a strange-looking man had come to their home and talked privately with her husband. From that time on, she felt, he had acted queerly and talked increasingly little to the family. This had been three months before his disappearance. In going over his private papers afterward, this paper with its strange figures and message had been found.

On the top of the paper were traced two lofty mountain peaks. Sharp-pointed, like the ends of knife blades.

Under them were written:

Ten rivers up Usumacinta and turn west. See two peaks, between which runs ancient Indian trail into Valley of Darkness and the Lake of the Mist.

THE WIFE EXPLAINED that it was her belief that the dark-faced stranger had given her husband a paper on which these words had first been written in Spanish, and that her husband, in making a copy, had written in English. When she first found this paper, she had been puzzled, but now the voice of her husband coming from the Usumacinta jungles left no doubt in her mind but that his disappearance must be linked with this strange message.

Leybren had smiled grimly when he saw the name Usumacinta on the paper. He knew the dreary wilderness of impassable jungle that lay in the path of this great river—a jungle whose green blanket of dense undergrowth had hidden, for centuries, the countless ruined cities of the great Maya civilization.

Explorers had called this region, "The Land of the Sleepless Dead." Many had ventured in, but none had come out to tell what strange mysteries this wilderness held. Even the famous explorer Stephens had shrunk from entering the country, unwilling to face the insurmountable barriers of unknown terror.

But Leybren had embarked upon the dangerous undertaking. In less than a month he was on the first leg of the perilous journey.

At Campeche he was met by Von Schlossman, who had entered the picture unknown to him. He was a tall, thin-faced man somewhere in his fifties, with cold gray eyes and a manner that indicated cunning and craftiness.

He had a cablegram from Mrs. Hillright requesting him to assist Leybren. Von Schlossman explained that he had been a great friend of the missing husband and that he was ready and willing to do anything in his power to help in the search. In fact, he had explained, he already made all the arrangements for the trip, having secured a crew of *mestizos* and a stock of provisions. Leybren cabled Mrs. Hillright and she confirmed Schlossman's words.

They had plunged into the great jungle from Laguna de Terminos, following the Usumacinta until they had come to the tenth tributary, which was a small jungle stream, and then had slipped into the vast darkness of the unexplored wilderness.

Three nights out Leybren knew that Van Schlossman would strike. He knew by then that Schlossman had picked his *mestizos* carefully. And it was five against one, with the one lone man powerless to turn back, powerless to do anything but wait until the blow came. Von Schlossman's actions told Leybren beyond a doubt what was in store for him.

AND NOW LEYBREN dozed, standing against a tree. By deliberate will power he coaxed himself into a sleep, his body still resting in a standing position against the tree, his hand on his automatic; and so he remained until the dawn broke slowly through the impenetrable gloom of the forest.

Wearily Leybren lifted his head and looked around. Above him was a rustle of wings. A huge bird, whose plumage was gorgeous, flew through the trees. It was the *meleagris,* the wild turkey of Yucatan and Guatemala, one of the most beautiful birds of those forests. Leybren looked at it and grinned. It was food, but right now he was not worrying about food.

After a quick dip in the river and a frugal breakfast from some of the canned meat, Leybren threw the supply pack over his shoulders, fastened the straps, and then, without a look behind at the bodies of the dead *mestizos,* he plunged into the jungle—heading toward the interior of that dark and unexplored region. In those hours he had slept, his mind must have come to the decision to go on; for when he awakened at dawn the idea was firmly planted in his brain.

The first move was made!

CHAPTER III

VALLEY OF DARKNESS

A WEEK LATER, Leybren came out from the fringe of jungle undergrowth and stood on a plateau that shot upward toward a great range of mountains in the distance. His face was lined and thin, his eyes sunken, and his cheeks hollow. His body leaned forward as he staggered up the plateau, as if weighted down by a weighty load, but the pack on his back was no longer heavy.

Days before, the last of the canned goods had been eaten, and all that remained to him now was a few pounds of ammunition and quinine, and the hammock.

All during that week he had savagely beaten and cut and thrashed his way through the jungle undergrowth. His face was lashed and streaked with welts where the high grass and the vines had beaten it unmercifully; his clothes were torn to strips and his body was discolored from the *piume* flies that infested the swamp grass and the deadly *inata* mosquito, found only in the Yucatan jungles.

The torrid, suffocating heat had sent his senses reeling time and again until it seemed that all sanity would leave him, but he had pushed on, relentlessly and grimly. During those first days the pack had retarded his progress, but as little by little the supplies were consumed, the pack lightened and he was able to make better time.

He traveled without a compass, but he kept the sun a little to his left,

pushing southeast, basing his hopes on the fact that the jungle river's source lay in that direction. To follow the river was out of the question. And yet it was somewhere at the source of that river that the two peaks were located, and beyond the peaks lay the Valley of Darkness, his goal.

And now he had come to the edge of the jungle and within sight of an unknown range of mountains. His eyes widened with wonder at what he saw. Rising majestically at towering heights were giant *cendellas* of a virgin forest; at places the trunks of the trees reached diameters of twenty feet. And under those great trees animals roamed unmolested as they had done since the beginning of time: gorgeous birds with gorgeous plumage hovered in the air.

LEYBREN STAGGERED INTO the cool shade of the trees and sank to the ground.

During the week he had traversed the flood country, where neither man nor beast lived; he had had no fear of attack. But now, he knew, the situation was different. Here would be the added peril of unknown Indian tribes to contend against, as well as jaguars and other beasts of prey that infested the jungles.

But as he lay on his back, his body weak from lack of food, and every part of it stinging and swollen from the bites of the *piume* fly, he cared nothing for dangers from savages or beasts. His one overwhelming emotion was hunger. He realized the folly of a shot in the forest—but he also knew that unless he got food, death from starvation inevitably faced him.

So after resting his exhausted body for a while, he got to his feet, slipped the automatic from his holster and walked slowly through the great trees that towered over him. As he plunged deeper into the forest, the matted jungle growth around the trunks of the trees thinned perceptibly, and finally he was wandering through a wood where only flowers grew under the trees—the great bushes of the *dahlia maxonii,* with their starry pink and white blossoms; the long vines of the yellow orchid-shaped blossoms that crept high in the trees, giving forth the fragrance of bananas; and the large blue violets that dotted the earth everywhere.

Monkeys chattered and jumped among the trees. Small deer darted among the bushes and a tapir crashed through the undergrowth.

It seemed to Leybren that he was walking in a sylvan forest, such as had the kings of old. The air was cool and refreshing and his brain cleared; and the blood coursed back through his veins with a renewed vigor.

But he was famished and his body was weak. He came to a small clearing. Reckless of danger, he shot a tapir with his automatic. He skinned it and cut a steak from the rump and ten minutes later was broiling it over a fire.

And then when he had eaten his fill, he doused the fire and stretched his hammock between two trees and laid down. His exhausted body had hardly straightened out before he fell into a dreamless sleep.

How long he slept he did not know, but once again that ever alert sixth sense flashed the alarm through his nerves and he woke up fighting.

BUT THIS TIME he had no chance to reach for the automatic strapped on his knee. It seemed to him that the lid of hell had blown up and hit him squarely in the face. All he knew was that over him, around him and under him were fierce, inhuman devils. He was on the ground, shooting his left viciously, kicking his feet at the same time, and with his right hand trying to reach for the automatic at his knee.

He had no idea whether the weapon were still there, and even if it had been, his right hand was blocked by snaky arms and black torsos grappling with him. And more and more of these bodies were piling on him, grabbing at his throat, battering his head in the ground with fists, knees and feet. Fingers were gouging at his eyes and the sharp click of biting teeth was near his face.

WITH A SNARL of rage, Leybren raised himself by a superhuman effort to his knees, heaving bodies up with him. With a wrench, he threw them off. Powerful punches shot out from his shoulders, hitting the groins of the attackers with dull thuds. There were yells of anguish, but suddenly new assailants leaped at him. His right and left continued to shoot out wickedly, methodically, connecting with perfect regularity on the black groins. At every blow, he twisted his body, facing a new opponent at his right, partly evading his last attacker who clutched frantically at his back and his throat.

     THE BEST OF THRILLING ADVENTURES

He made no attempt to aim his blows. They shot out, landing where they might, high or low, and at every smack a black shape doubled up and fell writhing and gasping to the ground. Around him now was a huddle of twitching bodies, hindering his actions but capable of no return blows. Fighting with ponderous power but with uncanny speed, he was like a bear surrounded by wolves, his fists going out with deadly precision and chopping his enemies down.

But fight as he would, he could not protect all sides at once. Behind him an enemy, fresh in the fray, leaped on his back and clutched wiry fingers around his throat. Leybren brought his chin down with a jerk and broke that grip; and then grabbing the arms around his neck and hunching his back powerfully, he hurled the attacker over his head. The man's body hit the ground, but Leybren was grimly holding on to the arms; then jumping instantaneously to his feet, he whirled the astonished assailant around, gaining momentum as he did; and using the man as a human bludgeon, he swung him around and around, battering down every opponent within six feet of him.

From the unwilling acrobat came yells of pain and fear and from the savages floored by the swinging legs came another medley of screams. Grinning wildly, his blue eyes glazed with fatigue and his mop of blond hair wet from the exertion, Leybren whirled the man. It couldn't last forever, but while it did, he was safe.

Then suddenly there came a sharp piercing yell—this time not a shout of fear, but one of command—cold and hard and vibrating. The yell stopped the incoherent clamor of the attackers as if a sword had suddenly cut their lives away in one sweeping stroke. Even Leybren, caught by it, stopped swinging the human form around. He let the man fall to the ground, but he kept his fingers tightly around the wrists.

THROUGH A BLUR of fatigue, Leybren for the first time saw two things. The first was surprising. Dawn had broken and the sunshine was beginning to penetrate the forest. In the fury of the battle he had not realized what time it was or how long he had slept.

The second thing he saw was an old man. In all his experience among savages he had never seen one that looked quite like this one. He was tall, but his body was shriveled and gaunt. His face was a bronzed yellow, but the usual heaviness of the savage features was not there. It was the face of a man with a keen intellect and an active mind. The lines were finely drawn across the mouth, and the eyes were a steel gray—cold and piercing and calculating.

He was dressed in a cotton robe, snow white and embroidered with gold lace. The robe—a work of exquisite beauty and art—held Leybren's eyes as the old man surveyed him slowly and coldly. Downward over the fighter's build, the steel gray eyes wandered, taking in every feature of the tall, powerful frame— the broad shoulders, the heavy chest muscles, the long arms and the heavy fists—fists that were still closed around the wrists of the half-dead human bludgeon that lay on the ground. The eyes of the old man scrutinized the face, the mop of blond hair and the blue eyes, the well formed mouth.

ALL DURING THAT survey no one spoke, no one so much as moved. Leybren, badly battered and out of breath, seized the respite to regain his breath and clarify his mind. In the stress of the combat he had paid little attention to his attackers.

Now he looked at them. They were Indians, but like the old man, their faces were thin and intelligent, lacking completely the animal look that is to be found among the savages of the jungles. Their bodies were tall and straight, and most of them wore a cotton blouse that was wrapped around their waists and up over their shoulders like the *saris* of the Malay country. A few of them, those who had come up with the old man, carried long spears; but those who had surrounded Leybren appeared unarmed.

Leybren let his eyes wander back to the strange old man. His body stiffened and his eyes widened at what he saw. The old man was staring at him, and in those steel gray eyes was terror—stark terror of some strange fear; and the shriveled body, covered by the gold laced cotton robe, was shaking and trembling as if in a fit.

"Martikatasi!" came shrilly from his mouth.

And at the sound of that word, utterly foreign and unknown to Leybren, the old man was on the ground, his body prone at the feet of the American. The strange word acted like a shock of electricity to the other Indians. With groans and lamentations that filled the great forest, they fell forward on the ground.

Leybren stared at the sight in an almost stupefied amazement. Slowly his hands released their grip on the wrists of the man he had used as a swinging club. This man rolled over on his stomach and crawled painfully to the feet of Leybren, and his groans and jabbering rose above the others.

For minutes this weird groveling on the ground continued, and then the old man rose to his feet and threw his arms high in the air, as if supplicating the heavens for aid. Leybren wondered if he were in a dream or if his brain had not snapped and he was the victim of a hallucination.

"IT IS MARTIKATASI," the old man sent up to the heavens in a fear-stricken voice. "It is HE whom we have awaited these many circles of the moon. HE has come and we have smitten him."

The words came in the Mayan language, which Leybren understood well. The other Indians remained prone on the ground and in a chanting, wailing chorus they repeated: "HE has come and we have smitten him."

Leybren looked at the old man and then at the bodies at his feet. His mind, still a little dazed at the strange sight, was unable to register properly what was going on.

He had known when he plunged into that dark and unexplored wilderness that there would be danger of unfriendly savages. And here he had met them, had been practically overpowered, and now they were groveling at his feet, bringing to the end of the fight almost a comic opera touch.

He had no idea who this Martikatasi was, or the occasion for such great lamentations over having attacked him, but he saw that as long as the Indians believed he was this Martikatasi, no harm could come to him.

THE INDIANS ROSE to their feet and at a command from the old man, they surrounded Leybren. While they were doing this he saw his gun on the ground and he surreptitiously picked it up. Then the Indians moved on in procession through the forest, with Leybren walking at the head beside the old priest.

Like a somber funeral cortege, they advanced. The sun was already high in the sky, but the great forest was cool and the fragrance of the flowers filled the air with a sweet perfume.

For over an hour the march continued, but then suddenly the forest ended and they came out on a great rocky plain—the base of the mountain range.

Leybren's lips went tightly together and a cold smile came to his face. Rising far up in the air, their sharp points lost in the clouds, were two peaks, with the summits like the points of knives.

The peaks drawn on the paper! Between them lay the secret Indian path that led beyond the mountains into the Valley of Darkness, and to the Lake of the Mist!

CHAPTER IV

CITY OF GOLD

THROUGH THE LONG weary hours of the morning, with the sun mercilessly baking the flint of the narrow trail—a trail worn a foot deep by the countless footsteps that had trod it for centuries—the procession moved forward. Upward it went, slowly winding in and out of the huge boulders along the steep grade of the slope, until at last they were high upon the mountain.

The heat from the sun caused Leybren's head to reel and his senses to wander. The fight had destroyed what little strength the tapir steak and the night's sleep had given his body, and he staggered forward, blindly at times, until he thought every part of his body surely must collapse. But silently, like phantom beings at his side, the strange Indians, with their aged leader, moved at his side.

At noon the procession stopped and Leybren threw himself down in the shade of a large rock. The Indians brought out some goat skin canteens of water and maize bread. He was given all of the bread and water he desired, and though the food was meager and the water very warm, it gave his body a little much-needed strength.

From where he lay under the rock, Leybren could see, far below, the great forest he had passed through. Over the tops of the tall *cendellas* stretched the jungle—vast, impenetrable, and brilliantly green, even from that distance;

and in this blanket of green was a thin thread of a river, winding in and out like a twisting snake.

He wondered if that were the source of the river he and Von Schlossman had followed from the Usumacinta. They had taken the tenth tributary, which was specified in the instructions on the paper, and this tenth tributary was supposed to bring them to the two peaks, under the shadow of which he now lay.

These thoughts, however, were brought to an abrupt end. The Indians had gotten to their feet and the leader approached Leybren, his face still twisted with some strange fear.

"We go now into the Valley of Darkness," he said, "and from that Valley of Darkness into the Lake of the Mist and beyond these we will find *Her*."

LEYBREN WAS TOO weak, too utterly bewildered by the fantastic proceedings of the morning to take much interest in what the old man said. It would have made little difference to him if he had been told they were about to enter the center of the earth. Somehow it seemed that he was in a dream—a wild, improbable dream, from which, after awhile, he would awaken and find himself lying in his hammock. And nothing that was said or done mattered, for when he awoke it would be over.

Once again the procession started. The Indians now headed for the great rocks that jutted out from the mountain side. The ancient trail led into these rocks and suddenly Leybren was conscious they were in a huge cave and that the air was damp and cold. They walked on through the semi-darkness of the cave and then everything became a stygian black as they advanced further into the underground passageway.

The clammy air turned to a bitter, freezing cold. His clothes, which now were not more than a few strips on his body, gave him no protection from the cold and his body trembled and shook with chill.

But after what seemed hours to him, the air suddenly became warm again and he could feel the sun on his half-naked body. The sound of a great rock being moved came from before him. Then he walked out into the brilliant light of day.

The glare blinded him for a moment and he stood, trying to adjust his eyes to the daylight again. Then as his eyes grew accustomed to the light, he stared—bewildered and dazed at what he saw.

Spreading away from where he stood on the mountain side was a great crater-like basin, with the tops of the jagged cliffs surrounding it lost in the clouds. At places these cliffs rose hundreds of feet into the air.

And in the center of the crater-like basin was darkness—a vaporous darkness that shifted and moved and changed from a dull black to a soft gray and then to a yellow haze. Changing, moving, wavering, the vapor was ghost-like and terrifying.

"The Valley of Darkness," the aged leader of the Indians said to Leybren. "It is through the Valley of Darkness that we must go, to find what lies behind it."

DAZED, AND CERTAIN now that he was

walking in a weird dream, Leybren wordlessly went with the Indians down the narrow trail that was soon lost in the mist. The darkness proved, when Leybren got down in it, to be nothing more than a dense, blinding fog, but he could see the outlines of the Indians in front of him, walking silently and in single file, and he had no difficulty following them.

Down and down they went. The fog covered his body with a cold moisture, and then the fog was no longer around him, and he was following the Indians down into a region of eternal twilight— the soft, cold twilight of coming night.

In the gray shifting shadows of this light he could see the rocks and the ground. From somewhere far ahead came a dull, thundering roar. This roar increased—angry, sinister—like the growl of some prehistoric animal in the bowels of the earth.

And then suddenly he was standing at the brink of a great lake, a lake of dark-blue waters. Three great boats were tied to the banks—canoes hollowed out of the trunks of giant trees. Still without a word, the Indians got in, and the old leader escorted Leybren into one with him. The canoes were pushed away from the banks and a powerful current swung them along without the necessity of using their paddles.

SILENTLY, AWESTRUCK, LEYBREN watched the dark-blue waters. Overhead was the dense fog which hid the lake, and emerging from the depths of the waters was the mighty, thunderous roar, increasing in volume as the boats raced on, carried forward by the mysterious current.

The speed increased. Leybren saw the Indians gripping the sides, their bodies leaning forward tensely and their faces grim and set. Then suddenly everything went dark. The roar increased to a deafening thunder. And through a bank of jet black darkness, Leybren felt himself flying. He was conscious that the boat was under him, but he seemed to be no part of it.

He closed his eyes. On and on he went. He wondered if he were being taken into the very bowels of the earth. He opened his eyes. A brilliant light appeared far ahead. It died away. Then it came back again, rushing toward him at an increasing speed, growing larger and larger.

THE ROAR DIED away; their speed perceptibly lessened. And soon the boat was gliding slowly over still and sparkling waters. The darkness disappeared, and to Leybren came the familiar blindness from the sun. This lasted only a moment, and when he was able to see again, he found that the three canoes were being paddled by the Indians with an ease that was astounding in view of what they had gone through.

Leybren looked at the river. It was wide and the water was blue and clear. The banks were covered with a soft blue grass, over which towered tall and ancient trees. He raised his eyes. He was in a great valley. Several miles to his right and left rose gigantic granite cliffs, cliffs that towered two and three hundred feet in the air.

Down the river the boats glided easily and swiftly. Leybren watched the landscape on either side. It was not the landscape of a jungle. It was a countryside dotted with fields of corn and wide roads and giant trees. Every part of it denoted the presence of a highly civilized people.

The river took a sudden turn and there burst upon his eyes a sight that made his body stiffen and his eyes open in wonder.

It was a city—a beautiful city of shining buildings, buildings whose walls gleamed in the sunlight as if they were constructed of gold and silver, mixed in shimmering waves. From a distance moving on toward it, Leybren watched as if he were looking at a city of old taken from the Arabian Nights.

He stared, awestruck, but now his mind was functioning normally. He realized that the city in front of him was none other than the famous hidden city of the Maya civilization, the city for which explorers and historians had searched for countless years. He realized that this was no myth, no fantastic dream. It was simply that through a series of impossible events he had stumbled accidentally on the ancient city which so many other men had sought in vain.

Certainly there must be paths that led out of those granite cliffs; but the Indians finding him had taken the most baffling and hidden way to enter the valley where the city was located. The entrance he had gone through, Leybren realized grimly, was one which would elude the search of centuries.

AS HE APPROACHED the city, he saw rising in the center of it, gleaming snow-white in the afternoon sun, a magnificent structure. It seemed to be an almost exact replica of the famous Temple of Warriors, uncovered and restored in the ruin of the famous Mayan city, Chichen Itza, in Yucatan. The temple was built on the top of a pyramid that rose upward some forty feet in four receding terraces. A wide stairway wound up the east side to the edifice.

Leybren could see the pair of great feathered serpentine columns, standing some fifteen feet high, which divided the entrance into three doorways. The lofty walls of the temple were covered with freizes and sculpture.

And surrounding the pyramid and the temple was a broad terrace of many acres on which stood thousands of high columns, symmetrically laid out. It formed a great court where gold robed priests could be seen wandering slowly about, absorbed in their devotions.

Around this great temple were the other buildings of the city—smaller temples, market places, ball courts, astronomical towers—all of which covered an area of over a square mile. Beyond this area were smaller houses, all snow-white like the temple, the homes of the Indians.

The valley was broad and flat. In all it covered some ten square miles, with the huge granite cliffs rising over it and shutting it completely out from the outside world. The river passed through the center of the city, alongside the great court of round columns. And as the boats neared this place, the old man with the cotton robe of embroidered gold rose to his feet and called out in a loud voice: "Martikatasi has come!"

The boats came to a stop alongside a stone wharf. Tall priests, wearing feather cloaks, walked solemnly to greet them, while Indians, apparently court attendants or guards, clothed in jaguar skins, ran down to the wharf and threw out long *pissaba* ropes to make the canoes fast.

Leybren was escorted up the time-worn stone steps and onto the Terrace of the Thousand Columns. Above him rose the temple, a piece of architecture that would have been a gem in any civilization. And then suddenly he was conscious of the great crowd that had gathered around them. He could catch a few words of the muttered exclamations from the Indians. He heard blue eyes and blond hair mentioned.

WAS IT HIS blue eyes and his blond hair that had attracted the attention of the Indians in the forest and caused them to fall prone at his feet?

But he had little time to pursue this thought. The crowd had broken, and two priests with gorgeous feathered cloaks came toward him. They dropped to their knees, and as they did the crowd followed their example. From all parts of the city, as if the news of his arrival had spread like wildfire, people came running to the court. They remained at a distance, staring at him in wonder and amazement; and after they had seen, they, too, fell to their knees.

The whole procedure was bizarre—childish and foolish to Leybren; but he held his tongue and played the part of a god, if that was what he was supposed to be.

The priests and the crowd finally got to their feet. Then two priests led Leybren to a low house behind the temple; a house that looked like a miniature temple in itself. Inside the building was a large room, with a great couch covered with jaguar skins. Indians brought luscious bowls of fruit, and inviting food of every kind.

Without a word the two priests backed out of the room and left Leybren alone.

CHAPTER V

A VOICE FROM THE SHADOWS

LEYBREN WAS HUNGRY to the point of starvation, and the first thing he did was to eat. There was meat, deliciously boiled goat meat, and bread and soups and the fruit. For fifteen minutes he ate and gave no thought to the fantastic situation in which he had so suddenly found himself.

And after he had eaten, he lay down on the couch, and stared up at the ceiling. The food, the first real nourishment he had had for days save the tapir steak, gave his body a feeling of relaxation, of complete indolence that was not bothered by the conflicting thoughts in his mind. But after lying there for some time, he began to think.

The process was wholly unsatisfactory

and without results. So he got up and walked around.

THE ROOM WAS large, about twenty feet by thirty. The walls were of a white granite, in which had been sculptured, in alternating panels, grotesque human masks, and the gruesome looking serpent bird. The body and wings and feet were of a bird, while the head was that of a huge snake with a forked tongue, with a human head clamped between the serpent jaws.

The sculpture did not add anything to his peace of mind. He walked to the door and looked out. The temple seemed more than ever an enchanted palace from some fairy tale—a mirage created only by the fantasy of forgotten time.

Leybren shook his head weakly. Was he still dreaming? Slowly he went back to the couch and laid down again.

Outside the sun was going down and twilight was filtering through the city, making the white buildings look ghostlike and eerie. An Indian came in and lit two lamps, lamps of wicks floating in oil; and the flickering light played against the white walls in spritelike shadows that danced and leaped and twisted over the feathered serpents sculptured on the walls.

It was weird—inhuman and uncanny, the semi-darkness of the ghostlike room. Leybren picked up a robe that lay on the couch. It was for—

His body stiffened and turned. Somewhere in the dark shadows of the room he had heard a voice. It had come to him faintly, as if emerging from a great distance; yet when he heard it he thought it was only a few feet behind him.

" 'Ullo—'ullo there," the urgent voice called. *"Move that loose rock in the rear of your room and come down here, Martikatasi."*

LEYBREN'S BODY REMAINED stiff and his thin face knotted in muscles. It was the voice of a white man, a man speaking English. With a spring he was at the rear of the room.

"Move that rock and come down here," the voice continued. "Don't try to answer me or they will hear you."

Leybren was down on his hands and knees.

The dirty, yellow light from the burning wick did not penetrate so far back into the room, and the darkness was intense. His hands moved over the wall. They found a large stone that jutted out an inch from the others. The rock moved as he pulled on it; it moved softly and easily, as if soaked in oil.

Leybren strained it softly, strongly out, and then he was staring into a dark opening, the opening of a passageway that led down into the earth.

He twisted his body through the narrow aperture and plunged into total darkness, having no idea where the passage might lead or what he would encounter at the other end. It was a low, narrow covering, and he had to crawl on his stomach through it, feeling ahead with his hands. Suddenly it shot downward at a steep grade and he let his body slide, keeping his balance and guiding himself with his arms.

For a long time he slid over the rock floor, until it seemed to him that he must be fifty feet below the ground, when, without warning, without seeing the gleam of the small wick lamp ahead, he rolled out into a small, dungeon-like room. Slowly and warily he got to his feet. At first he saw nothing save the shadows from the lamp that danced on the cold and damp walls of the cell.

Then he heard a dry, hollow laugh behind him. He turned and as he did, his body twisted a little and his teeth came together with a sharp click.

Sitting on a pile of old straw with wrists and ankles chained to the wall, was an old man. He was in tattered rags. At first, Leybren could see nothing but the shaggy hair and the great white beard, unkempt and knotted, that covered the face. Then he saw a pair of gleaming eyes—and the face was that of a white man.

"Well, Martikatasi," the old man said dryly, "I thought you might hear me and would come."

Leybren, his face set and his eyes filled with amazement, studied the tattered rags that covered the broken body. Then he relaxed and smiled grimly.

"I take it," he said, "that I have the honor of talking with Thorton Hillright, one-time professor at Harvard and now lost in the Mayan jungles." The eyes of the man studied Leybren coldly—impersonally. The body seemed to contract a little and pull against the chains that held him to the wall.

YES," CAME FROM the man, "you are speaking to Thorton Hillright. But this is quite interesting. I have been here for twenty years waiting for the coming of a white man, and the first one to come knows me by name. Very interesting, indeed!"

"You sent a message to civilization," Leybren replied. "The message finally got to your wife. She came to me, hired me to come and find you."

"My wife," the words fell from Thorton Hillright's mouth in gasping sounds. "My wife—Martha—and she hired you to come into this cursed city of the dead—to get *me.*"

Leybren shrugged. The discovery of Hillright had unnerved him. He squatted on the floor and watched the mere shell of a man in front of him.

Hillright returned the stare and then his body started to shake and tremble and the white bearded face fell forward. His body was shaken with loud sobs. It was as if some tense cord within his mind, a cord that had been strained and held taut for twenty years, had suddenly snapped, and the pent-up emotions of the years burst forth at last wildly and uncontrollably.

AT LENGTH THE sobs stopped and the exhausted body went limp. The tired eyes stared at Leybren pitifully. Leybren understood and said nothing, waiting for Hillright to regain control of himself.

"You—you came in answer to my call," he whispered. "You came to take me—from this hell I have—have—"

The voice quivered again, but Hillright threw his head back and the half-frightened, half-startled look left his eyes.

"We must work quickly," he said, his voice and his manner undergoing an almost miraculous change. "In ten or fifteen minutes you will have to return to your room. Should the priests enter and find you gone, I would be killed for speaking to you. You know very little, I am sure, of the real story of my disappearance twenty years ago.

"Two months ago an aviator, flying over the city crashed. His plane was broken to pieces and he was killed, but in the wreckage I found a wireless set. Wireless had been a hobby of mine years ago. I tried to send a message, not knowing whether it would ever be received by the outside world. The Indians caught me sending it, and the set was destroyed, for they believed it to be some evil spirit."

Hillright smiled. Through the great mass of his white beard, Leybren was able now to see the outlines of his face, strong and intelligent.

"No, I am not chained down here all the time," he continued. "Only at night. I am supposed to be crazy—possessed of evil spirits. But among these aborigines, there is a legend that ill luck attends those that kill or sacrifice an insane man. That has saved my life for twenty years; yet some day it will not suffice and I will be killed.

"Now approaches the month of Karaiti, the god of the harvest, and on that day there must be sacrificed to this god a human life. It may be I, for the witch doctors can, at any time, declare that the evil spirit has left me.

"Twenty years of this living hell, Leybren—chained to these stone walls at night. And in the daytime, as I wander out, the people curse me and pelt my body with stones. And each feast day that comes brings the danger of death.

"A living hell—but you have come! It almost seems that the hand of a just God gave you those blue eyes and that blond hair, for that is why you have been taken for Martikatasi."

LEYBREN REMAINED SQUATTED on the floor, his eyes watching the pallid face of Hillright. The professor was talking rapidly now, in an excited, nervous manner.

"First I will tell you of the legend of the God Martikatasi," he continued. "You are, as you perhaps now realize, in the hidden city of the Maya.

"It is ruled over by a queen, the most beautiful of all women. I have seen her only a few times, but her beauty, you can be assured, is a thing that has never been equalled.

"She is a descendant of the great Queen Kinich-Kakmo, wife of famed King Chaacmol. I have not time to go into the story of this famous queen, but she ruled over the far-flung cities of the Mayas in centuries past.

BUT A GREAT evil visited her family and they were murdered by the nobles, all save a little girl that was spirited to safety by a trusted servant. When this girl grew up, she gathered around her a few loyal followers. She came into this valley and founded this city, and the present queen is a daughter of this girl.

"It was said then by the gods that out of the north would come a blue-eyed, blond-haired god to lead the Mayas back to the greatness they had known, and this god would be called Martikatasi."

Leybren listened, a little bewildered, as Hillright continued the legend of this strange god, of the marvelous deeds expected of him when he came. He would be of super-human strength and he would slay the enemies of the queen. The people would know no want and the harvest would be always bountiful.

"Sorais, the old priest, found you in the forest and saw your blue eyes and your blond hair and believed you were Martikatasi," Hillright explained. "But soon you will have to go before the queen. She will study your face and consult the witch doctors and they will have to convince themselves that you are really the god that is to lead the Mayas back to their one-time glory.

"I was brought into the city the same way as you. But my eyes are not blue and my hair is not yellow. I did not know their language or anything about Martikatasi. I failed to convince them that I was a god. Because of my hardships in the jungle, my brain snapped and I was a little crazy for a while. Had I not been crazy, I would have been taken to the great sacrificial stone and my body hacked in many pieces.

"But with you, it is different. Your eyes are blue and your hair is blond and you can speak their language; and greater than all that, you now know the legend of the Coming God. You can easily convince them that you are Martikatasi."

Leybren smiled grimly and nodded.

"I can take care of that O.K.," he said, "but my job is to get you out of this city. But you might as well tell me why you came. It wasn't your interest in Mayan ruins. Too much happened to me after your wife gave me the copy of the paper you had hidden in your safety deposit box!" Hillright stared at him, his mouth gaping open a little.

"A copy of a paper in my safety deposit box?" he said. "A copy of a paper with twin peaks—"

"Just that," Leybren interrupted. "It was the only clue your wife had as to where you might be."

"And after you got that paper, someone tried to kill you—"

TRIED VERY HARD." Leybren laughed grimly. "Only a week ago in the jungle a man named Von Schlossman tried to have me killed. He escaped with the canoe and all the supplies. I was left in the jungle to die."

"Von Schlossman." Hillright's eyes left Leybren and fell to the floor. "Von Schlossman coming up here?"

Leybren nodded.

"Sit down," Hillright said weakly. "Sit down and I will tell you the secret of my coming here. The secret for which that man tried to kill you."

The yellow flame from the lamp flickered and started to die out, Hillright moved the wick with his finger and the flame rose slowly and again cast the weak light over the darkness of the dungeon.

"Even when I was a student at Harvard," Hillright began, "the mystery of the Maya civilization intrigued me.

I had delved far into such meager knowledge as historians had been able to discover. Three years before my disappearance, on a pretext of going to Europe, I came down here to study the ruins of the cities in Yucatan. Studying these ruins, I made the discovery that started me on my final tragic quest.

THE MAYAS HAD reached a stage of civilization almost equal to the civilization of ancient Greece. They were a rich race: yet nowhere in all the ruins of the cities was found one trace of gold, one gem of any value. What happened to the wealth will never be known. I think sometime it will be found buried beneath the ruined temples. Or perhaps the jungle, creeping up to claim its own, has hidden it from human eyes forever.

"But I thought then that if, in the vast jungles, could be found a Mayan city of the old civilization, unlimited wealth would be there."

The old man looked up at Leybren and stopped talking.

He shook his head sadly, and stared at the floor, a habit he had acquired through the lonely years of his captivity.

"At that time," he continued, "I was young and foolish. I had a good position at Harvard, but I craved wealth and independence. This overwhelming thought of finding an ancient city, still inhabited, fascinated me. Then I first learned of the strange story told the explorer Stephens in 1850 by the *cura* of Quiché, an Indian village in Guatemala. This *cura,* according to the story, had wandered forth alone, and had gotten lost in the great mountain range that could be seen from his village, a nameless range that came out of the land of mystery.

"Briefly: in his wanderings this *cura* came to the top of the range, at the top of the very cliffs that surround us now, and looked down upon this city, the last remaining one of the Maya civilization. And standing there he saw what you have not yet seen. The great pyramid of gold glistening in the sunshine on the far side of the temple.

"He followed the cliffs around until he came to the twin peaks and there saw the ancient Indian trail. He followed it, and somehow he discovered the hidden passageway through the mountain, something no one else ever has done. But when he came to the Valley of Darkness, he became frightened and hurried away. He followed the jungle river down to the Usumacinta, where some friendly Indians gave him a boat and supplies. He finally arrived at Campeche, more dead than alive."

Again Hillright stopped talking and looked at Leybren quietly.

"The story seized my imagination and made me lust for this wealth," he confessed bitterly. "I went to Quiché to see if I could find some of the relations of this *cura,* someone in whom he might have confided his experiences."

THE *CURA* HAD refused to give Stephens any idea of the location of the city, claiming that he could not remember; but I knew the cunning of these Indians and I was certain that the secret of that city could be found. I knew the *cura* was dead, but I had a wild idea that somewhere in his papers or with his relatives, if he had any, would be the data about the city.

"I talked to a nephew of the *cura* and told him what I believed. I offered him five thousand dollars if he could discover any such information and deliver it to me at my home in Cambridge.

"It was on my way home, on the ship, that I met Von Schlossman. He was a young man then, well versed in the history of the Maya civilization. He was intelligent and we struck up an acquaintance, but at no time did I like the man. But I was foolish enough to repeat to him the story of the *cura* and to further say that I had been at Quiché.

HE APPARENTLY BELIEVED that I had found the information, for he made an attempt on my life before the ship got to New York. Made it in such a subtle way that I could prove nothing against him. Later he came to my home and demanded point blank if I had the location of the city. I told him no, but he did not believe me.

"Well, when the nephew appeared two years later and gave me the parchment paper with directions to the hidden city on it, something snapped in my brain. Here was the key to hidden wealth. I would go alone, secure the endless gold, and then return to my family. I could not tell my wife, for she would have believed me insane.

"So I disappeared one night and came down here. I was young and very foolish. I did not realize the utter impossibility of finding the city and getting the gold and escaping with my life. I followed the instructions on the parchment paper and finally came to the forest where you were captured.

"And there I was seized and taken for Martikatasi, just as you have been—"

Hillright raised his manacled hands suddenly.

"Quick," he whispered, "they are coming to your room. If they find I have talked to Martikatasi, they will kill me like a dog."

Leybren jumped to his feet. His ears strained to hear a sound but none came. He looked at the old professor.

"For twenty years," Hillright said, "I have listened to footsteps coming and going in that room. I can hear what you cannot. Hurry and get back there. We can plan further tomorrow night."

Leybren turned quickly, dropped on his hands and knees, and started up the narrow little passageway that led to his room far overhead. He crawled rapidly, more certain of his way in the darkness now.

Near the top he stopped and lay flat on the cold, damp rock floor. Above him, coming from his room, he heard voices—low and excited!

He had moved too late! At first he considered retreating back into the dungeon. But that would do little good. He would soon be discovered with Hillright and that would be the end.

If he went forward, they would also know, unless—

He rose to his hands and knees and crawled forward through the darkness. He came to the small opening in the wall of his room. He could hear the voices distinctly now.

His jaws set with a clicking sound: his body was tense as he pushed his way through the small opening and fell to the floor of his room, his body still partly hidden by the shadowy darkness that the feeble rays of the wick lamps could not reach.

CHAPTER VI

GOLD PYRAMID

LEYBREN LAY ON the floor, his body tense and every muscle alert and ready for action. The lamps threw their yellow glow over the room, and in this shadowy light he could see two men standing near the couch. Outside the building the two guards remained.

From his prone position, he could not see the faces of the men. One was clothed in a white robe. The other appeared to be a servant or a warrior, wearing, as he did, the white *saris* around his waist and shoulders.

Suddenly the man in the robe started toward him.

Leybren was on his feet with a spring. His right hand went back to drive a paralyzing blow in the face of the man, but the blow died before it started.

THE MAN STANDING in front of him was the old priest, with the shriveled body and steel-gray eyes, the one that had found him in the forest.

"You have found," the priest said quietly, "the man with the face of white."

The old priest bowed, and in the presence of Leybren his body trembled a little.

"He is possessed of the evil ones," the old man continued, "and if he has talked to Martikatasi, he must die: for no evil can touch you whom we have awaited so long."

Leybren walked over to the couch and sat down wearily. The reaction had unsteadied him.

"My friend," he said, "if I have come from a distant land to lead you-"

"You are Martikatasi," the old man cried and fell to his knees. "And you have come to lead us back to our ancient glory—"

"And yet your men smote me," Leybren answered dryly. "But no one knows that you did this."

The priest rose to his feet and gazed bewildered at Leybren.

"If it is your wish, Martikatasi," the old man said, "that no one knows Timkanti, the evil one, has spoken to you, my lips will not speak of it. But he will not speak to you again, for it was ordered last night that Timkanti die in three suns on the festival of the god Karaiti."

"That he die!" Leybren gasped.

The old priest nodded.

"When the sun will have passed beyond the cliff three times," he said, "he will be sacrificed to the god of the crops."

Leybren stood up and his face paled.

"And you," the priest continued, "will on that night be taken to our queen and be declared the god of our forefathers— the god to lead us forth again."

Then the old man and his attendant, whom Leybren recognized as one of the warriors of the woods, bowed and left the room.

For the next three days Leybren was showered with all the attention, all the homage that could possibly be bestowed upon a god. He was permitted to wander over the city and he went far out among the corn fields that stretched in every direction over the valley.

Despite the cloud of death that hung over Hillright, the city of the aboriginal Mayas fascinated him. The fields were cultivated by hand, and the corn indicated a large yield. The Indians were aided in their farming by the priests who, from the towers, kept them in touch with the different astronomic phenomena that forecast the prospective weather changes. THE CITY ITSELF represented a civilization and a development of the arts that rivaled the Greeks. The temple and other buildings were elaborately sculptured and many of them brilliantly painted. Wood carving, jade cutting, feather work pottery design, weaving, painting, and other arts were carried on successfully.

But the fascination of the ancient city did not prevent Leybren from using every effort to discover some avenue of escape, some outlet through those granite cliffs that kept him and the valley safely guarded from the outer world.

He studied the current of the river running through the city, the river that had shot him out of the bowels of the earth and into the valley. The current was strong, but he knew that, somehow, the Indians had gotten those boats into the lake of the Valley of Darkness.

IT WAS UNDOUBTEDLY done by trained and skilled paddle men, who could take the canoes through the underground passage where the river shot down into the earth from the lake. But to a person inexperienced and untrained it would be utterly impossible.

It was on the second day that he discovered the famous Pyramid of Gold, near the palace of the queen.

The palace was situated on a high terrace court, a beautiful building constructed in white marble. On its walls were sculptured friezes of human heads; and the feathered serpent was there, stretching along the wall, with its reptile mouth holding a human head.

Wide and impressive marble steps swept from the ground to the doors of the palace.

South of the palace, rising some twenty feet in the air in five small receding terraces, was the Pyramid of Gold that the bewildered *cura* had seen from the top of the cliffs. In the sunlight it shone with a dazzling, brilliant glitter that could be seen for miles.

Leybren tried to estimate the value of the gold in the structure, but the figures got so high that they startled him. No wonder the poor *cura* had gazed in awe and wonder at what he saw: no wonder poor Hillright, hearing of this fabulous fortune in the wilderness, had left family and home to secure it. And the mystery of why Von Schlossman was willing to commit murder was no longer a mystery.

DURING HIS WANDERINGS around the city, Leybren saw Hillright, his shaggy white beard falling far down on his chest, and his unkempt, snowy hair falling over his shoulders, running and darting around like a beaten and haunted dog. Dirty rags hung over his long body and his feet were bare. The Indians jeered after him, threw rocks at him.

All during those two days Leybren saw nobody go near the poor old man, save to pelt him; no human voice talked to him, save to curse and abuse him. Hillright, playing the part of a demented man that his life might not be taken from him, jumped and groveled on the ground and screamed wildly.

For twenty years this had been his role. The very terror of it, the utter brutality struck Leybren with a force that sickened every part of his mind. He wondered that Hillright had retained any semblance of sanity; yet through all these years his powerful will, encouraged by hope that could not die, had kept his mind alert and keen.

Any communication with him was impossible. Two attendants were at Leybren's side at all times, and wherever he went the people—men with the *saris* over waist and shoulder and women in the embroidered dresses of white—flocked after him and fell to their faces on the ground when his eyes met theirs. Had Hillright sought to come near Leybren, he would have been beaten to death by the people.

Thus the three days passed, and Leybren was unable to convey to Hillright the plan that had been forming in his mind.

But on the third night, as twilight was filtering over the white city, Leybren lay on his couch. His face was tense and his eyes narrowed a little. Near him stood the two attendants. He had found out from his friend, the old priest of the woods, whom he learned was called Sorais, that it would not be until the moon was high in the heavens that he would be taken to the queen. And it would not be until dawn that the sacrificial ceremonies would call Hillright to the stone slab to be killed.

THE PLAN THAT had formed in Leybren's mind was desperate—almost absurd; yet it was the only one he could conceive. He had come up here to save Hillright and if he was going to do that, the break would have to be made *before* he was taken to the queen. He wondered if the poor professor had yet been told of the doom that the dawn would bring him.

His eyes watched the tall, bronze-skinned attendants that stood mutely at his side. The muscles on their bodies rippled as they moved their arms. Each carried a spear. Leybren smiled coldly. He would have the advantage of striking first, and by that advantage he might be able to put one of the guards out of business before the other one was upon him.

Outside the silence of the night was eerie and oppressive. It would be over an hour before the girls would come with the fruit and food bowls. But there was always the chance that some priest might wander in and if he did—

Leybren's eyes wandered to the part of the rear wall where the stone had been pulled out several inches. He had a file

          THE BEST OF THRILLING ADVENTURES

and a hammer, both crude implements, and with them he hoped to break the chains that held the professor.

Leybren's body moved slowly, stealthily off the couch. He was on his feet. The two attendants were several feet from him, in front of the couch. One of them turned his head slowly.

And as he did, Leybren's right shot through the air like a piston rod and caught the man flush on the jaw.

CHAPTER VII

THE BLACK RIVER

THE BLOW LANDED with a loud smack and the man went to the floor with a dull groan, falling face forward, as if every muscle had suddenly gone limp and useless; but before the body had hit the floor, Leybren was sending his left through the air at the second attendant.

The man ducked the blow and jumped back, his eyes terrified with fear at seeing the white god turn against them. For a split second the man stood there and stared at Leybren, and that split second was all Leybren needed. Rising on his toes, his right went against the man's chin, backed by every ounce of weight in his body, with every ounce of his strength behind it.

Like the first attendant, this man crumpled to the floor in a limp and senseless heap. Leybren was tearing one of the cotton robes into long strips, and with deft and sure hands he bound and gagged the two unconscious men.

Quickly he dragged them to the shadowy end of the room and thrust them into a darkened corner.

Then he plunged down the narrow tunnel passageway to Hillright's cell. Hillright looked up in amazement and fear as Leybren's body hurtled into the dungeon room.

"We've got only minutes to get out of this hole, Hillright," Leybren said brusquely. "I've got an Indian file and a hammer to break your chains."

Hillright drew back, his eyes flashing anger.

"Fool," he hissed. "What good will it do to get out of here? Where will we go?"

"LISTEN," LEYBREN SAID grimly. "If you don't know the news, I'll break it to you now, and not gently. When dawn comes you are going to be sacrificed for the benefit of some fool god that makes the corn grow."

Hillright's body stiffened and terror came in his eyes.

"The month of Karaiti," he gasped. "I am going to be killed—"

"The priest Sorais told me," Leybren answered. "And for three days I have been unable to get the word to you. Now we've got to act."

"But—but where can we go?" Hillright groaned weakly. "For twenty years I have been trying to find some path out of this hole—"

"We'll talk about that when we get out of this dungeon," Leybren broke in quickly. "I've got my automatic, and that'll get us somewhere!"

He had the file and hammer out, and was working rapidly on one of the chains.

"Escape!" Hillright straightened suddenly. "God, escape from this—here. I'll show you how to break these chains—give me the hammer. Escape! We can go through the underground passage that leads from this dungeon out under the courts of columns, and from there we can hit the river. The river will carry us somewhere—maybe to death—but it will at least mean freedom. Escape! God, escape!"

The sudden change in Hillright's demeanor filled Leybren with fresh hope. The two men hacked and filed and beat the iron links. From overhead in Leybren's room there came no sound. But any minute some priest might enter the room, discover Leybren gone and the insensible attendants tied and gagged on the floor.

One of the links broke. Feverishly—with an almost insane energy, Hillright assisted Leybren. Another link broke and now the professor's hands were free. The iron band around his right ankle came open easily, but the left band did not yield to the file and hammer. Hillright tore and hammered against it, ripping his skin without any apparent feeling. Blood spurted from his ankle and ran into the filthy straw.

But finally one of the links gave in the chain and Hillright was on his feet.

"This way," he whispered, starting for a darkened door of the dungeon.

Overhead came a sudden babble of voices. Leybren looked at Hillright and smiled grimly.

"They have found the god is gone," he said. "Quick. Which way are we to go?"

HILLRIGHT DARTED OUT through the door of the dungeon, with Leybren close on his heels. The voices coming from Leybren's room were shrill and excited now. Someone was hurtling down the narrow tunnel that led from the house above into Hillright's dungeon.

But neither Hillright nor Leybren paid any attention to the person coming behind them. They ran madly through the pitch darkness of the corridor which was outside the cell. Leybren followed the little dots of white, which were Hillright's tattered clothes. He crashed into a wall and was thrown back. He heard Hillright's voice ahead of him and he sprang to his feet, progressing less hastily through the darkness, feeling with his hands.

"Look out for these steps," Hillright cried. "After the steps we will be under the court of columns surrounding the temple. Then we will have to make a break for the river." Leybren felt ahead in the darkness with his toes. He touched a step and then he was racing up them, three at a time, trying always to keep the white of Hillright's rags in front of him. It seemed to him that the underground passageway had suddenly become a babble of a thousand voices. The voices raised in shouts echoed and re-echoed through the maze of black tunnels behind them. But he continued up the steps, not allowing the pursuit to deter him.

He came to the top of the steps, stumbled through the darkness and nearly fell, but Hillright's hand grabbed his shoulder and straightened him up.

"The current of the river will carry us beyond the city," Hillright whispered. "It may carry us to our death. But it is our only hope. Don't use your gun unless absolutely necessary, as it will bring the whole city down on us."

Cool air came through the darkness, and far ahead Leybren saw a small square of bluish moonlight. The end of the tunnel, and after that—the river! He set his jaws with a click as he dashed for the opening.

Hillright stopped and yelled: "They are coming from the front!"

LEYBREN CRASHED INTO the old man, and as he did he saw pass across the little square of moonlight ahead, two forms, shadowy and dark. Far behind them in the darkness of the underground passage, the pursuing Indians were yelling.

A trap of death! For a moment Leybren looked back of him and then in front. His body was now naked to the waist. He had discarded the gold robes, and all he wore was the remains of his trousers. Even his shoes, torn and cut from his trip through the jungle, had been thrown away.

In that passing moment he made his decision.

"We'll get to the river," he said to Hillright. "I'll take care of the two men in front of us."

HE ADVANCED SLOWLY now, with body leaning over and arms swinging at his sides, ready for action. His gun was stuck in the belt around his waist to be used only as a last resort.

Hillright kept at his side, his breath coming in short gasps from the exertion of running. The opening of the tunnel seemed to be coming to meet them. It grew larger and the darkness around them was broken by the faint moonlight that penetrated the opening.

There was a swish of air. Hillright groaned. A spear hit the rocks and its metallic twang echoed weirdly down the tunnel.

With a snarl and a curse, Leybren's body lurched forward, his right coming up in a vicious, paralyzing undercut. The blow cut up through empty air, but his body hit the man that had thrown the spear and they went together to the earth, snarling, fighting, cursing.

The man was powerful and Leybren had difficulty in keeping him under. Near him he could hear another struggle, but he had no time to turn his head to see how poor Hillright was coming out. Against a young Indian the old professor could last but a few seconds.

Leybren brought his right crashing down to the face of the man under him. He heard the crunching of bones as the blow landed on the Indian's mouth. Again the right came down; again there was a crackling of bones. And suddenly the body under him went limp.

Leybren was on his feet with a leap. A struggling, fighting mass hit his legs and knocked them from under him. He was thrown violently backward. He heard the gasping groans of Hillright as he hit the floor.

Leybren's body came up slowly, resting on his hands and knees. He lurched forward and grabbed at the indistinct, seething mass of human flesh. His hands caught the white beard of Hillright, and with a vicious pull, he had the professor away from the Indian and threw him back against the wall.

A FORM ROSE above Leybren with the speed of a tiger, but Leybren remained on the ground. He rolled over the floor and grabbed the feet of the Indian standing ready to pounce. With a hunch of shoulders and a sudden raising of his body, Leybren threw the Indian over his shoulder, hurling him through the darkness against the wall.

"Come on!" he yelled at Hillright.

Without stopping to see what had happened to the unlucky assailant, Leybren and Hillright dashed madly down the passageway for the little patch of blue moonlight that indicated the opening. They came to it and fairly flew out into the open. Five feet ahead of them could be seen the waters of the river, gleaming brightly in the moonlight.

Leybren's dive for the waters started the minute he left the opening of the tunnel. His body hurtled across the five feet and hit the river at the edge of a stone wharf. And as he did, he heard another body splash alongside him.

His body sank under the still waters. He went down and down. At first he seemed to sink naturally and slowly, from the force of the dive. But suddenly something gripped him, something that seemed to have the power and strength of a giant deep-sea octopus. The next second he was being twisted and dragged and thrown in churning, maddened waters.

He struggled wildly against this gripping, tenacious power that was tearing him down and down. He was conscious that he was being hurled through the water at a terrific rate: the sickening thought flashed through his numbed mind that he was in the throes of an underwater current, so powerful, so deep that no man could ever hope to come out of it alive.

His lungs were bursting for air. His senses reeled. One second—two seconds—three seconds. He could not hold out much longer. Every part of his body cried for air. His jaws were set in the vise-like grip of death. The minute he opened them—

Water was rushing through his mouth, filling his lungs and stomach, and then his body began to sink lower and lower.

That was the last he remembered— the water filling his lungs and his body going down and down. After that merciful unconsciousness came over him and thoughts ceased stabbing through his tired brain.

CHAPTER VIII

THE HOUSE OF SILENCE

LEYBREN CAME TO slowly, his eyes still closed and his lungs filled with shooting pains. He was lying on something soft, but he did not have the strength to open his eyes. He wondered vaguely, in a dazed manner, if he were at the bottom of the river. He had been sinking when consciousness left him, but if he were on the bottom of the river how could consciousness return?

Crazy, distorted thoughts flashed through his mind. Then even these thoughts left and he felt tired to death, and his mind sank slowly back into the oblivion whence it had come.

When consciousness returned again, his head was clearer. He opened his eyes. Forms—dark forms were standing over him. Somewhere a soft light was glowing dimly; everything around him was shadowy and spiritlike. Then slowly the forms around him took shape. They were men—Indians, and the face nearest him was that of his friend, Sorais, the priest. The old man was staring at him with fear and terror registered all over his shriveled and yellow old face.

Leybren smiled at him and muttered: "What are you doing here?"

"Martikatasi," the old man breathed weakly, "the evil one talked with you, and those he talks with die. We saved you from the waters of the river by throwing a net across it."

Leybren sat up. Now he remembered all that had happened, He and Hillright jumping into the river and the undercurrent pulling them down. He had been saved from the river—but Hillright?

"You saved me," he said to Sorais, "but Timkanti—did you save him?"

Leybren saw now that the room was filled with priests and warriors. They stared at him with the same fear and terror in their faces that Leybren had seen in the face of Sorais.

"The evil one was saved to die at dawn, Martikatasi," Sorais said. "He will die to satisfy the god Karaiti, and never again will he bring evil to others. When we pulled the net up and found you, you were dead. But our doctors brought you back to life, for you cannot die."

A SICK, WEAK feeling spread over Leybren. He thought for a moment that unconsciousness was coming back again. His body swayed. But a priest came up to him and gave him an earthen jug to drink from. The liquid was sweet tasting and it brought strength back to the American's body, and dispelled the last vestiges of weakness.

"The moon, O Martikatasi," Sorais cried, "is high in the heavens now. And now you will go to tell *her* that you have come to lead her people to the glory that once was theirs."

Leybren looked around him, his lips pressed tightly together, his mind working coldly and rationally. It would be some hours before Hillright died, and in that time some escape might present itself.

Any move now would be found to end as tragically as had their attempted escape. So Leybren got up slowly and motioned with his head to Sorais that he was ready for his visit to the queen.

OUTSIDE THE MOON, high in the heavens, flooded the temple and the court of columns with a bewitching bluish haze: in this soft moonlight the whiteness of the buildings seemed ghostly and unreal. Slowly and solemnly, the procession of priests and Indians, escorting Leybren to the Palace of the Queen, moved through the night.

Two Indians with jaguar skins around their waists went ahead, holding burning torches high above their heads. Behind them walked the priests with the feathered robes, their faces covered by masks and in their hands earthen jars of burning incense. And then walked Leybren, now clothed in a robe of pure gold. Sorais walked at his side, silently, as if in a hypnotic trance. At the rear came other priests.

The procession wound through the court of columns and then came out in front of the temple. Up the wide, snowy-white stairway that climbed the four receding terraces to the temple, Indians were moving about slowly. And at the top, lights were burning in preparation for the sacrifice to the god of the harvest.

The procession ascended the marble stairs to the great doors of stone that were rarely opened. At their approach these doors, as if operated by some electric switch, opened slowly and noiselessly to permit their entrance inside the sacred portals.

A soft, fragrant light of wavering red greeted Leybren as he stepped into the palace. At first he could see only this wavering red light, and then as his eyes pierced the haze he could not suppress a gasp of utter wonder. In all his life he had never seen anything quite as exquisite, quite as enchanting as the beauty of that room.

Gorgeous blood red rugs lay over the floor, and in the light—a light that seemed a representation of the very blood of life—these rugs presented an appearance of a lake of bewitching scarlet waters. Around the room were sculptured pieces—human bodies, great feathered serpents, and animals—each of which would have been considered a beautiful work of art in New York or Paris. On the walls were friezes done in a style that would have caught the attention of connoisseurs in any country or civilization.

The whole room, with its soft red light, its gorgeous rugs, and its sculpture and paintings seemed to Leybren to be a floating, enchanted land far removed from anything human or real. THE TWO TORCH bearers had remained outside the palace and with them stayed the priests and Indians who had comprised the procession. Only Sorais and the two men bearing the incense jars had entered the front doors with Leybren.

Slowly Sorais led Leybren across the blood red rugs and to the far end of the room. Here he stopped in front of a second door, fell to his knees, and cried: "O Queen of Beauty, hear thy servant, the humble Sorais, for he brings to you Martikatasi, whom you have awaited so long."

SILENCE, EERIE AND deadly, followed those words. Leybren had remained standing, his mind and his body in a daze of bewilderment.

Slowly the second door opened. Sorais rose to his feet. "You go alone," he said to Leybren. "The queen awaits you in her own room."

Leybren walked through the door, walked as if he were floating in some fantastic dream of a magician's creation.

He tried to smile, but no smile came to his face. He wet his lips and wondered if he had entered some strange world in the misty vale beyond life.

The click of doors behind him, as they closed, brought him to his senses. He looked around.

He was in a smaller room, and here the wavering light was a soft blue—a hazy mist that passed before the eyes softly and gently. In this blue light he could see the multi-colored walls of the room and a domed ceiling suspended, it seemed, in the clouds.

For a moment he stood, wondering what he was supposed to do. Then softly, as if from afar off, he heard a voice whisper: "Martikatasi."

He swerved quickly, stood as if he had suddenly been riveted to the floor, and stared in utter amazement and wonder at what he saw.

He was looking at a woman, such a woman as he had never before dreamed could exist. She was standing before a throne that sat back in the wall, her graceful body swaying a little as if she were floating in the cloud of blue that surrounded her.

A long gown of snow-white fell over her body, but Leybren saw nothing but the face that was gazing at his. It was the face of a woman, of a bewitching, divine beauty—a face that some Greek sculptor must have hewn from a marble white as snow. The face, the eyes, the nose, the mouth—every feature was utter, beautiful perfection. Over the ex-quisite shoulders long yellow hair fell gracefully and softly.

For a moment it seemed to Leybren that every part of his little act to prove that he really was Martikatasi had fled from his mind. He stood gaping in wonder at the beauty of this woman, his mind a complete blank.

And then he realized that the queen was looking at him, and that those eyes were watching every move he made. She must make sure that he was a god and not an imposter.

He advanced toward her slowly and then he fell to his knees at her feet.

"Rise, Martikatasi," she said in a voice that was soft and tender. "Why wouldst thou kneel before a poor child of human blood, such as I?"

Leybren rose slowly. He wasn't quite sure that he was doing what a god should do. He shook his head a little to disperse the bewitching spell the queen's beauty had thrown over him.

"Even to Martikatasi, O Queen," he said slowly, "thy beauty is a wonder never glimpsed before."

THE QUEEN LAUGHED, a quick, nervous little laugh, and sat down.

"Flattery is also the weapon of a god, Martikatasi," she answered. "You may call me Esterais. But come closer that I may see you—your eyes and your hair, and your face."

Leybren advanced until he was standing within a foot of the queen. Her eyes studied him closely, and he knew that his life was hanging on a thin thread. But even faced with death, he felt no fear, no nervousness in her presence. Only utter amazement that a woman could be so beautiful, so entrancing, and still be human.

BUT THE AMAZEMENT passed and cold reason returned. Leybren was conscious that the eyes of Esterais were sapphire blue and her hair was yellow. What connection this could have with the coming of a blue-eyed, blond-haired god mystified him.

"Your eyes are blue," she said softly, "and your hair is yellow, as it was written that the eyes and the hair of Martikatasi would be. Your face is thin and your features noble, as also were to be the features of Martikatasi when he would come to lead us to the glory that was ours. Ours before the evil one struck and slew those who were noble and wise."

"And I see also that your eyes are blue and your hair is yellow, O Queen," Leybren said in the soft, slurring accents of the Mayan language. "As it was written that my eyes were to be the color of the skies and my hair the color of gold, so it was foretold to me that I should wander the face of the earth until there appeared a queen of the Mayas whose eyes and hair were a like color. A queen of a beauty that was not of this earth."

A tremor passed through the queen's body, and then she swayed in the throne-like chair. She rose stiffly, and with a moan fell at the feet of Leybren, her body quivering and sobbing.

Quickly he reached down and touched the soft flesh of her delicate shoulders and raised her to her feet. Her eyes were closed and her body was still trembling, and she moaned: "It is Martikatasi. He has come—he has come!"

He helped her back to the marble chair and rubbed her wrists nervously, but her eyes remained closed and her lips quivered.

Then she opened her eyes slowly, and her white, delicate hand went out to caress his hair. He was on his knees in front of her, staring helplessly up into the soft blue eyes and the white face. It was as if she held him in a hypnotic trance—a trance that left every part of his body numb and helpless.

And in that moment he renounced everything. Outside the poor old professor was being prepared for the sacrifice to the god of the harvest, but Leybren had forgotten him.

The professor, the world, the gold—everything had fled from his mind, as he kneeled in front of the queen, a helpless victim before the beauty of her face.

CHAPTER IX

THE SACRIFICE TO A GOD

THE HAND OF Esterais left his hair and Leybren rose to his feet, his mind still dazed and bewildered. But through the bewilderment gradually seeped the slow realization of his tremendous task.

"You have come, Martikatasi," Esterais said softly, "and together we shall strike my enemies and once more lead my people forth. You have come just as I thought it was too late. But now I cannot speak of those that are seeking to undermine my rule and my life. You must go before the priests and the wise men, and they must be convinced that you are Martikatasi."

"When the dawn breaks," Leybren said quietly, "there will be a sacrifice to the God Karaiti, and the man you have called Timkanti, the evil one, will be sacrificed to this god. It is my wish that this man be not sacrificed. For he is not a man of evil but a man who can help us."

The queen looked at him and shook her head sadly.

"It has been ordered by Kankomo that the evil one shall die," she said. "Kankomo is powerful. Timkanti is evil. There is nothing I can do to save his life."

LEYBREN PRESSED HIS lips tightly together and his eyes narrowed.

"If the man of white hair and white face dies," he said, "a friend and helper dies. For he is not a man of evil, but one who wishes to work with me—"

Esterais interrupted him with a short, nervous movement of the hand.

"Kankomo has ordered his death," she repeated. "Kankomo is the high priest of the palace, a man who would be king. His influence over my people is great and I am helpless to save this man. Enough!"

Leybren smiled grimly and said: "Then Martikatasi will save him, for it is written that Martikatasi must save all who are white of face and hair."

Esterais looked at him, her soft blue eyes unfathomable and mysterious, and he wondered what thoughts were passing behind those eyes. Then suddenly she leaned forward and again a flashing gleam came in her eyes, and on her face came a look of triumph.

"Thus it is as I have long wished," she whispered. "Only one man can defeat Kankomo and that man I have known would be Martikatasi. For ere you can lead us out into the glory that has passed, you must first slay those who fight within our ranks."

Behind them the doors to the room suddenly opened. Esterais rose slowly and whispered: "Kankomo."

Leybren turned quickly. He saw the doorway fill with priests, headed by one who was tall and powerful of build. THE PRIESTS FELL to their knees and the tall leader's body was prone on the floor.

The queen stood in front of the marble throne, her body straight and her eyes flashing at the form prostrated in front of her.

In the hazy blue light of the room the whole procedure looked bizarre, unreal to Leybren. He stood silently at one side of the throne and watched Esterais.

"Arise," she called out in her low, melodious voice. "Arise, ye that kneel before your queen, and behold the god Martikatasi come to us."

Slowly, moving in perfect unison, the ten priests and the leader rose to their feet and gazed at Leybren, and in that passing stare he saw the face of Kankomo, the high priest of the palace. The face was a fitting complement to the powerful, highly muscled body. It was a face of utter cruelty and cunning; a face heavy with the passions that surged behind it, with eyes of a savage, beast-like ferocity.

And in the passing second that his eyes met those of Kankomo, Leybren sensed a struggle, a struggle between himself and this high priest, that could only end in the death of one of them.

"Kneel, thou fools," came from Esterais in a sharp command. "Kneel, for thou art in the presence of the god Martikatasi—the one foretold by the great father, the king of kings, Chaacmol."

Down the priests went, this time flat on their knees, with Kankomo striking the floor before the others. For a long time they lay there, and then Esterais looked at Leybren and nodded.

"Arise," Leybren called out in a loud voice. "Arise, ye mortals of clay!"

His words sounded foolish and he had an impulse to laugh aloud, but he kept his face serious. But the speech had an electric effect, for the priests were on their feet with a spring.

Leybren watched them closely. He was convinced that he had passed for a god in front of the queen, but the cunning look he had seen in the eyes of Kankomo told him that a greater test was yet to come. A test of two wills, each seeking ruthlessly a different end.

TO KANKOMO THE presence of Martikatasi would mean increased power for the queen: to Leybren his successful passing as a god meant the life of the man he had come into the jungles to save—the life of a white man.

Kankomo walked up to Esterais, his long robe of gorgeous feathers trailing on the floor. On his head were other feathers, placed in a band that circled his forehead. His face was twisted in an anger that he could not completely dissimulate.

"If thou, O Queen," his voice was cunning and low, "will take the advice of a poor, humble subject whose whole life and whose every move is for thy safety and thy love, you will first make sure that he who stands here as Martikatasi, the god that is to come to you from the wilderness, is really the god.

"Be certain that he is not one of these white men of the north who slew our people—our women and our children— with savage lust, when our people lived in great cities that stretched even unto the endless waters of life, that led to where no man knew."

It flashed through Leybren's mind that Kankomo was speaking of the Spaniards who had come with Cortez, and destroyed the few Mayan cities that remained at that time. Kankomo's tactics had a certain sinister danger that Leybren knew would grow rapidly, if not cut off before they got under way. He further realized that Kankomo was not talking so much to the queen as he was to the ten priests behind him. It was obvious that his words were taking effect on them.

HE TURNED QUICKLY, his face tense and his hand resting on the golden robe over his automatic.

"Queen of Beauty," he said to Esterais in a voice that was low and piercing, "who is it that questions thy word and the word of Martikatasi? Martikatasi who, as was foretold even when Mayapan was a great city and on the throne sat the Queen Kinich-Kakmo, wife of the great King Chaacmol, has appeared to lead you and your people to a glory that was denied the Mayan people. Because in that city were evil ones—nobles and priests who slew the king and the queen, and destroyed the city.

"Tell me, O Queen, who is this man that dares to speak evil in the presence of your beauty and your goodness?"

Leybren's eyes bored into Kankomo relentlessly as he spoke, and he saw the heavy face of the high priest pale and his body tremble, as Leybren told the story of the City of Mayapan, a story every student of Mayan history knows well.

And then when he ceased speaking, a silence oppressive and terrible followed. Esterais stood in the misty blue light, her eyes flashing fire and her face pale with the great triumph she knew now was hers. She waited for the high priest to answer.

Kankomo's face was still twisted with fear and rage, but finally anger and cunning won out in that heavy face, and with a wicked smile, he turned to Esterais.

"O Queen," he said, "the strange one speaks with wisdom of our people; yet such wisdom could be learned by the great white race that came out of the wilderness of waters to slay us. If this one be Martikatasi, let him then throw from his body the robe.

"If he be a god, his body must needs be without a blemish; but if he be a human creature, as we are, there may be a weapon, a knife or an axe that he has carried to protect himself from animals of the forest."

Leybren's body stiffened and the muscles contracted around his mouth. His hand went to his automatic. The trickery of Kankamo was obvious. If Leybren unrobed and they found the gun and the money belt, in which was still the paper Mrs. Hillright had given him, these things would prove powerful weapons toward Kankomo's case.

And as he stood there, his right hand resting on the butt of his automatic, his body tense and his eyes riveted on the face of Esterais, watching what move she proposed to make, it flashed through Leybren's mind that Kankomo was working his plan with a confidence that could not spring from his mind alone.

THE HIGH PRIEST of the palace was playing a lone hand—a hand that carried danger and death to him, if there was one slip up. He was an Indian, steeped in the superstitious lore of his race, and no matter how much he regretted the coming of Martikatasi, every part of his makeup should cause him to fall on his face and worship the god.

His suggestion that Leybren disrobe, Leybren was convinced, was made with absolute confidence that on the so-called god would be found something to his absolute undoing. It was obvious to Leybren now that Kankomo paid little attention, and cared not at all for what Esterais might believe or say; every move he made, every word he uttered, though addressed to her, was meant as propaganda for the priests.

But how could this Mayan Indian priest, isolated in this aboriginal city, knowing nothing of what lay beyond those granite cliffs, have information sufficient to make the daring request that Martikatasi unrobe? A request that threw a direct challenge in the face of the god.

These thoughts flashed through his mind as he watched the pale face of Esterais, and as they did, another thought came to him, a thought that caused every muscle in his body to jerk and his eyes to narrow to pin points.

But Esterais' next move gave him little time to follow up this last thought. Her chin went up and a look came to her eyes that caused the priests—all but Kankomo—to shrink back a little.

"On the face; thou fool, Kankomo," she screamed. "Wouldst thou question the belief of thy queen, daughter of Tinchtum, descendant of the great Chaacmol? Speak! Thou dog, thou unbelieving vandal of the woods. Speak! Or when dawn breaks thy body shall go on the sacrificial stone, and thy blood shall atone for the evil that has come to thy body. Speak!"

KANKOMO WAS ON the floor before the words of Esterais were finished, and he crawled to her feet, covering them with kisses, and his face went up to her in supplication.

"A humble servant would die at thy feet, O Queen of my people," he cried. "Strike him dead new, that the evil in his soul may die forever. I only question such things in life as will bring happiness to thee and to thy people. If I have spoken evil, I would that a dagger shall pierce my heart."

Esterais looked at him and with her foot she pushed him away.

"Arise, fool," she said, in a voice that was deadly in its coldness. "Arise and go forth, and nevermore question what thy queen believes or death shall strike thee."

Kankomo was on his feet, and without a word he walked out of the room. The other priests stared at Esterais a moment, as if unable to decide what to do. Then they turned quickly and followed the high priest.

"We have little time to work," Esterais said to Leybren, her eyes flashing anger. "The priests have gone out with Kankomo. We must move quickly and against great, almost impossible odds, if we are to save the life of the white man."

CHAPTER X

AN UNSEEN ENEMY STRIKES

TWO HOURS LATER Esterais, escorted by a procession of priests and warriors, walked out of her Palace with Leybren, headed for the temple where the sacrifice to the God of the Harvest was to take place. The first streaks of dawn were breaking over the tops of the great cliffs whose bases were still hidden by the darkness of the night.

At Leybren's side was Sorais. The old man's shriveled face was tense and his eyes darted around nervously. During the two hours after Kankomo had left the Palace, Leybren and Esterais had estimated their possible forces and realized that the odds were stacked ten to one against them.

With the ten priests ranged on the side of Kankomo, it meant that only those few with Esterais had remained faithful. It meant also that the warriors of the city would go over to Kankomo.

It was a small, pitifully small, group of faithful followers of the queen that made up the procession. Leybren had his gun and that was about the only advantage they held in the coming conflict. But the few shells he had could not hold off the horde of warriors very long.

Grimly and silently Leybren walked along. Already he could see the fires burning in the temple. He wondered if Hillright were already there; he wondered if the old man had accepted his fate calmly. That would help a great deal.

Leybren's faith in his power as a god was not great. He realized that the queen had accepted him as such, as had Sorais and her followers. But somehow he felt that Esterais, driven to hopeless desperation by her continuous war with Kankomo, had been ready and willing to accept as a god anyone who might bring relief and aid to her followers.

HE LOOKED AT her. In the night she appeared more like a phantom of beauty than a girl in her early twenties. She walked with head up and body erect, with an ease and grace that was enchanting. Her fairness, the blue eyes and blond hair and white skin, was puzzling to Leybren.

Yet he realized that among historians the identity of many of the Mayans was a moot question. Some contended that the ruling families of these Indians had been a European race that had filtered down through the Bering Straits and into Mexico and Central America. The color and eyes of Esterais confirmed this belief.

The procession, moving slowly and solemnly, with the torch bearers ahead and the priests with the incense behind them, turned a corner and walked on into the court of columns; and as they did, the city, which had appeared asleep when they first stepped out of the palace, came startlingly to life.

Over the great cliffs far above the city the gray shafts of dawn were breaking rapidly, and the darkness of the night was lifting. In its place was the cold, shifting mist of daybreak.

SUDDENLY FROM OVER the city there burst forth chanting and singing, a barbaric melody that was savage and nerve racking to hear. People came running across the squares and plazas, placing themselves in front of the great temple in which would be the sacrifice to the god Karaiti. The din increased to a deafening roar. Undisturbed by the noise, the priests escorting Esterais to the temple moved forward with the somber silence in which they did all things. Esterais was apparently oblivious to the noise and the wildly running people; her face gazed straight ahead, body erect, and her eyes flashed a look of subdued excitement.

They came to the bottom of the long stairs that led up to the temple. Above them the great pyramid, with its four receding terraces, rose up grimly and gleaming in the gray mist of the early morning. Priests walked up and down the stairs, robed in jaguar skins, feathered cloaks and embroidered cotton stuffs, their bodies half lost in the clouds of incense that swirled around them.

At the entrance to the temple, beside the two columns of the feathered serpents, tall Mayan warriors were leading a small man, clothed in a robe of laced gold, with stooped shoulders and a stiff walk, into the doorway.

Even from the bottom of the steps, where the barbaric splendor of the scene held him enthralled, Leybren saw that the small man, ironically robed at last in a gorgeous cloak of gold, was poor Hillright; and he recognized the tall, powerful body of Kankomo striding behind the professor.

ESTERAIS STOOD AT the bottom of the great stairway. She threw her hands high over her head, and as she did, there came from all parts of the temple the wailing cry, "The Queen."

Priests, warriors, and Indians fell prone on their faces, and slowly, with the majesty of a true queen, Esterais started up the steps. She ignored completely the groveling human beings at her feet. Leybren followed behind her, his eyes moving slowly over the forms that lay prone on the stairs. As the queen passed, the Indians rose to their feet, and the din of the barbaric music continued.

At the top of the stairs, Esterais turned. Her face was pale and drawn, but her body seemed animated with a strange fire of vitality. Her voice rang out clearly over the vast throng that moved on the stairs and stood in the dense crowd at the foot of the steps.

"Hear ye, O my people," she cried. "There has come to us the god, Martikatasi, whose advent, through the cycles of time, since the great Chaacom ruled our race in splendor, we have awaited. He has come, and the prophecy of the ages will be carried out.

This god, with eyes of blue and hair of yellow, will bring to us great harvests.

"He will lead us from this valley and we will build great cities, and there will be abundance and happiness for all.

"Kneel thou, for thine eyes are now gazing on Martikatasi."

Her arms swept to the right and her finger pointed to Leybren, and from the vast multitude there rose a chanting, a wailing cry of exultation. Then the great crowd fell to their faces, their bodies writhing and twisting.

For a long time this weird, grotesque sight filled Leybren's eyes. Then, from a command of the queen, the Indians rose and threw their arms high in the air and chanted: "He has come! Martikatasi has come to lead us to the land of food and plenty! He that we have awaited since the cycles of the moon have been three hundred fold, he has come. Our God—our leader."

THE CHANTING CRY rose to a shrill, insane scream. It was powerful in its effect—weird—fascinating in its very savagery. Leybren stood, transfixed at the sight, not knowing exactly what he was supposed to do. It seemed to him that a god meriting such homage should say a few words, especially when this god was facing a struggle for life wherein the only hope lay in his power over the Indians.

So he walked to the edge of the top step, threw his arms high in the air, and cried out:

"Ye children of Chaacom, of Kantachici, of Mayapan, of Kulkulkan, who have lived since the first cycle of the moon when the earth was a vast land of desolation, hear me and listen to my words! I have come to lead ye forth, to make again your race the great race of the world.

"And if ye follow me, life and abundance will be yours; if ye do not, the sun will burn your crops and ye will die for lack of food, and desolation will visit ye.

"And your city will be a ruins, so that the god of life, wishing to hide the sight from the eyes of the sun and the moon, will cause grass to grow over your temple, and rock and dirt to cover your city from that day.

"Follow me and I will lead to the glory that once was yours."

He stopped and let his arms fall to his sides. It was about the third speech he had ever made in his life—the second having been in front of Esterais—and he was surprised at the melodious quality of his voice and its carrying power, which had borne his words to all parts of the great crowd far below.

For a moment a deathlike silence followed his words; then from the Indians came an answering dirge, as if from childhood they had been prepared with certain words for Martikatasi when he came. The words came in a chant that was monotonous and ghastly in its wailing quality.

"You have come, O Martikatasi, and we will follow you, that we may have food and riches, and that our cities may again be great and cover all the land even to the land of the waters."

LEYBREN RAISED HIS arms to the skies again, and then turned and with Esterais entered the temple. The excitement of the scene outside passed at once, and his face again was set and hard. His eyes looked around him coldly and penetratingly.

His reception by the Mayans had been successful, but now he was to face Kankomo. Without any doubt he felt that in dealing with this cunning Indian, he was not dealing with a primitive soul who could be moved by mere superstition of a god.

The front chamber of the temple was a long colonnaded hall whose twelve sculptured columns were painted with a dazzling brilliancy of riotous color. Through this long hall the queen's procession filed, and then they came out into a large room, filled with priests. At the rear of the room against the far wall, was a huge altar of stone, supported from the floor by small statues of human figures with hands raised above their heads, sustaining the weight of a great flat rock. This was the top of the sacrificial altar.

LEYBREN'S EYES TOOK this in at a glance. He saw the priests standing near the stone. Two of them wore strange masks and their bodies were covered by long, purple robes. The huge knife each held told Leybren that these were the priests of the sacrifice.

And standing between them, his body broken and his eyes glassy, was Thorton Hillright. He was wearing a long gold robe, interlaced with white, and his hair seemed to have been combed down with some kind of oil and his long white beard was clean. His preparation for the sacrifice had been complete.

But his body seemed to have shriveled up and his face, around his eyes, was haggard and drawn.

His eyes saw Leybren, but they failed to register either recognition or surprise. He seemed like a condemned man, who in the hour of waiting for death, had started to die, and only the shell of a broken body remained.

Leybren signaled him with his eyes and the old man's body straightened a little and color came back slowly to his face. Leybren embraced the situation at a glance. Kankomo was there, seated on the right of the stone chair where Esterais had taken her place. Behind the high priest stood several gold-robed men who wore masks of serpents over their faces.

The entrance of Esterais in the room was the occasion for more kneeling on the part of the priests, but this time Leybren did not play his little act of being Martikatasi.

He realized grimly that the time for action had finally come. Every priest in that room, except those that had come with him and Esterais, was loyal to Kankomo and nothing he might say or do would change their attitude.

Leybren had no time to try to figure out just what Kankomo's plan of attack would be, but the cunning look the high priest gave him indicated that he knew what Leybren planned and had prepared himself for the test of power that was at hand.

THE PRIESTS SUDDENLY started an inhuman chanting—the chant of death. Far down at the foot of the great stairs that ran up to the temple, the Indians took up the chant, and it rose to a terrifying crescendo. The two purple-robed executioners had picked Hillright up and laid him on the sacrificial stone. Now they turned and looked at Esterais, as if awaiting the signal for the sacrifice.

Weirdly, like the chant of thousands of ghosts, the wailing song of death continued, and then came the beating of drums on the terrace in front of the temple. The drums and the death dirge held Leybren with a strange power. It was barbaric—savage—brutal. He looked at Esterais. Her eyes were blazing and the fine nostrils of her nose rose and fell, as if her very soul were in that threnody.

The robe had been stripped from the body of Hillright, and the old and broken body lay exposed on the slab, helpless and inert. The weary face stared lifelessly up at the ceiling.

Leybren came to himself with a spring. The priests had raised their knives, and as they did, his hand went for his automatic.

Then shrilly, over the noise of the

chanters and the drums came Esterais' voice.

"Martikatasi," she cried. "The god sent by our fathers would speak." The chanting of the priests ceased and a silence fell over the room. Outside the temple, the drums continued to beat and the unearthly chanting rose to a frenzied roar.

Esterais was standing in front of her throne, her body leaning forward a little and her face pale. In her lovely eyes was a look of determination—of power and authority that caused the priests of Kankomo to stare at her helplessly. Even the purple robed executioners let the knives drop at their sides, and their eyes flew to Kankomo.

The high priest was on his feet with a snarl of rage.

"Karaiti," he cried, "the god of the harvest, of food, of life commands this sacrifice! Strike, that the blood of the evil one may run down the steps of the temple to appease the anger of Karaiti."

The voice of Kankomo brought his priests to their senses, and the two wielding the knives of death turned and raised them over their heads. The knives cut through the air and came down in a flashing arc toward the body—the inert, helpless body of the unconscious Hillright.

BUT AS THEY did a leaping flame of white smoke shot through the air. The roar that followed filled the room. The knife of the first priest fell to the floor and the priest screamed in anguish and grabbed his wrist. Again the leaping flash of white smoke and again the explosion of Leybren's automatic, and the knife of the second priest was on the floor. The man doubled up and fell face forward against the sacrificial altar.

Leybren had backed to the throne and was standing to the right of Kankomo, watching the high priest from the corners of his eyes. He was breathlessly aware of the turmoil and consternation that had followed the shots. Even the beating of the drums and the wailing dirge had ceased outside. A silence, oppressive and ominous, followed.

Then suddenly Leybren felt something hard pressed in his back, and he heard a voice behind him, a voice that spoke a cold, precise English.

"Well done, Martikatasi," the voice said, "but drop your automatic. Your little game is over."

Leybren's body stiffened and the muscles around his mouth contracted. Without looking around he knew from whom that voice came. He had heard it many times before. It was Von Schlossman!

CHAPTER XI

THE BATTLE FOR THE PALACE

A COMPLETE PICTURE with every detail fitted in perfectly flashed through Leybren's mind when the voice of Von Schlossman came to him out of the deadly silence that followed the reports of his automatic. Ever since Kankomo had called upon him to disrobe, he had suspected somewhere in the background the master hand of Von Schlossman.

How the German had got into the city remained a mystery, but now it was certain that he had. Finding Leybren hailed as the god Martikatasi, he had been able to convince Kankomo that he could destroy this new god that threatened the power and the hopes of the high priest.

It was all very plain: every move Kankomo had made now showed the advice and cunning of Von Schlossman.

But knowing those things were of little aid to Leybren as he stood near the altar with Von Schlossman's gun in his back. Von Schlossman had been one of the three masked priests behind Kankomo. Whether the other two were the *mestizos* that had escaped with the German, Leybren had no way, at that moment, to discover. If they were, it was three armed men against one, and that one was standing in front of the three with a gun stuck in his back.

SUDDENLY LEYBREN'S BODY twisted a little to the right—just enough to throw Von Schlossman's aim off, and then he was on the floor of the room with the swiftness of a tiger. The twist of the body was an old trick when a gun was in a man's back; it was flirting with certain death if the twist and the subsequent movement of the body were not done with the very speed of lightning. But it had worked now! Von Schlossman's gun roared and the bullet cut over Leybren's back and struck the marble wall with a sharp twang. And then before Von Schlossman could fire again, Leybren's arms had gone around his legs.

Together the two white men went to the floor struggling, fighting, kicking and gasping. In his struggle Leybren had no chance to see what was going on around him. He heard screams and the sounds of bodies crashing back and forth. He had no time to see if the other two masked men were the *mestizos,* for his one job was concerned with getting his arms around Von Schlossman's body so that he could crush the German to the floor and overpower him.

Something crashed on his head. It was a sickening, paralyzing blow, and for a moment every part of his body seemed numb. Pains shot down his neck and over his back; and in that split second, Von Schlossman threw Leybren's body over on its back and sent a crash right down on his jaw. Through blurred eyes, Leybren saw the tall German reach for his automatic, which had fallen on the floor.

With a shake of the head, a violent, desperate shake that sought to halt his fleeting senses, Leybren was on his knees. Carefully, with perfect aim, he shot out his right, throwing behind the blow his last remaining ounce of strength. It caught Von Schlossman flush on the jaw. He went face forward to the floor, an inert, helpless mass.

MEN WERE SCREAMING over Leybren. He rose to his feet unsteadily, and as he did, bodies hit him, struggling, snarling, fighting bodies. He was carried along with them, unable to stop the onrush, or to fight against them. He was crushed against the wall. And then suddenly he seemed to be alone. He let his head clear before opening his eyes, and when he did, he gasped in amazement.

The first thing he saw was Thorton Hillright, his white hair and beard caked with blood, his body naked as it had been on the sacrificial stone, standing a little way from him, swinging one of the huge knives that the priests in purple had held in their hands. The old man's eyes gleamed with diabolical fury. Around him lay priests with their bodies cut and bleeding.

Beyond Hillright, he saw Sorais, wielding the other knife, keeping the onrushing priests back from Esterais, who remained standing near her throne, her face calm and her eyes watching the scene coldly.

And on the floor, near the throne, where Leybren had grappled with Von Schlossman, lay the tall German, still unconscious from the blow to his jaw. Lying near him, on his back, with head crashed in by a blow from Hillright's knife, was one of the *mestizos* that had escaped with Von Schlossman. An automatic lay near the body.

WITH A LEAP, Leybren got into action again. He dove for the automatic, reaching it with his fingers, just as a great yell came from the front room of the temple, and the next moment warriors carrying spears horizontally over their heads, burst through the entrance of the altar room.

Leybren was at the side of Esterais, and he stood with his body protecting the queen. Slowly, and with deliberate and careful aim, he fired at the onrush of Mayan warriors. Four times the gun in his hand spit fire and four warriors crumpled to the floor, writhing and twisting. The barking, roaring weapon of death caused the others to stop, and some turned and fled. But the voice of Kankomo, coming from somewhere back of the warriors, caused their ranks to close up again.

"The other room," Esterais said to Leybren. "We must force our way out there, for from there we can escape through a secret passageway to the palace."

Leybren smiled grimly. They might as well have been miles from this passageway, for the warriors were massed in the doorway, their spears poised overhead. Behind them the voice of the high priest rose, exhorting them forward.

Sharp, quick orders came from Leybren to Hillright and Sorais and their followers. The work of Hillright and Sorais with the huge knives had cleaned the room of all the priests loyal to Kankomo. And then Leybren, flanked on each side by Hillright and Sorais, forced a flying wedge; with Esterais at their rear, protected by her priests. Leybren fired the two remaining cartridges from the automatic. Two warriors crumpled to the floor. The others hesitated, their eyes stark with terror at this strange weapon that sent death through the air so mysteriously.

And in that split second of hesitation, the flying wedge hit them. Hillright and Sorais hacked and wielded the executioners' knives with a fury that sent the warriors back in dismay. And in the center of the wedge was Leybren, his right and left shooting out like pistons, sending warriors to the floor before they could get their large and unwieldy spears into action.

LIKE AN IRRESISTIBLE moving object, the wedge plowed through the warriors. Far to the rear could be heard the shrill, enraged voice of Kankomo. But now the words of the high priest had no effect on the bewildered and fear-stricken soldiers, and the few that remained suddenly broke rank and ran.

"This way, quick," Leybren heard Esterais call to him. "Kankomo will return with more warriors."

He turned. The queen had left the flying wedge and was running between two brilliantly painted columns, with Hillright and Sorais and the priests following her. They came to the far wall. Esterais touched something with her fingers, and slowly the wall opened. A great marble slab moved outward on the floor, disclosing the entrance to a secret passageway.

Esterais entered the passageway and Hillright and Sorais and the others followed after her. Leybren waited outside. He had slipped another clip in his own automatic, having thrown away the one picked up from the body of the *mestizo*. He started to enter the passageway, but as he did, there was a swish of air over his head and a spear clanged against the wall with a loud metallic ring.

And then through the columns came a horde of new warriors, this time bloodthirsty and unterrified by the sight of a weapon that spat death like a serpent spat venom at its victims.

LEYBREN BACKED AGAINST the wall. His gun brought down the leader of the onrushing horde. Twice more his gun barked and the two men behind the fallen leader fell face forward. Again the gun roared. Leybren was watching the last of the priests dart into the opening, and when they had disappeared, he emptied his gun into the bodies of the warriors and made a dive for the passageway. Slowly the huge marble rock started inward. Spears hit it with sharp, ringing sounds; the brown bodies of the warriors grabbed for the marble slab, but slowly, relentlessly, it closed, crushing bodies with it.

Fifteen minutes later Leybren and Esterais and their followers entered an underground room of the palace. They mounted a dark flight of stairs, following it for some distance; and then taking a narrow stairs that branched off from the main steps, finally coming out into the cerise-colored room, the front room of the palace.

Sorais and Hillright, both grim and silent, went to the great stone doors of the palace and Sorais peered out through a small hole in the wall that was placed there for just such an emergency.

"Kankomo is surrounding the palace," Sorais reported. "His warriors are coming across the Court of Locusts below."

Esterais laughed coldly and in her laugh there was no weakness, not the faintest trace of fear.

"His warriors can beat their bodies against the walls of my palace," she said, "but never will they enter. We have food

　　　THE BEST OF THRILLING ADVENTURES

and supplies here to last us for many nights and days.”

BUT AFTER THAT, Leybren questioned.

“Sometime the food must give out, and sometime Kankomo may succeed in breaking through a secret passage.”

Esterais looked at him and smiled wearily.

“Thou dost not speak as a god, Martikatasi,” she said with a sigh.

“Thou speakest as one of us, who in time will get hungry and weary, and long for death to relieve us of our sadness.”

Leybren’s mouth was grimly set and his eyes were narrowed.

“I speak as one, Esterais, who is willing to die for your beauty,” he answered. “And if I can do that, I believe that then will I be a god.”

Her hand reached out and gripped his, and her eyes looked at him sadly.

“Thou art a god, Martikatasi,” she said, but I have led you to destruction. I did not realize the power of Kankomo until too late. I did not believe that all the warriors that have fought for me so long would go to him. There are a few servants in the palace, and a few old men, but we would be cut down like corn at harvest should we venture out on those stairs.”

“We would be if we walked out now,” Leybren replied. “Kankomo is in command of the city. But when night comes we can attack with some hope of success.”

“Attack with a few servants?” Esterais laughed. “I am afraid Martikatasi, that you underestimate the fighting qualities of my warriors.”

“I am depending on the faith of your warriors,” Leybren said. “Right now a new Martikatasi has come to your people and if my blow to the jaw didn’t bust his face completely, I believe you will see him being paraded very soon as the god you all have awaited these cycles of time.”

A strange look came into Esterais’ eyes. A sad smile lit her face and her hand pressed Leybren’s firmly.

“There is only one Martikatasi for me,” she murmured, “and you are he.”

“I hope you have made no mistake,” Leybren said quietly. “The first thing we better do is to take a count of our forces and see just how many men we can count on.”

They went into the throne room and sat around a low stone table that had served as counsel table for Esterais in her meetings with the priests and wise men of the city. The table was a large flat stone held up from the floor by a number of small human statues, as was the great sacrificial stone that had embraced the body of Thorton Hillright. **THE CHANGE THAT** had come over Hillright was almost a miracle. As if a cord had been cut and a great curtain had fallen suddenly, it seemed that the twenty years of shrinking and brutality and terror had been shut out from his eyes forever. There was no fear left in his clear eyes. Again he was a man, quick of mind and erect of body. He had tasted freedom and that one small taste had brought back all the courage, all the desire to live that he had possessed before his twenty years of a living hell.

Leybren lifted the body of his enemy over his head.

And while Sorais and the faithful priests went through the palace gathering such servants as had remained, and checking up on the number of spears and men available for an attack on the forces of Kankomo that night, Esterais and Leybren and Hillright sat around the conference table and considered the situation they were facing.

On the whole, their plight was neither favorable nor hopeful. For over an hour they discussed it from every angle, and they were still so engaged when Sorais brought back the report that Kankomo

 THE BEST OF THRILLING ADVENTURES

was parading a white man through the streets of the city and proclaiming him the great god Martikatasi.

THE IRONY OF the situation caused Leybren to smile bitterly. Now it looked like a struggle to see who was to successfully pose as Martikatasi. Undoubtedly, as far as prestige and victory were concerned, Von Schlossman was the successful Martikatasi for the time being.

But there was little irony in the position Leybren and Hillright found themselves, with the queen and her few faithful followers. There might be food for a few weeks in the palace, but at some time that food would give out. And by that time Kankomo could be in supreme commander of the city.

Both Leybren and Hillright impressed upon Esterais the need for striking quickly before her people believed her dead and before Kankomo could proclaim himself king with the aid of the new Martikatasi.

Esterais saw the logic of their arguments, and was ready and willing to leave the whole matter to Leybren. For a long time she was unable to accept Hillright, who but a few hours before had been Timkanti, the evil one, a dirty groveling human being that even the dogs in the street bit when he appeared. Slowly his keen mind and his powerful personality won her over and she listened to him, a little bewildered and amazed, with almost the same confidence that she listened to Leybren.

Sorais had rounded up some thirty men in all and had armed them with spears and knives, many of the weapons coming from the royal kitchen. Most of the thirty were old and trusted servants of the palace, men little accustomed to battle. Theirs was a sorry looking army to go forth and fight the powerful Mayan warriors that were now under the banner of Kankomo and Von Schlossman.

There was, however, one thing in favor of the thirty priests and servants. Old as they were, they were ready and willing to die for their queen, and their love for her made them soldiers that would fight with an insane fury. But the insane fury, however sincere, of thirty men could avail little against the strength and brutality of the hundreds of men Kankomo commanded.

Leybren spent a great part of the morning examining the vast rooms and passageways that lay under the palace in the center of the pyramid on which the structure sat. Great store rooms held an abundance of food, and a spring of clear water ran through that one of the rooms which acted as a sort of refrigerator for the food supplies.

THEN IN THE afternoon he went to the front room of the palace and spent a long time watching the forces of Kankomo mobilizing at the base of the temple pyramid. Twice he saw Von Schlossman, clothed in a gold robe, being paraded in front of the Indians as the new god.

The German was received with great shouts. The Indians fell to their faces in tribute to the new Martikatasi. Late in the afternoon Leybren saw a small Indian being led to the stairs of the temple, and after a time there came the weird chanting wail he had heard just before the scheduled sacrifice of Hillright. Kankomo was not forgetting the god Karaiti, and he was leading a native victim to the temple to be murdered.

This move carried with it greater dangers than anything else. The sight of blood, the sacrifice to the god Karaiti would work the Mayans up to a frenzy of lust that would make it impossible to win any of them away from Kankomo. It promised to make any pitched battle a short, bloody affair, with the few loyal servants of the queen slaughtered before they could even get down the great stairway that led from the temple to the ground.

The hours of the afternoon passed slowly. With each passing moment Leybren realized the utter hopelessness of their situation. When the sacrifice to Karaiti would be completed and the bloody body of the poor victim thrown down the stairs of the temple to appease the god of the harvest, the city would be in such a state that any attack would be almost foolhardy.

But as the hours wore on, a plan, daring and dangerous, began to form in Leybren's mind. A grim smile came to his face as he thought of it, but he kept his own counsel and waited for darkness.

CHAPTER XII

NIGHT AND DEATH

NIGHT FELL OVER the city with an orgy of barbaric ferocity that reached heights of savage frenzy. The sacrifice to Karaiti had been made and the body of the victim thrown down the long stairs, where his blood flowed to satisfy the anger of the god Karaiti. The sight of blood had acted as a goad of insane fury to the Indians.

The chant of death, which had been a low, monotonous roar that morning, was now a screaming, piercing dirge. Everywhere in the city great bonfires lighted the squares. Around these blazing fires Indians gyrated and whirled and yelled until they fell exhausted on the ground.

The festival of Karaiti was under way! AND OVER IT all, supreme and confident, stalked the tall form of Kankono with the gold robed figure of Von Schlossman at his side as the god Martikatasi. Everywhere they went people fell prone on their faces and proclaimed the new god, and already the murmur had gone through the crowd that Kankomo had been ordered by Martikatasi to be their king.

Around the base of the palace pyramid stood the warriors of Kankomo, with their spears ready and their bodies alert and tense. It was as if they expected, with the falling of night, the great doors of the temple to open that they might dash up the stairs and enter the house that through all their lives had been the great House of Silence to them.

The warriors took no part in the celebration. Grim faced and stolid, they stood their watch, waiting for the first sign of battle; and among the Indians that groveled and yelled and fell on their faces was the expectation that the night would yet end in a great battle. It was to be hoped for; it would mean more blood and more hysterical excitement.

At the door of the temple Esterais stood with Leybren, and through the holes in the thick walls they silently watched the mad threnody of the Indians.

Finally Esterais said: "My servants will die for me, but it is useless. We have no hope now. Kankomo has wisely chosen the night of the festival to Karaiti, and my poor people, insane with the celebration, know not what they are doing."

"If we wait, Esterais," Leybren said, "tomorrow will be too late. Kankomo will be declared king and the palace will be stormed. Your doors are of stone, but time and men can break them down. If we strike swiftly, while your people are in the fury of the feast, there may yet be hope."

ESTERAIS' HAND RESTED on Leybren's arm. Her face was drawn and tired looking.

"We will strike when you wish, Martikatasi," she said. "I will go forth and lead the few of my faithful followers. If death must be mine, it is my wish that I die at the hands of my own people, whom I love."

"You will remain in this palace," Leybren broke in curtly. "What fighting there is to be done will be done by myself and the men."

Esterais patted his hand, smiled and said nothing.

Leybren turned and with Esterais walked back into the throne room. Hillright was there waiting for him. He still held the huge executioner's knife in his hand.

"The sooner we start," Hillright said to Leybren, "the better it will be."

Leybren turned to Esterais.

"Sorais will lead your faithful few into the battle," he explained. "Hillright and myself, with five of your best men, will go forth into the city while the battle rages."

A sudden terror-stricken fear came into Esterais' eyes.

"You go forth into the city," she gasped. "O, Martikatasi, they will kill you—"

"No quicker there than on the stairs," Leybren broke in quickly. "While Sorais and his men attack from the front we will attack from the rear."

"There are a thousand warriors out there," Esterais said. "Of what avail will you and the small army of Sorais be against such a force? You will be swallowed up in death—and then I will be alone. If you go, I go with you!"

Leybren could not repulse with a curt order the pitiful, pleading look that came into the blue eyes of Esterais. Her white face with its alluring beauty was pale and sad; her body, graceful and delicate looking in the long, white gown she wore, seemed to slump forward brokenly.

Taking her hands, Leybren said: "You must put your faith in me, Esterais. We are not going into the city wildly. We are going to wipe out the evil that has crazed your people. We are going to bring your people back to you; but if we die in the attempt, know that we have died for you and that the death we experience will hold no terrors—no fears."

TEARS CAME TO Esterais' eyes. Her hands went to the face of Leybren, and the soft white fingers traced lines on his cheeks.

"Go," she said softly, "and if death finds you I will be at your side. Together we will go into the vast vale of night where have gone those of my blood since time started the cycle of the moon. Go, and know that I will be with you, even though my body remains in the temple. Go with my love that will be even greater in death."

Leybren's body swayed. A feeling came over him that he had never experienced, before. He felt humbled before the very beauty of Esterais; yet as his body swayed, it seemed that those eyes, blue and sad and eternal, held him up, as if they contained a power, a strength greater than any human power.

For a long time—ages it seemed to Leybren, his eyes were held by the sheer beauty of Esterais, held in a trance from which he could not break away. But suddenly he heard Hillright's voice telling him that darkness had fallen, and with a quick turn of his body Leybren swerved and walked away from Esterais. He did not dare to look back at her face.

A half hour later the great stone door of the palace opened, and to the astonished eyes of the warriors at the bottom of the white stairs, Esterais' small army burst forth, led by Sorais.

CARRYING SPEARS AND knives they advanced down the marble steps in a wide thin line—advanced slowly and relentlessly toward the warriors who had been waiting throughout the day for their appearance.

The great bonfires of the city cast a flickering, grotesque light over the stairs, a light that made the small army led by Sorais look like toy figures of brown moving forward on a lighted stage.

For a full minute the warriors of Kankomo stared at the pitiful little army. The very absurdity of the attack startled them, but suddenly from behind came the shrill voice of Kankomo—now eager and triumphant in its brutality.

Kankomo, with Von Schlossman, stood a little to the rear of the soldiers, directing their movements with sharp, vicious commands. His army, spurred on by his voice, leaped for the stairs.

And then the battle began.

But Kankomo's warriors did not cut Sorais' men down like corn at harvest time. There were two good reasons why they didn't. In the first place they met a silent, stubborn fury at the hands of the few faithfuls of the queen; fury that refused to give ground and that thought only of slaying as many of Kankomo's men as possible before death should strike them.

ALSO THEIR POSITION on the stairs helped a great deal. They were shoving their spears downward and slashing with their knives from a superior position, and their flailing weapons struck before the enemy could charge advantageously and destroy them.

Yet despite this advantage in position, despite the silent fury that drove Sorais' men on, theirs was a losing battle. It

    THE BEST OF THRILLING ADVENTURES

was only a question of time. The first onslaught of Kankomo's army was repulsed and bodies of Indians lay strewn over the stairs.

The second onslaught met with the same result, but among those bodies that lay in death were a number of Sorais' small force; and each onslaught was weakening them.

While the battle raged on the marble stairway, raged grimly and silently with only the clash of spears and knives breaking the weird silence of the night, and the fire from the great piles of wood scattered around the city cast its yellow, flickering rays over the gruesome sight, Leybren and Hillright, followed by five powerful Indians, were running through an underground passage that led from the temple to the center of the city. In the hands of the five Indians were long *machete*-shaped knives. Leybren carried his automatic, with four bullets left in the clip, and Hillright was lugging the huge executioner's knife with which he had wreaked such damage in the altar room.

On through the pitch-black darkness they dashed, giving little heed to what they might crash against. They came to a stairway and took the steps up two at a time. Dashing through the stone door at its end, they emerged into the night at a point near the river, some two hundred yards from where the battle was raging on the stairs of the temple.

To the right and left of them the great fires were burning and Indians were moving around, silently now, their eyes turned toward the temple where the hideous clash of spears and knives rent the air. There was no hope of hiding or slipping up to the battle lines on the part of Leybren and his men; so they dashed openly, fearlessly across the Court of Columns, waving their long knives and shouting in stentorian refrain.

When they got to the rear of Kankomo's men they saw that the thin line of Sorais' army was slowly breaking and, spurred on by victory, Kankomo's warriors were pushing their way up the stairs, intent upon murdering the remaining bodyguard of the queen. In a few minutes it would all be over.

BUT SUDDENLY THE air was rent with savage yells, yells that broke over the din of the battle, and then came two sharp reports from Leybren's automatic. The two captains leading the men on the stairs grabbed their throats and fell backward, rolling awkwardly down the stairs.

Then with the fury of demons, the five Indians with the long *machete* knives were up the stairs cutting and slashing Kankomo's warriors from the rear. Dazed and bewildered by this sudden assault behind, the warriors turned. They tried to fight back but the five knives cut them down as if they were straws of wheat.

While the fierce battle raged, Leybren and Hillright were darting behind the battle lines surrounding the base of the pyramid. Hillright, with the huge knife high in the air, was leading the way, his eyes gleaming like two dark burning coals.

With a piercing yell of rage, Hillright

made a flying leap at a body of warriors standing around two men—Kankomo and Von Schlossman. His knife came down in a vicious curve and one of the warriors went to the ground, his body sliced in half from the right shoulder down.

AND IN THE next second Leybren was in the midst of a milling mass of brown bodies. He saw the knife of Hillright go up in the air: he heard it whiz down again with a sickening crunching of bones and torn flesh. Then he saw the professor make a leap for the tall figure of Kankomo, who had stood surrounded by his warriors, watching with fear and fury the unexpected retreat of his army.

Then Leybren had time to see no more.

Two powerful bodies came down on him. His automatic barked twice from his crouching position, and the bodies rolled off him, lifeless. He was on his feet. A searing, belching flash of orange red shot through the night at him but he was diving to meet the flash of red before it had died away.

His body hit Von Schlossman, and as it did, his right shot out and knocked the gun from the German's hand. Von Schlossman's left came up in a paralyzing uppercut and caught him on the jaw. His senses reeled and his knees started to buckle under him. He grabbed for Von Schlossman's body to hold on until the effects of the blow wore off. Like pummeling jabs from a machine, Von Schlossman's fists went into his ribs, trying to break the hold.

Leybren's brain cleared and he jumped back. He shot his right out and caught Von Schlossman behind the ear. The blow was delivered with all the power in Leybren's body, but the tall German shook his head, groaned a little, and then bored in. Back and forth across the narrow space the two white men fought, fought for life and death.

The Indians looked on in awe and amazement at the two gods fighting, fighting in a way they had never before seen. No one made a move to interfere. The great struggle on the stairs was neglected. The clash of steel could still be heard, but no attention was paid to it.

Like two beasts of the forest the two men fought back and forth across the plaza. Leybren did not see the body of Kankomo lying at his feet; he did not know that Hillright had dashed up the temple stairs to take part in the battle that was still raging, a battle now made more grim by the fact that Kankomo's men had been reinforced, and slowly but surely the five Indians with the *machete* knives were being backed up the stairs toward the Temple doors, leaving a welter of bodies in their backward retreat.

LEYBREN KNEW NOTHING, save that in front of him was the man that had tried to kill him, the man who aimed to destroy the power and the life of the lovely Esterais.

A hard right from Von Schlossman caught Leybren on the neck and knocked him back. With the savage lunge of a tiger, Von Schlossman was on Leybren, his fingers reaching for the throat and his knee looming up in a hard kick to

 THE BEST OF THRILLING ADVENTURES

the groin. Leybren ducked and his left shot out, burying itself in Von Schlossman's stomach.

The German doubled up and his hands went for his waist, and as he did, Leybren, with every ounce of power left in his body, sent his right, in a blow that started from his toes, to the jaw of Von Schlossman. There was a sickening crack and the German rolled forward on his face, his body crumpled and inert.

Leybren stood like one dazed and stunned. He was conscious that around him Indian faces were raised with awe—looking at the Martikatasi that had won.

Then there came to his stunned senses the sound of a voice, clear and distinct above the noise of the battle. His body turned as if a shock of electricity had shot through it.

STANDING AT THE entrance of the temple, her arms outstretched to the battling warriors below her, was Esterais.

"O, my people," her voice pleaded, "why dost thou slay each other for naught? If it be thy will that your queen shall die, slay me and end this slaughter that will suck the blood from the veins of my people."

Her voice carried to all parts of the great stairs and down to where Leybren was standing.

With a quick movement Leybren reached down. He lifted the body of Schlossman over his head and pushed his way through the crowd. He had seen the dead body of Kankomo but he paid no attention to it. On the stairs the carnage of death had suddenly ceased at the words of Esterais. With Schlossman hanging over his shoulder, Leybren made his way over the mass of dead bodies and up to where Esterais stood.

"Martikatasi," she cried. "Martikatasi, you still live!"

Leybren turned and stood at her side. His gold-laced robe was in tatters. The warriors on the stairs, the great crowd of celebrating Indians, stared up at him silently.

WITH A MIGHTY heave of his arms Leybren raised the body of Von Schlossman, still covered by the robe of Martikatasi, high over his head, and then he hurled the body of the German down the stairs into the midst of the soldiers of Kankomo.

"Martikatasi speaks, thou unfaithful," he called out in a voice that sent a chill through the crowd. "Ye wouldst slay thine own queen. Look yonder on the floor of stone and ye will see the body of the traitor, Kankomo, the man that led ye from the queen that loves ye and who would lead ye to happiness. Look at that body in death. Below my feet I have hurled the white man who would come to steal thy gold and thy jewels, who would pose as Martikatasi and scheme with Kankomo to destroy your city. Those that defy the queen will die, for now Martikatasi speaks."

His speech produced an electric effect in the crowd. Already the word had passed out that Kankomo was dead, and the presence of Esterais on the stairs had worked another wonder.

With cries of rage, the former warriors of Kankomo and the Indians below the pyramid seized the body of Von Schlossman and carried it away.

"My people," Esterais cried. *"My people!"*

And then a great hush fell over the night and every man, woman and child in the great throng fell forward on their faces in humble homage to the queen that had risked her life to speak to them.

In that silence Leybren stood by the side of Esterais. He felt her hand reach for his and heard her whisper softly: "Martikatasi."

Three days later Leybren and Hillright stood on the far side of the mountain, beyond the twin peaks, at the edge of the great forest that led to the jungle river and to civilization. Five Indians were carrying a boat on their shoulders, a canoe hollowed from the trunk of a tree, and other Indians were carrying an abundance of supplies for Leybren and Hillright's trip back to Campeche. The Indians would take them as far as the river and then they would return to the city.

Esterais was there, still clothed in the long white gown. Her face was sad and her eyes looked at Leybren pleadingly.

"Thou returnest to thy people," she said softly. "Thou hast said thou art not a god, yet thou came and slew my enemies. And now thou leavest me forever!"

LEYBREN LOOKED AT her, and his lips were white and tightly pressed together.

"Esterais," he pleaded, "your face is white and your eyes are blue and your hair is yellow. You are of my race, and if you return to my country I shall make you happy, a happiness born of love."

She smiled wearily and her eyes moistened, but she shook her head slowly.

"Countless ages ago," she said, "my people came out of that great land of waters from a country far, far away. The legend says that they were white and blue-eyed and that they found the race of brown Indians and taught them the art of building great temples and of planting crops. And the Indians heralded them as their kings. Even then my people awaited the coming of Martikatasi, who would lead them back to a glory that had died.

"And thus must I return to my city and await the coming of Martikatasi, for now the people with brown skins are my people and I am their queen and I must await the prophecy of countless ages ago. Go thou to thy people and be happy, and because I wish only that thou be happy, take a small gift from me."

SHE TURNED AND motioned to two Mayans behind her. They came forth, carrying boxes. Esterais took these and handed them to Leybren and Hillright.

They were boxes made of gold, and when Leybren lifted the lids he saw the dazzling brilliance of hundreds of beautiful jewels—rubies, diamonds, sapphires.

"You white men fight and die for such things," Esterais said. "Thus they must bring happiness to you and you shall take them with you to remember me and the love that I cannot give you, but which is as much a part of me as life itself. Go now, and please do not look back."

Leybren turned slowly. The look in

   THE BEST OF THRILLING ADVENTURES

Esterais' eyes told him the pain more words from him would give her.

He followed the Indians carrying the canoe down to the edge of the great forest; he followed as if walking in a trance. He was not conscious of the gold box in his hands.

He was conscious only that on the side of the mountain stood Esterais, watching him go out of her life forever. ONCE, ONLY ONCE, he paused to look back.

That was from the great forest trees, where she could not see him, and as he looked back, he saw her white form outlined against the mountain side, her arms outstretched towards him in humble pleading.

Then, slowly, her white form was lost in the mist that was falling over the mountain, and Leybren slowly walked on through the shade of the sylvan forest.

The Pearl of Death

BY **LIEUT. SCOTT MORGAN**

The Avenger of Lo Chang On the Trail in San Francisco's Mysterious Chinatown

LARRY WESTON'S FACE was covered by a thatch of straggly beard; his eyes were bloodshot and his face pale through the tan. It had been a long grueling task, this searching out the pearls of Lo Chang, and there had been dead men strewn along the pathway to their recovery.

As he stood on the Embarcadero, staring out at the vast expanse of San Francisco Bay, over which gulls circled and screamed as they followed the ferries back and forth, his eyes were very thoughtful.

He lifted his arm, pulled back the sleeve and stared at the slender cicatrice, a wound which had been made by the Lo Chang, in a monastery in far Tibet, when he had became a brother of the tong by mingling his blood with that of the priests of the temple.

There he had taken the vow to bring back the pearls which had been filched from the hand of the Buddha in the secret room of the monastery. He was here in San Francisco now to recover the last of three pearls.

Two others had been returned to him—a man was long since dead in Shanghai who had possessed one of them for a brief space—a second had been left unconscious on a boat from Dover to Calais—and the third, whose name was various—George Furness, Caleb Thane, Joshua Horne, depending on where the man was and what he did—was supposed now to be somewhere in San Francisco.

AND SAN FRANCISCO would hold many of the Lo Chang in its Chinatown. Here, at least, Larry Weston would be able to summon the genii of the ring which Lo Chang had given him, that queer ring which, shown to brothers of the tong, evoked their absolute loyalty, called upon them to give him every support, even to the risk of their lives.

Yet just now he felt very much alone—one man pitted against the mysteries and dangers of a great city.

Where should he begin? The trail of Joshua Horne—the last name the man he pursued seemed to be using—had ended on the docks at San Francisco, where the great city had swallowed up the man, caused his trail to vanish.

One more pearl to get—and his vow would have been kept. The other two pearls—priceless in themselves, greater in value than the ransom of a dozen kings when the three were together— were on his person now.

He wondered, with a wry twist of his lips, what the people who passed him with averted faces, as though afraid he would ask for the price of a cup of coffee, would think if they could know his possessions, vast enough to have paid off the tax burden of San Francisco. In specially constructed little holsters,

the two pearls reposed in his armpits— where policemen sometimes carried their weapons.

He sighed a little. Nothing had happened for several weeks, since he had left Dane, the possessor of the second pearl, on the Dover-Calais boat, unconscious. He ached for action, and the fulfillment of his vow.

And he must begin somewhere. He had so little to guide him. Just a name on a passenger list, an almost illegible scrawl—and the memory of a face with deep-sunken, murderous eyes.

He turned away and was lost in the crowd.

CHAPTER II

THAT NIGHT, DOWN on Pacific Street at one of San Francisco's most famous night resorts, a smartly dressed man, with the beginning of a mustache and the rudiments of a spade beard, pushed his way through the standing throng of sweating humanity to the end of the long hall, above which rose tiers where men and women—the women of the place who took a percentage on drinks—sat and looked warily into one another's eyes.

Larry Weston was casually interested in a Eurasian woman who did a snaky dance for the benefit of pop-eyed men who cared about such things. She did her act behind a taut rope against which men of all sorts leaned heavily, as though the better thus to see her writhing convolutions. She was a beautiful woman, with hell in her eyes. She met the gaze of many men and stared straight at and through them. She made Larry Weston shiver.

He could fancy her, even in the midst of her dance, thrusting a knife into a man from the back. She seemed a creature without mercy.

Larry Weston pressed forward against the rope while his eyes roved over the faces of those who came to watch. So closely was humanity packed that when one person moved, even to breathe, all the others moved, too, to accommodate the original movement.

This was the sort of thing which would interest Joshua Horne, he felt. It was as good a place as any to begin. ONE THING ONLY troubled him. Nobody molested him, yet he had known from the beginning that his interest in the pearls of Lo Chang was known to the man he pursued. That man was one of three who had looted the Tibetan monastery, after which they had separated, each with a pearl, to make recovery difficult if not impossible, planning to get together in a year to divide the spoils from the sale of the pearls.

And now, where was Joshua Horne?

Larry Weston, through force of habit, shrugged his shoulders, to make sure that the two pearls he had already recovered—and which must have cost the lives of many men down the ages since their first discovery and bringing together—reposed in the little pouches he had made for them.

They were there.

He was watching the dancing girl and remembering others he had seen—the Nautch girl of Benares, the Egyptian girls with the lower part of their faces hidden by provocative *yashmaks*—and comparing this girl in San Francisco's once famous Barbary Coast with them.

It seemed that all the meaning, all the innuendo he had read into the movements of the others, in the far places, was incorporated into this girl's dance.

Smoke from cigars and pipes and cigarettes clouded the room. Faces pasty white, yellow, brown, even piebald, were fastened on her—and then Larry Weston knew: this girl was all the others; their dancing she had made her own: their twistings and writhings, created to appeal to the eyes of men, she had copied and improved upon—hers was the age-old lure which made fools of men.

Something touched him behind, at the shoulder blades. His coat, light for summer wear, became flabby across his back. He whirled. He had been too long on strange missions not to know when exploring fingers touched him. What he saw when he whirled was a strange thing.

It was a woman who had been directly behind him. She was a beautiful woman, with dark eyes, with little fires deep down inside them—eyes which showed no hint of fear, but only, now, glints of the devil's mockery.

The woman was thrusting something into the bag on her arm.

ONE GLANCE TOLD Larry Weston what they were—the two pearls of Lo Chang which he had been at such pains to recover!

He realized, with a sudden flash of

thought, that a razor-sharp knife had taken the back out of his coat, that a hand had retrieved the pearls from their resting place, that he had lost them. But at the same moment he knew exactly where they were: the woman was dropping them into her purse.

Split seconds were needed for the flashes of thought. They came and went even as he turned and looked. There went a year of labor, of passing through danger, always with the knowledge that brothers of the Tong watched his every movement to make sure that he played square with the priests who really owned the pearls—which they held in trust for Buddha himself.

He did the automatic thing. He thrust forth his right hand to clutch at the leathern twin bags—and the whole roof of the resort seemed to descend on his head.

Stars danced a crazy rigadoon in the blackness which descended over him. He felt himself falling, while the woman seemed to be receding from him. Her shapely white hand was falling to her side, the pearls were safe in their appointed resting place.

"I mustn't pass out," he fiercely told himself. "That way leads to the door. That way is out. But why must it be so dark? I've lost my eyesight. I've got to get those pearls back."

HE DUCKED HIS head. Another blow struck him between his bare shoulders, which the slashing knife had made naked. That blow had also been intended for the top of his head. He had avoided it by pure chance.

He knew, in a dim sort of way, that two blackjacks were being aimed at his skull. There might be many innocent ones here. That didn't matter. Just now they hampered his efforts. He couldn't see where his blows went and it didn't seem to matter.

He began to fight. He surged forward on rubbery legs, knowing that the blackjacks still strove to bring hem down.

He sent long lefts straight ahead, felt them crash against faces—of whom he didn't know—and followed with savage, murderous rights. The mob ahead of him, few perhaps of whom had had anything to do with the daring robbery, tried to give back.

Women screamed that a madman was loose in the crowd. He knew that the Eurasian had ceased her dancing, that she had pressed to the ropes and was urging the mob, in a monotonous, quiet voice, to make way for the crazy man, let him through, so that she could go on with her dance.

There was nothing to worry about, really.

He wondered what had become of the blackjack wielders. They would be conspicuous in such a place. They, too, were probably fighting their way to freedom, with better chance for success than himself, perhaps, because their weapons were more savage.

He lunged forward. The crowd swayed away from him. His teeth were set in a snarl as he lashed out, left, right, left, right—left and right again—and each time he struck he surged forward, using husky shoulders to force a way.

He felt that once he gained the street that the light would give his eyes back to him, that a miracle would happen and he would see the woman who had taken the two pearls of Lo Chang.

THEIR LOSS MIGHT well mean his death—for the Lo Chang were watching him every minute. It didn't matter that the pearls had been lost through no fault of his own.

His life was forfeit, by the terms of his vow, if he failed in his mission—and the arms of the Lo Chang were long enough to reach around the world many times over.

Forward he surged again—taking one step—two—and now he found his voice.

"The woman in white! She has robbed me! She's getting away. Stop her, some one!" It was plain that he couldn't see. It was plain from his blind advance, from his stumbling gait as he fought forward toward where he thought the door which gave on Pacific Street ought to be. Now hands tore at him and he knew that his already damaged coat was gone entirely from his torso, together with his shirt and undershirt.

The blackjackers had probably made good their escape, because they must still have the sight of their eyes.

And they might be in league with any number of men here. All that must have been secretly planned in advance.

Maybe the woman who had taken the pearls had been following him as long as he had been following the evasive trail of Joshua Horne. It didn't matter now; nothing mattered except the woman, the return of the pearls, and the recovery of the still missing third pearl of Lo Chang.

HE DIDN'T KNOW why he did it—it was more of a hunch than anything else—but even as he shot forth his hard fists, he turned that strange ring he wore so that its insignia was inside his palm. There was no reason for so doing—it would mean nothing to anyone except the Lo Chang—but he did it just the same, never guessing that it was that ring which would save his life.

When a blast of cold air struck the left side of his face, when he had fought until he could fight no more, he turned to bring the breeze against his face, stumbled out through the open door unmolested—and collapsed on the concrete sidewalk, half in and half out of the gutter.

Far up the street a taxicab, bearing a beautiful woman in white, turned a corner and vanished.

CHAPTER III

STRANGE THINGS HAPPEN on Pacific Street and Larry Weston never discovered how it happened that he could be picked up from the gutter and taken away, without his captors being molested by any one, even the police.

But this much he did know: he regained consciousness to the odor of incense in his nostrils, incense and opium, of birds' nest soup and sharks' fins—of jasmine tea and queer candies—Chinese odors.

He knew by the feel of the bed that it was not a bed, but a *kang*.

From somewhere beyond the walls he sensed surrounded him, he heard shrill voices raised high in sing-song cadences.

There were the voices of men, the sweet melodious voice of a young girl.

He opened his eyes.

The room was small, with a low ceiling, and the walls were covered with many scrolls and pictures of sober Chinese. He knew that only the dead were pictured in old-fashioned Chinese homes. So he was probably staring at the dead and gone ancestors of the people whose voices he heard through the wall.

He tried to move.

He could not. He stared down at himself, his head reeling with pain, blackness threatening to flood over him again, to find himself bound hand and foot with small, stout cord. He tested out his bonds a bit and found he could do nothing with them.

They did prove, though, that he was in the hands of enemies. Friends did not cover one with lengths of stout cord that could not be broken.

The room rocked and rolled and seemed to shake on its foundations. That was because his head spun like a top and his brains felt, he thought to himself, "like, the yolk of a fried egg."

Then he called weakly.

"Will somebody be so kind as to tell me where in the devil and Tom Walker I am?"

The voices outside ceased. He heard tapping steps, the footfalls of slip-slopping sandals. A narrow door opened at one end of the room and two men came in.

One of them was very old, with face covered entirely by wrinkles, the other was young, hard of face, deeply black of eye, and with the look of the professional hatchetman about him. Both stared at Larry Weston with baleful orbs.

"Just what," asked Larry Weston, "is the big idea? How did I get here?"

"I brought you!" said the younger man. His voice was toneless, the words came forth casually as though the speaker didn't care a tinker's dam whether or not he answered.

"Why?"

"We received word, my father and I, that you were an enemy of Lo Chang. We are Lo Chang. So—"

THE CHINESE SHRUGGED his shoulders as though that said everything.

"Who said I was an enemy of Lo Chang?" demanded Larry Weston.

"One does not know. But the word came by mail, a letter without a signature."

Larry tried to rise to a sitting position, while sweat burst from every pore and his body went hot and cold by turns.

"Where was that letter posted?"

"How should I know?"

Larry settled back. It was plain that neither of these two intended to release him. The younger was probably a college graduate, the old one knew only Chinese. Chinese families in America were often like that.

"So, Horne tried to have me slain by locating Lo Chang here and telling them I was an enemy, eh? Well, if I prove to you that I am not only not an enemy, but am, indeed, a brother of the tong, what then? Will you help me?"

He smashed his feet against the side of the hatchetman's head.

The eyes of the younger man widened. He spoke to the old one in the speedy sing-song, after which the eyes of the old one narrowed.

"How does it happen that a foreigner speaks of being brother of the tong? It has never been done!" stated the younger man flatly. "The brothers do not admit foreigners to their secrets."

"Yet if I were to tell you—"

"We would say that you lied!" snapped the younger Chinese. "It is for the Lo Chang to decide."

"But I have proof!" said Larry Weston.

He looked at his right hand, which had worn the queer ring which had been given him at the monastery in far Tibet—and the ring was missing! When had it been taken? There was no way of knowing. Only the white circle on the finger proved that he had ever had it at all. And he had no proof, beyond that ring, of his vow of blood brotherhood with the tong.

"Let me up," he said coldly, "and tell me where that letter was posted, if you know. And then I swear I'll find the proof that I am brother of the tong."

"That will be proved tonight, my son," said the old man, suddenly speaking

     THE BEST OF THRILLING ADVENTURES

out in mandarin, "when the American brothers of the tong meet. If you are an enemy—"

THE OLD MAN looked at his son. That worthy's right hand fell to his waist, where a squatty hatchet hung. The fingers played over the sharp blade with a loving caress. Larry Weston, panting, tried to relax.

"I *can* prove it," he said, "given half a chance. But if I must wait to be tortured—can't you loosen these thongs a bit? They are biting into my arms and legs, cutting off circulation."

"Perhaps if they were tightened," said the younger man, "we would have less work tonight to prove that you are an open enemy of our tong. You know, my friend, enmity to the Lo Chang means death."

The younger man came closer to the bed, grinning a little as though enjoying the suffering of Larry Weston. He leaned over the bed and examined Larry's bonds. Larry Weston acted then, knowing that he forfeited his life if he failed.

HE DREW HIS knees up with the speed of a serpent striking—and smashed his feet against the side of the hatchetman's head. The Chinese fell without a sound. As the old man plunged through the door, slamming it shut, screaming for help in a high falsetto, Weston rolled off the bed, turned the unconscious man over with his feet—and rolled against the razor sharp edge of the hatchet. The bonds fell free.

There was a rush of feet outside as Larry Weston bent over and slashed at the bonds which held his feet. His ankles were free, but for a moment he swayed. Nausea bit at his stomach. His hand went to his head to find it dotted with lumps that were egg-size. The people who had smashed him with blackjacks had done a thorough job of it.

Larry caught up the hatchet, swung it back over his shoulder.

Men came through the door, hatchets in hands of some of them, snub-nosed automatics in others. This old man was well guarded. Larry stood, legs wide apart, over the body of the man he had downed.

"Attack me, my friends," he said, "and I'll drive this hatchet through the skull of this man!"

He knew that no threat against the newcomers themselves would have been as effective. They had him beaten in advance, by the sheer weight of their numbers. They would know that. The old man answered:

"He has forfeited his life anyhow by allowing himself to be tricked by an enemy of the tong!"

Larry Weston decided on a bold move.

"I have told you I am not an enemy of the tong, but a blood brother," he said quietly. "A year ago, far up in the Tibetan mountains beyond Darjeeling, up beyond Nepal and Bhutan, the Lo Chang made me a blood brother. I took a vow—"

"What was the occasion of this meeting with the Tibetan Lo Chang?" parried the old man, while the others edged forward, aching to charge and overpower this upstart who had forfeited the life of one of their number by out-witting him. "What was the vow? And where is the sign that the words you speak are true?"

"I cannot tell you until I know for a certainty that you are Lo Chang. But I had a ring, in which was set a certain design—"

HE BEGAN TO describe it. The old man held up his hand. On it was a ring.

"Is this the ring?" he asked. There was something ominous in his voice, his eyes were hard—and Larry Weston knew that the old man was setting a trap. Larry studied the ring as best he could from where he stood. He dared not move closer.

"It was not like that," he said slowly, "though that ring comes very close to being a replica. These, are the differ-ences—"

He went on to describe them faithful-ly. And when he had finished he knew he had won, for the old man said:

"There is a possibility that you speak truly, yet in this land where men are hanged by the neck if they take even the life of an enemy, one should be careful. If you can produce proof of your words—then you shall be given the chance.

IF THERE IS a mission for the Lo Chang, it is our duty to aid that mission. What can we do for you? If we do aught at all, a member of the Lo Chang will always be close enough to drive the bit of a hatchet into your skull."

Larry Weston sighed his relief.

"That letter you say you received," he said. "I wish to find the writer. Send out your men to aid in the search. That writer has precious possessions of the Lo Chang which he would, in time, barter for money—and those posses-sions are the world's richest, belonging to Buddha himself."

"We will help you find this man. But how are we to know him? Is he a for-eigner, or a Chinese?"

"I do not know for a certainty. When I last saw him it was among the shadows of the monastery about which I have hinted—the headquarters of the Tibetan tong. I only know one thing about him—that his eyes were cat-slitted; their pupils, instead of being round, were ovoid, like those of a cat. Find all the cat-eyed men in San Francisco. Turn the town upside down."

"That eye marking is unusual, but I have seen it several times," said the old one. "Is there nothing else? There may be several cat-eyed men."

Then Larry Weston, taking into con-sideration all the details of the recent robbery, the fight at the resort, and his subsequent awakening here among people who had been warned he was an enemy, thought he had some inkling of the kind of man Horne might be. So he said:

"The man will be wearing that ring I just described to you—"

Something like fear overspread the faces of the Chinese.

"If this is so," said the old man after a moment of tense hesitation, "then we are bound to help *him*, for if he possess-es that ring it is proof that he is blood brother of the tong."

"But if he does not wear it on the middle finger of the right hand? Where do foreigners wear their rings? The left hand—and that's where he will wear it, thus proving himself an impostor. To him it will be just a ring."

A long hesitant pause. Then the old man nodded.

"You may depart, but you will return here this evening. You must always return here when sent for—and remember, my friend, that there is always the blade of a hatchet within reach of your skull. If you are a brother in very truth, then, later, we will express to you our sorrow that you have been so illy treated by us. We will make full amends. But if you fail, the hatchet will strike!"

"It is agreed. You have a telephone? Then, listen: I shall telephone here for news every half hour I am away."

CHAPTER IV

LARRY WESTON HAD no idea how many Lo Chang there might be in San Francisco, but that there must be hundreds, perhaps even thousands, seemed a certainty. Lo Chang were almost as numerous as Buddhists. Their creed, or faith, had lived through the centuries—since the three pearls had first been brought together.

And Chinese were notoriously prolific. That meant that the offspring of even one family, in the course of centuries, might cumber the whole earth. So Larry Weston felt safe in believing that when the old man had given his word that the Lo Chang of San Francisco would help him, it meant something.

But what—just to be supposing—if Horne knew of the necessity for wearing that strange ring on the middle finger of his right hand—and the Lo Chang accepted him, instead of Larry himself, as the blood brother of the tong?

He knew he would die with great speed, his slaying so carefully covered up that his body, even, might never be discovered.

THERE WAS ONE break in his favor: that the Lo Chang had even listened to him at all. That had been, he knew, because he had managed to describe the identifying ring with great exactitude. That had saved his life.

But supposing—

He made an end of supposing as the Lo Chang, taking him by a narrow passageway which gave him no chance to see the room, led him out of their dwelling. When he saw a patch of light from which came the roaring of traffic, he submitted to a blindfold.

He went out, felt the touch of pavement under his feet, was thrust into a taxicab by men who laughed immoderately, as though they were playing some joke. And the cab driver received his blindfolded fare in that spirit. Or maybe he knew his Chinatown, knew it was indiscreet to ask too many questions.

As someone gave directions to the cab driver, one of the Chinese leaned into the cab and spoke to Larry Weston:

"Remember the hatchet. The Lo Chang are everywhere."

But when the cab drew away he knew

that he was alone, or thought he was, until he tried to remove his blindfold. Then a voice said:

"Not yet."

It came from the floor right below his feet and he knew that one of the Chinese had crawled into the cab with him, unseen by the cabby. If he were to raise his feet and kick—but even as he thought this, as though the other had read his thought, something sharp, razor-sharp, pressed against, his ankle. He knew it for the bit of a hatchet and made no further move. The man chuckled. Larry Weston leaned forward and spoke softly.

"We are brothers," he said. "I shall prove it yet."

"We are not brothers," came the low-whispered reply, "until you have produced the proof."

They traveled for what Larry Weston judged to be fifteen minutes. The way led downhill. Finally the cabby stopped, laughed a little, spoke to Weston.

"I guess this is where the joke either begins or ends. It's where I was supposed to bring you."

Larry now lifted his hand to the blindfold without hindrance, then stared down at the floor of the cab in amazement. He hadn't heard the car door open, nor felt the breeze of its opening on his face—yet the hatchetman of the Lo Chang had vanished. Larry Weston climbed from the cab, stood for a moment on the street.

AS HE STOOD, wondering what to do next, two young girls passed him. He caught at the threads of their conversation:

"Lord, did you ever see so many Chinks on the street—outside of Chinatown, I mean?"

"No, but ain't some of 'em handsome—that slender one we just met."

And then they were gone, and Larry Weston's heart was beating high with excitement. The Lo Chang were abroad! He looked back up the street, which he discovered to be Van Ness Avenue.

A half block back a young man stared in at a window. His hat was pulled down to his ears. His occidental clothing could not disguise his yellow skin. He didn't even seem to be conscious of the scrutiny of Larry Weston, but Larry, studying the man, estimated the distance to him. A good hatchetman could throw a hatchet that distance with deadly accuracy.

HE SHUDDERED A little. The Lo Chang meant business. How much did they know of his mission? In the end he would probably have to tell them the whole thing. If he failed, well—he kept thinking of the distance from himself to that young Chinese, how a hard arm could send a hatchet hurtling swiftly to its goal.

He shrugged. The old one was keeping his promise to keep Larry Weston under surveillance. Larry was as much a prisoner as though he had never won free of his bonds. If he called a policeman—but how could he ask for the arrest of a Chinese who merely stared through a window at American food?

He decided on the downtown district, along Market Street. But first he looked at his watch. It was three o'clock in the afternoon. Lord, he'd been out a long time—since last night. His quarry might be hours out of the Golden Gate now, traveling to some other hiding place. Unless he felt sure that the Lo Chang would unceremoniously dispose of Larry Weston.

He stepped to the curb, called another taxi. He ordered himself taken to Market Street, near the Civic Center. He peered back through the rear window. The Chinese before the restaurant window was also calling a taxicab. Larry Weston turned back to watch the road they traveled. As the cab whirled him along he studied the people on the street. Every tenth man seemed to be a Chinese!

And was he mistaken, or did they gaze slantwise at every man they met, seeking the man with the cat eyes? Lord, the whole city was acrawl with yellow men! How many of them hid hatchets under their coats? How many deaths would eventuate before he regained possession of the pearls of Lo Chang?

He thought of many places he had visited—because, having inherited two millions of dollars he could go wherever he wished—in which he had seen the way yellow men operated. He'd seen them in Lhassa, in Golokwa, in Altan Buloc, everywhere—and always they had been the same: stalking nemeses of their enemies.

They were like that now. He wondered how many Americans on the streets of San Francisco noticed the increase of strolling Chinese, how many of them even sensed the dynamite held in leash by men trained for centuries to hide their feelings under philosophic calm.

He quitted the cab.

HE STRODE DOWN Market Street half a block and he looked back. A Chinese, not the same as the one before the restaurant, followed easily along behind, blandly ignoring Larry Weston. But Larry knew that, for the moment, this man was his "trail." He was half-minded to go back and ask the fellow what the hell he was after, but thought better of it, because he knew.

He looked at his watch. Three-thirty. He stepped into a cigar store, called the number the old one had given him. A girl's voice answered, the soft, melodious voice of the girl whom he had heard through the partition of the room of his captivity.

"Yes, Mr. Weston?"

He hadn't said a word. He gasped. She had called him by name.

"How did you know?" he asked.

"You said every half hour. I kept the time. I knew you would call. Three calls have come in from—from—our people. Two men with cat eyes have been found. One is a very old man who walks on crutches and talks to himself."

"He isn't the one."

ONE IS A young man who runs a garage on Sutter Street."

"No. I'll call back again at four o'clock."

But when he tried to call back at that time the line was busy. It was busy for ten minutes, and when the girl answered again her voice was high-pitched with excitement.

"Two more men have been found. Both have offices on Market Street, two blocks from the Ferry Building. One wears a ring like—like the ring of which you seem to know. The other is negroid. Both men are being watched by three of the Lo Chang. The three travel together, like students in animated conversation."

Larry's heart leaped with eagerness. He liked the sound of the girl's voice. He told her so. Her answer was sharp.

"If you are what you claim," she answered, "you are a brother—and could not show undue interest. If you are not, you are an enemy of my house. Do not speak compliments again. It is not mete in either case."

But he felt, despite her coldness, that she was laughing at him.

"After I have finished my mission," he said boldly, "I shall no longer be a blood brother."

Her answer was sharper still.

"Once a brother, always a brother of the tong. Vows are not taken so lightly among us."

THE GIRL CLICKED up the receiver. Larry Weston went out onto Market Street, the south side. He was four blocks from the Ferry Building. He hadn't asked the girl on which side of the street to look, but the traffic scarcely obstructed his view, so he knew that he would easily spot three Chinese walking together, even across the street.

But he didn't have to cross the street—for three Chinese, laughing and chatting easily, and gesticulating as Chinese did—one even made a character in his hand to elucidate the meaning of something he was chanting in shrill Cantonese—came out of a department store and turned toward the Ferry Building.

Ahead of them was a broad-shouldered, lowering individual, who waded through pedestrians, giving way neither to the right or left, like an ice breaker through skim ice. Larry Weston hated the man instantly for his obvious ill nature and truculence.

But, when he came to think about it, he could scarcely blame the man. Larry Weston had been trailing him for months, keeping his nerves on edge, so that it was little wonder that the man was almost savage.

Larry Weston overtook the Chinese without glancing at them. When, almost abreast of the hulking brute, he looked back, the three Chinese had become four. The three had been joined by his tail. Larry grinned to himself at their elaborate show of disinterest in himself or the striding man.

Larry came abreast of the man. The fellow's lips were twisted in a snarl. His eyes were bloodshot and wild. But as he walked he suddenly lifted his left hand and stared at it—and Larry's heart jumped again. There was his ring!

And this man was Joshua Horne, one of the deadliest of the men whom Larry Weston had followed halfway around the world. How did one go about handling such a one, here in crowded Market Street?

He didn't know. If there were trouble, and the police came in, there would be complications. He would have to tell about the pearls, which had been smuggled in.

HE'D NOT BOTHERED to declare his because he intended returning them to their owners. He knew men of Horne's ilk well enough to know that the hulking brute would have laughed at the idea of declaring a pearl worth a million dollars.

What could he do? He decided on a long chance. Walking abreast of the big man, who glanced neither to right or left, he spoke out of the corner of his mouth:

"What would you say, Horne, if I were to say that I was a brother of the Lo Chang?"

Even as he spoke, Larry Weston turned his head away, before the other could look at him squarely. At the same moment a man of almost Larry's size and build shouldered between Larry and his quarry—and Horne spoke.

"This is what I would do!"

He knocked the perfectly innocent man into the gutter, then broke into a run for the Ferry Building.

CHAPTER V

THERE COULD CERTAINLY be no doubt now that the man was Horne, the man who held the third pearl of Lo Chang which Larry Weston had vowed to return to Tibet. And—it just came to Larry—he was probably the man who had been the power behind the girl who had robbed him last night on Pacific Street.

It was barely possible that Horne might have had no connection with that robbery. And yet—no, no one else could ever have known that he had the other two pearls.

However, the near future would tell. But that man who now raced for the Ferry Building was undoubtedly the one whom, in the darkness of a secret room, in the high mountains cradling a Tibetan monastery, he had been attacked by. As a result Larry had forfeited his life to the Lo Chang, and it had been spared him only when he had vowed to bring back the pearls the man had stolen from the upturned palm of the great Buddha in the temple.

Larry Weston had got two of the pearls. The third was in the possession of that running man—and maybe the key to the location of the others. Yet Larry dared not run.

Horne had not had time to recognize him, if Horne had ever even seen him face to face—for it had been dark in the monastery, though not so dark that Weston hadn't noticed the peculiar shape of the pupils of Horne's eyes.

To run after him now would be to attract undue attention, inasmuch as Horne was looking back over his shoulder, obviously expecting pursuit.

But when Horne had vanished into the building Weston raced across the clearing where street cars turned to go back up Market Street, slowly to a walk when he entered the building. A ferry boat whistled. It was preparing to cast off for the run across to Oakland or Berkeley.

Larry Weston must get on board. He couldn't depend too much on his disguise—which consisted solely of the rudimentary mustache and the sprouting spade beard. But he wasn't too sure that it mattered any longer, with Chinese all over San Francisco—and of course the bay cities—on the lookout for the man with slitted pupils. Horne hadn't a chance to escape.

Larry's one fear was that the Chinese themselves would take more than an active hand and defeat his purpose entirely. They might not even be Lo Chang—and to them the pearls would be priceless possessions indeed. THEY, IF NOT Lo Chang, might guess that the quarrel between Horne and himself involved something precious which would be of use to them. But he cast the thought aside as unworthy. Knowing Chinese, he didn't have the usual occidental distrust of them. They were honorable—at least as honorable as the average occidental.

He raced for the gangplank of the ferry, got aboard. He was strengthened in his belief that Horne was aboard by the fact that two Chinese moved unobtrusively—but with deceiving speed— up the gangplank ahead of him. He felt that they, too, were on the trail of Horne.

Larry Weston searched the first deck as the boat pulled out. Just away from the slip, gulls began to scream over the ferry. Passengers tossed out bits of biscuits, remnants of noonday lunches of people who commute to Frisco from the bay cities.

Weston shook himself, considering all that had befallen him since he had last watched the gulls with a show of interest.

"If Horne got cornered he wouldn't be above throwing the pearls into the bay," he decided. "I wonder if gulls would catch them before they hit the water—and wouldn't I have a sweet job following the right gulls to get them back. That *would* be a job for the Lo Chang."

He cast out such whimsical thoughts as, finding that the man he sought was not on the lower deck, he climbed the stairs to the upper deck where tired shopgirls and clerks were catching the evening breeze. He passed from bench to bench, studying the faces of the men—seeking Horne.

But it seemed that his search was to be fruitless. Just as he was about to give up, one of the Chinese who had preceded him onto the ferry, passed him and spoke slantwise out of motionless lips.

"The Lo Chang watch. The man you seek is aboard. Look sharply!"

The yellow man was gone before Larry Weston could see his face. Now Larry's hand went to his pocket; but he remembered that he had no weapon. The Chinese had come from some place aft—and Larry guessed that he must just now have seen Horne.

SO WESTON TURNED about, retracing his steps, looking into all the nooks and crannies where a man might make himself inconspicuous during the crossing.

And in a corner near a lifeboat he found the man he sought, leaning on the rail, apparently deeply interested in the ducking and diving of the gulls. Unobtrusively, Larry Weston slipped

THE BEST OF THRILLING ADVENTURES

to the rail beside him, looked over the side. Horne did not even notice him. He remained where he was for a minute or two.

Weston finally faced Horne squarely, spoke:

"It's a swell day, isn't it?"

Horne snarled at him.

"What the devil if it is?" he demanded.

Larry took the plunge.

"I was just thinking what a fine day it would be for you, Horne, to return to their proper owners the pearls of Lo Chang!"

At the same moment a sudden outcry came from forward. Shrill cries in Chinese rang through the boat. Passengers eager to satisfy their curiosity, were rising from their seats, racing to the point of excitement.

At the same time four Chinese appeared, running silently toward Weston and Horne. Horne took in the situation at a glance. His right hand darted to his pocket.

"So you're the guy that's been following me for a year, eh? Well, I'm a different customer than the chaps you got the other two pearls from, see? I won't give them up to anybody without a fight!"

"Then fight it is, Horne, or whatever your real name is," said Larry grimly, "for I mean to have the pearls, all three of them."

THE LAST WAS a shot in the dark, but Horne did not dissemble in the least.

"Well," he snarled, "try and get them!"

And his hand snapped forth, gripping the butt of an automatic. Weston jumped at Horne. His right hand dropped down to the muzzle of the automatic before Horne could pull the trigger. He grabbed the barrel.

Horne's right forefinger was on the trigger. Weston twisted the weapon back so that it pointed along the back of the man's hand. That left the trigger finger of Horne fastened tightly in the trigger guard. He was a prisoner—or almost any other man would have been, for this trick was a crippling one.

With a little jerk Larry could break the man's finger as he would snap a twig. He saw sweat start from the cheeks of Horne. But Horne, in spite of the agony of a finger bent back upon itself to almost the breaking point, aimed a savage left hand at Larry's chin.

Larry twisted the automatic quickly, secure in the knowledge that Horne would not fire it, or if he could that the bullet would fly off across the bay.

BY JERKING THE man he pulled him closer, and that cruel left-hander went harmlessly around Larry's neck. Horne swore furiously. The four Chinese, with glances back over their shoulders to make sure that their countrymen were still keeping the passengers interested, grinned at the struggling men—and Larry Weston saw approval of himself in their grins.

He was making good in their eyes. There was no collusion in the meeting of Horne and Weston, which they might previously have suspected.

They knew now that he was a brother of the tong.

But Joshua Horne was a hard man. He wasn't finished yet. For sheer nerve the next thing he did was the best Weston had ever seen. For Horne, knowing that he would break a finger, suddenly yanked away. The finger snapped. The trigger guard of the automatic raked the skin and flesh from the man's finger, clear to the broken bone.

But Horne was free. With a snarl on his lips, even as Weston reversed the automatic for a shot at Horne, the killer-bandit turned away—hurled himself at the rail of the ferry, went over the side in a great leap. "Follow!" snapped Larry at the Chinese.

HE HIMSELF VAULTED to the rail and dived, hurling himself as far as possible in the direction of the circle of waves where Horne had gone down. He swam swiftly under water when he struck, and went deeply down. Even as he came up he kicked out strongly, away from the path of the ferry. He had no wish to be caught in its mechanism.

But he was risking even that to make good his capture of Horne—and the pearls. That Horne had them he was quite sure, else Horne would not have taken such desperate chances to win free of his pursuer.

Larry Weston came up immediately after Horne did. The lights of the ferry were receding. Apparently their plunge had attracted little or no attention. The Chinese had managed that somehow, with skill.

Weston, while Horne trod water and awaited his attack, hurled himself through the water at Horne. Horne waited to meet him. He was swearing bitterly, savagely.

"I can handle you with both hands broken, whoever you are!" snarled Horne.

"I'll tell you who I am, though I'm sure you know. I was the man in the temple in Tibet. I'm the man that caused the death of your partner in Shanghai, the man who got the second pearl from your second partner aboard the Dover-Calais steamer. And I'm here to get you in the same way!"

He pounced for Horne with both hands. Horne struck at him as savagely as he could manage. But Larry ducked, and with his head under water to avoid the blow, acted on impulse. He dived, fastened his arms around the legs of Horne, dragged him into the depths. He doubted if Horne were in as good physical condition as himself, could stay under water as long.

So he swam downward as long as he himself could hold his breath, then rode, side by side with Horne, to the surface of the bay. Down there he had felt the terrific pull of the current, and it had come to him that even if he whipped Horne, and got the pearls, he had barely a fighting chance of getting to the mainland with them.

He recalled stories he had heard of prisoners trying to escape from Alcatraz, and losing their lives in the treacherous currents.

HORNE WAS ONLY half conscious when they floated again on the surface, Larry Weston swimming heavily because he had to support himself and Horne, too.

The killer-thief didn't seem to care now whether he lived or died. And then his eyes opened and he seemed to become aware for the first time of the vast expanse of the darkening waters which surrounded him.

With a sudden cry of fear he flung his arms around Larry—and they went down again, while Larry fought with might and main to jerk free of entangling arms and legs.

He managed it finally—managed it when the under water world was becoming a black hell shot through and through with spots of red light—and beat his way back up, holding fast to Horne's coat collar.

This time when they floated he kept Horne's back to him—and spoke savagely, shaking the struggling man as a terrier shakes a rat.

"Give me the pearls! And don't drop one of them or you sink, here and now."

"What does it matter? No matter how much I help you," Horne was gurgling, proof that he had taken aboard plenty of the bay's waters, "we still can't swim all that distance to the shore."

But Weston remembered what he had said to the Chinese aboard the, ferry—and that Chinese were resourceful. They would manage somehow to help him. He shook Horne again.

"Quick, Horne, the pearls!"

"Inside pocket of my coat, if they haven't been lost in the bay!" gasped Horne, all the resistance gone out of him. Taking a firm grip on Horne's coat collar, and twisting it until he had shut off the man's breath, Weston felt around the big man until his hand delved into the inner right pocket of his coat. With his fingers he felt a bulge; three of them.

There were the leathern shapes of the little holsters in which he had carried two of the pearls under his arms. He managed to place the holsters in his own pocket.

THE THIRD PACKET was the right size and shape—and it seemed to be a bag of yellow silk. He dared to maneuver the mouth of the bag, to open it slightly, until he could see the third pearl. He knew the other two by their feel. He thrust all three into places of safety.

"Now, Horne," he ordered grimly, "lie flat on your back, don't mind a few waves wetting your nose, and we'll see if we can make it. Kick your feet a little to help."

Horne was obedient, docile, but Weston didn't trust him. The man might conserve his strength while Larry used up his, then turn on him with a savage attack, and regain the pearls of Lo Chang.

And when they were almost within hailing distance of the shore, Horne did exactly this. By this time appalling darkness mantled the waters of the bay, so it was little wonder that Weston hadn't noted the small boat creeping up on them. Nor did he think of small boats as he found himself fighting tooth and nail against Joshua Horne, there in the water. Horne's fists were heavy and Horne had regained all his strength. Larry was in the grip of a deathly fatigue. He felt himself start sinking as a savage blow landed squarely on his jaw.

Hands explored his clothing. He clamped his right arm hard over his pocket. And then—something happened: the small boat, with a shadowy figure in the prow holding a long oar upright, materialized beside them out of the night.

The oar crashed down atop the head of Horne. For a moment Horne rested on the surface of the waters. Then something gleamed in the shadows. A streak flashed from the hand of a second man—and ended at the skull of Joshua Horne.

With his last strength Larry Weston clutched at Horne, found his left hand, dragged off the ring, and slipped it onto the middle finger of his right hand.

Then his fingers went nerveless and Joshua Horne slipped away from him.

Strong hands that were friendly grasped him under the arms—one of which, the right, still clamped down tightly over his pocket—and pulled him aboard the small boat.

He passed out.

When he regained consciousness it was to discover himself far at sea, aboard a steamer bound for China, with the pearls intact. Chinese were clever. Later he stood at the rail, staring out at the heaving waste of waters. His lips moved.

"When I've returned the pearls," he told himself, "I'm going in for something not exciting—say hunting black leopards in Malaysia!"

The Terror of Siberia

BY **LIEUT. SCOTT MORGAN**

Plundering Hordes and Valiant Deeds in the Frozen Wastelands of Russia

CHAPTER I

SINISTER SCREAM

KARA SEA AND the Arctic had given birth to that wind; through Rand's sheepskin jacket was three-quarters of an inch thick, it stabbed through like a knife cut. He ploughed through the knee-deep snow, a dozen feet behind "Swede." The long, narrow street was deserted—and desolate with the peculiar air of space and loneliness which characterizes Siberia.

At the end of the street, Rand could see the yellow lights of Tominoff's *traktir.* Warm there, at least, and raw vodka has its virtues. He kept his eyes on it—and his mind almost pleasantly occupied cursing the smooth-talking Russian in Constantinople who had convinced them of the glorious opportunities offered American airmen by the Soviet authorities in Siberia. In a moment of madness, they had taken him seriously.

Cursing the Russian was some satisfaction—and it helped to pass the time away. Rand did it fluently and thoroughly. He ran out, eventually, of cuss words in English, French and Malay, and was making fairly good progress in Boer Dutch, when Swede O'Hara's bulky figure came to a halt. Rand bumped into him, wiped the ice out of his eyes and inquired profanely what was the matter. "I thought," said Swede, "we were the only two nuts in Siberia out in the open."

"Well?"

"Look—to your left."

Blurs, darker shadows in the semi-darkness of the alley a bit ahead and to the left of them. Men—perhaps a dozen of them. Rand strained his eyes, crouching forward.

He could not make out precisely what they were doing, but there was sinister significance in the abrupt, vicious crack of a revolver.

Swede's eyes, red-rimmed from the bitter wind, questioned him eagerly.

"It *might* be interestin'."

Rand shrugged. "Curiosity isn't a healthy habit. But—let's investigate."

SWEDE BEGAN CROSSING the street—and suddenly broke into a run. From the blurs in the alley came a scream.

A woman's scream—high-pitched, hysterical. It ceased abruptly.

Rand followed, slipping off his right mitten. Whoever the men might be, they were up to some deviltry.

He yanked out his big .45 automatic, jammed it into the side pocket of his sheepskin. Easier to get to it there; and he'd seen times when that split fraction of a second meant the difference between life and death.

It did then. Swede had entered the mouth of the alley—perhaps a dozen feet ahead of Rand. The man who leaped upon him had been crouching against the wall. A niche there of a sort, for neither had noticed him.

And Swede would have never noticed him. Or anything else—had that knife reached its mark. The three things happened almost simultaneously. The black figure leaping out. A powerfully-built man, fully as big as Swede. A huge knife in his right hand, uplifted, some unseen light reflected on the polished steel.

Swede turning, having heard the movement behind him. The knife swooping upward still higher, and then—downward. And a sickening feeling in the pit of Rand's stomach that Swede couldn't make it. That he could not possibly evade that sure, swift lunge of the knife.

And then Rand pressing the trigger of the automatic. No time to take aim. No time even to bring up the gun. A desperate yank, then two shots. Blind shooting. A race whether the slug would reach the man before that ten-inch blade had buried itself in Swede's back.

The man with the knife froze. A statue of stone, for a fraction of a second. He collapsed abruptly—on his knees, then flat on his face. Swede grinned. He waved his hand nonchalantly.

"Good shootin', kid!"

"Behind you, palooka!" Rand yelled, leaping forward.

Another man, also appearing abruptly out of the darkness, hurled himself at Swede. Knife in hand, murderous blade driving downward. But now the blond giant was ready. Smoothly, his magnificent body swung into action.

A sidestep, perfectly timed. The knife passed beneath his armpit. A hoarse scream of pain as Swede caught the man's wrist. The knife thudded softly on the snow. Another sharp wrench, and the man's feet left the ground.

SWEDE SLAMMED HIM against the wall. His right fist created a short arc. The sharp crack of bone striking bone—and Rand knew that the man with the knife would be indifferent to his surroundings for a while. Men generally were—when Swede's big fist connected.

Someone further in the alley, one of the group, shouted hoarsely in Russian.

"*Petrov!* Son of a dog, for what are you waiting?"

An orange flash stabbed the darkness. Rand recognized the report—a high-powered rifle. And the rifleman knew his business. The bullet struck the wall an inch from Rand's face. It ricocheted off with a vicious whine.

"Down, Swede!" he shouted. "I'll take care of that baby!"

Swede dropped flat on the snow, rolled over toward the wall. Rand raised the automatic to the level of his eyes, waited. The tattle-tale flash of the rifleman's next shot would seal his death warrant.

AS HE CROUCHED there against the wall, he cursed Swede's suggestion. The men might be members of G.P.U., the dreaded Soviet secret police. Making an arrest, perhaps. When Swede and he had burst upon the scene, they probably assumed it was a rescue party. Which meant that the two of them would never get out of Siberia alive. For one of the men was already dead—dead from a .45 slug of his automatic.

It had been a question of Swede's life or the other man's—of course. Only a bullet would have stopped that knife from entering Swede's back. But Rand knew perfectly well what weight his plea of self-defense would have in a Soviet court. If it ever got to a court.

"So damn stupid," he muttered. "Mixing into something which has nothing to do with us. Killing and getting killed maybe—and without the faintest idea what the hell it's all about."

He shrugged. Too late to retreat now. A rifleman out there in the darkness, alert, waiting for some betraying sign from him. To veer away from the protecting darkness of the wall meant swift death.

A minute dragged. Another. Then another orange flash. Rand gently squeezed the trigger. There came a high-pitched, screaming curse of a man mortally wounded. For a second it lingered, suspended in the darkness. Choked off.

"Got him, kid!" Rand heard Swede's voice.

"It isn't a compliment!" he snapped back. "Stay where you are!"

His eyes tried to pierce the darkness. Black silence. He sensed, rather than saw movement—darker shadows among the shadows. Too vague for accurate shooting, though. And Rand had no desire for further killing. He waited, crouching forward. Nothing else to do.

Twelve shots in three seconds—
screaming men clawed the snow.

A woman's voice came suddenly from the darkness—low, tense.

"Don't shoot. They're gone. I'm going to strike a match."

"Very well," Rand replied in Russian. He added, under his breath, to Swede, "Start creeping forward, big boy. May be a trap."

THE BLACK BLOTCH on the snow that was Swede moved slowly, like a huge snake. Rand followed, shoulder scraping the wall, automatic ready. Foot by foot, they advanced. Then—a scraping sound, and the tiny flare of a match. Rand jerked away from the wall. Again the woman's voice, a bit frightened now.

"Don't shoot! Please!"

She was on her knees, one hand

     THE BEST OF THRILLING ADVENTURES

holding the match, the other supporting the head of a man; no one else, so
far as Rand could see, within twenty
feet at least. He heard movement at his
left—Swede getting up.

"Stick to the wall!" he said sharply. "A
shadow there. Step out in the middle of
the alley—and you'll be a swell target."

A low, relieved laugh from the
woman. A touch of hysteria in it.

"You are English?" She spoke in
English.

"Americans," said Rand.

"Thank God!" she whispered fervently, lapsing back into Russian.

The match went out. Complete darkness again.

"Say," Swede complained, "I'm gettin'
tired o' this. Looks like to me those birds
are gone."

"They *are* gone!" the woman said, speaking almost perfect English. "But," she added bitterly, "they'll be back."

"One moment," Rand said coldly. "These men *I* had in mind wouldn't have left so conveniently. Those boys don't quit easily. Something damn funny here; and I am suspicious of things I don't understand."

"But," the woman insisted, "they *have* gone."

"HOW DO YOU know?" Rand snapped. "You can't see through the dark. Who were they, anyway?"

"Don't ask me now—please! It's a long story, and time may be precious. My father is hurt. Will you help me carry him up to our room. You've done so much; won't you do a little more?"

There was a pause.

"Well," Swede said truculently, "what you hesitatin' about?"

"Don't be a sap all your life!" Rand replied impatiently. "We may be in one hell of a jam right now. We ought to scram out of here—and pronto! Before we get in any deeper."

"But there's no harm helpin' the woman."

Rand shook his head. "I don't like it. It's very nice to be a gentleman—sure; but a Russian prison doesn't appeal to me right now, and a wooden kimono even less. Come on; let's get out of here."

The woman said abruptly, "Yes, I think you'd better. I'm sufficiently grateful to you as it is. I suppose I'll manage somehow. He isn't very heavy, and it's only one flight of stairs."

"I'm goin' to help her carry her old man up," Swede growled. "If you ain't got the guts to come along, I'll meet you at Tominoff's."

Rand laughed shortly. "You're reacting exactly as the lady figured a big boob like you would. When it gets through your thick skull that you owe me an apology, I'll take it. All right, pick him up. I'll trail along with this automatic here."

"The door is behind me," the woman said quietly. "The stairs are at the left."

Swede stood still.

"Well?" Rand snapped.

"I'm thinking," said Swede. "It comes hard. I'm generally wrong when it comes to using my head. If you still wanna scram—well, I'm ready."

Rand grinned in the darkness. "Ever read 'Service,' big boy? He made a crack: 'A promise made is a debt unpaid.' You may as well go through with it now. I'm kind of beginning to get curious as to what this is all about. Go on—pick the old guy up!"

CHAPTER II

BLACK SILENCE

THE WOMAN LED the way up the narrow, ill-smelling stairs. Swede followed, easily carrying the unconscious man in his big arms. Rand brought up the rear, half-crouching, automatic ready, every sense alert, A trap, maybe, cleverly arranged by the woman; but he meant to make every shot in his automatic count before he went down beneath some murderous knife or bullet.

The silence—the dead, black silence of the house—was oppressive, sinister. Either no one lived there, or bitter experience had taught the occupants to mind their own business. Rand found himself wishing he had adopted a similar philosophy. One lived longer thus—and kept out of trouble.

"A turn here," the woman said softly. "Be very careful please."

A metallic sound—evidently she was fumbling with her keys, then the squeaking of rusty hinges as she opened the door.

"Better let me go in first, kid," Rand said quickly.

Swede stepped aside. Rand brushed by him. His left hand reached out, caught the woman's shoulder.

"We'll go in together, if you don't mind," he said coolly.

"You don't trust me?"

"No!" Rand replied bluntly.

His hand on her shoulder, they entered the room. With an abrupt gesture, Rand jerked his left arm over, then around her body. He swung her close to him, moved to the left. He felt his back touch the wall. Her body tensed, but she offered no resistance.

"Okay, Swede. Now do just what I say. Lay the guy down first."

"These precautionary measures aren't necessary," said the woman, a tinge of contempt in her voice.

"Maybe not," Rand agreed. "But I'm alive today because I seldom forget them. You put him down, Swede?"

"Yeah."

"Close the door. You ought to be standing near it."

A SHORT PAUSE, then the squeaking of the hinges again.

"Okay, Larry."

"Put your back to it."

"Right."

Rand raised the automatic.

"All fight, strike a match!"

Another pause. Swede's big body abruptly leaped into relief as he struck a match. He raised it over his head. Rand's eyes searched the room. A glance was sufficient. A small, bare room. A bed along one wall, a washstand in the corner, an old bureau, with a smashed glass, to the right of it. Nothing else.

"Satisfied?" asked the woman.

"Yes," said Rand.

He released her. Swede lighted another match. She ran across the room to the bureau. An oil lamp stood on its scarred top. She lighted it quickly, turned down the wick, replaced the glass chimney. Grace in her movements; quick efficiency.

Rand suddenly found himself wondering what she looked like. Hitherto, while she was a threat, a possible danger, he hadn't given her personality a thought.

She turned away from the bureau, holding the lamp in her right hand. Rand caught his breath. He forgot Swede. Forgot the man on the floor. The fight a few minutes ago. Himself. Forgot everything except the flaming beauty of the girl facing him.

She held the lamp at the level of her

shoulder, the yellow light accentuating her face as a cameo. An exquisite cameo. A dark, proud face. Beauty there—and yet more. Character, breeding. The rough peasant clothes she wore failed as a disguise. She was an aristocrat. Born so—and would ever remain so.

She spoke to Swede.

"Will you please put him on the bed?"

It broke the spell. Rand frowned, annoyed at his absorption. Women had left him two souvenirs: gray hair on the temples and a memory. He intended it to remain—a memory.

"Well," he said sharply, "you heard what she asked you to do."

The blond giant shook his head. He picked up the unconscious man, carried him to the bed. His eyes never left the girl's face.

"Hell," Rand said to himself, half-grinning, "this is getting serious."

He strolled to the bed. A glance convinced him that on one point at least the girl spoke the truth. The old man on the bed was her father. No doubt about it. The same features, the same proud expression. A handsome old man, though privations and suffering had left their marks on his face.

A SHALLOW GASH ran across the right side of his forehead. Blood still trickled at the lower end. The girl, returning from the washstand with a wet cloth, bathed the wound. Almost immediately the old man showed signs of returning consciousness.

"Won't be long now," said Rand. "And if he isn't hurt anywhere else, you've got nothing to worry about."

The girl smiled bitterly.

"Nothing to worry about, eh?"

"Implying," said Rand—"what?"

She did not have time to answer. Swede, standing ten feet away, suddenly threw himself in a flying tackle. His shoulder hit Rand on the hip. Two hundred pounds of bone and muscle behind it. Rand crashed into the girl. Both slid a dozen feet across the room.

A PERFECTLY-TIMED, BEAUTIFULLY-EXECUTED muscular reaction. A tenth of a second, perhaps—but it was sufficient. A man outside the window had jerked the trigger of the revolver a tenth of a second too late. A mad splintering of glass. A slapping sound as the bullet buried itself in the plaster wall in the precise spot against which Rand's body had been.

The man on the ladder outside the window cursed hoarsely. With a single vicious blow of the revolver's barrel he smashed the remainder of the glass.

Rand saw that bearded, animal face turn in his direction. Slanted, piggish little eyes, venomous with hatred, glittering with blood lust. The barrel of the revolver swinging around. Swiftly, surely. Another fraction of a second, and it would be spitting swift death.

Desperately, Rand reached for his automatic, back in his shoulder holster, beneath the sheepskin.

"Won't make it," he said to himself. "Can't!"

The barrel of the revolver swung around. The target only fifteen feet away. Rand's hand now on the butt of the automatic. He rolled over convulsively, half-sick with the conviction he couldn't make it. The other would get in one shot at least.

The shot came. Crack! Something hot—like the burning tip of a cigarette—touched Rand's left ear. And then the automatic in his hand roared its message of death. The man outside the window threw up his arms. For a moment he seemed suspended in midair, mouth open, twisted to one side. His body toppled backward. A scream, choked off abruptly.

Rand leaped to his feet. He ran to the window. Below, a black blotch on the snow. Arms and legs sprawling out. Like a big black spider. As he watched, other figures materialized from the darkness.

Rand's thin lips twisted grimly. He ignored the hot blood trickling down the left side of his neck. The automatic made a short arc. Centered. Then spurted flame. One of the figures below twisted around like a mad dervish. The others scurried away like rats. Two blotches on the snow now. Two big black spiders.

"Damn 'em!" Rand said under his breath.

HE LEANED FURTHER out of the window. He thought he saw movement in a doorway at the very mouth of the alley. Savagely he aimed at the center of the door. He did not have an opportunity to squeeze the trigger. Steel fingers gripped his shoulders, swinging him around and away from the window. Swede's bronzed face towered over him.

"Let me go!" Rand said coldly. "Damn you, *will* you let me go?"

The giant shook his head.

"Easy, kid! I know you, when you get started that way. You don't scare me."

The devil was on Rand's thin, dark face. He said slowly, dropping the words out of the corner of his mouth: "For the last time, palooka—let go!"

Swede picked him up, shook him like a terrier might shake a rat. He kept it up. The girl watched him, wide-eyed. He lowered him.

"Thanks," said Rand. "I'm all right now." The killer's look had gone out of his eyes.

"HANGIN' OUT THE window the way you was," Swede said apologetically, "you coulda been popped off like that." He snapped his fingers. "Besides, I thought you oughta go easy on the few shells left in that gat o' yours. They might come in handy gettin' outa here. For once, I kinda used my head. Brother," he added, grinning, "you're the most cold-bloodedly cautious guy I ever seen, but when you go haywire—" He shook his head.

Rand touched the side of his neck. His fingers came away moist, sticky. The girl approached him, holding a white cloth. She gestured for him to lower his head. Rand obeyed indifferently.

The emotional reaction had left him weak, cold. He was glad it didn't happen often—that snap in his brain when he turned killer: coldblooded, merciless killer. Some day, he knew, it would cost him his life. For the chances he took during those moments were suicidal.

The girl bandaged his head. As he straightened, he caught fear in her eyes. Fear of himself. It annoyed him.

"I am all right now," he said sharply. "How is your father?"

The girl's eyes widened. She whirled to the bed. The old man, forgotten during the murderous interruption, was sitting up, his back against the head of the bed. He was smoking a long Russian cigarette, and seemed extraordinarily cool and composed.

He gestured carelessly with the cigarette.

"I am also quite normal—thank you." Like the girl, he spoke perfect English. "That was excellent shooting my friend."

Rand grinned. The old man's coolness was genuine; Rand liked him instantly.

"Had to be—accurate. The gentleman lost because his wasn't—by perhaps a quarter of an inch."

"I appreciate that. I assume that you're also the gentleman who did that magnificent shooting in the alley. I lost consciousness a few seconds after you directed a bullet through Petrov's filthy carcass. It saved the situation—temporarily, at least—for myself and my daughter, I am very grateful to you."

Rand waved his hand.

"One of those mad impulses," he said coolly.

The old man flipped the ash off his cigarette.

"Exceedingly mad, if I may say so. I shall explain by introducing myself first. I am Feodor Vladimir Pavlov, Grand Duke, related by blood to the house of Romanoff. This is my daughter Vera. As my execution has already been commanded, your speaking to me now will alone probably earn for you indefinite lodging in our palatial Russian prisons."

"Interesting," Rand murmured.

"QUITE," SAID THE old man. "That, however, should be the least of your worries. The Government doesn't know my whereabouts. Others, who have nothing to do with the Government but who are, nevertheless, equally interested in my person, do know. I am referring to the rats in the alley—Gurin and his gang of cutthroats."

"And who, pray," said Rand, "is Mr. Gurin?"

"A crook—of international prominence. Being a clever devil, and realizing that further public disturbance would probably bring the police, resulting in my arrest and ruination of his plans, he retreated. It wasn't, I assure you, cowardice."

"I am afraid," sighed Rand, "I still don't understand."

The old man nodded. "You shall—presently. First, I wish to acquaint you with the identity of the animal in the window. He is—was Kiok, brother of Agur. Agur is the chieftain of Kalmuck bandits who rove the plains a hundred miles north of here."

"The significance of which is—what?"

"That your lives," said the old nobleman, "aren't worth a kopeck. Agur will avenge the death of his brother. Sooner or later, you'll be kidnaped, tortured and, eventually, butchered.

"And I know precisely what I am saying. Messengers probably going to the chieftain this very moment. I am not a fatalist, but—my reason tells me to bow to the inevitable. Your life—the lives of everyone of us aren't worth a kopeck."

"How tremendously interesting!" Rand murmured.

CHAPTER III

KALMUCK REVENGE

SILENCE FOR A while. Bitter cold seeped through the smashed window. The oil lamp began to splutter, running out of kerosene. Rand lighted a cigarette, puffed on it thoughtfully. The old man might have spoken the truth. But he could not see the story as a whole. Fragments here and there, weaving a fantastic pattern.

An internationally-known crook— Kalmuck bandits. The old nobleman and his beautiful daughter. What were they doing in Northeastern Siberia, anyway?—Kalmuck revenge. "You will be kidnaped, tortured and eventually, butchered." Damn dramatic, but—

"Hooey," Rand said to himself.

On a sudden impulse, he strolled to the window. Looked down. He turned away with a frown. The two bodies were gone! It spoke of others—many others.

Swede's eyes met his. Questioning. Rand could not answer his questions. He turned to the old man.

"What are your plans?"

"I have none."

"Quitting?"

"Yes."

"And your daughter?"

"I know. But what can I do?" He sat up straighter. "Gurin is working hand-in-hand with the Kalmuck chieftain. Every exit from the town is watched— that I know. Should I venture out openly to seek outside help, someone will recognize me. It means—execution." He leaned forward. "Gentlemen, I'll make you a proposition."

He paused. Rand said nothing.

"WE'RE ALL IN the same boat now, as you Americans would say. You too have *got* to get out of Siberia now. None of us probably will—but you, at least, are in a position to make an effort. I am stopped—on every side. Would you help us?"

"You said—a proposition," Rand drawled. There was hard suspicion in his eyes.

"Yes. The mouth of the Ob River, where it forms its delta into the Gulf of Ob is only three hundred miles north from here. A Russian whaler, captain of which is an old friend of mine, is awaiting us there now. Get us to it, and it's liberty—life for all of us; and fifty thousand dollars apiece for you. That's my proposition."

"You mean," Swede cut in, incredulously, "you have all that money with you?"

"No. I should have explained. Two months ago, I realized I had to get out of Russia. My family has been for centuries one of the wealthiest in all Europe. I gathered our valuables—family heirlooms, mostly, and rather priceless paintings, the total easily amounting to several millions of dollars—placed them in a trunk and buried it near my country estate.

"THE SERVANT WHO had helped me fell into the hands of Gurin. Under torture, he revealed the secret, but died before he had a chance to describe the precise spot where the treasure was buried. That's what Gurin wants; I shall die before he gets it."

"I am beginning to understand," said Rand.

The old man smiled bitterly. "My original plans were excellent. I'd made arrangements with the captain of the whaler. Ordinarily, I wouldn't have many difficulties reaching the Coast. Terrible privations probably, but I'd make it.

"The whaler would bring me to some European port, I'd get in touch with some men I can trust in Russia, tell them the burial place of the treasure, and they'd smuggle it out of Russia to me. But—Gurin caught up with me here. You've seen what happened."

The girl spoke abruptly. "You'll help us? Oh, I know you will. We need you."

"Vera!" the old man said sharply.

"But we do!" she cried.

Swede touched Rand's arm.

"What do you say, kid?"

Rand rubbed the stubble of beard on his chin. He looked at the girl. He thought of the two bodies in the alley—removed. The old man *might* have framed the Kalmuck vengeance story—as well as the treasure yarn—in order to get help, but Rand doubted it. He knew men.

"It looks to me, Swede," he said quietly, "we just have no other choice. We've got ourselves into a jam—and this seems to be the only way out." He turned to the old man. "All right, we'll see what we can do."

"My daughter and I thank you, gentlemen," the old man said with quiet dignity.

"Save it until we get you out," Rand said curtly. "We'll leave you now. For an hour, maybe. Don't believe that gang would be back so quickly. Anyway, it's a chance you'll have to take. Got a gun here?"

"Yes."

"Good. Use it. Come on, Swede."

"Brother," Swede murmured as they descended the narrow stairs, "you sure don't believe in wastin' time."

"We've got to work fast, if we're to get out of this damn country alive."

"She's a swell looking jane," Swede put in irrelevantly.

"That's not why I'm doing it," Rand snapped.

"No?"

"You go to hell!" said Rand.

CHAPTER IV

SOMOLOV

RAND SLID OUT of the door into the alley. He hugged the wall, moving along it. At his right, a swishing sound. Swede, making the same progress. No other sound, except the howling of the wind in the chimneys above. Darkness, silence.

If spies watched their movements, they were well concealed and knew their business. Rand strained his eyes, fingers gripping tightly the automatic. No sign, no sound of life. They were alone in the alley, apparently.

Gradually, they worked their way to the mouth of it. Out on the street now. Rand relaxed. Replaced his automatic. The Kalmucks—Rand feared them now more than their Russian leader—seemed to favor the knife. In the middle of the street, comparatively light, back-stabbing was difficult.

"WHERE TO NOW, kid?" asked Swede, catching up to him.

"Somolov. Let's find out if that plane arrived. If it did, we'll load on the old man and the girl, throw the damn mail out and bee-hive for the coast. It'll be a cinch."

"Yeah, but what if the plane didn't come? They've been promisin' it to us for the last three weeks."

Rand shrugged. "Then we'll have to hang around until it does. No other choice. Though I'll admit we'll be running a sweet chance of getting our skins perforated."

"Which same don't appeal to me."

"You wouldn't kid me, would you?" Rand murmured.

Two men crossed the street ahead of them. Rand slipped his hand beneath the sheepskin, fingers caressing the butt of the automatic. The men disappeared in one of the houses. Rand relaxed. Swede grinned. "Jumpy, eh?"

"Cautious," Rand replied shortly.

They paused before one of the better houses. Somolov's home. Yellow light filtered through the curtained windows. The President of Workers Council of Kurlov was evidently at home.

Swede banged his fist against the massive door. Again. Footsteps within. Clanging sound of bolts drawn aside. The door swung open. An old woman looked out, one yellow hand at her throat clutching the folds of an old Russian army overcoat. She stared at them with the dull apathy of a Russian peasant.

"Somolov," Swede growled. "We want to see Somolov. Tavarisch Somolov."

Still no sign of comprehension on the old woman's face. But she stepped aside. Swede swaggered in, Rand behind him. Anton Somolov sat writing behind a huge desk. He did not look up.

Swede scraped his feet, coughed. The fat Russian continued writing. Swede clenched his fist, then relaxed. Nothing left to do but wait—until the Russian deigned to recognize them.

Rand wasn't watching the commissar. Three soldiers sat on a bench along the right wall. One held a short carbine across his lap. The other two were armed with revolvers. The flaps of their holsters were pinned back.

A significant detail in itself—as well as their presence. Reason for it: The Russian had expected them to drop in that evening. Rand didn't like it. He tried to remember how many shots he had left in his automatic.

SOMOLOV LOWERED HIS pen with an important flourish, looked up.

"Ah, my American friends! I am glad you have come. I have news."

"Good!" said Rand. "You've got the plane?"

The Russian shook his head. "It is with much sorrow and regret that I must inform you of the message which I have received from the Executive Council at Tomsk. The plans for air mail have been changed. The War Department at Moscow is unable to spare the necessary airplanes."

"Is this final?"

"Unfortunately—yes."

"Well, I'll be damned!" Rand exploded. "We come six thousand miles upon the invitation of your Government. We're supposed to risk our necks flying air mail across Siberia for you birds—for a thousand a month. Your War Department suddenly changes its mind. What the hell are we supposed to do now? How're we to get back?"

"You may take up the finances for your return transportation with the Executive Council at Tomsk."

"But, damn it," Swede cut in savagely, "Tomsk is eight hundred miles from here."

The Russian smiled. "Americans—they are noted for their ingenuity. I repeat—I am sorry; the matter is now out of my hands."

"Oh, yeah?" Swede said grimly.

With two tigerish strides, he approached the desk, towered over the Russian.

"So it's outa your hands, eh? Why, you—"

"Look behind you, Swede," Rand interrupted quietly.

The three soldiers were on their feet. The carbine covered Swede. The revolver in the hand of another. The third had the ugly snout of a German Luger trained on Rand. And the expression on the faces of each unmistakable. They were merely awaiting a command from Somolov.

The Russian stood up. He pointed to the door.

"Get out!"

"May as well, big boy," said Rand. "We haven't got a chance."

AS THE DOOR slammed behind them, they heard the Russians laugh.

"The little fat pig!" Swede panted. "I shoulda pasted him one anyway."

"Yeah, and get a slug through you just about a second later. It wasn't worth it. After all he was probably just acting under orders."

They walked on a while, the soft snow crunching beneath their feet.

"Well," said Swede, "this kinda gums up your plans. What now?"

Rand shook his head. "Trust to luck, I guess. Big boy, now we are in a jam!"

Swede grinned. "It ain't the first time. How about Tominoff's joint. A drink generally helps."

"Lead the way, Sunshine," said Rand.

CHAPTER V

FIGHTING GIANTS

TOMINOFF'S *TRAKTIR* WAS low, long, dark, and saturated with the indescribable odor of unwashed bodies, cheap tobacco and alcoholic fumes of raw vodka. From a side table in the rear, Rand gave the orders to the fat proprietor. Tominoff waddled away.

"Another fat pig," Swede commented

disgustedly. "I feel like punchin' him in the nose—just for the hell of it. Come to think of it, I'm in a kinda nose-punchin' mood." "Yeah?" Rand grinned. "Well, lay off! Save those big mitts of yours until there'll be need for 'em. And I can promise you *that*."

He looked around. Men in various stages of drunkenness sat, leaned or slept at the dirty tables. Peasants, a sprinkling of soldiers. Here and there, a better dressed man—who might be anything.

At the two tables across the room from them, a number of Kalmucks. Broad, squat, powerful-looking little men. Dressed in roughly-sewn furs from their moccasins to the wolf caps. Brown, bearded faces, flat-nosed, a Mongolian slant to the eyes. Tough little devils.

They paid no attention to Rand. Or else were mighty good actors. The white man at the table at their immediate left did. A burly, red-headed man, with the fleshy face of a brute, long, gorilla-like arms, powerful torso. He caught Rand's eye, stared. Then stood up jerkily.

Rand kicked Swede under the table.

"Here's where your mitts go to work," he said out of the corner of his mouth. "Got a hunch who this gent is. And he's got a mean look in his eyes."

Swede grinned happily.

The red-headed Russian reached their table. Towered over it—a great bulk of a man. A brutish twist to the side of his mouth, cold menace in his eyes.

"I believe," he said slowly, in English, "I've—er—encountered you gentlemen before."

"Possible," Rand murmured.

"An hour ago, perhaps?"

"Perhaps."

"In," the Russian added softly, "a certain alley?"

Rand lowered his glass. His eyes interlocked with the Russian's.

"Yes—Mr. Gurin."

Silence for a moment—hot, tense.

"Meddlers," said the Russian, "generally get in trouble. Serious trouble, sometimes. Trouble which might cost them their necks."

RAND SENSED THE Russian's body tensing. Saw the Kalmucks, across the room rise. A dozen of them maybe. Anticipation already in their eyes. Hands already reaching for their knives. Savages about to be in on a kill. A pack of wolves closing in on its prey.

Rand smiled at the Russian.

"A warning?" he asked gently.

"A prediction," said the Russian.

Rand lunged to the right. Gurin was a fraction of a second too late. He'd thrown his body against the table, hoping to pin Rand to the wall. The table crashed over. Rand tried to straighten. Slipped. He fell in the arms of a drunken peasant at a neighboring table.

The man awoke with a frightened grunt. He sat up—and sighed suddenly.

Something resembling a big black wasp appeared square in the center of his forehead. A bullet—intended for Rand.

THE PEASANT COLLAPSED, sliding sideways out of the chair. Rand rolled over desperately, but the second shot did not come. Swede had gone into action.

Head down, hard fists hammering. A magnificent fighting machine.

A smashing uppercut sent Gurin staggering backward. Swede lived because the Russian dropped the revolver. No time to pick it up, for Swede was upon him. A right, a left, a right again. Another man would have gone down; the Russian merely shook his head. He came weaving in, gorilla-like arms outstretched, fingers hooked talon-wise.

The two giants had the floor. The Kalmucks stood back, their eyes glittering. Rand got up, crouched against the wall. A touch of the trigger of his automatic—and Gurin would have gone down with a bullet through his heart. But that which held the Kalmucks from leaping with the long knives kept Rand from firing.

The thrill of contest. Who was the better man? The blond, broad-shouldered giant or the great Russian bear? Again and again Swede's big fists found the Russian's face, his body. Blows which could be heard clear across the room. Bone striking bone. Again and again, they snapped the Russian's head back. Sent him staggering backward, an animal-like rumble in his throat.

Swede fighting coolly, scientifically, a contemptuous smile on his lips. Making each blow count. Wearing the Russian down. Playing with him. Gurin's face becoming a bloody horror. And still, in the dead silence, he came boring in.

Swede—as everyone else in that room—knew Gurin's object. The Russian was a wrestler. Once he got his gorilla arms around Swede, the blond giant—big as he was—would die with a broken back. But Swede demonstrated another science—new to that savage audience. The science of boxing.

His big body was a melody of grace as he leaped in and out. On the balls of his feet, half-crouching—and big fists ever punishing. Cutting the skin, bruising the flesh; gradually forcing the inevitable.

IT CAME ABRUPTLY. Crack! A long right-cross, two hundred pounds of bone and muscle behind it. It landed behind and below Gurin's ear. The Russian's head snapped sideways. For a moment, his big body tottered—like a tree undercut by a woodsman's ax. His knees stiff, he fell flat on his face.

And then hell broke loose. A savage yell from the Kalmucks. Long knives glittering. Wild faces, further distorted with bloodlust. Fur-clad bodies leaping forward. Kill, kill, kill!

No time to think. To plan action. The little brown men were upon Rand. The first died with a bullet through his skull.

A sidestep, as the ten-inch blade in the hand of the second sought Rand's throat. The man wielding the knife crumpled. Blood clung to the butt of Rand's automatic. The force with which he had brought the gun down on the Kalmuck's skull almost sprained his shoulder.

He leaped forward to meet the third man. Swung out with the heavy butt. Missed. The Kalmuck came up. A flash of steel. The razor-like edge made a clean slit in Rand's sheepskin. His left hand flashed out, caught the other's knife wrist. Swiftly, he jerked up the gun. And then the Kalmuck's free hand caught his wrist.

So they stood there, panting, glaring at each other; cold gray eyes, slanted black eyes.

Swede's voice rose above the bedlam. "All right, you rats! Come 'n' get it!"

Rand risked a glance over his shoulder. The giant had swung up a heavy wooden table. He whirled it over his head, and then in a great circle at the level of his waist. In his hands, it was a terrible weapon. Men went down screaming. Broken bones. Smashed skulls.

"The crazy palooka!" burst from Rand's lips.

Swede had cleared a circle. But he wasn't content with that. He leaped forward. Another step. Still another. And over the table swinging, smashing everything in its path. The Kalmucks scattered like rats.

AND THEN RAND'S mind jerked to the man before him. For he felt the knife wrist slipping out of his fingers. Oil on the Kalmuck's body. As he tried to wrench the automatic loose. Realizing he could not hold on much longer to the slippery wrist, the Kalmuck brought up his knee. Jabbed it just below Rand's belt—a vicious, experienced blow. A red glare danced before Rand's eyes.

He suddenly realized that his left hand no longer held the knife wrist. And then saw the knife. Saw those ten inches of steel going up and back—the backward swing of the pendulum which would end in his death. Triumph in the slanted black eyes. The look of an animal about to kill.

Another Kalmuck at his left. Another knife, plunging forward. But not at himself. For a moment, Rand thought he went mad. For the second Kalmuck had buried the knife in the heart of his tribesman.

It wasn't an accident. Done deliberately. The Kalmuck flashed his white teeth. Rand looked down stupidly at the man at his feet. When he looked up again, the Kalmuck who had averted the death blow had disappeared.

Swede loomed up before him, still clinging to the gory table.

"Come on!" he panted. "Follow me!"

RAND'S HEAD CLEARED. He followed Swede, automatic ready to flame death. It wasn't necessary. No one tried to stop them. In thirty seconds, they were outside. Out in the clean, cold air.

"Well," Swede said exultantly, "I call that a scrap!"

"It isn't over yet," Rand snapped back, jerking around with the automatic.

The Kalmuck running toward them waved his arms wildly. Rand lowered the automatic.

"That's right!" said Swede. "Save him for Mrs. O'Hara's son."

"Lay off!" Rand replied. "That *hombre* saved my life two minutes ago. Though," he added with a frown, "I'll be damned if I can figure out why."

The man approached them, the palms of his hands raised in midair.

"Friend," he said in the odd Russian used by the Kalmucks.

Rand nodded. "Of that," he replied in Russian, "I have had proof."

He saw now that the Kalmuck was an old man, though he still retained the vigor of youth.

"I am Kusslo. You are my friend."

"Good," said Rand. "But why am I your friend?"

"You have killed Kiok," the Kalmuck said simply. "Kiok killed my son. You are my friend."

"That's three times you're his friend, Larry," grinned Swede, who understood enough Russian to follow the conversation.

"At one time," the Kalmuck continued with quiet dignity, "I was chief of the tribe. I go to the great war. When I come back, my people do not welcome me. Agur and his brother Kiok poison the minds of my people. Into the back of my first born Kiok stabbed with his knife. Ay, into the back. For my son was a great warrior. You have avenged him. Kusslo is grateful."

Rand looked thoughtfully at the old man. His mind raced. The Kalmuck spoke the truth. No doubt about it. Hence he could be trusted. But would he do it? Would he risk his neck—out of gratitude?

"You have paid your debt of gratitude, Kusslo," Rand said gravely. "But will you do even more?"

"Speak," said the Kalmuck.

"I desire a sled and ponies. Of these can you provide?"

"Ay, that I can," Kusslo replied promptly.

"I desire a driver who knows the country, for I wish to reach the waters which never freeze." Rand pointed north.

"It is Agur's country—and you have killed his brother," the old man said significantly.

"That it is," said Rand. "And Agur may seek to stop us. And even so, Agur may die."

The old Kalmuck's eyes glittered.

"Then again I shall be chief, and my son after me, and the son of my son."

Rand nodded.

"I SHALL DO it!" the Kalmuck said slowly. "Yes, I shall do It. My son will help me. My years are many; if die I must, it is good to die so. When do you wish the sled and ponies?"

"We have no time to lose," said Rand.

"And that we shall not. You will come with me?"

"Yes," said Rand. He turned to Swede. "Get our trunk, kid. Haul it up to the girl's room. It's only a little ways, and they won't take any action until Gurin comes to, at least. Which won't be for a while yet. Break out a couple boxes of these .45 slugs, and put our Winchester together. Come on, brother; move! We'll give those *hombres* a run for their money."

CHAPTER VI

SNOW TRAIL

LIKE STILL WHITE death were the Siberian steppes, locked in the grip of winter. Smooth white surface, so far as the eyes could see. Snow, ice. And God-forsaken loneliness equalled only by the Great Barrens of Northern Canada.

The Kalmuck, Pavlov and his daughter rode in the square sled. The Kalmuck stood upright, almost constantly cracking the twenty-foot whip. The old man and the girl sat in the bottom of the sled, wrapped in furs. Swede, Rand and a younger Kalmuck followed, running easily on wide-webbed Kalmuck snowshoes.

Far to the south, gray Arctic dawn was breaking. Already six hours on the trail, yet none of the running men showed fatigue. Swede O'Hara's body did not know the meaning of the word; Rand's slim body was as tough as old hickory, and he'd spent years on northern trails; the Kalmuck had been doing it all his life. And the three shaggy little Siberian ponies had the endurance of the gray wolf."

No one spoke. The great silence discouraged it—and breath was precious. One by one, miles slipped by.

Occasionally, Rand would glance over his shoulder. No doubt in his mind that Gurin and the Kalmucks were on their trail—a trail on the soft snow that a child might have followed.

No attempt had been made to stop them when leaving the town, but slanted eyes had watched them go. Fur-clad figures running to report even before they'd gone out of sight.

On the trail, running men can outdistance horses. Constantly able to take advantage of short cuts. Occasional snow-covered dunes, too steep for the ponies to drag the sled over, yet, which the Kalmucks could easily cross. Thus ever gaining, closing in.

And the shaggy little ponies, though tireless, had to plough through snow fully a foot deep in places before their hoofs reached the under-crust.

Only a matter of time. Then it would be a running fight—clear to the coast. Facing odds of perhaps ten to one. Bandits to whom fighting was second nature. Fierce little devils who could not be bluffed, who'd fight until their last breath. Clear to the coast—if they ever reached it—

RAND SHRUGGED. WITHIN the next few hours, hell would break loose. They might be lucky—

More hours dragged by. The runners of the sled sang on the snow. The sled creaked. Bullet-like reports of the twenty-foot whip in the old Kalmuck's hands. The ponies snorting, waving their bushy tails, tossing their manes. The snow scrunching softly beneath the snowshoes. And the great silence hemming them in. A silence one could hear. When the sun was high in the sky, marking the half-passage of the short Arctic day, Kusslo stopped the ponies.

"We rest," he said to Rand. "We eat. The trail is long."

Rand nodded. He approached the Kalmuck again as he squatted over the tiny fire.

"You are sure you know the place he spoke of?" He pointed to Pavlov, tramping about on the snow, stretching his cramped limbs.

Kusslo smiled. "When boy, I speared

the walrus there. Ay, my friend, I know it well."

"Good," said Rand.

HE WALKED AWAY. He was restless, uneasy. Glancing back over their trail, the white emptiness failed to reassure him. Swede's big body loomed up alongside of him.

"What's the matter, kid?"

"Nothing," Rand said shortly. "But I've got a hunch. In fact—"

He gripped Swede's arm, pointed. The wise old Kalmuck had stopped the sled at the top of a long incline. From there they had visibility of several miles. Far away, almost on the horizon, tiny black specks now dotted the white. The pursuit was drawing near.

"Won't be long now," Rand said grimly.

Swede tried the bolt of his Winchester.

"Oh, what the hell!" he grinned. "It'll break the monotony, anyway. I'm kinda gettin' bored."

Rand gestured to the Kalmuck. He pointed down the trail.

"Yes," the old man said simply. "Pretty soon, they catch us."

Rand stroked thoughtfully the stubble of beard on his chin. He looked up the trail to his left. The incline continued upward for perhaps another mile, then the land leveled sharply. The black specks, when he looked down the trail again, were already larger. The Kalmucks were making good time.

Rand jerked his thumb to the sled.

"All right, Kusslo," he said sharply, "we make trail again."

The Kalmuck nodded, ran to the sled.

Two minutes later, his whip cracked savagely. The ponies threw themselves against the traces. Snow flew beneath their sharp little hooves as the runners clung to the snow. The frozen runners jerked loose. With a lurch, the sled was off.

Fifteen minutes—and they were over the crest of the incline. Two hundred yards further, Rand ordered a halt.

"Come here, palooka!" he shouted to Swede. He motioned the Kalmuck and Pavlov also to join them. Then he spoke in slow, simple Russian that Swede could understand. "You"—he poked his finger in the Kalmuck's chest—"go ahead with the sled. And make much speed. You," he looked at the Russian—"can you use a rifle?"

Pavlov nodded.

"Good," said Rand. "You stay behind. And you two." He gestured to Swede and the younger Kalmuck. "That's four rifles. Now when they come over the crest—"

The old Kalmuck grinned. Respect in his eyes when he regarded Rand. Without another word, he got up and ran to the sled.

The younger Kalmuck caressed the stock of his Russian army rifle, his black eyes glittering.

"I think," Swede said, slowly, "I'm goin' to have lots o' fun."

PAVLOV WALKED QUIETLY to the two rifles the Kalmuck had thrown out on the snow before he drove away, picked up one, worked the bolt. Rand, watching him, said to himself,

"The old boy's all right. Plenty of guts—and he's used a rifle before."

     THE BEST OF THRILLING ADVENTURES

He raised his voice. "All right, gang. Break out the ammunition. Fifteen clips a piece. I want plenty of lead spilled—and spilled in one hell of a hurry!"

Again minutes dragged. They waited, spread out in a line. Each man on his knees, a small pile of cartridges ahead of him. Rifles ready, faces set, grim. When the Kalmucks appeared over the crest, death would go on a rampage.

Rand turned to the younger Kalmuck, kneeling at his right.

"How many warriors think you are coming?"

The Kalmuck clenched and un-clenched his hands five times.

"Fifty?"

"Yes."

RAND SHOOK HIS head. He discarded his original hope—that enough Kalmucks might die when they came over the crest to cripple their force. Inducing the others, perhaps, to give up pursuit. Especially if their two leaders—Gurin and Agur—were among those killed. But fifty men cannot be annihilated by five—no matter how clever the ambush. Ten, maybe, fifteen, twenty. Still enough left to carry on.

The younger Kalmuck hissed softly. "They come."

Rand listened. Heard nothing. His ears weren't as acute as the native's. He gestured to the other men. Four rifle butts jerked to four shoulders.

"Not," he cautioned, "until I give command to fire."

Now other sounds disturbed the silence. Scrunching of snow beneath many feet. A guttural voice. A laugh.

And then the first line appeared over the crest. A dozen men, crouching forward, running swiftly on their snowshoes.

Amazingly, several seconds went by before the four kneeling men were noticed. Now a second line had come over the crest. One of the Kalmucks yelled shrilly, jerking around to unsling his rifle.

"Let 'em have it!" Rand shouted.

The four rifles cracked as one. Again. Still again. Twelve shots in three seconds—and at least eight men writhed on the snow. Murderous shooting. They kept it up. Firing quickly, yet with cold deliberation. Making every shot count.

The twin line of Kalmucks dissolved—as if struck by a tornado. Screaming men clawed the snow. Others stumbled over them—and died. The Kalmucks did not have a chance.

Nothing could withstand that steady, deliberate stream of lead.

The remaining handful alive made a dash for the crest—to run into the third line of Kalmucks, pressing forward, excited by the shooting. A mad confusion reigned. And ever the four worked the bolts and triggers of the hot rifles. And men continued to fall screaming, clawing the snow.

Rand saw Gurin's bulky figure in the second line. He was the last man on the right, tugging violently at the revolver on his hip. Rand swung the rifle around. With savage deliberation, he lingered, the Russian's broad chest clear in the sights. Then gently squeezed the trigger.

HE CURSED UNDER his breath. A Kalmuck, racing madly for safety back over the

A shallow gash ran across the right side of his forehead.

crest, lurched against the Russian. It cost him his life. Again Rand worked the bolt, pressed the trigger—the Russian's chest in the sights. A click—the hammer striking an empty shell.

Feverishly, Rand slipped a new clip in the magazine. Snapped back the plate. Worked the bolt. And jerked the rifle to his shoulder. Too late. The Russian had retreated beyond the safety of the crest—taking the last dozen feet in a magnificent dive. The remaining Kalmucks followed his example.

"Like the old days in France, eh?" Rand heard Swede's voice.

"I'll say!"

   THE BEST OF THRILLING ADVENTURES

At least a score of men lay dead or dying on the snow. Several of the wounded tried to crawl to safety. A single shot rang out. Another. A third. Kusslo's son finishing the wounded. Fierce exultation on the Kalmuck's face. A savage completing the kill.

Rand opened his mouth to stop him. Then shrugged. Too late. Besides, the wounded would have frozen to death anyway. The others would not pause to take care of them. Only death stops a savage on the blood trail.

He stood up.

"Let's go. A few minutes before they organize and rush us. Then it'll be with ready rifles. Which might mean another story. Come on!"

They ran after the sled. Every hundred yards, another man paused, keeping the rest covered against a rifleman crawling over the crest. None came, however. Not the Kalmuck style. Sneaking up on their victim in the dead of the night, then a long knife, burying into the enemy's throat, was more their way of fighting. MINUTE AFTER MINUTE they ran on the wide snowshoes, Rand in the lead, the others trailing single file. On both sides, the parallel ruts of the sled.

Rand knew that in addition to reducing the enemy's forces one half, they accomplished much more. Slowed up the pursuit. Taught the Kalmucks respect for the deadly efficiency of their rifles. They'd investigate now every possible place for ambush before venturing recklessly across it. A loss of time.

They soon sighted the sled. The old Kalmuck driving obeyed orders. He waved his whip triumphantly in reply to the shrill whoop from his son, but did not slow up. The girl, standing upright too, waved something white.

"Sayin' hello to me," said Swede, running alongside of Rand.

He flourished his rifle. The girl waved again, unmistakably in reply to his gesture. Swede smiled happily.

"Didn't I tell you?"

Rand frowned. The blond giant was a child. Rand had knocked around the world with him eight years. They were as close as only men could be who had time and again faced death together, who had saved each other's lives. Rand did not want to see him hurt. There was a look in Swede's eyes as he waved again to the girl he did not like—

CHAPTER VII

THE BLIZZARD

THE OLD KALMUCK stopped the sled. Rand ran toward him.

"It is a bad place to make camp," he said angrily.

"I do not stop to make camp," said Kusslo. "Look!"

Rand followed his outstretched hand. The old man was pointing northeast. Rand was puzzled for a moment. Then he understood. He hadn't noticed the black clouds. 'Way off on the horizon, they hung like a black pall. And even as he looked, Rand could see the black curtain spreading: ugly, sinister.

"Storm?" he asked quickly.

"Ay. Great wind pretty soon, and much snow."

"Good!" said Rand. "It will cover our tracks."

The old man shook his head.

"When the great wind come and the snow, men must find shelter. Or they die. Their faces turn black and they do not feel their fingers and the fingers of their feet, and soon they want to lie down on the snow and sleep. They never awaken."

"Isn't that sweet?" Rand murmured in English. He said, "Know you of shelter here?"

"The hunters make *kanus* in the summer—huts where a man may crawl in when the great wind comes. If we find one, we live. If none we see—" The Kalmuck shrugged.

He picked up the reins. The twenty-foot whip cracked. Again the sled lurched, creaked—and the runners sang on the snow. The trail again. But now an impending blizzard to face.

"Lady luck," Rand murmured whimsically, "smile. Boy, how we need you!"

The air began to rustle. Softly at first, then with an ever-increasing velocity. The Arctic wind, giving warning of the frozen hell to follow. The old man now lashed the ponies—skillful flicks of the long whip. The younger Kalmuck constantly veered off, now to the right, now to the left, like a bloodhound anxious to pick up a scent. Sometimes he would disappear for minutes at a stretch.

THE WIND BROUGHT a new sound. A sound incredibly lonely—a sound which made Rand's spine tingle. The howling of the wolves, greeting the coming of the storm. The enormous gray Siberian wolves. They were now entering their territory—the tundra stretches, the home of the reindeer.

The black pall spread. The sky adjoining it became murky gray. Swiftly, it grew darker. Still darker. And ever the wind increased in velocity.

Until it soon shrieked across the plains like a lost soul in torment. Until progress against it became a bitter fight.

It had scooped up tiny particles of ice in its mad dash across the snows; they lashed the skin like thousands of tiny needles, adhered to eyelashes, blinded.

"Ain't this fun?" Swede panted to Rand.

Rand smiled grimly.

Abruptly, came the snow, driven by the terrific wind. The world became a swirl of white madness. In five minutes, Rand knew, they would not be able to see ten feet ahead of them. In an hour, they would be frozen corpses. For the temperature had been dropping steadily, mercilessly.

The younger Kalmuck appeared suddenly out of a snow flurry. He waved his arms excitedly, then leaped to the center pony. Pulling its head down and to the left, he swung the sled off the trail. Fifty yards. Fifty more. He paused.

They were before a dome-like structure, low, squat, resembling a hillock of snow. Kusslo jumped out of the sled, and together they dug in the snow—fifteen feet or so away from the hillock. They lifted a square mat of woven branches. The old Kalmuck motioned to the black opening. His gesture unmistakable, it was the entrance to the dome-like structure—the entrance to a Kalmuck *kanu.*

THERE SEEMED DISAPPOINTMENT in the savage shriek of the wind.

Quickly, Kusslo threw the harnesses off the ponies. They lay down immediately, their tails to the wind. Again the old man pointed to the black opening.

Rand climbed in first. It was a six-foot well, at one side of which a narrow passage went off at right angles. He wriggled into it crawled forward on knees and elbows. Black darkness, but Rand guessed the construction of the *kanu.* The other end of the tunnel should lead into the hut itself.

It did. Rand crawled until he reached a step. He crossed it, raised his hand overhead. He found he could stand now. Hearing someone else crawling through the passage, he tore off his mittens and struck a match. It revealed Vera's lovely face, emerging from the black hole. It was gray with fright.

She scrambled to her feet. Threw her arms about Rand, forcing him to drop the match.

"It was a—a cold thing," she half-sobbed. "I could see its eyes. It crawled."

Her arms tightened about his neck. Rand felt her soft body against his. Inhaled the perfume of her hair. He crushed her in his arms.

SOMEONE ELSE, STRIKING a match. Swede O'Hara, looking at them, his eyes blue flame.

"First chance you got, eh?" he said softly.

Rand released the girl. He returned coldly the blond giant's glare.

"Grow up, you big sap! You're not a kid—the girl was frightened. Jealous, eh?"

Swede leaped forward. His big hands closed on Rand's throat.

"Well?" Rand said coolly. "Going to strangle me?"

He could have reached for his automatic. He didn't. Just stood there, waiting, bitterly wondering whether those fingers would squeeze. He was sick at heart. Buddies for eight years—

Swede stepped back.

"What's the matter?" Rand asked bitterly. "Didn't have the guts?"

The giant struck a match again, now touching the flame to the tip of a cigarette. His bronzed face was set, coldly expressionless. He did not answer.

The others now crawled through the opening—Pavlov, the two Kalmucks. The latter dragged in sacks of food and the rifles. Kusslo returned to close the surface opening.

Holed in now. For a day, three days, a week. Perhaps even longer. Depended upon how long the blizzard would rage. Suicide to venture out while it lasted.

Black darkness in the hut. Cold, yet a livable temperature. They made themselves comfortable on the earthen floor. No one spoke. Now they were conscious of fatigue. Could feel now the strain of those weary hours on the trail.

Rand sat with his back to the wall, listening to the wind howling outside. It fitted in with his mood—cold, savage. He could not forget the expression in

Swede's eyes. A woman had wrecked his life once. And now a woman had smashed a friendship of eight years' standing. Rand no longer cared whether he reached the whaler. Did not matter now. Nothing mattered any more.

His head dropped on his chest. Like slow poison, fatigue claimed his body. The howling of the wind became fainter, more distant. Rand slept.

He awakened several hours later, called out the old Kalmuck's name, and asked for the water canteen to be thrown over to him. He drank, smoked a cigarette, then went to sleep again. The wind still howled.

WHEN HE AWAKENED again, he felt fresh, rested. He lighted another cigarette, and heard the girl's voice.

"Can you spare one, please?"

"Yes," he replied.

He could hear her crawling toward him. He gave her a cigarette, lighted it. She curled up alongside of him. Rand wondered what Swede was thinking.

"I don't give a damn!" he said to himself, savagely.

CHAPTER VIII

MOCKING LAUGHTER

IT WAS ON the third day—so far as Rand could judge—that the wind ceased howling.

"Think you, Kusslo," he said to the Kalmuck, "it is safe now to make trail?"

"I do not know," replied the old man. "But my son shall be our eyes. Urlop!

Make a circle, as big across as a man can run in three hours. Perhaps Agur and his warriors perished in the great wind. Then you bring me his head, and it shall hang in our lodge."

The younger man replied a guttural assent. Rand heard him work his way through the passage, his trailing rifle bumping the walls.

"Will not the snow weigh the cover so that a man could not raise it?" he asked curiously.

"No, my friend. The wind is too great. It sweeps the snow. Never does it become deeper than the width of ten fingers."

Rand frowned. He'd imagined that the blizzard would bring snowfall of several feet deep, thus almost totally obliterating the huts. To get out, he thought they'd have to pierce the roof. But the width of ten fingers—six inches, perhaps—would still leave the huts in full sight. If the blizzard had already quieted sufficiently to permit the Kalmucks to take the trail, they could not help stumbling across them.

"And it's a cinch they'll take a look-see if we're in one of 'em," he said to himself. "Hell, we'll be caught like rats in a trap! Won't even have a chance to put up a scrap." The seed, once planted, took root, flourished. With each passing minute, Rand's nervousness increased. His jaw set grimly, he stared in the darkness. Death held no terror for him, but to be caught, helpless, in a black hole—

"Damn it," he said aloud abruptly, "the ponies!"

"What about the ponies?" Pavlov's voice questioned in the darkness.

"Nothing," Rand said shortly.

No use frightening the girl. Besides, the younger Kalmuck may return any moment now, with the happy news' that the coast was clear. That it was safe to venture out. Nevertheless, Rand could not stifle the thought of those ponies. On their feet probably now, sharp little hooves digging the snow for the green moss underneath. Their brown hides, against the white background, visible for miles literally. The Kalmucks had good eyes.

"Five minutes more " Rand said to himself, "then I'm getting out of here. I want a run for my money."

A sudden pounding on the side of the *kanu*. Rand leaped to his feet, his hand darting to the butt of his automatic. "What is that, Kusslo?"

"Urlop opening the wall door," the Kalmuck replied calmly. "Better so to get out. The storm is no more."

A LINE OF light now streaked horizontally across the side of the hut. Two more vertical lines. A two-foot square section, already cut out, was slowly being pushed into the interior of the hut. More and more light, harsh to the eyes used now to darkness. The section thudded to the floor. A square opening, like a rough window, through which they could see falling snow.

"Urlop!" the old Kalmuck called sharply. No answer. No one at the opening. A sinister silence.

"Urlop!" the old man repeated, his right hand reaching for the rifle against the wall.

Still silence. Then—laughter! Guttural laughter, swiftly increasing in volume as more and more men joined in. Mocking, savage laughter. The Kalmucks gloating over the capture.

Swede moved to the opening, rifle at his shoulder.

"Stand back!" Rand snapped. "You'll only get your fool head blown off."

Swede hesitated, stepped aside.

A SHARP COMMAND. The laughter ceased. Gurin's mocking voice.

"I think," he said, speaking in English, "we have reached the end of the trail—eh, Your Highness? Or, perhaps you *still* disagree?"

"My dead body is all that you shall have for your troubles," Pavlov replied quietly, picking up his rifle. "That what you seek you shall *not* get."

"You value your gold more than the life of your daughter?"

Pavlov glanced at the girl. She shook her head.

"You heard my answer," he said shortly. "I've nothing more to say."

A short pause. Then Gurin's voice again, coldly menacing.

"You're a stubborn devil, old man; I give you a last chance to reconsider. If you're putting up a bluff, let me remind you that the five of you haven't a chance. I command to fire through the walls of the *kanu*. Thirty rifles. It wouldn't take long."

"You have heard my answer, Gurin!" the old man repeated.

Silence for a moment. A muffled command. Then a terrific volley. Thirty fingers touching the triggers of thirty rifles. Mad splintering of wood, flying earth. Six feet above, the level of the earthen floor, light streamed through dozens of jagged edged holes ripped through by the heavy slugs.

"That," said Gurin, "will give you an idea. For the last time—reconsider! Tell me where the treasure is buried—your word is sufficient—and you shall be set free. At liberty to go where you please. You and Vera. She is too beautiful to die beneath Kalmuck rifles!" he added dramatically.

"What about the others?"

"This is out of my hands. The two Americans have killed Kiok—and many more. Their lives belong to the Kalmucks. They will be tortured, and I shall contribute to that of the big one. The two renegades from the tribe shall, too, feel the bite of hot iron. Why should their fate concern you?"

Pavlov looked around the hut. His eyes passed from face to face. They lingered on his daughter's. She shook her head.

"No, damn you!" he shouted savagely.

Gurin cursed. "Very well; I've given you your choice."

"Down!" Rand whispered. "Quick!"

He dropped to the earthen floor, the others following his example. As he lay there, Rand was conscious of the futility of it. Sooner or later, the hungry bullets would find their targets.

They waited—awaited the hail of death.

SECONDS DRAGGED. WITHOUT—SILENCE! Heavy silence, tense, sinister.

"Well," Rand thought fiercely, "what the hell are they waiting for?"

Now he heard a murmur of voices. Gurin's guttural laugh. His voice, audible now to those within the *kanu*.

"Well spoken, Agur. Bullets *do* kill quickly, and lack the thrill of slow torture." He raised his voice. "Pavlov!"

"Yes?"

"Agur has just made a suggestion—splendid suggestion," Gurin drawled, speaking in English now. "Your food is in the sled. Time isn't pressing. I'm curious whether the sight of lovely Vera dying of starvation may change your mind." He laughed again.

Rand understood the Russian's motive. Pavlov's death in itself was little compensation for his troubles; above all, he wanted the location of the treasure. He now hoped that the suffering of the girl might induce the stubborn old man to give in.

THE KALMUCKS HAD another motive. The bodies of those in the *kanu*, riddled with bullets, did not interest them. The same bodies, lashed to the torture stakes, did.

A cruel bunch of devils, they would delight in squatting on their haunches, watching the kanu. Knowing that those in it were slowly dying of starvation. Knowing that sooner or later their bodies would be too weak to offer resistance—too weak to lift the deadly rifles. Then—capture! Live bodies to feel the bite of hot iron. The savage has patience. "Hell!" said Rand. "Like rats in a trap."

A mad fury possessed him. He snatched his rifle, crept to the opening. A sudden thought arrested him. Sanity crept back into his eyes. Hope. He remembered Urlop, the old Kalmuck's son. Gurin had said, "The five of you." Didn't know, then, the younger Kalmuck was not in the hut. Still snowing. It had covered his tracks. The young Kalmuck was out there somewhere. Free! Gurin and his gang could not possibly expect outside help for those within the hut. Hence would be off their guard. Urlop had courage and brains.

"Our last chance!" Rand said slowly. "Our *only* chance!"

CHAPTER IX

TENSE MOMENTS

DARKNESS SLOWLY CLAIMED the day— the long Arctic night, jealous of the few hours of light. Rand stood to the right of the opening, hugging the wall. Outside, he knew, a guard squatted on his haunches, rifle across his lap.

Rand had heard Agur's instruction to the guard. They were curt, grimly eloquent. Shoot first—investigate afterward. Shoot at the first suspicious move. His own life would pay for the escape of the captives.

"Under torture!" Gurin had added.

Cautiously, Rand looked out. The guard jerked up his rifle. Cold warning in the slanted eyes. Rand withdrew his head. He might have shot the guard. A snap shot with the automatic. But they had nothing to gain from the death of one man. The next would simply be more cautious. A sense of failure, of defeat now gnawed at Rand's heart.

Hours now since their capture. Weary hours, waiting, hoping. And still no sign of the younger Kalmuck.

The young tribesman may be in the neighborhood somewhere, waiting. Waiting with the patience of a savage for an opportunity to creep into the camp. A logical explanation. But equally logical was Rand's growing conviction that the Kalmuck had turned back when he saw the capture of the others. Turned back to save his own skin.

Swift Arctic twilight passed, leaving blackness. Several hours yet before the sky would blaze with the glory of the Arctic night. A prolonged, dismal howl somewhere in the distance. The gray wolf greeting the night.

The sound grew louder, louder, raising the dog-hair on Rand's back. The leaders calling the pack together. If luck was with them, by morning they would taste the lifeblood of some stray reindeer.

In the complete darkness within the hut Rand found he could peer out of the opening now without being seen by the guard.

At the left, the Kalmucks slept around the huge fire built from one of the *kanus*. THE HOWLING OF the wolves did not disturb them. They lay there, dark patches on the white expanse of the night. Half-buried in the snow, which still fell gently. Like the shaggy little ponies. And as comfortable.

Rand's mind drifted. He wondered where the Kalmucks had found shelter during the blizzard. Would Kusslo's son come? What will be Pavlov's final answer?

He thought of the girl, and cursed under his breath. Poor kid! Born the daughter of the Grand Duke Feodor, with everything the world had to offer at her feet. Only to find death on lonely Siberian steppes. Snow, ice. Bleakness. Poor kid!

His body tensed. He thought he saw a shadow behind the guard. A black figure, coming around the side of the *kanu*. It was Urlop, long knife in his right hand. He paused over the squatting guard. Rand saw the knife in Urlop's hand swoop downward. In—in to the hilt in the Kalmuck's throat. A sighing sound—so soft that Rand, who expected it, barely heard it. The guard slumped forward.

Urlop grinned, showing his white teeth. He motioned Rand to come out.

Rand crawled out. Stood on the snow now, caressing his rifle. A fierce exultation possessed him. Go down fighting—that's the way a man ought to die.

"And still," he said to himself, "while there's life there's hope. Still a chance—"

The others now stood behind him— Swede, Pavlov, the two Kalmucks, the girl. Faces grimly determined, resolute. Rand sensed their acceptance of his leadership. They were awaiting his commands.

The Kalmucks around the fire slept on their rifles. Peaceful enough now. But let one awaken. A cry of alarm, a shot—and hell would break loose!

Rand's eyes failed to see Gurin or the chieftain. They probably slept in one of the *kanus*. Kusslo nudged him.

"We go with our knives, my son and I," the old man whispered. "We kill with the silence of the wolf."

Rand frowned, shook his head. Thirty men cannot be knifed, one after another, without at least one giving the alarm before he died. And savages awake like animals, alert, instantly in full possession of the senses.

RAND'S BRAIN RACED. Attack the Kalmucks now, while they slept? Kill as many as they could—and then make a run for it? He decided against it. The odds were too great. For open fighting anyway. An ambush, perhaps, later on. Further north, where the country became rough, rocky. They'd have more of a chance.

"Think you, Kusslo," he whispered to the Kalmuck, "you can get the ponies up without awakening the men around the fire?"

"Yes," the Kalmuck replied promptly. "They will recognize their master."

"You are sure?" Rand insisted.

"Ay, that I am!"

Rand's hands gripped tighter the rifle. "Let's go!" he hissed to the others. He strapped on his snowshoes, padded softly out of the *kanu*, stepping over the guard's dead body. The others followed, their wide-webbed Kalmuck snowshoes making no sound on the soft snow.

Rand led to the left, skirting the ring around the fire as widely as he dared without wasting precious time. They paused at the sled, half-buried in the snow. Swede lowered his rifle. Bent down. His big hands gripped the cross bar between the two runners. He pulled upward. Again. The frozen runners came loose.

RAND WHIRLED TO the fire, rifle butt at his shoulder, his heart pounding. There had been some noise. But the men around the fire, their bodies weary from the long hours on the trail, slept.

Now Kusslo and his son moved toward the dark patches on the snow which marked the ponies. They bent over them, their hands stroking the shaggy hides. The ponies stirred, stood up. Quietly permitted themselves to be led. Sweat poured down Rand's face.

He didn't think the trick could be done.

He motioned Swede to pick up the loose traces. Pavlov helped in the rear. Foot by foot, they slowly moved the sled. Further and further away from the fire. Twenty feet, fifty feet, fifty yards. They paused.

The two Kalmucks leading the ponies joined them.

They worked quickly, efficiently. In sixty seconds the ponies were hitched to the sled, ready to take the trail.

Kusslo threw back and over the hide covering the sled. Leaned over, fumbling with something at the bottom of the sled. Rand waved his hand impatiently. Time was precious.

The Kalmuck grinned. He straightened, holding a large leather water bottle. He grinned again, turned—and Rand almost cried out. The old man was padding softly toward the ring of men around the fire.

Rand cursed, softly but with a terrible intensity. What was the old fool up to?

They hadn't a moment to waste—and to take that frightful risk! He moved after him, then stopped. Impossible to head him off now without awakening the devils around the fire.

Now a dozen feet from the sleeping men, the Kalmuck stopped. Rand saw him pick up a long wooden pole, used in the construction of the *kanus*. Kusslo lashed the bottle to the forked end of the pole. He approached closer the circle of men. Swung the pole around and over them. Then, moving very slowly, he proceeded to spill a few drops of the liquid in the bottle upon the snowshoes of every fifth man or so as he went around the circle.

Took time to complete that circle— and Rand, in his mind, a dozen times strangled the old man. "Medicine water" probably in that bottle. Given the superstitious native by the local *shaman*.

"Supposed to lead astray the feet of the enemy," Rand guessed, grinning wryly. "Magic water. And the old fool has enough faith in it to risk his neck—and everyone else's." He shook his head.

KUSSLO COMPLETED THE circle. He moved toward the *kanu* where the others slept. He spilled more of the liquid beneath the opening. It made a huge brown stain on the snow. Rand breathed easier when, still grinning, the old man returned to the sled.

"You are very lucky, Kusslo," he whispered fiercely. "You are also an old fool! Come! Already death has shown too much patience."

The grin remained on the old man's lips.

"I know what I am doing, my friend. You will understand later. And then you will say that Kusslo is a man of much wisdom."

"Yes," Rand repeated bitterly pointing—"of much wisdom!"

One of the Kalmucks at the fire sat up. Stared at them now. A shrill cry of alarm lingered for a moment in the still air. Ceased as the bullet in Swede's rifle found the Kalmuck's heart.

"Get going!" Rand yelled savagely, unconscious that he spoke in English. The twenty-foot whip cracked. The sled lurched off.

"A man of much wisdom!" Rand panted, running behind it. "Hell!"

CHAPTER X

THE HOWLING WOLVES

KUSSLO DROVE THE ponies to the right. There the land dipped sharply. They were over it, running madly down the incline before the Kalmucks had a chance to open fire.

Constantly the long whip lashed the backs of the ponies, driving them at a killing pace that Rand knew they could not keep up much longer. The snow was too soft.

And then Rand saw the old Kalmuck's object. In a few minutes they were on the bed of a frozen creek. The terrific wind had swept it clean of snow. Hard surface for the sharp little hooves of the ponies. Not too slippery—and the shaggy little animals were as sure-footed as cats. Here they could easily outdistance running men.

But Rand noticed something else. The creek winded like a huge snake. Sticking to its bed, they were forced to travel fully half as much again as their pursuers, who could easily cut across every loop. Only a matter of time. An hour, two, three. Then they'd be surrounded, forced to fight it out.

He shrugged. The pace the old Kalmuck had set up forbade thinking. He devoted his attention to the trail.

A new sound now, too, to occupy the mind. The howling of the wolves. Faint, at first, then louder and louder. And then Rand began to see the gray forms running swiftly through the darkness. Now on their right, now on their left. Huge, gaunt gray forms. The Siberian gray wolf, who with a single slash of his fangs can rip the throat of a three-hundred pound reindeer. The largest, the most vicious of the breed. Kusslo no longer had to use the whip on the ponies. The gray shapes were sufficient impetus for speed.

A cold hand suddenly gripped Rand's heart, squeezed. For the howling of the wolves abruptly took a new note. First, at the right—a volume of sound which seemed to increase every second. Madness now in the howling of the wolves. It spread. Now at the right. Now in back of them.

"God Almighty!" Rand whispered. "There are thousands of them!"

AS HE RAN he unslung the rifle. But the gray shapes on either side had disappeared. Rand thought he had the explanation. A herd of reindeer picked up by one of the packs. The others rushing back to be in on the kill.

Kusslo abruptly swung the sled to the right. Off the bed of the creek, on a tiny clearing, backed by a huge wall of a granite cliff. He stopped the trembling ponies, leaped out of the sled. He gripped Rand's arm. "You shall see," he shouted. "You shall see if Kusslo is a man of wisdom."

The mad howling came closer and closer. Berserk madness in it. Not just howling. The wolves had gone mad! Rand dropped on one knee, raised the rifle. Kusslo nudged him.

"No," he said, shaking his head. "They shall not harm us."

"What do you mean?" Rand snapped.

"Wait! You shall see."

SHOTS NOW MINGLED with the mad howling of the wolves. Rapid fire. Rifles emptied quickly. And then a grim tableau abruptly unfolded itself at their left. From around the bend of the creek a dozen Kalmucks came running. Running swiftly. And running still more swiftly, scores of gray shapes came hurling around the bend.

The Kalmucks stopped, turned. They had time for one volley. Then the wolves were upon them. It was over in two seconds. Gaunt gray bodies leaping through the air. White fangs slashing. A man's piercing scream. Then a horrible snarling. A fight for the meat. The kill was over.

The gray bodies paused motionless as fresh howling came from the left somewhere. They joined it, racing madly through the night.

"Let me see that bottle!" Rand said suddenly, turning to the old Kalmuck. Kusslo nodded.

"I think my friend is beginning to understand."

He walked to the sled, found the leather bottle, threw it to Rand. Rand jerked out the stopper. He poured a bit of the liquid on the palm of his hand, smelled it. He wiped his hand on his trousers and threw the bottle back to Kusslo.

"Yes," he said quietly, "I'm beginning to understand. Kusslo *is* a man of much wisdom, and deserves to be chief of his people."

"In Heaven's name," cried Pavlov, "what happened? What was in that bottle?" Rand smiled.

"An old trick—though I doubt whether it has ever been used for *this* purpose. That bottle contained alcoholic liquid that has the scent of a she-wolf mixed with it. Trappers sprinkle some of that liquid on a rag and make a trail by dragging it several hundred yards. At the end of the trail, they set a trap. Any wolf which crosses it will instantly follow that trail—but no longer cautious. And invariably he'll be caught in the trap."

"I see," Pavlov said grimly.

"It isn't difficult to understand. A number of the Kalmucks had that scent on their snowshoes. Taking constant shortcuts to catch up with us, they'd left these trails for miles. Wolves—as most wild beasts—have an instinctive fear of man; but the Kalmucks carried with them the scent of a she-wolf. These wolves were pretty damn hungry. So— well, you've seen what happened."

"Which means," said Pavlov, "that—"

"That nothing stands now between you and the coast," Rand said coldly. "We'll reach it in two days."

PAVLOV SAT DOWN on the edge of the sled. He twisted his fingers.

"I am not a religious man, but—thank God! Liberty—life!"

"Thank Kusslo here," Rand said curtly. "All right, let's get started. May as well get it over with."

He glanced at Swede. The blond giant had one arm around the girl. Her head on his chest. She was crying. "Come on!" Rand shouted savagely. "Let's go!"

Again the runners sang on the snow. One by one, miles slipped by. Rand ran behind the sled, his eyes down on the trail ahead of him. Looking up occasionally he would see Swede's broad back ahead of him.

"Now why," he asked himself fiercely, "should I give a damn? The hell with the big dumb palooka!"

They paused twice for food and a few hours of sleep.

"Not far now," Kusslo said, grinning triumphantly.

It failed to thrill Rand.

SIX HOURS LATER, the old Kalmuck stood up in the sled waving his long whip. He pointed. Rand, who had fallen behind, caught up with the sled. He followed the direction of the pointing whip.

A long, white incline. The ocean where it ended. And to the right, resembling a child's toy ship, three masts of a schooner. The trail's end!

Men came to meet them long before they reached the schooner. Men who embraced Pavlov, carried him on their shoulders. Rand lingered behind and spoke to Kusslo. He shook his head when the captain invited him aboard. "A little later—maybe."

The Russian captain looked at him curiously, shrugged and returned to the others, waiting at the dory drawn up on the icy beach.

Rand motioned to the Kalmuck. Kusslo cracked his whip. And then Swede came running, waving his arms wildly. At a command from Rand, the Kalmuck stopped the ponies. Rand waited.

"Well?" he said coldly when Swede approached him.

The blond giant hesitated.

"I—I just got a kind of a present from Vera." He opened his clenched right hand. "These are black pearls, perfectly matched, and worth maybe ten grand." Rand glanced at the treasure on Swede's broad palm.

"They're worth a damn sight more than ten grand," he said curtly. "Well, what about them?"

"Half of 'em is yours, ain't it?"

"Not if it's the little girl's dowry," Rand drawled.

Swede stared at him.

"Dowry? What the hell!"

"Isn't it?"

"No!" Swede exploded. "It's a gift, I tell you. From the girl. The old man will have a hundred grand credited to our account at the Bank of France in Paris as soon as his stuff is smuggled out to him. I gave him our names."

"That's swell," said Rand. "Well—I'll be seeing you!"

Swede clenched his big fists, un-clenched them slowly.

"I'm goin' to bawl," he said. "If you don't stop it, I'm goin' to bawl like hell. Where you goin'?"

"I made arrangements with Kusslo to drive me to Turukhansk, on the Yenisei," Rand replied coolly. "Then, I guess, I'll drift into China. A swell revolution going on there now—and I know just the boys to approach."

"Good," said Swede. "They'll be tickled pink to get a couple of airmen."

RAND SHRUGGED. "MAYBE. I'll write you a letter."

"*Will* you stop it?" Swede said fierce-ly. "You know that when it comes to usin' my head, I just *ain't!* Listen, kid! How's chances o' me-kinda—well, kinda comin' along?"

Rand smiled happily.

"You're a damn nuisance, you big palooka, but—I guess so! It'll be a few months before we can start spending those hundred grand. In the mean-while—I heard it's a *swell* revolution."

Dogs of Shallajai

BY LIEUT. SCOTT MORGAN

A Pulse-Stirring Drama of Flailing Fists and Savage Foes in the Peril-Packed Wastelands of the Gobi

CHAPTER I

SINISTER WARNING

THE CHINESE GENERAL who commanded the Beiping garrison was visibly trembling. And there was plenty of reason. For he looked down into the stark dead face of the general to whom he had intended reporting. The dead man's throat had been cut from ear to ear. On his chest was a piece of thin rice paper upon which Chinese characters had been done in red paint.

General Hsa Lo Pe had just translated those characters for the benefit of the languid appearing young American adventurer to whom he intended entrusting the most important—to the general—mission of his career. The general's life hung on the success of that mission. He had just told Larry Weston, free lance of fortune, the meaning of the characters: "This is the Ta Kuei's vengeance. Let all other tyrants beware!"

Larry Weston flicked his trousers leg with his cane—inside which was a razor sharp sword.

"And you were saying what, about

the Ta Kuei, that it can have no real connection with this murder?"

"Just that. Our enemies, whom all the world knows, are using other means to bring China to their feet—a reign of terror. General Ya Che is the first to be murdered.

"THERE WILL BE many others, of that I am sure. The warning shows it. I may be next. High officials at Nanking may be next. We may all go at once, as this officer went. And not even the boldest newspaper in the world would dare lay the blame at the doors of our enemy. Why? Because it is so obviously the work of the Ta Kuei."

"Just what, may I ask, is or are the Ta Kuei?"

Hsa Lo Pe shrugged.

"Nothing more than a Mongolian religious dance! How can a dance have anything to do with this?"

"Maybe little, maybe much," said Larry Weston softly. "The dancers in this particular ceremony, if I know anything of your more uncivilized compatriots, will all be masked?"

"Of course."

"And anybody can hide behind a mask!"

"Quite right. You can't tell Mongol women from men. Matter of fact, they are often stronger, greater fighters than men. And they are big people.

"Whoever hides behind their masks, to take part in the ceremony, must be big, too. Smaller men would be instant-ly discovered. The dance this year, as usual, will be held in the very shadow of Bogdo-Ula, near Urga—and for an outsider even to look at the ceremony may mean death."

Weston leaned toward the frightened general.

"You have your suspicions? You have some idea of the identity of the man or men who did this?"

Hsa Lo Pe looked around as though he feared that the walls had ears. Then he whispered to Larry Weston.

"I know of a professional killer, who understands all the arts of the dacoits of India. Nobody knows the number of his kills. He is highly paid, and he commits murder as other men take on an ordinary task for pay. The identity of his victims mean nothing.

"He would even slay his most recent employer if another were found who would pay him more.

"I KNOW ALL this because Ya Che left me a note. I found it in a desk. He expected something like this, which is why he sent for me, instructing me to bring you with me if you were in Beiping. In the note was a name, and a description. The name means nothing. The killer may have many names. But his descrip-tion is something else again. He has saber scars on his face, relics I think, of Heidelberg, but the name he is last known to have used scarcely suggests Heidelberg. It is—Sergei Popov."

Larry Weston sucked in his breath at the sound of the name. He had heard it several times in his life. He had heard it whispered in the secret councils of the Lo Chang of Tibet. He had heard it among the Goloks of the high plateaus, in Manchuria and Korea, wherever in the Orient his adventurous feet had led him. A dread name. The name of a man no single man could destroy, a man who had outwitted a myriad of would-be nemeses.

"The use of the name of the Ta Kuei is a challenge," said Weston. "At least that's my hunch, and I always play my hunches. I'm taking on the job of getting this Popov. Tell me more about him."

Hsa Lo Pe complied, ending with the ominous statement:

IF HE HAS taken up with the Mongols, which he might well do since he is known to have a weakness for Oriental women, he will have their power behind him. And that can be terrible. Have you ever heard of the dogs of Shallajai?"

Weston nodded grimly.

"They are tough to handle if a man is thrown to them, bound and gagged, with broken arms and legs, or even if he is merely turned loose on the desert among them."

"I'll take my chances," said Weston. "You will deposit ten thousand dollars to my credit in the Bank of Taiwan at Shanghai?"

"Of course."

"Thanks," said Weston, grinning, "it won't be necessary. I just wanted to see if you would haggle. That you don't proves your sincerity. I don't do this sort of thing for money. I do it because I like adventure—and hate cold blooded murderers. Besides, I have a crow to pick with this Sergei Popov. I'll be on my way. Keep your nose clean!"

From the shadows at the foot of Bog-do-Ula, Larry Weston, whom not even his friend would have recognized as Weston, stared out at the weird dance of the Ta Kuei, where Mongol men and women moved slowly and sinuously, not particularly gracefully or beautifully, to the strains of weird Mongolian music.

There was hell in the strange dance— hell and death and murder, though on the surface the dance was one which honored the Living God, the Dalai Lama, worshiped in the flesh by the Mongols of Urga and the surrounding desert.

During the day outsiders had been admitted to the dance, but they had gone with the setting of the sun and the real orgy began. Over the place of the dance rose the stench of unwashed bodies, of skin clothing—for the Mongol seldom bathed and wore his clothing until it rotted from his body. When this last occurred he merely donned a new robe over the old one and waited for the old one to fall apart inside the new one.

Weston tried to distinguish men from women, but found it impossible. He knew that the average Mongol woman was the match for almost any man at rough and tumble, that they were without fear in the usual sense, without morals of any kind, and even looked like men when their faces were exposed—hard, cruel women who asked no odds of any man they didn't make themselves.

IF LARRY WERE discovered here he would be torn to pieces. He knew that he walked close to death. But he wasn't afraid. A thrill of anticipatory excitement went through him.

Hell would doubtless break loose if he

     THE BEST OF THRILLING ADVENTURES

The dogs came out of the shadows, circled the fighters.

were discovered; but somewhere among all the dancers, he was sure, was the man known as Sergei Popov—for the man followed such rituals as these for a purpose: such dances always brought to view the wealth, in jewels and precious stones, of the dancers. And Mongol women—all Mongols were rich—wore their wealth upon their persons. It would take a man with courage to try to steal from the Mongols, but Sergei Popov, by reputation at least, had no fear in him.

Larry Weston, his last work completed on his Mongol dress, straightened. One could never have told him from a Mongol woman, from a Ta Kuei dancer.

There was one thing. He did not know the ritual or the responses, and few words of their dialect. But there would be ways of getting around that, he was sure. He never doubted the surety of his own native wit.

He rose, sauntered toward the place of the dance, down a narrow path which led from somewhere in the heart of Bogdo-Ula. It was no difficult matter to get into the place, for couples were constantly entering and leaving.

The jungles all about the depression in which the dance was held were given over to secrets at which he could guess with little trouble. A haven of opportunity for a man like Sergei Popov.

A man came out of the woods to Larry's right, stumbled down the trail as one far gone in liquor. He was alone. Larry darted aside, into the woods whence the man had come... and found, just off the trail, a Mongol woman, stripped of her wealth, dead, with her throat cut from ear to ear.

Sergei Popov was busy, it seemed! And he had just seen his quarry. Quickly Larry retraced his steps, knowing there was nothing he could do for the woman; that if he were caught near her, he would be accused and destroyed without a hearing.

He all but overtook the tall man at the edge of the dancing space, was so close to him that it would seem the two had returned together to the dance.

LOUD OVER THE place rose the wails and cries of the dancers, which sounded like those of souls in torment. Torsos and hips moved to the strains of hellish music. Faces were covered by hideous masks set in satanic smiles that never changed—huge heads, bulbous noses, earless horrors, the faces of animals such as had never walked on the face of the earth, faces born of the nightmares of mask-making artisans whose brains must have crawled with the maggots of insanity.

Weston's own mask was a devil's head, with short horns and a fixed leer meant for a smile. He had attained it in Beiping, from a temple at the foot of the Western Hills, in the shadow of the Temple of Azure Clouds. There were others here so nearly like it that he knew it would pass muster.

BUT HE MUST make no mistake. He must unmask his man and get him away alive, killing him only if it were absolutely necessary. He had no compunction about killing the man, none whatever. He was so many times a murderer that death constituted but slight punishment.

If for nothing more than his latest killing, done in cold blood on a woman who had been too kind and careless and for the sake of her trinkets, Sergei Popov merited torture and death. Weston didn't go in for torture, but if he were to take the man back to the tender mercies of Hsa Lo Pe—

He tried to imitate the movements of the dance, thankful for a photographic memory. But through the eye slits in his mask he kept his gaze on the man he had followed out of the shadows under Bogdo-Ula.

He edged his way through the half-crazed devotees, inching his way toward the killer who was one with the dancers of Ta Kuei. Closer and closer he came, making plans as he went.

One swift blow to the button, and he would grab his man and try to get away with him, trusting to the suddenness of his action to stun the dancers and give him a few seconds of grace.

The killer's face was covered by the usual devil's mask, and he was taking a chance that the man upon whom his attentions were centered was not the right man—but even as he reached him, the man lifted his hand, moved aside his mask —and Larry Weston saw a white face underneath, scored by saber scars—the face of Sergei Popov!

CHAPTER II

TERROR BY NIGHT

THEN LARRY WESTON moved. He never believed in waiting. There seemed no possibility that he could lose. His next move would be dictated entirely by what transpired after the blow was struck. He knew it would have to be a terrific blow, for Sergei Popov was supposed to have a jaw of iron, had in fact once been a fighter of some note. But even the hardest-jawed man would drop if belted by Larry Weston, when he did not expect a blow. The end justified the means.

So Larry faced his quarry and swung a wicked right to the man's jaw, aiming to strike just below the devil mask. His aim was true. His fist spatted against the flesh, and instantly he knew that he had made a mistake. Fist against flesh did not sound or feel like fist against flesh.

The man dropped with a sigh—his devil mask rolled off. The face of "Sergei Popov" also rolled off, to disclose itself as a flesh mask in the form and fashion of the man Weston sought, while under it was the brown skin of a Mongol!

The music stopped with a weird shrieking. The dancers paused in whatever postures the happening found them. A woman, in the midst of the dance, had struck a man with her fist and knocked him out.

Mongols did not, necessarily, use their fists. They wrestled their opponents down, broke their backs, ripped out their eyes, or mangled them in other ways.

So the savage blow was in itself a give-away. And a man's voice lifted in a sudden burst of dialect. Larry could understand no word—but when, immediately after the words were spoken, they came in English, he knew that he had been unmasked.

"It is not a woman, but a man, a foreigner—and a spy! Take him!"

For a brief moment Larry was bewildered. It flashed across his mind that the man he had knocked out had some connection with Sergei Popov. Popov, expecting pursuit, had laid his plans carefully.

He must have guessed that someone would be sent against him, who would seek him out among the dancers, and so had merely used a killer, instructed him in his own methods, and an innocent Mongol woman, avid for forbidden adventure—only it was not forbidden among Mongols—had paid for curiosity anent a stalwart stranger. Larry was only sorry that his blow had not been brutal enough to cause death.

HIS HANDS WENT to his garments, which had been constructed for just this emergency. In a thrice the clothing of Mongolia slipped from him, leaving him in nondescript khaki, with the remnants of "Ta Kuei" in folds about his feet.

His devil mask he did not remove for a moment. As well keep his identity secret for a time. They already knew he was a foreigner and that could not be hidden.

And now a high cry rose from the Mongols. He understood no word, but menace has a tone which is unmistakable, no matter in what language it be couched.

There was a surging among the dancers. The voice rose again, even as Weston hesitated for a moment, seeking among the Mongols for the man who had shouted in English—which not one in a hundred of the Mongols would understand.

The shouter had depended on the drama about Larry Weston to hide the fact that he too was a foreigner. Besides, he probably had privileges among the Mongols. Sergei Popov had, and the speaker had probably been the slayer Larry Weston wished to lay by the heels.

They hurled themselves at him then, as though a command had been given—which it had—as though all had been puppets pulled by strings in the hands of a single prompter. There was no fear in them.

Gleaming blades appeared from under the weird garments of the devotees, eager all of them to wipe out the sacrilege which the presence of Larry Weston had brought to Bogdo-Ula, the sacred mountain.

Larry darted away, knowing that his chances were very slight. Out here in the open every Mongol knew the lay of the land better than Weston could possibly know it. He would be tracked down. They were too many for him, would tear him limb from limb. But back among the buildings of Urga— THAT WAS THE place. It was a long race, in which he would compete with running men and men on fleet Mongol ponies, but for the moment he had his freedom and felt reasonably sure of keeping it.

He plunged into the woods, while the crashing of brush behind him told him that the Mongols were in swift pursuit, their knives eager for the taste of his blood.

He did not think of himself as running away, but only as picking the place of combat. He was thankful beyond measure for the fact that he always kept himself in the best possible physical condition.

He ran with the fleetness of a deer. The shout rose again. He didn't understand, but the resultant sounds, the cries of the devotees told him what was happening. While the first pursuers were beating the bushes for him, riders were racing for their horses to surround the woods and catch him if he came out. HE TURNED ASIDE, determined to keep to the edge of the woods, to break from cover at the first opportunity. His hands were before his face, so that he should not knock his brains out against the harsh bolls of trees. He hurled aside the devil mask with a sigh of relief.

A huge form came at him suddenly— two of them—he knew that one was a man, one a woman, whom he had all but surprised in the shadows. They had understood the cries from the clearing, knew that a defiler had been unmasked in the shadow of Bogdo-Ula.

Weston scarcely paused in his running. His left went to the face of one.

He crossed his right even as the one fell—and he didn't know whether it was the man or the woman. The second one—here he did not pause either.

He lowered his head and smashed with all his weight, straight into midriff of his enemy. Both were down, groaning. One was unconscious from his blows. And now a voice pursued him, again in English. He appreciated the guile of the man—whose words could well be taken for those of the man they pursued.

"Hsa Lo Pe chooses his men with little care! You must know that there is no chance for you!"

Larry Weston did not answer. There were too many beaters back whence the voice had come for him to await the arrival of the shouter. Better try the old Roman trick of scattering his enemies and defeating them in detail.

He ran on. Loud now over the other sounds, rose the stampeding noise of racing horses. The riders of Mongolia were on the way. Scores of horses were in pursuit, scouring the edge of the woods.

Larry kept close to the fringe, racing in the general direction of Urga. Horses passed him, so close he could have seen, almost touched them, had it not been for the woods. He must distance his pursuers on foot a bit further before he made his next move.

He increased his stride, held his racing speed for five minutes. He guessed that he had traveled all of a mile. To his left were still the sounds of many horses, the shouts of men and women who thought they had discovered him among the shadows.

He broke from cover, hiding in the darkness. Out across a plain he could see the horsemen, fantastic figures under a pale moon. Many dashed back and forth, covering every inch of the woods. One must eventually come close to the edge of the woods where he stood.

A horse shied away, smelling him. The rider, understanding that something was amiss, whirled the animal on a dime, lifted a gleaming weapon to strike out among the shadows. And Larry Weston moved.

IT WASN'T EASY to reach a Mongolian pony, but the animal was held in tight rein by its rider, which gave Larry Weston his chance. With a single leap, arms flung wide, he got his hands on the rider, used the man—or woman—as a lever by which to vault atop the animal behind the rider.

This done, so quickly that none of the other riders could have seen exactly what had happened, Larry did two things—he snatched the weapon, a gleaming short sword, from the hand of his adversary, and knocked that one from the horse with a savage blow behind the ear.

Then he set himself the task of handling the horse. Fortunately it was already headed toward Urga, and in its maddened fear it had the winged feet of Pegasus. It was away like the wind, running low with its belly to the ground.

Larry leaned over the animal's neck, urging it to speed and more speed. Behind him rose a thin wailing cry, and he knew that his recent adversary had given the alarm.

He looked back. Shouts followed him, shouts which the horse understood, for it hesitated a moment in its stride, as though to slow down, or turn back in answer.

LARRY HATED TO do what he next did, but between cruelty to an animal and his own life there could be no hesitation as to choice. He pressed the point of his sword against the animal's rump. The brute squealed with pain and surprise—and was again in headlong gallop toward Urga.

His pursuers, some of them, were bunched behind him and coming on like the wind. Others, on fleeter horses, were swinging away to the left, as though to pass and head him off.

Grimly he set his teeth. His lips were a firm straight line, his eyes glowing with excitement. He held the sword point against the animal, and the little brute responded with alacrity. Speed—speed—the sandy plain rolled behind him like a gray sea.

The pursuers were not gaining, he noticed when he looked back—but the swift outriders were distancing him. If they closed before he reached the doors of Urga, he was done; but they wouldn't, he promised himself that.

Rifles spoke behind him and from the flank, but their noise only served to make the horse travel faster, when already it seemed strained to the limit of its endurance.

Now ahead he could see the sullen lights of Urga, obscured by a strange sort of haze. His heart jumped, for he knew the meaning of that haze—that the winds across the Gobi had turned in the direction of Urga, lifting sand from the face of the ancient desert.

In a matter of hours a sandstorm could rise which would blot out the heavens and the stars, and lash the skin from the bodies of men. But such a storm would be a godsend to Larry Weston. He was glad that they were a frequent occurrence at Urga.

Closer and closer came the houses of Urga. Closer came his pursuers and the riders on the flank. He could see that they would all reach the town's outskirts at almost the same time.

And several times he had heard a shout in English which told him that Sergei Popov was among his pursuers.

That was as it should be, exactly what he wanted, so that events might shape themselves, or be shaped by him, to his advantage. Nothing pleased him more than to match wits and brawn with real fighters.

JUST AS HE would have swung into the first street which came under his eyes; just as his horse staggered with fatigue, the Mongols closed on him from the side—and his short-sword swung aloft in his hard hand, swung up—and down, and a man toppled from a horse with a thin cry. Another charged in.

Again Larry tried to use his sword, but it was knocked from his hand. The hand became a fist on the instant to drive full and true to the jaw of his enemy. Then Larry was up, running.

He went through the first door he encountered. Shrieks greeted him as sleepers awakened. But he didn't pause. He went through a window—then through a second window into another house, while behind his pursuers hammered at the door he had entered.

CHAPTER III

THE CLOSING JAWS

LARRY WESTON LEFT the second house, found himself in a narrow alley. There was little difference between alleys and streets in Urga. Both were dark, usually untouched by the glow of light from windows perpetually shuttered against the bite of wind-driven sand.

Through the second house Larry raced away, trying to keep his sense of direction, until he should locate the dwelling where for two days and nights he had hidden, making his plans for the capture of Sergei Popov.

He felt reasonably sure that his presence there had never been discovered. The house belonged to the dead Ya Che, who went there at certain periods to be near his mines beyond Bogdo-Ula, near the Siberian border village of Altan Buloc, "City of the Golden Key."

Ya Che must have stood in well with the Soviets for his residence had not been molested. Hsa Lo Pe had told him where to find it, that there he might live while he sought for news of Sergei Popov.

That he had done, with not even a servant—he didn't trust even those whom Hsa Lo Pe trusted with his life—to keep him company. Through the shutters he had watched the life of Urga. If he could get back there—

He had the sense of direction of the born flyer, though he had never gone in for flying, believing that the greatest excitement was to be found on the ground—and he hadn't the slightest

doubt that he would be able to find his house again, given half an opportunity. HE DASHED AROUND the corner, and almost into the arms of a man coming in the opposite direction, with head lowered against the drifting sand which was gaining in velocity as the wind grew stronger. The man looked up, uttering an ejaculation— His mouth opened wide, and his eyes bulged as he noted the white skin of Larry Weston. The man was a Mongol.

Larry drove out with a savage right. It cracked with triphammer force against the man's unprotected jaw. Larry hadn't time for the niceties of sportsmanship.

The man fell, rolled to his back, his hands lifted ludicrously, as though in his unconsciousness the Mongol assumed—too late—an attitude of defense.

Then Larry raced on. Behind him his enemies were shouting, going into and out of houses, rousing the inmates. The whole village would be at his heels in a matter of moments. It was a race against time—and the rising storm would play its part, too.

And then, out of the night, away to the west and south, came a long-drawn howl, rising into the wind, becoming a part of it—and Larry Weston shuddered, recognizing the sound.

The dogs of the desert, those savage scavengers which some people claimed were hybrids caused by interbreeding wild dogs and bears, were aprowl in the sandstorm, seeking their grisly feasts of whomsoever the storm might drag down.

Mongols fed their dead to these animals—and threw to their slavering jaws the living bodies of their enemies.

If Larry were caught those dogs would howl for him, too. But he gritted his teeth grimly—he wouldn't be caught.

He ran with the speed of a great athlete, thankful beyond saying that he was always in top condition, as his hazardous calling made necessary.

The sounds of pursuit died away, but they were still following him. He knew then that he would never be able to hide for any great length of time in the house of Ya Che.

SERGEI POPOV WOULD know of it, certainly, and in the end, even if it were done at the end of a house to house search, the Mongols would find him, drag him forth and tear him limb from limb. It was to the best interests of Sergei Popov that this should happen to him.

He was gaining on his pursuers, and now was out in a narrow street, racing straight toward his objective. Realizing that if they guessed where he was going, they would go directly to the house of Ya Che, he suddenly turned aside and ran to his right for all of a minute, then cut back toward the residence of Ya Che.

Several people met and passed him, saw his face, but next moment he vanished into the shadows, or into the thickening horror of the rising sand—and their shouts rose after him, directing the pursuit, as he desired.

Now he felt that with his enemies looking for him in one section of town, he dared to go to his own hideout, and accordingly, taking more care now that none see him, he headed directly for the place.

ONCE HE MET a man face to face—a Mongol. This one he dropped with a savage blow. From the man's torso Larry Weston yanked his heavy garments, evil with the odor of poorly cured skins and the stench of an unwashed body. He draped it over his own shoulders as a possible disguise, but had gone no more than a couple of blocks before he could stand the odor no longer—and hurled the garment aside with a snort of disgust.

Now, ahead in the gloom, dimly discernible through the screen of sand, he could make out the outline of the house which had sheltered him, must shelter him again for a little time. There were no lights, naturally. The front of the house gave on a busy street. For weeks no human being in Urga had seen anyone enter that place.

Larry Weston had gone in at night, from the back way—and hadn't even opened the windows. It was stale and musty from disuse, but it had served, must serve again.

Larry circled the house, looking carefully at three sides of it, knowing that none would have entered it from the front, else right now the street beyond the house would be packed with the curious.

Then Weston moved up to the window by which he always entered the place. It was just as he had left it on his journey to the ceremony of Ta Kuei. As far as he could tell nobody had meddled with the fastenings. He lifted his hands to them—crawled through the window without sound, and breathed a sigh of relief.

To his left as he entered was a bedroom, but he would have no need for that. He would not sleep again until his quest ended. Here he would rest for a moment before going out again, long enough only to allow the fever of pursuit to abate somewhat, if ever religious fever abated in the hearts of worshipers of the Living God.

Then Larry Weston came to pause. There had been no sound while he strode forward to the center of what he knew to be a large room; but his scalp prickled oddly. He distinctly sensed the presence of another human being. He listened with straining ears for the sound of breathing. But the sound did not come. Whoever was here held his— or her—breath, or breathed with the softness of a stalking cat. Larry swung his arms wide. They encountered only empty space.

Again he was safe, for if the skulker were beyond the length of his arms, he was not a menace. Larry stepped quickly aside to make absolutely sure that he was not outlined against the window, and thus an admirable target for a thrown knife or a pistol bullet. He listened.

Dared he lift his voice? He decided to risk it, hoping for some reply that would give him the location of the one who lay in wait, or would prove to him that his senses, this once, were wrong. "Who's there?"

HIS VOICE, LOW, tense, sounded hollow in the sparsely furnished big room. He waited—while the darkness of the world seemed to creep upon him like a tangible thing, and sand hammered against the shutters outside, against the walls and the roof, like the sound of hard, small, scampering feet.

There wasn't anyone then. He started moving forward again, confident he had been mistaken, despite the fact that his hunch still held the feeling that he was not alone. And then, the answer came, in surprisingly good English, with the startling suddenness of a thunderclap on a day of sunshine.

"You are looking for Sergei Popov? I heard so. I am here, waiting.

The voice was harsh, savage, with nothing human in it. There in the darkness, Larry knew either close to him or far away, but never beyond the comparatively narrow limits of the room, was the man he had come for—the man who had murdered Ya Che for some person or persons not yet discovered—the man who had murdered many others, who had procured the murder of the woman under Bogdo-Ula without the slightest sign of mercy.

"Good," said Larry Weston softly, "then you are ready to go back with me, Popov?"

A low chuckle was the answer.

"That depends," said Popov.

"On what?"

"On whether you can take me!"

"That's what I came for."

"I merely waited for confirmation of that. You can't do it."

SILENCE AGAIN. THE floor creaked. Larry

stepped swiftly aside—and something spatted into the wall far behind him.

He had stepped aside just in time to avoid a knife thrown by his enemy. And Weston carried no weapons. He did not believe in killing except to save his life, and then only when he was sure that his life did depend upon the life of an enemy.

The affair in the house of Ya Che, in the heart of Urga, became a strange game of stalking. Twice again, within ten minutes, knives zipped past the face of Larry Weston, one of them coming so close that it barely touched the lobe of his right ear.

Then he dropped to his haunches, waiting—waiting for the killer to find him, wondering if he would be able to reach the man's knife hand before his throat was slit from ear to ear. Popov would seek him out without fear, whether he moved or remained still. Popov had caution, but no fear whatever. THEN, AS THOUGH hurled at him from a catapult—making Weston think for a moment that his opponent had the eyes of a cat—a huge body crashed against Larry Weston, bowling him over.

He rolled aside as he struck on his back, but was up in a flash. He hurled himself at where he now knew his adversary to be.

His left hand touched cloth, the cloth of a human torso. His left hand moved with unerring accuracy, grasped a mighty wrist that was covered with hair—like that of a great ape.

Instantly he swung into a disarming hold, swinging his right arm under the man's elbow, over to grasp the wrist with his right hand.

Usually one could break a man's arm with this hold—but the best that even Larry, powerful though he was, could do, was to make Popov drop the knife. It clattered to the floor, and then Larry Weston was locked in a back-breaking hug. His eyes bulged. Blood rushed to his head. He had to work fast.

He butted with the top forward part of his head, a trick he had learned from darkies in the South—and the arms about him loosened for a moment.

Then he fought free, driving rights and lefts to the face and body of his enemy, striking off the flailing arms, battering away, knowing that he risked broken bones in his hands if his blows did not go true.

The big man staggered. Then Weston himself almost went down from a pile-driver right, which did not break his neck only because it was a glancing blow. He staggered back. His lips were tightset, his eyes straining to see the outline of his enemy without avail.

His fists were bloody, the skin of the knuckles broken, but he seemed to be making little headway against the big murderer.

He was growing weaker with the extreme effort—while Sergei Popov seemed momentarily to be growing stronger. He put all he had into a savage right. Sergei screamed, made for the window and was gone—with Larry in pursuit.

THE BEST OF THRILLING ADVENTURES

CHAPTER IV

GOBI JUDGMENT

THAT THERE MIGHT be some trick behind the rout of Sergei Popov, Larry Weston didn't doubt, but that did not keep him from following. He had come to Urga to get the murderer, and there he was, vanishing through the window.

He caught but the barest glimpse of the man's face—as though for a moment the moon had managed to peer through a rift in the storm of sand, and then the murderer had dropped to the ground.

Larry was out and away, after him, carrying no weapon but his fists. If the Mongols were still searching for him he could not tell by the sound, for by now the sound of the sand, driven in a brown wall—which was black in the gloom—before a mighty wind, had risen to a shrill whine.

Sand hammered like hail against the roofs of houses. Not even religious frenzy could have kept the Mongols outside in this blistering smother of sand.

The particles smashed against the face like needlepoints. Larry Weston knew that his face would be pounded to the consistency of beef steak in a matter of minutes. But he lowered his head against it, made out the retreating form of Sergei Popov through the smother and was away after him, fleet as a deer.

Sergei, for some strange reason, was heading straight out into the desert.

Maybe he had been driven mad by the pounding he had suffered at the hands of Weston. Maybe he, too, was a fugitive from the wrath of the devotees of Ta Kuei.

Maybe—Larry Weston knew that one guess was as good as another, that but one thing was certain—Sergei Popov was heading straight out into the Gobi— out of which, rising with its shriek, part of the noise of the storm, came the ululating baying of the dog-bear scavengers of the waste.

Larry shivered a little, thinking of the food which was customary for the evil brutes that ran in packs across the face of the Gobi.

In his time he had seen them drag down and devour weary pilgrims across the sands. He had seen half destroyed carcasses of Mongols on the evil surface of the Gobi, victims of the snarling, roving packs—and now Sergei Popov, for some crazy reason known only to himself, was leading Larry Weston directly into the desert, into the storm, into the land of the dog-bears.

WAS IT A trap of some kind? Were there Mongols out there waiting to take Larry Weston and throw him to the black brutes? He shook his head as he ran.

He was sure of his belief that the Mongols would not now be abroad in the storm. They in their turn, ceasing to hunt for him, would believe that he too would remain under cover during the storm, and that the hunt could be resumed when the storm was over.

No, there was only Sergei Popov and Larry Weston, pursued and pursuer, heading into the waste.

Larry wondered what he would do when he overtook Sergei, if he were so fortunate as to subdue him and make him captive.

But there would be only one thing to do—knock him out, or punch him dizzy, bring him back to Urga, and then find some means of getting him to Peiping and the justice due him for the slaying of General Ya Che.

He speeded up, his eyes peering from under his lowered brows at the broad retreating back of the murderer. Sergei Popov ran with ease almost as effortless as that of Larry Weston himself. His back was visible through the curtain of sand, never dimming, never becoming more distinct.

It was as though Popov intended for Larry to keep him in sight, to follow him, into that trap which Larry's fancy had made him think might await him out in the desert wastes—had not reason told him that such a trap was impossible.

OF COURSE THERE were the dogs, but they would no more be allies of Sergei Popov—or any other man—than they would of Larry Weston. The animals would drag down anyone, white or yellow or black, and devour their flesh with equal gusto.

But a strong man could keep them off—as long as he remained on his feet and guarded his throat against their slashing fangs. They were somewhat like Alaskan huskies, which devoured the falling loser of a fight among their own kind.

Larry Weston feared the dogs, but he wouldn't turn back from his pursuit of Sergei Popov for all the dogs in the Gobi—or for all the gold in Christiandom.

He speeded up. He could not tell whether Sergei looked back, or knew that he had increased his stride, but the fact remained that Popov speeded up, too, keeping just beyond Larry's reach.

Larry began to have a sneaking admiration for the endurance of the murderer—as Urga dropped behind them and the desert grew into being under their feet.

On and on raced Sergei Popov, while now the baying of the dog-bears came from all sides. Sergei must have heard them, but if he feared their warnings he gave no sign.

LARRY ALL BUT stopped as a shadow—two shadows—three, suddenly appeared to the very edge of his semicircle of visibility. Black animals, almost bear-size, they were visible for a second, then were gone.

But like roving wolves they paralleled the way which Sergei and Larry took into the desert. They would not come close to powerful men, but they would trail them tirelessly, until the men staggered. Then they would close in—and when a man fell—their fangs would be buried in his soft flesh.

That was their method of attack, as Larry Weston knew. Strange, the pass to which his hunt for the murderer had come. To follow him into the waste, both of them running like crazy men, their way guarded by the racing packs of the Gobi. Larry laughed into the teeth of the storm.

He glanced back over his shoulder, The sand hammered at his briefly unprotected neck. Urga had vanished into the wilderness of the sandstorm whose crest might have been miles above the desert floor.

This sand, Larry knew, when it traveled toward Beiping, often covered the floors of houses in the ancient capital to the depth of an inch or more in a few hours. There it was known as Beiping dust.

HE'D OFTEN HEARD of dust settling on the decks of vessels, a hundred miles at sea, and countless scores of miles from the desert, yet borne on the wings of the wind from the heart of the Gobi. Down the centuries the Gobi had scattered her harsh dust to the winds of the world, and almost to its uttermost corners.

He judged they were at least two miles outside Urga. For a moment his heart sank as he thought of what it would be like to retrace his steps. Only a man with his sense of direction could ever hope to return to Urga alive.

He couldn't backtrack, for the wind had erased his tracks as fast as he made them. The same with those of Sergei Popov.

But even that could not be considered until he had had a settlement with the arch murderer. Now he raised his voice in a shout to the killer—but the wind caught at his words, jammed them back down his throat—and he tasted the gritty sand on his teeth.

But Sergei, though he could not have heard the shout of his pursuer, suddenly stopped. Never once had he been out of Larry's sight. Larry had not been duped once, knowing all the time that Sergei Popov had some purpose in leading him into the desert, even though the purpose might be a crazy one.

Larry slowed to a walk, glad of the chance because the sand had been dragging at his feet as he ran—and approached Sergei Popov warily. The noise of the storm was higher than ever. Again and again Larry saw those skulking black shapes of the dog-bears.

Sergei stood with his legs far apart as Larry approached him. And Larry saw, when he finally stopped, within a stride or two of the murderer, that Sergei Popov was grinning.

Moreover, his chest scarcely rose and fell with his breathing. He had made the long run, into the teeth of the gale, without causing him to breathy faster than normal. And Larry Weston, powerful as he was, in such marvelous physical condition, was breathing with difficulty. He stared at his enemy, noting through the awful gloom the livid saber scars on the man's right cheek, noting the huge bulk of him.

"Well, Popov?" he shouted, to be heard above the storm. "Just what is the big idea?"

Popov raised his hand, signaling for silence—a strange gesture in the storm that could never have been silenced save with the power of the Almighty.

"Listen!" he cried.

Through the storm came the baying of the dogs—a myriad of them by the sound, close in, just beyond the curtain of the walls of sand.

"Get the picture?" asked Sergei Popov. "Get it, Weston? Oh, I know your name. I make it my business to check back thoroughly on any of my little jobs. General Hsa Lo Pe told me before I killed him!"

IF POPOV SPOKE truth, then he had moved with greater speed than Larry Weston, to kill Hsa Lo Pe after Larry had left Beiping, then to have reached Urga—but no, Larry had spent two days in hiding before venturing forth.

"What are you driving at, Popov?" asked Larry Weston.

"Just this, gullible fool! Do you think you could possibly beat me with your fists? I could have killed you any time I liked, with nothing but my bare hands. I intended to do that, but the baying of the dogs gave me a different idea. I like my little jests, Weston. Here it is—I shall whip you within an inch of your life, until you cannot stand on your feet—and then I shall leave you here, to the tender mercies of the scavengers of the Mongols!"

Larry laughed, even though the thought gave him a moment's pause. What Popov stated was not only possible, but a sure result if he were beaten and left behind. But he was not afraid, even though this man had proved himself of vast endurance and durability.

"I'm ready," he said, "when do we start?"

Popov answered by hurling himself forward, his hands in an attitude of attack and defense, the sure stance of the boxer. His fists were huge, twice the size of those of Larry Weston. Weston's eyes narrowed. He must beat this man with speed of movement, or lose—and fall to the fangs of the dogs.

He ducked as Popov sent in a pile driver right—and even as he did so he spoke.

"I'm not going to do *you* that way, Popov," said Larry. "I'm going to prove to you that I can beat you—and then I'm taking you back to Beiping, if I have to start from here, without food or water, and carry you all the way on my back."

But Larry did not believe in his own words. He knew that the whole thing would be settled, here and now, within the next few minutes—and that only one of them, if either, would go anywhere from this place.

HE SENT A straight left to the nose of the killer. Sergei's head snapped back—and quick as a flash Larry darted in and smashed a savage right to Popov's jaw.

The man sagged, tottered, started to fall—and Larry struck again, eager for the kill. Popov dropped to his knees—and out of the gloom came two black shapes, hurling themselves at the body of the fallen man. Larry jumped in, yanked Popov to his feet, laughed in his face.

"Who do you think now will be fed to the dogs?" he shouted.

Popov straightened, fought out, sending in blows from all angles, trying to land a laming blow to the groin with his knees—and Larry smashed him again. It came to him then that this was fit punishment for the murderer, if he could bring it off.

THIS BEAT EVEN torture Hsa Lo Pe might

have devised—and Sergei Popov had set the trap for himself.

Even as Larry thought this, a numbing blow struck him on the chin and he fell as though pole-axed. Even as he fell, with the roaring world spinning about him, flooded with darkness deeper than dark, Sergei Popov roared with satanic laughter—and several shadows leaped out of the storm at Larry Weston.

As he covered his throat with his forearms, fangs bit into his clothing. He hoped that the cloth would prevent the teeth from touching his flesh. Even that might mean death for him eventually.

Popov jumped in, to give him the boots—and Larry Weston rolled aside, scrambled to his feet, groggy, swaying, fighting with all the desperate fury of the man who hates his prospective conqueror and refuses to be beaten. His fists became mallets at the ends of his arms that grew weary with punching.

And now, as both men staggered from blows that both were too tired to guard against, when blows that were hurled hurt more to land than to receive, the dogs came out of the shadows and did not go back again.

They circled the fighters, their mouths open, red tongues lolling, and now and again, their eyes glistening with hellish fires, they lifted their noses and bayed at the storm. They were beasts out of some awful nightmare—and Larry Weston fought like a madman, as did Popov, to cheat them of their prey.

Once Larry even considered a truce with Popov, so that both might fight their way back to Urga through the storm, each helping the other against the dogs. But he refused to more than consider it. Popov had started this horror, and here it must end, one way or the other.

They met, chest to chest, their breath coming in sobs through lips that were mashed and bleeding—and their fists working tiredly, but working—on and on.

The dogs were close enough to touch, darting about them. Larry felt a pain in his thigh. The dogs were bolder, knew their meal was ready for serving, and were impatient.

Larry redoubled his speed—and Sergei Popov did a foolish thing. He started to cut out of the fight, to race past Larry toward Urga. Larry struck him again and again.

THE MAN'S EYES, in the midst of a face which had been chopped to pieces by Larry's fists, as Popov's fists in turn had battered the face of Larry Weston, were wild. He chattered with an access of fear, pushed Larry aside when Larry would have grappled with him—got past.

He fell! The dogs charged in. Larry jumped into the midst of them, reaching to jerk Sergei Popov to his feet. He managed it. Popov staggered. The dogs drew back. Larry struck the big man again. Again Popov turned, tried to flee—and again he fell.

This time Larry was no longer fighting off the dogs. He knew he dared not weaken himself too much, fighting the dogs off Popov, for he would need all his strength to escape the beasts himself.

AGAIN HE OPENED his mouth to suggest an alliance—and dropped in his tracks as Popov smashed him on the temple. He rolled to his stomach, hoping that his clothing would keep off the dogs until he could get some breath into his body.

Popov did not jump on him, as he expected. Larry whirled again, scrambled to his feet, struck out at twin shadows which rose through the air toward his throat—and saw Popov, twenty feet away, in the direction of Urga—flat on his face, motionless. Larry raced to him, turned Popov over.

What he saw reminded him of the throat of General Ya Che as he had last seen it. A dog, emboldened by the man's apparent weakness, must have jumped at Popov just before he had fallen—and the animal's fangs had ripped his life away.

Larry stooped, searched for a weapon in the clothing of the dead man, found none. Of course, if Sergei had retained a weapon he would long since have used it himself.

As Larry Weston stumbled back toward Urga, his strength returning swiftly now that his fight with Popov—the most brutal he had ever had with man or animal—was over.

"Trouble with my business is—there's no excitement in it—"

But when at last he saw the outline of Urga ahead, and the dogs were drifting away, howling their disappointment, he regained control of himself, became ready for any eventualities—for the world would have need, he knew, of the wit and the strength of its Larry Westons in the years to come—and he wouldn't have changed his occupation, even then, for all the wealth the world could offer.

The Sultan of Hell

BY **CAPT. KERRY McROBERTS**

Singing Steel and Blazing Guns in a Swift-Moving Novel of Breathless Combat in Kiruchu and Borneo

CHAPTER I

STREET OF HEAVENLY LIGHT

FRED TANDEN TURNED down the little street that led from the Pagola Square in Kiruchu to the jungle stream flowing along the edge of the town. He walked rapidly, his body leaning forward a little, one hand shoved in the coat pocket of his whites. Darkness—gray, sullen and dank—spread around him as he entered the alley-like thoroughfare.

It was called the Street of Heavenly Light. Narrow and winding and filthy, it was overhung in the daytime by the mists that rose off the jungle river, and at night by the darkness that filtered through this mist. Mud, ankle deep and slimy, sent up putrid, sickening waves of stench.

Tanden had turned down this street for no particular reason. All the other streets that led through the native quarters had the same ankle deep mud, the same putrid stench, and the same unbearable heat.

The name of the street caused a grim,

cold smile to spread over his sharp features. To Tanden, the time he had spent in Kiruchu and Borneo had failed to disclose anything to him that approached being heavenly.

Mud and filth. A damnable heat that covered everything like a suffocating blanket; fevers that came from the mist rising off the jungle stream, from the fetid and hot smells that emanated always from the jungle and the mangrove swamps; sudden death from the murderous Dyaks; loneliness, more terrible than death or fevers, because with it, stalked the constant dread of a crazed mind.

That was Borneo for you—and Kiruchu. Hell on earth, in perfect reproduction. Tanden knew it and hated it, with a fury based on more than the heat and the stench and filth.

The year before he and an American engineer, Fred Morley, whom he met in Singapore, had come to Borneo to look for gold. Far up in the mountains, after months of hard work, they had found it.

But neither of them then realized the power and the ruthlessness of the great unseen hand that struck death so swiftly and so certainly to all that opposed it. The hand of El Karim, the brown Malay sultan who ruled, thanks to the Dutch, the territory around Kiruchu!

Smiling and courteous and fawning, the Sultan had received them in his palace up in the hills from Kiruchu. He gave them every assistance—until they found gold.

AFTER THAT MORLEY had died in the palace from a strange fever. Tanden had escaped from Kiruchu more dead than alive, his body filled with wounds and the doctors giving him no chance to live. For five months he lay between life and death in the hospital in Malacca, before he started to get well.

And now he was back in Kiruchu, fighting single-handed against the shadowy power of El Karim. A hopeless struggle to anyone who knew Borneo; but to Tanden it was a grim, stubborn battle to avenge the murder of his friend and to regain the gold concession which El Karim had stolen away from them.

As he walked down the little street, his lean face was tense. Thin lines ran away from the corners of his mouth and lost themselves in his bony face. His fingers were clutched around the automatic in his coat pocket. Around him, through the misty darkness, furtive forms moved, forms that would gladly slash his throat for the price of a cheap drink.

But those worried him little, and he continued on rapidly. His intention was to cross the river, where he could hide out in his old cottage until such a time as he had gathered enough evidence against El Karim to force the Dutch authorities to act.

A cold smile came to his lips as he thought of the wildness of this latter hope. It was more probable that the forces of El Karim would discover his presence. When they did, it would be only a matter of hours before a knife would be sent through his heart.

Suddenly he stopped. Not more than twenty feet ahead of him, two furtive, indistinct shadows moved. From the darkness, another came to join the two.

The figures looked ghostlike in the night. From their hands long kris knives gleamed dully. They moved like animals, their bodies crouched low as they crept toward the wall of an old building. Tanden could see nothing against the wall, but he guessed that a human being stood there, waiting for the death that was to strike him.

A native killing!

AS TANDEM'S EYES grew accustomed to the gray darkness, he saw that the three crouching figures were half naked Dyaks, with *sarongs* around their waists. Slowly, relentlessly, they were edging their way to the wall, knives gripped firmly in their hands.

There was no hurry, no excitement, no nervousness in their manner. Their movements were certain and relentless—a slow, deadly narrowing of the semicircle around their victim.

In a few minutes it would all be over. A swift movement of a black hand—a scream of death as the knife found the heart of the victim. And after that the grim, unearthly silence of the night, and the body of a dead man lying in the mud. The grisly death tableau so often enacted on the Street of Heavenly Light!

Then suddenly from the wall came a low, muffled cry. A gasp of surprise and startled alarm.

It brought Tanden's gun from his pocket with a jerk; it sent his body forward with a frantic leap. But even as he leaped forward his mind was dazed, stunned, for the cry had cut through his senses like a rapier.

Again the cry came. Tanden caught a fleeting glimpse of something white moving in the darkness, the end of a long robe. The three Dyaks had closed in on their victim. A knife went up in the air.

TANDEN FIRED FROM the hip as he dashed toward the scene of the struggle. A leaping, darting flame of orange red cut through the darkness. Then the knife fell with a splash in the mud, and the tall, black body of a Dyak swayed a moment, then crumpled in a lifeless heap.

But before the body hit the ground, Tanden had collided with an onrushing Dyak. There was a flash of steel over his head. The knife was only inches from his throat. In the split second of action that followed, he had no chance to swing his gun again.

He saw the leering, snarling face near his; he saw the row of ivory teeth in the black mouth, teeth that glistened in the night.

Tanden's head ducked. The knife cut down across his shoulder, ripping his coat. His right fist shot out like a piston, caught the black body full in the stomach. The man doubled up like a ball, groaned weakly, and then crashed backward against the wall.

Tanden moved with the swiftness of a tiger. There was a *swish* of a knife near him. His gun had dropped from his hand, but even if he still held it, there would have been little chance to use it. **THE THIRD DYAK** closed in on him, the

*"Pigs of Satan, get back! Do not use
this place to kill a white man!"*

long, powerful arms crushing him to
the mud. In that powerful grip, Tanden
was completely helpless.

His face went into the slimy mud; the
sweating, stinking body of the half-naked Dyak was over his head. Helplessly
he struggled to get his breath, to lift his
face out of the suffocating mire.

The Dyak momentarily released his
powerful hold around Tanden's body,
fingers seeking for his victim's throat.
In that fraction of a second, while the
long black arms moved swiftly for a
death hold, Tanden came to life.

His legs and his body lurched out in
a violent leap, breaking the agonizing
grip. In the flash of a second, he was
on his feet. The huge body was rising
slowly to grapple again with him. But
as it came upward in the darkness—a

　　　　THE BEST OF THRILLING ADVENTURES

grotesque, inhuman looking thing in the night, Tanden's right shot out. With every ounce of strength and weight in his body behind it, it traveled ahead for three or four inches, and cracked against the jaw of the rising native.

The Dyak slumped, fell face downward in the mud. He remained there, limp and unconscious.

From the wall came a low, soft laugh.

Tanden stood swaying in the darkness, his eyes fixed stupidly on what he saw. AGAINST THE DARK wall was a girl. In the darkness Tanden could only see the white outlines of her dress, the silhouette of a face, hair falling down over the shoulders.

"I am sorry," he heard her say quietly, "that you have interfered. It would have been much better if you had not."

Tanden stared transfixed at the white face, phantomlike in the darkness. He wet his lips and shook his head, as if trying to dismiss an illusion.

The voice he heard was that of an American girl. The American twang was so distinct and clear that there was room for no possible doubt.

An American girl on the Street of Heavenly Light! An American girl anywhere in Kiruchu, wandering around alone at night! The idea was almost fantastic.

A sound at his feet brought Tanden back to his senses with a snap. One of the Dyaks was struggling to get up. Tanden whirled quickly, but the man was already on his feet, running madly down the street.

"Quick," the girl cried, with a trace of hysteria in her voice, "You must run also. You do not understand. You—"

Tanden faced her, his thin face tense and grim.

"Running is something that won't do me much good now," he said. "I'll put a lot of questions in one, to make things brief. Who are you, and what in the name of God are you doing on this street?"

The girl moved away from the wall, took several steps toward him.

"They'll be back any minute," she said quietly. "You might fight three—but you can't fight a hundred. So please leave me. My running won't save me now. Nothing will."

The sucking of mud far down the street broke the black silence. Voices, wild and savage, rang out, and the night was suddenly filled with a horde of dark forms.

Tanden reached out, grabbed the girl's arm, and started up the street toward the Pagoda square. Madly he raced away from the Dyaks who were coming from the other direction.

CHAPTER II

A DESPERATE GAME

WHITES SPATTERED WITH mud, face covered with rivulets of perspiration, Tanden dashed across the little court of Loy Son's hotel at the far end of the Pagoda square. He clattered up a short flight of stairs and into a room that overlooked the court.

The girl was close behind him, breathing heavily. Her dress was now black with mud, and her hair hung over her shoulders in a disordered mass.

Tanden closed the door, locked it, then turned really to look at the girl for the first time. When he had seen that face in the Street of Heavenly Light, silhouetted in its ghostly whiteness against the wall of the old house, the thought had occurred to him that there was a girl from Tar Sonken's dive, some unfortunate creature who had wandered into that street.

When he had heard the American voice, he was prepared for anything— anything but what he was now gazing at, stupidly and with bewilderment. The girl was young, still in her early twenties. Hers was a strange beauty, a coolness that made one think of flowers and things fresh and clean, yet was at the same time baffling and indefinable.

The face was thin, sharply featured, with somehow the touch of the spinster about it. The wide set eyes were blue and very much alive; the skin, ivory white and pale; the body slim, delicate in its perfect grace.

She was looking at him and smiling. A very charming smile, yet one that touched her lips alone—not her eyes. These, in contrast, seemed baffling and deep, like windows lighted by some far, unseen source. A strange, bewildering smile, all the more attractive because of the ivory cheeks and the sharply featured face.

"American?" she asked quietly, as if nothing had happened to ruffle her soft, perfect composure.

Tanden nodded, looked at her through eyes contracted a little. He walked to the window, looked out on the court, then smiled grimly as he returned to her side.

"They have followed us here," he announced, "and we won't have much time to talk. Perhaps I can help you."

"You can't," the girl said quietly, positively.

TANDEN SHRUGGED AND said nothing further. He studied the face of the girl carefully, still bewildered at the look he saw in the blue eyes.

"It was kind of you," she hastened to say in her quiet, calm voice, "to have come to my aid in that street. I *should* thank you, but really, it has proved a bit annoying."

"I'm sorry," Tanden replied dryly.

"But you see, it is the custom, when—"

"I understand all that," the girl interrupted, "but I am going to ask you not to interfere any further. They are waiting for me outside now, and in a moment I will go to them.

"I prefer it that way."

It came to Tanden very suddenly, with something of a shock, that the girl must be insane—that the look in those deep blue eyes, the strange smile that played on the lips, the ivory color of the face—all were the results of a disordered mind. Yet with this thought came another, more compelling and more convincing.

He felt that this American girl was grimly and hopelessly playing a desperate game, waging a losing fight, against the lurking, unseen powers of Kiruchu; and that somehow and in some way, she was connected with his danger. A fantastic thought, he admitted, yet it stuck in his mind.

"You know that going out there means your death," he persisted quietly.

The girl shook her head slowly.

"They do not want to kill me," she answered. "They want to take me where I want to go. Oh, I know it all sounds silly—crazy. But it's hard to explain, because there is so little of it I can tell."

"You are an American and so am I," Tanden replied. "I want to help you if I can."

The girl smiled—again with her lips only.

"You can help," she said, "by leaving this room at once. You can go out that rear door and they won't bother you—"

There was a flash of steel over his head.

"And leave you alone with these murderous Dyaks!" Tanden shook his head. "That's asking too much."

"Asking a stranger not to interfere with your private affairs is hardly asking too much," came back coldly, sharply at him. "And that is all I ask."

Tanden flushed angrily, bit his lips to hold back the feelings that suddenly surged over him. In the court he could hear the muffled voice of someone talking low, then on the steps outside came the soft sound of a footfall.

"YOU WON'T HAVE to go out there," he

     THE BEST OF THRILLING ADVENTURES

said curtly to the girl. "They'll come in after you, in a moment or so. When they do, it won't be to take you any place."

"If I tell you why I came to Kiruchu and where I want to go," she questioned calmly, "will you promise to leave this room—before it is too late?"

"It would be interesting," Tanden acquiesced.

The girl looked directly at him and in that quiet, unwavering look Tanden sensed a will that was strong and stubborn—a will equal to his.

"I came to Kiruchu," she began, "with only one purpose! Tonight I went to the famous dive of the old Mohammedan, Tar Sonken, and asked him to do what he could for me. I asked him to get me some kind of work in the palace of El Karim—"

"The palace of El Karim," Tanden repeated, in a hoarse whisper. He stared blankly at the girl.

THAT IS WHERE I am going," she said determinedly. "Tar Sonken wouldn't send me, but the minute I stepped out of his place I was followed. At first I was frightened and then I realized that it was El Karim's men following me.

"In the Street of Heavenly Light I stopped. All would have been well if you had not interfered."

Tanden looked at her, a thin, humorless smile on his lips.

"The palace of El Karim," he mused. "Funny, that is what I came to Kiruchu for. But when I go, I must be prepared. Because it will be his life or mine."

The girl's eyes opened wide.

"You, going to the palace?" she gasped.

"Yes, I am going," he said slowly, firmly, "but you are not."

The girl was on her feet, her face flushed with anger.

"What do you mean?" she cried.

"I mean that you are not going," Tanden replied quietly. "I don't know what foolish—or romantic—idea you have in trying such a thing. But if you went up there alone, you wouldn't want to stay two hours. And when you wanted to leave, they would drug you, a little each day, until you didn't know what you were doing. You'd wind up by either killing yourself or going crazy."

The girl laughed coldly.

"Sounds very dramatic—and exciting," she said. "Really, you must think I'm a fool, a mere child, to talk to me like that."

Tanden struggled to hold back the impulsive anger that was fast getting possession of him. It struck him that the girl should be taken over the knee and given a good spanking. She was obviously a foolish young woman, letting her stubbornness carry her on to a sordid doom.

But mixed with his anger was the thought that all this strange bluff and front on the part of the girl was not born of stubbornness; that those eyes, blue and silent and baffling, seemed to hold some message they wanted to tell, yet couldn't. With an effort he controlled his rising temper.

"You are going out that rear door with me now," he said incisively. "If we make our escape and live until tomorrow, you are boarding a ship and returning to the

States. You're *not* going to the palace of El Karim—not while I am here and alive."

The girl gave a quick, sharp laugh and turned. She moved with a speed that was almost faster than the eye. Before Tanden could jump into motion, she was at the door of the room and out into the night. With a curse he dashed after her.

OUTSIDE THAT DOOR, on the little balcony that rose a few feet above the court, hell broke around Tanden! Hell in the form of black, snarling bodies and kris knives that whistled through the air. He heard the muffled scream of the girl, from somewhere in the court. Two bodies crashed against him, threw him back against the wall of the hotel. Knives gleamed dully in the night, over his head, cutting the air in sharp slashes.

Twice his gun roared. A black body crumpled to the balcony at his feet. Again and again his gun belched fire, straight into the surging mass of Dyaks closing in on him.

Then his gun clicked on an empty barrel, and he let it drop to the floor. He ducked with lightning speed, then came up with the same rapidity. His shoulders hit the black legs and arms closing around them in a vise-like grip, and as his body twisted upward, he brought the struggling, screaming Dyak with him.

Tanden stepped backward along the right of the wall, whirling on his toes, using the big body of the half naked Dyak as a human bludgeon. The body crashed into the black forms closing in on him.

The night was filled with curses and howls of pain. As if by prearranged signal, the Dyaks moved away from the swinging bludgeon and disappeared downward into the court.

The human club fell from Tanden's arms with a dull groan, and lay inert on the balcony, With a wild leap Tanden was over the bodies lying in front of him, down the steps and across the court.

But in the court all was silent, save for the groans of the wounded Dyaks above on the balcony.

Tanden dashed out into the street, but the same still, misty darkness greeted him. Nowhere did a form move. There was only silence and the gray night that had suddenly and completely swallowed up the American girl whose blue eyes had so strangely looked at him.

CHAPTER III

DOLORES

TANDEN DARTED BACK in the shadows of the buildings along the street. Out of the misty gray that covered everything with the sweltering blanket of heat came the *sihk,* the native police, rushing toward the hotel court where the shooting and fighting had taken place.

Tanden watched quietly, knowing he had little to fear from them. They would find the bodies of the dead Dyaks on the balcony, and cart them away. That would be the end of it all, as far as the *sihk* were concerned.

DEATH AND MURDER were too common

 THE BEST OF THRILLING ADVENTURES

on the muddy stifling streets of Kiruchu to concern them greatly. The customary report would be made to the Dutch authorities and the Dutch, reading that several Dyak killers had been found dead, would file the report and promptly forget about the matter.

But as he stood in the shadows, Tanden realized grimly that now there were plenty of other things to worry about. First and foremost was the fact that by now El Karim undoubtedly knew of his presence in Kiruchu. It would be only a short time before the lurking power of El Karim would reach out through the darkness and mow him down.

The totally unexpected entrance of the girl upon the scene was the second source of worry. If El Karim were taking her to the palace, her presence there would be of little aid to Tanden, should he be compelled to play the desperate game of stalking the Sultan in his own quarters.

Tanden's first impulse had been to dash into the gray night, searching anywhere, everywhere, for El Karim's Dyaks and the girl. But common sense showed him the utter futility of trying to find them in the dark muddy streets of Kiruchu, and reluctantly he abandoned the idea.

The strange actions of the girl mystified him. One part of his brain still saw her as a foolish, stubborn girl looking for adventure; yet in another section of his mind, he revisualized the strange blue eyes, the hidden secret in them, and the desperate, hopeless look on the white face.

Then suddenly his body stiffened, as if some powerful, overwhelming thought had come to him. A gasp of astonishment escaped his lips.

The native police had left the street and Tanden walked out of the darkness. He turned to the right and progressed quickly, body alert and every nerve taut. TEN MINUTES LATER he stopped in front of the two story frame building, with its latticed porch and queerly shaped roof, that housed the notorious dive of Tar Sonken. In a land where dives abounded in every form—where the lowest scum and riff-raff of the earth foregathered to talk, and plan and execute every known crime on the calendar—Tar Sonken's place had the reputation of being the lowest of them all, from Borneo to Wenchau.

For a moment Tanden stood outside on the street, gazing at the building. Lights came from the open windows, and the whining thrumping of a native orchestra broke rudely on the stillness outside. Then he walked up the steps, across the porch, and kicked open the door.

The sweet, sickening smell of opium greeted him as he stalked inside. Mingled inescapably with it, a part of the very atmosphere he breathed, was the odor of rancid *ghee* and stale tobacco, and the many other smells peculiar to the far East.

A haze of smoke rose slowly to the ceiling of the large room. Through the fogginess, Tanden regarded the motley gathering of humanity that sat around the tables.

Malays, brown of body, naked to the waists, with their multi-colored *sarongs* standing out vividly against their brown skins, were there. Dyaks, tall and powerful, with snarling, murderous faces, squatted on the tables like black buddhas, smoking opium pipes.

There were the lithe Singhalese, moving like sneaking animals from table to table; Chinese, their faces expressionless, smoking the ever-present opium pipes; Japanese and Lascars; renegade whites, most of them Eurasians.

Humanity in every racial form—with all that was vile and evil in it.

Tanden walked across the floor, past the tables, his eyes darting keenly to right and left. He knew that of all places in Kiruchu, death would strike quicker in Tar Sonken's dive than anywhere else. It was here that El Karim saw and watched through the eyes of his numerous henchmen and killers.

At the rear, Tanden sat down and ordered a *stengah*. At a table not far from him, a Malay got up and disappeared into the crowd. Another signaled to someone in the front of the room and followed after the first. There was a sudden movement behind him, a shrill laugh, and a woman said: "Ze Americano! You weel buy Dolores a drink, *n'est-ce-pas?*"

TANDEN TURNED SLOWLY, grinned maliciously as he looked at the woman behind him. Her type was to be seen in every dive from Borneo to Shanghai. Dark and swarthy, with the slanting eyes of the Oriental, her face was that of some half caste white breed. Hair long and black and straight, parted in the middle and combed back over the ears; teeth ivory white and perfect; black eyes that flashed with volcanoes of hate and passion.

A human dynamo of mixed emotions—sometimes good but usually evil—these are the worst of all women.

In them is the slinking, subtle mind of the oriental, combined with the evil there is in the trace of degenerate white blood.

She slid into a chair beside Tanden, easily and gracefully, her dark eyes watching him closely.

"*Ze* good *Monsieur* will buy me a drink?" she invited.

THEN HER BODY moved forward a little, with the angling movement of a snake. Tanden stiffened. His hand shot under the table, closed around the wrist of the woman with a twist that sent her body over the table with a muffled groan. A knife fell to the floor and rattled ominously.

"El Karim," Tanden said dryly, "has many strange ways to kill people, but this is not a new one to me.

The body of Dolores still lay across the table, her right arm pulled down straight by the grip Tanden retained on her wrist. Her eyes darted flashes of black hate at him, and he laughed coldly. Gradually he released his hold on her wrist and allowed her to sit up.

There was a lull in the babble of voices around them. Two Dyaks had gotten to their feet and were looking at him suspiciously. There was a sharp order in Malay behind him.

    THE BEST OF THRILLING ADVENTURES

"Where is Tar Sonken?" Tanden said quickly to Dolores. "Talk fast, or a bullet will go through your sweet body."

Dolores sat up, her eyes filled with the terror of an animal that strikes in the dark, fails, and is cornered. Her words came viciously, almost congested with rage.

"You are ze fool," she snarled. "Very soon, you will be dead."

Tanden was on his feet in a thrice, his hand jammed in his pocket as though grasping a gun. The lull, ominous and deadly, continued in the room. A surging mass of humanity was silently moving toward the table. Tanden backed to the wall, remained there grimly, as the tension was suddenly broken by the cries of the surging Malays and Dyaks.

Dolores had jumped to her feet. Loudly she screamed that she had been insulted by the white man, and her cries brought the brown faced Malays to a pitch of frenzied anger.

Tanden sidled to the right, making for a door that led to the rear of the house. He moved slowly, stealthily, unwilling to provoke a rushing attack. As he paused at the door, a kris knife came hurtling through the air, striking the wood over his head. The room became a veritable bedlam of cries and rushing bodies.

And then out of the door came a short, fat man, clad in a long white robe.

"*Peri Pehuimn,*" came shrilly from the man. "Pigs of Satan, get back! Do you think Tar Sonken's place is to be used to kill a white man? Back, pigs of Satan, or I'll blast you to Hades."

THE CROWD STOPPED, gasped in fear, and then fell back. Tanden darted through the door and ran down a narrow hallway. He came to another door, opened it, and dashed into a large room. The door closed behind him upon the entering footsteps of another person.

"*Mynheer* Tanden," a voice behind him said, "is like all fool white men—walking straight ahead into death."

Tanden turned and smiled into the round, greasy face of Tar Sonken. The small eyes of the Mohammedan looked at him from behind layers of fat, with something like a twinkle of humor in them.

Tar Sonken was neither a noble nor a law-abiding citizen. Yet with all his crimes and his reputation, Tanden had always felt a certain admiration, a certain friendliness for the old Mohammedan. Cunning, Tar Sonken was, playing his struggle with life carefully and astutely, taking no more chances than were necessary.

BUT HE POSSESSED one attribute that was remarkable in a soul so steeped in murder and lust. That attribute was his word.

Inviolate, he kept it, giving it seldom, but when he did, it was as good as a bond of gold. And Tanden knew that the minute Tar Sonken had refused to send the American girl up to El Karim as a dancer, some cause lay behind it that would make the old Mohammedan a valuable ally.

"I came to see you," Tanden said to him, "and the reception was not very pleasant."

Tar Sonken smiled thinly, without humor.

"You are a fool, my friend," he said, "to walk into my place. You are a fool to return to Kiruchu—"

"I'll admit that," Tanden cut in quickly, "but I risked my life to get into your place. I want to find out, from you, why that American girl is so anxious to get to the palace of El Karim."

"Ah," Tar Sonken said softly, "you are speaking of the one with eyes of the heavens and hair of gold. Charming—exquisite. A jewel of rare beauty."

"All right—all right," Tanden broke in dryly. "We know all that. You haven't answered my question."

"Allah be praised," Tar Sonken raised his hands upward in a weary shrug. "I am but a humble old man who wishes to help his friends, but you ask a question that only a wise man can answer."

"You're the wise man, Tar Sonken," Tanden laughed shortly. "Answer that question any way you wish, and I'll understand."

"My advice to you, my friend," Tar Sonken said slowly, "is to forget your foolish idea of revenge. You are young, and youth must forget some things. The little wealth you have lost is nothing compared with life and the pursuit of real happiness."

"Thanks for your advice," Tanden replied, "but I am here. When I leave, El Karim and his white advisors will have paid for the murder of my friend—or I shall be dead. This question is the only favor I have asked you—and I am quite sure you also will not mourn the downfall of El Karim."

Tar Sonken smiled craftily, with a cunning that spread over his great face.

"I know no more than you, *Mynheer*," he replied. "Yet Allah gave me eyes and with those eyes I have looked; and Allah gave me a brain and a memory, and with that memory I have gone back over the years. And I have seen that face again—the pale cheeks, the sharp features and the strange blue eyes.

"BECAUSE I HAVE used my memory, I know why El Karim wishes to get the girl in his clutches. If you would do the same, you also would know."

Tanden stared at Tar Sonken, not a muscle of his face moving. His eyes were partly closed and the hands at his sides clenched convulsively. Then he smiled, a cold, deadly smile.

"The same thing came to me, a few minutes ago on the street." His voice was hard. "But I had to risk coming here to make sure. I had to know definitely."

"I am very sorry for the girl," Tar Sonken said, "but there is nothing I can do to save her. Youth is headstrong and foolish. Those who follow its impulses walk quickly to a grave."

Tar Sonken got up slowly and walked to a red covering that hung on the wall. He pulled it back and disclosed a door.

"You are young, too, my friend," the old Mohammedan said. "And I think you, too, are going very quickly to your grave. But depart hence from this door, for I do not wish you to leave this world in my home."

Tanden walked to the door, stopped and patted Tar Sonken on the shoulder, then laughed.

"Thanks for all you've told me. I'll try to repay your kindness—by not getting killed in your place."

CHAPTER IV

THE RULE SINISTER

LATE IN THE afternoon Tanden, on horse-back, turned a sharp curve in the narrow mountain trail and came in full view of the palace of El Karim. It was a cluster of white buildings, with flags flying from the turrets and soldiers standing guard at the gates.

It was a pleasant place—at least for Borneo—with its gardens, its artificial lakes, and the resplendent luxury made possible by the Dutch government. The chief interest of these worthies was to keep the conquered sultans satisfied and they accomplished their purpose by allowing the native rulers completely to enjoy themselves.

In the vast territory surrounding his palace, the Sultan's word was law. Because he was isolated, and because the Dutch did not want to interfere, he was able to rule, when he so chose, with a sinister hand of murder and death. And El Karim could do that in a way that was most neat and effective.

Isolated in a little valley, surrounded by scrawny peaks of a great mountain range, the palace looked regal and stately—from a distance, like a minia-ture fort. The green of the mountains ran down into the deeper green of the jungle; the buildings of the palace gleamed very white in this setting of brilliant vegetation.

But the beauty of the place did not deceive Tanden. He was completely aware of what lay hidden within those charming buildings. Too well he knew the power of El Karim and the murder-ous cunning of the brown-faced Malay ruler.

Deep and dark underground passage-ways honeycombed the earth beneath the buildings. Death in a hundred forms lurked in the luxuriously furnished rooms: death by poisons, by fevers, by hidden traps, by knives thrown from concealed panels in the walls. Death in every form imaginable—and it struck with the speed of a cobra.

In going to the palace, Tanden was acting on an impulse. It was mad, il-logical, perhaps, if studied with careful scrutiny; but nevertheless, under the circumstances, it remained the only possible way for him now.

HE REALIZED THAT his only chance lay in a bold, aggressive front; in direct, swift action. Any cautious tactics, any attempt at evasion or secrecy, would be utter folly. The power behind El Karim was far too great to allow him to fight that way.

The sun was falling beneath the saw-toothed mountain range to the west when he rode up to the gate and jumped off his horse. A flaming tree, with a huge fan-shaped top, threw a hundred different colors over the gate and gave the place an air of exotic brilliancy.

A tall, heavily decorated guard took his horse, and an officer of the Sultan's court came through the gate to greet the visitor. The small brown-faced Malay, walking like a monkey standing upright, led Tanden directly across the court. He seemed to have been expecting him, and to have received orders where to take him.

TANDEN KNEW THEY were headed for the card room, where the Sultan would be passing the time with his two white advisers. A grim smile came over his face as he thought of these two white men. There was more to fear from them, in some ways, than there was from El Karim.

Van Duren, resident at the palace, was a heavy, flabbily fat man, with the soul of a snake. A middle-aged man who laughed a great deal, but whose laugh hid murder as well as humor.

He was in the pay of the Dutch government, but that was only a small part of the money he received for his work for El Karim.

His running mate at the palace was Multao, a half-caste Portuguese, a man evil from any standard. This man was the professional henchman and killer for El Karim.

The three men were together when Tanden was ushered into the room. The Sultan, a short dish-faced Malay, with small flashing eyes, threw the cards on the table and rushed to greet his visitor with a great show of affability. He was in evening dress and looked very much like a monkey dressed to order.

"Welcome, *Mynheer* Tanden." His voice was thin and boyish, oddly disagreeable. "It is good to see you again. It has been a long time since you have visited us."

Van Duren laughed heavily and proffered a huge hand to Tanden.

"We have rather been expecting you, Tanden," he chuckled. "Yes, we rather expected you."

Tanden looked at him, grinned coldly, and said: "I *thought* you'd be wanting to see me."

He turned to the Sultan.

"Your Highness, could I speak with you—alone?"

The Malay shrugged, looked at Van Duren and Multao.

"Why, certainly," he replied to Tanden. "Van Duren, you will excuse us for a moment."

"I'll dash along, Your Highness," Van Duren chuckled, his eyes on Tanden. "Be careful, Tanden, if he offers a rubber of bridge. He's a fiend—a perfect fiend—with cards."

He went out of the room. Multao remained standing, his sharply pointed olive face expressionless. His dark eyes stared at the Sultan as he awaited orders.

"I'll see you later, Multao," El Karim said softly. "In a very little while."

Multao nodded and walked out of the room.

"Your Highness," Tanden began quietly when they were alone, "I intend to be your guest for a little while. It may be for several weeks, or it might even be for only a day."

IF THERE WAS any surprise behind El Karim's yellow masklike face at this announcement, he showed it neither by word nor action.

　　　THE BEST OF THRILLING ADVENTURES

"You are always welcome, *Mynheer* Tanden," he said. "It is a pleasure to have your company."

"I thought it would be," Tanden retorted dryly.

Little lumps of muscles rose on his jaws and his eyes studied the Sultan coldly. El Karim did not reply for a moment, and the two men gazed at each other in silence. The air was heavy with conflict, between two men whose wills were diametrically opposed.

One, the silent, mask-faced Malay Sultan, deadly as a cobra, shrewd and sinister; the other an American, roughly dressed, ready to fight his battles in the open, carelessly, almost foolishly unafraid of what might happen. Two men that represented the complete extreme of human wills. Neither could ever hope to understand the other; there could never be any common ground for meeting.

IN TANDEN'S EYES smouldered a hot fire—a fire of impulsive, uncontrolled anger; in El Karim's eyes was only imperturbability. Yet each man knew the power of the other; each gauged and respected the other without illusion.

"I have a very great and very pleasant surprise for you, *Mynheer* Tanden," El Karim said with a cold, vague smile. "One of your countrywomen—a most charming, delightful girl—a Miss Contillo—"

"I know all about her," Tanden broke in curtly. "That is one reason that I came."

"And the other reason?"

"We will wait until the girl is safe, before we discuss that," Tanden snapped. "I am here to see that no harm comes to her—and to take her away when she is ready to leave."

The Sultan made an impatient gesture.

"My friend," he answered, "you speak very foolishly indeed. What harm could come—"

"As a liar," Tanden said easily, "a yellow face is damned hard to beat."

The Sultan smiled, a weary, fleeting smile.

"Perhaps you have not dined, my friend," he said in his thin, reedy voice. "You have ridden far and this air makes one very hungry."

"I will eat—later," Tanden cut in sharply.

Again the Sultan made an impatient gesture.

"You have spoken about the girl," he said. "Perhaps you can inform me just what you mean to do?"

Tanden smiled grimly and seated himself on the edge of the card table.

"She is young," he said, "but that fact will have little influence with you. She is an American girl—headstrong and with the foolish idea that she can outwit you. That's why I came. It would be very sad if she were stricken with a strange fever—as my friend was, last year."

"A very unfortunate circumstance," the Sultan replied, "The young man was sick when he came here. We did everything possible for him, yet he died. A very sad—a truly unfortunate—case."

"There was a gold concession," Tanden said dryly. "I hardly believe the

Dutch government knows the whole truth about that concession."

"Is that a threat?"

"No—not exactly. The matter is simply this, El Karim: I came back to Kiruchu to settle a score with you, and discovered an American girl who had come for the same purpose. My first duty is to see that nothing happens to her."

The Sultan nodded and a smile spread over his face.

"PERHAPS," HE SAID, with an odd wistful twinge to his voice, "perhaps, after you have dined and refreshed yourself, you will return and honor me in a game of cards or a string of billiards. I have always found it very pleasant to deal with an honest man, whether he be friend—or adversary."

Tanden slid off the card table and stood up.

"It will be a pleasure, Your Highness," he said. "I may return later."

CHAPTER V

TENSE MOMENTS

UPSTAIRS, ALONG A narrow hallway carpeted with a blood red rug, Tanden moved swiftly and silently through the half darkened corridor. His body hugged the wall and his fingers were clasped on the butt of his automatic.

He knew the Sultan was in the card room downstairs with Van Duren and Multao. Tanden was still playing his cards on the aggressive, direct attack. He knew that El Karim would first consult with his two advisers before making any decision toward getting him out of the way.

It wouldn't take the three long to make that decision, but the few minutes it gave Tanden were minutes of life and death to him.

He came to a turn in the hallway, stopped quickly and threw his body against the wall. In front of him was the door to the Sultan's harem, and to the right were the doors to the guest rooms. His body remained hard against the wall, but his hand shot down to his coat pocket and jerked out the automatic.

Fleeting and darting, a mere shadow in the semi-darkness, the body of a tall, powerfully-built Malay, a syce in the palace, had moved in front of him and disappeared through a door.

Tanden moved away from the wall, crouching, his muscles bunched for a spring. He advanced noiselessly, rapidly, over the thick carpet. He completed the turn in the corridor, making it slowly, head and shoulders leaning forward a little to see what lay beyond.

There was a whish of air near his head. A knife fell to the floor behind him. His head ducked and from out of the darkness a long, brown arm moved and then a body.

The gun went back into his coat pocket; a shot now would bring the whole palace down on him. Tanden did the only thing he could safely do.

He lunged forward, sending his body through the air in a perfect flying tackle. He had leaped blindly, knowing only that somewhere in front of him, close against the wall, the Malay killer waited. It seemed to him that his body was flying for many long seconds before his shoulders hit the wall. As he landed, he saw the darting shadow of the Malay move.

But the man had been a split second too slow. Tanden was on him, pulling him to the floor, in a thrice. He held his right hand over the man's mouth to prevent him from yelling.

The man was powerful and slippery. Tanden could not use his right or left to deliver a paralyzing blow. He caught the man around the neck with his free left arm and crashed the head to the floor with all the power in his arm and back. **THE MAN GROANED** dully and gasped for breath. Before the Malay could realize what had struck him, Tanden had raised himself to his feet, still holding his death grip around the man's neck. He threw the yellow body against the wall and then with a short, vicious uppercut, a blow that traveled with the speed of lightning, he sent the Malay's head back with a snapping crack.

There was no groan from the yellow man this time; only a sagging of the body, a stupid, glassy stare in the eyes. The man's knees buckled and he went to the floor in an inert heap.

Tanden looked up and down the hall. No other shadows moved in the semi-darkness. With speed and deftness he tore the inert Malay's *sarong,* then tied and gagged the man.

He dragged the body to a small alcove in the wall of the hallway, threw it back in the darkness. Swiftly he moved ahead, crouching now on hands and knees until he reached a door. For a tense moment he remained still and alert, ear against the panel.

HE COULD HEAR someone walking back and forth inside, walking with a soft, pattering step. His arm reached out and opened the door noiselessly, fractions at a time. A wall of jet black darkness greeted him. With the deadly swiftness of a tiger, Tanden was inside the door, still crouching on his hands and knees.

Then his body rose, swung forward at the same time, arms flailing. In the darkness a form stiffened, went backward with a weak grunt, and then crumpled to the floor. Tanden was over it. The butt of his gun crashed down on the head of the dark form. The unconscious man jerked once and then lay still.

Tanden continued on through the darkness, his outstretched arms guiding him. He came to a second door, passed through it, and found himself in a large room, with long windows that overlooked the court of the palace. Through these windows came the soft, misty light of the night that had, by this time, fallen outside. In the gray mist that came in the room, everything looked ghostlike and weird.

He saw a great bed, with a deep canopy over it. The ever present netting, used to keep out the insects of the jungle, fell from the top of this to the floor, giving the bed a white, phantomlike look. Tanden crossed the room with long strides.

There was a movement in the bed, a

short, startled cry. Someone came to a sitting position, stiffly and quickly.

"Miss Morley," he said in a whisper.

"Oh," came weakly from her. "It's you."

Tanden threw the netting back and sat down, looking closely at the girl.

"You certainly got your wish," he said dryly. "Here you are, in El Karim's palace."

With a spring she was out of the bed, fully clothed, wearing a blue sport suit. She stood in front of Tanden and stared at him in amazement.

"You—you," she whispered hoarsely, "know my name. You know now why I came."

Tanden smiled grimly and remained seated on the bed.

"Blue eyes that never smile," he said. "I was a fool not to have understood at first. It came to me after the Dyaks captured you; I went to Tar Sonken's to confirm it. It was brave—foolishly brave for you to have come here, but a girl trying to outwit El Karim is a pathetic sight."

"Fred Morley was my brother," she said softly.

"AND I WAS his partner," Tanden replied. "He was murdered by fever—and I was shot full of holes in Kiruchu. Last week I came back from the hospital to settle the matter with El Karim. It would have been much easier for us both if we had stopped last night to introduce ourselves."

"You—you—were Fred's partner," Grace Morley gasped. "The man he was working with—and you came back to avenge his death?"

"All of that," Tanden said, jumping to his feet, "but we have little time to talk now. What did you come up here for?"

"To find evidence that Fred was murdered," Miss Morley said. "I know he was. If I can find a book I gave him just before he left home, the evidence will be in it."

"A book?" Tanden questioned.

"You see, Fred was sentimental in many ways and a great lover of poetry," she explained. "When he left, I bought him a fine copy of Keats, with a secret cover. I made him promise me that if anything happened, he would write it all out and put it in that secret cover.

"That book is somewhere in this palace. I was waiting until everything got quiet, and then I was going down to the library to look for it."

"El Karim and his white killers are down in the card room now," Tanden said. "We have one chance in a hundred of getting down to the library. But we'll have to take that chance."

"I HAVE IT all located," Grace explained. "It is on the floor below. The side stairway leads to one of the doors."

"Okay," Tanden said.

Quickly they quitted the room, walked through the little anteroom and out into the hallway. Grace led the way to a narrow corridor that branched off the main one.

Silently and swiftly the two moved through the semi-darkness. They came to a stairs and went down it rapidly, coming out in a dark hall. They followed this for some distance, came to a door, and went through it into a long, narrow room.

Bookshelves lined the walls. Elegant furniture—chairs and tables and smoking stands—filled the room. At the far end, French windows opened out on the court of the palace.

Tanden moved swiftly, on tiptoe, across the heavily carpeted floor to the large double doors that were the main entrance to the library. His body jerked back and his muscles bunched. Outside the door was the sound of someone walking.

THE FOOTSTEPS CAME indistinct and subdued. Muscles tense, Tanden waited, but the footsteps died away. Strain his ears as he would, there was only a deadly, ominous silence. He turned and saw Grace looking through the book shelves. Suddenly she stopped, reached up for a book. Tanden was at her side.

"Here it is," she whispered weakly. "It's Fred's book of Keats."

Her hands went for the cover frantically, nervously. She opened it, pulled out some papers, stared at the writing. For a moment her body swayed, but she caught herself and looked at Tanden, her face pale. "It is there," she said. "It's his handwriting and I've read enough to know what it is. Evidence to hang the man that murdered him!"

"That is," Tanden whispered, "if we get out of this palace alive. Sneaking down to the library is one thing, and escaping is another. El Karim doesn't care where we go inside the palace, but outside—"

He stopped abruptly and looked at the French windows. His face lightened as he moved across the floor. Opening one of them, he motioned for Grace to go out on the little, balcony.

"If El Karim is still in the card room," Tanden said, "we have a chance—a very slim chance."

Out on the court the moon cast a soft light over the flower gardens and artificial lakes. Grace started out of the window, but suddenly she stopped.

Tanden's body stiffened and he swerved around.

Somewhere behind there had been a muffled step. Someone was walking in the library, walking noiselessly, quickly.

Tanden stopped, facing the door, and his jaws locked with a snap. Coming toward them was Multao, his olive-skinned face expressionless—and his right hand on the gun in his pocket.

TANDEN STARTED TO move for his own gun, but halted the motion of his hand with intention. He looked at Multao with eyes grown cold and deadly. Common sense told him that the use of a gun now would inevitably mean his death and Miss Morley's; reluctantly his hand came away from the pocket of his coat, and hung motionless at his side.

Multao's face in the shadowy darkness was immovable. Tanden searched it closely to see if there were any intimation that he had overheard any of the conversation; but on the thin, olive dark face was nothing save the blank, lifeless expression that was habitually there.

"His Highness," Multao said in French, "would see you in his private quarters, *Monsieur* Tanden."

Tanden balanced his body on his toes, looked at Multao for a moment before speaking. The muscles in his face contracted in thin ridges, and his jaws were locked so tightly that the muscles around them rose up in lumps. *"Alors,"* he answered also in French. "I will see His Highness in his own quarters—in a few minutes."

Multao bowed and walked out of the room.

"Running would be suicide now," Tanden said grimly to Grace Morley. "We'll play their game and see what happens. Remain close to me and keep your eyes open. Say nothing, no matter what happens to me or what I say!"

CHAPTER VI

A CONFERENCE

TANDEN AND GRACE Morley walked out into the hall. A syce was waiting for them. Silently, with bows and motioning arms, he led them through the hall, up a flight of stairs, and then down a narrow, dark corridor. Their walk came to an abrupt end at a great teakwood door.

The door opened slowly and the two Americans entered a large room, furnished with a splendor and grandeur that caught even their breaths. It was the Sultan's private room. Silk pillows, of colors rare and startling, lay strewn over the room; hangings of gorgeous, exotic patterns covered the walls.

Teakwood chairs, hand carved and examples of an art found only in the East, stood around the walls, in company with cabinets of the same wood; silken couches, blood-red and low, were set upon Oriental rugs of priceless value.

And with all this, the soft, bewitching odor of incense and perfumes made the air scented and almost hypnotic.

El Karim himself was seated on a large couch. At his side was Van Duren. The Sultan had discarded his evening clothes and was dressed in native robes of white, with a gold belt around his waist. Tucked in the belt was a curved scimitar, in a sheath of ebony.

El Karim rose quickly and walked forward to greet Grace and Tanden. His yellowish face was wreathed in a pleasant smile.

"Ah!" His thin voice sounded nervous and a little more shrill than usual. "You have brought Miss Morley with you, *Mynheer* Tanden. That is excellent. Now we can all talk together."

Van Duren remained on the couch. He wore clean whites; his round face was all abeam with smiles of friendship.

TANDEN LOOKED AT the Sultan coldly, a grim, bitter smile on his lips. He reached over, grasped a black teakwood chair and motioned for Grace to sit down in it. He saw that her face was pale and her body trembled as she looked at the face of El Karim; in those blue eyes flashed a light Tanden had not seen before.

The chin was up a little, but there was no false stubbornness, no cocksuredness in the American girl's expression now. Coldly and calmly, with a hatred that sprang from every part of her being, she looked at the yellow-faced Sultan. Looked at him without a tremor of the eyelid. There was no panic, no threatened hysteria in that gaze.

El Karim was conscious of her eyes. The brown man's face went mask-like, as if suddenly the look of the girl had frightened him, made him ill at ease.

Tanden took a chair near her and sat with his legs stretched out in front of him. His hand in his coat pocket gripped his automatic. The silence was oppressive, charged with a ton of high explosive that seemed as if it might go off any minute.

Tanden saw that the eyes of El Karim were still on Grace and that Van Duren, too, was watching her closely.

Neither of the men was paying any attention to Tanden.

Suddenly the Sultan shrugged.

"We were about to have coffee, *Mynheer* Van Duren and myself, Miss Morley," he said, "certainly you and *Mynheer* Tanden will join us?"

"Thank you, I do not care for coffee." The girl's voice was so quiet, so calm, that it seemed to ring in that room of deadly tension.

Again the silence. Somewhere a clock ticked. Van Duren had reached his hand into the coat pocket. Tanden grinned at him and said nothing. The Sultan backed to a couch and sat down near Van Duren, fingering his sword hilt nervously.

"You wished to speak to me, Your Highness," Tanden interjected. His words broke the silence rudely.

"Ah, yes," El Karim replied softly. "I thought it would be well—you understand—for us all to have a little understanding."

"I thought I had that understanding with you earlier this evening," Tanden replied. "I told you I was here to see that no harm came to Miss Morley. She has decided she wants to leave at once, and I am taking her back to Kiruchu."

EL KARIM LOOKED at him with eyes that gave no expression of his inner feelings or thoughts.

"Come, now, Tanden," Van Duren said jovially, "we are all grown people, the four of us. This little matter can be adjusted in a friendly manner. Naturally, you understand we know all about the purpose of Miss Morley's visit here.

"We knew she was coming before she left Singapore. His Highness thought it would be best to have her come to his palace, where we could discuss the matter in a friendly, quiet way. If it's reparations—"

"We are quite willing to talk reparations," Tanden broke in calmly. "We are willing to listen to any terms His Highness wishes to offer."

A sharp gasp came from Grace. Her lips trembled and she started to speak, but Tanden gave her a quick look and then said: "You must excuse Miss Morley, gentlemen. Naturally, she feels very keenly the unfortunate death of her brother."

Grace wet her lips and sat back in her chair.

"I can assure Miss Morley," El Karim said, "that that unfortunate death has been a source of great worry, great anguish to me. Naturally, I wish to make such amends that—er, well—are within reason. Though, of course, I feel in no way responsible for her brother's death. "MISS MORLEY, I believe, has assumed another name in coming here, but we will forget that name. Her brother stopped over one night, a very sick man. We did everything within our power to save his life, but the fever was too far advanced. There was nothing—"

"Your story," Tanden broke in dryly, "doesn't interest us, Your Highness. How much are you willing to pay?"

The Sultan shrugged and looked at Van Duren.

"Really, now, Tanden," Van Duren said good-naturedly, "a bit crude, the term, 'willing to pay.' His Highness feels very much distracted that the young man should have died in his palace, but after all, everything within human power was done to save his life.

"Of course, if you have any evidence that Fred Morley died of anything other than fever, we will be glad to hear it."

Tanden's face remained tense, expressionless. He knew all this conversation and delay was simply an effort on the part of Van Duren and the Sultan to find out if Miss Morley had any damaging evidence against them.

"Perhaps," Tanden said coldly, "His Highness would be willing to pay, say— well, we'll make it reasonable. Fifty thousand pounds, payable in gold!

"Not a big price, considering everything, Van Duren—the gold concession and the prospects of your necks hanging at the end of a rope. Rather cheap, I'd say."

"Fifty thousand pounds," Van Duren gasped. "Let's confine our talk to reason—"

"That," Tanden cut in sharply, "is our price. Take it or leave it."

The Sultan gave Van Duren a quick, nervous nod. The fat man slapped his knees with his huge hands and laughed jovially.

"Well, well, Tanden," he remarked, "looks as though you get your price."

"It will be cheap all around," Tanden drawled easily, his eyes on the automatic in Van Duren's coat pocket. The Dutchman had not let his fingers wander once from it during the interview.

"Then it's all settled," Van Duren said, getting to his feet. "Have a smoke, Tanden. A smoke on the successful settlement of an unfortunate affair."

HE HANDED TANDEN a cheroot, a long, spindly-looking cigar, the kind smoked by the Sultan. Tanden grinned as he took it. His eyes wandered again to Van Duren's gun and to the knife in the gold girdle around the Sultan's waist.

"Sure, we'll smoke to our success," Tanden laughed.

He lit the cigar, puffed weakly on it and blew the smoke up toward the ceiling.

"Not a bad cigar, Your Highness," he said. "Import them from Holland?"

"A special brand I furnish His Highness," Van Duren put in. "We Dutch, you know, have a knack about making cigars."

Tanden looked at Grace. Her face was still pale, but she looked at Tanden and smiled.

Suddenly Tanden's face twisted queerly. His eyes went glassy, and his fingers fumbled weakly at his throat.

For a second his body swayed crazily on the chair, then he toppled face forward to the floor.

Van Duren leaned back and laughed, heartily and very boisterously.

"The cigars, Your Highness," he said, "work very fast."

ON THE FLOOR in front of them, the body of Tanden stretched out on his face, limp and helpless.

Grace gave a startled scream and jumped to her feet. But with the speed of a cat, Van Duren was off the couch, his great hands grasping her slender shoulders.

"No more foolishness, Your Highness," he said. "We can put the girl out of the way now without making a great mess. Before Tanden comes to, a knife can finish him."

"It is a very excellent idea," El Karim said quietly. "These white men like Tanden make a great ado and kill many people—unless, a little poison puts them out."

Grace screamed again, weakly. She was utterly helpless in the powerful grasp of Van Duren's great hands. The Dutchman threw her on the couch, and brought his automatic out of his pocket. His full face was distorted with the insane lust of killing; his eyes gleamed wildly.

His fingers started to press the trigger of the automatic. And as they did, something hit him, hit with a resounding smack that carried to every part of the room. With a dull groan the killer slipped to the floor; he rolled over on his face and lay hunched and still.

But before he did that, the body of Tanden had swerved to the right. Catching the brown-faced little Sultan in his two hands, he raised him high in the air, bringing the monkeylike body down on the floor with a crash that sent all consciousness from the Sultan's brain.

Van Duren's body moved and with a bellow of rage the huge man was on his feet. His eyes burned in a pale face. His right hand was still grasping the automatic; the gun came up with lightning speed and filled the room with a deafening roar.

Tanden had twisted to the left in the split second it took Van Duren to bring the gun up. The bullet nipped the side of his shoulder and bored into the wall.

He dropped to one knee, bringing his own gun up, but before he could pull the trigger he heard Van Duren's gun click on an empty barrel. The huge body of the Dutchman sprawled over him, carrying him backward. There was a sickening, deadly crash against his jaw and the next thing he realized he was on the floor, against the wall.

Weakly, he pulled his knees under him, attempting to rise to his feet. His head was reeling insanely and every part of his body felt numb and half paralyzed. He heard a second bellow of rage, saw the body of Van Duren lunging toward him. He tried to raise his right, but the arm refused to respond.

TANDEN FELL TO the floor, face down. With a feeble lurch forward, he caught the ankles of Van Duren, jerked them toward him with the little strength left in his body. The Dutchman went to the floor, on his back, with a heavy thud.

Tanden struggled to his feet. His head was clearing rapidly from the effects of the blow to the jaw. Van Duren lay on his back, a pool of blood forming under his head where it had struck the floor. His eyes were closed and his breathing was heavy and jerky.

"Quick," Tanden shouted to Grace, who stood pale and trembling in the center of the room. "Tear enough of the Sultan's clothes off to tie and gag him. I'll take care of Van Duren."

A FEW MINUTES later Van Duren and the Sultan lay under the great couch, their hands and feet bound and their mouths gagged. Tanden looked down at Grace grimly, his steel-gray eyes cold and expressionless.

His chest rose and fell with his still labored breathing.

The girl smiled at him weakly, questioningly.

"You seem," she said quietly, "to get over poison very quickly."

Tanden smiled humorlessly.

"There are several ways of smoking a poisoned cigar," he said. "I played them for just such a trick. The Sultan likes to do his murders quietly—without too much ado. It was safer to wait and let them play their hand, then catch them by surprise. Any more on my part, before, would have meant death before I got out of the chair."

"All right," Grace said quietly. "That's that. Now, what are we going to do?"

"Get out of this palace—alive," Tanden replied.

He turned and walked to the black teakwood door, Grace close behind him.

His hand went to the knob, turned it, and pulled the door open.

But as he did, he jumped back. Grace gave a muffled cry. Standing in the doorway, his dark face leering and murderous, was Multao. Massed behind him stood a dozen powerfully built *syces*.

CHAPTER VII

MULTAO

TANDEN'S SHOULDER WENT against the teakwood door with a bang, closing it in the face of Multao and his Malay killers. Before the enraged group could hurl their bodies against it, Grace slipped the long bolt lock as Tanden held the door shut.

"That's one way we won't escape," Tanden said grimly. "Take this gun of Van Duren's. I've reloaded it, and don't be afraid to use it."

There was a violent pounding on the door, and the muffled cries of the men on the other side came through the teakwood. Tanden ran to the window, drew aside the heavy drape and looked out; then he let the drape fall back into place and returned to the center of the room. "Sit down," he said quietly to Grace.

She sat in the black teakwood chair she had used before. Tanden took out a package of cigarettes.

"Have one?" he asked.

Grace took one, tapped it on the back of her hand, and then leaned forward to light it from a match in Tanden's hand.

"Sad but true," he said with a hollow

laugh. "It's a good twenty feet to the ground from that window. They're waiting for us below, and the minute we show ourselves we'll be dead. So that's that!"

The pounding on the door increased to a terrific din. Suddenly it stopped, and the heavy thud of some object being used as a battering ram jarred the very ceiling.

"It won't take them long to break through the door," Grace said. "Perhaps there is a hidden door leading to the harem, or some such place."

Tanden shook his head.

"If there were such a door," he answered, "they wouldn't be knocking that one down to get in here. A Sultan's private quarters has only one entrance. It's safer that way when he sleeps."

Under the couch Van Duren or the Sultan was moving on the floor. The great scarlet covering waved a little.

"We'd be safer if they were dead," Tanden said grimly. "If we have any chance it won't amount to much if they are freed by Multao."

Grace shook her head.

"I can't do that," she said softly. "You understand."

TANDEN NODDED AND looked at her. For a long time they gazed at each other without words, each realizing grimly the utter futility of their position.

Finally Tanden said: "There is one chance—and I'm taking it!"

He got up and approached the door. The heavy thud of the ram, which had stopped momentarily, now recommenced. He listened for a moment, then returned to Grace.

"We are only two," he told her. "Two against a palace full of guards. If I were alone I'd try to fight my way out—but with you, it is different."

"I'd rather fight than die—like this—"

"You'll have plenty of chances to die," Tanden interrupted. "Don't let a little thing like that bother you."

"It's silly—and quite useless," she whispered, "for me to say I am sorry to have gotten you into this mess."

He smiled down at her, this time with his eyes as well as his lips.

"This is no time for last regrets," he said. "Now, listen to me. You are going to remain here, while I go out in the hallway."

She looked at him rebelliously.

"You—alone—"

"There is only one chance," he said. "And that is—Multao."

"Multao?"

"Multao is a killer and everything else that can be called evil," Tanden explained, "but he has sense. He *might* listen to reason—"

"Listen to reason?"

"You'll have to let me handle this myself." Tanden was firm. "We can't kid ourselves. That door will break down in a few minutes—and then you know what will happen. I'm going out there alone.

"If you hear more than three shots when I am gone, you can take this pistol of Van Duren's and do what you wish. I advise you to save one shot for yourself."

He handed Grace the automatic he had taken from Van Duren.

She looked at it helplessly, turned it over, and then looked up at Tanden.

"Whatever you say is right with me," she said. "I realize this is no time to be silly, but—it isn't easy to see you go out there—alone."

"If you went with me, it would only make matters worse," he answered. "I can handle the situation better alone."

"But you have no chance, facing those killers."

"The chance is slim—too damned slim, but it will be our last bold stroke. After that, well—"

THE HEAVY THUDDING on the door stopped again. Tanden darted across to it, with Grace at his side.

"When I get out, close the door behind me and throw the bolt lock," he said. "I can stop the ram with my gun, long enough for you to do this."

He drew the bolt, pulled the door open a few inches, and slipped out into the hall. He heard the door slam behind him, and the bolt go back with a click.

And the next second he was conscious that in front of him was a sea of yellow faces. The sudden maneuver of a man slipping through the door caused the Malays to gasp in surprise and wonder. It required only that fraction of a second for Tanden to get into action.

Ten or more *syces* were carrying a log up to use as a battering ram. One shot from Tanden's automatic, a shot that cut the ceiling over their heads, caused them to stop dead. They stared in fear and wonder, holding grimly onto the great log that was taxing every ounce of their strength.

FROM BEHIND THEM came an order, uttered in a sharp, shrill voice. The log was lowered to the floor, and Multao advanced swiftly, in the slinking manner habitual to him.

"*Entendez,*" Tanden called out to him in French. "I'm going to give you your choice, Multao, of being a dead fool or a live hero. El Karim and Van Duren are out. Their little play is up and the reckoning with the Dutch authorities is not far off.

"You can go the way they have gone—or get out of this mess with a whole skin. Keep those yellow savages off me for five minutes and at the end of that time you can do what you wish. You know we can't get out of here alive."

Multao's dark, olive face remained cold and expressionless.

"Where is the girl?" he asked.

"In the room. She'll be safe there for five minutes."

Save for the cruel lines of brutality that were always there, the face of the half-caste Portuguese did not show a flicker of expression. He seemed to ponder for a moment, then he smiled craftily, shrugged.

"Fool," he hissed. His right shot out with lightning speed for Tanden's gun. Tanden caught the movement in the split second that Multao's hand shot forward. His gun went up, away from Multao's blow and then the *syces* surged forward.

TANDEN'S GUN ROARED once. A Malay screamed, grabbed his throat and fell face downward. A sharp blow across Tanden's wrist knocked the gun out of his hand and the sea of yellow faces and yellow arms was on him, snarling and yelling and biting.

     THE BEST OF THRILLING ADVENTURES

Tanden dropped to his knees. He was pushed against the wall, but his right and left shot out with the speed and precision of a steam piston, landing on yellow groins with loud smacks. Yells and screams followed and yellow bodies doubled up and rolled over on the floor, holding their stomachs.

Tanden's fists continued their deadly blows. Though many bodies rolled away from him, yet relentlessly—like a great surging sea, still others came on. Tanden's arms were numb. His back was now tight against the wall. Yellow hands were reaching for his throat and shoulders.

His blows were stopped by the flood of onrushing bodies. His arms were pinned to his waist, and slowly he was being crushed to the floor. He struggled against the overpowering weight over him, struggled fiercely, then with declining powers. The weight of the bodies suffocated him and pinned him to the floor, helpless to move so much as a hand.

Then the crushing load lifted, and he was rolled over on his face. Bereft of all strength, Tanden made no further effort to resist. His mind stopped thinking at this point. He was conscious that his hands were being pulled up across his back and ropes were tying them together; he felt ropes going around his ankles.

After that he was lifted up and carried along the darkened hallway. He could see the *sarongs* of the *syces,* who were carrying him, and that was all. He heard Multao giving orders to the Malays and he caught enough of the orders to know that he was being carried to some kind of dungeon.

Then suddenly the air grew damp. The walking *syces* stopped. He heard a door open, and the next thing he knew he had been thrown into a dark room, his body landing on a cold, stone floor as a door closed behind him.

CHAPTER VIII

COMBAT

TANDEN LAY ON the floor, face downward, unable to move a hand or a leg. He lay there for some time, and then slowly his brain cleared. He found by a supreme effort he could move his hips and waist, and after several futile attempts he managed to roll over on his back.

Darkness—jet black and dank—was all he could see. The air was foul and soggy. Lying on his back with his arms doubled under him was tortuous; he succeeded in rolling over on his side and lay partly on his right shoulder and partly on his face.

Grimly and bitterly he reviewed what had happened. There was no time for regrets now; no point in worrying about what might have happened. He had taken the only chance left—and had failed. To him, the failure was ignoble.

Tanden was too far underground below the palace to hear anything overhead, but he knew that by now the teakwood log must have battered the teakwood door down. Grace had the revolver; one shell of it would be for herself.

A groan, not of fear or pain, escaped his lips, a groan of desperate anguish at the thought of the girl. What might happen to him was a secondary matter, making little difference now; he gave it little thought. Tanden had lived too long within the shadow of death to worry greatly about it when it finally came. It brought him now a surprising feeling of relief, a feeling of complete forgetfulness.

He twisted his body over on his side a little more and as he did, he felt his wrists give a little. He jerked against the ropes. They were loosening with each jerk. He rolled over on his face to give his hands more freedom; then slowly he worked his wrists back and forth. The flesh tore away, but slowly, surely, his right hand worked out from the rope.

He succeeded in getting as far as the knuckles, and there it stuck. The skin came off as he pulled frantically. Finally the hand slipped out.

Tanden's weariness slipped away with returning hope. He sat up and reached down to his feet, pulling at the cords with his free hand. His left arm was still doubled up against his back, making movements of his shoulders and right arm difficult and awkward. The ropes around his ankles were tied tightly; so he gave up trying to loosen them and went to work on his left arm. He rolled over on his side, using his free arm as best he could.

FINALLY HE TORE the ropes away from the left wrist and used both hands on the ties around his feet. He had gotten them half free, when suddenly the door to the cell opened.

Tanden fell on his back quickly, with his arms under him. A light broke into the jet black darkness, a light feeble and flickering, and in its glow he saw the face of Multao, sneering, mocking, very dark in the yellow light. In the half-caste's right hand was an automatic, and it was pointed directly at Tanden's head. "I THOUGHT," MULTAO said quietly, "that you would get those ropes loose. I tied them myself and fixed them so you could escape them in time."

Tanden looked at him and said nothing.

"Fool," Multao said with a snarling laugh. "Your proposition sounded fairly good to me. But *mon Dieu*, such pig-like stupidity, to yell it out in front of the *syces*. Some of them, *mon ami*, speak and understand French."

"What's happened to the girl?" Tanden asked hoarsely.

Multao shrugged and smiled coldly.

"The girl," he said, "might still be in that room—and she might not. I have said that your proposition interested me. Since El Karim and Van Duren are in that room, I am in command of the palace.

"I have seen to several things to enable us to get away—providing, of course, that you agree to my terms. But we will have to work fast. As I came down here I heard the *syces* battering on the door again.

"The door will hold five minutes or

ten—but no more. I have taken the guards away from the bottom of the window out in the court, and you can get her down that way now. I can control the *syces* only so long, and unless you agree to my terms, you will both be dead in an hour. But I think you will agree to them.

"My price for all this is the girl. You can have the rest."

Multao laughed coarsely. His body relaxed and he lowered the gun to his side. And then Tanden lurched forward, his body remaining close to the ground. His right hand shot out with the speed of lightning and caught Multao's ankle. Before the astonished half-caste realized what was happening, he turned a backward somersault and landed in a corner of the dungeon.

The old wick lamp fell to the floor, the gun following. Tanden lunged forward, his bound feet dragging. His hand went for the automatic, secured it between his forefinger and thumb as Multao, springing to his feet with the agility of a cat, came plunging at him.

The gun was snatched away from Tanden's fingers, but Multao, unable to stop his headlong plunge, hit the floor, crashing with his full weight against Tanden's shoulder. The American groaned, twisted his shoulder, and barely managed to pull away from under. The half-caste was on his knees, the gun coming up to a level with Tanden's head.

It happened in the matter of a split second, and it was the difference between life and death for Tanden. He pulled his bound legs up under him, brought his body to a kneeling position, and then struck out blindly—desperately with his right. All the weight of his body went behind the blow.

HE HEARD A crunching of bones. A sharp pain shot through his fist, and then Multao fell backward. The half-caste was unconscious from the blow that had caught him under the jaw, flush on the right side of the neck.

Tanden wrenched the gun from the unresisting hand. He took a stiletto knife from Multao's belt, and with a slashing movement cut the remaining ropes from his ankles. He struggled to his feet, reached down, raised the oil wick lamp and stood over Multao. His automatic covered the dark, bestial face that leered even in unconsciousness.

Finally Multao moved, opened his eyes, and looked up at Tanden with a blinking, dazed stare.

"Now, Multao," Tanden said dryly, "we will talk business. *Your* terms do not interest *me*."

"Stupid pig," Multao muttered. "How long can you live, without my help?"

"TURN OVER ON your stomach," Tanden ordered. "I'm going to do you the same favor you did me. I'm going to tie you up, in such a way that you can work your ropes loose in time to make a getaway. I told you up in the hall that the game was up for El Karim and Van Duren—and for you.

"You didn't kill me up there and you made it possible for me to work the ropes loose, but what you intended to do after that is something I don't like.

Roll over on your stomach. A shot down here won't be heard."

Multao went over on his face, and quickly, with certain deftness, Tanden tied his hands and ankles with the ropes taken from his own body. "How do I get out of here without going up into the palace?" he asked Multao.

The half-caste watched him through cunning, half-closed eyes.

"Go out in the corridor, follow it to a little stairs and then turn to your right. You will come out in the court," he said. "I have taken the men away from the window. That is all I could do."

"You can work your hands loose in time," Tanden said, "and by that time I may be dead. If I am, your own chances of living won't be very high. El Karim and Van Duren are still under that couch, if the *syces* haven't broken the door; you'd better get out of here before those two are released."

Without waiting for Multao's answer, Tanden walked out of the dungeon door into the jet black corridor. The wick lamp cast a shadowy light before him, falling on walls, old and black with the mold of many years.

He walked quickly. He had no choice but to follow Multao's instructions, and in time came to the small stairs. He went up them to a landing and then turned to the right. Up other steps he went, through a darkness that even the yellow light failed to penetrate deeply.

After what seemed to be hours of walking upward, he finally came out into the open on the court. A pale moonlight cast a ghostly haze over the garden and the artificial lakes.

Tanden stood under the cover of the vines that hid the opening of the underground passageway, his body tense and every nerve alert. The lamp lay at his feet, the flame snuffed out.

Then from overhead came a shot, followed by wild yells. The outburst emanated from a window above him—the window of the Sultan's private quarters—the room where he had left Grace. HE HEARD GRACE'S scream pierce the night air; after that came the recurrent thud of something crashing against the great teakwood door.

Tanden threw all caution aside. Frantically, though without hope, he went up the vines that crept to the second floor of the palace. The yelling above him increased, but he no longer heard the screams of Grace.

The green ladder protested under his weight. He saw from the corners of his eyes that they were removed some feet from the window, and that there was nothing but bare wall between the window and the vines. But up and up he went, the vines breaking under his weight, sagging down rebelliously. When one broke, he grabbed another, until slowly he got up even with the window. WITHOUT HESITATION HE leaped through the air, throwing his hands out frantically for the narrow sill outside the window. His fingers touched the cold stone, almost slipped as his body fell under them. He gripped desperately, with an almost insane fury. And then he was hanging onto the lower part of the window.

   THE BEST OF THRILLING ADVENTURES

With the same insane fury, the same desperate energy, he strained his body up.

He rested his weight on his right hand after he had risen over the narrow ledge, and smashed the glass with his free left.

Tanden virtually fell into the room, his hands and face bleeding from the broken glass, his body sprawled out in a heap on the floor. For a moment it seemed that the superhuman effort of pulling himself up into the window had taxed his last remaining strength to a breaking point. He groaned a little. All around him was a bedlam—a fury of sounds.

He came to himself with a spring and was on his feet. He held his eyes partly closed, as if afraid to see what had happened to Grace; but when he opened them, he saw her standing in the center of the room.

Her face was pale and her body rigid as she stared at the teakwood door. She held Van Duren's automatic in her right hand.

Thump! Thump! The great teakwood log was slamming against the door. It was finally breaking. Already the hinges were loose, and from the other side came wild, exultant yells of the Malays.

In the bedlam of noise filling the room, Grace had not heard the breaking of the window. She knew nothing of Tanden's presence until he grabbed her around the waist and carried her to the window.

"We're going out that window," he said grimly. "Don't ask me any questions now."

He turned and ran over to a couch, pulled the huge red cover off it. He threw the cloth out of the window, after tying one end to the massive teakwood cabinet.

"Go down that," Tanden instructed her. "You'll have to drop ten feet. Then run as fast as you can for the stables."

There was a deafening crash behind them, a splintering of wood and steel and plaster as the great teakwood door fell to the floor. The mob of infuriated *syces*, their faces twisted with hatred and fury, came rushing into the room.

Twice Tanden's automatic roared. Two of the onrushing *syces* crumpled to the floor. The others hesitated, staring with terror at Tanden's belching gun.

"For God's sake," he yelled to Grace, "get out of the window and to the ground!"

THERE WAS A bellow of rage from the sea of yellow faces. A kris knife came through the air, striking the wall within inches of Grace's disappearing figure. Tanden's gun roared again. The man who had thrown the knife lurched forward, stiffened, and then went to the floor.

Tanden was out of the window, his hands gripping the scarlet red cover. Below him he saw the body of Grace hurtle through the air, hit the ground and lay there inert and still.

Down the cover his body slipped. He came to the end, let go with his hands, and fell ten feet through the air, landing close to the limp body of Grace Morley.

CHAPTER IX

A RACE WITH DEATH

TANDEN ROSE TO his feet, momentarily stunned by the fall. Grace stirred, got weakly to her feet and stood swaying beside him. In front of them the blue of moonlight cast the soft, fleeting glow of a dream over the court.

Across the court, beyond the artificial lakes and huge flower beds, stood a low, one-story white building, the stables of the Sultan's palace.

But before Tanden could say anything, before his brain cleared and the blood flooded back through his numbed body, the air above them was filled with yelling, screaming yellow forms. The *syces* were following out of the window, sliding down the red silken cover.

A booming voice rose above the yells of the Malays. It was Van Duren, yelling orders from the room. Mingling with his deeper tones came the thin, shrill voice of the Sultan.

Tanden grabbed Grace by the arm and started for the stables. It was a wild, frantic race with death for both of them. There was no time to turn and fight. Every fraction of a second meant either life or death to them.

Around the artificial lakes they raced, following the winding stone walk that took them through the labyrinth of gardens and flower beds. Behind them came the yelling, screaming mob of yellow bodies, knives waving above their heads.

Tanden saw the door of the stable.

There would be guards in there. Perhaps not more than two, but two men in front of them with the yelling, surging mob at his back, could easily have the power of a hundred.

He and Grace came to the door of the stables, gasping for breath, stumbling helplessly forward, with the *syces* close on their heels. As Tanden leaped through the door of the stables a form moved out of the darkness.

There was the cold gleam of steel as Tanden brought his automatic up and pulled the trigger. He was conscious of a sudden dull pain in his arm, a pain that seemed to numb his right shoulder and the fingers of the hand that gripped the gun.

He knew what it was, but he dared not think of it. The knife had buried itself deeply in the flesh and was still sticking there. A yellow, writhing form was at his feet.

Grace screamed as she saw the knife.

"Keep quiet and *pull the knife out!*" Tanden cried to her.

Her face distorted with pain and anguish, she grabbed the knife, pulled it out and let it drop to the floor.

By that time the horde of charging men behind them had reached the door of the stables. Tanden knew that he was weak; he knew that every part of his body was numb. He felt the warm flow of blood as it dripped out of the wound. But he steeled himself.

"Get two horses," he said to Grace, "and if any guards appear, shoot hell out of them. I'll take care of the men at the door."

GRACE MOVED AWAY from him swiftly, without a word, without protest. He heard the movement of horses behind him; then all he was aware of was the roar of his automatic, firing point blank in the mass of yellow bodies that was crowding to get in the front door of the stables.

The *syces* dropped back, as they always did, in the face of lead. Tanden heard the bellowing, roaring voice of Van Duren behind them. He saw the huge form of the fat man, his face distorted insanely in the pale moonlight, push his way through the crowd. There was a roar of rage from him and his gun jumped in his hand.

The bullet cut within an inch of Tanden's head. His own gun roared. Van Duren stumbled forward, as if someone had suddenly pushed him in the back, fell to his knees. His mouth gaped open, his right hand jerked to his neck. THERE WAS A rattle in his throat—the weird, ghastly rattle of death. He toppled head first to the ground, his jerking body gradually going limp.

Behind Tanden, Grace called out. He swerved and, through the gloom of the stables, saw the two horses she had bridled. There had been no time for saddles—and they weren't necessary.

In front of them the brown-faced Malays were staring down at the lifeless body of Van Duren, unable to grasp for the moment what had happened. Tanden backed to the horses, put his hand over one of the animal's neck, but found himself suddenly helpless. Every part of his body seemed suddenly cold and paralyzed from his wound.

A shout from the door startled him. There, surging forward now, knives gleaming in their hands, was the yellow horde. At their rear came the shrill, thin voice of the Sultan, sending them forward with a new frenzy.

Tanden gathered himself together, summoned up every force in his body, and clambered to the back of the horse. Grace was already astride her mount. A knife came hurtling through the air.

Tanden put his hands on the side of his horse's bridle, leaned forward over the animal's neck, and, with a sharp kick, sent the pony through the darkness of the stable. Grace raced along beside him, hugging her horse's neck and sending him forward with soft words and pats on the neck.

The horses—fleet Arab ponies—took them through the darkness at a terrific speed. Suddenly they were outside the stables, the horses shooting through a door at the rear.

Out into the haze of moonlight they raced, leaving the palace and the court behind them. The horses' sharp hoofs clattered on the rocky ground of a mountain path. Tanden had no idea in what direction they were going.

He hung on grimly, his left arm around the neck of the pony. His brain reeled; there was no sense of feeling in his body. His pony swept around a curve and he reeled dizzily, all but going off headlong. But he felt a little better and his brain cleared.

On over the narrow mountain pass, bathed in the soft moonlight, the horses raced. They cut around the spur of the mountain range and started down into the valley that led to Kiruchu. Far behind them came the sound of pursuing horses. Then suddenly Tanden's horse slowed and broke into a limping walk. Grace's pony raced on ahead and then it, too, slowed down and walked with short, jerky steps.

TANDEN WAS OFF his horse, falling weakly to the ground. With difficulty he raised himself slowly; his shoulder was shooting sharp pains through his entire body. Grace had sprung off her pony and was running back to him.

"The horses," she gasped, "are lame."

"Multao!" Tanden replied grimly. "He cut the muscles of their legs. He figured we would make our escape on the horses, and prepared against that. And by now he is loose, and perhaps—"

Tanden's words came to an abrupt stop. His hand went weakly for his gun. Directly in front of them, standing in the middle of the road, was the leering, sneering half-caste himself, the gun in his hand pointing at Tanden and Grace.

"I have been waiting for you," he said with a sneer. "I expected you would escape on horseback; I had the horses fixed so that they wouldn't go very far."

HE LAUGHED BRUTALLY, his olive face cold and repellent.

"You were very kind, *Monsieur* Tanden," he continued, "to tie my hands so loosely. I was able to free myself and get up here, by taking a secret path, even before you made your escape. And now I have come to take my part of the bargain."

Tanden's body stiffened. The shooting pains had abated to a dull ache. He looked at Multao and clenched his fists impotently.

Multao's part of the bargain! It was very simple what that would be. A bullet would end Tanden's life, and then—

"You need not fear El Karim," Multao sneered. "I did not want that monkey-faced Malay to interfere with my plans, and their horses were fixed the same as yours. I was desirous of completing my little part of the bargain all alone."

"And the first part of that bargain?" Tanden questioned.

"A bullet through your heart, *Monsieur* Tanden," Multao snapped at him. "There is no time to gloss things over. You are a man and you understand."

A muffled scream came from Grace Morley. She sprang forward between Tanden and Multao, her white face quivering and her blue eyes flashing.

Tanden's right arm went out with the speed of lightning, caught Grace around the waist, and threw her back as Multao's gun roared. Tanden's body dove forward, in a headlong plunge.

The bullet cut over his head, whined dismally among the trees. Grace gave a muffled scream. Tanden's body hit the waist of Multao, driving him to the ground with the fury of an enraged beast.

The gun fell from Multao's hand, but the body of the half-breed twisted, came up with a quick, powerful heave, throwing the weakened body of Tanden to one side. A knife gleamed in Multao's hand. It went up in the air as Tanden struggled to his feet, coming down toward his throat.

Tanden laughed, a cold, desperate laugh.

His right hand went up, caught Multao's wrist, and then he rose to his feet, sending every ounce of weight and strength of his body against the knife.

For one tense, deadly second the hand of Multao, gripping the knife, hung suspended in the air. In that moment the strength of two men met in a grim, bitter death struggle.

Then slowly the hand and arm of Multao went backward, the last ounce of power in Tanden's body behind it. THERE WAS A dull cutting thud, a ripping of cloth and then flesh. Multao's face went blank, dazed; a film came over his eyes. Then he sank to the ground, blood gushing from his mouth, fingers reaching feebly for his throat but closing on air.

Tanden stood over him, body swaying back and forth. The bloody knife was in his hand. Behind him Grace sobbed weakly and turned her face away from the last quivering of Multao's dying body.

Tanden stared at Multao. The half-breed coughed weakly and then his body stiffened and relaxed in death.

"Quick," Tanden cried to Grace as he swerved. "The Sultan's men are coming."

Down the road came the beating hoofs of horses. Tanden and Grace fell into the brush as the horsemen came around the turn in the road, brought their ponies to an abrupt stop, hoofs skidding over the road.

"Come on," Tanden whispered weakly to Grace. "I don't know where we are going or how long I can last, but we have to get out of here."

CHAPTER X

PEACE IN KIRUCHU

HE COULD HEAR the *syces* jabbering and moving around excitedly on the road, over the body of Multao. Over this din the movement of Tanden and Grace's bodies through the brush could not be heard.

They lunged on blindly through the darkness. The bush slashed their faces, tore at their clothes, but they went on. Tanden led the way, trying weakly to push the brush away from Grace's face, his body and brain numb.

Behind them the voices of the *syces* had ceased and they had spread out, fan shape, and were combing the woods. Tanden slowed down. He was far ahead, but any noise now would lead the oncoming Malays to them.

He and Grace came to a little valley and an open space. They raced across it and back into the dense undergrowth again. The *syces* came on relentlessly, deadly in their purposefulness.

Tanden knew that running was out of the question, that El Karim's men would hear the noise of their bodies and it would only be a matter of time until they were surrounded.

He stopped, sat down near a little stream, and struggled to keep unconsciousness from overcoming him. Exhaustion and pain—he had fought these for a long time, and slowly they were overpowering him.

"We'll have to take our chances hiding," he said to Grace. "If we run, they'll hear us."

Behind them came the *syces,* closing in on them. Tanden lay flat on his stomach, Grace at his side. The brush moved and crackled a few feet from their heads. Men moved beside them. A foot scraped Tanden's arm.

And then he remembered no more. Lying down, his senses had reeled and he could no longer control them. When that foot touched his arm, the last thin thread of reason left him.

He came to with the feeling of something cool on his head. He opened his eyes. Arms were around him. He tried to struggle free but consciousness left him.

When he opened his eyes again, his senses had cleared. He heard Grace's voice and he knew that she was bathing his head with water. Moonlight was flooding the ground around him. A few feet ahead was a little stream.

Tanden smiled and sat up.

"You got me here?" he said to Grace. **"THE *SYCES* HAVE** left," she answered. "They walked right over us and then I dragged you in a little ravine. When they came back they passed the ravine and went back to their horses. The last I heard they were taking the body of Multao back to the Sultan."

"I see," Tanden replied. "And now we are in the woods—without food and with me wounded and a long way from Kiruchu.

"It's been so long since I have had food," Grace laughed, "that I have forgotten all about it. I was afraid to eat in the palace for fear of being poisoned."

Tanden had stood up and was peering through the moonlight.

"It's only fifteen miles and there are native huts along the way," he said. "We can make it back to Kiruchu if we take it slow."

FIVE DAYS LATER Tanden, shoulder bandaged and face pale, stood in the office of the Dutch Governor in Malacca. Grace Morley was at his side, her eyes flashing in her drawn face. Across from her, surrounded by guards, was El Karim, brown face expressionless and eyes fixed on the governor.

The governor, a short, fat man, with red cheeks and a tight smile, sat behind his desk. Grimly he read the papers that Tanden and Miss Morley had taken from the book of poetry found in the Sultan's library.

He finished reading and looked at Tanden.

"These papers," he said, "give a complete story of a cold blooded murder. So complete, that there can be no question of what happened to young Morley, or of the real ownership of the gold concession."

Tanden started to nod agreement. But in that moment, El Karim came to life with a snarl and leaped from his chair.

"This is an insult," he cried. "I, El Karim, Sultan of Kiruchu, accused of murder. You have taken our lands and now—"

THE BEST OF THRILLING ADVENTURES

His hand went to his belt with a speed almost faster than sight. A curved blade flashed in the air, and before Tanden could lunge forward, the knife was coming directly at his heart.

In that split second he could do nothing but swing around, placing his right side in front of the oncoming blade.

There was a swish of air, a tearing of cloth, and then Tanden felt a sharp, piercing pain in his right side, under his shoulder.

A gun roared, the thunderous explosion filling the room. In the blinding haze of smoke Tanden saw the body of El Karim crumple to the floor, roll over on its back, and then lie still.

"Are you hurt?" the fat governor cried to Tanden.

Tanden moved his arm and grinned weakly.

"The blade cut through my clothes and ripped some skin," he said. "Nothing more."

The two men looked down at the lifeless form of El Karim. Over the erstwhile Sultan stood the guard who had fired the shot.

"THE BEST RIDDANCE the Dutch could hope for," the governor said grimly. "Now that El Karim is no more, we may hope for some peace and prosperity in Kiruchu."

"The only way you would ever have gotten it," Tanden replied.

"And when you decide to work that gold concession, *Mynheer* Tanden," the governor smiled, "you can expect the utmost cooperation from us. We feel under great obligation to you and Miss Morley for enabling us to get El Karim, a thing we tried for years."

"A job I don't want to have to repeat," Tanden laughed.

He and Grace Morley walked happily out of the room.

Orchid of Doom

BY **LIEUT. SCOTT MORGAN**

*An Intrepid Adventurer Runs
a Mad Race with Death in the
Weird Depths of the Jungle*

CHAPTER I

WHITE INDIANS

LARRY WESTON WAS in the Canal Zone on a vacation. A vacation, he hoped, from righting and adventuring. This was the last place in the world, he decided, where anyone was likely to call upon him to exercise his peculiar talents.

Therefore he thought nothing of it when a seedy individual sidled up to him, as he was taking his morning constitutional along Gatun Locks.

"Lis'en, bo, how about stakin' a poof devil to coffee and beans for one meal?"

Larry Weston paused, stared at the man in white ducks. The fellow had ragged clothes, straggly hair, and appeared to have gone long unwashed. His eyes were wild, staring. His toes were visible through holes in his shoes and socks. He looked like a man who had been through hell.

Larry's nose wrinkled with disgust. A serious expression crossed the face of the beachcomber. He lowered his voice.

"I don't really want anything," he said softly. "But I do want to know this: are you Larry Weston, whose name was registered yesterday as a new arrival in Colón?"

Weston's eyes widened in surprise. He wondered what sort of a game was being played on him. But he nodded, his interest quickening.

"Yes, I'm Weston," he said flatly.

"Ever hear of the 'Dawn Lady?' " asked the beachcomber.

Larry shook his head. The fellow went on:

"You've heard that Panama is known as the 'home of the orchid?' Well the 'Dawn Lady' is an orchid. Some call it the nightmare orchid. No scientist has ever been able to bring one out of Darién, not even myself, I discovered the orchid, but a mob of cutthroats drove me away from my find.

"They're in there now, gloating over the Dawn Ladies like misers over their gold. The first person to bring out one of the orchids will be world famous and can name his own price for exploitation, motion pictures, and so forth.

"I'm just one man, wasted by fever and other kinds of sickness, including, at times, the madness induced by the Dawn Lady. It needs a cool hand and head to go into Darién and bring out one of those flowers, Will you take on the job?"

Larry was surprised. The demand was abrupt and unexpected.

"But it will take money," he objected. "Why should I spend my own—"

He got no further. The beachcomber delved into his pocket and brought out a roll of bills—did it with some difficulty, because it was so big for his pocket. The top bill was for a hundred dollars. The man rapidly peeled off twenty bills exactly like the top one.

"It isn't much," he said apologetically, "but there is plenty more. I need scarcely warn you that if you take this on, your life isn't worth a nickel."

"In that case," said Larry Weston calmly, "I'll do the job. You going?"

"Yes. I'll see about getting the outfit together. We need some Jamaica blacks as carriers, and—"

"You take care of the details. But if I take it on, I'm the boss. From where do we start into Darién?"

"From the headquarters of the Yavisa River."

"Tomorrow?"

"Right. And watch yourself. I'll see you at your hotel. My name is Michael Badger, of the National Museum of Natural History."

THE BEACHCOMBER SIDLED away as furtively as he had approached, and with his going Larry Weston had the strange feeling that all Gatun, all Colón, had suddenly become a place of eerie mystery and danger.

He felt eyes boring into the back of his neck. He looked around him but saw no one save the workers at the locks, who were easing a big liner through into Gatun Lake for the run through the Canal. Any body in that crew, he decided, might have seen the passage between himself and Badger.

That Badger was closely watched—if he had told the truth—Larry Weston was quite sure. His expression became grim.

Again he was the righter of wrongs, the world adventurer, taking on all honest jobs that came his way.

Colón had lost interest for him. The jungle was calling, the jungle and danger. A mile from where he stood were the dark shadows of the brush filled with all manner of violent death. He would be facing it soon.

He looked like a soldier, tall, slender, stern of countenance, as he strode back to his hotel. Badger had vanished as though the earth had swallowed him. That he would reappear again, Larry knew quite well. At the hotel desk, he tossed one of the century notes to the clerk.

"That the real thing?" he asked casually.

The clerk fingered the note.

"I'd like to have two carloads of 'em," he said, grinning.

"Thanks," replied Larry.

He went to his room, turned the knob, entered—and hell itself seemed to hurl itself on him from the darkness.

His blinds had been up when he had left. Now they were down, and blankets must have been hung over the windows to make the room look so dark. He caught an alien odor, a wild strange odor, mingled of unwashed bodies and something his nostrils had never before experienced.

THEN HE WAS fighting for his life. His fists began to lash out. He felt his knuckles collide with flesh and bone.

He felt the bone give before the savage ferocity of his blows.

His feet moved in the darkness with the surety of the ballet dancer. He was a master fighter, even in the dark. His keen ears gauged distances by the barely audible breathing of his adversaries. He knew there were four of them, and that they attacked with knives.

Something hot slanted along his side, ripping coat, shirt and undershirt to ribbons. A knife blade had pinked him. He gauged the slant of the knife, knew exactly at what angle it had struck.

His hands darted out, caught the knife hand as it was raised to strike again. He yanked the man toward him with his left hand, and drove his right to where he was positive the would-be killer's face was. He had the satisfaction of feeling his knuckles strike full and true to the jaw of his enemy.

The man wilted in his hands. He allowed him to drop as softly as possible, unwilling for the noise of this fracas to reach the ears of the hotel people. The enemy, too, apparently desired to do all this in absolute silence, for they fought without sound.

THEY GAVE BACK now for a breathing space, and Weston realized under what a terrific disadvantage be was laboring. His enemies had been long enough in the darkness for their eyes to become accustomed to it. He had just come in from the brilliant sunlight and was virtually blind, would be for several seconds.

But he didn't wait. He was glad that his door had a spring lock. But he could always see anyone against the door if it opened, and get them before they got away.

He flung his arms wide and hurled himself forward. His right arm encircled a waist. It slid swiftly up to a neck, fastened in the throat of a rough garment. His left hand grasped a throat.

He stopped, held back by the inertia of the man he had grabbed. This put both of them slightly behind him. He had an arm fast to each. He gritted his teeth, exerted all his force, and brought the two of them together ahead of him before they could even have time to comprehend what he intended doing.

They came together with battering-ram force. Their skulls cracked against each other with a sickening smash. He dropped the two as though they had been hot pokers. Three out of the running. One left.

This one had plenty of courage, for now he hurled himself at Larry Weston like something shot from a gun. Larry knew that his knife was lifted, ready for a savage down-stroke, or that it was coming up from below in a disemboweling stab.

He crooked one knee ahead of him to protect his loins, held his left forearm over his face to shield himself against the stab.

A hand, a wrist, crashed down on his forearm. Larry allowed his arm to give a little with the blow. His right hand shot forward, under the knife arm of the attacker, then back over behind the elbow, so that his hand could grasp the wrist whose hand held the knife. Then, with all his power, he jerked.

A scream, instantly shut off as his attacker remembered, gurgled in the throat of the man. Larry loosed him and the man staggered back. Larry was on top of him, pounding away. His left shook the invisible enemy. His right drove savagely to the heart, and the unknown went down.

LARRY'S BREATHING WAS scarcely accelerated. He stepped to the window, yanked down the blanket, slid up the blinds. The brilliant sunlight poured in.

He came back, stared down at the four who had attacked him. They were all white men, with hair that was almost golden, blue eyes, and faces with rather rounded contours. They seemed typical Nordics, large and powerful, but it came to Larry Weston that there was something unusual and other-worldly about them, something strangely weird.

Weston remained quiet just for a moment. He could have called the police and sent them to prison, but he was curious.

That they were in some fashion connected up with his recent contact with Michael Badger, he knew very well. Certainly that man's enemies had wasted no time. Only fifteen minutes ago Weston had agreed to do a job, and already an attempt had been made on his life.

CHAPTER II

HOSTAGES OF HATE

THE MEN STIRRED, one after the other. All were very much alive, and quickly returning to consciousness. Weston ripped sheets from the bed, turned the men over, noted that each wore sandals, and bound their wrists behind them. Then he sat back and considered his next move.

It was obvious that, whatever the mystery behind this attack, the future was filled with danger if he went through with his promise to Badger. And he had no intention of not going through. He lighted a cigarette. His hands did not tremble, even after his tremendous exertion. They never did. He was always in perfect physical trim.

His telephone rang.

"Someone reported a disturbance—" began the hotel clerk.

"It's nothing," said Larry. "I stumbled over a chair." He clicked up the receiver.

One of his attackers returned fully to consciousness. He opened his eyes widely, but made no sound. He merely looked around him, as though orienting himself.

Then his eyes settled on Larry Weston. Something began to grow, deep down in those eyes. It seemed to be madness. The light in the eyes was flecked with little spots of gold.

Weston understood it. This man was actively hating him, and the longer he stared at Larry the more savage and bitter became his hatred. The anger increased until murder, plain, unadulterated, unhidden, glared satanically out at Larry Weston. In spite of himself, Larry shuddered at what he saw in that gaze.

But it wasn't this that troubled him, for he had seen murderous hatred in the eyes of men before now. It was the aura, the emanation, from the man, which was distinctly—well, *different*—the only word by which he could describe it to himself.

One by one, the four men returned to consciousness. Each, without making a sound, first oriented himself, then stared bitter hatred at Larry Weston.

Then the bound men, turning their heads slightly, exchanged glances. Their lips did not move, nor did their eyes. They seemed to be concentrating on something, and Larry had the uncanny feeling that, without words or gestures, they had clearly communicated with one another.

IT WAS A queer sensation. It came to him that they, all four of them, were invisible radio sending-and-receiving sets. The room literally filled with the tension of cruel, murderous hatred.

There was a knock on the door.

Larry's right fist was against his hip, clenched and ready for action, when he stepped to the door. He hesitated for a moment, then swung the portal open, moving aside just on the off chance that whoever knocked might instantly start shooting.

The man who came in was Michael Badger. The result of his arrival was strange. His eyes fell on the four bound men. Their eyes clashed with his. The four men were utterly still. Badger's face convulsed with fury. He hurled himself forward. His right hand came out, holding a knife. He was a man beside himself.

Weston flung himself on Badger, hurled him against the wall before he could stab one of the defenseless men. Then Weston stood before him, his face grim, his lips a firm straight line.

"I won't countenance murder, Badger!" he snapped.

"You would," croaked Badger. "You would if you knew what I know. Do you know what those people are?"

"No. They look like Swedes, Norwegians or Danes."

"They're not. They're white Indians from the heart of Darién, from the land of the Dawn Lady. No scientist save myself—and now you—has ever seen one of them and returned to tell about it.

"Some of them go into the outside world, passing for white, almost unnoticed. Only those with a faculty of tongues emigrate, and always they return to their own.

"Expeditions into their lands all vanish from the face of the earth. I am the only white man ever to go among them in their own territory and return alive—and they hate me beyond the power of white men to hate.

"They have sworn that none shall ever bring a single specimen of the Dawn Lady to civilization. Just now they are working with my enemies to prevent my return. When I have been done away with, my enemies in turn will be ruthlessly slaughtered."

"You mean there are others like these in the heart of Darién?" asked Weston incredulously.

"YES. I ESTIMATE their number at four thousand odd. They are protected by all other Indians—Chaco, San Blas and the like—against any encroachment by outsiders. The red Indians regard them almost as gods.

"They don't intermarry, zealously guarding the purity of their mysterious strain. Their women are gorgeously beautiful, but to look on one of them means death for a white man.

"God, Weston, I went mad when I saw them. If you hadn't stopped me from slaying them and I had knifed them, nothing on the face of this earth would have saved either of us from destruction!"

"But who would have known?" asked Weston. "Obviously, they came here unobserved. They wouldn't have been missed."

Badger's face worked spasmodically.

"They're stranger than strange," he said. "Stories, legends about them, have been current since the Spaniards first landed in Darién. They are credited—and rightly, too, Weston—with almost unbelievable powers of clairvoyance.

"I CAN TELL you this, right now: every white Indian in Darién knows at this moment what has happened here, and they have told their red brethren. These four have doubtless sent messages, by some telepathic means, to their people.

"If I had slain them—we couldn't get into Darién with an army! We'd be followed to the ends of the earth by their executioners, and no matter where we might be—in a Greenwich Village studio or a Park Avenue apartment—the executioners would find and destroy us."

"Then what do we do?"

"Turn them loose," said Badger.

"Then guard ourselves from every angle against murder at their hands."

Badger turned on the white Indians, spoke to them swiftly in a *patois* of which not a single word was comprehensible to Weston. They received his words in silence. Badger motioned Weston to stand back and cover the four with his automatic.

Then Badger swiftly slashed the bonds of the four killers. They rose to their feet. They seemed on the verge of resuming the attack on Weston.

Badger stood beside Weston. His own hand now held an automatic. The Indians hesitated, looked at one another in that wordless way they had. Then they stared at the window, then at the door. They went through the door as silently as cats. Weston and Badger looked at one another for a moment. When they went to the door, peering cautiously out, the four white Indians had vanished.

Nobody in the hotel reported having seen them. They had apparently disappeared into thin air.

THE TWO MEN were grim as they sat down to dinner that night. Badger, now dressed in the habiliments of civilized society, reported that he had prepared for departure the following morning at four o'clock. Weston took charge.

"You will act as guide," he said succinctly. "If our numbers permit, there will be advance guard and flankers, also a rear guard. For I'm telling you something, Badger: even if I'm all alone at the wind-up, I'm going into Darién and come back with a specimen of the Dawn Lady—if there is such a thing."

"There is," said Badger quietly. "I've seen it—them, thousands of them!"

"Then to procure one should be easy," replied Weston.

Badger shook his head. There was a fanatical light in his eyes. His next words made cold chills race along Larry's spine, despite the fact that the steamy heat of the tropics had bathed his whole body in clammy perspiration.

"I won't come back," said Badger. "I know that. They've told me, and they keep their promises. I've left twenty thousand dollars in a bank here, which will be paid to you when you produce a Dawn Lady—fully described by me to the bank's president—with the assurance that Michael Badger receives credit for its discovery and classification. You'll do that?"

Weston hesitated. He licked dry lips with his tongue. On the point of telling Badger that he wouldn't come back without him, Weston changed his mind, for it came to him as he looked at Badger that he saw a man already as good as dead. He shrugged.

"I think you're right, Badger," he said, and it was as though he added his own words to the sentence of death against the man. "I won't pretend to believe otherwise. Maybe you had better not go."

"You'll go anyhow, even if I don't. You'll bring back the nightmare orchid. The white Indians will blame me for your success. And whether I go or stay, or wherever I go, they'll find and destroy me. I'd rather die facing them and fighting them for what I regard as the most precious thing in my life."

     THE BEST OF THRILLING ADVENTURES

Weston marveled at the fanaticism of scientists like Michael Badger. He didn't try to understand the man, which wouldn't have been difficult—for Weston himself belonged to the strange tribe which would not take a dare, though he never worded it like that even to himself.

CHAPTER III

INTO THE JUNGLE

AND SO IN the steamy dawn of the next day, with a dozen carriers, Weston, dressed for the jungle—armed with guns, his hard fists and the canniest wits that had ever gone into the Panamanian wilderness—started out with his expedition. Four men—had been sent ahead the previous night, to have burros and additional carriers ready for them when they left the Yavisa Valley.

He went to Cristobóbal, thence down the Isthmus to Yavisa, where dugouts were waiting.

Now and again crocodiles splashed into the stream. Ocelots, pumas, jaguars screamed from the jungles at night, and sometimes stared with golden eyes at them from the limbs of overhanging trees. Tapirs, disturbed at their feeding, slipped into the stream and vanished. Badger explained that these animals walked along the bottom of lakes and streams as easily as on the ground above.

SNAKES SUNNED ON the banks. Bush dogs showed themselves, slinking figures in the jungle's gloom. Deer flashed through clearings like streaks of light. Huge boa constrictors sometimes were seen hanging from trees like fat lianas, waiting for the passing of unwary victims.

Death lurked in the jungle everywhere. Tiger fish filled the waters. For a man to fall overboard meant that his flesh would be stripped from his bones before he could ever be pulled in again.

They came to the place where they were to leave their dugouts; to the place whence, really, they were to start their grim dash for the heart of Darién and the valley where Badger said the Dawn Lady would be found.

Weston's eyes were grim. He seemed oblivious of the ghastly heat which shriveled the flesh even of the tropic-born Jamaican blacks. Nothing appeared to trouble him. He drove his carriers like a slave master.

The grim procession started away from the Yavisa. Badger looked back, said softly:

"My last look. I shall never see it again." Weston didn't answer, feeling again in his heart that what Badger said was true.

Three men went ahead as an advance guard. They were burly Jamaican blacks who ordinarily didn't fear anything that lived. But their faces wore that sickly, fish-belly color which shows when a black man is deathly afraid. They carried rifles in the crooks of their arms, and went on with many backward glances over their shoulders.

All the carriers were likewise armed

with rifles and each man had been supplied with plenty of ammunition.

One hour passed one hour during which the procession dropped the valley of the Yavisa behind them.

Ahead, blue with distance, showed the peaks of the mountains which masked the mysterious land of the San Blas, where no foreigner might stay after sundown. Nearer at hand, somewhat lower down, was another mountain range. Between it and the first, according to historians and geodetic survey topographers, ran a mysterious river, along whose banks were the white Indians and their red brethren. All of them had remained aloof from the outside world for centuries, and had destroyed without mercy—as far as the world knew—every expedition which had entered their land.

THE MOUNTAINS THEMSELVES seemed to hold up their hands to bar the passage of Weston's expedition. They were a menacing rampart, thrown the length of a continent across the east.

The procession turned around an outcropping of land and came upon the three members of the advance guard. They were piled together, as though flung there by the hand of a giant or the blast of a hurricane. A poisoned arrow stuck from the throat of each. None had had opportunity to fire a shot.

The carriers looked, then whirled. They started back toward Weston, fright in their eyes. Instantly his automatic leaped to the fore, together with that of Michael Badger.

"Back to your jobs!" snapped Weston.

"We're going on. Don't turn your backs on the enemy or you're finished!"

Just what they would have done was to remain forever afterward a mystery, for at that exact moment, as though they had sprung from the soil, scores of red men appeared on all sides of the procession. Savagely painted, they were armed with ancient weapons and with bows, arrows and spears.

"Down!" barked Weston. "Throw your packs ahead of you as protection. Prepare to commence firing!"

WITH THE FIRST move of the procession, the Indians opened. Arrows smashed into the burros first, killing the entire train. Arrows, spears, bullets, streaked past the ears of Weston and Badger. Two carriers flung up their arms and crashed down, dying even as they fell.

Weston realized that even to be touched, to have one's skin broken by one of those arrows, spelled instant death. He flung himself down behind one of the dead burros, dragging Badger down with him. Badger was babbling:

"It's the nightmare! It's the nightmare!"

Weston turned on him without a word and slapped him cruelly across the face. Badger looked stunned, but something of the madness went out of his eyes.

"Sorry," he mumbled, "and you're quite right. My raving would make the carriers turn back in spite of everything you could possibly do. I had it coming."

Badger, there beside Weston, began to fire. The carriers, now under cover, such as it was, were unlimbering their rifles. "Shoot to kill!" barked Weston.

　　　THE BEST OF THRILLING ADVENTURES

His own automatic began to bark. He fired over the back of the burro behind which he was ensconced. He never once missed with that automatic of his.

The Indians were so close he could see the fanatical light in their eyes. He fired at one, saw a hole appear in the man's forehead, and held his breath when the man—who must already be dead on his feet—charged forward. With mouth open, eyes set in a blank stare, the man did not drop until he had stumbled over the burro from behind which Weston had slain him.

Weston's heart felt cold. If the Indians who still lived took it into their heads to charge, not all the bullets in the party could keep them from slaying every man in it.

"Rapid fire!" barked Weston.

He again fired. This time he shot twice at his man, once at the heart, once at the legs. The man went down, unable to charge. Weston hated to use two bullets on each man, but it wouldn't do for each to charge, even in death, upon him. One might destroy him with a poisoned blade or an arrow. Again and again his gun roared.

OTHER INDIANS CAME out of the woods to join the attack. Now the Jamaican blacks were firing rapidly and with deadly effect. They, too, got wise to the necessity of making sure that an enemy dropped when struck with a bullet, and concentrated on the knees of their enemies.

The Indians fell in windrows. Ten minutes of fighting and fully a score of the Indians had fallen dead within plain sight. Others, shot through heart or skull, had whirled and vanished into the jungles, to die beyond sight of the interlopers.

Then, as quickly as they had come, the Indians vanished, and utter stillness took possession of the wilderness. Weston rubbed his eyes. The Indians had taken away their dead and their wounded, doing it so quickly that he had scarcely been conscious of their actions.

Fearfully, the blacks raised their heads. Nothing happened. No arrows, spears or bullets came out of the woods. AND THEN, JUST as the carriers would have risen to their feet, a solitary figure appeared on the trail ahead, right hand upheld in the universal token of amity or truce. A voice spoke to Weston, calling him by name! The English was excellent!

"Your party wins for the moment," said the red man. "But it is impossible for you to go into Darién and live! One by one you will fall until none is left. Our people will die, gladly, to the last man, to make sure that none of you escape. Go back, and you will not be molested. Come forward, and you will die."

Weston looked at Badger. Badger's face was utterly white; but his eyes were filled with grim purpose.

"I go forward," he said, "whether I live or die." Badger raised his voice in answer to that of the Indian.

"We shall not turn back," he said.

The Indian vanished. One moment he was visible; the next moment there was a blank space where he had been standing, beyond which was the wall of the jungle.

The carriers were gray-white with terror. They rose to their feet, surged on Weston. He stood staring at them. Jamaica Jim, straw boss of the carriers, spoke to Weston with chattering teeth.

"We're going back, boss," he said. "Ain't enough money in the world to send us agin them red fellers."

"The families of each of the dead will receive five hundred dollars, Jim," snapped Weston. "The same goes for anyone who dies hereafter. And each of you who gets back receives a thousand dollars, in addition to your regular wages. Get your men going. Take the packs off the dead burros and increase the loads of your men to take care of the extra duffel. Get going!"

But the blacks stood their ground. Their rifle muzzles menaced Weston and Badger. Weston's eyes narrowed to razor-edge sharpness. Grimly, he moved forward. His right hand held his automatic at his hip.

"The first man to pull a trigger dies," he said softly. "I'll get him, even if I take a bullet through the heart at the same time."

He could see black fingers, trembling, tighten on triggers. But he moved forward. He stood facing Jamaica Jim. The black stared at him fixedly. The whites of his eyes were showing, red-rimmed with a horrible fear.

Casually, Weston pushed aside the muzzle of the man's rifle, stepped in and felled Jamaica Jim with a blow of his fist. Then he looked at the others.

"I'm not disarming you, because they may come back," he said calmly. "But you're going ahead with us."

JAMAICA JIM SAT for a moment. Then he rose to his feet, picked up his rifle and felt of his swelling jaw, which had almost been broken by Weston's fist. He grinned at the man who had downed him, and whirled on the blacks.

"What's the matter 'a you fellers?" he bellowed. "Didn't you hear Mista Larry say we go on? Get going before I sink my feet into you. Ain't a one of you wouldn't kill for a thousand dollars—guess you kin die fer that much, if you has to!"

The blacks hesitated. They rolled their eyes at Weston, looking for him to relent. But the grimness never left his eyes. His fist held his automatic in readiness. The blacks turned back, refitted their burdens, slung their rifles over their backs, and took up the trail again.

Three went ahead, when the trail at last came to an end, to cut a way through with *machetes*. Sweat poured from their ebon bodies. But something had gone into them. The determination of Weston, which took no thought of death, had been forced into them. It was as though they themselves had refused to turn back, even for death. Something of their leader's grimness of purpose became their purpose, too.

A half hour passed. Weston was driving the men without mercy, as though they raced against time to cheat death. Once, as they slowed for a breathing space, a gray streak flashed from the jungle. It struck a carrier. He dropped. His throat had been ripped open. He died with his hands at his throat, blood spurting through between his fingers.

THE BEST OF THRILLING ADVENTURES

CHAPTER IV

SCENT OF THE DEATH FLOWER

WESTON TURNED TO Badger. The scientist's eyes were wide with amazement.

"That was a jaguar," he said. "I never heard of one of them deliberately attacking a man. But I *know* what it is. It's the night—"

Then Badger remembered, fell silent. As the carriers, with a long look at their fallen member, again took up the trail, their speed still more accelerated, with no time out now for rest, Badger dropped in beside Weston.

"They're trying some other way," he said softly. "That animal was mad. It's the nightmare orchid again. To breathe of its odor means madness! That cat didn't know what it was doing, else it would have run away instead of striking."

As though in answer to his words, something streaked again from the jungle, this time from the other side, into which the jaguar had gone. Weston's automatic leaped forward, spat. The gray streak dropped into the newly cut trail. **THE CARRIERS STARTED** to look back. Weston barked at them to keep going. He and Badger paused beside the dead jaguar. Its yellow eyes glared at them. Its claws made convulsive movements, as though even in dying he would rip out their throats. A strange, giddy odor came from the dying cat.

"It's the orchid," whispered Badger. "The cat has been caged and literally bathed in the odor of the Dawn Lady. If we took time to go into the jungle, we'd find the cage from which the Indians released him."

Weston's teeth showed as though, like the jaguar, he snarled. But not once did he look back the way they had come.

"Will the Indians attack again?" asked Weston.

"No. They're smart. They know our rifles are too good for them, have too great a range. They'll turn the jungle against us."

But in spite of Badger's dire forebodings, nothing further happened that day until after the sun had dropped into the invisible Pacific and utter darkness possessed the world.

Then the carriers threw up a hastily built barricade of logs and brush, in the center of which they built a fire to keep off mosquitoes. Around it they huddled in wordless fear, their white-irised eyes never still as they searched the surrounding blackness of the almost impenetrable jungle. Tents were thrown together for Weston and Badger, but Weston knew that he would not sleep.

He had started to enter his tent when one of the carriers screamed, jumped to his feet, and yanked something from his neck—something about two feet long which writhed sinuously. The black dropped it on the ground, where he started to stamp it to pieces with his feet. **BUT AFTER HIS** first frantic jump, his movements slowed, as though a mighty weight had been dropped suddenly on his shoulders. He staggered, stumbled to his knees, fell forward on his face—and the little snake which had bitten him in the neck crawled into the brush of the barricade and vanished before it could be slain.

"I saw it come into the barricade," said Badger, running up. "It came sailing in, end over end. But thank God none of the carriers saw it come. I just happened to be looking in the right place. If they blamed that on our enemies, not even our automatics could keep them from bolting."

"We've got to play fair," said Weston. He raised his voice to the carriers. "That snake was thrown in, fellows," he said. "If any one of you want to go back now, he is at liberty to do so."

The blacks did not answer for a moment. Then Jamaica Jim spoke for them all.

"You'll go with us to see we gits back safe?"

Weston shook his head.

"When I go back, it will be with the thing I came for."

"Then I guess we has to go with you," said Jamaica Jim simply; and forever thereafter, no human being would ever be able to convince Larry Weston that color had anything to do with the shape and form of a man's courage.

Weston hesitated.

"Break camp," he snapped. "We can't stop now until we've done our job. If we stay here, we may all be dead by morning."

As though to emphasize his words, queer sounds came out of the jungle. The first was the far muttering of drums. The next was the muted screaming of men. And in and through these sounds went others which were oddly like the screaming of frightened women, or the squalling of newly awakened babies.

BADGER SEEMED TO be cataloging these latter sounds. Weston watched the moving of his lips.

"Pumas! Ocelots! Jaguars!" Then Badger turned to Weston. "I know what they're doing," he said. "They are either capturing, or driving before them, all the jungle cats they can gather. And the time will come when, in some fashion or other, they'll turn them all against us."

Weston sighed with relief.

"We can cope with things we understand," he said. "It's the unknown that frightens people. The blacks won't be afraid of the cats!"

Grimly Badger shook his head. In less than five minutes the camp, so recently made, was dismantled. By the light of flaming torches, which afforded any enemy excellent targets—though not a man was fired on during the ghastly, grueling night which followed—the procession cut and hacked its way through the lianas and underbrush which guarded the way into the heart of mysterious Darién.

Once a negro took a sleeping boa for a liana and struck it with his *machete*. Instantly it whipped around him, and the man was dead before the others could slash him free of the constricting coils. The other blacks scarcely bothered about it. Boas were common, a way of dying they all understood. They drove themselves as mercilessly as Weston had been driving them.

And all the time, as they drove forward and upward—the last proof that they were ascending the mountain which would take them into the valley which no man had seen and returned to tell about—the drums kept beating in the night. The darkness was filled with the shouts of men, the beating of spears against shields, and the screaming of Panama's big cats.

AND SO, FINALLY the sun started out of the east, signaling its coming by a crimson streak which was the color of blood. Scarcely had the dawn started breaking than a ghastly thing happened. A strange, terrible, heady odor came through the jungle, rousing it to eerie, mad life.

Badger pressed in close against Weston and whispered:

"It is the time when the Dawn Ladies open their petals," he said. "All the jungle goes mad when it smells the odor—all save the red and white men who live here and are accustomed to the nightmare orchid!"

The carriers became erratic. One sang a song, dancing as he moved forward with his burden. Two began to fight. Weston, himself, resisting a desire to scream with laughter, hurled himself at the fighting blacks.

With blows to the chin he knocked them out. Then he kicked them in the ribs until they returned to consciousness—and they laughed in his face like fools as they rose and staggered on.

"We've *got* to resist the desire to go mad," whispered Badger, "or we'll scatter into the jungle and the natives will get us, one by one."

Weston nodded grimly.

He was everywhere at once. Every time a black man tried to break free of the procession, as though to run wild in the woods, Weston, now dripping with perspiration and panting like a spent runner, drove him back with his fellows.

They paused once for a few minutes. Badger and Weston, both chattering nonsense until each called the attention of the other to his chattering, secured the packs to the ebon backs so that the carriers could not throw them away. Then, with feet and fists, they forced their men on; while every minute, as the sun climbed higher, the odor of the nightmare orchid, possessing all the jungle, became more and more overpowering, more conducive to the craziest, wildest fancies.

They reached a hilltop and Badger pointed. Directly beneath them was a valley, formed like an amphitheater. And its floor was covered with nodding stems, topped by flowers—which were visibly opening—with petals as red as the blazing orb of the rising sun!

Badger screamed and started forward. He ran past the carriers without seeing them, forgetting even Weston. Weston watched him go. The carriers stood, or danced, or sang—depending on the effect of the ghastly odor of the flowers on each individual—and watched the scientist race into the very midst of the vast area of Dawn Ladies.

CHAPTER V

WALL OF FLAMES

"GREAT GOD!"

The exclamation burst from the lips of Larry Weston in a great explosion. For now he understood the devilish cleverness of the men against whom he had, at Badger's request, arrayed himself.

Tongues of flame were shooting up from the hillsides all around the valley. The tongues joined. In a few seconds, the valley was walled in by the rising fire. And the nodding stems of the Dawn Ladies, dry and brittle, would burn like tinder!

"AFTER HIM!" YELLED Weston. "We've got to reach Badger!" Driven forward by blows and kicks, the whole procession raced after Badger. He was babbling when they came up to him, with his arms filled with the crimson flowers he had picked; his face was buried in them as though he deliberately drank of the nightmare.

And at that exact moment, Weston realized the full extent of the catastrophe. For in and among the underbrush on the hillside, in and among the nodding stalks of the orchids, flashed countless cats—ocelots, pumas, jaguars!

They wouldn't attack men of their own accord, but now, by the devilish ingenuity of the Indians, they were being forced to fall on the interlopers. For they were hemmed around by the flames, even as the interlopers were; and the flames were closing in, their heat forcing the jungle cats closer and closer to Weston's expedition.

Neither Weston and his men, nor the cats, could penetrate those flames. In the end, all would be destroyed—but not before the cats, driven mad by the flames and the odor of the Dawn Ladies had torn every last man asunder.

Grimly, Weston decided on the only course open to them as he saw it. He yelled at the blacks:

"Grab as many of the flowers in your left hands as you can hold. Then gather around me. We're going back out, understand? Two of you grab Mister Badger. He doesn't know what he is doing."

Two men hurled themselves at Badger, but the scientist, utterly mad, screamed like a great cat himself and dashed straight away from them, running with the speed of a deer. Before the eyes of them all, he ran full tilt into a jaguar which was pawing at flames that bit into his fur. Badger went down, his precious flowers flying in all directions, and over his body the screaming jaguar went mad.

Now Weston formed his men into a sort of flying wedge, turned them about. They cast their packs from them, ripped them apart, kept only the pieces of canvas in which their duffel had been wrapped. Weston led the charge.

The carriers carried flowers in their left hands. Their rights held their rifles. They raced toward the closing wall of flames.

The cats they encountered charged at once.

WESTON'S AUTOMATIC SPOKE repeatedly. The black men fired when their rifle muzzles actually touched the bodies of ocelot, jaguar or puma. Two men were dragged down, torn apart. Weston wondered if the Dawn Lady were worth all this, realized that many lives—in the name of science—had been given for orchids far less important and mysterious, gritted his teeth and rushed on.

Now the flames were almost against them. Weston yelled to his men to cover their heads with the canvas and dash into the wall of flame. They obeyed. Their screams as the fire touched their skin were ghastly. Weston himself suffered the torments of the damned.

But they were through. The wall of flames was as thin as paper. The carriers flung themselves down, clawing at their burns.

The Indians who had planned all this charge, were driven back by bullets from the rifles of the maddened blacks, the automatic of Larry Weston.

And Larry Weston made a strange discovery.

NOT A CARRIER had succeeded in getting through with a single specimen of the Dawn Lady; and of all he had plucked himself, his left hand held but one. He tucked this one into his shirt and buttoned the material over it, thus shutting off some of its odor. But already it was almost imperceptible, and he knew why: the Dawn Lady closed its petals when the sun had entirely risen.

Then began the race back. Once, a mile from the valley of hell, a shout came from the woods in the voice of the Indian who had given them the first warning:

"You shall all die this side of the Yavisa! Badger is dead. His enemies have served us and they, too, are dead!"

But Larry Weston did not believe in failure.

One week later, with three black men who looked like scarecrows, he re-entered Colón. Scarcely pausing in his stride, he went to the bank, took the Dawn Lady from his shirt and showed it to the bank president. Without a word the official placed a fat packet of bills in Larry Weston's hands. Weston turned to the blacks, one of whom was Jamaica Jim.

"I can trust you to divide this properly among your people?"

"Yes!" And Larry Weston knew that Jamaica Jim had gone through too much to consider cheating anyone. He had learned how unimportant life was, how simple and sudden death might be.

Weston gave the whole packet of bills into the black hands of Jamaica Jim, thrusting them at him as though the bills were impregnated with the venom of all the reptiles in Panama. Then he shook the hand of the faithful, courageous black.

Later Weston went to his hotel. He spoke grimly to the hotel clerk.

"Listen," he said. "I'm going to sleep. I don't wish to be disturbed."

"Yes, sir, Mister Weston! You are enjoying your vacation?"

There was a queer light in the eyes of Larry Weston, just finished with one of the most amazing experiences he had ever undergone, as he answered:

"Oh, definitely! And, listen, mister, don't even send up the mail or newspapers—and if anybody else asks if I am enjoying my vacation, tell 'em you don't know. Tell 'em to go to the devil, tell 'em anything—but don't tell any of 'em that I am anxious to make expeditions into Darién!"

Lost Treasures of Eden

BY **CAPT. JOHN POWERS**

The Glamorous, Astonishing City of Flaming Swords—Untold Wealth Hidden Under the Weight of the Centuries—And Stirring Combat With Denizens of the Unknown!

CHAPTER I

A PLEDGE WITH DEATH

I SEARCHED PROFESSOR Gregory's face carefully, I knew, though he held himself staunchly upright, with the cold sweat streaming from his face, that he had only a very short time, to live. Malignant malaria might carry him off at any moment. He had to talk rapidly.

He had, in a few brief minutes, turned back the hands of the centuries almost six thousand years, by Biblical reckoning!

"You know, of course," he said, "the story of the exodus from Eden?"

"Of course. Who doesn't? Eve was tempted by the serpent and ate of the apple, and she, with Adam, was driven from the Garden of Eden with a flaming sword in the hand of an angel of the Lord. It was their punishment. And since that time nobody has ever been able to locate the idyllic garden of the first man and woman."

Professor Gregory leaned forward tensely.

"I know where the Garden is!" he told

me. "And I know that if Adam and Eve were driven out—and I would never deny Holy Writ after all I have seen—they crept back later, or their children did, and remained in the Garden until their death, leaving it to their descendants to the end of time. They have occupied it uninterruptedly ever since."

NO, THE MAN wasn't mad. He had taken an expedition into the vast lands of Yucatan—lands which were guarded by Indians who never allowed outsiders to spend the night in their domain. Now, the only survivor of the expedition, he came out claiming he had found the Garden of Eden!

I suppose I was the first person to see Gregory and not to laugh at him. I had a hunch, which was why I had called on him in his hotel. Gregory was pitifully eager to talk. The ridicule he had received at the hands of his fellow scientists had eaten into his very soul. If ever a man had been sentenced to die of a broken heart, that man was Professor Alexis Gregory.

"You believe me?" he asked. "I tell you I have seen the city that stands in the Garden of Eden, inhabited by men, women and children as white as you or I. The city is surely the oldest in the Western Hemisphere. It is like a monster beehive, but marked by domes and minarets which glisten like gold in the sun—because they are gold! Their leader is a first daughter of Eve! Their symbol is the flaming sword.

"The city rests in a deep valley which is like an amphitheater. Outside of the valley, guarded on all sides, at every approach, by lost descendants of the Aztecs, are the hills which no outlander, except myself, has ever passed and lived. I have been in, and have come out. I returned to find someone to take up my work and prove my story; I found shrugs and disbelief. They think me mad. I've been through enough to make me mad."

I looked at him again, and he wasn't mad. My heart hammered with excitement. Gold beyond computing! Diamonds, too, mined through the centuries from the changeless hills!

"I know all about you," he told me finally. "I would like you to go into the place, study it, confirm my stories of it, and make preparations to enter with a scientific expedition, open it to the world. You'll do it?"

It didn't take me long to make a decision. To rediscover Eden! To look upon a city forever lost to man!

I extended my hand to him. He caught my fingers and clung. His eyes stared into mine with fierce intensity. Then, slowly, his fingers relaxed, he sat back—and Professor Gregory was dead.

At that moment, I had the feeling that nothing in the world could stop me from keeping faith with him. I had clasped hands with death and made an agreement.

I STARED AT the dead man for a moment. Then I rose to my full six feet, and went to the small black handbag which he had explained held all his data and whatever money I would need. The whole thing was in a big envelope, marked with my name. Gregory had known I would accept his proposal.

I shivered a little, recalling what he had told me of the gift of prophecy possessed by these people. Had he had some of it himself?

I counted the money and whistled softly to myself. There were forty new bills of one thousand dollars each. Enough to keep a man in comfort for a lifetime, but for one thing—that potential storehouse of wealth beyond man's wildest imagining. If I hadn't known of the professor's golden city, this forty thousand would not have seemed, by comparison, like a few pennies jingling in the bank of a child.

I called the hotel authorities, reported the death of Gregory. As soon as the medical examiner pronounced his death natural, I slipped out. Times Square seemed a place apart, somehow alien, for beyond and through the lights I could see that sun-drenched city of gleaming roofs!

Making inquiries, I found that the first steamer for Puerto Cortez left in three-quarters of an hour. I headed straight for the docks. I had money to purchase what I needed. By going alone, and immediately, I guarded my secret.

THE STEAMER FAIRLY crawled southward. Many times I cursed myself for not having flown. But I spent the time planning ahead. Of the Yucatan jungle. I knew only that it was filled with snakes, poisonous orchids, ocelots, jaguars. But inland, beyond, the valley of lost rivers, I knew nothing of the land. Neither did any other known living white man.

I docked at Puerto Cortez, hurried from the steamer, and bumped into a short white man.

He had blue eyes, fair skin, and yellow hair. The bumping, I thought, was accidental, I started to apologize.

"To go into Eden is to die!" he said softly.

I didn't stop to think, I just grabbed at the man. But many people were moving down the gangplank, jostling me, and he slipped through my fingers. It wasn't a retreat, for there was nothing in the man's eyes even remotely resembling fear.

His eyes warned me. They were malevolent.

I started after him, but he moved away. To run after him would be to court too much attention, to bring my name into prominence. I didn't want any publicity, so I had to let him get away.

How could this man have been there, ready?

How could he have known of my coming?

Dread suspicion gave me cold chills. The "people of Eden," Gregory had said, could see things at a distance! Absurd!

But Gregory had believed in it himself.

The man on the dock had known of Gregory, of course; had seen stories of his death in the newspapers, stories in which my name had been mentioned. Knowing Gregory, the fellow must have guessed what Gregory would do, and had watched incoming steamers for my appearance.

I wasn't ready to accept people who could see things at a distance. There were plenty of things in the world beyond my comprehension—but then I remembered: had not Jehovah said to Adam and Eve:

"But the tree of knowledge ye shall not eat of it!"

"I must be crazy," I told myself, "to believe in this nonsense!" But what if, as Gregory had said, the first man and woman had come back in the olden time, and eaten of the tree?

My thoughts were leading me into all sorts of mental absurdities. But I couldn't get that white fellow and his warning out of my mind. It stuck to me, and his face went with me in memory, during all my preparations for the trek into the south.

First, I found a beachcomber who had once fought with me in a revolution in Nicaragua. The man's name was Mestizo Jaime, and he might have been any nationality.

"Into Yucatan?" he asked when I told him. "Sure, I'll go. I've heard a lot of stuff about that place. Any fighting?"

"Absolutely," I replied.

"Then I'm on."

"You may get killed," I said.

In a second they would have
torn me limb from limb.

    THE BEST OF THRILLING ADVENTURES

"What of it? I can't live forever."

"If you are captured you may be tortured or sacrificed to some heathen gods."

He grinned. His mouth was full of gold teeth, his only assets.

"They'll know they've been in a fight!"

TWO DAYS LATER, with a group of twelve additional men and four burros, we started out of Puerto Cortez and headed straight toward the heart of Yucatan, following a route Gregory's notes had laid out for us. Our crew contained seven blacks and five white men, the latter beachcomber friends of Mestizo Jaime whom he had gathered together.

From the very beginning we had our work cut out for us. The jungle was matted, and we had to cut our way through with *machetes*. Mosquitoes descended on us in countless hordes, filling our veins with malaria. I dosed everybody with quinine, including myself, until our heads rang like temple bells. Only the burros did not seem to mind.

MESTIZO JAIME RULED the bearers with a heavy hand. They obeyed him without question.

"Get the lead out!" I kept urging them. "This is a race against death!"

At last, after what seemed endless hardships, and dangers which had taken the lives of two of our men, we stood at the uttermost limit ever reached by any expedition. This was the jumping-off place. I lifted my eyes and peered ahead, debating with myself. That warning rang in my ears louder than ever:

"To go into Eden is to die!"

As I stood beside a tree, scanning the way ahead, I heard a light thud. I turned, startled. An arrow had imbedded itself in the tree. Nobody saw it but Mestizo Jaime, who happened to be with me. There was a piece of paper tied around the haft of the arrow. I unfolded it.

Amazingly, the message was in English, a mere scrap of words that meant nothing. The paper was torn, and raggedy. Then I recognized the handwriting. It was that of Professor Gregory! It said:

northeast corner of the Garden of Eden.

It looked to be a page torn from a diary. In itself it meant nothing. The arrow was the warning. The handwriting told me our unseen watchers knew who we were and why we were there.

Mestizo Jaime and I looked at each other in silence. The jungle was suddenly silent as the grave, as though all the world had paused to listen, and to wait for what would happen next.

There was nothing miraculous about this, I reassured myself. Gregory had kept notes while a prisoner in the city about which he had told me. To himself he had probably called the place the Garden of Eden, and this note was merely something he had written to remind himself of some spot in the city, some location perhaps, or some hiding place.

"Well, Jaime," I said, "do we go on or go back?"

"What do you say?" he answered.

I gritted my teeth.

"I go on if I have to go alone."

"I go with you," he said simply. "Let's put it up to the others."

I took the arrow and went back to our resting men. I spoke to them briefly.

"To go on may mean that every last one of you will be wiped out. To go back means only to get through the dangers of the jungles—the normal ones. To go on means plenty of money for you if you live. To go back means to forfeit any rights in whatever this expedition develops. What do you say? Remember, now, once we have traveled ahead for just one hour, you're committed to the trip, no matter what happens. It will be too late to turn back. I give you fifteen minutes to decide."

TO A MAN—SO well had. Mestizo Jaime chosen our crew—they agreed then and there to go ahead, and we started.

I expected almost anything to happen. But nothing did, as we went deeper and deeper into the jungles which now mounted toward the peaks of the second range behind the mountains ramparting the sea.

We built a barricade that night and set double guards. The jungle was silent. I slept. I wakened to hear a mad, wild chattering, in which there was nothing that sounded human. I jumped from my hammock, thinking we had been attacked.

Three men, who had been sleeping were dead. Over the nostrils of each was a poisonous orchid—the Midnight Lady!

CHAPTER II

LANCETS OF GOLD

BUT AS I had already told my men, it was too late to turn back, nor would I have done so, even had I been offered all the gold about which Gregory had spoken. I knew that every last man might die before we ever glimpsed the Garden, but that didn't deter me, either.

We pushed on, after burying the three dead men, as we had buried the others who had died. And now I knew why the jungle had not showered us with enemies. They were around us all the time, lying in wait, prepared to destroy us as they chose. I had walked my men straight into their trap. As we advanced, the blacks, with flaming torches of wood, led the way. They fought at the lianas with *machetes* until sweat poured from the laboring bodies. When the ever-expected onslaught did not come, I cursed our unseen enemies with all the evil words I knew. Not to attack was worse than any attack could have been. The suspense was ghastly.

It was around two o'clock in the morning when we lost our first burro, but we couldn't blame that on human enemies. A boa constrictor swinging from a tree, and looking like a liana, wrapped himself around the animal and squeezed it to death before we could kill the reptile. Mestizo Jaime shot the snake. It might just as well have gotten one of our men.

The boa, however, didn't fall onto the ground after Jaime's bullets had smashed its head. It merely hung straight down from the fatal tree limb, its loosening folds dropping the contorted burro to the ground.

I looked up and shivered at what I saw. The most dangerous folds of the boa constrictor, the last few feet of the tail, which he had to fasten onto something to bring his other coils into play, were fastened about that tree limb with a liana.

He had been placed in our trail by some human agency.

He couldn't thus have trapped himself.

"They must be all around us!" I told Mestizo Jaime.

I looked wildly into the blackness of the jungle. To me, now, it was peopled with the very imps of Hades. As we went on, we watched for all sorts of traps, for anything the mind of man might imagine. The snake had gotten under my skin, for it made me think again of Eden, in which Eve had listened to the evil counsel of a snake and been banished for her failure to resist.

"Keep going!" I yelled at the men, already traveling their best.

NEAR MORNING WE stood on a cleared space on a shoulder of the last mountain range westward, and looked into the south and east. The sky, in that direction, was streaked by a strange glow. The glow was as if it came from a city lighted with electricity, but I knew that was absurd. Such a glow, I told myself, might have been caused by a vast flame reflecting itself from some smooth substance, say a mighty glass reflector.

Or it might have been reflected from burnished gold!

Gold going to my head: but in that direction, I knew, was the place we sought, if Gregory had been as sane as I thought him, and if his maps and notes were even approximately correct. We had followed those directions minutely.

That the light was of human origin I knew before I took another step, for the glow suddenly vanished as though it had been switched off, and the night sky, where it had been, became as black as Erebus. I judged the light had been three miles away—three Yucatan jungle miles, each of which was as far as the moon. But I hammered at my men.

WHEN MORNING CAME, after hours during which I watched the sky for the reappearance of the light, we stood on another eminence and looked down into a valley. Gregory had said that the true valley was guarded by Indians. We saw no such guards.

On the valley floor—and what a fortress the valley was!—were tumbled masses of rock, which were shaped in what seemed to be beehives of mighty proportions, or like pyramids with abutments of some sort. The buildings looked as old as time itself. They covered the valley floor almost to its edge, where the hills rose. In between them were growing things, gorgeous foliage born of the tropics.

Here was a paradise. It didn't seem to be inhabited. I saw no living thing that moved—and yet, as I looked, the sweat burst forth on my whole body. I trembled and was afraid. Not afraid of anything

Scores of men poured forth, fiery swords gleaming.

There must be people somewhere, for this city showed evidence of intense, inspired cultivation. Near the abutment of one of the buildings I saw something move. It seemed to be a huge man, but it was gone so quickly I couldn't be sure. It was as though it had caught my glance and ducked back.

And then—suddenly—the sun came out of the east, rising like a red ball of fire, and splashed its light over the roofs of the city. I gasped. I couldn't seem to catch my breath, for when the sun's rays struck the city, the city's roofs struck back at the sun with lancets of gold that were brilliant as those of the sun itself. The whole city seemed to glow, a golden glow of unimaginable splendor.

Were those roofs sheathed with gold? I think my men must have thought so, for they swore softly, in low voices, and their eyes did not blink as they stared, as though they feared to miss something for an infinitesimal second.

They got out of hand. They forgot hardships and warnings, and acted like men who had gone mad.

"Take it easy!" I cautioned. But they paid me no heed.

THEY BUNCHED THEMSELVES and charged down the mountainside. I wouldn't be left behind. After all, this was the place I had set out for, and I was going down into it at any cost. I became as bad as the rest; I raced after them, took the lead. All of us gripped our weapons. The burros with our duffel and our food were left

I could touch, but afraid of a nameless something I couldn't comprehend.

A warning had come to me from this place. I hadn't heeded it. Yet here was power, plainly indicated, which dwarfed my own to pigmy size. Had I been able to conceive of this place, I wouldn't have dared to move against it with less than an army!

behind, forgotten.

"Look to your guns!" I snapped.

At the beginning of the city, I managed to call a halt. Before us were streets. There were spots in their cobblestones which glistened when the sun struck them as the roofs of the city did. And there were spots where the ground was not covered by stones at all. In these bare spots showed the footprints of human beings—bare feet, and feet covered by sandals.

"Good God!" It was an exclamation, almost a prayer, from Mestizo Jaime.

There were people here, all right, but where were they? Not one was visible. I followed Jaime's gaze and read the answer. On the hill where we had stood were men aplenty. They seemed to be soldiers in extended order. I studied them more closely, and knew they were Indians, the guardians of the passes Gregory had mentioned.

YET THEY HAD allowed us to pass through. I felt a chill at that. It meant that we were to be handled by the people of the city; that there was no escape for us. I followed the rim of the valley with my eyes, and knew that every foot of the way out was guarded—by men who merely stood, dots against the jungle, and stared at us in silence, bows and arrows gripped in their murderous hands.

"We're trapped," I said flatly. "But we're still alive. Nothing shall stop us!"

I sent two men ahead as point, to give us warning if enemies waited around the next corner. I watched the two men go. They turned a corner, moving with utmost caution. Then we advanced. But when we reached that corner, no more than a minute later, the two advance men had vanished—and there were spots of blood on the cobblestones.

I looked at Mestizo Jaime, and he looked at me. Jaime grinned. He would have grinned at anything. But I didn't feel like grinning.

"Listen, Jaime," I said. "I don't intend to be played with. Here we stay until something breaks."

We leaned against a wall which seemed to shut off a dwelling of some sort, and waited. We waited for two minutes by my watch. Nothing happened. Then, something did. It was a simple thing, until one recalled that two of our men had disappeared as though miraculously snatched into nothingness.

The something was the musical sound of a bell. I listened, and my head swam. The earth seemed to whirl and spin under my feet like the deck of a boat in a heavy sea. No need to tell me of what metal, or what alloy, that bell was made.

"Listen to it," I told Jaime.

He nodded, his eyes wide. He, too, had guessed.

The bell was made of gold. It was being rung by a man, or woman, of great power. Its great volume penetrated all the mysterious city, all the valley. It was threatening, savage, commanding.

Then a cry rose from the hills—the guardians making answer: an answer which traveled all around the valley's rim, a cry that chilled the blood.

THE BEST OF THRILLING ADVENTURES

With a creaking sound, many doors opened. White faces peered forth. I looked back the way we had come, between high walls—and the way behind us had been closed by a third wall which had dropped silently into place, or had been raised into place from the ground.

CHAPTER III

MOVING WALLS

TO SAY THAT we were startled, would be to put it mildly. The way back was effectively blocked. We whirled around again, in a body—and there a fourth wall had risen. We were now blocked in by four walls, all of them higher than we could reach with our fingertips when extended to their greatest reach. And two of the walls were closing in on us, to smash us out flat.

The slow moving of the two walls reminded me of the ponderous moving of the leaves of the great Panama Canal locks. Those walls were heavy; they must have weighed tons. My men were swearing. Their eyes were big with fright.

I stared from one moving wall to the other—and my stomach turned. Those walls were stained significantly with gruesome black splotches which could mean but one thing: other men had seen this treatment before. I fancied I could even see their shapes, painted by the stains of their own blood, on the jaw-like walls closing in to crush us.

THE IRONICAL PART of the whole thing was this: we were going to be crushed by gold! The two walls were literally plated with it, and it glistened even through the hideous stains. It was as though the people here had known why we came, and were mocking us by showing us pounds and pounds of gold, before that precious metal spread us out flat and killed us. I could have laughed hysterically over the irony of it—but some action was necessary. I hated to die like a rat caught in a trap.

"Get hold of yourselves!" I yelled at my terrified men. "Form for wall scaling!"

Mestizo Jaime quickly took charge, dividing them into four parties, one for each wall. He formed his men in the usual pyramid, facing the wall that closed on us from the front. I took three negroes and the wall to my right, which was a fixed wall. We climbed up. Jaime got onto the moving wall with his men. Two of them sat astride, reaching down their hands to one man who remained at the base. He took two steps backward, and prepared to run and jump, holding up his hands for his comrades to grasp.

"Hurry!" I yelled at him.

But he missed his grip, and by this time there was no chance left to jump again. The closing walls were within two feet of each other.

The man himself knew he couldn't make it. His hands were uplifted as though in supplication. His eyes were starting from his head as he watched the tops of the two walls—those tops now so close together that he could see them both at once, five feet above his head.

"Goldlemighty!" moaned Jaime.

Then the opposing walls touched their victim, while his arms were still stretched to their utmost above his head. I stood there, horrified, turned to stone. I wanted to turn my head away and could not. The walls were flattening him out. The resistance of his body did not stay their slow march at all.

A ghastly scream burst from his lips, rose in a terrible agony and died away into the silence of death.

Even then the walls continued to close. When they finally stopped, one could not have inserted a finger between them at the top.

No wonder there were stains on those walls!

"Run!" yelled someone. "Get away from the walls!"

I REGAINED CONTROL of myself, whirled atop my perch to look about me. Things had gone bad indeed for us. Mestizo Jaime's men had dropped beyond the wall they had scaled, or so it looked. I was alone on my wall, for the three whom I had helped out of those ghastly jaws had dropped into a sort of compound beyond.

Now they were racing like madmen toward a tall door in the face of a building. I don't know that I blamed them, for the jambs of that door shone in the morning sun like a thousand eyes.

"Where in God's name did they come from?" I asked myself, as I looked at those eyes.

Diamonds? I didn't know. Rubies? Perhaps. Whatever they were, whether precious or semi-precious, there were hundreds—thousands—of them set into the stones of that doorway. Were my men racing to twist those stones loose—or were they racing for the door merely because it seemed to suggest a way of escape?

I soon had the answer, for they yanked the door open. They dashed through it and the door slid closed silently behind them. Only silence answered when I shouted,

"Where the devil are you?"

I STEPPED OUT onto the wall over which Mestizo Jaime had gone, looked down the "street" where, a few minutes before, we had stood before the walls began to advance. Mestizo Jaime and the three with him had vanished also. Then I stepped to the wall which had been to the left, peered over into another courtyard. It was empty of any living soul.

The rest of my men, save only the one whom the wall-paws had caught, had been swallowed up by this beautiful city of gold and precious stones. Prisoners? Who knew, save the inhabitants of the place? I didn't know what to do next.

"Come and get me, too!" I shouted, but only silence answered.

I stepped back to the position on the right wall where I had watched the closing of the doors, I stood there because that spot alone somehow seemed to belong to me. It was little enough to possess, but it seemed oddly like a place of refuge.

"Where are my men?" I raved. "Where is Mestizo Jaime? I've found a city of gold, yet have not one person with whom to share it. And now that I have it, what good is it to me; what can I do with it?"

I gripped my rifle in readiness. I searched the city with angry, sick eyes. If I could spot so much as a moving body, I would fire. I would teach these people to make a mock of me. But nowhere could I spy a living soul.

Well, one compound was as good as any other. I dropped into the one which had swallowed the three men who had scrambled out of the trap with me. And for the first time I was cognizant of the beauty of that compound. It was planted with all kinds of gorgeous flowers and shrubs, their odor sweet to the nostrils.

Then I stared down at the material of which the winding walks were composed, and felt a little sick. They were made of human bones worked into red sandstone, to form beautiful, brilliant mosaics—so that, I thought savagely, the owners of this place walked always in contempt over the enemies they had slain.

My bitter meditation was broken by a sound I had heard before: the ponderous grating sound of those moving walls. They were drawing apart, their work done. Warily, my rifle at the ready, I started for the door which had swallowed my three men.

I reached the door, and the two broad steps which led up to it. Both steps were slightly hollowed out in the center, as though by the footfalls of the centuries. Then my eyes flashed to the door jambs, and the glistening stones set into them. I wasn't an expert in stones, but I would have sworn that this one doorway—in a city which must have had thousands of doors—was worth a fortune in itself. And some of the stones had been cut! If only those stones could speak!

HOW COULD I pass the portals of this place? I studied the building. There seemed to be no windows; certainly none I could see. But there were cornices on the roof, and I was startled as I noted their decorations. Animals, done in metal, marched down the ridges on the roof.

Maybe the idea had come from China, or the traditional animals on Chinese roofs had been modeled after these, but there they were—ocelots, pumas, bush dogs—all done in gold, or gold plating! The place must be a shrine of some sort, or the home of some important dignitary.

I knocked and yelled: "Open up, whoever you are!"

Then I drew back the butt of my rifle and banged it savagely against the door, several times. The sound of the banging seemed to ring through the whole city. I heard it boom muffledly through the thick door.

THE BANGING GAVE me an idea. I stepped aside, smashed my rifle butt against one of the stones stuck into the doorjamb at the height of my eyes. The stone jumped out with the force of my blow. It was a many-faceted ruby, larger than a big man's thumb-ball.

I thrust it into my pocket, and was instantly conscious of an aura of menace that seemed to flow out at me from all over the city. I could feel thousands of eyes on me. Then, the door slid open noiselessly and I stepped across the threshold and into a room that was as light as day, because the sun came through great skylights in the roof.

Reaching to the roof from the floor was a mighty black figure. It might have been a statue of Buddha, but for one thing—the body of it was covered with coarse black hair at least two inches in length. Directly beneath it, and about four feet from the floor, was a stone basin. Here was a mighty idol to whom the inhabitants of this place made sacrifice.

I had ghastly proof of this, for I was staring, horrified, at such a sacrifice. Lying at either end of the great sacrificial basin, their headless necks slanting into it, their bodies nude and bathed in the brilliant light of the sun, were two white men. They were my two point men who had vanished so mysteriously!

Could this ghastly place be the Garden of Eden in very fact? If it were, then the sons of Adam who had crept back into it, forsworn by their God, must have forsworn Him in their turn, setting up in His place this mighty black monster whom only human blood would satisfy.

I did a foolish thing, then. I raised my rifle to my shoulder and fired twice, aiming at where the thing's heart would have been had it been semi-human as it seemed.

The thunderous echoes of my fifing fairly rocked the place. The result was immediate and horrible.

CHAPTER IV

SONS OF ADAM?

FROM BEHIND THE figure, coming from right and left, lumbered two huge creatures, larger than the biggest man I had ever seen. They looked like apes. They looked like giant negroes. They looked like either, neither, both. Their little red eyes were fixed on me with dreadful intensity. They were tiny replicas of the statue into which I had fired.

With arms outstretched, they plunged at me. I yelled and fired at the foremost. I heard the bullet smash into his body, but the thing came on. His huge hands grabbed my rifle and wrested it from me. In savage anger the maddened brute brought it down across his chest and bent the steel barrel double.

Then both brutes had me down. In a second they would have torn me limb from limb, but there came an interruption. Scores of men, all perfect specimens, poured into the vast audience hall in front of the black statue. They were led by a girl dressed in something white which looked like a Roman toga, her golden hair drawn back from her forehead with a circlet of gold encrusted with gems that, even in my extremity, made my mouth water. The girl's feet, tiny and beautiful, were shod with sandals, made of golden thread, studded with brilliants.

Her face was grim as she said something in a strange tongue. Instantly the two monsters drew back from me, left me panting and weaponless. One of them lumbered to the sacrificial basin where the headless bodies lay, and dropped my ruined rifle into it. Perhaps it was his idea of offering up a sacrifice.

It was no surprise to me that the girl addressed me in English, Gregory had been a long time among these people, and there may have been others before him. Now, at this writing, I know that these people unsuspected, travel throughout the world as sailors, tradesmen, whatever other white men do, and learn all of its secrets; but that always they return home, and keep their own secrets and that of their abiding places. "What are you doing here?" the girl asked.

IT WAS A facer. But I could lose nothing by telling the truth.

"I come to open earth's most beautiful city to the world, which has too long been denied such loveliness," I answered.

Her face flamed with anger, the anger of a goddess who listens to words of defilement. "Who are you who dares thus to address the first daughter of the first woman?"

My heart almost stopped beating. What was this woman trying to tell me? That she was a first daughter of Eve?

"But that is impossible," I stammered. "By Biblical reckoning the first man passed to his rest over six thousand years ago."

"Yea, and the God of Heaven did say to him that he should not eat of the Tree of Eternal Life, lest he, like Jehovah, live forever. But he did not forbid the daughters of him who was called Adam."

"And you did eat, and have lived since that time?" I gasped.

My brain whirled. Did this woman count her age in centuries, her beauty growing with each passing year? For she was the most gorgeous woman I had ever seen. It was absurd, impossible. But could I tell her that she lied?

"I come only to look upon wonders," I temporized.

"And wealth?" she asked.

"And wealth. What good is it to you, who never use it?"

"But it is ours. We mean to keep it. Down the centuries our people have guarded it, protected it. Men of your race have come to us, have despoiled us, have gone among us with flame and sword. We have never seen one of you in our own land that did not mean death to many of our number."

"I did not come to bring death," I assured her.

"Then why did you come with weapons in your hands?"

I COULDN'T VERY well answer that one. Her beautiful face hardened. I guessed that she was either a priestess of the temple or the queen of the city.

"And you have violated the temple of our god, the Black Avenger," he continued. "You have raised your hands and your weapons against him. For this you will undergo the greatest punishment we can bring to bear against you. There is no escape. We are guarded by thousands of our Indian slaves. You cannot get through them. They obey us because we are their gods. Had you taken heed of our warnings, which began when you landed in Puerto Cortez, you would been spared this."

I bowed to her. "It is worth dying," I said, "to be able first to look upon a woman so beautiful."

But that didn't get across very well. Her face formed into an imperious, displeased frown.

"It is not proper thus to speak to Mene, priestess of the temple," she said. "It augments your punishment."

"I would not retract the statement if I could," I answered.

A MUTTER OF protest rose from the lips of the men who stood around me, clear-complexioned men with blue eyes and the inevitable yellow hair, men who showed signs of unusual intelligence and courage.

"Let him die at once to appease the wrath of the god he has wronged!" one of them cried in English.

I don't think it would have surprised me had some of them addressed me in Latin or Sanscrit. I had discovered a highly cultured civilization, a lost tribe, a lost city, in the heart of a country which was almost on the doorstep of my own!

"Where are my people?" I asked.

"Those who live are prisoners," said Mene. "You will see them soon. They, too, have been condemned to sacrifice. But first, they must work out their atonement."

It didn't take me long to understand what she meant by atonement, for half a dozen men laid violent hands on me. I was led from the temple by another way, into what appeared to be a vast hothouse. Towering beams upheld its quartzite roof, through which the rays of the sun came to bring life to the luxurious plants which filled the place.

All around the inside of the vast building were urns which must hold fires at night—and so I knew the meaning of the glow I had seen against the sky, though I wondered why the fires were lighted.

I was soon to know why, for in that great hothouse I found my fellows laboring among the plants and flowers, stripped to the waist and clothed in sackcloth, and guarded by "angels of the Lord."

That phrase leaped to my mind without thought on my part. I couldn't fail to think of it, for the guards in this place were armed with long swords with snaky blades, and the swords were plated with gold that shone like the sun. When the swords moved, the blades seemed to be of living flame. With such a sword had the first man and woman been driven out of Eden!

I noticed that the backs of my men were bloody, but I didn't wonder about it long. Immediately I, too, was stripped to the waist, and then beaten across the back with the flat of half a dozen swords until I gritted my teeth in agony and fell to the floor on my face, with the sweet odor of gorgeous flowers in my nostrils.

"Oh, God," I prayed silently to myself, "save me from this torture."

LYING ON MY face for a moment, I was enabled to see under the plants in the storehouse—to see the thousands upon thousands of glistening eyes! Those eyes were precious stones, of a value beyond all computing, and they glistened because, as any man who is familiar with stones knows, life gives brilliance to gems. Actually, those who worked here, worked to keep the stones "living."

The breath of the plants, and the life of them in that hothouse, literally kept the stones alive—so that, since we were slaves of the plants, our hearts' blood, literally, fed the life of the stones.

Here, then, was the lost treasure of Eden. And there was no end to the power of Mene and her fellows, if they had, centuries ago, broken the divine command and eaten of the Tree of Knowledge!

They *must* have eaten, and so learned all things—learned where earth's treasures were to be found, so that their slaves might dig them out of the ground and lift them out of the sea, that all might be gathered here to be kept alive by the exhalations of the slave-tended plants. Since Mene knew the abiding place of all earth's treasures, she had but to fetch them at her whim, and this lost city probably held scores of hothouses like this one, each with its countless hoards of living stones tended by miserable slaves. MY BRAIN WHIRLED with the fantastic suggestions of it all, even as the flat of the swords were laid across my quivering back.

The guards kicked me to my feet. I fought savagely, and instantly the points of two swords touched my throat. So much did they resemble living flame, I could almost feel heat emanating from those tips.

Then the guards drew back, and one called to me in English what I had to do. I fell to with my fellows. They were carrying huge rocks from a pile at one end of the place, building a big rock fountain in the center of the green-house. Each of those rocks would have required the work of three men to lift, but we were forced to lift them, roll them, move them any way we could, one man to each rock. And when we moved too slowly the swords were laid across our backs again.

That night the fires were lighted, turning the whole greenhouse into a blazing, sweating hell. We labored on, without food or water or rest, our eye-balls starting from our heads with pain.

Near morning a man fainted. He was Mestizo Jaime, who hadn't said a word to me since we had been thrown back together. He believed, now, as I believed, that the most fortunate man among us had been the one whom the walls had crushed. They carried Mestizo Jaime away, and he did not come back.

I heard a whispering among the guards, whispering I was meant to hear, because it was in English. Mestizo Jaime had been taken to the temple to be offered as a sacrifice to the Black God when the morning sun sprayed the broad ebon breast of the statue with its lancets of gold.

Desperately, I attacked the guards, calling on my men to help me, intend-ing to rescue Mestizo Jaime. I was beaten senseless for my pains.

When I regained consciousness I was working. I must have been working while in delirium, for there were just five men left of us. The others were gone. The five told me through horribly cracked and bleeding lips that the missing men had followed Mestizo Jaime, and that we were slated to go in turn. They were driving themselves to keep their feet, because even in this hell there was a certain sweetness in living. I WAS TO be the last, they told me, punished by watching my men being led to the slaughter, because I had brought them here and deserved the greatest punishment. I would go to the temple, too, in time—and for three whole days would be tortured, to lose my head finally in the sacrificial basin.

"We'll stop it," I said. "There must be a way out. We'll each take a guard when I signal by straightening my back. Take his sword away from him or die trying. Then split up, smash your way through the greenhouse walls, and every man will be for himself. Try to meet me on the coast where we started."

They agreed. In desperation they would have agreed to anything. It was days later—I have no idea how many—before I decided that the time was ripe. Near morning, when even the guards were sleepy with watching, I gave the signal—or tried to. But I had stooped so long over my labors I could not straighten my back. I cried out in despair. Guards came running with lifted swords of flame. "Now, for the love of God!" I yelled. "This is the signal!"

CHAPTER V

FACT OR FABLE?

WITH HOARSE SHOUTS my men charged the guards with me. My hands were hard claws, broken and burning with blisters I expected to carry with me to my grave. I thrust out those claws at the first man to reach me. I was almost a madman, and he couldn't have stopped me with any weapon.

"Strike and die!" I yelled at him.

I struck aside his thrusting sword with my right hand, slid in, kept the sword away from my body with my left arm, and drove a savage blow to his jaw with my right, In that blow went all my hatred for the oppressors, all my eagerness to win free. The man went down.

It was every man for himself. One of my followers missed in his effort to push aside the sword of his attacker, and was run through the body. Next moment I had caught up the sword of the man I had downed, and had lopped off the head of the killer. I got savage satisfaction out of watching his head roll on the floor, as the heads of some of my men had rolled into the sacrificial basin.

I whirled back to the other four. They had somehow eluded the guards. Each was going off in a different direction.

"Follow me!" I yelled.

They didn't turn, didn't hear me. In the city outside I heard the commanding notes of the great golden bell, and knew that the denizens of the place were waking from sleep and hurrying to aid our guards. I dashed for the nearest wall of the place and went through it head foremost, still bearing the flaming sword in my hand. I cut myself on the glass, Great slabs of it crashed down behind me. If I had been stayed for a second any one of those slabs would have cut me in two.

I dashed straight ahead. I didn't realize that I had managed at last to straighten my tortured back. I just ran. Shouts and cries were rising all over the city. From the hills surrounding the place came a bedlam of weird, far cries, as guardians of the passes shouted promises to their white gods that no prisoners would get past them.

I gritted my teeth and ran on. Once let me get atop one of the walls and I would make my escape, at least out of the city.

BUT THE WALLS were high, too high to reach.

Then I thought of the hilt of my flaming sword, and as I ran I tore cloth from my rough garment, wrapped it about the flaming blade. When I came to the first wall I jumped, holding the blade in both hands, and tried to fasten the sword hilt over the wall's top.

I missed as a thousand lights, signal fires, flamed on all over the place. I jumped again. This time the hilt caught, held, and I clambered up.

Now I stood limned in the light of all those fires, which glowed from a thousand windows like great searchlights. Behind each one was a reflector made of gold and studded with precious stones.

Arrows began to whiz about me as I raced along the wall. Once I stopped and looked around. One of my men was racing along on the wall behind me, a sword in his hand. Then a score of arrows struck him, buried themselves in his body, toppled him off the wall.

Nowhere could I see the others. I whirled and ran on.

"Come and get me, you pariahs!" I screamed as I dropped down into a compound which was dark.

Maybe the building in its center was deserted. I circled it cautiously, ran into a *cul-de-sac* where wall and building merged, went up and over into a street—the same, I guessed, by which we had come to this place.

I RAN LIKE a scared rabbit. Somewhere ahead was one of those moving walls which had trapped us. Suddenly I saw it rising out of the street, of which its flat top had been a part. It was rising swiftly, but I was close.

I cleared the rising wall, yelling as I jumped, while every tortured nerve and muscle cried out in protest at the pain I was inflicting on myself. Behind me a noise as of countless demons shouting inspired me to greater speed.

I was running through dank verdure which gripped at my legs. I stooped as I ran and pulled some of it with my right hand, to stuff the green, wet stuff into my mouth. It tasted like nectar of the gods.

Instantly heartened, I plunged on, knowing that I would still have to run the gauntlet of the guards at the rim of the valley. But I didn't head for that part of the rim down which we had come into the valley.

Once or twice I looked back. The city seemed to be in flames. I knew that the rest of my men were being hunted down, but evidently my escape hadn't been noticed. I hadn't deserted those men, but I couldn't have helped them in any way whatever. They knew it and I knew it.

With a heavy heart, I turned to the right, running the long way of the valley, straining my tortured eyes on the rim, looking for signal fires, or the shapes of Indians against the moon. I saw nothing. The valley was a bedlam of shouting furies. Soon I heard pursuit behind me, and settled to run myself into the very ground if need be, to escape them.

Drops of rain began to fall after a few minutes, and I found time to be thankful for an overcast sky. As I ran I held my mouth open to catch the splashing drops of moisture.

I ran like a man in a nightmare.

When I reached the incline of the valley, leading out, I was panting hoarsely, but I wasn't stopping yet, not even with that precipitous climb ahead of me. With my sword in front of me I started swiftly up.

WHEN I REACHED the summit, I looked back. I heard men shout behind me, from three different directions, and knew that at least three of my men had gotten out of the city. It would be useless for them to make for me. I raised my voice in a terrific shout that was like the cawing of a crow:

"Make for the place I told you!"

That shout, which was answered from three directions, brought the Indians leaping through the dark. Arrows winged past me as I darted away. I whirled. A man closed with me and I sliced at him savagely with my flaming sword—which even in the dark seemed to glow with a strange fire—and felt the blade bite through bone and muscle and sinew. The man fell. I heard him roll in the brush. Other arrows came, but none touched me. I ran on.

Twice more I had to strike with the sword, and I struck each time as though I myself had been an avenging angel, punishing once more the inhabitants of Eden. Somehow I got through them, though from both sides I heard their shouts and the patter of their feet, as they converged behind me. I banged against the bolls of trees, almost knocking out my brains. I caromed off, ran on.

I decided to race at top speed for three minutes, then stand and take whatever might come to me. Nobody can imagine what I suffered as I desperately carried out this scheme.

Then I stopped, beaten. I could go no further. I looked aloft. It was hopeless to climb a tree; I didn't think I had the strength, and the pursuers were close behind me. Nevertheless, I started up.

How I got up I don't know, but the branches finally hid me. Rain pelted through the leaves, and I hoped that water, cascading down the tree trunk, would erase my tracks. I crawled to the very top, where I fastened myself to limbs with parts of my ragged clothing until I was almost naked.

There I stretched out with my face to

the black sky, with my mouth open and my tongue sticking out, and gloried in the pelting rain against my body, which absorbed the water greedily. It was ambrosia!

I heard men racing through the jungle under me, quartering their tracks. I heard arrows whang into trees all around me, some of them into my own. But none touched me. Then I slept.

HOW LONG I slept, I have no idea. But when I wakened, my whole body was burned and blistered by the sun, which must have been bathing it for hours—days, for all I knew.

I felt I would die of the pain, but I had suffered so much that sunburn was anti-climax. I straightened stiffly. Slowly and painfully, still grasping my snaky sword, I went down.

The sun was low in the west. I took my bearings on it and started. Nobody followed. Momentarily I expected a trap. Often I went into trees when I detected suspicious sounds. My ears seemed preternaturally keen.

I went on. Again I found myself in the jungle. Vines and brush tugged at me as I forced my way slowly forward. There, were times when I had to use the sword to chop the tangled growth from my path.

As night approached, the jungle became a place of unseen menace that lurked insidiously all about me. The slightest rustling in the brush made me pause more than once and look about me anxiously. I had not forgotten that this was the domain of the Indians, nor could I be sure they were not stalking me now.

BLACK DARKNESS OF a cloudy night descended. I found that I could go no further. I sank down with my back resting against the trunk of a big tree. The flaming sword lay within easy reach beside me. For what seemed ages, I sat there.

I suppose that finally I must again have fallen asleep. It was all hazy, almost like a weird dream. But I opened my eyes to find it was once more daylight. My body was a mass of throbbing muscular aches.

I again went on. Finally I reached the trail that had been made by my men when we had advanced toward Eden. It was far easier to travel through the brush from here on, but always there was danger lurking in the shadows all about me.

I circled the sleeping places of boas. Twice I stood like a statue when stalking jaguars roamed near me. Finally I came to believe my enemies had given me up for dead.

Sometime later—I will never be able to estimate it in actual hours or even days, because time stood still—having lived on fruits and water from streams, I stood at the jumping off place, the last shadowy outpost of civilization.

I saw marks of three sets of footprints in the dirt. My men had beaten me out. They hadn't waited. I followed them back to Puerto Cortez, but I haven't seen them to this day. Doubtless they fled as fast and as far as they could, hoping never again to hear of me or the land into which I had lead them.

TODAY I AM a broken man, my body

slowly mending. I think that I shall never again be tempted to go adventuring—but I don't know. Adventure is in the blood of men. As I grow stronger, my eyes turn at times to the sword with the curving blade over my fireplace, glowing like the flames below it. It seems somehow like a giant finger, pointing back, as though beckoning me to return to the city of flaming swords. Will I, in the end, heed the call?

I have thought long though lately. How can it be possible, I often ask myself, that Mene be truly a first daughter of Eve? Who has ever known of such longevity?

Once I studied the flaming sword closely, and found an inscription on it, written in tiny letters which seemed to be holy fire. I copied the inscription and sent it away to learned theologians to be translated. The translation came back, but whether in jest I have no way of knowing, and this is what it read:

I am verily that flaming sword of the Angel of Jehovah which drove the first man and the first woman and their children from Eden.

Maybe the translations is true, maybe not. But I think of the fabulous treasure of the city of Mene, and the slaves who tend the plants which give life to the treasure, and I wonder.

Doctors say I wander mentally, but they are liars. And the day shall come when I will prove it to them by opening Eden to the world; or, if it be not Eden, its counterpart—fully as beautiful, thrice as miraculous and filled with such treasure as Eden never knew!

If I live, I shall some day discover the truth—now that I know so much no man has known before me.

The Lagoon of Monsters

BY **JOHNSTON McCULLEY**

*Shanghaied Aboard a Yacht
of Mystery, An Intrepid Texan
Plunges into A Roaring Maelstrom
of Savage Battle and Desperate,
Breath-Taking Peril in a
Sinister Outpost of the Orient*

CHAPTER I

TROUBLE IN SINGAPORE

THROUGH THE SWIRLING clouds of stale tobacco smoke and the haze of dust, Joe Parkner caught sight of him again—the foul-looking, evil-visaged half-caste derelict who seemed to be watching him malevolently.

He was shuffling forward beneath the reeking hanging lamps, with his shoulders hunched and his long arms dangling at his sides like a great ape. He finally dropped on a bench not far from that upon which Parkner was sitting.

His beady eyes seemed to glitter as he watched Parkner. He growled at a waiter who had the temerity to ask for an order, and did not glance toward the stage where one of the dancing girls was twisting and squirming in time to the weird music. Parkner took his eyes off the man a moment to glance around the room—and was startled to behold another of the ilk watching him closely also. To the left, a third was thrusting his way roughly through the jostling crowd; and, advancing toward him furtively from yet another direction, came a fourth.

Parkner became doubly alert now. He saw the four glance at one another in signal. One grunted an order. And suddenly all were on their feet, standing fan-fashion a short distance in front of Parkner and glowering at him. They began a slow and cautious advance.

That settled it!

With sudden decision, Joe Parkner sprang to his feet and kicked the bench back out of his way. He half crouched behind the table. His six feet of broad-shouldered, well-muscled young body was tensed like a fine steel spring. His hands became fists at his sides, and his lower jaw was thrust forward pugnaciously. And so he waited for the attack.

For there was not the slightest doubt about it in Joe Parkner's mind now—he was to be the object of a murderous assault. The four were concentrating on him, their purpose unmistakable. Parkner knew of no reason for it. And there was no time to ask.

Here he was, in this low dive in the most notorious and lawless part of Singapore, where many a man would engage to slit a throat for the price of a drink. He had come here with Pelican Jones, his boon companion these days, for sightseeing only. Pelican Jones had left him alone to slip out into the semi-dark little garden and make love to one of the dancing girls. And so, alone, Parkner faced the suddenly perilous present.

Why he should be subjected to an attack puzzled him. He had not been flashing money foolishly, for he had none to flash. His clothes certainly did not stamp him as a man worth robbing. And none of these assailants, creeping upon him like hungry wolves upon a wounded stag, was a personal enemy.

He never had seen any of them before.

Parkner retreated until his back was against the wall. The four followed, deliberately closing in on him, and making not the slightest effort to hide their purpose. One thing was a pleasant surprise for Parkner—no knives gleamed in the streaky light that came from the reeking hanging lamps.

He was glad for that! He carried no weapon himself.

Then they rushed.

Here was the welcome relief of action after a period of uncertainty and tense waiting. Parkner sprang forward, and his fists came up. Screams of rage ripped from four throats as he hurled himself at the men before him, carrying the fight straight to them and meeting them more than halfway.

THE BLATANT MUSIC of the native orchestra ended in a sudden discord. The dancing girl on the stage stopped her gyrations abruptly, and the other girls screamed and ran toward a corner. Men sprang up from benches and stools to crowd back against the walls and watch. But no profane bouncers appeared to put a swift and violent end to the disturbance.

That surprised Parkner—made it appear that the management had anticipated this trouble, and had sanctioned it.

Somebody was bellowing orders to Parkner's assailants, cautioning them not to injure him and to take him alive.

Parkner had a fleeting glimpse of him—a white man, plainly of the seafaring type.

He had no time to wonder what the unusual order might mean. It was as mysterious as the reason for this attack. And now, though certainly not needed, reinforcements arrived for the enemy. Two more men rushed into the fray from tables where they had been watching, to cut off the possibility of Parkner's escaping to either side.

Joe Parkner's Texas blood was at the boiling point now. This attack for no reason at all, plus the overwhelming odds, enraged him. He roared in a frenzy of wrath—and hurled himself forward again.

Parkner could use his fists with telling effect, and he did so now. They thudded into faces and against breasts, and his elbows jabbed. He was hurled back against the wall but rebounded at his antagonists, smashing into them, while they screeched and howled in his ears.

He was trying to get out of the dangerous corner, and was wondering whether Pelican Jones would hear the row and come to his assistance.

And, at the crucial moment, Pelican Jones arrived. He announced his descent with a strident shout that rang above the din:

"Stand to 'em, Texas! New Hampshire is comin'!"

PELICAN JONES CAME with a rush—a short, squat, uncouth individual with squinty eyes and a wrinkled face, whose age was perhaps fifty. Pelican Jones prided himself on being what he termed an international tramp. The ports of the seven seas had known him.

Strange and dangerous adventures were to him but the ordinary bread of daily life.

That his physical strength had not been entirely wrecked by the years and his mode of existence, Pelican demonstrated now. Deftly, he unbalanced one of the assailants and hurled him aside, floored a second with a blow to the face, and won through to a position near Parkner.

"Make for that window, lad!" he shouted. "Smash the dogs! Right at 'em, Texas!"

Side by side now, they fought fiercely to get to the open window. Parkner's fist crashed against a nose and brought a deluge of gore. He snatched up a heavy stool, and used it to help stop the next rush. As their enemies gathered for another advance, Pelican Jones went through the window headlong, and Parkner went tumbling after him. They found themselves in a pitch-black alleyway between two rows of dark buildings.

The window behind them immediately spewed angry men.

Wild cries of insane rage assailed their ears.

"This way, Texas!" Pelican Jones shouted.

"Comin', New Hampshire!"

"Hold out a hand in front. It's so

blamed dark—can't tell what we might run against."

So they began their flight. Behind them was an immediate pursuit. Nor were they to be allowed to remain in protecting darkness. Lights appeared, brought from the resort they had just quitted, and revealed them.

Some of their pursuers ran ahead of the others, spurred on by a bellowed promise of reward made by the seafaring man Parkner had noticed.

Parkner and Pelican Jones found that they would have to stop and fight them off again.

They retreated slowly as they fought side by side, working back along the narrow alley and preventing their foes from getting behind them.

But suddenly they found that they could retreat no more. Their backs were against a wall.

"Look for a door—a gate," Parkner panted.

Pelican Jones' reply had a tone of finality in it:

"We're caught in a blind alley, Texas. Here's where we stop."

"We don't stop till they down us, Pelican. That ain't Texas way!"

Then events occurred so swiftly they were bewildering! Guns barked, and deathly blades of steel were lifted evilly!

" 'Tain't New Hampshire way, either. Smash 'em, lad! Beat off the rats!"

With their backs against the wall, they fought as well as they could. They felt that they could expect no mercy after the terrific beating they had given some of this riffraff. And from the darkness another offer of reward was bellowed—a reward for taking the pair alive.

Parkner reeled as a stiff blow caught him on the side of the head. His fists thudded into the blur of faces before him.

He saw Pelican Jones go to the ground beneath a couple of his adversaries.

And then, as he tried to go to Pelican's assistance, another blow came, and with it oblivion.

CHAPTER II

PUNISHMENT

TO JOE PARKNER, the first intimation of a return to consciousness came from a terrific pain in his head, accompanied by a nauseating taste in his mouth and a dull roaring sound throbbed in his ears.

He tossed and moaned, and immediately felt a hand upon his brow, and heard the welcome nasal twang of Pelican Jones, at first as from a far distance.

"Good lad, Texas! They couldn't kill you with an axe. Take a swig of this."

Parkner felt a supporting arm around him, half lifting him, and managed to sit up. Nausea claimed him a moment. He made no attempt yet to open his eyes, for things seemed to be swimming around even with them closed. He felt the rim of a glass against his lips, and gulped liquor which went down his throat like fire.

"That's prime stuff, lad," Pelican Jones was telling him. "Let it hit bottom, then take some more. You'll be on your pins again in a jiffy."

Parkner gulped more of the liquor. The pain in his head grew less sharp. He heard a distant, regular throbbing, and became conscious of a rising and falling sensation that needed no explanation. He was aboard some ship.

He opened his eyes slowly, averting his head from the bright light. He found that he was in a berth, and swung his legs over the side. Pelican Jones sat by him, keeping an arm around his shoulders.

"Lad, that was a scrap!" Pelican Jones announced. "Best I've had since a couple of years ago in Liverpool. Too many for us, though."

"What was it all about?" Parkner asked.

"Don't you know?" Pelican Jones' surprise was genuine. "I sure don't. I never saw any of 'em before. Heard the row, and came runnin' when I saw you in it Thought that you'd mixed it with 'em for some reason."

"They just jumped me, Pelican. I don't know the why of it. I thought they might be some of your old pals tryin' to square accounts."

"It's right peculiar. Didn't even turn our pockets inside out. Wouldn't have got anything if they had."

Joe Parkner

"Where are we now?" Parkner asked.

"We're aboard some ship, but that's all I can tell you. Haven't heard or seen anybody. Found myself stretched on the floor with that bottle of prime stuff beside me. Somebody probably figured that we'd need it."

WITH PELICAN JONES helping him, Parkner got to his feet. He reeled, and braced himself against the wall. His face had been bruised, the clothes half torn from his body, and Pelican Jones was in a similar state.

"I've got it!" Parkner said. "I know the answer, Pelican—we've been shanghaied!"

"The devil you say! Take a look around," Pelican ordered, "and then guess again. We're in a fine cabin—mahogany trim, beveled lookin'-glass on the wall, and other fancy fixin's. Men who get themselves shanghaied are generally tossed right into the fo'cas'l."

"What do you reckon the idea is, then?"

"I've stopped askin' myself questions, lad. We were doped after bein' smashed on our heads—the taste in my mouth when I woke up told me that. Maybe jabbed with a needle, then brought here. How long we've been asleep, I don't know. It's still night—but maybe not the same night."

Parkner lurched across to the port and looked out.

He could see a wide expanse of tumbling, moonlight-drenched water, and nothing more.

He began a methodical examination of the cabin. On the mahogany lintel of the door had been carved a Chinese character he did not understand, and a word: *Soha.*

"Look at this, Pelican!" Parkner exclaimed. *"Soha!* I'm bettin' that we're on the yacht owned by Wu Chang, that millionaire Chinese pirate."

"What?" Pelican Jones betrayed sudden interest.

"Soha is the name he gives to that mysterious island he claims he found, and which nobody else can locate. And his yacht is named *Soha,* too."

"You're right, lad! But why should we be on Wu Chang's private yacht? We ain't his friends—and what's a long sight better, we ain't his enemies. And why are we here in a fancy cabin, 'stead of for'ard?"

"You're askin' yourself questions

again," Parkner said, grinning.

They examined the door, to find that it was fastened securely on the outside. But now they heard a key scratching in the lock, and the sound of a bolt being withdrawn. The door was opened a few inches, and eyes gleamed at them.

"Oh, come right on in!" Parkner invited, sarcastically. "We might as well get acquainted. Don't be afraid—we never harm children."

The door was opened wider. In it stood framed a giant of a man, who regarded them fiercely. His shirt was open at the throat to reveal a hairy, barrel-like chest. His sleeves were rolled above the elbows, and bulged with biceps. His hair was close-cropped; his florid face was seamed and wrinkled and scarred.

Behind this man, two others were standing in the semi-gloom of a companionway. They were Chinese, and were holding revolvers. In their belts were wicked-looking cutlasses. They peered piercingly at the pair revealed in the bright light of the cabin.

LOOKS LIKE A gang of pirates," Pelican Jones growled.

"Step along, you!" the giant in the doorway ordered in a rumbling voice. "Don't make a wrong move, or you'll be food for sharks."

He motioned up the companionway, and Parkner and Pelican Jones went before him, following the two Chinese. When they came to the deck, the fresh air smote them pleasantly, and they drank in deep gulps of it.

Pelican Jones

The yacht was wallowing through the moonlight-tinted sea. A glance at the nearest life-preserver on the rail confirmed the belief that she was the *Soha,* owned by Wu Chang, a somewhat mysterious and fabulously wealthy Chinese with headquarters in Singapore and elsewhere.

Parkner and Pelican Jones were conducted aft. Here a silk canopy had been stretched, and the deck beneath it covered with thick rugs and studded with heavy carved furniture. Shaded lamps cast eerie streaks of light. Incense was burning in a large brazier, the cloud of scented smoke trailing toward the stern.

THEN THEY HAD their first sight of Wu Chang. He sat in a huge chair, motionless save for ever-shifting eyes set in a

THE BEST OF THRILLING ADVENTURES

Lottie Marchand

dollars gold to have them carried away?

They had no opportunity to discuss it. Snebley motioned to the two Chinese, and they thrust Parkner and Pelican Jones forward urgently into the light.

Wu Chang bent his head slightly and made a swift inspection of them. His eyes blazed, but not at the prisoners. His voice was low and even again, however, when he spoke:

"A good brain may evolve perfect plans, and poor hands ruin them. There has been a regrettable error, Snebley. These are not the right men."

"What?" Snebley cried.

"Not the right men," Wu Chang repeated. "And I promised my friend that I would attend to the affair properly. Now I am in shame before him. To whom did you entrust the capture of the men I wished to get?"

"I gave the job to Baxton."

"Baxton has been careless. There can be no excuse for this. I cannot endure carelessness in carrying out my orders. A careless man is always dangerous. I believe we can get along without the further services of Baxton. Those two men behind you, Snebley—have them attend to it at once."

Snebley gestured; the two armed Chinese slipped away silently through the shadows, Snebley got out a revolver and stood on guard behind the prisoners. Wu Chang bent forward again.

"Who are you, gentlemen?" he asked.

yellow mask of a face. He clung to the old order of things, even to wearing a queue. Rich Chinese garments shrouded his form. Jewels gleamed on his fingers.

"Bring the two men before me at once, Snebley." Wu Chang gave the order in a low voice. "I am eager to see the pair so dangerous that I am paid ten thousand dollars in gold for carrying them away."

So Snebley was the name of this giant who had taken them from the cabin. Parkner had heard of him as one of Wu Chang's trusted men, a white renegade the Chinaman had saved from prison and turned to his own uses.

But what was this about Parkner and Pelican Jones being so dangerous that somebody would pay ten thousand

"I'm Joe Parkner, American."

"And I'm Pelican Jones, another American. And these here are fine goin's-on, I must say! When two gents goin' about their business are jumped on—"

"I regret the incident very much, gentlemen," Wu Chang interrupted. "You have been subjected to annoyance. But the man Baxton shall be punished for his mistake, if that is any satisfaction to you."

"Where are we bound?" Parkner asked. "We've got business back in S'pore—got jobs promised us."

"We are bound for the island of Soha, gentlemen. Perhaps you have heard of such a place? I contracted to take two certain men there and keep them, for they were in somebody's way. Through an error, I have you instead. Truly, we are but acorns driven by the winds of chance. But you are fortunate, gentlemen. Suppose my orders had been to have the two men slain?"

"Who were the men you were supposed to kidnap?" Parkner asked.

NOBODY KNOWN TO you gentlemen. Two bright young Englishmen who accidentally learned too much regarding the business methods of a merchant of means. They were threatening to cause him trouble with the authorities. He merely wished me to remove them from his vicinity, and insure they would not return. I gave my promise—and I failed. It is regrettable."

"You mean that we've got to go to this island of Soha and back, and in that way lose a lot of time?" Parkner asked.

Wu Chang

"You must go to Soha, gentlemen, since that is where this yacht of mine is bound," Wu Chang replied. "But you are not coming back."

"How's that?" Parkner cried.

"Save for the few trusted men aboard this craft, nobody is allowed to come back from Soha. Thus is its location kept secret."

"You can't do this, Wu Chang!" Parkner cried. "You can't get away with it! We've got influence! We've got friends—"

"But none of them know where you are. You were smuggled aboard the yacht while unconscious. You have simply dropped away out of sight."

"Let me tell you—" Parkner began. **BUT HE DID** not have an opportunity to tell it just then. Further speech was interrupted by a piercing scream some-where forward. It was not an ordinary scream, but the terrified cry of a man who looks a horrible death in the face and knows that he cannot possibly escape from it.

There were sounds of a violent strug-gle, another wild cry of despair, and then an ominous silence which was broken only by the rush of the wind and the gentle slap of water against the yacht's sides.

Wu Chang seemed to be listening intently. Parkner and Pelican Jones kept silent, wondering what had happened.

There was another jumble of chat-tering voices, and they thought they heard a splash.

Almost immediately, the two Chinese came shuffling back into the circle of light cast by the largest lamp, their faces wooden. One was holding a knife stained with fresh blood.

They bowed before Wu Chang, and one muttered something. Wu Chang gestured, and they retired again.

"It is well," he said. "The man Baxton will make no more annoying errors."

CHAPTER III

THE CAGED BEAST

THE INCIDENT DID not seem to disturb Wu Chang to any appreciable degree. He merely wafted more incense smoke into his nostrils and settled himself in his silk cushions. His face remained a yellow mask.

Parkner and Pelican Jones fought off their feeling of horror, trying to match the inscrutability of the Chinese. They felt that this was not a time to exhibit symptoms of fear. Perhaps Wu Chang was waiting for just that.

Parkner tried to keep his voice firm as he spoke:

"Can't you put back and land us, Wu Chang? We'll lose the jobs we've got promised us if we don't show up on time—and jobs are hard to get."

"I'll see that you have jobs for life," Wu Chang said. "Your future is assured."

"We'd rather you put back and land us."

Wu Chang smiled slightly.

"I'm sure, gentlemen, that you're kind enough to credit me with having common sense," he purred. "Put back and land you, after what you have wit-nessed? I feel certain that you could not avoid talking about it."

"Yeah, and I suppose we can expect a dose of the same kind of medicine, when you get around to dishin' it out," Pelican Jones put in.

"Not unless you give me cause, gen-tlemen."

"What are you goin' to do with us, then?" Parkner wanted to know.

"Take you to the Island of Soha, and keep you there. It is a paradise. The climate is good, the food plentiful, the natives brew an excellent potent drink, and the brown women are charming. What more could a man ask of life?"

"It ain't our fault that we're here," Pelican Jones pointed out. "Can't you take us back if we promise—"

"Not that, gentlemen. But I'll do my best to make amends otherwise. I'll even begin at once, by furnishing you with some amusement. Sit in those chairs over there, please: I hope you enjoy the performance."

Wondering what was coming, Parkner and Pelican Jones sat down as directed. Wu Chang motioned to Snebley, who disappeared. On a table before them, Parkner and Pelican Jones found liquor and cigars, and some little cakes; and at Wu Chang's gesture they helped themselves.

"Have you gentlemen ever heard of a man called Sam Hagadan?" Wu Chang asked.

"Sure!" It was Parkner who replied. "Everybody knows about him. He's a tough guy—modern pirate. Owns a dirty little schooner and prowls around in her."

"THIS SAM HAGADAN is jealous of my success along certain lines," Wu Chang explained. "He has annoyed me on several occasions. Now, he has become unduly interested in my mysterious island. And he has foolishly played right into my hands. Listen!"

From forward came sounds of a terrific battle. A gun was barking, and the shrill and angry cries of Chinese mingled with the stentorian roar of a male voice on the rushing wind. There were grunts and gasps, a scream, the sounds of blows, then a peculiar sound as of chains clanking.

Parkner and Pelican Jones sipped their drinks nervously, and glanced at each other in apprehension. Then, along the deck and toward where Wu Chang was sitting beneath the silk canopy came a strange procession.

A huge man with red hair, his face cut and bruised and half covered with blood, his clothes almost torn from his body, was being forced along between Snebley and another man and with some of the Chinese of the crew behind.

The red-headed man was loaded with chains. A foot of heavy links connected the old-fashioned handcuffs with which he had been manacled. Another foot of chain fastened his ankles together. There was a heavy chain around his waist. But, despite the shackles, and the terrific fight through which he had just passed, he was walking erect and with a look of defiance about him.

Parkner had seen him once in Singapore, at a gambling table with stacks of gold coins before him, roaring drunk, flinging his money broadcast, making seemingly impossible bets and always winning.

This was Sam Hagadan, who had the reputation of being guilty of almost every crime known to law. He had served two short prison terms. Pearl poaching, slavery, woman stealing, open piracy and wanton murder were attributed to him.

THE UNUSUAL PROCESSION came to a stop a short distance in front of Wu Chang. Sam Hagadan's bruised lips were twisted in a sneer.

"Well, Wu Chang, you yellow rat, your bums caught me," Sam Hagadan said. "I sent a couple of 'em to hell before they did it, though. And I notice that you wasn't takin' any part in the fightin' yourself."

Wu Chang ignored the insults.

"I fight only with worthy and honorable opponents," he replied. "You are very foolish, Mr. Hagadan. Curiosity has brought you to this end—an eagerness to see my property."

"Yours? Maybe it's yours—and maybe it belongs to anybody who can handle it."

"Your poor schooner is unable to trail my yacht to *Soha*. Three times you have smuggled one of your men aboard, but none lived to return and tell you where Soha is located, and what I have there. Now, you have tried it yourself. Foolish of you, Mr. Hagadan! We knew when you sneaked aboard, and where you hid yourself—and, when we were ready, we simply hauled you out."

"WELL, WHAT ARE you intendin' to do about it?" Hagadan asked.

"Not have you killed instantly, as you probably expect. You are so eager to see Soha that I'll take you there. Afterward—we shall see. Snebley, is the cage prepared?"

"The men are just finishin' puttin' it up."

"Excellent! Mr. Hagadan, you cannot expect me to let you run loose. You have an evil reputation, sir. It is said that you delight in killing persons, and I have no wish to die at your hand. So, you must be caged."

"What blasted nonsense is this?" Hagadan roared. "If you're goin' to have me shuffled off, do it! It's what I'm expectin'. You'd better kill me now,

Wu Chang, while you've got the chance. If you don't, I'll get you!"

"Sometimes, Mr. Hagadan, death is preferable to life," Wu Chang hinted. "It may be so in your case. When we get to Soha, perhaps we'll play a little game. But, just now—the cage."

Wu Chang gestured again, and the men started to take Sam Hagadan away. Though he could have no hope of victory, he began putting up a fight. They laughed at him, mocked him, tripped him, pulled him along the deck and forward like a lifeless thing.

Parkner and Pelican Jones had remained silent, and continued to do so. Presently, one of the Chinese slipped aft and whispered to Wu Chang, then slipped away again like a shadow. Wu Chang arose, and beckoned Parkner and Pelican Jones to accompany him.

FAR FORWARD, A big steel cage, probably fashioned originally for the confinement of some jungle beast, had been fastened to the deck. In it was Sam Hagadan, the manacles and chains still on him. Wu Chang went close and looked at the prisoner.

"A beast in a cage—very appropriate," he said.

"I'm tellin' you again, Wu Chang— you'd better kill me now, while you've got the chance!"

Wu Chang turned away.

"Snebley, do not forget to feed and water the beast," he smiled thinly. "I want him in good condition when we reach Soha."

Wu Chang turned and strolled aft again, with the lurid oaths of Sam

Hagadan following him. Snebley walked over to where Parkner and Pelican Jones were standing.

"You can get along now, gents," he said. "You know where to find your cabin. Make yourselves comfortable—you're guests for the present. Prowl around all you like, except in Wu Chang's private suite. And just a hint—better keep away from this here caged wild animal."

Parkner and Pelican Jones strolled aft a short distance and stood at the rail. Two members of the crew were at work swabbing the deck. Remembering Baxton, the man who had made one mistake too many, Parkner and Pelican Jones did not need to be told why they were so engaged.

They talked in low tones for a time, but there did not seem to be much to say. Wu Chang had said it all in a few words—they were going to the Island of Soha, and they were not coming back!

Joe Parkner's Texas blood was boiling again. But he knew that this was not the time for a display of wrath. It was a moment for remaining quiet—and planning.

"No Chinaman who ever lived, or white man either, can keep me on any island if I don't want to stay there. Not unless he kills me first!" Parkner muttered.

"Maybe that's the way he aims to keep us there," Pelican Jones suggested.

"We can't do anything about it now, Pelican. We can't very well grab the yacht, just the two of us, and put back to Singapore. We aren't that good."

"I'd sure hate to be in Sam Hagadan's place," Pelican Jones said. "Wu Chang will be thinkin' up some special things to do to him, and they won't be pretty. They've hated each other for years."

"Our own case is plenty bad enough," Parkner reminded him. "There ain't as much as a pocket knife on either of us. We've got to get hold of weapons. It'd be foolish for us to make a move now. We'll just act pretty—and wait."

CHAPTER IV

BULLET-PROOF

FOR SEVERAL DAYS the yacht Soha plowed the green sea with nothing unusual occurring.

Parkner and Pelican Jones found themselves ignored except by the man who carried food to their cabin, where they ate alone. When they spoke to anybody, they received only the shake of a head in reply. They knew that they were being watched continually, and were careful in speech and action.

They did not see Wu Chang, who seemed to be keeping to his cabin. Snebley was the yacht's navigator, they found. The crew were Chinese. There was but one white man besides Snebley, now that Baxton had paid for his mistake—the chief engineer, a dour man named Lorch.

Sam Hagadan was kept confined in the cage like a wild beast, and subjected to continual taunts. There were times when he seemed to be going almost insane, and howled curses into the wind. The yacht ran into heavy seas, and the cage was deluged repeatedly and Sam Hagadan half drowned.

"That baby's just storin' up hate," Pelican Jones said to Parkner. "If he ever gets a chance at Wu Chang—"

"But Wu Chang isn't fool enough to give him the chance," Parkner replied. "Maybe if Wu Chang is busy fightin' his private war with Hagadan, he'll grow careless about us."

"What are we goin' to do, lad? I don't aim to stay on that island of Soha all the rest of my life. It wouldn't agree with my New Hampshire constitution."

"It wouldn't fix in with my Texas temperament, either, Pelican. But we don't want to get in a hurry and make a wrong move. We'll have to watch for a chance to do somethin' about it."

IT WAS EVENING, and they were standing at the rail smoking. From somewhere forward suddenly came a screech of fear from one of the Chinese, then the bark of a gun. There was a scream, a groan, then silence again.

Members of the crew began calling to one another in voices of excitement. Bare feet pattered along the deck. The stentorian voice of Snebley could be heard as he demanded to know what had happened.

"Sounded to me like that shot was near the cage," Pelican Jones whispered to Parkner. "You don't suppose that somebody's shot Hagadan, do you?"

"Not when Wu Chang wants him alive."

And now they knew that nobody had shot Hagadan, for they could hear him roaring:

"You come here, Snebley, and let me out of this damned cage! Come runnin'! If you don't—"

"HE'S GOT A gun!" somebody forward was yelling. "Stay back! Hagadan's got a gun!"

"How could he get a gun?" Pelican Jones whispered to Parkner. "We can't get one, and we ain't caged."

"Stay here," Parkner cautioned, as Pelican Jones would have started forward. "We don't want any of this. We've got troubles of our own."

A gun cracked again, and a scream of pain answered the shot. Bare feet pattered along the deck once more, as one of the Chinese hurried past the pair at the rail and disappeared down the companionway.

"He's gone for Wu Chang, I betcha," Parker whispered.

Hagadan continued his bellowing, damning his enemies and roaring a general challenge. The members of the crew were jabbering wildly. Parkner slipped slowly a short distance along the rail in the semi-darkness, with Pelican Jones close behind him, until they got where they could see.

Two members of the crew were stretched on the deck, their bodies sprawling lifelessly in the moonlight. Snebley was crouching behind a ventilator, and others of the crew had sought cover where they could find it.

"Snebley, make one of your confounded rats come here and open this cage, if you're afraid to do it yourself!" Hagadan bellowed. "If you don't, I'll plug everybody I see!"

Parkner suddenly pressed Pelican Jones back against the rail, into a darkened area. Wu Chang had appeared. He was walking forward slowly, as though taking an evening stroll, passing through the shadows of moonlight. He stopped within plain sight of the cage, and Hagadan grew quiet.

"What is all this tumult, Snebley?" Wu Chang called. "It disturbed my meditations."

"Hagadan's got hold of a gun somehow. He's shot two of the crew. Better get under cover."

"I do not run from a rat," Wu Chang said.

His voice carried, and Hagadan heard. From the cage came a streak of flame, and the gun cracked. Evidently, the bullet failed to strike Wu Chang. He did not make a move to dodge to cover even then.

"How did he get the gun?" Wu Chang demanded.

"Don't know," Snebley replied. "I caught sight of it—it's an automatic. He didn't have it on him when he was put into the cage."

"Then somebody aboard this ship gave it to him. The guilty man must be punished. Who has been near the cage?"

"Several men," Snebley answered. "Trouble is, we don't know when he was given the gun. Maybe tonight—maybe yesterday."

THE GUN CRACKED again, and one of the Chinese gave a yell. He had carelessly exposed a leg, and Hagadan had demonstrated his marksmanship.

"We must get the gun away from him. He is hurting too many men," Wu Chang said.

"He'll shoot anybody who gets in range," Snebley warned. "I'll have the steam turned on him."

"But I do not want him cooked," Wu Chang protested. "It is my wish that he reach Soha in good condition. Two things must be done at once, Snebley— disarm Hagadan, and find the man who gave him the gun."

Hagadan began howling again:

"Get me out of this cage, Wu Chang! You're standin' out in the open. I can drop you—"

"You cannot harm me," Wu Chang interrupted, his voice ringing. "I am coming straight to the cage."

THE YACHT WALLOWED on. None of those on deck watching the scene spoke now. Parkner and Pelican Jones bent forward to watch closely. Wu Chang commenced walking slowly through the shadows, the wind whipping his robes about him.

Hagadan ripped out a curse, and the gun spoke. Wu Chang walked straight on, neither quickening stride nor slowing. Through the eerie shadows cast by the moonlight and the ship's lamps he went. Hagadan fired again.

It seemed to Parkner and Pelican Jones that Wu Chang reeled slightly and they thought that he had been hit. But he did not fall, did not even falter. He walked on.

"You cannot hurt me, Hagadan! Your gun is useless against me. No bullet can harm me!" Wu Chang's voice rang.

A stream of curses volleyed from Hagadan's lips, and a stream of bullets from the gun he held. Wu Chang was so close to the cage now that it seemed impossible for the infuriated man in it to miss. Snebley was pleading with Wu Chang to get under cover. The Chinese of the crew were muttering, superstition heavy upon them.

Hagadan began screeching like a wild man. They could see him lift the gun again in both his manacled hands, and aim it carefully. It barked, and spat flame and bullet again—and Wu Chang walked on calmly toward the cage.

"I hit you, blast you! You're dead, and still walkin'! Fall, curse you! I hit you twice—"

Hagadan was screaming, shouting like a maniac.

Again the gun cracked, and then: "His weapon is empty now, Snebley—I have counted the shots. Get that gun away from him," Wu Chang ordered. "Bring it to me aft."

Snebley bellowed orders, and men rushed to the cage. They waited until Snebley unlocked the door. Then they pulled Hagadan out, tore the empty gun from his grasp, roughed him up, and tossed him back and locked the cage again.

Parkner and Pelican Jones had remained in the shadows at the rail, watching and listening.

"Wu Chang's sure got nerve," Pelican Jones whispered. "I'll give the yellow devil credit for that."

"There's somethin' mighty funny about it," Parkner declared. "Blamed strange he wasn't hit even once. Thought sure that he'd got it one time."

"Maybe he's wearin' bullet-proof underwear," Pelican Jones suggested, laughing.

"Pelican, maybe you've guessed it. Even so, he sure took a chance. Suppose Hagadan had aimed at his head, his face? Bullet-proof underwear wouldn't do him much good then."

"Speakin' of faces—" Pelican began. "His was like a mask—I noticed it. But he was in the shadows most of the time. Kind of a set expression on his face, what we could see of it. Like he was concentratin' his mind, or somethin' like that."

"Some of that Oriental mystery stuff, huh? Whatever it was, it sure wrecked Hagadan's nerve."

"And Hagadan's wreckin' the crew," Parkner pointed out. "Killed two of them in that first fight when they caught him, and killed two and wounded one just now."

"Lad, I don't like this layout at all. We're up against somethin'. Even that danged island is a mystery, and what Wu Chang does there. And we sure don't aim to stay on it the rest of our lives."

"We sure don't," Parkner agreed.

Snebley summoned them aft, where Wu Chang had gone to sit in his big chair beneath the canopy. All were there except the man at the wheel and those of the engine room crew.

"WE HAVE A traitor among us," Wu Chang said. "Somebody gave Hagadan that gun. Until that man is found, we cannot trust one another. I have examined the gun. It does not belong on the yacht, nor is it one I ever issued."

"How about these two men?" Snebley asked, pointing to Parkner and Pelican Jones.

Wu Chang shook his head negatively.

"Don't be foolish, Snebley," he demurred. "Study human nature. If either of these men came into possession of a gun, he certainly would not give it to Hagadan. He'd use it himself."

"One wise guy!" Pelican Jones muttered.

The identity of the man who had given Hagadan the gun remained a mystery. Hagadan only grinned when asked.

No evidence was found to point to the guilty one.

The yacht wallowed on through the green sea.

On another evening, Parkner and Pelican Jones were standing at the rail when Lorch, the dour engineer, stopped beside them and asked for a match.

"We'll be at Soha tomorrow," Lorch said, as he lit his pipe. "It's right queer how you gents got mixed up in this. Baxton was sent to get a couple of men, and all he had to go by was a description. Somebody must have pointed you two out to him by mistake."

"And he had his gang grab us. It was a sad mistake for Baxton," Parkner said.

Lorch lowered his voice.

"Baxton was my friend," he said.

"I'm understandin'," Parkner told him.

"You'd better understand this, too—Wu Chang is absolute master at Soha. He's got the power of life and death—in Soha and on this yacht as well."

"So I noticed in the case of Baxton."

"Baxton's mistake made Wu Chang lose face, so it called for quick action. Other cases might be handled slower."

"Meanin' that somethin' may happen to us if we don't be careful?" Parkner asked.

"Maybe not somethin' exactly like that. There are other ways. Human bodies are scarce sometimes—and the monsters must be fed."

"What are you talkin' about?" Pelican Jones demanded.

"I'm talkin' too much about everything, and that's right dangerous hereabouts. Remember what I said, gents—Baxton was my friend. And I ain't feelin' exactly happy at the manner of his takin' off."

Lorch walked on along the rail and disappeared.

PARKNER WHISPERED TO Pelican Jones:

"There's a gent who'll throw in with us when the proper time comes."

"Yeah, I gathered that much. But what's all that talk about monsters havin' to be fed?"

"Don't know, Pelican. But I've sure got an idea now about one thing. I think I know the name of the man who slipped that gun to Sam Hagadan."

CHAPTER V

THE ISLAND OF SOHA

EARLY THE NEXT morning they sighted, far ahead, a swirl of mist along the horizon, with a dark streak extending along the bottom of it.

"That'll be the Island of Soha," Parkner said.

But it was late in the afternoon before they finally neared it, for the speed of the yacht was greatly reduced, and a man in the bow heaved the load continually. The yacht seemed to be weaving in and out through a maze of treacherous reefs.

Soha was similar in appearance to scores of other small islands. There was the usual lagoon, and on shore a group of buildings like those of an ordinary island trading station a distance back from the beach.

The yacht did not enter the lagoon but was anchored outside close to the mouth, which puzzled Parkner and Pelican Jones. A power launch was dropped overside, and Wu Chang got into it with some of the crew. It sped into the lagoon and toward the shore where the natives were gathering.

Then Parkner and Pelican Jones saw something which startled them. The water of the lagoon suddenly was churned into a froth. Those in the launch seemed to be heaving something into the green depths. The launch sped on to land.

"This here situation begins to look hopeless to me," Pelican Jones said to Parkner, sure that nobody could over-hear. "This island ain't on any chart, and nobody's ever been able to trail Wu Chang's yacht here. Some people think that there ain't no such place."

"But here it is," Parkner replied; "and nothin' is hopeless, Pelican. I'm right down surprised at a New Hampshire man havin' sentiments like that. Wait till we find out about things before you start cryin' about it bein' hopeless."

"Who in blazes is cryin'?" Pelican Jones demanded.

The launch landed Wu Chang and returned immediately to the yacht. Snebley approached the pair at the rail.

"Come along, gents," he ordered. "You're goin' in this trip, with me. Don't worry about your baggage." He leered at them.

They got into the launch, and it was cast off, turned and driven toward the beach. Parkner was thinking that Lorch, the engineer who had been Baxton's friend, was the only white man left aboard with Sam Hagadan in the cage. That might result in something, if the Chinese of the crew were not watching too closely, and the two had a chance to talk.

The launch was being driven slower this trip.

"Look down, gents," Snebley said.

They looked off overside. The water was crystal clear, and they could see bottom except where depth caused darkness. Down there was a beautiful marine garden studded with castles of coral, with schools of brilliantly-hued fish playing through it.

"This here is called the Lagoon of Monsters. The natives named it that," Snebley explained.

THEY SAW WHAT he meant. Scores of gigantic man-eating sharks were swimming below, surging up toward the launch at times as though anticipating food.

"This is their little playground,"

Snebley said. "And that ain't all, gents. Under them submarine cliffs are some of the finest and biggest devil fish in the old sea. This spot is filled with interestin' things like that. Wu Chang encourages them to stay here. They might take a notion to go travelin'—if they didn't get morsels of fancy food now and then. Watch, gents!"

Snebley took the paper off a package he had brought from the yacht, and showed a chunk of ship's pork. He stood up and threw the meat as far as possible from the launch.

From a score of directions, and from far below, the monsters darted through the water to get the prize. The sea was churned into a froth as they fought for it. **"SPEAKIN' OF MORSELS** of fancy food, I didn't mean ship's meat, exactly," Snebley continued. "I trust you understand me. A fine chance a livin' man would have in that water, huh? Yeah, a fine chance! They'd tear him to bits. He'd be gulped down almost before he knew he was dead. Better remember that, gents!"

Then the launch came to the beach and ran its nose into the sand, and they went overside and splashed ashore. Parkner and Pelican Jones shivered when they thought what would happen to a man in the waters of the lagoon.

And they realized that the demonstration had been staged for their special benefit.

The natives had gathered before Wu Chang's bungalow, the largest building, and he had been speaking to them and giving them presents. Parkner had noticed the absence of canoes on the beach. There was no craft at all except the *Soha's* launch, and a clumsy raft of some sort moored a distance away.

Snebley conducted the pair to the foot of the veranda steps, and Wu Chang motioned for them to ascend.

"Welcome to Soha, gentlemen," he said. "This is Mr. Barwright, my manager here." He introduced a middle-aged, surly brute who bobbed his head. "I've explained to him about your misadventure. And this is Mr. Bill Donland, my diver."

"Diver! So it's pearls! That's the mystery," Parkner said.

"And such pearls! The greatest pearl oysters in the world are on the floor of this lagoon, guarded by monsters of the deep—yet we gather them."

"Seems to me the divers take a big chance," Parkner suggested.

"We have but one diver—Mr. Donland. In some queer manner, he conquers the monsters. With him, they are as playful as kittens. At times, to make it interesting, I have him take some other man along. But none ever comes back. It is regrettable."

Parkner and Pelican Jones shivered again. They did not need a fuller explanation. They understood all too clearly Wu Chang's conclusive method of punishing recalcitrants in this island kingdom of his.

"That small hut," Wu Chang indicated, "is yours, gentlemen. Make yourselves at home. The natives will serve you. Tell them what you wish, and they'll get it."

*Screams of rage ripped from four throats
as he hurled himself at the men.*

"Come along," Snebley growled at them again.

Parkner and Pelican Jones sat in the shade while some of the natives cleaned the hut. Food was brought them, and a potent native drink, and curious brown damsels stood a short distance away and made eyes at them.

"HERE WE ARE!" Parkner said. "Thousands of men would howl with glee for a chance at a life like this. Yet what we're thinkin' of is gettin' away."

"It makes a whale of a difference when you've got to stay in a place," Pelican Jones replied.

"When the *Soha* goes away from here, we're goin' to be on her," Parkner declared. "That's settled!"

"Just like that, huh?"

"Just like that! This here is Texas talkin'!"

"New Hampshire is trailin' right along."

The soft tropical night came down, and Soha grew quiet. The lights had been extinguished in Wu Chang's bungalow. Parkner and Pelican Jones decided to go into the hut and sleep.

But Bill Donland, the diver, came strolling toward them through the shadows. He was tall, lean, a man with a face not easy to read. He seemed to want to be friendly, yet was plainly on guard, feeling out the pair of newcomers and being careful what he said.

"THIS HERE SOHA ain't a bad place," Parkner suggested.

"Unless a man wants to get away," Donland replied.

"Won't Wu Chang let you get away?"

Donland shook his head.

"No. I'm the only man who can get out the pearls for him, so I have things pretty much my own way. He sees that I get particularly good care. But, even so, I wouldn't dare go too far."

"A man ought to be able to get away, if he feels like it," Parkner persisted.

Donland shook his head again.

"This island is unknown," he said,

"Not even a gunboat ever comes prowlin' around here. Wu Chang won't let the natives have a canoe—it's death to be caught makin' a boat. Perhaps, when the pearls are gone, he'll kill all but his favorites of the crew, and sail away."

"How are the pearls holdin' out?" Parkner asked.

"No need to worry about that. If I worked hard every day for fifty years, I wouldn't be able to get up all the shell. So. I've got a life job at no wages. You never saw such pearls!"

"How'd you come here? Wu Chang fetch you to do his divin'?" Parkner asked.

"Shipwreck. I was here for several years, livin' with the brownies, before Wu Chang happened to find this island on one of his cruises. I'd collected some pearls, and I tried to trade him some for passage to Singapore. That was my first mistake. He learned how I got them, and he wouldn't take me away. Took charge of the island and kept me here to get up the pearls."

"Why don't you strike?"

"I'VE BEEN HOPIN' that he'd market so many fine pearls that they'd attract attention, and he'd be followed here by somebody who'd rescue me. Then there's another reason—the girl."

"Girl?" Parkner questioned.

"A white girl, here with her old father. Wu Chang gave orders that they weren't to be harmed because he's superstitious about 'em for some reason. But he may change his mind, so I'm standin' by."

"What's a white girl and her father doin' here?" Joe Parkner then asked.

"The old man is Dr. Marchard, a scientist studyin' tropical diseases. His daughter is named Lottie. 'Bout a year ago they were travelin' between islands and got caught in a storm. Their boat lived through it. Got blown far off the course and landed here. Wu Chang protected Dr. Marchard and the girl, and tossed the natives into the lagoon. The Marchards live in a little bungalow down the beach."

Parkner got up to stride back and forth restlessly.

"It's a lot of confounded nonsense!" he exploded. "The idea of this Wu Chang lordin' it over everybody! You're entitled to the pearls you get, Donland. You made the discovery, and this island is uncharted and unclaimed."

"That doesn't help me any," Donland said.

"Him tellin' men they have to stay here the rest of their lives! If the three of us aren't men enough to lick a bunch of Chinamen and the white renegades with 'em, and get away, and save that girl and her father—"

Out of the soft night came a disturbing chuckle. Through the bright moonlight and toward them walked Wu Chang, with Snebley and Barweight close behind bodyguards.

"A chivalrous thought, Mr. Parkner!" Wu Chang said. "But, as a friend, let me caution you to curb your tongue, and advise you not to indulge in silly mutiny. After you've been here a few days, you'll realize the futility of it. And the monsters in the lagoon are always hungry, remember."

CHAPTER VI

DOOMED

WITHOUT FURTHER REMARK, Wu Chang returned through the shadows with his bodyguard. Bill Donland spoke to Parkner and Pelican Jones in soft tones.

"Better be careful," he advised. "Wu Chang will have you watched now. That yellow devil can be everywhere at once, and he sees and hears everything."

Then Bill Donland departed, and Parkner and Pelican Jones went into their hut and got to sleep. They slept soundly that first night on shore, and awakened only because of a din down on the beach.

The sun already had popped up out of the sea. Two native women were waiting outside the hut with their morning food. The launch was in from the yacht, and almost everybody on the island had gathered at the landing.

"What is it?" Parkner barked at one of the women.

She grinned at him and rolled her eyes, feeling a superiority because she knew some English.

"Big beast in cage," she said.

"That means Hagadan," Pelican Jones muttered.

"Yeah! And it means that we stay right here and eat breakfast and 'tend strictly to our business. The less we call Wu Chang's attention to us, the better. We'll mix in the fringe of the crowd later."

They ate while the two native women served them and jabbered at them until Parkner told them to be quiet.

But from their hut they could see what was happening.

The big cage had been brought in on the launch, in sections. Hagadan, in chains, was in the launch also, closely guarded. The natives, urged to it by some of the white men, were taunting the prisoner.

The sections of cage were carried ashore, and it was erected again in the clearing fastened securely to the ground. Hagadan was taken from the launch, fighting like a wild man, and hauled up the beach toward the cage.

They had some difficulty getting him into it, despite his shackles. But finally Snebley locked the door, and gave the key to Wu Chang, who in turn handed it to Barwright, his Soha manager.

PARKNER AND PELICAN Jones finished their meal and drifted down toward the cage, the native women following. The few whites were grinning as they listened to Hagadan's profane threats, and the natives were laughing and chattering, and hurling sticks at the bars.

Then they were quiet, for Wu Chang had come forward. He peered in at Hagadan, and spoke:

"You wanted to see Soha, Hagadan, and here you are. From that cage, you can see the colony and witness what goes on. You'll learn what interest I have here."

"I ain't dead yet, Wu Chang," Hagadan raved. "You'd better kill me now, while I'm chained and helpless. If you don't—"

Wu Chang lifted a hand for silence. "SPEAKING OF DEATH reminds me, Mr. Hagadan," he purred, "of the pleasant little game I have arranged for you. To kill you immediately—that would be nothing. Your suffering would be over too soon."

"What's your game?" Hagadan snarled.

"You are to die, but you will not know the time or method of your death. Perhaps a shot when you are least expecting it. Perhaps a knife-thrust as you sleep. Perhaps poison in your food or water. Perhaps today, perhaps not for weeks or even months."

"Blast you—!"

"I am interested in watching a strong man like you under such a strain," Wu Chang continued. "I wonder how long before you break and beg me to have you killed? You'll dread to eat or drink. You'll fear to go to sleep. Every time a man approaches your cage, you'll wonder if he is the executioner. I promise you one thing, however—death will not be in your first meal. Feed the beast well, Snebley. He'll need strength."

With Hagadan's oaths ringing in his ears, Wu Chang went on toward his bungalow. The two men who had slain Baxton, Wu Chang's executioners, remained on guard.

Parkner and Pelican Jones drifted away when the crowd began breaking up. The native women still followed them, until Parkner drove them away.

"Speakin' of cruelty, this here Wu Chang is a master at it," Parkner said. "But we ain't got any call to feel sorry for Sam Hagadan. If a man ever merited death, I reckon he does. Just the same, it's a devilish layout."

"Shows us what we can expect to get, if we ain't careful," Pelican Jones replied.

"I reckon our game is to keep quiet. But we want to get hold of some weapons if we can, and maybe hide 'em till they're needed."

"That's goin' to be a job, lad. You can lay a bet that Wu Chang don't allow guns and knives to be scattered around promiscuous. All numbered and accounted for, maybe."

They glanced toward Wu Chang's bungalow, and saw that the natives were drifting in that direction. Snebley and Barwright were with Wu Chang. Two natives carried a big chair down from the veranda and put it at the bottom of the steps, and Wu Chang sat in it.

"What's comin' off now?" Pelican Jones muttered.

"Looks like he was goin' to hold a session of some kind," Parkner said.

"Glance at what's comin'."

Parkner turned quickly to look where Pelican Jones indicated. Then he had his first glimpse of Lottie Marchard.

SHE WAS COMING along the beach, clinging to the arm of an elderly man who stumbled as he walked. The girl was about twenty-five, Parkner judged—tall, lithe, graceful. Her brown hair was blowing about her face. Her scant clothing, whipped around her by the wind, revealed a charming form. "Dr. Marchard and his daughter," Parkner whispered. "The old gent looks about all in."

"Comin' to welcome Wu Chang home, I suppose."

"Double blast that old pirate for orderin' around folks like them!" Parkner growled. "They're our kind, Pelican. We've got to help 'em if we can."

"Oh, sure!" Pelican said. "I s'pose you'd be just as keen about it if the girl happened to be bent and old and ugly."

"They're white folks," Parkner persisted. "It's got my Texas blood boilin'."

"I'm feelin' a little itch in my New Hampshire veins, too," Pelican admitted.

THE MARCHARDS WERE coming directly toward them along a path that curved past them and went to Wu Chang's house. Parkner and Pelican Jones stepped aside. The girl was helping her father, who was evidently extremely weak. Her clear eyes surveyed the newcomers to Soha.

Parkner reached to remove a hat that he had forgotten was not on his head. He flushed, and bowed.

"I'm Joe Parkner, miss," he said. "This is my friend, Pelican Jones."

"I'm not interested, sir." The girl's voice was like ice.

"Don't get us wrong," Parkner said. "We don't belong to this crowd. We were brought here against our will."

"Yeah, and we ain't goin' to be kept here, either," Jones added.

"If the chance comes, and we can help you—" Parkner began.

Her lips curled with scorn.

"I suppose Wu Chang told you to speak like this, try to get us into some plot to escape, and then say we've violated his hospitality," she said. "He's promised punishment if we're caught breaking rules."

"You think me and Pelican Jones would have any part of that yellow devil's schemes?" Parkner barked at her. "I'm from Texas, ma'am! I'd help a nice woman any time, anywhere—yeah, and her father, too."

"Even if you are sincere, you can do nothing," she told him. "And I don't think you are sincere. We don't have many gallant knights coming to the island on the *Soha*."

Parkner would have protested again, but there came an interruption. From the thick jungle and into the clearing rushed a scattering of excited natives, Then two of Wu Chang's Chinese guards appeared, dragging a native along between them. Parkner and Pelican Jones heard Lottie Marchard give a cry of pity, and turned quickly to find her eyes bulging and her face chalky.

"They've got Nugago," she was saying to her father. "Oh, we must hurry!"

"What's the trouble now?" Parkner asked.

"Nugago—he's been kind to us, has tried to help us. The guards have him. If you only knew—"

Then she was urging her father to hurry on along the path. Parkner and Pelican Jones followed slowly. From every direction, natives were hurrying toward where Wu Chang sat in state, with the white renegades of Soha at his back.

The screeching native was pulled roughly along the ground by the two guards. Parkner and Pelican Jones quickened their step and got to the edge of the throng. The native prisoner grew quiet when he was taken before Wu Chang. All spirit seemed to leave him. He looked around at the others wildly, then bowed his head.

"WHAT IS THE man's offense?" they heard Wu Chang say.

Barwright replied:

"This is the man I spoke to you about, Wu Chang. We've been holding him since yesterday in a hut back in the jungle. The guards caught him in a cove on the other side of the island, building a boat."

"Building a boat? We have a penalty for that. Can there be any question of his guilt?"

"He's guilty," Barwright replied. "He was watched a couple of days. Buildin' a canoe big enough to carry several people. Had it almost done."

Wu Chang gestured, and the guards hurled the native to the ground at his feet.

"Are you guilty?" Wu Chang asked. The native nodded confession.

"Why should you want to get away from Soha? You're a Soha man. Your people are here. Were you building the boat for somebody else?"

THE NATIVE SAID nothing, did not move. One of the Chinese guards kicked him cruelly, but still he would not answer.

"You know the penalty," Wu Chang said. "The monsters must be fed."

The native gave a wild cry and prostrated himself in the dirt. Other natives began whimpering, but a shout from one of the guards quickly silenced them.

Then Lottie Marchard had thrust her way forward to a position in front of Wu Chang.

"He was doing it for me!" she cried. "For me, and my father. We want to get away from this dreadful place. It's my fault. I begged him to do it. He's Nugago, the best canoe builder on the island."

"So you, too, are guilty," Wu Chang said.

"I'm as guilty as Nugago. I paid him to do it."

"That does not excuse him. He knew the penalty. He must be fed to the monsters."

She began to plead for the native's life. Parkner gripped Pelican Jones' arm until the latter flinched. To see such a girl pleading with a yellow pirate—

"Enough!" Wu Chang ordered. "I cannot change the law."

"Throw me to the sharks, too. I'm as guilty as he," the girl was crying.

Her father was clutching at her, fear in his old face, trying to get her to be quiet.

"You are too valuable to be tossed to the monsters," Wu Chang said. "You must live, yet you must be punished. I shall give you in marriage, by lottery."

She reeled back from him, looking wildly around her.

"Married to a man of Soha, you will not be so eager to get away, perhaps. Your husband, home interests, all will be here then," Wu Chang purred. "Out of special consideration, however, only men of your race may compete for you."

"Men of my race!" She laughed wildly. "Scum of the earth! Renegades!

Disowned by their own kind and looked down on by yours!"

Parkner glanced at the men behind Wu Chang, all of them leering, grinning. The giant Snebley, the beast Barwright, Bill Donland, Lorch the engineer.

"I'll kill myself!" Lottie Marchard cried.

"We'll have you guarded carefully until the affair is settled," Chang said. "Afterward, it will be your husband's task to keep you alive. But we attend to this man first."

CHAPTER VII

DEATH—AND A BRIDE

THE DOOMED NATIVE, his wrists lashed behind his back and ankles tied together, was carried down to the beach. Wu Chang walked there with his bodyguard, white and Chinese, around him. The natives of Soha, silent now, followed. Lottie Marchand and her father had been taken away under guard.

Parkner and Pelican Jones followed the crowd, a little behind. Pelican Jones was growling something that could not be understood.

"Careful," Parkner warned. "We can't stop this, Pelican. The native knew what he risked, I reckon. But that girl—we'll have somethin' to say if—"

"And we'll die if we make a move," Pelican cut in. "Lad, how I'd like to get a chance at Wu Chang!"

"Maybe we'll get one. Just got to wait, Pelican."

THEY PASSED CLOSE to Hagadan's cage, and he was howling curses at Wu Chang. Hagadan looked as though he had spent a terrible night. He eyed Parkner and Pelican Jones askance, possibly wondering if they were to be his executioners. The Chinese guard motioned them to keep their distance.

The launch had been started, and had picked up the clumsy raft Parkner had noticed the day before. Now the raft was being towed a hundred feet behind the launch. It was swung toward the shore, and men caught and held it.

The doomed native was tossed to the middle of the raft.

Not a sound came from those on the beach as the launch started slowly out into the lagoon, towing the raft behind it. Two men in the launch began tossing out chunks of some kind of meat. Fins cut the surface of the water as the monsters fought for the tidbits. The launch circled the lagoon, the sharks following it.

Now the sea monsters were around the raft, churning the water. The launch cut the raft loose and let it drift.

Those on the shore could see the terrified native as he crouched in the middle of the raft, helpless, his wrists and ankles bound.

The sharks seemed to be in a frenzy. The raft began tossing and tipping as they nosed it, swept against it, cut the surface of the water so the doomed man could see their little, beady eyes. The native tried to keep balance, finally dropped to his knees.

The launch had turned again, and now it went forward slowly until it bumped against the raft, and the monsters of the lagoon were swirling around it, too. One of the men in the launch put a boathook against the corner of the raft, and depressed it.

The native screamed as he slipped toward the depressed end, his bare feet sliding on the soaked surface of the raft. He screamed again as the man with the boathook gave a quick shove. An instant he balanced there, then lurched over into the water, his last wild cry ringing to the shore.

There was a wild tumult in the churned water, a maze of tails and fins and snouts. The surface of the lagoon suddenly was stained. The launch caught the raft again, and towed it back to its resting place.

On the shore, the natives filed away silently, going to their huts. Nugago, their friend, was gone, food for the lagoon monsters. Parkner and Pelican Jones would have slipped away, but Wu Chang called to them.

"You gentlemen are eligible for the lottery," Wu Chang announced. "So are Snebley, Barwright, Lorch and Donland. Notice that I put five black pebbles and one white one into this bowl. I hold it above my head—so. One by one, you will draw. The man who draws the white pebble wins a bride."

"I DON'T WANT any of it!" Pelican Jones said.

Parkner gripped him by the arm.

"Oh, take a chance, Pelican," he said. "If we've got to stay here the rest of our lives, we might as well be settled right.

White women are goin' to be very scarce, I can see that."

The Chinese were grinning. Snebley was laughing raucously; Barwright looked eager; Lorch and Donland's faces were expressionless.

"Draw!" Wu Chang ordered.

Snebley drew first, got a black pebble, cursed and tossed it away. Barwright had no better luck. Donland and Lorch drew black pebbles also.

"One of our newcomers is to win the prize," Wu Chang said, smiling slightly. "Draw, gentlemen!"

PARKNER DREW—AND GOT the white pebble.

"Congratulations!" Wu Chang said. "You will claim your bride, Mr. Parkner, and move into the Marchard bungalow. No doubt your friend will not be lonesome long. He can find a companion among the brown women."

"Come along, Pelican, and help me get settled," Parkner said.

Lottie Marchard and her father had been detained at the edge of the clearing, and Parkner started toward the spot with Pelican Jones beside him.

"Some good luck!" Parkner whispered. "Gives us a chance to protect her. And a chance to find out all about this island of Soha before we make a move. And the sooner we make a move, the better."

Two of the Chinese were guarding the girl, and her father. Parkner tried to flash her a message as he approached, but the Chinese were watching closely. Wu Chang called to them to let the girl go, that she now belonged to Parkner.

"Which one of you—?" she began, as the pair stopped before her.

"Oh, I'm your new husband!" Parkner said, motioning for the Chinese to leave.

"If you think—" she began.

"Act up!" Parkner hissed at her. "Put up a fight so Pelican will have to help me take you home. Don't you understand? This is a good break for you. I won't harm you any. But we've got to make it look good to Wu Chang."

Her eyes flashed as she understood, and her father began whimpering. She pretended to fight when Parkner grabbed her and acted as though trying to kiss her. Pelican Jones put on a show of helping his partner carry home his bride.

Holding her by the arms, they took her along the path, her father following.

From the distance came the laughter of those who watched.

The Marchard bungalow was a small, neat affair in a grove of palms. As they went toward it, Parkner talked swiftly, telling of what had befallen him and Pelican Jones.

"We're goin' to get away, all right, and we'll take you and your father with us," Parkner said.

"Useless to try it, I'm afraid," she said. "It'll only mean for you what Nugago got."

"We know a few things that I ain't tellin' now. And we'll have help," Parkner assured her. "Fast as you can give it to me, I want all the information you can peddle out. All about how Wu Chang lives here, how he's guarded, what he does. There's only one way—get control of the yacht and sail away, leaving most of them here, and send a gunboat back."

"GET CONTROL OF the yacht—you two men?" she asked.

"But I'm from Texas," Parkner told her.

"Yeah, and I'm from New Hampshire," Pelican Jones added.

Dr. Marchard began whimpering again. His daughter urged him to keep quiet, and to say nothing of what he heard.

"He's breaking fast," she whispered to Parkner. "He's in continual fear—especially for me. His health isn't good—tropical fever once."

"We'll get him away in time," Parkner assured her.

But he knew he had a job ahead of him. In the bungalow, while Lottie got a meal ready, and Dr. Marchard sat on the veranda to watch if anybody approached, Parkner held speech with Pelican Jones.

"We've got to get in touch with Lorch, Pelican. I know he'll throw in with us on account of what happened to his friend Baxton. And don't forget that he's chief engineer of the *Soha*. We'll need him."

CHAPTER VIII

THE MASK

LATE IN THE afternoon, Parkner strolled down toward the beach. Pelican Jones had gone there long before, and had been circulating with the men, laughing about his partner's "marriage." He flirted with one of the brown women, and strove to create the impression that he and Parkner had no thought of getting away.

The natives were taunting the caged Hagadan. Snebley and Barwright had been drinking heavily. Bill Donland was out in the middle of the lagoon on the raft from which Nugago had plunged to his horrible death.

"That baby's sure got nerve!" Pelican Jones commented. "He's been divin' and fetchin' up shell. Sharks don't seem to bother him."

"That's just another peculiar thing about this place," Parkner said. "Have you seen Lorch?"

"Saw him go into the storehouse but didn't get a chance to talk to him."

Parkner went to the storehouse and negotiated for a pipe and some smoking tobacco. Lorch was there, talking to one of the natives.

"So you're gettin' to be a regular citizen, married man and everything," Lorch said.

"That's the way of it," Parkner replied, grinning. "Not bad for a starter. Soha ain't such a bad place, after all."

They strolled outside, and went down to the beach. Parkner pretended to be interested in Bill Donland's diving.

"Do they leave the launch ashore nights?" he asked.

Lorch glanced at him swiftly. "Sometimes. I'm goin' aboard to spend the night, but the launch will come back to be here in case Wu Chang wants to board the yacht. The Chinese engineer sleeps in her when she's ashore."

"You handle the engine room gang, don't you?"

"I can always get along in the engine room—if the deck is bein' handled."

"Three men ought to handle the deck, and the crew, if Snebley was ashore, huh?"

"Yes," Lorch said. "Which three?"

"Me and my pardner, and maybe that diver."

"I see. There's Sam Hagadan to be remembered, too. If he was loose, he might keep some folks busy."

"Yeah, if he was loose," Parkner agreed. "I wonder how much you can be trusted?"

"Baxton was my friend."

"CHECK!" PARKNER SAID. "I've got a notion to spend my weddin' night prowlin' around Wu Chang's bungalow. And— anything might happen."

"Two Chinese on guard there at night," Lorch warned. "Good luck, Parkner! Maybe I can do somethin' before I go aboard. And I'll be bossin' the engine room—in case anybody wants to take a sea trip."

Parkner had no definite plan. He wanted to get into Wu Chang's bungalow, explore its possibilities. If he and Pelican Jones could get weapons, and seize the launch, they would have a chance of getting out to the yacht and leaving the more dangerous adversaries ashore.

He believed that Bill Donland would help. He guessed that Donland had not turned in to Wu Chang all the pearls he had taken, but had saved a nest egg for himself, and was eager to get away. There was the problem of Lottie Marchard and her father, too. They must be taken out to the yacht.

PARKNER WAS NOT underestimating the perils of the situation. He realized what failure would mean. He was thinking of that as he joined the group around Sam Hagadan's cage and stood beside Pelican Jones. One of the Chinese had just brought food to Hagadan, and Wu Chang was standing in front of the cage.

"Are you afraid to eat, Mr. Hagadan?" Wu Chang asked. "It may be poisoned, you know. Did you sleep well last night, Mr. Hagadan? Were you not afraid that a bullet or knife might come out of the darkness and put an end to you?"

Hagadan replied with a volley of lurid oaths, and wolfed down the food. There was a wild look in his face, and his eyes were bloodshot. Wu Chang laughed a little, something unusual for him, and went on to his bungalow. His two Chinese guards shuffled along at his heels.

Lorch approached the cage now, bent over, and squinted as he looked at Hagadan.

"Here's a plug of tobacco, you bloody pirate!" Lorch said, tossing it through the bars. "I'd be careful usin' it, if I was you. Might be poisoned, you know. If it ain't, maybe chewin' it will help you keep awake tonight, so's you can watch nobody slips up on you."

Parkner felt the significance in that speech, and wondered at the tobacco. Sam Hagadan cursed Lorch the same as he had the others, but retained the gift. Lorch laughed and walked on, and Parkner went with Pelican Jones toward the path that ran to the Marchard bungalow.

"We'll get together late tonight, Pelican. We're goin' to pay Wu Chang a visit."

"There's nothin' like fun," Pelican Jones said. "I'll prowl around meanwhile, and see if I can learn anything important."

"The launch will be in, and the yellow engineer sleeps in her. If we can get weapons, and get out to the yacht in the launch—"

"It's a big order, lad, but maybe we can fill it."

"You turn in at the usual time. I'll drift along some time durin' the night."

"Careful, lad! Don't let your hot Texas blood run away with your common sense."

"And don't let your New Hampshire conscience keep you from smashin' this offal if we get the chance."

"You don't have to worry about my conscience. I put it away in moth balls years ago."

Parkner explained his plan to Lottie Marchard. He did not know what might happen, he said. But he wanted the girl and her father to get up and dress when he called to them during the night, and slip down to the beach unseen, getting as close to the launch as possible. If he called, they were to hurry to the launch. Otherwise, they were to get back to the bungalow.

IT WAS PAST midnight when Parkner knocked on the door of the girl's room. He heard her answer, then got quietly out of the bungalow. In the darkness he crouched silently for a time, watching and listening.

He was afraid that Wu Chang might have put a guard over the bungalow, but he did not see or hear anything to indicate this was so. But he crept stealthily through the deeper shadows to the jungle's edge, and circled toward the hut where Pelican Jones was living.

Pelican was awake and waiting. They went together around the edge of the clearing, and approached Wu Chang's bungalow from the rear.

"Two Chinese guards," Parkner whispered. "We've got to locate 'em and put 'em out of business. And we can't make any noise doin' it."

THEY WERE UNARMED save for clubs they had picked up on the way. The Chinese guards, they knew, would be heavily armed, and probably would shoot at the first indication of anything wrong. It was the task of the advancing pair to dispose of the guards without awakening Wu Chang and giving him a chance to prepare to defend himself.

They got against the wall of the building where it was pitch dark. Keeping close to the wall, they crept to the corner of the veranda. One of the guards was pacing back and forth on the veranda silently.

Pelican Jones tapped lightly with his club on the wooden floor. The Chinese slipped swiftly along the railing, bent over to investigate. Parkner's club crashed down upon the back of his head. Pelican Jones reached up and pulled him over, straddled and throttled him to insensibility.

They bound him swiftly with pieces of rope Parkner had brought from the

Marchard bungalow, and gagged him with a length of cloth. Then they rolled him against a veranda post and lashed him there.

"That's one of 'em," Pelican Jones whispered. "We're on our way, Texas."

"Let's get goin', New Hampshire."

They went up the steps; crossed the veranda to the door. As they reached it, it was opened. The second guard was coming out, probably to visit with the other.

Again, Parkner's club crashed. Pelican Jones caught the man as he fell, and eased him to the floor. The guard was bound and gagged swiftly, and tied to another veranda post. Then Parkner and Pelican Jones slipped inside the house.

They were on dangerous ground now, they knew. They had no light, nor did they care to make one. They wanted to locate Wu Chang and subdue him, and also get weapons.

Along a narrow hallway they crept, toward where a door stood open for a few inches, with light streaming through. Parkner reached it first, and peered in. Wu Chang was sitting beside a table, reading. This room seemed to be a sort of study.

There were some books, chemical apparatus, a small safe, a workbench strewn with miscellaneous items.

Parkner touched Pelican Jones on the arm, and their eyes met. There was a wild dash as Parkner kicked the door open wide. Startled, Wu Chang sprang from his chair, his hand going toward an automatic pistol on the table. Parkner's

club struck him down before he could reach the gun.

They bound and gagged him swiftly. Parkner closed the door. Their victim was propped up in a huge chair, to take his time about returning to consciousness.

THEN THE PAIR began a swift search of the room. They broke open a cabinet, and found arms and ammunition.

Taking two guns each, they stuffed them in their pockets with cartridges.

"Commencin' to feel human again," Pelican Jones said. "A gun makes a heap of a difference when you've got it yourself."

"We've only started, Pelican," Parkner reminded him. "We ain't out to the yacht yet."

"Look!" Pelican's gasp caused Parkner to whirl toward the cabinet again.

He, too, gasped in surprise. Pelican Jones was holding up a mask of Wu Chang's face. It was a perfect likeness, made of bulletproof metal and padded on the inside.

The exterior was tinted the color of flesh.

"That's why he wasn't afraid of bein' shot," Parkner said. "Wearin' that thing, and bulletproof underwear, maybe, he could take a chance."

"He's wakin' up, lad."

WU CHANG HAD opened his eyes. Parkner strode over to the chair. "Can you hear me, Wu Chang?" he asked.

The Chinese nodded, his eyes glittering at them.

"We gave you a chance to take us back to S'pore, and you wouldn't. So we 've got to use our own methods. Maybe we'll send somebody back for you and the others, Wu Chang—a gunboat, maybe. Then you'll have a lot of explainin' to do."

"Let's get goin'," Pelican said.

"I've got an idea how to make the job easier," Parkner said. "Me, I'm goin' to be Wu Chang. I'm goin' to make a few lordly gestures and have my way for once. With this mask, and some of his robes—"

Pelican Jones gasped as he caught the idea. Parkner put on the mask and fitted it into place.

He dressed in some of Wu Chang's garments.

"Turn up the collar of that robe," Pelican said. "The devil wears a queue, remember. Lad! Passin' through the moonlight and shadows, you look enough like the old boy to give me the shivers."

Wu Chang was glaring at them. They took him from the chair and tied him to the leg of the massive table.

"Somebody'll find you in the mornin'," Parkner said, "You're marooned, Wu Chang. Your own orders are bouncin' back at you. Now don't you wish it hadn't been against your law for anybody to go ahead and build a boat?"

"Let's get goin'," Pelican Junes said, restlessly.

They slipped out into the hall and closed the door. To the rear of the house they went, and got out there, to keep in the shadows listening for a time. A few natives were around Hagadan's cage, and the one Chinese night guard was squatting a short distance from it. None of the white men were to be seen. Lorch was aboard the yacht. Donland, according to word Pelican Jones had got to him, was to be near the launch.

Snebley and Barwright probably were sleeping heavily because of the liquor they had taken.

"Walk beside me, and have a gun ready, Pelican," Parkner said. "I'm Wu Chang, and I've decided to take you aboard the yacht."

THEY WALKED SLOWLY forward, Parkner imitating Wu Chang's stride as well as he could. His head was bent slightly, but in the mixture of moonlight and shadows that mask made it appear that the master of Soha walked there.

Hagadan caught sight of them, and began cursing Wu Chang. The Chinese guard sprang to his feet and stood ready to receive orders. The few natives fled.

"Straight to the launch," Parkner whispered to Pelican. "Start talkin' about somethin', and I'll pretend to be listenin' to you."

CHAPTER IX

DISASTER

IT HAD BEEN an unusual plug of tobacco that Lorch, the engineer, had given to Hagadan.

Some time prior to the gift, Lorch had been drinking with Barwright. The latter always relaxed and drank heavily when Wu Chang was in Soha. And it had not been difficult for Lorch to get from Barwright the key to Hagadan's cage.

He had purchased the plug of tobacco at the storehouse, gouged it out and inserted the key, made it look like a perfect plug again. Sam Hagadan had known there was something important about that tobacco, from the way Lorch had spoken, and because Lorch had slipped him the gun on the yacht.

Hagadan had found the key and secreted it. And now, when Parkner appeared and was taken for Wu Chang, and the guard was watching him and the natives had fled, Hagadan swiftly and unseen unlocked the cage, hid the lock and key in a pocket of his ragged trousers, and waited for the proper moment.

He had no weapon. But he thought possibly there would be help, once he was outside. His eyes burned as he watched the man he thought was Wu Chang. His hatred for the Chinese surged through him. His humiliation had half-crazed him.

The guard's back was turned. Sam Hagadan threw open the door of the cage and sprang out. As the Chinese guard moved, Hagadan crashed against him. His fury gave him added strength. In an instant, he had choked the guard into insensibility, and had torn out of his belt cutlas and revolver.

"Now, Wu Chang, blast you—!"

Parkner and Pelican Jones heard that wild cry as they neared the water's edge, where the launch was waiting. They were near victory, they thought, but did not quicken their steps. They saw Bill Donland slipping toward them through the patches of moonlight, and Parkner was about to make a signal which would attract Lottie Marchard and her father.

Hagadan's wild cry caused Parkner and Pelican Jones to stop and turn quickly. It rang over the clearing. The gun Hagadan had taken from the guard barked, and a bullet whistled past within inches of Parkner's head.

Then events occurred so swiftly that they were bewildering.

Snebley and Barwright suddenly appeared from one of the huts. They saw Hagadan free and charging down toward the beach, a blazing gun in his hand. They saw a man they supposed was Wu Chang, with Pelican Jones beside him, in danger of being shot down.

Snebley whipped out a gun and fired, and Hagadan turned an instant to return the fire. Barwright was howling as he rushed forward.

"Get to the launch," Parkner whispered to Pelican Jones.

The Chinese engineer of the launch had been awakened by the tumult. Parkner made a gesture at him, not wishing to speak if it could be avoided, and hoping the man would take the gesture to mean that he wished the launch started.

Sam Hagadan fired again at Snebley and Barwright, then began running toward the water.

"You won't turn bullets aside this time!" he screamed.

PARKNER DID NOT know whether to tear off the mask and show Hagadan his mistake, or hold his peace. Perhaps the infuriated man would not realize the set-up in time, and join their forces. And Parkner did not want to shoot Hagadan if it could be avoided.

It was a bullet from Snebley's gun that cut Hagadan down as he fired at Parkner again. He reeled, and dropped the gun he held. Then Snebley and Barwright were on him, beating him, throttling him.

"Get to the launch," Parkner whispered to Pelican Jones again.

"They'll think that's funny. They will be expectin' Wu Chang to give orders about Hagadan."

"We've got to get away," Parkner said.

"Donland's hangin' back because he thinks you're Wu Chang. And that girl and her father won't come now, thinkin' the same."

Back at Wu Chang's bungalow a shrill voice began cutting through the night.

"It's that lousy Chinese pirate! He's got loose," Pelican said.

"Quick! The launch!"

WU CHANG, MIRACULOUSLY free, was screeching at Snebley and Barwright. They heard him, understood, and charged down upon Parkner and Jones. The pair turned toward the launch. Parkner flashed his gun at the Chinese engineer.

"Get her started!" he barked.

The strange voice, seemingly coming from the body of Wu Chang, startled the superstitious engineer to a state of inaction. His eyes bulged, his jaw dropped. Parkner and Pelican Jones were splashing in the water, trying to get aboard. Parkner fired once at Snebley and Barwright, and Pelican Jones added a shot of his own. But neither scored a hit.

Then Wu Chang's men were at them. Evidently, Wu Chang had given orders to take them alive, for Snebley and Barwright risked bullets to clash with them. Each fired once. Pelican missed, but Parkner's shot hit Barwright in the shoulder. It did not prevent the clash. There was no doubting Snebley's strength or ability in a rough-and-tumble fight. He clashed with Parkner, knocked the gun from his hand, fought him back to the ground. Hindered by the robes he wore, Parkner was at a sad disadvantage. Snebley crashed through his guard and put across a blow that sent Parkner to the ground, unconscious.

Pelican Jones and Barwright were on even terms for a moment. Then Snebley came to Barwright's assistance. Pelican Jones, too, was soon stretched on the ground.

Wu Chang came running down to the beach, half dressed, his usual inscrutability shattered. Swiftly, he explained what had occurred. He got possession of the mask, issued swift orders.

"Put them in the storehouse and guard them. Let them not be harmed. They shall both fish for pearls with Mr. Donland tomorrow while we watch. Look to Hagadan, and save him if possible. Call some of my countrymen—and have them who failed to protect me."

Then Wu Chang marched back across the clearing.

CHAPTER X

THE SHARK MASTER

"PELICAN, I THINK we're done for now," Parkner said.

Dawn was stealing through the windows of the storehouse where they had been confined. Outside the door, armed guards made sure they could not escape. They had no weapons, not even tools with which to commit suicide had they wished to.

"It's a terrible end, lad," Pelican replied. "But it'll be over quick. I'm wishin' we could have gone on. We'd have been great pals."

They looked at each other an instant; then their hands clasped in a tense grip. Then, side by side, they faced the door, which was being opened.

Armed Chinese were there. They rushed the prisoners, hurled them back against the wall, bound their wrists behind them, then led them forth.

Everybody in Soha had gathered at the beach except Lottie Marchard and her father. Parkner supposed they had learned what had happened. He felt sorry for the girl.

SAM HAGADAN WAS in his cage again, a bloody bandage across his shoulder. He was still howling curses and insults at Wu Chang, probably hoping that Wu Chang would order him killed and make an end of it.

Wu Chang, dressed in his finest robes, approached the pair where they were being held.

"I congratulate you on your courage, gentlemen," he said. "But I cannot congratulate you on the outcome of your attempt. You would have made good citizens of Soha. Here you could have lived in peace and plenty, in a lazy happiness. But the outside world called you—to death."

"Cut it short!" Parkner growled.

"I have decided that Mr. Donland shall take you pearl fishing. He will conduct you, one at a time, to that little hut you see far out on the coral. That is where he prepares for his pearling. You will conform to the ceremony he uses. You'll be stripped of clothing, and taken out on the raft—and dive for pearls. You first, Mr. Parkner. I am truly sorry, but nothing else may be done. It is regrettable."

A feeling of utter helplessness assailed Parkner. It would avail nothing to attempt a fight. He could not hope to gain much, with his wrists lashed behind him. He caught of a sudden a peculiar look on Bill Donland's face.

"Good-by, New Hampshire!"

"Good-by, Texas! It's tough, lad!"

"Come along, you!" Bill Donland growled.

He grasped Parkner roughly by the arm and hurried him down the beach. Those left behind made themselves comfortable to watch.

There was a little hut far out on the ledge of coral, and toward that they went.

"Do just as I say, Parkner, and don't make any mistake," Donland said, as they hurried along. "Pretend to pull back once in a while—that's it! Now, listen! There's a trick about this stunt. I learned it when I was a kid. My dad was a no-good guy gone native, but my mother was white, too. He got bumped off when I was a young one, and the natives raised me. They taught me this stunt."

"What is it?" Parkner asked.

"You'll see. Do just as I say, everything will be all right. I'll save you and Pelican Jones."

"Save us? How can you, with that crowd watchin' back on the beach?"

THEY REACHED THE little hut, and entered. A stench assailed Parkner's nostrils. Working swiftly, Donland untied Parkner's wrists.

"Strip, quick," he ordered.

Donland began removing his own clothes, which were few. Parkner, wondering, stripped also. Donland shifted a few planks and some chunks of corals, and unearthed a battered old bucket filled with a greasy, sticky mess.

"Glad I've got enough," Donland said. "I suppose you're a good swimmer?"

"I can swim like a fish."

"Great! Listen, now. We go out on the raft. I'll pole it along the edge of the lagoon. See these chunks of rotten fish? I slip 'em over the side, and that gets the sharks fussin' around. Hold your hands behind your back, like they were still tied. I'll give the raft an extra hard shove, and you pretend to fall off. I'll dive after you—"

"And that's the end for me," Parkner said. "I reckon you're tryin' to brace me up, give me some hope, but it's no good. Thanks, Donland, but I know the answer."

"NO, YOU DON'T! Get busy and grease yourself with that stuff, from head to feet. Smear it on thick. Hurry! When you go into the water, drop right down. Then come up slow. Don't worry if the sharks brush against you. They won't try to make a meal."

"Why won't they?" Parkner demanded.

"It's an old secret of the natives. They've got a word for this stuff—make it of decayed shellfish and vegetable oils. When you're in the water, it gives off a freak phosphorescence. Maybe the sharks smell it, too—some say they can. Funny stuff—doesn't scare 'em exactly. They'll come close, but won't attack. Can't you take my word? I use it all the time gettin' out shell, don't I? Hurry and grease yourself!"

Half dazed, Parkner did as he was ordered. He smeared himself with the smelling mess, while Donland did the same.

"Hurry, or they'll be wonderin' what's keepin' us," the diver said. "Nobody ever comes to this hut, and I don't want 'em to. Wu Chang's orders now that they keep away."

"But I can't stay under water—" Parkner began.

"Slip off the raft where I show you. Swim around the lump of coral and crawl out and hide. I'll tell Pelican Jones the same. Stay there until night. I'll come to you—and we'll swim out to the yacht. No need to worry about the sharks. No devil fish on this side of the lagoon."

"If you're tellin' me the truth—"

"I am. We'll swim out and grab the

yacht or maybe take the launch if she's ashore. I'll get word to Miss Marchard and her father. We'll get 'em away, all right. Anyhow, we can try. I'm willin' to take a chance—sick of this. I've got some pearls cached away. Come on!"

DONLAND TOOK HIM by an arm again, and Parkner put his hands behind his back. They got on the raft, and Donland put the chunks of fish near the edge, where he could kick them off.

"Look to the left—that big hump of coral. Swim around it," Donland said again, "and crawl out. You'll be safe there till night. It'll be plenty hot—"

"I won't worry about that, if I ever live to get there."

Donland shoved off some of the fish with his foot as he poled the raft along the edge of the lagoon. Up came the monsters, to churn the water as they fought for the bait. But they did not seem to be trying to get at the men on the raft, as they had done in the case of Nugago.

Parkner began having some hope. But he could not convince himself that he could get out of this alive. He felt sick as he watched the monsters playing around the raft.

"Now's the time," Donland said, "when I give the word. Swim where I said, and crawl out."

He shoved off the remainder of the fish. He pretended to lurch toward Parkner as the sharks surged upward again.

"Now!" he said.

Parkner felt that his heart was standing still. It took courage to drop into that crystal clear water. But there was nothing else to be done. It was a chance, and he had no possible hope otherwise.

With the idea that Donland had been trying to make it easy for him, he slipped off the raft. Down he went, eyes open and watching. Two gigantic sharks swooped at him—and swerved. Another did the same. Parkner began coming up slowly, kept just below the surface, and swam.

Each instant he expected to feel the bite which would mean the end. He swam as slowly as possible, letting out little bubbles of breath. Another shark dashed at him, and away again.

He made for the hump of coral, and found a tiny inlet around it. Into this he went, breaking to the surface. The water grew shallow suddenly. He cut his knee on the sharp coral. And then he was out, sprawled on the rock in the hot sun, panting and almost exhausted.

CHAPTER XI

A RUINED CAREER

THEN HE WAITED. He could hear distant shouting on the shore but did not dare lift his head above the lump of coral to see what was happening. Gradually it grew quiet. He wondered whether Pelican Jones was passing through the ordeal. Pelican was a stubborn cuss. Maybe he would refuse to do as Donland directed, or be foolish enough to put up a hopeless fight.

Parkner drew down to the edge of

the water and watched. And, after what seemed an eternity, he saw Pelican Jones swimming toward the hump, saw him come into the tiny inlet and break the surface. A moment later he had Pelican by the arm and was pulling him to land.

They were speechless for a moment. Pelican broke the silence.

"Didn't expect to see you again, Texas, this side of Heaven or the other place. Got a new lease on life," he growled. "Wu Chang and his gang think we're in shark's stomachs by this time. How in the world did that Donland guy do it?"

"Some trick he learned from the natives. I've heard of it," Parkner said. "Never believed it till now. It's that mess he smears himself with. Nobody but the natives know what it is—the natives and Donland."

"It sure smells," said Pelican Jones agreeably, "but it does the work. And now what?"

"Nothin', except to lay low and wait for night. I could do with some food. But I reckon we should not complain."

IT WAS THE middle of the night when Bill Donland finally came to them over the coral.

"They think you're dead," he reported. "I got word to the Marchards that you're alive. Wu Chang was makin' fun of the girl bein' a widow so quick, and sayin' that he'd raffle her off again in a few days."

"What are you plannin'?" Parkner asked.

"We've got to seize the yacht. I've got one automatic—had it hidden for a long time, waitin' for a chance. And a couple of good knives. It may be hot work."

"We can do it," Parkner said, "if we can get to the yacht."

"We'll swim out. Here's a bucket of grease. You needn't be afraid, gents."

"If we can get to the yacht, Lorch will help us," Parkner explained. "He'll handle the engine room crew. Pelican is a navigator. There's probably charts in Wu Chang's cabin, so we can get the ship through the reefs. But, how about that girl and her father?"

"Get command of the yacht first," Donland suggested. "The launch is ashore. Maybe they'll come out to see what's wrong."

THEY GREASED THEMSELVES again, and each of the partners fastened a knife around his neck with a thong. Donland wrapped the automatic and an extra clip of cartridges, all he had, in a length of cloth, and fastened it around his head, turban fashion.

"Just take it easy, and follow me," he said. "And don't worry any."

They were in the water again, swimming slowly and easily through the mouth of the lagoon. They could not see into the depths now, but a couple of times Parkner fancied that he felt a body brush past him.

The phosphorescence worried Parkner. He was afraid somebody aboard the *Soha* would see the trails they made through the water. But no hail came from the yacht. Discipline there had relaxed while the craft was in port.

Finally, the three men were resting beneath the bow, holding to the anchor chain. No sounds above them told of a member of the crew beings on watch.

A loud jabbering came from the forecastle.

Parkner went up first, slowly, laboriously, and got aboard. He crouched in the shadows until the others were beside him. They rested a moment, and got their weapons ready.

"Let's get to Lorch's cabin," Parkner whispered. "Let him know what's up, and we'll have that much more help. He's got a gun, probably."

They were almost to the companionway when they bumped into one of the Chinese. His squawk of fright was cut short when Pelican Jones knifed him. But it had been heard.

Chinese came tumbling on deck. Donland began firing at them, and they scattered. Parkner plunged down the companionway, howling for Lorch, and the engineer, half-dressed, came rushing out, rubbing his sleepy eyes.

"We're here—the three of us! Get a gun and come runnin'!" Parkner cried.

He rushed back to the deck, and Lorch came bellowing after him. The two blazing guns drove the Chinese into the forecastle. Lorch led the way to where the engine room crew was coming up from their quarters below. He bellowed orders, and they rushed below again.

"We've got the yacht, and now what?" Pelican Jones demanded. "There's four of us—"

"And the launch is putting off from the shore," Lorch interrupted. "Better let me handle this, gents. I'll coax 'em aboard."

The other three crouched out of sight. The launch came on full speed, circled, came up to starboard.

"What's goin' on?" It was Snebley's voice.

Lorch showed himself.

"Hello, Snebley!" he hailed. "Had a little trouble with the crew. Had to drive 'em into the forecastle. Maybe you'd better come aboard and help me straighten it out."

"I'll straighten them lousy skunks out quick enough!" Snebley roared. He had come out in the launch alone with the Chinese who ran her. Now he came hurrying to deck. As he sprang aboard, he found Parkner and Pelican Jones confronting him, with Donland just behind them.

SNEBLEY WASTED NO time in speculating how Parkner and Pelican happened to be alive and on the yacht. He roared a challenge and reached for his gun. They hurled themselves upon him. Snebley fought along the rail after they had got the gun away from him. He tried to break free, and they took after him.

He could not get to a cabin for another weapon. He turned and raced back, intending to get to the launch. Parkner made a dive for him. Snebley lurched backward, swung a terrific blow, lost balance—and fell.

There was a splash at the yacht's side. Bill Donland and Lorch were tumbling into the launch, overpowering the Chinese. Snebley started swimming toward it.

BUT SNEBLEY HAD not been stripped and treated to a coat of that mysterious grease. The others saw his arms flash in the moonlight as he swam, but only for a moment. One arm flashed straight up; Snebley's body shot halfway out of the water; one terrible scream came—and then he was gone.

"Sometimes, they hunt at night," Bill Donland was saying, softly. "They're queer—nobody can understand 'em. Don't ever believe anything anybody tells you about a shark. They're always changin' some of their habits."

"Snebley had it comin' to him," Pelican Jones said. "One devil in human form—that was Snebley."

Then it was quiet, except for the infrequent howls of the Chinese imprisoned in the forecastle. There were hails from the shore, but no replies from the yacht.

"We'll wait a little longer, then pick up that girl and her father," Donland said. "I told 'em what to do—slip out along the edge of the lagoon and get to my hut. If they were able to do it, they'll be waitin'."

The men waited almost an hour, then got into the launch and ran slowly into the lagoon. But they did not go to the beach where a curious group was waiting. The launch turned in to the fringe of coral, nosed it and stopped. And Dr. Marchard and his daughter came hurrying toward them through the shadows.

They were on the yacht when dawn came. Lorch was mastering his engine room crew. Pelican, Parkner and Bill Donland were on deck. Wu Chang's cabin had been rifled and charts found, and Pelican surveyed them carefully.

On the shore, they could see Wu Chang, the others grouped behind him. There he and Barwright would remain, completely helpless, until a gunboat came to take them off and to punishment. Wu Chang's own orders were responsible for his being marooned now. The fate he had so cunningly contrived for others was inevitably his own doom.

A derisive screech from the yacht's whistle, and the craft started slowly away from Soha. Carefully, she was nursed through the maze of treacherous reefs. And late in the afternoon she was free, and took up speed.

"WE'LL BE RUNNIN' across a gunboat in a few days," Pelican Jones said. "Lad, I never thought I'd skipper a fine craft like this. This time yesterday I was figurin' I'd never skipper anything."

"Everything's lovely," Parkner said, grinning. "Wu Chang and his pals, and Sam Hagadan, are where they can be picked up any time. Donland's got a couple of bunches of pearls that'll make life easy for him the rest of his days. You can go on bein' an international tramp. Miss Marchard and her father can go home and startle the folks who think they're dead."

"AND WHAT DO you get out of it?" Pelican Jones asked.

"A chance to work my way back to Texas and see it again. Only, maybe I won't have to work my way. Donland's goin' to claim that pearl bed by right of discovery, and go at his fishin' lawful under government supervision. Nobody can dispute the claim. Wu Chang sure won't be in a position to do so. And

  THE BEST OF THRILLING ADVENTURES

Donland's cuttin' us two and Lorch in on the company and profits."

"You'll be needin' pearls—anyhow, maybe a rope of 'em," Pelican Jones said.

"How's that?" Parkner asked.

Pelican Jones was grinning. Parkner turned to see Lottie Marchard walking slowly toward him, smiling at him.

"She thought you might be a scoundrel, and you turned out to be one of them knights after all. She'll never quit till she gets you, Texas. You might have made a fine international tramp like me. But not now. Women—they've ruined a lot of fine international tramps by marryin' 'em and makin' 'em settle down."

World of Doom

BY RAY CUMMINGS

Captured by Mysterious Denizens of an Asteroid, Ralph Owens and Jack Clark Are Pitted Against the Mighty Power of Weird Forces of Destruction!

CHAPTER I

"THE EARTH IS MENACED!"

"I SENT FOR you, Jack," Professor Owen said, "because I think that the earth is menaced."

Jack Clark, reporter of the *American Press*, started across the professor's dim, shadowy library. Owen was leaning forward in his chair intently, His thin face drawn.

"What do you mean by that?" Clark demanded.

"I mean a menace from space. I think that—last night—weird beings from another world landed upon earth. I have a statement to make to the press—scientific facts to back it."

The aged Professor Owen's voice became solemn, and more grim than ever.

"This attack—if it should come, Jack, it could devastate the earth."

It sent a shiver through Clark to hear a calm, precise man of science make such a statement. Weird beings from another planet attacking the earth! He shuddered at the gruesome thought.

It was midnight—the night of August 10th. Clark had received an urgent summons to Professor Owen's home on a mountaintop in New Hampshire. He had come by plane—the professor's private landing field was beside the house, lighted with floodlights now. And nearby was the dome of his private astronomical observatory.

"I don't understand—" Clark began.

Ralph Owen, the professor's son, spoke earnestly.

"We'll explain quickly enough. This asteroid thing—"

Young Owen and Clark had been good friends in college. Owen was plainly under stress now, grim as his father.

"I'll explain it to him, Ralph," the professor interjected.

He turned to Clark. "You know, Jack, that some three months ago an incoming asteroid was discovered, out near the orbit of Jupiter?"

"Yes, I know that."

"A dark little world. It has, we think, a diameter of about two hundred miles—a circumference of some six hundred. It's been coming in toward our sun, on an elliptical orbit like a comet. It probably will round the sun, like a comet, and go out again."

"And it's passing the earth now," Clark nodded. "I've read all about that."

"Exactly," the professor agreed. "It's too small to affect us in any way—and it's moving too swiftly for the earth to draw it to us. Tonight, it is some five hundred thousand miles away, at about its closest point. That's pretty close,
astronomically speaking. Only about twice the distance of our moon."

"Ever seen it?" Ralph Owen asked Clark.

"No. But I read that, to the naked eye—"

"Come here, I'll show you."

THEY STOOD AT the French windows. To one side of the dark and silent grove of trees, a big patch of purple-velvet, star-strewn sky was visible. The stars were clear and sparkling here at this altitude.

"Out there," young Owen indicated, "midway from the top of that left-hand tree to the zenith—"

Clark could hardly be sure that he identified it. Certainly it looked harmless enough—a little pinpoint of blazing light—just one of the myriad of smaller stars. But they were all blazing suns, thousands of light-years away, and this asteroid was very, small and very close. Dark and cold—like our earth, and Venus and Mars and the moon. No light of its own. Shining only by reflected sunlight.

They sat down again.

"The public isn't very interested, of course," the professor continued. "But, Jack, that little world has an atmosphere. Air envelopes it, like our earth. The surface can't be seen because the clouds hang too thickly."

"Until tonight, Father," young Owen said—and Clark heard a strained hush to his voice.

"Yes, until tonight," the professor repeated heavily. "I was at my telescope. It's small, compared to the big observatories, but adequate for this job."

CLARK KNEW ABOUT the professor's telescope. It was of a new type, an electro-telescope. Small of lens, it yet had remarkable power. Its electronic current sent from its barrel a narrow jet of violet radiance into the sky. That small violet beam was visible now, slanting upward from the observatory dome toward the asteroid. Clark had noticed it a moment ago when they were at the window.

"As I was at my telescope tonight," the professor said, "there suddenly was a rift in the clouds around this asteroid. I saw down to the surface. I saw small metallic mountains—but there was vegetation growing. Signs of water, ice melting, because now the little world has come into our sun's warmth. It is warming up from what must have been a devastating cold. I saw all the necessities of human life—"

"And life itself," young Owen exclaimed. "Things moving—"

"Just a brief glimpse," the professor added, "and then the clouds closed in again. But I saw what I think is human life."

Interesting! But what could be so frightening in this? It seemed that Owen interpreted Clark's thoughts, for he said:

"Frightening, Jack, because last night Father thought he saw something approaching our earth. I mean really close—just above our atmosphere. Fifty miles away, maybe. A tiny, swift-moving blob. It crossed the field of the telescope so fast that he barely saw it—and he could never pick it up again. But it could have been an interplanetary vehicle."

Owen's words were tumbling over one another with a swift vehemence.

"Something coming down from the direction of this asteroid, to land upon our earth. It could have been that. And last night there was a small news item in the papers—naturally, you probably didn't notice it. A farmer and his family near here were all found dead. Little burned black patches on them—as though they had been struck by lightning.

"As a matter of fact, there was an electrical storm near dawn. But that probably was just a coincidence. They were all indoors, and the house wasn't struck. And Father thinks—"

"I think," the professor said slowly "that I actually did see an interplanetary vehicle about to land on the earth. The beginning of an attack from this asteroid. Weird beings—God knows what they can be like—things intelligent—perhaps more intelligent than we are—perhaps not even in human form."

IT TURNED CLARK cold. He was a big fellow, this Jack Clark, blond as a Viking, afraid of no man. But things inhuman—a quiet man of science saying things like this! The shadowed library here suddenly, to his startled imagination, lurked with menace. These opened French windows—that shadow over there by the piano—

He felt a cold sweat starting from every pore. He shook himself to free his mind of those crazy thoughts.

"But look here—" he objected.

He got no further. Vague fears leaped suddenly into realized ones. The silent house rang with a woman's scream of terror.

Clark and his two companions leaped to their feet.

"Good Lord, that's Annie, our cook!" young Owen ejaculated.

THE TWO YOUNG men found Annie in the kitchen. The young negress lay sprawled on the floor, dead. Unquestionably dead. But killed—how? Not stabbed, or shot. There was no wound upon her. No sign of violence.

"Look!" Owen yelled suddenly. "Look, here on her arm!"

Stark terror was in his voice. The white sleeve of the girl's waist was ripped; and blackened, charred! The flesh of her arm had a little burned spot—like one who has been struck by lightning. Clark's mind swept back—that farmer and his family—they had been found dead like this, last night.

The menace from the asteroid! Weird beings, perhaps not even in human form. They must be here—now!

They had been bending down over the dead girl. Clark sprang to his feet.

"These—confounded things from space—here? They must have been here, Ralph. Just a minute ago."

And suddenly they thought of Professor Owen. The old man hadn't followed them in their rush here. It was a hot night. The kitchen door and windows were open; the serene starlit night brooded outside. Clark started toward the door, then turned.

"Got to get back to your father," he jerked.

They ran. On the floor of the shadowed living roomy the blackened body of Professor Owen lay there crumpled. Dead!

Clark's brain whirled. These enemies—were they invisible? There was nothing here. The room with its opened French windows seemed empty. But was it?

Owen stood stricken, gazing down at his father, forgetful of everything in the face of this terrible, unexpected tragedy. Clark shook him.

"Got to do something, Ralph. Death here—to us also."

The living must fight, not stand helplessly mourning the dead. Owen suddenly snapped out of his trance, his pale face contorted, his dark eyes blazing with the desire for vengeance. Both he and Clark were unarmed. On the table was a heavy bookend and Clark seized it for a weapon. Owen, still confused, stood with clenched fists.

Was there a rustling in the room? Clark thought so. No, it was outside the French window. He ran to the window, leaped upon the window box, and with a bound landed outside on the grass. Owen was directly behind him.

Nothing out here. In the starlight, with the dark shadowed grove of trees close at hand, they stood peering.

Nothing here?

THEN CLARK SAW the accursed things. With a chill running like ice through his veins, he stood stiffened, gripping his companion—both of them staring, wordlessly, almost paralyzed with disbelief.

Under the trees, things were moving. The patterns of starlight showed them, upright brown things, with legs short and squat. Travesties of humans, with

heads, and waving arms. Things some four feet tall. The eyes of them showed as moving green points of fire in the darkness.

"Why—why—look—" Owen muttered.

Close at hand there was a rustle. In the starlight of the open lawn, not ten feet away, one of the squat brown things stood upon its jointed legs, its multiple arms waving like tentacles. Insect? Human? The shell-like jointed body was garbed with clothes. Weapons dangled from a belt.

The thing stood with a single eye gleaming balefully from its travesty of a face. And then it leaped forward upon the two men!

CHAPTER II

FORTY MILLION MILES

CLARK FLUNG THE bookend, but it went wide of its mark. The attacking brown shape struck against him. It was light

The little tentacle arms flailed; the bent and useless
little legs kicked against Clark in abject terror.

in weight and he hardly staggered. But brown tentacle arms enveloped him. A huge pincer gripped his shoulder; it cut through his leather jacket, squeezing, pinching his flesh.

A leering face, with a wide, slitlike mouth in a gaping crescent, stared up from the height of his chest. The goggling round single eye gleamed with a green phosphorescence.

Instant impressions. Clark struck with his fist into the gruesome face. His fist sank deep as it cracked like an eggshell. He felt, on his fist and wrist and part way up his forearm, a horrible gluey, sticky ooze. The thing screamed—an eerie cry, half animal, half human. Its gripping pincer loosened; the enveloping tentacles fell away so that Clark jerked his fist from the ooze and staggered back, free of it. The wounded thing sank to the ground, writhing.

But others were here. A ring of them now, surging forward, closing in. The stench of the broken thing at Clark's feet was nauseating. At a little distance, on the ground, he saw Owen rolling with a brown cluster of the things upon him, a mass of tangled bodies and threshing tentacles. One of the brown shells crushed under the weight of Owen's heaving body. Owen was a small fellow, but he was lithe as a cat. He was fighting like a cat now.

The ring around Clark was closing in. It seemed, in the dim starlight, to be a ring of phosphorescent eyes. He saw waving weapons; scientific devices, undoubtedly. But none of them were being used.

Thoughts are instant things. The impression came to Clark in that second while he stood there panting, glaring at his antagonists, that these strange beings wanted to capture him alive. Then a tiny bolt flashed, like an updarting, inverted flash of lightning. It spat high, went up through the tree branches. A warning bolt, to show him what could be done.

The brown things around him were standing inactive now. But Owen, on the ground, was still fighting. He shouted:

"Jack! They're flimsy. Smash them! I can—" His voice went off into a gurgle. Clark swung and leaped toward the struggling group.

"Stop it, Ralph! Don't fight—they'll kill—"

WITH A RUSTLING surge, the brown things came at him. They swarmed over him. His flailing fists cracked them in a tumult of horror. He waded through the broken, oozing bodies, flung them off, but others came. Fearless things. The death of one had no effect upon the others. The starlit grove rang with their blood-curdling screams.

Then it seemed that from the pincer-hand of one of them, a metal cylinder was squirting fumes into Clark's face. The smell was heavy, sickeningly sweet. He held his breath. He caught the cylinder, ripped it away, and crashed it through the face of the, thing which had been wielding it.

But he had breathed the drug fumes. His legs and arms suddenly felt heavy. His head was roaring; he felt his body bathed in a sudden outpouring of sweat.

     THE BEST OF THRILLING ADVENTURES

He was still fighting—but abruptly it seemed like a dream. He saw Owen's inert body being carried away under the trees by a staggering group of the brown creatures.

WAS THIS THE end? As though in a nightmare, Clark tried to keep on fighting, despite his fading senses. Then the starlit vision of the tentacles around him deepened into blackness. He felt himself falling. The roaring in his head grew into a great torrent of sound, enveloping all the world. Then it, too, faded, as all his senses slid away into a black and soundless abyss of unconsciousness.

Clark recovered his senses to find himself lying on a metal grid-floor. Owen was sitting beside him, bending over him.

"Oh—you're all right now. Thank God for that!"

"Yes. All right. I guess so." With returning strength, he struggled to sit up. "Where—where are we?"

They were on a space-flyer, quite evidently. In a small and dark, cell-like room. Neither of them was greatly injured. They had been drugged and now it was wearing off.

They were alone in the room. A few pieces of strangely fashioned furniture were here. There was a metal door-slide but it was locked; Owen had already investigated that. In one wall, opposite the door, was an oval bull's-eye pane. Brilliant starlight was streaming in. It was the only light in the room.

"We're in space," Owen muttered. "Heading for that confounded asteroid. Come here, I'll show you." He gestured toward the window.

Dizzily Clark gained his feet. He was horribly weak, his head still heavy and whirling.

"I was knocked out, like you," Owen tried to reconstruct events. "But I came to—Lord, it seems hours ago. A day maybe. Nobody has been here. But we're moving through space, all right."

The room was vibrationless. There was no sense of moving, but a distant hum and throb were audible. The vehicle's mechanisms were in operation.

The sight from the window was amazing. Freed of earth's hampering atmosphere, the stars shone with an amazing blue-white brilliance, against a firmament dead-black. Illimitable distance stretched here. Black infinity of space, star-filled. The stars were everywhere—overhead, and to the sides, and underneath.

"I figure we must be near the stern of this ship," Owen said. "The sun must be forward. We're heading toward it. You can't see it from here. I figure that's the earth there."

He pointed.

THE EARTH! OF course it was. A reddish-silver disc, level with the window. Clark had his wits now, and he was puzzled. The earth, off there, was visually no more than the size of our moon. And there was the moon itself, a tiny light-point, hanging near the earth-disc.

"But, good Lord!" Clark expostulated, "how did we get so far away, just while we've been unconscious? For the earth to be that small, we must have gone a great many million miles. The asteroid was only half a million. Where the devil are we heading? Where is the asteroid?"

"Darned if I know," Owen scowled. "But I can guess. Say, aren't you pretty hungry?"

Thinking of it, Clark was. And thirsty. And very strangely weak.

"My guess is that the drug we breathed threw us into catalepsy," Owen said. "Suspended animation, out of which we've just recovered today."

"Today?" Clark gasped.

"Sure. Today. I think we've been unconscious a week of earth time. Maybe longer."

IT WAS TRUE. The asteroid had been passing the earth the night they were abducted. It was only five hundred thousand miles away, but by the laws of celestial mechanics, every instant its velocity was accelerating. The space vehicle was chasing after it now, and taking days to catch it. Already the vehicle had crossed the orbit of Venus, and was well in toward the orbit of Mercury.

The two men had been at the window perhaps five minutes when there was a noise behind them. They swung, tense, alert, to see the door-slide moving. In the dim aperture, a squat brown thing stood peering. With an outstretched tentacle-arm holding the partly opened door-slide, it gazed in at the two prisoners. And they stared back at it.

Clark saw it suddenly not as an insect, but as a human. A travesty of a man. Jointed legs, short and bent; with a garment of grey fabric draped across the hips and up over the shoulders.

Four tentacle arms. A body, with bulging chest. A neck, thin and spindly, supporting a round head. A face, with a single eye over the nose, and a slit of mouth beneath. And flapping ears at the sides.

But still it seemed human. The voice mumbled words in a strange tongue. It was harsh and guttural; but there was intelligence in the sound.

Then the man—Clark could think of it as a man now—came slowly into the room. One of his hands—not a pincer on this arm, but flexible fingers—fumbled at his belt.

Clark said tensely:

"If you understand English—don't try to kill us. We don't want to fight."

The English words evidently were unintelligible. But the hand came from the belt and proffered a small cylinder of red-brown polished metal.

And Clark relaxed.

"Good Lord, Ralph," he said, "I guess it's something to eat or drink."

He took the cylinder, shook it; a liquid swished inside. At the door now, others of the little brown-shelled men were standing. They held weapons in their hands—small projectors of metal. But they were all smiling, the slits of mouth upturned into the mockery of a grin. And the one in the room made a gesture of drinking.

"Thanks," said Clark. He put the open end of the cylinder to his mouth, and drank a heavy sweetish liquid. But it was refreshing, queerly strengthening. Almost at once the weakness he had felt left him; his normal strength came quickly back. An elixir.

A cylinder of it was given Owen. Then food was brought.

A DAY PASSED—THEN another. Days of accustomed earth time, to be measured now only by hunger intervals, and times when Jack and Ralph went to sleep. Except when one of their captors brought food, the men were left alone. Two mattresses were given them to lie on—fabric coverings stuffed with something soft, redolent as incense. And the shining round disc of the earth dwindled steadily in visual size.

Another meal. They tried to calculate how far they might be from earth now, forty million miles perhaps. They were discussing it when abruptly the silent interior of the vehicle sounded with voices and the scratching tread of men.

The door-slide opened. The man who had been bringing in their food and drink signed for them to come out. They were accustomed to his gestures now, and followed him docilely along a narrow vaulted metal corridor into a larger room which was in the bow of the vessel.

A GROUP OF the weird-looking little men was here. Through every contact with their captors now, the two young prisoners were increasingly aware of the little brown creatures' human aspect, for all their weird appearance. And an ironical thought struck Clark so forcibly now that he laughed aloud.

"Heavens, Ralph—we look as queer to them as they look to us!"

It was true enough. The group here in this long narrow apartment—it seemed the control-room of the vessel—crowded forward to see the huge, strange earthmen. They plucked at them, felt their strange solidity of bone and muscle, meanwhile jabbering with guttural rapidity. And their stares were composed of awe and fear. Truly, to them these strange giants were things to be afraid of, and to watch closely.

Clark saw that he and his companion were certainly being carefully watched. Several of the men, with projector weapons held alert, were always close beside the captives. Beyond that, after the first few moments, the earthmen were ignored.

Brilliant light was streaming in one of the left-hand windows. Gigantic sun now. Huge ball, leaping and crawling with color. The flames of the corona—monstrous tongues of fire—licked outward into space. And the asteroid was here, close in advance of the ship's bow.

It showed as a titanic half-moon, dark on one side, painted with sunlight on the other. Huge, unreal, it stretched half across the visual firmament. Even to the naked eye now, its heavy dark cloud masses were visible.

Hours passed. A meal of the strange food to which they were growing accustomed was served the prisoners. Swiftly the asteroid grew in visual size. Presently it stretched and blocked all the forward hemisphere of space. Its clouds held solid. Then the clouds and all the starry heavens swung in an arc, as the vessel altered its course. To Clark came a new viewpoint.

The tumbling vapor-masses of the

asteroid's atmosphere were under the space-ship now. The ship was dropping down into the clouds. Then it was in them. A solid grey fog, luminous with radiating sunlight, enveloped all the bull's-eye windows.

There followed an hour's descent, with the men at the controls watchfully regarding their banks of dials and in-dicators. An air of excitement now was upon all the little men. Soon they would land, triumphantly bringing home the captive giants whom undoubtedly they had been sent to earth to secure.

JACK'S MIND SWEPT back to that night in Professor Owen's mountain-top home. It seemed so long ago. He realized now that this vehicle had been attracted by the violet beam of the telescope, whose penetrating radiance had streamed into space. And the floodlights of the landing field had brilliantly illumined the house and its vicinity.

The bull's-eye windows in the floor of the room here had suddenly brightened. The ship had come down through the clouds into a grey, flat twilight.

The new world! It lay spread beneath them, weird, strange, bizarre beyond anything they had ever imagined.

CHAPTER III

THE BRAIN IN
THE CHAIR

FORGETFUL FOR THE moment of their own situation, Clark and Owen peered down through the aperture at their feet. The ship was descending from what seemed now an altitude of no more than twenty thousand feet. Overhead, the sky was sullen with dark, misty clouds.

Below, the surface of this little world was visible—a tumbled region of grey-black mountains.

Desolate vista! Bleak naked crags. Spires and pinnacles of shining me-tallic rock, some of them smooth and burnished, gleaming with a dull sheen in the twilight.

The vehicle dropped lower. The convexity of the little world was clearly apparent. The horizon was close; the sharp curvature obvious. To one side, where a bank of little mountains rose in serrated ranks, what seemed water was visible.

It was a painfully barren landscape. And where were its people? None were visible here. Then Clark saw that the tumbled and scarred surface was pitted with cavernous openings. A honeycomb of grottoes in which, undoubtedly, the people lived.

And then he saw things moving—blobs on the rocks.

A succession of new details. The two earthmen could hardly encompass them, so strange was it all, so swiftly changing as the spaceship dropped down. Against the horizon, to the right, a red glare showed, and rising smoke. A volcano? Now vegetation was apparent. Vines, low on the rocks. Little patches of soil, lying like water in the rock-hollows, and in the soil, small, stunted trees, blue-white.

And then Clark saw that the vines

were crawling on the rocks. Vegetation, swiftly growing with visible movement!

The twilight was fading. It was evidently late afternoon in this little world with a day of only three earth hours. The night came swiftly; the scene plunged into sudden darkness. Weird world!

FROM THE WINDOWS where now they could see only vague spots of moving light, the fascinated spectators were presently plucked by their captors. The ship was preparing to land. Clark and Owen were shoved back into the dim windowless corridor. Beside them stood their four little guards. Flimsy humans. Flimsy as huge insects.

"I could smash all of them with a blow," Owen murmured.

"But don't try it," Clark warned. "We can't kill everyone on the ship. And everyone on the asteroid. What's more, we couldn't navigate the ship—even if we had control of it."

There was a thump as the vessel landed; grinding sounds as the heavy windows and door-slides were opened.

Air of the new world! Heavy air—heavy with strange smells. The guards shoved the two prisoners forward. Out of the ship. Down an incline.

To the pair it was a phantasmagoria of weird flickering lights—shadowed rocks—crowds of the small insect-men plucking at them, pushing them forward, staring awed at these giant beings from another world. And a chaos of sounds. Jabbering voices; cries of command; the scratching of insect-like feet.

They stumbled forward. A rocky ground was underfoot. Then they were in a cave—a tunnel, descending. It was dimly lighted with spots of blue light placed at intervals along its ceiling. The jabbering voices echoed with a muffled roar.

"Queer that the gravity is almost like the earth," Owen said suddenly.

They felt almost normal. A little lighter, but not much. The density of this small asteroid was amazing. Of what metal the rock might have been, no one will ever say. But undoubtedly, it had an immense atomic weight.

The underground corridor broadened. As they passed a branch corridor, a group of the brown-shelled men, brandishing metallic fan-shaped swords, herded all the crowd into the diverging tunnel. There remained only the two captives and a dozen of their guards. Diffused light showed ahead—a dim radiance, blue-white.

They emerged at last into a fairly large underground apartment. It was queerly blue—the radiating blue light which came from a hidden source; a padded blue floor; walls and ceiling draped with blue fabrics. At first the two men could see very little. The blue radiance, though not intense, strangely dazzled them. They moved forward, shoved by their captors, who prodded them with the projector weapons.

THE APARTMENT SEEMED empty, queerly silent. The jabber of the men had ceased, and the padded floor muffled their scratching tread. The room was some fifty feet long. At its end, on the floor, a few strangely fashioned chairs were placed. Beyond them was a raised platform—a padded dais some three feet high.

No one here? Clark's eyes were becoming more accustomed to the blue radiance now. With a sudden pounding of his heart, he saw a small, wide, padded armchair on the dais. In it, sitting motionless, was a man of this weird world. A man? Clark's reason had to call the thing a man. Ruler of the asteroid? It seemed so.

The little insect-men, to whose gruesome aspect they had in a measure grown accustomed, shoved their captives to the foot of the dais. The earthmen they had been sent to get. They stood silent, expectant, as they brought the earth-giants for their ruler's inspection.

And Clark and Owen, with pounding hearts, stared at the man in the chair. He was just about level with them as they stood on the floor before the dais.

Owen gasped out a startled oath. Clark murmured an aside.

"Easy! Don't make a move. If we frighten them, they can kill us in a second."

The man in the chair had a head of perhaps twice normal earth size. A single-eyed face, with a slit of mouth. A spindly neck, upon which the huge head wobbled. His body was small as a five-year-old earth child—the bulging brown chest clothed and hung with metal ornaments like a profusion of medals, to dignify his high office.

He sat wobbling in the chair, his four tentacle arms gripping the chair sides to steady himself. His small jointed legs hung down, not touching the floor.

A MAN ALMOST all head. And now as Clark stared, he saw that the huge hairless skull was transparent. Not bone. Not even a shell. A head of bloated membrane, bloated by the brain inside it. Transparent membrane. The huge brain within lay visible—palpitating, twisting like a tangle of worms.

The single eye was regarding the prisoners steadily. To Clark the silence became insupportable. He burst out impulsively:

"Do you speak? What do you want of us?"

In the hush, his voice burst out like a bomb. It startled the ruler in the chair. And the guards beside Clark leaped, seized him with their pincers. Their weapons came up, leveled at his head; and then as, for a tense moment, he did not move, the guards relaxed.

Owen expelled a long breath.

"Gosh, you tell me to be careful, Jack!" he murmured. "Don't do a thing like that again. That head up there—"

THE MASTER BRAIN! A gigantic intellect dominating this little world. Undoubtedly, it was that.

Then this ruler spoke softly in his own language to his men. One of them leaped lightly to the platform. And now Clark saw, on a rack up there, a row of what seemed to be large test tubes. There were ten, with wires connecting them. The light shone on them as the guard carefully lifted them and hung them like a necklace around the spindly neck of the ruler in the chair.

The connecting wires looped and fastened them; the tubes in front dangled on his bulging chest.

The light from over the dais shone more clearly on the test tubes now. Clark saw that they were filled with a grey, palpitating substance. Living brain tissue! Brain of this ruler which his bloated head could not contain, nurtured in the test tubes!

A wire was placed now around his bloated, quivering forehead. The brains in the tubes were connected with the brain in his head, so that now he might use all his mentality in dealing with these strange prisoners.

Suddenly Clark saw that other wires from the necklace of brain tubes were tossed by the guards over the dais front. A guard below picked them up. Two wires. A looped electrode was at the end of each. And the guards were about to fasten them to the foreheads of the prisoners.

Owen winced. He muttered an oath of protest. But he was seized, menaced. He stood, belligerent, gazing wild-eyed at his tormentors.

Clark's senses whirled. Was this some weird form of electrocution? He felt the electrode touch his forehead. His whole instinct was to cast it off. To fight—to go down fighting.

But that was sure death. This might be something else. He stood stiff and tense, watching the wire fastened now around Owen's head. The young man was panting, his face pale, his fists clenched.

The electrode was cold on Clark's forehead. It snapped together with a click. The guard stood away.

The brain in the chair had a hand on a switch lever. And slowly he pulled it.

CHAPTER IV

THE ATTACK ON THE CAVE

CLARK FELT A sudden reeling of his senses. Every muscle in his body was taut, braced against the shock. On earth, in the electric chair, the condemned criminal doubtless is taut like that as he waits for the shock of dying.

But Clark felt only a wave of dizziness. The vision of the dais and the weird ruler in the chair reeled before him, but he was not dead. Not even harmed. He saw Owen standing, still wild-eyed—and then on his face, when he found he was still alive, an expression of wonderment and—great relief.

A minute passed while neither of the prisoners dared move. Clark was aware of the hum of a current, vague, as though it were not audible to his ears, but sounding in his head. Everything was vague; and abruptly he was conscious that his thoughts were wandering. Dulled.

He fought to think clearly. But it seemed as though this current were sapping his mind, draining it, so that he was blunted, passively quiescent, almost stripped of his ability to think.

This current, draining his mind! Taking, from the brains of him and

Owen, thoughts and stored knowledge and transferring them to the vast storehouse of the brains in the test tubes and in the bloated head of the ruler in the chair.

WHAT IS THE evanescent thing which we call a thought? A vibration? Electrical? Perhaps it is that. No human intellect on earth ever has been able to fathom the nature of a thought.

But here, now, upon this weird asteroid world, human knowledge was brought into the realm of science. Controlled. Transferred over wires, through tubes, and manipulated by what other strange mechanisms no one will ever know.

The ruler had moved the switch again. The current was off now—or at least altered to a lower intensity. And out of the silence the ruler's low, guttural voice was saying:

"I—have it now. Your—strange language."

English! It came from his wide slit of mouth haltingly, with a queer accent. For his physical vocal equipment was different from that of the earthmen, inadequate correctly to pronounce the words—but the words themselves were correct. Clark gasped.

"You can talk to us!" he said unbelievingly.

"Yes. Talk to you now. Your knowledge—added to mine."

He passed a hand across the bulging membrane of his forehead. There was a surge of movement within his head; and in the test tubes around his neck, the brain tissue was writhing.

"Your knowledge—confusing to me at first," he said slowly. "I will have it sorted in a moment."

There fell a silence. Strange necromancy of science. But Clark now had accepted it as a weird actuality.

The instinct of life, of personal safety, is strong in every human. His thoughts swept into questions of how he and Owen might escape out of this. If only they could get control of that space-flyer; if only—

But his brain was still connected with the brain of the ruler. He had forgotten that. The ruler's mouth was upturned now in a monstrous ironic smile.

"But you cannot escape," he said.

"What do you want of us?" Owen burst out. "We never harmed you."

"I wanted—your language. I have it now. And the knowledge of the things in your strange world."

His voice droned on. He talked slowly, carefully, as though his purpose were not so much to inform his prisoners as to practice for himself the use of these queer English words.

"I am about to conquer your earth," he said. "I can realize now how easy it will be. My expedition is ready, waiting my command. Survival of the fittest. I notice you have a phrase like that. Your people must die to make room for mine."

HIS SLOW RECITAL was horrible in its calmness. Quietly he explained.

The asteroid—a wanderer in space throughout all the known history of its inhabitants—was heading now for the sun. It was rapidly warming. Soon it would be fiercely hot. And the barrenness of it was changing.

Heated by sunlight, vegetation here which for centuries had been dormant in the cold, was springing into life. Amazing life. Menacing! The little brown-shelled people were fighting it now. And other things were springing into life. Things formerly microscopic were hideous now with gigantic size. Most of the asteroid already was overrun with them.

THE LITTLE WORLD was doomed. Fertile through ages past with frozen dormant life, it all was springing now into lush growth and movement under the unaccustomed heat of the approaching sun! A tiny world, loaded with hideous microscopic life ready now to overwhelm it.

And the internal fires of the asteroid—through past ages just enough to support this human life against the frigidity of outer space—were spreading now. Inflammable gases were expanding under pressure in caverns far underground. At any moment they might ignite and burst forth.

Doomed little world indeed! And so the earth had been selected for an exodus of these asteroid people. A conquest of earth—the survival of the fittest.

Clark stood amazed, listening. But under the flow of words, his thoughts were clear. An expedition of space-flyers, ready to start now for earth! It must be stopped. He and Owen must escape, get out of this. That space-flyer in which they had arrived—if only they could seize it!

Wild, hopeless plans! But they were better than none; and in them Clark presently seemed to see a rationality. A course of action, desperate, but at least possible of success. He asked, when presently the ruler paused:

"Where are these space-flyers which you say are ready to leave?"

"They are quite—near here. You would call it—on earth—a mile."

"The one we came in," Clark persisted, "is closer than that?"

"No. It has been moved to join the others. I will take you there soon—everything is ready."

"And your idea?" Owen exclaimed, "is to devastate our earth?"

The ruler nodded calmly. "Of course. Your people must die," he said, "so that mine may live."

Primitive reasoning. But to him it seemed natural, quite obvious. His face twisted into a monstrous smile.

"I have the weapons. All in a moment—I can kill a million—of your people. And my people will want your earth—in peace and security. For that, I must kill all of you."

Again Clark realized that his thoughts were open to this antagonist. Up to now, the asteroid ruler had been so interested in his narrative that his mind probably had not yet become aware of Clark's thoughts. But Clark was afraid of that. What might come!

"This wire on my forehead?" he said abruptly, "it keeps my mind all confused. Take it off." He flashed Owen a warning glance.

Owen took the hint.

"You've got enough of our knowledge, haven't you?" he asked.

The huge head nodded.

"Yes, I think so." The ruler signed to the guards, and they removed the wires.

"Thanks," Clark smiled. Queer, how much more clearly he could think now! A chance to escape—if he could manage it. HE SAW OWEN eyeing him, puzzled, realizing that he had some plan. But the ruler spoke English now, and Clark could do no more than give his companion another significant glance.

"You want to know how I will devastate your earth? My electrical weapons would not do it very quickly—you have perhaps seen our flashguns operate? Not with flashguns, but with the disease, I will kill you."

Clark was hardly listening. If only he and Owen could be alone here with this ruler. Huge brain—body of a child. Helpless physically. He did not seem even to have any weapons. If they could seize him—

Clark gestured at the group of guards who stood close at hand, curiously watching the scene. He was trying to think of some plausible reason for the ruler to dismiss them. He said, smiling:

"I'm afraid of your men. They stand so close."

"We will leave here presently," the ruler spoke impatiently. "We—"

HE STOPPED. HE turned his great head as though listening. He had heard something that the earthmen could not hear. And the guards were aware of it. They stirred uneasily. One of them mumbled with fear.

The sound, obviously, was swiftly intensifying. Clark heard it now—a distant commotion. Eerie screams of the asteroid people. Weird rustling and scratching. The hiss of flashguns.

An attack upon these caverns! A tumult of frenzied strife! It grew rapidly in volume. Approaching—

The ruler in the chair tried to stand upon his little feet. His wide spread of face was contorted with terror. He shouted at the guards. But they, too, were in terror, running—scattering. All in a moment, they had vanished from the cave room.

Clark's chance! This doomed world! It had brought the opportunity he was seeking.

With a bound he was on the dais. The little ruler was wobbling on his feet. Owen followed instantly.

"What's the idea?" he demanded breathlessly.

"Got to get out of here!"

"But we don't know the way!"

"He does," Clark reached down and seized the ruler's little shoulder. The shell bent inward at his touch.

The ruler screamed. "You hurt me!"

Clark relaxed. "I didn't mean to. Can you walk?"

"Yes. A little. I am not—"

"You know the way out of here?"

"Of course. All these doors. But there is an attack—you hear it? These things accursed—"

"We'll have to break through them." THE WILD COMMOTION was much closer now. It came from the left-hand side of the room, where doors opened into corridor tunnels.

Owen gestured. "We can go the other way. There's a door there, and we—"

He suddenly stopped, staring down the length of the room. Clark followed his gaze. From the dais they could see the full stretch of the empty, blue-lit cave.

At the distant door through which they had entered, a huge blue-white leafy thing came slithering. A growing vine. Its leaves and tendrils spread forward over the room floor. Its growth was amazing. New lengths of it were springing into being every moment. New leaves, new tendrils, reaching, seeking something to grasp.

That way of exit was cut off.

"Can't stay here!" Clark snapped. "That thing will fill the room in a minute!" He reached down. With his left arm he scooped up the little ruler. The great head sagged on the spindly neck. The test tubes clinked together; one of them smashed. The little tentacle arms flailed; the bent and useless little legs kicked against Clark's side. The voice screamed:

"You hurt me!"

Physical pain. It produced an unnatural terror in this being whose body had become useless, with intellect too great for it. He screamed again.

"You hurt me! Put me down!"

"If I do, you'll be killed here," Clark said, grimly, swiftly. "And you've got to show us the way to the space-flyers. I'm trying not to hurt you."

Owen already had leaped from the dais. "Come on!" he shouted. "We'll be trapped here! That cursed vegetation—"

The leafy mass of the invading vine already had spread over half the room floor. Its tendrils were thickening, reaching up toward the ceiling, waving and thrashing. The whole farther end of the room was solid with it now.

Through the doors to the left, abruptly came sprawling figures in screaming combat—the brown-shelled asteroid men, with things double their size attacking them. Clark had only a glimpse of things six feet or more in height— shapeless—not human—indescribable masses of living pulp, blood-red.

The silent blue-lit room suddenly was a chaos of horror, over which Owen was shouting:

"Jack—come on—this way!"

With the struggling brain-man under his arm, Clark leaped from the dais. He and Owen sped from the gruesome turmoil of the cave, through a doorway, and plunged into the dimness of an ascending tunnel.

CHAPTER V

END OF A WORLD

THEY RAN. THERE seemed a pursuit behind them, but ahead lay only a dim silence of upward slope. Owen led the way. Clark followed with his squirming captive under his arm. The brain-man was far lighter than an earth child. Fifteen pounds, perhaps.

Once Clark bent down. "You stop struggling. I can kill you with a squeeze of my arm. You know that?"

"Yes—I know it."

"And if I let you loose, those things—whatever they are, chasing us—you couldn't escape them."

It silenced his captive. "I want you to direct us to your spaceships," Clark added. "Will you?"

"Yes."

"The end of the tunnel," Owen called. He stopped, and in a moment Clark was beside him. A dark night spread before them—a dim vista of rocky distance. To one side, half a mile away perhaps, there was a confusion of moving spots of light. In the silence came the distant sounds of a turmoil. And then the hissing of flash-guns, and the near horizon of the convex surface was illumined with brief puffs of glare. A combat off there.

"Which way?" Clark demanded.

The head under his arm said:

"Hold me up. Let me see where we are."

Clark held up his captive.

"This way." One of the tentacle arms gestured. "A mile or less, you would call it, from here. But there is vegetation—newly grown—"

CLARK'S EYES, BETTER accustomed to the darkness now, saw trees fairly close at hand. Tall, spindly growth, some fifty feet high. They waved in the night breeze—eerie, ghostlike.

"That way?" he demanded.

"Yes. But that is newly grown—" Terror was in the ruler's voice.

Owen said sharply:

"In the tunnel—things coming."

From the tunnel behind them, weird, oncoming cries were audible. Screams? Not that, for these sounds were indescribable—the cries of things unnameable.

They plunged off. Within a minute they were in the forest. Solid blackness was here, save that on the tree branches there were luminous pods radiating a green phosphorescent glow. The tree trunks were porous—flimsy. They rose high overhead, with thick, entangled branches—a blue-white leafy mass, lurid with the green phosphorescent radiance.

The rocky ground held an earthy soil now. There was an underbrush, thin at first, but within a minute as they ran forward, it grew thicker.

SUDDENLY OWEN WAS shouting: "This confounded vine!" He was ahead of Clark, invisible momentarily with tree trunks between them. Then his voice turned to terror:

"Jack, help! It's—got me!"

The startled Clark crashed into the thick tree trunk. It smashed with his weight, came down, splintered around him. He leaped over it.

"Jack, help!"

He saw Owen struggling in the grip of a huge vine. A leafy python wrapped around him, squeezing him, with a myriad of smaller tendrils writhing to clutch him.

Clark dropped his captive burden. He leaped, dashing into the vegetation—ripping it—kicking, flailing. Unlike the tree, the vine was sinewy. It writhed. Every branch of it which he touched, at once flung tendrils at him. Almost a thinking antagonist.

A minute or two of flailing horror, then Owen was released. The two men kicked themselves free. They saw, near at hand, their captive trying to run, his great head wobbling. In a bound, Clark had seized him. They ran onward.

Eerie passage! From every side now, in the greenish darkness, it seemed that giant tentacles were lashing, trying to grasp these human fugitives. The soft loam underfoot grew sandy, then spongy and wet as quicksand. A morass here. They sank sometimes knee-deep.

It seemed an eternity as they fought their way forward. Panting now— winded—thrown down by an entangling vine—ripping it apart—gaining their feet again and stumbling on.

Then, abruptly, the ground hardened. The trees thinned. The underbrush and the slashing vines were gone. Ahead of them again the rocky darkness showed, with a red glare. There was smoke off there. A sulphurous smell.

THEY EMERGED FROM the gruesome forest; stood on an open rocky expanse, panting, struggling for breath. Behind them in the woods cries resounded, cries of pursuing things from the tunnel. But the two men did not heed what was still behind them. They stood staring at the turmoil ahead. A rocky amphitheatre was here. It was painted red by the distant lurid glare.

The expedition of spaceships ready to depart for the conquest of earth! It had been that, a few hours before. But what a turmoil was here now!

In the bowl-like depression, the lip of which was close at hand, some fifty space vehicles were racked. Gleaming cylindrical ships of several sizes and shapes. Decks covered with transparent domes—the armada of the little asteroid. But it was in distress now. Giant vegetation was slithering from the darkness, entangling the ships at the outer edge of the bowl.

It was a chaos of turmoil. Myriad shapeless things of human size were everywhere leaping and pouncing. A thousand, perhaps, of the asteroid people were here on the ships and on the ground between them. A thousand individual combats. A wild chaos of screams.

One of the ships rose drunkenly into the air. Its deck, under the transparent pressure dome, was black with the struggling figures. It rose no more than a hundred feet, wavered and crashed back, smashing two other ships in the wreckage. Fire broke out in the litter.

The flames illumined the interior deck of another ship on which was a huddled group of the little brown-shelled asteroid people. Monstrous blood-red shapes of things inhuman rolled and surged and pounced upon them. Devoured them. Turned, palpating for other prey.

A tremendous heat was here. Breath of the distant fires, surging now from the ground. Incandescent gases, wafted on the night breeze. Owen was suddenly coughing.

From under Clark's arm, the asteroid's ruler panted:

"The doom—it—has come."

"Things—behind us—" Owen gasped.

Clark barely turned. Shapes of red things, coiled like hoops, were rolling out of the forest.

"This way, Ralph," he panted. "One ship—near here—"

Over the lip of the cauldron, one of the nearer ships seemed momentarily deserted. It was a small vessel, with only thin tendrils of vegetation entangling it. They fought their way to it. A doorway in its side was open. They plunged in. IT WAS A ship no more than thirty feet long. The little corridor was illumined. Horrible passage! The walls and grid-floor were splattered. Leprous broken shells of what once had been asteroid people were strewn here, half de-voured—and the invading things had gone.

Ah empty ship! With food tubes! Triumph swept Clark. They came to the control room. It was small with transparent vizor-panes on three of its sides. The controls were here. Clark set the asteroid ruler down before them.

"You have all knowledge—you can operate this?" he panted.

"Yes—I can operate it."

"Do it, then! Close the ports. Raise us. Your life—and ours—"

THE RULER'S FOUR little tentacle arms reached for the levers. The ports slid closed with a grind. Through the vi-zor-pane Clark saw that the dawn was coming, a swift twilight merging into grey daylight. The three-hour night of the asteroid was over.

Two other ships rose, and crashed. The cauldron was a litter now. The vines were spreading everywhere—a tangle in which the myriad blood-red shapes were lurking. But the turmoil was soundless, shut away from within the little spaceship.

Seconds of apprehension. They seemed an eternity to the breathless Clark and Owen, bending over the bobbing head of the asteroid's ruler as he worked the controls. Would the ship operate? Could it break from the entangling vines? At the window ports, gruesome red shapes were crowding now, thumping futilely against the heavy bull's-eye panels, smearing against the windows in a blurring crimson ooze.

The current hummed. The bow lifted. The little vessel jerked against the ham-pering vines, then broke free!

Free! They were rising! The glare and the turmoil fell away. Overhead was daylight, and a spread of grey clouds.

Clark breathed again.

"We did it, Ralph! Safe!"

Safe? In the control room behind them, they heard a thump. Clark whirled. Owen stood with hands out-stretched before him, gaping with horror. The asteroid ruler turned and sucked in his breath with a gasping whine of fear.

These red things—Clark had seen them only at a distance, caught brief glimpses. But one was here in the control room now. The crimson, grue-some horror was shut up here with them, in this small room. An antago-nist. A menace that must be killed, now!

Through a second of stricken fixity Clark stared, bathed in sweat, his blood seeming to run like ice through his veins, a constriction in his chest as though fingers of fear were squeezing his wildly leaping heart.

The thing had come rolling into the control room; a looped crimson thing like a great hoop. At the door it straightened into an oblong, upright shape—a cylindrical rod two feet thick and six or seven feet high—a mass of crimson pulp. It stood palpitating, bouncing, as though to maintain balance. An oozing, pulpy mass of semi-solidity!

A disease germ!

A little rod of red, Clark had once heard such a thing as this called by a learned man of science; and through a microscope he had seen a squirming group of them. Infinitely tiny. Far too small to be seen by the naked eye.

And here was a single one, grown monstrous. The germ of tuberculosis, though of a nature different from earth, doubtless. Disease here—visible, ponderable human disease, insidiously microscopic no longer, grown gigantic, hideous, revolting beyond human conception.

The thing lurched forward, and in an instant they were engulfed in it!

THROUGH A BLUR of horror, Clark felt his hands ripping the sticky mass apart. It clung, gluey, writhing, wrapping itself around him. Then, all in a moment, he and Owen had strewn it over the room. Sickening, stenching litter here, in the midst of which they stood panting, senses whirling.

But the thing was dead. And Clark was aware that the asteroid ruler had neglected his controls. The ship was lurching.

"Steady us!" Clark gasped. "Never mind this—we're falling! Steady us!"

The brain-man swung back to his task. Clark, bending down, watched for a moment how the controls were operated, asked a few questions.

The ship righted, rose higher. The surface of the asteroid, lighted now by flat grey daylight, lay spread beneath them. Gigantic battle-ground! The rocks were all covered by the leafy, crawling vegetable growth, through which the monstrous disease germs were surging, seeking out the few remaining little humans to be devoured. A single last flashbolt spat from the horizon, as though to mark the end of the struggle.

The ship rose higher. Far to the right, Clark saw the red-yellow fire mounting into the air, with a rolling cloud of dark volcanic ash.

"Jack! Look out!"

Owen's startled, warning voice sounded. Clark swung, and saw that the brain-man had left the controls. He stood against the wall of the room. His bloated head wobbled; his crooked little legs bent and shook under his weight. One of his tentacle arms held a gleaming cylinder which evidently he had snatched from a wall-rack over his head. His single eye gleamed with a baleful phosphorescence.

IRRATIONALITY! INSANITY! ON the monstrous travesty of the face, Clark saw it plainly. The test tubes of brains around his neck were all smashed now. Within his transparent membrane head, the brain tissue was writhing.

Intellect gone mad! Deranged by the

terror of this revolting, pulp-strewn room! His guttural voice rasped.

"You cannot take me prisoner! Alone, I can conquer your world! I am the Master Intellect."

His waving cylinder spat forward. But the flash went high, sizzling against the metal room ceiling. Owen had leaped, and Clark was hardly a second behind him. They struck the bloated membrane head almost together. Mashed it, with the tiny shell-like body, against the wall of the room. The brain-man's voice split with a chilling scream, mingled with a gruesome squash as the head burst and splattered.

The two men picked themselves up. They did not look again at the mashed thing against the wall which a moment before had been a human madman.

AGAIN THE RISING little spaceship was out of control. Clark sat at the levers. He had watched the asteroid ruler; and watched, also, the control of the other ship as they were nearing the asteroid from earth. The panting Owen bent over him. "Can you work it?"

"Yes. I think so."

A moment of experimentation. Then the ship steadied, rising normally again. The lurid surface of the asteroid was far down now, the heavy cloud masses close overhead. And suddenly there came a rift in the clouds. Fierce, dazzling sunlight struck through. Not the sunlight familiar to earth. This was infinitely hotter. Gigantic sun, so close now!

The sunlight beat in great shafts upon the asteroid's surface. And like the ray of a burning glass, it shriveled the monstrous vegetation. All in a second, upon the distant horizon, titantic jets of inflammable gases were ignited. Huge tongues of red-yellow flame shot forward, tremendous, spreading fiery incandescence.

A rolling, tumbling sea of fire was down there now. Doomed little world! Gigantic pyre, to mark its end!

Smoke rolled up in vast dark columns. A titanic chimney of heated air was surging up. Like a tiny blob of metal in a furnace blast, the ship was whirled upward, through the tumbling cloud masses, and hurled into space!

ON EARTH, ON the morning of August 11th, there appeared in the newspapers a small item which noted inexplicable deaths of Professor Owen and his negro servant. Ralph Owen, son of the professor, and Jack Clark, of the *American Press*, were missing.

But the item caused very little public comment.

Nor—weeks later—was the public more than mildly interested by the news that the wandering asteroid had rounded the sun, come out again and at last was gone, back into the remote realms of interplanetary space from whence it had come. Harmless wanderer! The few imaginative souls who had been excited over its presence—those days in August—realized now how foolish they had been.

But in November, the entire world was startled. The captain of a Pacific passenger liner, midway from San Francisco to Honolulu—saw something come wavering down from the sky one placid starry night. It was the little spaceship which, during all these weeks, Clark had been struggling to navigate back to earth.

But the captain of the liner did not know that, of course. He stared, amazed, as the small cylindrical thing wavered drunkenly and struck the placid, starlit ocean surface only a few miles away.

The gleaming metal shape sank in a moment. But the captain's glasses disclosed, bobbing on the surface, what seemed to be two swimming figures. He sent a boat and picked them up.

THUS CAME THE end of an adventure which for a time electrified the world. Then the world forgot. The asteroid had done no harm and was gone.

And everyone had his own troubles to worry over.

But to Jack Clark, pondering the amazing fantasy through which he had lived, there often came memory of the doomed little asteroid; of its struggling humans, beset by every adversity of hostile Nature. Survival of the fittest! Thus it had been meant to be. Thus it was!

The Web of the Green Spider

BY **CAPT. KERRY McROBERTS**

Torture and Terror Stalk Menacingly Through the Wild Sierra Tuscomnia—the Jungle of Inpenetrable Depths!

CHAPTER I

DEATH JUNGLE

THE THREE INDIANS came out of the blackness of the jungle swiftly, crawling on all fours like animals. Their bodies looked, in the shafts of pale moonlight of the camp clearing, like grotesque creatures from hell.

Fred Kermac, lying in his hammock, heard a twig break. With a leap he was on the ground, his automatic coming out of the holster strapped around his leg. Behind him came a piercing, wailing scream of anguish. He swerved. At the hammock next to his, he saw the Indians. A knife gleamed in the air. The body of a white man rose slowly and then sank to the ground.

Kermac had no time to reach the man. His gun roared twice at the Indians over the body; then he turned, fired two shots into the crouching savages closing in on himself. One of them went to the ground, groveling crazily in the dirt.

The two others were on Kermac with vicious snarls, sending him staggering back, stumbling to the earth. A long arm reached for his neck. A gruesome face, with beady eyes and the jaws and mouth of a gorilla, appeared in front of him. He brought his automatic up, fired point blank into that face.

He saw the mouth gash open with blood. The savage fell heavily over him. Kermac kicked the lifeless body off and squirmed around, trying to rise to his feet. The third Indian was on him with terrific force.

Kermac pulled the trigger of his automatic. It clicked on an empty chamber. The Indian had him pinned to the earth, arms around his neck, pulling it back for the quick snap that would break a vertebra.

Kermac's knees went up, catching the savage with full force in the stomach.

The man groaned. The arms relaxed in their death grip. Kermac came up with his body and his fist, sending a right to the savage's jaw. There was a resounding crack. The round, bullet head of the Indian snapped back. Kermac's left caught the chin as the head came back in place.

The savage's knees buckled, then straightened again. Kermac was on his feet. The Indian bellowed strangely, looked at him, and then melted away into the darkness as if the jungle night had swallowed him up completely.

Kermac was over his hammock with a leap, at the side of the white man lying on the ground. The man's shirt was torn down the front, disclosing a chest covered with blood. Overhead the moon, sending its thin, weak shafts of light through the dense foliage, lighted the

face. It was thin, bloodless and weak. The eyes were closed; the mouth gaped open.

Every muscle in Kermac's body tensed. His mouth contracted into a thin line. His steel grey eyes narrowed and his lean face seemed suddenly to freeze.

On the forehead of the white man was printed the outline of a green spider!

The Green Spider! The strange mark of death for all white men who went into the mysterious Sierra Tuscomnia country that lay to the south of Venezuela, between the Sierra Tuscomnia Mountains and the Orinoco River. A vast desolation of impenetrable jungle, with countless streams and lakes.

Fourteen white men, Americans all, had died with the mark of the green spider stamped on their foreheads within the last year. All that was known of their death was what could be gleaned from the disjointed stories told by the Indians of the boat crews who had escaped. And they told weird tales of strange savages and death that came out of the bushes with the uncanny speed of a striking snake.

KERMAC, OF THE United States Secret Service, had been sent to Cuidad, Bolivia, to investigate the deaths of the American citizens. For fifteen years he had worked in the South American countries for the Service. He knew the language of the different natives and the *lingua geral,* the common language of all the savages of the Amazon country.

He had listened to the weird, incoherent tales told by the natives who had escaped the strange death. They spoke in fear of the destruction that came mysteriously from the bushes and of a white man called the Green Spider.

The last white man killed had been Bill Sprague. He had gone into the country of death with a partner in search of diamonds. Only the partner had returned alive. Philip Unger was his name—a thin, weak-faced individual with shifty shell-blue eyes and a tall, slim body.

Kermac had distrusted the man on sight. Unger repeated the story of the Indians. He admitted that he and Sprague had found diamonds, a fortune; but he had fled, leaving them hidden in the river.

The one part of the story Kermac believed was about the diamonds. There had been an attempt to kidnap Unger in Cuidad, Bolivia, by mysterious persons. Kermac got him out of the city, loaded him on a *mounterais,* a large canoe, and started for the clearing where Unger and Sprague had found diamonds.

Kermac knew that his line of action was reckless and foolhardy, but there was certain cold reason and logic to it. Unger's knowledge of where the diamonds were hidden made him a valuable pawn against this unseen hand of death.

But now—

Kermac was on his knees, hands ripping Unger's shirt away. He listened for some evidence of the man's breathing. At first there was none. Kermac wet his lips nervously. Then he caught the faint, indistinct sound of a feeble respiration; short, barely audible gasps that seemed to die in the throat before they reached the mouth.

THE MOONLIGHT ENABLED him to see the wound in the chest. A knife had entered Unger's left side, several inches below the heart. Kermac tore the shirt in strips, bandaged the wound as best he could. The breathing was coming heavier now, with more strength. Then he walked down to the river.

His big *mounterais* was gone, with his crew of bush Indians. That did not surprise him. The natives had long been ready to desert him, and the attack was sufficient excuse.

Suddenly there was a splash of water near the bank, at the feet of Kermac. Out of the blackness rose the head and shoulders of a huge Indian. He came out of the water, up over the slippery bank, with the speed of a water animal, standing upright in front of Kermac, the muscles in his naked shoulders and back rippling in the moonlight.

His face was heavy, with the high cheekbones of an up-country Indian and the heavy mouth and jaws of a Columbian negro. His body was naked to the waist. Below that were soiled white trousers. His feet were bare.

"Padrao," he said hoarsely, "me swim after boat, but bush Indians get 'way with supplies and food. Green Spider men scare them away."

Kermac smiled wearily and nodded.

"I know, Agrillo," he answered. "But the white man is dying."

A puzzled look came over Agrillo's face. His eyes looked at Kermac in the manner of a dog looking at his master. Agrillo had been more than a faithful dog to Kermac for five years. He had worked for him, gone with him every place he went, ready and willing to risk his life at Kermac's slightest wish.

"Green Spider strikes very fast," Agrillo said now. "If white man dead, we no find Green Spider."

Kermac turned and walked back to the hammocks. Unger was still lying on the ground, his breath now coming in jerky heaves. Agrillo went to his knees over Unger's body, examining his wound.

Finally the Indian turned.

"Knife cut edge of lungs," he said. "Maybe white man die and maybe he no die."

A muffled groan came from one of the savages lying on the ground. His body twisted and then stiffened. There were no more groans. The other savage lay on his face, rigor mortis already setting in.

Agrillo's eyes darted through the darkness, his head moving slowly about.

Then he turned to Kermac.

"We got little time to work," he said. "Me make bed for white man. We carry him through jungle."

Kermac wasted no time talking now. He started, an inventory of the camp and while he did this, Agrillo, using his *machete,* cut the limbs of the *luira* trees, and with *pissaba* vines as ropes, made a stretcher for Unger.

By the time the Indian had completed this job, Kermac had finished his round of the camp. In a hidden cache,

a precaution he had taken against such an emergency, he found two canteens of water, some rice, and canned meat. The bush Indians had taken most of the other food in their flight.

Unger was placed on the improvised litter. He was moaning now and his eyelids jerked. From a flask of whiskey he carried in his pocket, Kermac gave the man a small drink. Agrillo had gone into the jungle, returning with some peculiar-looking leaves. These he formed into a wet plaster and placed over Unger's wound.

"Jungle medicine cure wound," he said. "We keep going into death jungle?"

Kermac nodded determinedly, His voice was firm.

"We cut across the jungle," he said to Agrillo. "We'll have to take a chance of striking another tributary and finding an Indian village. If we do, it will be your job to steal a canoe. Our food will only last a few days, and we must save most of it for Unger."

AGRILLO GRINNED BACK at him, his white teeth shining in the night.

"*Padrao,*" he said, "me steal canoe easily."

The grin remained on his face. Without further words he reached down, slipped the *pissaba* rope at the end of the litter over his shoulders. Kermac did the same to the rope at the other end. They lifted the litter up.

Agrillo started out of the camp clearing, his *machete* in his right hand, cutting and slashing vines and underbrush away.

CHAPTER II

HOSTILE COUNTRY

A MONTH LATER, in a native canoe hewn out of the trunk of a tree, Kermac and Agrillo paddled up a narrow, shallow river of the Sierra Tuscomnia country, far inland from the Orinoco River. Under the thatched roof of the small house constructed in the center of the canoe, Philip Unger lay on a bed of *plantillo* leaves. His wound had healed and strength had returned to his body. The knife thrust had cut along the edge of the lungs, not penetrating deep enough to cause a serious hemorrhage.

Agrillo's treatment, using the jungle herbs, had helped it to heal rapidly. The rice and the canned food Kermac had taken from the camp gave the wounded man back his strength, but he lay on his bed of leaves, staring up at the roof, his eyes glassy and filled with a haunted look of terror.

Kermac and Agrillo had been forced to live off the jungle. Kermac's clothes were torn and his body bruised and swollen from the ravages of insects, and the constant wading through jungle grass and crawling through underbrush.

For over two weeks, after leaving the camp, they had beaten and hewn their way through the jungle. Agrillo acted as the jungle cook, and Kermac was fed dishes that often caused his face to twist and his stomach to rebel.

There had been baked ants and boiled caterpillars. From the yucca roots Agrillo had baked something that looked like bread. From other roots he had boiled a jungle tea, bitter to taste but refreshing. Kermac had managed to kill a *pecari* when it seemed that he could stand the gnawing hunger no longer. They had feasted on this meat for more than two days.

Then they had come to a river. By this time Unger had recovered, but he refused to walk, forcing Kermac and Agrillo to carry him on the stretcher.

Kermac, unwilling to risk Unger to the dangers of the jungle, had done this without protest.

When they came to the river, Agrillo disappeared for two days, coming back one evening with the dugout canoe and some Indian food. Then they started up the stream in the boat, following it until they came to a larger tributary. They continued on this for five days, cutting off finally, at Unger's advice, on the narrow shallow stream they now were on.

THE ATTITUDE OF Unger worried Kermac. The man lay under the little house, speaking only when addressed directly. Then his voice was hoarse and frightened.

His shell-blue eyes, weak and shifty, watched every move Kermac made with the cunning of an animal watching its captor.

It had been the same way in Cuidad, Bolivia, when Kermac had first questioned him. Unger had not protested against going back to the clearing, yet Kermac sensed that behind his silence was part of the story yet untold about the death of Sprague.

Kermac, knife in his hand, again backed to the stone wall with his two companions at his sides

These things passed through Kermac's mind as the shallow canoe skimmed over the reddish water of the river. Kermac sat in the front and Agrillo in the stern, guiding the boat through the treacherous rocks that filled the stream. Behind them could still be heard the subdued roar of a rapids they had come over; ahead of them the water was still and glistened a bluish red in the late afternoon sun.

They were out of the low country. The air was clear though the sun beat down with a scorching heat. Overhead spread the branches of the giant *cendralles* that towered like grim, silent sentries over the green forest. The matted foliage that clung to their trunks, forming an impenetrable wall of green along the river banks, crept up the trees for several feet; above this, continuing the climb, were the heavy *liana* vines that went to the top of the trees.

On these vines were flowers; yellow orchids that gave the air a scent of bananas, and other jungle flowers, a multitude of colors, that lost themselves in the great spreading branches. Among

     THE BEST OF THRILLING ADVENTURES

them gorgeously plumed birds flew, sending down cries of anger at the human beings that had intruded on their solitude.

THE CANOE CAME to a turn in the river. The banks seemed to draw together and the water became redder. A great rock protruded from the center of the stream and a little distance ahead a sand bar jutted out from the bank.

From the thatched house came a wild cry from Unger. He was crawling toward Kermac, his face twisted with fear.

"This—this—is the river," he said in a strangled voice, "I remember that rock and that sand bar."

Kermac turned, yelled an order back at Agrillo. The canoe made for the bank, gliding up alongside the sand bar. Kermac jumped out, grabbing the prow of the canoe and pulling it up on the sand bar. Agrillo waded to shore, helping to shove the boat up.

Unger got out slowly, walking with shoulders slumped and face pale. He had recovered his strength, but he found walking, at first, a little uncertain. He made his way slowly to the bank and sat down.

Kermac covered the canoe with brush while Agrillo carried what few supplies remained to the shore and into the dense foliage. The Indian cleared a small space for a camp. UNGER WALKED INTO the small clearing as Kermac came up from the sand bar.

"Agrillo," Kermac said, "you stay here with the canoe. Unger and I are going to take a look at the clearing where Sprague was killed."

Unger turned on Kermac savagely, his eyes flashing hatred and fear.

"The clearing?" he cried. "My God, man, you're crazy. That place isn't human. Confound it, we won't live five seconds—"

"There isn't any place along this river that will be human for us," Kermac replied quietly. "We can hide the canoe and this camp for one or two days, possibly, but after that our lives won't be worth a nickel."

A smile twisted Unger's thin lips. His face drew up with a look that was both malicious and greedy. His eyes narrowed slightly.

"Now that we are here, Kermac," he said coldly, "we might as well start calling a spade a spade. All this hokum about your being a Secret Service man doesn't convince me that you came up here for anything but those diamonds. I came with you because the Green Spider would have killed me in Cuidad, Bolivia—he would have followed me to the end of the earth. Why he would isn't important now—"

"I came here, Unger," Kermac

Agrillo

admitted, "to get those diamonds, I want them for two reasons. The first is the more important. The Green Spider wants them and the minute we start after them, we are going to come face to face with his natives. It is quite probable that the Indians will kill us since they are hundreds and we are only two. But we have a chance—remote, I admit— and I am taking that chance!

"The second reason why I want those diamonds is that one half of them belong to Sprague, and his family is destitute. The other half will be yours."

Unger laughed coldly.

"And you think," he sneered, "that I believe all that and that I will lead you to the diamonds? After you get them you will kill me just as the Green Spider would, I'm no fool."

Kermac's face remained

Kermac

"Padrao," he said to Kermac, "you no come back from clearing alive."

"This boat and what supplies we have, Agrillo," Kermac said, "are too important to leave alone. You watch them. We will be back."

Agrillo shook his head, started to say something, but shrugged and walked away.

CHAPTER III

THE ENEMY STRIKES!

KERMAC MOVED ON hands and knees through the matted green foliage of the jungle, his right hand reaching out to push the vines and brush away. His face was bleeding and his flesh torn by the vines and grass and brush.

Ahead of him, a few feet, Unger crawled, his face and body bruised and bloody from the same jungle foliage. Unger moved forward slowly, desperately, never so much as stopping or looking around. He brushed the jungle growth from in front of him savagely, with only a muttered oath now and then to break the eerie silence.

OVERHEAD, HIDDEN FROM the earth by the branches of the trees that intertwined themselves into a roof of green, the sun was slowly falling below the western rim of the jungle. It left only a shadowy light of purple grey, which did not penetrate through the trees overhead to where Kermac and Unger were moving like animals over the ground.

Suddenly Unger stopped, drew himself

expressionless, as if he had not heard Unger's words. His eyes looked at the quivering man without either hatred or friendship in them.

"You are going to the clearing with me, Unger," he said calmly. "I don't give a hoot what you think. You are taking me to those diamonds—and you are going to prove to me that your story about the death of Sprague is true."

A look of animal cunning came to Unger's eyes. A cold, sneering smile came to his lips.

"You think I murdered Sprague," he said hoarsely. "You are a fool. I will go to the clearing with you. You will see the death that comes from the bushes. It will strike you—but not me, I will go with you."

Agrillo sidled up to Kermac, his face worried.

up to a standing position. Kermac crawled up to him, jumping to his feet.

"There it is," Unger said quietly. "Sprague was killed in that shack and I guess his body is still there."

Kermac stared out at the small clearing, already half reclaimed by the jungle grass and brush that had grown up around a shack that stood in its center. Some forty feet from the shack was the river, a narrow, shallow stream, with its banks dug up and the dredging platforms still standing, just as Sprague and Unger's crew of workers had left it.

Kermac walked out of the jungle and onto the clearing, heading directly for the shack. Unger followed after him, keeping close to his heels. At the door of the shack, Kermac pushed the vines and the brush that had grown over it away. Then his body stiffened and his jaws clicked shut at what he saw.

He was looking at a bunk against the far wall. On it, covered by moldy blankets, lay a skeleton, the bones bleached white by the humid heat of the jungle. It lay crossways on the bed, the bones of the legs drawn up, showing that the man had died in a struggle.

Kermac took a step inside the shack. There was a movement behind him, a slight shuffling of feet. He swerved and saw, for one brief second, the leering, sneering face of Unger. Then something crashed against his head—a sickening, paralysing blow that sent him staggering over into the shack, his body falling over the bleached bones of the skeleton on the bunk.

Unger

He was on his feet in a flash, his head swimming crazily and a nauseating feeling at the pit of his stomach. He leaped for the door.

Across the clearing, near the river, he saw the darting, running Unger disappear into the jungle. Kermac dashed out of the shack, racing after him—but before he got ten yards, he made a headlong dive for a bush, landing under it on his head and shoulders.

From out of the forest, to the left of him, two Indians came running on the clearing!

KERMAC LAY UNDER the cover of the bush, his body hugging the ground. In his right hand his automatic was ready for use. The Indians, running in crouching positions, crossed the clearing and entered the jungle like darting animals.

For a full minute Kermac remained

Von Durkin

under the bush; then he crawled to his hands and knees. The clearing was deserted. The twilight was fast fading into darkness. Kermac was on his feet, darting for the spot where Unger had disappeared.

He stopped suddenly, every muscle in his body stiffening. From somewhere out of the jungle came a piercing, wailing scream that rose to an insane pitch, dying away in a muffled groan.

Hardly had it faded away before two Indians rose from the tangled grass of the clearing, rushing on Kermac with leaping bounds. The American's gun roared, the spitting, jagged flashes of flame cutting through the gathering darkness. One of the Indians reared backward, remained in that position for a second and then crumpled to the ground.

Kermac was across the clearing, plunging into the jungle. A spear came through the air at him, zipping past his head with a whining moan, losing itself in the green foliage. With a crash he broke through the jungle netting, landing in a mass of liana vines that hung down from the trees. HE TORE HIMSELF away from this net, crawling to the ground. Striking viciously with his right and left, he knocked the dense undergrowth away as he crawled in the direction the scream had come. Only silence, grim and sinister, greeted him; then somewhere in the vast desolation of the jungle a twig snapped to break this stillness. It was only a vague, indistinct sound; yet to Kermac it grated horribly, an ominous warning that death still lurked at his side.

Crawling and creeping, fighting frantically against the undergrowth in a darkness that was fast becoming stygian, he worked his way to a narrow trail that led into the mysterious region beyond the clearing. The shifting light of the coming night broke through the tree tops and covered the path with a blue haze. Through it he could see the soggy earth where bare feet had slopped through the mud.

With the coming of the night the *piume* flies swarmed over his blood-soaked body, biting into his wounds with a viciousness that, for a while, threatened to drive him insane. Mosquitoes came in thousands to aid in the work of the *piume* flies.

The coat and shirt had been torn from

Kermac's back; even his white trousers were mere strips of blood-soaked cloth. Every part of his body was covered with scratches and bruises from the vines and the impenetrable underbrush through which he had fought his way.

He rose to his feet, arms swinging wildly to chase the insects away. He started down the path, away from the clearing. He walked rapidly, head and shoulders leaning forward. His head still ached from the blow; at times he felt dizzy.

AROUND HIM WAS a dreary, ominous silence, more terrifying than the yells of a hundred Indians. Kermac knew that eyes were watching him—small black beady eyes of the strange Indians. With chilling clarity he realized that the stories told by the natives who had escaped the Green Spider death were all too true. Death had leaped indeed from the bushes.

A grim, bitter smile came to his face when he thought of Unger's warning back at the canoe. Unger had come with him, knowing what to expect. He had said that death would strike Kermac but not him. Kermac had half expected the attack from Unger, but had not believed it would come with such speed and viciousness.

Unger's natural greed had dictated that move. He wanted the diamonds for himself and was willing to chance death to get them. That partly explained the attack; yet Kermac felt certain that, behind all this, there was some strange relation between Unger and the Green Spider.

The path widened while darkness fell rapidly. Kermac was now walking through a haze of gathering black, able to see only dimly the trees at his right and left. He had no idea where this trail led, except that from somewhere in this direction had come the scream of death when the Indians had come out of the bush at him.

Then he stopped suddenly. The automatic came up in his right hand. Ahead, along the path, the darkness moved. A crouching figure had darted into the jungle. Kermac remained standing in the center of the path, every muscle tense and every nerve taut.

The darkness ahead of him did not move again. He started for the spot where the form had disappeared, his gun ready to spit fire. He walked slowly now, his eyes trying to pierce the deep mist ahead of him.

Above him a limb of a tree moved queerly, with a sharp, snapping sound. There was a *whish* of air. Then another snapping sounded, ending in a hiss.

These three sounds came to Kermac in the space of a second. He had no time to stop; not even a chance to turn his head in the direction of the noises.

For out of the darkness came an inhuman power to grip him around the body, pinning his arms to his body. He was jerked up into the air as if he were a mere feather.

Five, ten feet up he was pulled, dangling like a sack of flour. Higher he went; suddenly the upward movement stopped, and he hung suspended in the stifling, suffocating air, barely able to catch his breath because of the crushing power gripping his body.

CHAPTER IV

THE WEB OF THE SPIDER

KERMAC REALIZED QUICKLY what had happened. Walking over the jungle path, his head and shoulders hunched over, he had stepped into a native death trap, which, had it not been for the position of his head and shoulders, would have torn his head off.

A tall tree, the toughest wood of the jungle, had been bent over to the ground, with a *pissaba* rope curled into a noose. Through this noose he had shoved his head and shoulders before his foot had set off the trap that caused the tree to snap with the speed of lightning, taking his body up with it.

The matter of several inches had caused the noose to catch him around the shoulders and arms instead of around the neck where the sharp rope would have severed his head. Even now the rope was cutting through the flesh of his arms as he hung helplessly in the air, fifteen feet from the ground, unable to move either of his arms. Desperately he kicked his legs. This did nothing more than cause his body to swing around as the rope cut into his flesh, tightening every second in its death grip.

Sweat broke out on his forehead and face from the pain of the cutting rope. His right hand worked itself around until it slipped the knife from his belt. Slowly he bent his hand and wrist upward, but halfway to the rope the hand stopped, unable to go another inch higher. And after trying several times to raise the knife to the rope, Kermac let his hand drop helplessly.

HE STARTED KICKING again. In the darkness he could see the trunk of a tree near him. The kicking started him swaying back and forth. He kicked harder. His body was now swinging. His foot kicked against some brush, sending him away from it in a long, swinging arc.

He came back through the air, crashing against the trunk of the tree. His legs went around the tree, pulling his body tight against it; then slowly he worked himself up, the rope loosening above him. He twisted his shoulders, every movement sending stabbing pains through his head and neck and down his arms.

His hand, holding the knife, went up again. This time it got to the rope and he sawed it frantically. The tough fibre resisted the knife, but at last the blade ripped through it and his arms were free. He threw them around the trunk of the tree and started sliding down to the earth.

THE GRIM, EERIE stillness still pervaded the forest. It was unreal, unnatural; yet Kermac knew, as he had known when he and Unger first stepped into the clearing and sensed the unbroken silence that hung over it, that it was caused by the fact that human beings lurked in the bushes. Their presence chased the jungle life away, stilling all the usual noises.

In the darkness below him, Kermac knew that human eyes had watched him; had seen him step into the death trap that had jerked his body up. But as he slid down the tree, no form of life moved in the desolation of the jungle. No sound came to break the dreariness of the unearthly silence.

His feet hit the ground. His arms were still numbed from the cutting pains that shot through them, though he could move them freely. He stepped back from the path, his right hand gripping the automatic.

And then the jungle moved and came to life, noiselessly, viciously, swiftly. At first the darkness seemed to roll up and move toward him in a wave of black. The wave broke into short, crouching men and then swept up to Kermac with the fury of a tidal wave.

He stepped back, lurched out with his right hand. His knife sank into human flesh. There was a muffled groan. Then the wave of human bodies hit him, sending him to the ground under a mass of sweating, snarling bodies.

He struggled feebly, but his arms and legs were firmly pinned to the earth. There were excited jabberings going on over him. For some time he lay there, his arms and legs held to the ground, preventing him from moving any part of his body. The conversation continued; then at length this stopped and he was picked up.

His wrists and ankles were tied. Four natives carried him along the jungle path. There was no talking now.

HOW LONG KERMAC was carried through the jungle he had no way of knowing. To him it seemed ages. The numbness had left his body and every part of it ached; with the aches were the sharp, shooting pains from the torn muscles of his arms where the death trap rope had cut into them. And to add to these pains came the swarm of insects to feed on his body.

The procession left the jungle, marched up on higher ground, across an open stretch of waist-high jungle grass. There was no path here and the grass cut his face and lashed against the open wounds in his body. From the tall grass they entered a forest. The moon was up by this time, flooding the night with a silvery glow.

The forest seemed cool. There were giant trees and under them no underbrush grew. For over an hour he was carried through the forest and then suddenly the procession came to the shore of a large lake. In the soft moonlight the waters looked blue and clear, like glistening glass, without a ripple or any movement.

The procession stopped only a moment at the shore of the great lake. Tied to the bank were a number of shallow, native canoes, hewn out of the logs of *luira* trees—long, narrow boats built for speed.

Kermac was thrown in the bottom of one of them. From where he lay he could see the strange-looking Indians crawling into the other canoes. There were more than twenty of them, all powerful of body, with huge shoulders and strong, broad backs.

They moved swiftly, without any conversation or wasted movement. The fleet of shallow canoes swung out into the blue water of the lake, cutting across the surface like long sharp knives, sending a spray of water up around each of them.

Kermac twisted and squirmed at the bottom of the canoe, but the rope around his wrists and ankles held tightly. After a time he ceased his futile efforts and lay still, his mind trying to grasp the events of the night which had happened with such startling rapidity.

SUDDENLY THE CANOES slowed down. The paddlers straightened up, letting the boats coast over the water. They hit a bank with a quivering thud. The Indians leaped out, pulling the craft up on a bank.

Four of them lifted Kermac from his boat and carried him up on the bank. Here the *pissaba* rope around his ankles was cut, a cloth was tied around his eyes; and, blindfolded, he was marched ahead of the Indians, with the points of sharp spears in his back.

He was conscious of walking over sharp rocks and then down stone steps. An Indian went ahead, guiding him. He was taken through a door. A bright light struck the cloth over his eyes, seeping through a little. He was shoved forward for a few feet; then brought to an abrupt stop.

The cloth was torn from his eyes. A brilliant light blinded him for a moment. He blinked helplessly, trying to adjust his eyes to the new light. Finally forms began to take shape and then he was staring at the face of a white man seated behind a large table.

The face was hideous in the yellow-grey of the skin; it looked like the face of a dead man. The features were heavy, the face long, coming to a sharp point at the chin. The man's eyes were colorless, the eyes of a staring corpse. His face was expressionless as he looked at Kermac. The lips were a blood red, as if they had been painted.

His huge body was slumped over, elbows resting on a blackwood table. It was a gorgeous, hand-carved piece of furniture, such as one would expect had come out of medieval Italy.

"I must admit, Kermac," the man said in a hollow, lifeless voice, "that you are exceedingly adroit at walking in and out of death traps and remaining alive."

"I've been darn successful so far," Kermac retorted with a grim smile.

The man shrugged, without any form of expression coming to his grey face or his colorless eyes.

"You got out of the trap set for you on the Orinoco River," he continued. "Frankly, I didn't expect that. A very deadly trap, the *pissaba* rope and the *luira* tree. You are the first human being that ever escaped its almost certain death—"

HE SMILED, A peculiar twisting of the facial muscles forming such a grimace as one would expect to see on the face of a corpse.

"As for Unger, he acted a little too hastily," he said. "But—to get back to yourself. You are a man to be admired. I have heard of you and when I learned that you were in Cuidad, Bolivia, to investigate the death of Sprague—and to try to capture the Green Spider—I was interested. I always prefer a clever, courageous adversary. For over a year I have killed only the stupid diamond hunters who have come into my territory. Like killing sheep, it was uninteresting—boring."

Kermac's eyes flashed and his lips went tightly together as if struggling to hold back a sudden emotion of fury that had come over him.

"If you didn't give the others any more chance than you gave Sprague," he retorted, "I would say that such slaughter could hardly be interesting."

The man shrugged. He rose slowly to his feet, his huge, bony body towering high over the table. He waved his arm around the room.

"BUT VERY PROFITABLE," he said. "I have amassed a great fortune. Let me show you something of the treasures hidden in this room."

Kermac followed the arm with his eyes, and for the first time got a look at the room he had been led into. It was large, with chalk-white stone walls, indicating that it was either underground or carved out of a cliff of limestone. On the walls were beautiful paintings and gorgeous silk hangings.

The floor was covered with a deep red Oriental rug, one that must have cost a small fortune. The furniture was massive, luxurious, chosen with excellent taste. Along one side of the room was a large cabinet with many drawers in it. The man walked over to this cabinet, motioning Kermac to follow.

Behind Kermac stood eight or ten of the Indians who had brought him in the room. Kermac stared at them in amazement. It was the first time he had seen them in the light. Their bodies were tall, arms abnormally long, and shoulders broad and powerful. Their faces were ghastly in their hideousness—long, distorted faces, with beady eyes and the features of gorillas.

The white man opened several doors of the cabinet. Reaching in them, he extracted handfuls of gold, some in nuggets and the rest in dust.

"For twenty years," he explained in his hollow, lifeless voice, "I was a white trader, suffering the hardships of the jungle and profiting but little. Then it struck me that I had been a fool. Wealth is not achieved with the hands, toiling for it. It is gotten by brains.

"Look at the men behind you. Strange-looking Indians, abnormal creatures according to our white standards; yet those men had what I needed for success. In those bodies is a strength that can strike death with a speed quicker than the eye. One twist of those long arms and a man's neck is easily broken.

"I became their chief through tricks that are elementary and simple to the white man. With them I have plundered and robbed the Sierra Tuscomnia country. I have allowed the white traders to come up and find gold, and the diamond hunters to come and get diamonds. Then I have struck. Already there is a great fortune in these drawers. In five years it will be fabulous and then I am through."

Kermac looked at the strange man, at the ashen grey face and the distorted features. Then he looked at the Indians that stood near him.

"And now, Kermac," the white man said, "you are going to discover the little joke of the Green Spider. All those whom I have brought here to rob have discovered the secret."

CHAPTER V

THE PIT OF BONES

POWERFUL ARMS, ARMS that moved with inhuman speed and strength, took Kermac's wrists and pulled them behind him. He was fairly carried out of the room by the Indians, through a long stone corridor and into a large room, barren of any furniture.

Here other Indians were waiting. Three of them were prying up a great rock in the floor. One of these Indians, slightly smaller in body than the others, was lifting the huge rock by his own strength.

A rope was tied under Kermac's arms and he was pushed over to the hole where the heavy rock had been removed. He brushed against the Indian. Something cold touched his hand. His fingers closed around a knife. He looked up quickly.

Standing at his side, his face distorted into a likeness of the other faces around him, was Agrillo!

KERMAC GOT ONE fleeting look at the face of his friend; then his body hurled into the hole. At first he plunged headfirst into a sickly, yellow light. He went down in this manner several feet when the rope tightened around his body and he was lowered more slowly into the yellow pit below him.

He hit the stone floor in a sprawling heap, on his hands and knees. The rope was thrown down with his body. He got to his feet. The yellow light was coming from two tapers stuck in the sides of the stone wall. Kermac looked up. The hole was thirty feet above him, with no remote chance of his ever crawling up to the opening.

He looked around the pit, a shudder going through his body. It was filled with human bones, skulls, arms and legs. Several of the skeletons were intact, lying in huddled positions. The air was heavy and putrid from the carnage that had taken place in the yellow pit.

The bones told Kermac the grim, silent story of where the many white men captured by the Green Spider had met their death.

He looked up again at the gaping hole far above him. A shadow moved over it and then the ashen-grey face of the strange white man peered down at him, the features distorted with an insane hatred.

"So you came to destroy the Green Spider," the man sneered. "You are a fool, Kermac—a stupid fool. I knew you were coming when you landed at Cuidad, Bolivia. I set a trap for you, a trap that brought you here where no man has ever escaped alive. Fool— fool—"

The man's words died away in a weird laugh. Something dark came dangling down the hole. Kermac caught his breath. It was a spider, and as it came nearer, he saw that it was green.

The Green Turkiti! The most virulent of all jungle insects, found in the Sierra Tuscomnia district. A cross between a spider and a scorpion more deadly than the latter, its bite bringing instant death. It was an eight-legged insect, differing from the more common jungle spiders in that it had an elongated tail, at the end of which was a poison-laden sac. With deadly speed, this tail came under the body, striking out in front of the animal's head when it dealt death to its victims.

Kermac knew this creature of death well. He had made a study of the insect life of the jungle. He knew where the poison sac was and how death would strike him—but knowing that was little help to him now.

LOWER AND LOWER came the creature of death. Kermac's fingers closed around the knife Agrillo had slipped into his hands. A smile came momentarily to his lips when he thought of the faithful Indian. He had sneaked away from the camp when Kermac and Unger left, knowing that Kermac would face death.

How he had got into the mysterious stronghold of the Green Spider was a mystery to Kermac, but it made little difference. He had done his best. But the knife he had slipped to his *padrao* was little help against the sting of the Turkiti.

Kermac looked down at the bones of the men that had gone before him in the yellow pit of hell. Each of them had stood as he was, looking up at the leering face of the strange white man, with the green messenger of death being lowered at him. The only consolation in it all was the fact that death would be instantaneous when the Turkiti struck.

IT WAS ONLY two feet from Kermac's body. He knew the futility of running. The Turkiti would be on him in a flash, no matter where he was in the pit; so he remained standing under the hole, with the Turkiti descending on his head, being let down into the pit by a silken cord. The Yank's lean face was hard and tense; yet in his steel grey eyes came no fear. He had come to the stronghold of the Green Spider with his eyes wide open and he was ready to take the consequences.

A cold, bitter smile came to his face. He was thinking of Unger. The Turkiti was within inches of his head now.

"You fool," the man at the hole screamed, "that is a Turkiti. It is death when it strikes. Why do you stand there, gazing up like an idiot? Why don't you cringe and run like the others did? Fool! You will be dead in a minute."

Kermac laughed harshly, bitterly.

"That's one pleasure you'll never have," he taunted. "Seeing me run."

The man stood up, letting the silk cord down slowly.

It was within an inch of Kermac's head, bearing a grotesque, hideous creature of death.

Kermac's eyes turned up to the Turkiti, stared at it in amazement for a moment. Then his body stiffened and

There, bones bleached white, lay a grim skeleton!

his fingers closed around the handle of the knife in his hand. From above came a mocking laugh, but Kermac continued to stare at the green Turkiti, every muscle in his face set, his eyes cold and hard.

The hand that held the silk cord let it drop. The green creature came falling through the air at Kermac. It landed on the side of his face and in the next second Kermac's body went to the floor of the pit, a groveling, struggling mass of human flesh. From overhead came another mocking, shrill laugh before the great rock was thrown back in place with a heavy thud.

Kermac remained on the floor, but his body stopped groveling. A minute passed and yet he did not move. From the wall, directly in front of him, came a dull, thumping sound, vague and indistinct, as if it came from far off.

The thumping caused Kermac to move slightly. The Turkiti had fallen from the side of his head and lay on the floor on its back. The thumping on the rock continued. With a leap Kermac came to life, springing to his feet, the knife Agrillo had given him gripped tightly in his right hand.

He looked at the rock covering the hole, making sure that the aperture was covered. Then he looked down at the green Turkiti, smiled grimly, and kicked it to one side.

The green creature of death was dead! IT HAD BEEN dead when the man overhead had let it down into the pit. Kermac had seen that much as he had stared up at the insect, but he knew that the weird white man, letting it down into the pit, did not know that. So he had fallen to the floor, to prevent the human killer from knowing that the bite of the Turkiti had not been fatal.

The pounding on the rock continued.

With a leap Kermac was over at the wall, not wasting any time trying to figure out how it happened the Turkiti was dead. It was obvious that the thumping was a signal. He examined the wall.

The outlines of loose rock could be seen in the yellow, flickering light, a light that made the bleached human bones lying on the floor glisten weirdly. THE KNIFE IN Kermac's hand went around the edges of the rock, cutting the dirt out. He tried to pry the rock loose, but his knife made little impression. The air in the pit was fast becoming suffocating, lacking any inflow of oxygen. The air was stifling him and his head was swimming crazily.

The wounds in his arms, made by the ropes of the death trap, were burning and stinging; yet he worked on frantically, pulling and tugging at the loose rock, working his knife as deep in the crack as it would go. The rock moved, came out an inch from the prying of the knife. Kermac's fingers clutched at the inch of exposed sides.

The rock came out further. Kermac got a firmer grip; and then with a scraping, sliding roar the big rock fell out of the wall on the floor.

A yawning hole of black was exposed, a hole just big enough for Kermac's body to go through. His head and shoulders went into the gap, his body squirming like that of a great snake.

A gust of fresh air hit his face. On through the dark hole he crawled, through blackness so intense that he could see nothing. He came abruptly to the end of the passageway through the

     THE BEST OF THRILLING ADVENTURES

wall, his head and shoulders plunging down, carrying his body with them.

On through the void he fell, legs and arms dangling wildly. He hit something hard, the force of the jar sending his senses haywire again. But they came back to him in a flash and he rolled over on his back, staring into an impenetrable wall of darkness.

Something moved at his side. He was on his feet with a spring, the knife going back, ready for instant use.

"Padrao," came from that darkness softly, in a whispered voice.

"Agrillo!" Kermac laughed with relief. "What in blazes are you doing in this hole? I thought you were upstairs—or, anyway, guarding the canoe!"

From the darkness came a good natured chuckle from the Indian.

"Padrao," he answered, "you no safe without Agrillo. I hide canoe far in the jungle when you and white man leave. I follow you to clearing. See strange Indians. Know they try to capture you. Follow them to this island ahead of you. I twist face like jaguars. My big shoulders and body help."

"And you killed the Turkiti the Green Spider let down on me," Kermac cut in. "And how did you get down here?"

"Green Turkiti dies when it bites," Agrillo explained. "It bites anything when frightened. I in room with Green Spider and see Turkiti. I let it bite at piece of stick. It no die at once. The Green Spider no know this when he let Turkiti down hole. Turkiti die when coming down.

"White man named von Durkin,"

Agrillo continued excitedly. "I know him long ago. Bad trader that kill Indians. He Green Spider now and kill white men. We on island center of Lake of Blue. Von Durkin have island guarded by many savages and death traps. We have no chance to escape—"

"ALL RIGHT, ALL right," Kermac snapped back. "Von Durkin thinks I am dead and that will give us a small break—"

His words were cut short by a piercing scream of pain and death; the same scream he had heard in the jungle! It ended with a wailing, "God, don't!"

With a muttered oath, Kermac swerved and dashed through the darkness toward the tortured scream, with Agrillo close on his heels.

CHAPTER VI

THE SECRET
NEVER TOLD

KERMAC RAN AS fast as he could through the wall of black, hands in front to protect himself from colliding against a wall. His feet tripped over a rock and he went to the floor. Far above came the piercing scream again, this time weaker, ending in a muffled groan.

Agrillo yelled something about steps. Kermac was up, feeling his way carefully, his feet touching ancient stone steps. From far overhead came the shrill, piercing yell of Indians.

The yells echoed and re-echoed weirdly through the underground room of stone.

Kermac went up the stone stairs three at a time. He finally landed in a wide corridor dimly lighted by burning tapers stuck in the walls. Agrillo was at his side.

The two men raced through the smoky, yellow darkness. Kermac's eyes took in the walls. They were of stone, black and mouldy with age. The floor was stone, worn down by the tread of countless feet throughout the ages.

On the walls were strange carved figures, animals and serpents and, in one place, a row of women's heads. Kermac knew that he was underground in some form of cave on the island; yet the carvings on the stone and the beaten floor told him this cave had been used for untold centuries. It puzzled him completely.

The rooms were far enough underground to be hidden from the sight of anyone coming to the lake. It explained the secret of the Green Spider's hiding place, but the walls and everything about the place were utterly foreign to any tribe of South American Indians Kermac had ever known.

He came to the end of the long passageway. His body went sidewise, flattening itself against the wall. Agrillo did likewise, keeping close beside Kermac.

Around a sharp turn in the corridor, two Indians came, walking in crouching positions, faces twisted weirdly. They were inhuman-looking men, with bodies and arms more like those of gorillas than human beings. They went through a low opening in the wall.

The piercing scream had come from that opening!

With a leap Kermac was dashing for the gap. The knife gleamed in his hand. He ducked under the overhanging wall, going through the opening like a bullet.

He heard Agrillo at his side; and behind them, out in the passageway, men were jabbering and running back and forth. The opening was about ten feet long. Kermac covered that distance in a second, plunging out into a large, low-ceilinged room, lighted with the same ghastly yellow lights as the passageway.

For one brief moment Kermac's body stiffened and the muscles around his mouth contracted in thin lines.

IN THE CENTER of the room suspended by ropes from the ceiling, was the bent and contorted body of Philip Unger. Cords pulled his head and legs back. And above his head, within, a few inches, hung a long, silk cord, at the end of which was a green Turkiti!

Two Indians with spears were swinging Unger back and forth, using their long weapons to propel him. And as Unger went through the air, he came closer and closer, at each swing, to the green creature of death which hung there with its manifold legs moving and its head forward, as if it were struggling to bite into the human flesh that came so near it.

A pitiful scream burst from Unger.

"God, I'll talk," he moaned. "Tell von Durkin I'll talk. But—but—get that thing away from me. God, get—it—oh, God—" His words ended in a wailing, blood-curdling scream.

THE TWO INDIANS that had entered the room started to walk up to Unger.

Kermac stood with body tense, nerves taut. His eyes went over the Indians. Then with knife in right hand, Kermac plunged for them.

They heard his feet, swerved. Kermac collided with one. There was a ripping of flesh as his knife went into the man's body. The Indian sank to the floor with a groan.

Kermac swung on the other one, but before he could bring his knife up, the two powerful arms closed around his neck, bending it back with the power of a great steel vise.

Kermac let his body relax completely. It slumped down, and the powerful arm, forced to hold it up, stopped for the moment the backward twist of his neck, which would have ended in a broken vertebra. Then Kermac whirled to the right, brought his knee up into the groin of the Indian!

The savage groaned like a wolf snarling, and closed his powerful arm around Kermac's neck again. But with the speed of a tiger, Kermac twisted around, bringing the knife up, the blade ripping under the heart of the savage. The man stiffened, quivered and then plunged face forward.

Something crashed against the Yank's side, sending him staggering against the wall, the knife falling from his hand. He hit the stone, bounded away from it with a spring. He saw Agrillo struggling on the floor with one of the savages. And advancing toward Kermac was a fourth Indian, his face twitching with hate and his long arms reaching forward for his victim's neck.

Kermac sidestepped, brought his right up in uppercut that raised the savage inches from the floor. But the man came down, a fighting, infuriated beast of murder. His arms closed around Kermac's waist, powerfully and swiftly.

Kermac brought his knee up against the man's jaw, knocking the head back and loosening the grip of the arms. An overhand right, catching the savage flush on the mouth, caused blood to spurt over the face; but with a bellow of rage, the Indian came in, head down, long arms swinging.

Kermac had no chance to reach for the knife that lay on the floor. He was rushed against the stone wall and pinned there with all the force of that powerful body. He landed right and left on the black head, causing the knees of the savage to buckle under him. But the Indian came on for more, struggling to get the death grip on Kermac's neck.

Out in the passageway could be heard voices. Kermac fought desperately, hopelessly, knowing that the first sound of the fight to reach beyond the opening into the hall would bring hundreds of savages into the room.

HE DROPPED TO his knees, evading the long, swinging arms that had gone for his neck. He brought his fists up against the groin of the savage, putting every ounce of his weight and strength behind the blow.

The man doubled up, grabbed his stomach and danced around like a crazy man. Kermac was on his feet, lunging forward, right shooting over in a blow that had started from his toes. It landed on the savage's jaw with a loud smack. The man stopped dead, looked up at Kermac with stupid, glassy eyes and then rolled to the floor without even a groan.

KERMAC STOOD OVER him, swaying weakly back and forth. The savage quivered and then lay still. Kermac reached for his knife, grabbed it and threw himself in the direction of Agrillo. But Agrillo was standing up, looking down at the savage be had been fighting. This one's face was turning a sickly purple. He had stopped breathing and around his throat were the imprints of Agrillo's powerful fingers.

Overhead, Unger had stopped swinging and hung suspended from the ceiling, a foot away from the green Turkiti.

In an instant Kermac was on a large stone in the center of the room. While he cut the ropes that held the moaning man, Agrillo eased the body down to the floor.

Quick swipes of the knife severed the cords that pulled Unger's head and legs back. The limbs straightened out slowly in a stiffening movement, the body twisting in a reflexive effort to get the blood circulating again. Unger's eyes fluttered open, staring at Kermac in amazement. The parched lips moved, but no words came from them. The pale, bloodless face was drawn and haggard.

"Talk fast, Unger," Kermac snapped. "You know this place, and by this time you should know that von Durkin will kill you if you remain here."

A weak little smile came over the face of Unger.

"We might as well be in the middle of hell," he said in a hoarse whisper. "We'd have as good a chance to get out alive. We are on an island in the middle of the Lake of Death. If we could get to the lake—which we can't—we couldn't swim ten feet in it. Treacherous undercurrents would pull our bodies down.

"But we won't get to the lake. They will be on us in a minute and then it will be over. I was a fool. I thought I could play a game with von Durkin, but it's like playing with the devil. Only von Durkin is a little more powerful and a little more brutal than any devil."

"And the secret?" Kermac asked.

"I was ready to tell when you came in," Unger replied. "But telling him won't save my life now."

Kermac looked at the thin, weak face, smiled contemptuously, and shook his head. Unger's face became ghastly at the look.

"You are playing a game you can't beat," Kermac said. "You played it in the clearing when you tried to kill me. You should know it by this time, von Durkin is only using you—"

"I know it—now," Unger said hoarsely, "but it is too late."

"Where is von Durkin?" Kermac asked.

Unger laughed, a dry, lifeless sound that seemed to come from his stomach.

"We'll see him soon enough," he replied, "and when we do—"

THERE WAS A piercing yell from the low opening into the room. A shadow passed in front of it. The yell was taken up by someone in the corridor, and suddenly the underground dungeons became alive with screaming, running savages. They came through the doorway, swiftly, wildly, for the two white men and Agrillo.

Agrillo had picked up a spear from one of the dead Indians on the floor. Unger screamed pitifully. Kermac, with knife again in his hand, backed to the stone wall of the room, with his two companions at his sides.

Slowly and relentlessly, forming an encircling line, the savages advanced on the three men with their backs to the wall. In the sickly yellow light the faces of the gorilla-like Indians were ghastly in color—twisted, distorted faces of hate and lust.

SUDDENLY THE SAVAGES halted. From out in the corridor came the shrill, high-pitched voice of von Durkin, speaking rapidly in a language Kermac could not understand. The savages, hearing the voice, dropped their spears to the floor and stood there, some twenty feet from the three men, as if waiting for some mysterious thing to happen.

Kermac leaned forward. He considered the advisability of starting the fight, knowing that waiting for death was a sure way to receive it.

Unger's voice broke in on the eerie stillness, a gasping whisper.

"God," he said, "they are not going to kill us yet. They are—good God, the fiend—don't let him—don't—"

His words died in an anguished scream. Kermac swerved toward him, but as he did, there was a rumbling sound under him, a thundering roar. His body started to move upward. From the corner of his eyes he saw Unger going down into the earth.

Kermac gave a wild leap. The stone in the floor he had been standing on was opening up. His leap carried him to the edge of the moving stone.

He saw the distorted faces of the savages in front of him.

Then he went downward through darkness, with arms and legs dangling through what seemed to him endless space.

CHAPTER VII

UNDERGROUND HELL

FROM THE PIT of black below him, a growling, savage roar rose to meet Kermac as he fell headlong. Then there was a cold splash over his body and he was sinking under water. The long, powerful tentacles of some grim monster seemed to grab out and suck him under, whirling him around crazily. He came to the surface, still going around and around. Another body hit him. His right arm went out, encircling this person and drawing him close to him.

Then Kermac dived, forcing his body down through the insane, churning water. As he did this, he realized what had happened. Von Durkin had let the three men down into a raging *cenote*, an underground river of Central and South America—deadly, raging torrents that roared under the earth with the fury of a thousand beasts.

Down and down he sank, his body twisted and spinning around as if it were a mere straw. The man he was clutching at his side went around with him. Kermac's lungs were bursting for air. His head was dizzy. He could stand it only a moment longer.

Then suddenly he was out of the water. The force of the current threw him high above the surface; then its deadly tentacles of fury reached up to grasp him and draw him back into the roaring pit of underground hell that would carry him to death far below the earth.

But in that split second, with his eardrums almost bursting from the terrific din of surging water, Kermac drew on his last ounce of strength and threw himself to the right, carrying the limp body in his arms with him. The current grabbed him, took him through the stygian darkness at a speed of better than a mile a minute.

For one brief second his body traveled at this rate. His ears rang crazily; his senses seemed to be going around as fast as the whirlpool of water. His lunge had carried him far to the right. He hit a stone wall with a sickening crash, and then he was floating in still water, the deafening roar of the river still at his left.

He swam weakly away from the din until he came to a rock ledge. His legs touched bottom and he rested there, gasping for breath, with the person he had grabbed in the underground river lying at his side. It was too dark to see who it was, but Kermac knew by the feel of the thin body that it was Unger.

For a long time the Yank lay on the rock bottom, getting his strength back. His dive to the bottom, letting the whirlpool shoot him back above the surface, giving him a chance to throw himself out of the deadly current, had saved him from certain death in the fury of the river. His knowledge of the South American underground rivers had told him the only hope to escape their death was to let them carry the body down and with the current, the very force of which might throw a person out in the pools of still water along the river's side. THAT WAS WHAT had happened, but Kermac realized grimly that this offered little hope of life. He knew he was far underground, with no possible hope of getting out.

From the pitch-black darkness came a faint cry.

"Padrao," Agrillo was calling, his voice almost completely drowned out by the roar of the river.

Kermac turned and swam in the direction of the sound, carrying Unger with him. He found Agrillo in the same pool, hanging on to a rock ledge.

"Quick," Agrillo whispered hoarsely, "opening over us."

Kermac looked up. Far overhead he could see the misty light of a moonlight night through a hole in the ground. His heart gave a leap. That hole was beyond the underground stronghold of von Durkin. It might still lead out to the island, but, free from the great cave, there was hope of escape.

   THE BEST OF THRILLING ADVENTURES

Unger came to life with a stiffening of his muscles in Kermac's arms. He, too, saw the opening in the earth above them. The hope it offered revived his ebbing strength and courage and he stood up, staring at the avenue of escape.

Agrillo started up the steep, damp wall of rock. It went almost straight up, with only a few ledges and protruding rocks for footholds. Kermac followed, holding on to Unger's hand.

Slowly and silently, with the grimness of death hovering over them, the three men worked their way up the slippery wall. Kermac held on to Agrillo's hand and Unger on to Kermac's. One slip by any of the three and all would be hurled back into the river of death; the further up they went, the more certain it was that a fall would land them out into the current of the river.

AGRILLO CLIMBED WITH the agility of an animal, but Unger slipped several times. After they had gone thirty feet, the moonlight flooding through the opening lighted up the wall.

Kermac saw that the last twenty feet offered little possible footing. Agrillo continued to work up, however, his free hand gripping the stones and his bare feet digging into the thin ledges offered for footing.

They got to within fifteen feet of the top. Unger's foot slipped and his body swung out into the darkness, pulling Kermac down with him. For one deadly second the three men hovered over the pit of raging hell. Kermac's body started to slip, but he held onto the swinging Unger.

Agrillo clung to the narrow rock ledge he had reached with the tenacity of a steel cable. Unger swung out over the river once and then his feet came back to the wall, finding a footing.

THEN AGRILLO STARTED upward, silently and pulling the two men with him. Kermac clung to the slippery wall, working his way up even with Agrillo helping him. There was a fairly wide ledge six feet from the top. Kermac reached it, pulling Unger up alongside him.

"You'll get out first, Unger," he said. "You're the lightest and we can heave you up."

Unger made no protest. Agrillo and Kermac pushed his body up the remaining six feet. Unger caught hold of a scrub that grew near the hole, pulling himself through the opening. Agrillo went next, being helped by Unger from above and Kermac from below; and then, with Agrillo leaning out of the opening, Unger holding his body, Kermac was raised through the last few feet.

He fell on the ground weakly. At a glance he saw that they were still on the island, at the extreme western end. The land, from where he lay, looked like a great boulder, dome shaped. And under it was the headquarters of von Durkin.

Kermac raised himself to look across the island. On the south shore, the shallow dugout canoes were moored to the bank. He started to crawl toward them, with Agrillo and Unger close behind him. And then they saw, standing near the canoes, three savages, armed with *machetes* and spears.

The three fugitives got across the dome shaped boulder and onto the stretch of earth between the rock and the shore. Kermac rose to his knees; muscles and nerves taut. It was thirty feet to the boats and the guards.

Crawling across the open space without being seen was, obviously, out of the question.

He motioned to Agrillo and Unger and then, with a spring, he was on his feet. He started for the three guards and the canoes, but as he did, savages rose to his right and left. Piercing screams cut the night. Indians came out of the boulder like rats from a flooded hole, swinging their spears and closing in on the three racing men with the fury of beasts.

Kermac was sent to the ground from the force of the charge. He tried to raise up, to fight desperately. He saw Unger go down from a blow to the head with the flat side of a spear. Agrillo was fighting like a cornered jaguar. He sent three of the savages to the ground, but five others were on him.

All this Kermac saw from his prone position on the ground, through the squirming bodies over him. With a quick twist, he turned over, rising on his arms and knees, sending the savages on him to the ground.

He got to his feet. From the corners of his eyes, he saw the body of Agrillo on the ground, limp and still.

A blow caught Kermac on the side of the head, from behind. It sent him staggering forward with his senses in a whirl.

He fought back at the savages around him. Another blow caught him on the head. His knees buckled under him. He sank to the ground helplessly, consciousness leaving him in the sickening mist of total oblivion.

CHAPTER VIII

TORTURE CHAMBER

KERMAC REGAINED CONSCIOUSNESS with a feeling that he was soaked with perspiration. He opened his eyes, saw a blur of shifting light; then closed them, conscious that every part of him ached and that he couldn't move an arm or a leg.

From the midst of the blurry yellow light came a mournful, inhuman chant. There was a shuffling of feet. Kermac's brain cleared. He opened his eyes again. At first all he could see was the smoking, yellow light, but in its brightness forms took shape: The grotesque outlines of savages, their faces and naked bodies streaked with white and blue paint and on their heads strange feathered hats.

They were moving around Kermac in a circle, chanting in low, monotonous voices as they moved. Kermac's eyes penetrated the light further and he saw the ancient, black walls of stone. He looked down at his arms. He was tied to a great stone chair that sat in the center of the room. At his right he saw the limp, unconscious Unger, supported by the ropes around him.

To his left was Agrillo, his head up

and his thin, brown face twisted with pain. It came to Kermac in a flash that the savages had preferred to capture them alive for torture rather than kill them.

"*Padrao*," Agrillo said hoarsely, "we no get out this trap alive. We far underground and Indians painted for torture death."

A cold, dry laugh came out of the haze of yellow in front of Kermac. The dancing Indians stopped, falling to the floor on their faces. And then out of the flickering light von Durkin walked up to the three men tied to the chairs, his ashen-grey face expressionless and his colorless eyes mirroring a cruel hatred.

"So you get out of all death traps, Kermac," he sneered. "Well, try and get out of this one. I didn't intend that you would die this way. It is not advisable to let these savages work their crazy torture ceremony too often. It's a bad habit to get them into, because it works up their insane fury against all white men." The savages rose to their feet. There was a wild beating of drums somewhere in the room. The chant rose to a mad, weird din. Von Durkin, his face worried, stepped back to a stone chair that stood in front of the three victims.

The gyrating dance of the savages continued, reaching a deafening climax, their faces staring up at the three bound men as they continued their unearthly dance around the chairs.

Then, as suddenly as it began, the dance of death stopped. The savages threw themselves on the floor, groveling and twisting like dying creatures.

From the stone chair von Durkin spoke slowly and clearly.

"AN INTERESTING FORM of torture these beasts have," he explained. "A year ago I found their mysterious stronghold on this island, quite by accident. I was brought here to be tortured as you are to be, but instead they made me their chief. That is a separate story. The hatred of these strange savages against the white man is diabolical and they have reason.

"In the year I have been here, I have studied their lives and their history. Once these hideous-looking men were a great race. That was centuries ago, according to their legends. They were a tribe of the Mayan Indians, living in a great city. The Spaniards came, looted and robbed them, killing many of the women and children.

"The men were tortured. The Spaniards were looking for treasure. One of the means of making the men talk was to place them on a great stone slab, stretching the arms and legs until those members were torn from their sockets. A ghastly torture. Hundreds of the Mayans died in this manner.

"THE FEW THAT escaped came through Central America to this part of the country, building their stronghold on this island. You will find here evidences of the Mayan work. These underground rooms and the stone structures are the work of Indians who had once known civilization.

"But interbreeding and the hatred handed down from generation to generation have produced this tribe of vicious savages, men little better than animals.

All that is left of their one-time culture is their insane hatred against white men. When they can capture one, they make him suffer as their ancestors did on the stone of death. You will be placed on the stone table, with great rocks tied to your arms and legs until they are pulled away from your body.

"It is done with ceremony and considerable brutality. I have been forced, on several occasions, to give them white traders for this sacrifice and I have watched it. Ghastly and brutal."

Von Durkin laughed—a cold, inhuman, cackling laugh. The drums started to beat again. The Indians rose to their feet and started again the dance of death. Their faces were twisted, inhuman and gruesome.

Despite the pain that shot through him and despite the horror of the death that hung over him, Kermac could not help feeling a wave of pity for the poor, soul-warped creatures below him, the victims of the white man's brutality and greed centuries before.

Once they might have been a proud race of Mayan Indians, possessing a culture that had risen to great heights. But now!

Kermac stared at the tall creatures, with their hideous faces. In their eyes were pain and suffering, the pain and suffering of hundreds of years.

Kermac's gaze lifted until it fell on the thin, grey face of von Durkin. Centuries before, white men had placed the curse of hate upon these Indians; now another white man was using them, nursing their insane hatred for the race that had done this, making of them murderers and plunderers.

Von Durkin met Kermac's gaze with the cold indifference of a man who is pleased that an enemy is about to die. He sat in a large stone chair, undoubtedly the chair set aside for the head of the tribe. Three savages, bodies covered with feathered robes, stood behind him.

Two others stood at each side of the chair.

The dance of the savages had again reached an insane frenzy, but a sharp call from von Durkin sent the Indians groveling to the ground. Von Durkin got to his feet, looked at Kermac with a mocking, leering smile.

"YOU ESCAPED THE death I intended for you in the pit of bones," he sneered. "Unfortunate, indeed, that you did that. These savages do not know that the Turkiti failed to kill you. If they did, you would be a god to them as I am. When the bite of a green Turkiti fails to kill a man, that man is a god.

"When I drop the green Turkiti down on white men, I do so with caution, knowing what would happen if these savages ever learned that a white man came out of that pit alive. When I let the Turkiti down on you, Kermac, none of these natives knew it. You are really a god among them; yet you don't know it and they don't know it. You have been bitten by the Turkiti and have lived—but now you are going to die."

Von Durkin jumped back. Two of the feathered savages behind him grabbed his white coat, tore it from him.

A look of bestial brutality came into

his eyes, the same look that shone in the eyes of the maddened savage dancers. **UNGER SUDDENLY REGAINED** consciousness, screamed weakly. Kermac looked at him and then at Agrillo. Agrillo was motioning to Kermac with his head and his eyes were trying to convey some message. Kermac followed his eyes to the Indian's side but saw nothing.

"*Padrao,*" Agrillo said in a low whisper, "my belt. Knife."

Kermac looked at Agrillo's waist. There, as a part of his wide belt, was a knife. Kermac shook his head, knowing that now a knife would be of little use.

He looked back at von Durkin. Over his body was a gorgeous feathered cloak, the cloak of the chief. On his head was a feathered hat, a grotesque, misshapen affair. Two of the savages were tying a green Turkiti around his neck, and the Turkiti was alive, its numerous legs crawling over the bare chest of von Durkin.

A grim, bitter smile came to Kermac's lips. The Turkiti was the basis of von Durkin's power with the Indians. If a man could wear the green Turkiti and not die, he was a god. Kermac realized that von Durkin was wearing a green Turkiti with the poison sac from its tail removed. This could be done by the mere cutting off of the deadly stinger under the body.

Von Durkin clapped his hands. He was no longer looking at Kermac. His face was drawn and distorted. He was the chief of the tribe. Now he seemed to be a part of them; the hatred that possessed them was written in his eyes and face and in every iota of his actions.

The drums started to beat with a fury that made Kermac's head whirl. The Indians groveling on the ground leaped to their feet.

From somewhere out of the yellow light six men came carrying a huge rock table.

The table was carried in front of Kermac, set down between him and von Durkin. Six savages, wearing black cloth gowns, leaped up on the chair to which Kermac was tied. From the dancing savages came a loud, drawn-out chant—a piercing wail, the lament of a cursed race.

Burning tapers were brought in the room, handed to the dancers. Swinging these flaming sticks high over their heads, the savages increased the momentum of their orgy of twisting, jumping, screaming gyrations.

It was weird, unreal, unearthly—yet it held Kermac with a strange fascination. But this fascination was short lived. Bitter reality came in its place.

The ropes that tied him to the chair were severed. He was picked up and carried to the great stone table and thrown on it.

FROM SOMEWHERE OUT of the milling, screaming savages came two Indians rolling the great weights that would stretch Kermac's arms and legs from their sockets. Hands grabbed him.

A great strap was tightened around his body.

Clear above the din came the shrill, taunting laugh of von Durkin.

CHAPTER IX

MARK OF A GOD

THE SHRILL LAUGH from von Durkin brought Kermac to his senses with a leap. The strap around him was tightening. With a frantic twisting of his body, Kermac was out from under it. He saw a lurid face leering down at him. In the hands of the leering man was a great club. Kermac leaped.

But the leap he made was a split second too late. The great club was descending on him with a speed and force that would break his back in one blow. Kermac doubled up. The club crashed down, but it hit him a rolling blow, sending darting pains in every part of his chest. In the next second he was off the stone.

All this happened with such rapidity that few in the room realized what had taken place. The savages in the wild dance saw nothing; their eyes were glassy and they leaped and screamed and twisted like animals gone mad.

Kermac's body crashed against the waist of the man with the club, sending him staggering backward over von Durkin and the three savages with him. Kermac was on his feet, fingers gripping the great club. He knew the utter futility of the move, knew that in a moment a cloud of black bodies would descend on him. Yet if he could die fighting, it would be far better than dying from torture, victim to the savages' ancient hatred against white men.

He swung the club around in a vicious half arc. The Indians not in the dance had seen his move and were on him. The great club sent them to the floor with muffled groans. Kermac gave one long jump toward Agrillo, grabbed the knife from his belt and in a swing cut the cords around his wrists. He had no time to do anything further with the knife. Agrillo took it as Kermac swerved to meet the onrush of yelling savages.

The dance had ceased. The shrill, infuriated voice of von Durkin was shouting orders. The savages, moving like crouching gorillas, crept up toward the three chairs.

Kermac was on one of them, his great club swinging in a complete circle, knocking the savages down as if they were pins in a bowling alley. Agrillo was free. He cut the cords around Unger's body, but Unger simply sank to the floor at the foot of the chair, a helpless, beaten human being.

With his giant strength Agrillo tore a slab of rock from one of the chairs and heaved it into the onrushing horde of yelling Indians. The rock sent them back in a snarling, squirming heap. He ripped another slab and hurled it at the attackers coming from the other direction, throwing them into momentary retreat.

Kermac kept his club working, sending savages sprawling as they neared the chair. The complete fury of his and Agrillo's attack caused the Indians to back away. Von Durkin's voice was yelling shrill orders, but for a brief moment his shouts fell on deaf ears.

 THE BEST OF THRILLING ADVENTURES

IN THAT SECOND of a lull, Kermac straightened up, called out in a loud voice that could be heard in every part of the vast room. He spoke the language of the *lingua geral,* the common language of the different Indians of South America, not knowing whether the savages could understand it.

"God of Turkiti," he shouted, "has bitten me, and yet I live. If you crush me, you are crushing a god and his wrath will bring destruction to all that is yours. If you doubt me, look closely and see that the bite of the green Turkiti brings not death to me."

There was a hushed murmur throughout the crowd. The savages stared at him in amazement. Kermac swerved with the speed of a tiger, fairly leaping across the space between him and von Durkin. And before the leader realized what move he was making, Kermac was in front of him.

With one swipe of the hand, he tore the green Turkiti from the neck of von Durkin, put it around his own. With a leap he was back on the chair, his neck bare and the Turkiti against his skin, with its small legs kicking in jerky, nervous movements.

FOR ONE TENSE, dynamic moment, the savages gazed up at him, at the green Turkiti on his bare neck, their faces bewildered and their eyes filled with a strange fear. In that deadly moment Kermac's eyes went to the face of von Durkin, who stood near his chair, every part of him trembling with the fury and fear that was surging within him.

Yet the leader made no move toward Kermac, knowing full well what would happen to any who might lay hands on a person accepted by the savages as a god. He was forced to stare at Kermac, confining his rage to the look in his eyes, realizing that Kermac had guessed his trick of the Turkiti with the poison robbed from its deadly bite.

"I have the Turkiti against my bare skin," Kermac cried out triumphantly. "He has bitten me but I live. A year ago a white man came in your midst as I have done. You ordained that this white man die; yet when, you put the green Turkiti on him, he did not die. So it is with all gods that come to you."

A murmur started through the crowd. It rose to a piercing chant and then the Indians threw themselves on the floor, faces hidden in their arms, and the chant continued, rising to a screaming din.

The face of von Durkin contorted bestially. He looked at the prone Indians around him; then with a curse, he darted out of the room.

Kermac was after him in a flash, racing down a long, dark corridor, following the sounds of von Durkin's running feet. He came to a flight of stairs, rushed up them to the floor above. Yellow tapers lighted this part of the underground stronghold. He saw von Durkin leap for a door. Kermac went through it a few feet behind him and once again entered the room where he had first been taken when brought to the island.

With a snarl of insane fury von Durkin turned on him, an automatic coming out of his pocket. Kermac jumped to one side as the gun roared, the bullet clipping the stone wall of the room. Then with a headlong dive, he went for von Durkin's legs.

The gun roared again. The bullet clipped the side of Kermac's shoulder as he hit von Durkin and sent the man to the floor, the gun dropping from his hand.

VON DURKIN BELLOWED like an enraged bull, threw his powerful shoulders over, sending Kermac back on the floor. Both men were on their feet at the same time. Von Durkin's right shot out, caught Kermac flush on the jaw. Kermac's knees buckled, but he bored in, shaking his head.

Back and forth across the room the two men fought grimly, desperately, each knowing it was a death struggle. Von Durkin's surprisingly great strength was backed by a cunning and a speed that made every movement of his dangerous. Kermac, smaller of body, was forced to depend on speed to evade the long arms of his opponent.

Both men were bleeding and their mouths gaped as their breath came heavy and labored from the struggle. Von Durkin was working his way to the great table. Kermac sent his right over to the man's jaw and then jumped between von Durkin and the table.

VON DURKIN'S HUGE fist crashed flush on the mouth of Kermac, causing blood to spurt from his lips. Kermac's head swam crazily. Another blow from von Durkin sent him back on the table, helpless.

Kermac gasped, slid off the table to the floor, rising on his hands and knees, blood dripping from his mouth. Von Durkin stood over him, swaying back and forth weakly, his face a mass of clotted blood and his right eye closed. Then suddenly he took two steps backward, reached in a drawer of the table, pulling out a knife. As his fingers touched the hilt, his eyes lost their glassy stare and his lips curled in a sneer.

Kermac was on his feet. Von Durkin came around the end of the table, knife in his right hand, shoulders crouching over.

"So you're a god," he sneered. "You wear my Turkiti and don't die. You came to capture the Green Spider. Well, here he is. Come and get him."

Von Durkin's right hand went back as he lunged forward. There was a whish of air, the gleam of a knife.

The two men went to the floor, rolling, twisting, fighting, snarling. Kermac's hand had the wrist that held the knife. The two men rolled over, von Durkin landing on top. The knife went up and then came down slowly, Kermac still gripping the wrist. Closer and closer to his body the blade came.

It touched his flesh but as it did, his knee came up, catching von Durkin in the stomach, sending him to the floor.

What happened next, took place in the space of a few seconds. As von Durkin's knife went back, Kermac went with him, his hand still grasping the wrist that held the knife. Kermac went up in the air, coming down on that wrist with every ounce in his body behind it.

　　　　THE BEST OF THRILLING ADVENTURES

The knife went down toward von Durkin's chest. Von Durkin screamed wildly. There was a ripping of flesh as the knife went into his heart.

He twisted once, quivered a little, groaned weakly, and then lay still. Kermac fell over him.

For a brief moment he lay there, gasping for breath, his senses a jumble of crazy ideas. Then he got up. The blood was still spurting from von Durkin's wound, but the man's eyes were open.

A guttural laugh came from von Durkin's throat. He struggled to his feet, a ghastly sight, body covered with blood and his long twisted face in the throes of coming death.

Kermac watched him helplessly. It seemed that he himself could make no physical move.

Von Durkin fell against the table. An insane laugh came from him.

"So you think you've killed the Green Spider!" he said in the hollow voice of death. "You have killed him, but I have planned for this moment a long time. You'll never get my diamonds or my gold. You—blast you, you'll never live to tell what you have done. You and the crazy savages—everyone will die as I am going to die."

KERMAC LEAPED FORWARD feebly. He saw von Durkin's hand go for a lever under the table. The fingers went around it, pulling it back.

Every part of that room of stone started to shake. There was a deafening explosion. Rocks fell from the ceiling. The walls bulged out crazily. The room was suddenly plunged into infernal darkness.

Kermac tried to leap back. He fell heavily to the floor.

CHAPTER X

JOURNEY'S END

HE LAY ON his stomach, gasping for breath. The rumbling roar had spread to all parts of the underground headquarters. The air was filled with a dust that cut his throat. Something fell on his leg, almost crushing it. Overhead and around him, he could hear the great rocks falling.

Screams came from every part of the underground rooms, pitiful screams of fear. Kermac tried to twist his body. He released his right leg from the force that was crushing it. The rumbling roar had ceased, but the dust still filled the air.

He crawled forward in the darkness, a darkness so intense that he could see nothing. His shoulder hit a huge rock. He turned and went in the other direction. Rocks had him hemmed in. His hands went out, feeling for some opening.

It was obvious now what had happened. Von Durkin had had dynamite planted under the great stones against a day when he might be captured. The pulling of the lever had set the charges off. The great rock ceiling had fallen in, but Kermac had lain at a point where the rocks had not touched the floor; where they had fallen in a great pile, supporting themselves and holding their weight off him.

His hands went against the wall of fallen rock. From beyond them he could hear the wild shrieks of the terrified Indians. The rocks had not fallen on him, but they had pinned him under them with no hope of escape. His fingers gripped at them wildly. The dust in his throat cut like sharp knives.

The yells from the Indians had ceased. It came to Kermac that over him were tons of rock and that he, with the others, was buried alive.

His shoulder went to a rock. He heaved against it frantically. The rock moved. Other rocks over it rumbled. Kermac pushed again, sending his body forward as the rock moved. His shoulder slipped off it and he went flying through the darkness.

His face scraped against another rock, but he kept crawling and fighting. It seemed to him that he had been moving through the blackness for hours. The skin was off his fingers; his cheeks were bleeding. Then suddenly he fell out into an open space.

A light was burning over him. He struggled to his feet. Agrillo was standing over him. Under his right arm the Indian held the limp body of Unger. It took Kermac a moment to adjust his eyes to the yellow light. When he did, he saw that he was in the corridor outside von Durkin's room.

The walls were still standing, though beyond them, in doorways, he could see piles of stone that had fallen with the explosions.

AGRILLO'S FACE WAS gashed and bloody.

His right shoulder was bruised and the skin had been scraped from it.

"Von Durkin," Kermac said weakly to Agrillo, "tried to blow us all to hell."

"Explosion kill Indians in torture room, but many escape," Agrillo replied. "I crawl with Unger out of rocks. Only rooms fall in and not hallways."

"Can we get out of this hole?" Kermac asked.

"Indians running out opening over torture room," Agrillo said. "Explosion make big hole and moonlight coming through it."

"Okay," Kermac said grimly, "but I came here to get the Green Spider and I want to make sure that I got him."

Agrillo let the body he held down to the floor. Kermac saw that there were no serious wounds on Unger and that unconsciousness was due to fright and fear. He grabbed one of the burning tapers that remained in the walls. Agrillo followed him back in the room where Kermac had struggled with von Durkin.

IT TOOK THEM some time, even with the aid of light, to get to where the table had stood and where von Durkin had pulled the lever. One look told them that the Green Spider was gone forever. A great rock had pinned his body to the floor and all that remained to be seen was an arm.

Kermac and Agrillo took one last look at the room. They saw that everything had been crushed with the falling ceiling, except a narrow lane through the center of the room where the rocks had piled on each other, leaving an open space.

It was through this that Kermac and Agrillo had entered and it was through this lane that they left the room of death. Out in the corridor, a grim, eerie silence had settled over the underground ruins. No voice came from the depths to break the stillness.

"Indians all run," Agrillo said. "They think the God of Turkiti destroyed their caves because they tried to torture white man that would not die when Turkiti bit him."

Unger had opened his eyes. He got to his feet, staring about him in amazement. It took Kermac only a few moments to explain what had happened and to tell that von Durkin was dead. A wave of relief came in Unger's eyes and the fear left.

"I was a fool, Kermac," he said. "I couldn't trust you because I have never given many people reason to trust me. I guess you are about the first white man in this cursed country that didn't try to doublecross me. And because you didn't, I'm willing to come clean with you. I'll take you back to the clearing and we'll get the diamonds."

"Half of them are yours, Unger," Kermac said. "The other half goes to Sprague's folks. We'll report the location of this underground place and the authorities can come here and get the diamonds and gold under that mass of rock—the diamonds and gold von Durkin stole from traders and diamond hunters."

"THERE WAS ONE thing, Kermac," Unger said, "that I couldn't tell you in Cuidad, Bolivia. I didn't think I would ever tell you. I was a partner of von Durkin in the murder of Sprague."

Kermac's face remained cold and expressionless.

"Yes," he said, "I figured that."

"The story dates back several years ago, to when von Durkin and I were traders in the jungles," Unger explained. "He was an evil man then. There was a murder. I had nothing to do with it, but he implicated me and I was in his power.

"A year passed and I saw nothing of him. Then he appeared in Cuidad, Bolivia, got in touch with me. I didn't know then that he was the Green Spider. That was several months ago. I know now that his murders had frightened white diamond hunters from this country. It was necessary for his success that white men come here.

"He told me of the great amount of diamonds to be found here. I was suspicious. He ordered me to interest white men in coming, and threatened me if I did not. In the end I came here with Sprague. It happens that Sprague suggested the expedition, but I should have warned him because by the time we had left, I had heard about the Green Spider and realized it must be von Durkin.

"Sprague and I hit it rich. I saw that the diamonds were hidden where no one could find them. I did warn Sprague, but it was too late. Von Durkin struck that night. I escaped with my life, but von Durkin followed me to Cuidad, Bolivia. I had the secret of the diamonds and he wanted them.

"When you talked to me in Cuidad,

Bolivia, I didn't believe you were a Secret Service man. I came with you because I wanted the diamonds, and needed help getting here. I thought you were after them also. But after my attack on you in the clearing, von Durkin's Indians captured me. I wouldn't talk, and they tortured me. And you know the rest."

Kermac nodded grimly.

"Without you, Unger," he said "I could never have gotten the Green Spider. So we'll call things even. You can go back to civilization and start anew. You will have money and you can play it straight."

"With my money," Unger said wearily, "I'm going back to real civilization, where I can know honest men. You won't have to worry how I live. I've had enough of stealing."

KERMAC TURNED TO Agrillo and motioned him to lead the way out of the underground dungeons. The Indian walked ahead, through the corridor and down to the torture room, where a great yawning hole opened up into the moonlight.

Outside, at the shore of the lake, they found canoes left there by the fleeing Indians. The three men got into one, took a last look at the island of death, and then paddled rapidly for the far shore—and civilization.

Sublevel Seventeen

BY **PAUL ERNST**

Amazing Thrills of the Future as the City of Golden Spires Faces Destruction at the Hands of a Fiend!

CHAPTER I

FIGURE OF EVIL

ZARBOLA!

Previous to the world war of 1961 the name would have meant nothing in any language. Now, in the world language, Xephon, it meant City of Golden Spires. It also meant North America: two hundred miles square, the City of Golden Spires housed most of the inhabitants of the continent.

Zarbola! Truly named City of Golden Spires! Formed of countless colossal buildings rearing their shafts at six-block distances, the space between was made into park and lighted by the life-giving, carbon dioxide daylight tubes.

In the center of this gigantic metropolis soared the seven hundred and twenty-six story Central Control Building. Under its dome, made of the glittering yellow metal, klingsite, as were all the other domes, was the office of the Head of the Control Bureau.

At his desk, on the afternoon of August fourth, 2361 A.D., sat the Head himself, Cell Raggan. He was studying a paper written over with the terse Xephon script; and as he read it, deep lines creased his forehead.

He got to his feet and paced the great room, gazing absently through the glass walls at the giant city that rolled out of sight in every direction. Then he stepped to his huge klingsite desk and pressed the telesite switch.

The transmitted image of a broad-shouldered young man leaped out on the telesite screen taking up the east wall of the office. This was Ornich Fax, secretary to Cell Raggan, powerful in the city's affairs in spite of his youth.

"Fax, summon Tenlow Hass and then come to my office, please."

"At once, sir," the secretary replied.

The screen went blank. Raggan took up his agitated pacing, the furrows in his brow growing deeper.

The buzz of the announcer told him that Fax and Hass were at the door. He spoke the combination releasing the lock, and sat down at his desk as the two came in, A gleam came to his old eyes at the sight of them, but was clouded at once with the stern look of the leader in an emergency.

Two giants, these. Ornich Fax, dark and slow-moving, was three inches over the Zarbola average of six feet two; and Tenlow Hass, flaxen-haired and

The neuron-rod flicked across them, heart high, with stunning shock.

lightning quick in thought and act, was only half an inch shorter.

"Hass," Raggan began bluntly, "how long has it been since you heard from Operative T45S6?"

"Two weeks and four days," replied the young Zarbola Secret Service Chief.

"You've had no word whatever from him in that time?"

"None whatever. His wavelength has been dead. I've had a special operator on it constantly, and not a syllable has come through."

"It is not the wavelength of T45S6 that is dead," said Raggan bleakly, "It is the man himself."

"What?"

"Yes." The Head handed him the paper he had been studying. Hass took it and he and Fax read:

Report of T45S6. To Head of Control Bureau. Duplicate to Chief of Secret Service:

I have discovered the source of that which you suspected. But in so doing, I have been myself discovered and captured. Able to communicate only in script. I have found a messenger in my dungeon which I hope can be relied on to get a message to your attention.

Headquarters for that which you suspected is in sublevel seventeen, building 126 F, northeast. Come at once, for God's sake, if you—

The message ended in a scrawl.

Hass gazed at Raggan, his blue eyes cold as ice.

" 'Duplicate to Chief of Secret Service,' " he quoted. "I got no duplicate."

"I know," said the Head. "If you had, you'd have reported here at once, of course."

"How did this come to you, sir?"

"An electrical worker from building 122 F, northeast, brought it."

"And he? Where did he get it?"

Raggan drummed on the arm of his chair. "Building 122 F, a tenement tower, is unsanitary enough to harbor rats, it seems. This man chanced to see one dragging along sublevel two, and noticed something white tied to it. He caught it and found the white thing was a message tied to the creature's hind legs, which themselves had been bound together so the rat could be captured. That message was this report."

"And the duplicate?" mused Fax. "I wonder where that is."

"God knows," replied Hass. "The rat that bore it may be dead in a sewer—or it may have been caught by one of the band we're after."

"In which case," said Fax calmly, "they know that we know—and anybody going to sublevel seventeen, building 126 F, will be warmly received!"

HASS NODDED. BOTH looked at Raggan.

"There's a chance," said the Head, "that the band didn't catch the second rat. We'll have to act on it. You, Hass, with a hundred operatives and neuron-rods, shall clear out their nest—"

"I wouldn't try that," a voice interrupted. It was a harsh voice, a mocking voice, the voice of none in that room. It came from the telesite screen on the east wall.

The three whirled around. On the screen showed a strange picture—a figure bulky but deformed under its white tunic, topped by a bearded, hook-nosed face in which were set gray-green, evil eyes.

"I wouldn't try to clear out my nest with a hundred times a hundred men," the harsh voice went on. "Because if you do, your city will be destroyed in less time than it takes to speak its name."

SPEECHLESS, THE THREE men stared at the image on the screen. How was this intrusion possible? The line went only to the Telesite Power Station, one hundred floors below. Over that line should come only pictures picked up on the master receivers.

And how was it that the reverse switch was open, allowing this hook-nosed man of mystery to listen in on a conversation in the Head's office?

The figure bowed ironically.

"Allow me to introduce myself. I am Boc Mornug—future ruler of Zarbola, and the rest of Earth. Hear my terms:

"Before ten o'clock tonight you, Cell Raggan, will publicly announce your resignation. You will announce as your successor—myself. You will instruct all Bureaus to place themselves under my control. You understand?"

"I understand I am dealing with a madman," snapped the Head. But his voice quivered.

"I think you know I am not mad," sneered the bearded mouth. "And I think you will obey my command."

"If I don't?"

"Then every building in Zarbola will smash to the ground at the stroke of ten tonight. You have until then to surrender unconditionally. My wavelength is RV3449B1/2. Gentlemen, good afternoon."

The burly, twisting figure faded; the gray-green eyes remained, mocking, sardonic, till the last.

Hass drew a long breath.

"And now we know," he said quietly.

"Now we know," nodded the Head. "The tremor that shook this building twice in the past three weeks was due to no natural cause. Boc Mornug did it."

"But—how?"

"The Head of the Science Board does not know."

"What can we do?" half whispered Fax.

"I think we—must surrender." The words were wrenched painfully from Raggan's lips. "Though perhaps Zarbola's destruction is preferable to deliverance to the terrors of mad, criminal rule."

He slumped down in his chair. "Please go. I have no orders, Hass, my son. This is beyond the Service—beyond all but the duties of my own office."

Hass started impulsively to speak. Fax shook his head silently. They went out.

"To the Telesite Station," Hass snapped to the elevator attendant. "I want to know how that devil got through to the Head's private screen."

THE MYSTERY WAS shortly solved. At the foot of the giant Station control board lay four dead men. Death, not treachery, had opened the Head's official line to the hook-nosed outlaw.

In spite of the horror of the sight, Hass knew relief.

The two descended to Secret Service headquarters on the two hundredth floor.

CHAPTER II

IN THE POWER TUNNELS

"LET ME HEAR of this," begged Fax, when they were in Hass' secluded, insulated office. "The Head has kept it secret even from me."

"And from every one else save from myself, the Head of Science, and Operative T45S6," replied Hass. "Well, there's no more need for secrecy.

"Four months ago there was a curious lessening of crime in Zarbola. I suspected at once that a master brain was banding the criminal element for some large-scale operation."

Fax nodded. "That much I know."

"Well, three weeks ago, and again a few days ago, a mysterious thing happened. This building, Number One Dome, swayed on its foundations. The movement was slight; only a few persons felt the tremor; but Dod, of Science, surveyed the foundation pillars and discovered that the building had settled about four-hundredths of an inch.

"Seismograph records were consulted. There have been no earth tremors for years serious enough to shake the building. What did it?

"Here, then, were two puzzles: a cessation of petty crime and the inexplicable tremor that had shaken the

Control Building. I linked the two together and, shortly after the first tremor three weeks ago, I sent Operative T45S6 to spy through the underworld and see if he could learn anything.

"I thought perhaps the master criminal, whoever he might be, was planning to shake down Zarbola's bank buildings and loot the wreckage. How far I was from the mark! How infinitely greater is the plan of this outlaw—whom we now know as Boc Mornug!"

"I begin to see why the Head wilted so completely at the man's threat," said Fax.

"Yes. He knew that the threat of leveling the city at its foundations was not an empty one."

"But who is Boc Mornug?"

"We know little of him. He was once assistant to Head of Science of the city of Gramshar on the Black Sea. He disappeared six years ago, after killing a man, and was presumed dead himself. Now—he turns up here."

Both were silent, reviewing the paralyzing situation.

Boc Mornug, outlaw scientist, had organized Zarbola's criminals. He had found a way of overthrowing the city's mammoth skyscrapers. Now the city must be turned over to him and his army of murderers—or be destroyed with all its dozens of millions of citizens.

Head of Control, Raggan, must decide Zarbola's fate before ten o'clock.

FAX GLANCED AT his electric watch and swore softly. It was now nearly six.

Absently he gazed through the wall, watching an African airliner settle down, watching passengers stream from its triple ports, watching workers begin to roll out klingsite casks containing, no doubt, the refuse clay of the diamond mines, from which science was just beginning to produce small amounts of synthetic radium.

"Well," he said finally, gazing at Hass, "we each know what the other is thinking."

Hass nodded. "If a large force goes after Mornug in sublevel seventeen, it will be easily discovered and the bandit will wreck the city. But two men might creep up on him undetected, where an army would spell doom. However—there's no reason for you to risk your life, Fax. This is a police job."

"As a civilian who would be one of the first killed by Mornug," retorted Fax, "I think I have a right to share this."

Hass hesitated, then flipped open a drawer and took out two dull metal rods. Neuron-rods, releasing a charge that acted directly on the neurons, or nerve cells, of any living organism. They were adjustable so that the cytoplasm of the neurons could be shocked to temporary insensibility, or completely disintegrated, which meant instant death.

Hass handed one to Fax and took the other himself.

"Any last messages you want to leave, old boy?"

"No," said Fax, "unless you think I ought to report to Cell Raggan."

Hass shook his head. "He'd command us not to try this. You know how the old man feels about us."

A softer look crossed Fax's face. He did know.

They went to the elevators. Miles to the northeast lay building 126 F, in the heart of the tenement district. Under the sinister, four hundred and fifty story pile lay destruction for Zarbola, a secret guarded by an army of cutthroats. Two against a horde, invading a literal underworld of tunnels holding secrets which even the designing engineers knew nothing of, Fax and Hass set out to pit their wits against the brilliant brain of Mornug.

"THE SUBWAYS WILL be watched, and Boc Mornug knows us now by sight," Hass mused as they emerged from the Control Building. "How will we get to building 126 F?"

"The power tunnels are supposed to be safe and secret," suggested Fax.

"They are. But we can't waste time walking to 126 F. We have less than four hours in which to work. We'll have to go by air, and try an old scheme of mine."

Openly they climbed into the maroon helicopter which Hass used on official business.

A figure skulked behind a nearby machine. "We're watched," muttered Fax. "Good," said Hass. "I want us to be."

The speedy machine rose rapidly. At once a second machine soared after them.

"Why not shoot it down?" ventured Fax.

Hass pointed. Behind the trailing machine another was rising. "Mornug is taking no chances!"

North and east Hass rocketed, till building 126 F loomed on the horizon.

"And now for the trick," said Hass grimly. He pointed at a dingy, old-fashioned tower. "At the rear of that building is a single terrace. We'll skim the side, round it quickly, and drop to the terrace. You understand?"

"But what of the helicopter?"

"I'll set the controls. It will go on empty—and our trailers, I hope, will follow it."

Fax nodded, his own jaw grim. He belted a pneumatic shock suit about him and unlocked the catch of the floor trap.

"Ready?" said Hass, a human ball in his own suit.

Fax nodded again, ready to draw his head turtlewise into his suit as he leaped. The building swept closer.

QUICK AS LIGHT Hass banked around the rear wall. The single terrace, littered with tenement rubbish, showed beneath. Setting the controls, he dropped through the trap, with Fax after him.

The two human balls bounced and rolled from one end of the terrace to the other. One stopped a dozen feet from the parapet wall. The other rolled half over it and, after an agonizing instant rolled back again from the threatened drop of four hundred stories—too much for any shock suit to withstand.

At once the two leaped for the terrace doorway. Just in time! Barely five seconds after they dove out of sight the nearest pursuit machine swept around the building on the tail of the helicopter. In a moment the third machine appeared; in a straight line the three roared northwest.

"To Alaska, I hope," Hass growled. "There's almost enough fuel in my machine to get it there."

The pursuit seemed to be shaken, the pursuers eluded. The two went through the terrace entryway into the building. BEFORE A METAL door in the littered, dirty corridor, Hass stopped and whispered the phrase that opened it. He motioned Fax within the revealed room.

"A little hideaway of mine," he said in a low tone. "Come on, change your tunic."

He produced two garments, dirty, smelling faintly of the sewers. They put them on.

"Now some local color."

He wiped his hand along the dirty floor, smudged his chin and Fax's cheek, and tousled his hair.

"That'll do."

Two choice bandits stepped from the room and slouched to the nearest bank of elevators.

"Sublevel ten," Hass said truculently to an attendant who incredibly managed to look frowzy in a new city tunic.

The cage shot downward, stopped before a blank door. The door slid back and the two got out.

"And now?" said Fax.

"Now for the power lane."

"But that's eleven levels below here!"

"I know," said Hass. "But I didn't want to go lower with that attendant watching us. No use taking chances. There'll be no one on the stairs."

True prophecy. Stairs were archaic in Zarbola, used by nobody, existing only in the older buildings. They reached sublevel twenty without seeing a soul.

Neuron-rod in hand, Hass opened the heavy door leading to the sewer system. A whiff of rank air touched their nostrils. He peered out.

"No one in sight."

They concealed their rods and stepped onto the narrow walk flanking the viscous river of the sewer. Here, in the vast system that drained the City of Golden Spires, furtively lived the criminal element; just as, if old records are correct, the criminals of ancient Paris lived in its underground drainage system.

MANY TIMES HAAS had raided the sewers to clean them of the human rats infesting them; but the ways were too intricate, the hiding places too numerous, ever to ferret them out completely. And now a master rat had crawled down here to threaten the mighty city's very existence.

"How do you get into the power tunnels?" asked Fax.

"The nearest panel is about a hundred yards ahead—"

Two men suddenly stepped from a branching passage and stood before Hass and Fax, barring the narrow walk. They approached, slowly, suspiciously.

"Where are you two going?" demanded one, in the argot of the underworld.

"What do you care?" snapped Hass, gripping his neuron-rod under his tunic.

The speaker started angrily forward, but his companion, a small man with shifty eyes, caught at his arm.

"Come on. Leave them alone. The Chief said everybody must report at once."

"I know," said the other thug. "That's why I'm wondering why these two are going away from 126."

"We've got private business to tend to, then we're reporting to the Chief," said Hass surlily.

"You'd better finish your private business quick, or the Chief will burn you alive," was the threat. But the two stood aside while Fax and Hass clambered past them.

More groups they encountered, all crowding toward 126. All eyed them, but apparently accepted them as fellows. In a moment Haas and Fax turned right, into a smaller sewer vault.

Hass stopped before a massive alloy panel and muttered a combination known only to the Service, some member of which always accompanied a worker when repairs were needed on the power lines. The panel slid aside; they hurried through the low archway; the door slid shut behind them.

"Now we ought to be safe," Hass breathed, climbing down a narrow flight of steps to the power level.

The power tunnels lacing the city at the lowest of all levels were walled throughout with a vitreous compound that was practically undrillable. The rare panels leading to them were unlocked by a phrase known only to a few. EVERY FOOT OF the tunnels was wired for alarm; and if a hand were laid on any section other than the doors, a squad of fighters was rushed to the spot. So efficiently were the all-important power cables guarded.

Down the six-foot tunnel, skirting beside a waist-high, metal-sheathed cable that stretched ahead endlessly in the steady light of the carbon dioxide tubes, ran the two. Toward 126 F and the secret menace beneath its bulk. It was nearly seven o'clock, and at ten—

Fax ground his teeth. At ten the Head would either turn Zarbola over to organized crime, or Mornug would topple those great buildings to the ground, burying their millions in a wreck of metal and glass and stone.

Fifteen precious minutes later, panting, they halted at a branch passage. Hass bent over the symbols stamped in the metal sheathing of a small cable looping away from the big one.

"126 F," he said, and made for the nearest stairway.

Over their heads swished the sewers. Over that were the two levels through which shrieked the foul air of the ventilating system. And above that was—sublevel seventeen, bottom storage level, three floors beneath the machinery levels, below which no honest citizen ever went unless he was a workman on a repair job, or a Secret Service man.

Sublevel seventeen! What mystery did it hide? And would they ever live to learn it and reveal it to Zarbola's officials?

CHAPTER III

DISCOVERED

THE ARCHAIC STAIRS from the sewer system up to sublevel seventeen were, for once, crowded with men. Fine specimens, these—crafty of eye, sneaking of manner, stamped with the pallor of prison and of life underground. And in their midst, carrying their lives in their hands, walked Fax and Hass.

With the rest they debouched into sublevel seventeen and turned into one of the vast storage chambers. The chamber had been cleared. Bare and bright under the daylight tubes, its space was broken only by occasional tremendous foundation pillars.

It grew breathlessly crowded. The last trickles of corrupt humanity drifted in; eight brawny thugs closed the doors and remained outside as guards. There was a hush. All eyes swung toward a door in the end wall. This door abruptly opened, and Hass and Fax clenched their hands.

Walking with a queer, twisted hitch, like an animal with a short leg, the man whose image had shortly before been pictured on the Head's screen, came down an aisle kept open for him and mounted a low platform. A moment he stood silent, his grey-green eyes darting over their unwholesome faces.

HE LOOKED LIKE a white-tunicked Satan reviewing an army of minor devils. And this thin-lipped ruffian, wanted for murder in Gramshar, capable of such enormities as wiping out a city— this was the man who aspired to rule Zarbola!

"Men," he began, his metallic voice reaching every corner of the great room, "I have called you here for two reasons. The first is to tell you that we are ready to strike. This afternoon, less than two hours ago, I delivered my ultimatum to the Head of the Control Bureau. I gave him until ten tonight to turn the city over to us unconditionally."

The mob roared. Pillage! Ransom! Excess! Mornug held up his hand; the roar stilled.

"The second reason I called you here was to tell you at last precisely how I am able to destroy the city in case Cell Raggan is mad enough to defy us. Some have doubted my power. Some have said the foundation pillars were too strong for explosives to harm and too well guarded for borings to weaken. Some say I am bluffing in spite of the fact that twice I shook the Control Building to prove my words to you."

The cold, gray-green eyes swept the men, and few were the eyes that did not flinch at their impact. Fax, finding the merciless stare on himself for an instant, could hardly repress a shiver. It seemed as though he had been read to the soul, his greasy tunic stripped from him as though it had never existed. "THIS IS HOW I can destroy Zarbola if I must:

"Science has produced synthetic radium. The process is closely guarded, but I am scientist enough to make my own." The great chest of the man swelled arrogantly. "Furthermore, I can make it by the pound, where others deal only in milligrams. And I have been so making it in the laboratory adjoining this storage chamber.

"Now, under the north side of every building in Zarbola save this which houses us, a pound of radium in a klingsite tube is buried. Every tube is wired to the great main power cable of Zarbola. The Secret Service believes this cable cannot be tapped, but I—I have done it!"

Breathlessly, almost forgetting their peril in their eagerness to hear, Fax and Hass leaned forward. Mornug went on:

"At the stroke of ten tonight, unless Cell Raggan surrenders all Zarbola to us, I shall throw the switch that directs all the tremendous power of the Central Power Plant into the radium tubes.

"That will cause the radium to discharge instantaneously the total energy it normally gives off over thousands of years. And that, my friends, will cause the collapse of all atoms of matter within a hundred feet of each radium tube.

"They shall be compressed to a tenth their normal bulk. Thus the north foundation wall of every building in Zarbola will drop ninety feet, and the building will topple as if a giant's hand had pushed it. You see—"

The uproar of the mob cut him off.

Bank buildings shattered and spilling their gold! Men and women who might escape, delivered to them as slaves! Later, terrified at Zarbola's fate, all other cities of the world given over to them!

For minutes the shouting stunned the ears. But finally Mornug raised his hand again. Tense silence followed the uproar. And now the gray-green eyes no longer roamed. They centered malignantly, icily, on two men. And the two men were Fax and Hass.

"It can't be that he's recognized us in all this mob," Fax muttered.

"I don't think so—" The sweat of relief gleamed on Hass's forehead. "There! He's going on with his talk."

BUT THE RELIEF was premature. "So you have been told of my plans and of how I can carry them through," the voice boomed on. "And now, having learned what you came here to learn, you will please follow me into my laboratory— *Ornich Fax and Tenlow Hass!*"

In stunned silence the two heard their names pronounced—heard also the hiss of indrawn breath from men beside them. Then shouts began.

"Fax! Hass! Secretary to the Head— Chief of the Secret Service!"

The two whipped out their neuron-rods to make a last stand. But the gesture was futile. In an instant a dozen men were fighting to strike them down, tear at them, claw them to pieces.

Through the din burst the bellow of Mornug.

"Back! Back, I say! The man who harms them shall burn alive!"

Torn between fear of the man with the snaky, grey-green eyes, and hatred of the spies from the upper world, the crowd receded. Helpless and unarmed, Hass and Fax stood in a close, living circle. Mornug sneered at them in cold triumph.

"Open a lane for them, men." The mob, mad to kill, was slow to obey. "Open, I say!"

A grudging lane was formed to the door from which Mornug had first come. Mornug strode down it, paused to see that Fax and Hass were duly being shouldered forward, then opened the way to his laboratory and stepped within.

More dead than alive, still stunned by the suddenness with which it had all happened, the two prisoners followed him. The door banged shut.

They faced their captor, the diabolical genius who had crept under the foundations of their city like a secret pestilence and who now showed his teeth for the first time.

"FOOLS, TO THINK you could invade *my* stronghold undetected!" Mornug sneered. "I know every move you made. The elevator man in the building where you landed from your helicopter is mine. He reported your downward trip at once. The instant you set foot in the outer chamber I was notified."

"Well," said Hass, white-lipped, "now you've got us you may as well kill us at once. For if you think we will turn traitor and help you—"

"You will help exceedingly, I think," Mornug interrupted. "Though not, perhaps, willingly." He smiled, and Fax could feel the hair rise on his scalp.

"Raggan will give his decision shortly before ten o'clock. That decision may well be, 'No.' He may decide that Zarbola might better be destroyed than surrendered, my men being what they are. Is it not so?"

Neither Hass nor Fax moved; but both knew the reasoning was correct. The Head was faced with a horrible choice: surrender meaning slow death and outrage in every form, defiance meaning quick destruction. Who could say whether he would surrender or defy, both evils being almost equal in magnitude?

"Very well," continued Mornug, as if both had agreed! "That is where you fit into my plans. When the Head tunes in on my telesite screen there—" he pointed to a standard screen amid a jumble of laboratory equipment—" he shall see you two bound to heavy klingsite chairs where you are standing now.

"He shall also see a semicircular screen of tungstone, the new insulator against the emanations of radium. Behind this screen will be synthetic radium stacked around you like cordwood.

"He shall finally see the tungstone screen raised and yourselves exposed to the emanations—to melt slowly to shapeless, blackened things. Unless, of course, he gives the right answer. Now you see why you were not killed when I denounced you a moment ago."

The grey-green eyes glinted malevolently.

"The threat to you two may be just enough to swing the Head's decision. Just the added pressure I have been wanting. For he loves you two as if you were his own sons."

Fax shook his head. "That is not true. We are only his subordinates, nothing more."

But he lied, and he saw that Mornug knew it for a lie. Raggan did indeed love the two younger men as if they were his sons. And the sight of them, tied helpless and threatened with exposure to raw pounds of radium, would do terrible things to him.

MORNUG SMILED. "WE shall try the experiment anyhow. And now we shall put you in a safe place for the several hours remaining before the Head communicates with me— Stop! Stand where you are!"

Both were leaping at him, hands clawing savagely for his throat. Vainly! Quick as thought a neuron-rod appeared in his hand. It flicked across them, heart-high. Fax felt a stunning shock, then things began to go black. He felt himself hit the floor, felt Hass pile on top of him, and after that knew nothing.

CHAPTER IV

FLYING FURY

RECOVERY FROM A neuron-rod shock is painful. The shocked one quivers and trembles while every nerve in his body feels like a red hot wire. The brain is clear in spite of a blinding headache; but the body is a thing of torture.

Fax recovered first. He gazed at Hass and saw the Service man stir too and open fluttering eyelids.

"Where—" began Hass.

Both, trembling as though with palsy, gazed around. They were in a cavern, evidently a burrow outside the foundation walls of the building, with a metal door separating it from sublevel seventeen proper.

"Look!" whispered Fax, pointing.

Near Hass was a shriveled, blackened tunic. Lying on it was a shining metal disc with the symbols T45S6 stamped on it.

"The place where your man wrote his last note," Fax gritted out. "He got the fate Mornug was threatening us with, if the look of that tunic means anything."

"Burned alive," quoted Hass. "Radium rays—ripping through flesh and bone— destroying and disintegrating—" He controlled his shivering a little. "Wonder what time it is."

Fax glanced at his watch. It had stopped, of course. A neuron shock, while not harming metal, strongly magnetizes it. Another horror was added to their situation—uncertainty as to time. Had they lain there ten minutes, or two hours? Fax was inclined toward the latter guess.

Several rats crawled through holes near the door and ran squealing across in front of them.

"How the devil did T45S6 catch them?" Fax wondered idly.

By now their convulsive shuddering had worn off. They got to their feet, stretching their arms.

"What can we do?" Hass put the question both had in mind.

The walls of their dungeon were of native rock. The door, sole exit, was of heavy klingsite. They had only their bare hands as weapons.

"There isn't even a loose rock to throw at whoever comes in for us," Fax sighed. "If only we had some missile, some shred of hope—"

Hass glanced suddenly at him, blue eyes icy with concentration.

"That's it! A rat! Help me catch one. Quick!"

"A rat? Why do you want—"

"Don't waste time—help me!"

Mystified, Fax helped him. He took off his tunic and held one end while Hass held the other. They went to the largest rathole and knelt, one on each side, with the tunic poised like a net above it.

Minutes passed and no rat appeared. Fax had no notion what was in Hass' mind, but that it was urgent he could see by the tense mask of his face as they listened for the scrabble of paws. AT LAST THEY heard it. Both held ready. A pointed, small snout emerged from the hole, followed by the repulsive body of its owner. The rat squealed as it saw the two, turned, but was enveloped.

"Now," said Hass, his voice vibrating with impossible hope, "help me get the thing in my right hand so I can hold it motionless with my fingers around its jaws."

Easier said than done; but eventually the rat lay clamped in Hass' bare hand, trembling with vicious fear. The men sat down, with Hass hiding the rat behind him.

"When they come, Fax," he said, his eyes blazing, "be ready to jump!"

Finally there was a soft sound as the metal door began to slide open. Two men stood on the threshold. Not three, or half a dozen. Only two! Enough, of course, when the deadly neuron-rods were their armament. Fax saw Hass' eyes gleam brighter. The shorter of the two advanced warily, with neuron-rod pointed at the prisoners. The taller followed with a coil of wire in his hands.

"You!" snarled the man with the rod to Hass. "Get up and stand with your face to the wall."

Hass glared back at him. Also he stared covertly at the other man, and noted that both his hands were occupied with the wire. Only the one neuron-rod was covering them.

"Get up!" repeated the man with the rod.

Hass moved as though to obey. Then his right hand shot forward.

Now there are certain reactions in the complex world of men's minds that can be counted on pretty definitely. Hass counted on a definite reaction in this instance—and won!

HAD HE THROWN a rock at the man's head, the man probably would simply have ducked and then turned his neuron-rod on Hass. But there is something terrifying about seeing a huge rat, all snapping teeth and red eyes and clawing venom, flying through the air directly for your face.

The man shouted and instinctively threw up his hands, rod and all, to shield his face from the flying fury. The shout was still ringing in the little cavern when Fax's hands found his throat.

Fax rushed him back against the rock wall. There was a sickening crack as the man's head hit the rock; then he sagged to the floor.

Fax picked up the neuron-rod and whirled to use it on the other man. But he found that Hass already had him down. Hass' head jerked toward the coil of wire.

"Tie and gag him," he panted. And then, when this had been swiftly done: "Your man?"

"I think," said Fax evenly, "he won't need tying."

   THE BEST OF THRILLING ADVENTURES

Hass gazed at the figure by the wall, noted the queerly contorted limbs and staring eyes.

"Quite," he said briefly. "Come along." **THEY APPROACHED THE** metal door, gazed out. Before them stretched Mornug's laboratory—that secret room of science, of the existence of which no official in Zarbola had dreamed till now. It seemed to be deserted. They stepped into it.

Fax's elbow dug into his companion's ribs. He pointed.

Before the telesite screen a semicircular barricade of tungstone reared head-high. Behind that, they knew, would be the piled tubes of radium Mornug had threatened them with.

Beyond that was an inner barricade of tungstone—and then, no doubt, two klingsite chairs placed directly before the telesite screen. All was ready for them. They had not escaped an instant too soon!

Hass nodded toward the door leading to the great outer chamber which Mornug used as an audience hall. They started toward it.

The laboratory continued still and apparently deserted. The panel was partly ajar. No trouble about unlocking it.

"No, no, please!" came a calm voice behind them. "You must not leave so unceremoniously."

They swung around—to see Mornug and three of his men covering them with neuron-rods. Where they could have appeared from was a mystery—but there they were!

With an oath Fax jerked up his rod. It fell from his hand as Mornug, with easy accuracy, paralyzed his arm.

"Bind them to the chairs before the telesite plate," he said to his men. "Then we'll wait for our honored Head to get in touch with us and see what threatens these two he thinks so much of. He'll give in, I think—at least I hope he will. I'd rather rule a city than a heap of glass and klingsite and corpses."

CHAPTER V

RAGGAN DECIDES

SIDE BY SIDE, bound immovably to the heavy metal chairs, Fax and Hass sat facing the telesite screen. Circling behind them was the inner insulating screen, shielding them for the moment from the emanations of the stacked pounds of radium. They could imagine the precious stuff, piled head-high between the outer and inner barricades of tungstone.

Also they could see, by twisting their heads, that chains looped through pulleys in the ceiling were fastened to the inner barricade. Thus it could be raised by hands protected by the outer screen, to expose the two to the emanations.

Mornug gloatingly inspected their bonds—particularly the wire that fastened their arms to the arms of the chair. Fax's fingers clenched impotently at the near approach of the man. If only he could fasten those fingers on the throat that was so close as Mornug bent to see that the wire was tight! But his arms were held rigid.

Mornug nodded his satisfaction as he stepped away.

"That will hold them. However, we will gag them. They might try to shout secrets to Raggan when his image appears on the screen."

With death in his heart, Fax felt a heavy fabric band fastened over his mouth. Mornug had spiked, by that move, a very desperately cherished hope.

Hass was gagged too. Glancing sideways at him, Fax saw that he was pale as death. But no emotion was allowed to show on his face. It was a mask, every muscle admirably controlled.

But complete control, at the approach of death, is impossible. Hass' hands gave him away. His fingers moved jerkily, convulsively on the metal arms of his chair.

Fax sagged down against the bonds and waited, as did Mornug and the rest, for the picture of the Head of Zarbola's Control Bureau to appear on the telesite plate and his voice to sound from the transmitter behind it.

"Nine-thirty," said Mornug, gazing at his watch. There was a pause, timeless, eternal. Then: "Nine thirty-six— Surely he would not be so mad as to try to rush my laboratory, knowing that such a move would send Zarbola in ruins to the ground. No! He comes!"

And indeed it seemed as though the Head were coming in person, slowly materializing on the telesite screen. A misty figure quickly solidified into the well remembered body of Raggan and greeted the eyes of the bound men like a look into paradise.

THE HEAD OF Control was before them, his eyes wide and blank as he saw the two men wired to the chairs with Mornug standing beside them. Raggan was seated before his transmitting screen so closely that he filled the screen on Mornug's wall from side to side and top to bottom; a seated figure six feet across and six feet from abdomen to crown.

"Boc Mornug," sounded the Head's voice—cracked and aged seeming now, nothing like its usual, crisp self, "I am here."

"It is well that you are, Cell Raggan," said Mornug insolently. "In twenty-four more minutes you and most of the rest in Zarbola would have been dead, with your fallen skyscrapers as your headstones. Have you come to a final decision?"

There was a silence, then. A terrible, pregnant silence, in which the fate of millions upon millions of people was being weighed. Should they be given quick and merciful death, or slow torture and ruin?

TO WHAT A choice was this man, leader of the greatest of all great cities on earth, being driven! Hauntedly, helplessly, his eyes kept seeking the eyes of Fax and Hass.

Fax and Hass returned his gaze as stoutly as they could, trying to will him to disregard them and make his decision as though they had not been in Mornug's power. Fax kept his body still in spite of the agonizing terror that tore at his nerves. So, too, did Hass, save for the revealing small fluttering of his hands.

The silence was broken at last—by a

low moan from the Head's lips which he had not been quite able to repress.

"Why—are you holding Hass and Fax?"

Mornug smiled that satanic smile of his. He pointed to the tungstone insulating screen that surrounded them.

"You see that barricade, Raggan? Behind it are tubes of radium. Many of them. When the tungstone screen is raised your two young friends will be exposed to the full power of the emanations.

"It will be interesting to see what will happen to their bodies. Interesting for you, that is. I already know—I'm perhaps the only man on earth who does—precisely how a thousand pounds of radium acts on human flesh! I can tell you that the sight is not a nice one."

Raggan moistened his lips.

"Well?" came his cracked, unsteady voice.

"It is simply an extra argument for you to abdicate as I command," said Mornug suavely. "If you turn the city over to me, I guarantee life to them and to you. You shall have not only life, but positions of authority—if you recognize my rulership."

"I must think," groaned Raggan. "I must think."

The voice of Mornug cracked out, shedding some of its urbanity.

"Cell Raggan, why are you trying to delay? Why are you blocking the screen with your body? Who is behind you?"

"No one is behind me," said Raggan wearily. "That is, only a Xephon transcriber is here, taking notes which I can show to my people to justify any action I may be forced to take."

"Move aside and let me see."

The image on the screen shifted. For a moment it was clear, showing the office of Head of Control. In it to one side, a girl was seated, with blanched cheeks and horror-filled eyes, jotting down Xephon symbols on a square of paper. No one else was in the room.

"All right, Raggan."

The screen was again filled by Raggan's body.

"YOU HAVE LESS than twenty minutes, Cell Raggan," snapped Mornug. "Remember, at ten o'clock precisely I shall hurl your city to the ground if you do not—"

He broke off with a sharp cry.

"Raggan! Raggan—damn you—"

With utterly no warning the lights had gone out. Every light in the great room. And the faint humming of various of Mornug's machines was stilled, too. Utter silence enfolded the room, and absolute blackness.

"Raggan!" screamed Mornug, insensible of the fact that the telesite plate had also gone dead and there were no ears there to hear. "Raggan—I'm going to raise the tungstone screen from before the radium!"

A strangled exclamation tore from Fax's lips as he heard a preliminary creak of the pulleys.

Then he heard a frantic scuffling from Hass' chair beside him. Heard Mornug's voice: "Stop! *Stop!* Don't raise the screen! He's caught me! *I'm being held here—*"

Instantly Fax divined what had

happened in the darkness. Mornug had backed too close to Hass' chair. Hass' muscular fingers had gripped Mornug's tunic. The outlaw leader was being held so that he, too, would perish from the radium if the screen were raised.

"Don't raise it till I give the command!" screamed Mornug. "Don't—"

He tripped over Hass' feet in his effort to squirm out of his tunic. His head banged against Fax's chair. Fax felt hair sweep across his bound hands. His fingers clutched for it—and found it. An even deadlier hold than Hass'. Hair! A beard! His fingers twined in that beard in a grip only death could loosen.

AND THEN, ACROSS the pandemonium burst further uproar. The great door of the laboratory clanged open even as Mornug's men came running around the screen to aid their leader.

"Hass! Fax! Are you all right?"

"All right," Fax tried to say, into the heavy gag. Then he felt the beard tear loose, leaving much of itself in his fingers.

"Operative T61S8, with five hundred men," a voice said to Hass.

Then, a few minutes later, Fax was being unbound.

Back in the office of the Head of Control, Fax glanced from Raggan to Hass and back again.

"I don't understand this yet," he said plaintively. "It can't have been coincidence that the power station failed at just the right moment to rob Mornug of his power to overthrow the city."

"No," said Raggan with a tired smile, "it wasn't coincidence." He turned to the Xephon transcriber sitting nearby—the girl who had taken notes of the last talk between Mornug and the Head of Control. "Show him, my dear."

WITH A TWINKLE in her eyes, the girl handed Fax her pad of paper. On it he saw written:

Z.S.S. (Zarbola Secret Service.) Z.S.S. Shut down central power station. Mornug helpless without it. Mornug helpless without it. Z.S.S. Z.S.S.

Fax raised his head bewilderedly. "But we were gagged!" he exclaimed to Hass. "You couldn't have even whispered that message."

Hass grinned.

"Our lips were gagged—but not our hands. Didn't you hear my fingers moving on the arms of my chair? I was sending a tap-message, in the Service code. And this charming young lady, who used to be my private transcriber before she was promoted to this office, heard it, transcribed it, and rushed a teletype message to my floor.

"From there two messages went out. One to a force of men waiting in the power lane near building 126 F—just in the hope that they could do something, you know. The other to the central power plant. The men rushed the laboratory in sublevel seventeen just as the power was shut off—and here we are."

"And Mornug?" said Fax.

Hass sobered.

"Most of his men were killed in the rescue rush. He'll be with them in the morgue. There'll be no collapse of the City of Golden Spires—nor any reign of terror under murderers and thieves!"

The Curse of the Shining God

BY A. LESLIE

An Arizona Cowboy Barges into the Thick of Puzzling Mystery and Savage Battle in Mexico

CHAPTER I

A NEW JOB

WALT BOWMAN STARED, at the bartender of Watson's American-owned *cantina*.

"It's a job, ain't it?" he stated rather than asked.

The bartender, who had just offered what he evidently considered good advice, fumbled with a glass and glanced away from Bowman's hard grey eyes.

"Yeah, it's a job," he admitted. "But I'm sayin' again what I jest told yuh—don't take it!"

Bowman stared after him as the drink dispenser busied himself at the back bar.

"What's eatin' that jigger, anyhow?" muttered the tall young puncher. "An' why shouldn't I take a job ridin' for the—Rockin'-R, I believe he said it was. That old feller who called hisself Hunter looked to me like a square-shooter.

He leaned elbows on the bar, quietly sipping his drink.

Wham!

Walt instinctively lunged sideways. Quivering upright in the gleaming surface of the bar, so close as to touch his elbow, was a long knife with a rough horn handle. The keen blade glowed murkily in the light from the smoky hanging lamps. Walt whirled to face the room, hands hovering over the black butts of his heavy Colts.

Men, Americans and Mexicans at the roulette wheel and the card tables, were calmly attending to business, apparently not noticing the incident at the bar; but Walt caught the gleam of eyes slitting sideways. His own hard gaze studied the room and its occupants.

He reached behind him with his left hand, jerked the knife from the bar and sent it spinning into the air. Eyes came up at the gesture. *Crash!*

Walt's gun seemed to leap to his hand like a living thing. Fire streamed from its muzzle. The knife streaked through the air and clanged against the far wall. Walt's cold gaze flickered from one to another of the tables. Then, walking neither fast nor slow, he crossed the

Walt resisted fiercely as the savage creatures rushed madly upon him.

THE BEST OF THRILLING ADVENTURES

room and vanished through the swinging doors.

Curses and exclamations pattered through the smoke rings. A man slipped from his chair and picked up the knife.

"Good gosh!" he yelped.

The horn handle was ripped to splinters.

Men crowded around, examining the work of Walt's bullet. A sullen-faced individual with a mouth that was a cruel bloodless gash grunted a curse.

"Blast it, that's shootin'! Well—"

WALT BOWMAN, ARIZONA cowboy a long way from home, unhitched his horse and rode down the main street of Zacarra, the roaring Mexican cattle and mining town. He entered the office of the local *alcalde*. Of the two occupants of the room, one was an elderly cattleman with grizzled hair and beard; the other a dignified *caballero* who spoke the precise, stilted English of the educated Mexican. Walt nodded and sat down on a bench.

"He's workin' for me, Don Alberto," said the cattleman, jerking a horny thumb in Walt's direction, "Leastwise he was, 'bout ten minutes ago."

Walt grinned as he rolled a cigarette with slim bronzed fingers.

"Reckon I kin stand yore payroll for another ten minutes," he drawled. "Go ahead with yore talk; I'm jest waitin' to ride out with yuh."

The *alcalde* smiled and nodded.

"As I was saying, *Señor* Hunter, I have been unable to learn anything of value. I wrote to our governor asking that *Rurales* be sent to investigate the situation; but we are far from central authority here in the mountain lands of Sinaloa, and I fear we can hope for but little assistance from Culiacán. It is deplorable but, alas, true."

"Yeah, I guess yuh're right," admitted Jeff Hunter, "but it's shore raisin' the dickens with me. There ain't no sense in it, either," he added with an angry growl.

"Assuredly not," agreed the mayor, "but there are, among the ignorant of our people, those who fail to understand that it is to the good of our country to have in our midst energetic and enterprising *Americanos* such as yourself. That is, admitting that you are right in your surmise and it is some of our people who are causing the trouble."

"Who else kin it be?" grunted Hunter.

"There are many lawless elements here since the gold strike in the southern hills," said the *alcalde*.

"But what would that sort gain by runnin' me off my ranch?" Hunter countered.

The mayor shrugged resigned shoulders.

"*Quién sabe?* Who can tell?"

WALT AND OLD Jeff Hunter left town together and rode through the moonlight to the Rocking-R ranch house, ten miles west of Zacarra.

The ranch owner listened attentively to Walt's account of the happenings in the *cantina.*

"They ain't wastin' no time," he commented when the puncher had finished. "Givin' yuh a idea of what yuh kin expect if yuh stay on with me. Still figger yuh want the job?"

The big cowboy shrugged his wide shoulders.

"Why not?" he countered.

"Waal," grimaced Hunter, "they shore managed to scare the livin' daylights outa all my *vaqueros.* They quit me cold and I can't hire no more no matter what wages I offer. If I hadn't had the luck to git them two American waddies, Reynolds an' Waters, I don't know what I woulda done. Now, with you added to them, I may be able to git together a shippin' herd in time to keep from losin' my Gov'ment contract."

A light shone through the bunkhouse windows when they reached the Rocking-R.

"I'll be seein' yuh in the mawnin'," Hunter told Walt. "Come to breakfast with the other boys."

Walt put his horse away and walked to the bunkhouse. A glance through the window as he passed showed two motionless figures hunched over a table littered with cards.

"Them fellers don't seem to have much use for sleep," he chuckled as he shoved the door open. "Rise and shine, gents," he called. "There's a new poker expert in yore midst."

The figures at the table did not answer. Walt grunted his surprise and closed the door. He started across the room and suddenly froze in his tracks, staring with slitted eyes.

"No wonder they didn't say nothin'!" SILENT AND MOTIONLESS the two figures sat, their glazed eyes glaring at the littered cards, their lips drawn back in horrible, agonized grimaces. Protruding from the back of each was the rough horn handle of a long knife!

Walt did not touch the bodies.

"Better leave 'em right like that till the *alcalde* or the *jefe politico* looks 'em over," he told Hunter. "Yeah, I'm still hangin' onto the job," he added as he closed the door.

The *alcalde* and the *jefe politico*, chief of police, both rode to the Rocking-R next day.

"There is nothing we can do other than bury them," said the mayor. "I am distressed, greatly distressed, *Señor* Hunter, but what can I do? Yes, those knives are of Mexican manufacture, such as our *peónes* use."

AFTER REYNOLDS AND Waters were buried, Walt and old Jeff held a council of war.

"One thing's sartin," the ranch owner stated emphatically. "Yuh ain't gonna sleep in that bunkhouse. You leave yore blankets right here in the hacienda where yuh spread 'em last night."

"All right," Walt agreed, "but I got a little idea I'm gonna try out." Hunter smoked silently for some time. Then—

"I'm gonna ride over to the Triangle-D t'morrer an' see if Cal Rickey has had any more trouble," he said.

"Who's Cal Rickey?" Walt asked.

"He's American," Hunter explained. "He owns the Triangle-D an's int'rested in a coupla mines south o' here. He's a good *hombre*." Soon afterward Hunter went to bed. Walt sat and smoked until he felt the old rancher should be asleep; then he walked to the bunkhouse.

He lighted the lamp and undressed leisurely, crossing and recrossing the room before the open window. Then he blew out the light.

He redressed with swift, sure motions and slipped silently through the window. Keeping in the shadow of the bunkhouse and the widely spaced trees, he reached the ranch house. He placed a chair beside a window and sat down to watch. Hour after hour he kept the lonely vigil, his eyes heavy with sleep, his body aching from the unaccustomed strain.

"Dang," he grunted at last, "looks like I'm follerin' a cold trail. Reckon I'll—"

Crash!

Blinded, dazed, the puncher was hurled to the floor. Broken glass tinkled over him. His ears rang with the mighty roar of an explosion. A red blaze of light through trees and stables and corrals into startling relief against the black night. Then the darkness swooped down again; through it sounded the thud and rattle of falling objects.

Walt could hear old man Hunter shouting as he staggered to his feet. Soon Hunter burst in, followed by the cook, a stolid Yaqui Indian, bearing a lantern.

"What in blazes happened?" bawled the ranch owner; but Walt was already outside, running swiftly toward the bunkhouse, a gun in each hand. Hunter and the cook followed. Where the building had stood was a scene of wild confusion. Chunks of adobe and splintered timbers littered the ground. The iron stove lay in shattered fragments.

"What the—how—why—" sputtered Hunter.

"Dynamite," Walt told him briefly. "They figgered I was in there an' 'ranged a little house warmin' for me. I tell yuh, Boss, them jiggers is slick. I never took my eyes off that shack a minute an' jest the same they manages to slip up, plant dynamite, set her off an' scoot without me seein' or hearin' 'em."

Walt went back to the ranch house very thoughtful. On a table beside his bed lay the knives that had killed Waters and Reynolds. He picked them up, examined the horn handles, the finely ground blades, and laid them down again.

MEX STICKERS ALL right," he muttered, "an' that one in the *cantina* was Mexican and throwed like a Mexican throws 'em. But this business o' blowin' up a bunkhouse with dynamite ain't Mexican a-tall. It jest don't fit with the way *peónes* do things. Le's see, jest what did that letter they sent Hunter say?"

He rummaged in a drawer, found the rude scrawl and reread it:

The land of *Mejica* belongs to the *Mejicano.* The gringo must go. The land must return to the *peónes,* the people of the soil. We have spoken.

"Written in darn good Spanish, too," Walt mused. "Too darn good for ignorant *peónes.* But why would anybody else wanta run Hunter out? This range ain't nothin' extra, an' 'sides, there's plenty o' good land easy to git."

HE PUZZLED OVER the matter the following day as he rode the range and made plans for getting together the needed shipping herd. He was still puzzling over it when he entered the ranch house for supper. Hunter was talking with a visitor.

"Bowman, this is Cal Rickey who owns the Triangle-D. He rode in to talk things over."

Rickey was a big dark man with keen eyes and a heavy mustache. He acknowledged the introduction and shook hands with Walt. The puncher was impressed by his steely grip and the warm moistness of his big hands; but Rickey was cordial enough.

"Shore glad yuh was outa that bunkhouse last night!" he exclaimed heartily. "Yuh wanta keep yore eyes skinned, Bowman—these hellions down here are plumb bad. I got a bullet hole right through my hat yes-t'day."

He pulled the wide-brimmed J.B. from his knee and handed it to Walt. The puncher examined the punctured crown curiously.

"How'd this happen?" he asked.

Rickey swore with energy.

"Down on my south range. I was ridin' past a draw when a slug turned my hat sideways an' a couple more knocked dirt in my eyes. I didn't waste no time puttin' distance 'tween me an' them dry-gulchers."

Walt's grey eyes narrowed thoughtfully as Rickey lumbered out to wash up before eating.

"Now why did he go an' hand me a tall yarn?" the puncher mused. "The gun what made that hole in his hat was held so close it powder-burned the felt. I got a large-sized notion Rickey shot that hole hisself. But why?"

Rickey left shortly after supper. Walt and Hunter sat smoking while Huyan, the cook, cleared away the dishes.

"Ain't there anybody 'round here what would like to see yuh give the ranch up?" Walt asked. "That's a mighty rich gold strike they got down south o' Zacarro. Mebbe somebody figgers yuh got gold on this range an' wants to freeze yuh out?"

Hunter dissented emphatically.

"Nope, I usta be a minin' man myself. I've rode this range clean over to wheah *El Negro Infierno* begins—that's them sulphur colored hills—an' there ain't a sign o' gold or silver rock on it. Nope, it's jest them consarned pigheaded *peónes* with their newfangled idears 'bout liberty an' the-soil-for-the-people an' sich."

"*El Negro Infierno,*" Walt mused. The phrase caught his fancy. "That means 'The Black Hell,' don't it? Sounds interestin'. Reckon I'll hafta take a little ride that way."

Neither Walt nor Hunter saw the startled gleam that lighted the dark eyes of the Yaqui cook.

THE PUNCHER WAS surprised the following morning when Huyan came to the corral where he was saddling up. The cook spoke in Spanish. "*Señor,* ride not to *El Negro Infierno!*"

"Huh?" Walt exclaimed. "Why not, Huyan?"

"Because, *Señor,* it is a place of death! The Shining God dwells there and he slays in a way most horrible."

Walt stared into the unwinking beady eyes.

"Say, yuh're twirlin' yore rope too fast for me," he protested. "What yuh mean, the Shinin' God?"

"Long has he dwelt there," intoned the Yaqui monotonously, "and he permits no one to approach him. Those who do are seized and forced to serve him, and they die, most terribly."

Walt grinned.

"SOMEBODY'S BEEN HANDIN'" yuh a runaround, Huyan," he said. "Yuh oughta know better, too—*Señor* Hunter tells me yuh was educated over to the Mission."

"*Señor,*" said the Indian earnestly, "there was a man of my village. He rode into *El Negro Infierno.* One day, long afterward, he crawled back to our village. He had been caught by the priests of the Shining God and forced to tend him.

"The Shining God had stolen the very bones from his body. That man, *Señor,* was but a lump of rotting flesh that could not stand, that could not eat, that could only tremble and moan—and die."

Walt did not ride to *El Negro Infierno* that afternoon. He was altogether too busy. That day and the next and the next he and Hunter worked from daybreak to dusk in a frantic effort to get the needed shipping herd together. On the fourth day they had a piece of rare good luck.

Two *vaqueros* from the north rode up to the Rocking-R seeking work. Dark-faced young daredevils from distant Sonora, the threat of the local situation held no horrors for them.

"*Quién sabe?*" said Alfredo, the elder, shrugging with Latin expressiveness. "Tomorrow we die. Today we eat, and are merry! Knives, say you, *Señor?* Hah! I know a trick or two with the blade myself!"

"*Maldito,* yes!" agreed Felipe with a flash of his white teeth.

The work went faster after that; the number of *ganado* in the big corral increased rapidly. Walt and his two riders combed the outlying brakes for fat dogies that had been living high on the succulent grama grass.

Dusk one day found them in a narrow canyon, holding together a considerable herd they had collected.

"Yuh draw the fust watch," Walt told Felipe as he and Alfredo spread their blankets by the fire. "Call me if anythin' goes wrong."

He lay down and was instantly fast asleep. He was awakened hours later by Alfredo's hand on his shoulder.

"*Capitán,*" whispered the *vaquero,* "something is wrong."

Walt sat up, rubbing sleep from his eyes.

"Why yuh think so?" he asked.

"*Capitán,* there is a storm approaching and Felipe he does not sing. Besides, it is far past the time when he should have awakened me to relieve him."

Walt threw the blankets back.

"Come on," he ordered crisply. "Quiet now. Got yore guns?"

Swiftly the two cowboys drew on their boots.

"The *caballos?*" questioned Alfredo.

"NO," WALT TOLD him, "leave the horses; they'll make too much racket. You go to the right, I'll go to the—hell's-fire-and-damnation!"

Through the uneasy sounds of the night had burst a wild yell and a roar of gunfire. Followed the bellows of terrified cattle, then a low, terrible thunder.

"Fork yore bronc!" yelled Walt. "Hustle, feller, it's a stampede!"

Never in his life had Walt Bowman cinched with such lightning speed.

Death, a frightful death beneath slashing hoofs and goring horns, was swooping down the narrow gorge. To climb the rock walls was impossible. In headlong flight lay their only chance.

Walt swung into the saddle, held his frantic horse in check with an iron hand.

"I come, *Capitán!*" yelled Alfredo.

Wait gave the horse his head. Down the gorge they raced, neck and neck, that terrible thunder rumbling at their very heels. A jagged flash of lightning split the black heavens wide. In the blue glare Walt caught a glimpse of rolling eyes and tossing horns surging from wall to wall of the canyon.

HE LEANED FORWARD, urging on his

flying horse with voice and hand. Then he jerked the animal, staggering and reeling, back onto its haunches.

Alfredo's despairing yell ringing in his ears.

The *vaquero's* horse was down, screaming with a broken leg. Another glare of lightning showed Alfredo staggering to his feet.

"Hurry!" roared Walt, "they're right on top of us!"

With that wave of death sweeping down upon him, Alfredo took time to draw his gun and put the suffering horse out of its misery.

"Good man!" Walt applauded as he hauled the *vaquero* across the pommel. "Git goin', hoss!"

Mad with fright, the bronc shot forward. It screamed as a sharp horn raked its haunch. Walt could feel the hot breath of the roaring herd. His ears rang with the terrified bawls. He drew his gun and fired at the wild heads tossing on either side.

The cattle ranged away. The straining horse gained a yard—two—five! Like the shadow of a cloud fleeing before a lightning flash, he burst from the gorge and scudded across the open plain. Walt pulled him sideways in a long slant and brought him to a sobbing halt. The herd had passed them by and was already milling and scattering.

Alfredo dropped to the ground. *"Capitán,"* he said simply, "I thank you. And now," he added in a dry, hard voice, "we will go back and find Felipe."

"Yeah," agreed Walt, "what's left o' him."

They found what was left—a motionless body with the rough horn handle of a long knife protruding from the back.

"Slipped up on him, cashed him in, and then sent the herd down to finish us off," Walt deduced briefly.

"For which, *Capitán,* men—many men—shall die," said Alfredo.

"I hope so," agreed Walt, "but who?"

CHAPTER II

TANGLED THREADS

THEY BURIED YOUNG Felipe Fuentes on the lonely prairie, beside Waters and Reynolds. Old Jeff Hunter wiped the sweat from his face as he straightened up from setting the crude headstone. "Let's all ride to town," he suggested. "I feels the need of a drink an' I 'spects you fellers kin stand one."

"Suits me," said Walt. "You come along too, Huyan."

The Yaqui smiled, evidently well pleased at the invitation, but shook his head.

"Funny Injun," commented Hunter as Huyan departed with a load of mattocks and shovels. "Never touches it. Well, let's git goin'. Saddle me a hoss, if yuh don't mind, Alfredo."

Walt walked to the ranch house with Hunter.

"Got something to show you," he said. He handed the cattleman a short length of gold watch chain. The links at either end were broken.

"That was in Felipe's hand when I

turned him over," he explained. "Looks like he made a grab for the jigger what knifed him an' jerked his watch chain loose."

"**LOOKS THAT WAY**," admitted Hunter, "but it ain't much good, is it?"

"It's liable to give some sidewinder a dose o' lead poisonin'," said Walt. He hurried on before the other could interrupt:

"Hunter, no *peón* ever wore that chain. I even figger I kin go a bit farther and say no Mex ever wore it. That's an American-made chain an' I'll bet my last peso it was bought in the United States. You keep yore eyes skinned for a jigger wearin' a broken chain. Chances are he never noticed Felipe jerk it in the excitement See?"

Hunter nodded, but was not impressed.

"It's playin' a long shot an' danged little chance to cash in," he growled pessimistically.

But that very night Walt "cashed in" on the long shot, and was left even more bewildered than before.

Zacarra was roaring when the three cattlemen rode in. It was payday at the mines and the miners were celebrating. Cal Rickey's Tumbling-D riders were in town also.

Walt found Rickey seated at a table in the American-owned saloon where Hunter had hired him. He sat down at the ranchman's invitation. Rickey introduced his foreman, Squint Brenmer, a sullen-faced individual with a mouth that was a cruel bloodless gash.

Rickey swore angrily when he heard of the stampede and Felipe's death.

"They won't stop at nothin'," he grunted. "Somebody run a dozen steers over a cliff for me yesterday an' the boys found a fire jest in time to keep one o' my stables from goin' up in smoke. I'm thinkin' seriously o' sellin' out an' leavin' the country. Well, reckon I'll be ridin' back—it's gittin' late."

Brenmer pulled out a large gold watch, consulted it and rose to his feet "See yuh again," he grunted.

For long minutes Walt Bowman sat staring at the swinging doors through which the cattlemen had vanished. He ordered *tequila* and downed the fiery stuff at a gulp. For more minutes he sat pondering what he had seen.

It was not unusual for men in the cattle country to use a rawhide thong in place of a watch chain. Brenmer had worn such a thong looped from buttonhole to vest pocket. But when he drew the watch forth, Walt had seen that the thong was not fastened to the stem ring of the watch—but to a short length of heavy gold chain!

"I'da swore they was the same big flat links, too," the puncher muttered. He downed another drink and left the *cantina*.

"The whole thing don't make sense," he growled as he walked down the crowded street. "What in tarnation would Rickey want with Hunter's range? It ain't noways as good as his own an' he's got too much land, now. But why did he lie 'bout that bullet hole in his hat? And right now, of all times, his foreman's wearin' a broken watch chain!"

WALT RODE ALONE the following day, through the wild and broken country that formed the western half of the Rocking-R range.

"I got a notion a lot of the dogies we ain't been findin' are holed up back in these hills," he told his tall roan gelding. "Seems ev'body's got a mighty pore opinion of *El Negro Infierno* an' keeps away from there. I bet this section ain't been worked over right for one long time."

As he bored farther into the hills, the surmise was justified. He found cattle, wild-eyed, truculent *ganado,* but in prime condition.

"This bunch is gonna have us settin' purty with the shippin' herd," he exulted. "Now what's that, a calf bogged down?"

His keen eyes had caught a floundering movement beside a low ridge of rock. He rode toward it, lids slitted against the sun glare.

"THAT AIN'T NO calf!" he exclaimed suddenly. "Danged if it ain't a *hombre!*"

It was a man, or had once been one, a man whose skin had originally been coppery-red, whose hair had been lank and black. Now the skin was a repulsive, dirty grey, the hair thin and dead. Walt paused a half-dozen paces distant, a chill of horror prickling his scalp. In his ears rang the words of Huyan, the Yaqui cook—

"—a lump of rotting flesh that could only tremble and moan—and die!"

That was all the dying Indian was—a lump of rotting flesh, toothless, trembling, moaning. The slow writhing of the body suggested the boneless movements of a torpid snake. It took all Walt's courage to kneel beside the horrible thing and pillow the rolling head on his knee.

"What happened to yuh, old-timer?" he asked. "Is there anythin' I kin do?"

He repeated the words in Spanish. The filming, lackluster eyes gazed into his, the quivering lips twitched and writhed. Words like the croak of a tortured frog seeped between the shriveled, bloody gums:

"El Dios de la luz!"

"The god of light—The Shining God!" Walt translated. "Say, what—how—"

The Indian suddenly rattled in his throat. The writhing body stiffened, quivered, relaxed. The shrunken jaw sagged.

But even in death there was no expression of peace for the tortured features. The glazed eyes still stared with horror in their depths. The thin lips writhed back from the bloody gums. The whole emaciated form seemed to cry out against some dread and agonizing fate.

Walt eased the body to the ground and stood up. For long minutes he stood gazing toward those gloomy, threatening hills that fanged the blue sky. He shivered in the bright sunshine.

"Heck, it's cold!" he muttered as he walked back to his nervous horse.

THAT NIGHT WALT Bowman fought a hard battle with himself. He had a hunch and he wanted to follow it. Back in those ominous sulphur-colored hills of *El Negro Infierno* there was undoubtedly some terrible thing of blasting horror.

Walt had been more amused than

impressed by Huyan's grim story. Now he had seen that tale of terror unfolded and brought to its awful conclusion before his very eyes.

"I don't know how I know it," he growled to himself, "but I'll bet all the *dinero* I ever hope to have that back in them holes is the reason why Cal Rickey, or somebody, is tryin' to run Hunter off this range!"

He was suddenly struck by an idea. "Didn't Huyan say somethin' 'bout the priests of the Shinin' God? Mebbe there *is* a Shinin' God an' his priests is sore 'cause Hunter came in here an' took up land they think oughta b'long to their god. If it wasn't for that phoney bullet hole and the chain, I'd be 'bout ready to count Rickey outa the deal."

Walt rode away from the Rocking-R at daybreak, alone. He shivered as he passed the shallow grave he had scooped out for the dead Indian the day before. Over him swept again that terrible feeling of oppression and deadly cold.

Hard of eye and grim of mouth, he rode on beneath the shadow of those lurid hills that seemed to reach out mottled skeleton arms to crush horse and rider. Far to the west the great somber cone of a slumbering volcano reared against the sky, a trickle of dark smoke slavering over its drooping crater lip.

The stricken Indian could not have traveled far, Walt reasoned. Somewhere at no great distance, doubtless within the confines of the Rocking-R range, lay the mysterious horror. Silver River, chafing against the westernmost hills of *El Infierno Negro*, marked the limit of Hunter's range in that direction. But within that half-score of miles lay the wild, rugged and little known Black Hell.

The faint cattle trail Walt had been following petered out altogether and the cowboy rode between frowning canyon walls that drew closer and closer together. Mile after mile he threaded the gloomy gorge, alert for danger but seeing and hearing nothing.

WATER MOANED OVER the rocks and from time to time a weird bird cry winged down from the saffron-flaring crests. The canyon ended abruptly in a blank rock wall.

Walt pulled up, eyeing the un-climbable cliff.

"Looks like we done mavericked inter nothin' at all," he told the sorrel. "Nobody ever clumb down them rocks."

Suddenly his eyes centered on a fissure in the frowning barrier. It was a mere crack in the rock, extending from top to bottom of the cliff. Had not the early afternoon sun been shining directly against the cliff face, Walt would have overlooked the rift altogether. He rode forwards and peered into the gloomy opening.

"If that don't look like the front door to hell, I hope I never see the real thing," he muttered. "Hoss, yuh can't go in theah, an' I ain't got no business goin'."

He turned the roan and rode slowly away from the cliff. In a little grove where there was grass and water, he dismounted.

"Jest stay here an' wait for a plumb

danged fool," he ordered. "An' here's hopin' yuh don't hafta wait too long!"

CHAPTER III

EL NEGRO INFIERNO!

SLITHERING AND WINDING, the fissure bored through the solid rock. Walt cursed heartily as he stumbled over loose stones and bruised himself against snagging fangs of rock. He was sweating profusely when the fissure opened into a gorge narrower and gloomier than the one he had just left.

This gorge was in reality little more than a cave with a crack in its roof. Walt groped along in the half light, an intangible apprehension clawing at his nerves. He tried to shake it off but it persisted.

An unfamiliar, irritating odor began clogging his nostrils. His eyes stung as if from heavy smoke. He glanced about, but could see nothing but the frowning walls of queer reddish rock.

He rounded a sagging corner and halted abruptly, staring with puckered eyes.

The gorge widened slightly and ended, a hundred yards or so distant, at what appeared to be the lip of a cliff. Beyond the lip was blue distance. Walt gave all this a passing glance and then devoted his attention to what lay nearer at hand.

The walls of the gorge were torn and gutted. Heaps of the strange reddish rock lay about. At one side and close to the cliff lip was a crude furnace built of stone blocks, through whose poorly filled niches seeped clouds of oily black smoke. Dark wisps blew back into the gorge from time to time and bore with them that strange, irritating odor.

"Had a notion I was crawlin' inter hell," muttered the cowboy, "but durned if I figgered I'd find one o' the cook pots goin' full blast!"

He walked slowly toward the furnace, alert for any danger that might threaten. He could see dark fissures gouging the cliffs, but no movement was apparent within them. The gorge seemed utterly deserted.

The smoke grew thicker as he approached the mysterious furnace. Walt coughed chokingly. His eyes stung. There was a peculiar constricted feeling inside his chest, as if an iron band were slowly tightening about his ribs. He hesitated a moment, then went on, bending low to escape the fumes.

As he drew nearer, he noted the peculiar construction of the furnace. It appeared to have upper and lower compartments. A wooden cylinder, evidently hollow, thrust out from the upper compartment, curved down and vanished in a shallow pool of water. CHANNELS CUT IN the smooth rock of the gorge floor led away from both pool and furnace. Walt moved in a little closer, and as he did so a gust of wind swept a great cloud of oily smoke down upon him.

Choking and gasping, he reeled back, pawing at his stinging eyes; and as he did so hands like vulture talons gripped his arms and legs and hurled him to the ground!

He struggled madly with the horrible figures that had darted, under cover of the smoke, from the dark holes in the cliffs; but his arms were wrenched behind him and quickly bound with rawhide thongs. He was jerked to his feet and dragged back out of the fumes. His eyes cleared and he glared about.

His captors were Indians, or what had once been Indians. Now they were frightful, toothless, hairless things that seemed mere bundles of rotting bones and stringy muscles. They stared at the prisoner with furious evil eyes, champing their flabby jaws, their lips writhed back from swollen, bloody gums. Their limbs jerked and trembled, their breath hissed out in incredibly foul blasts.

One of their number gave a sort of animal howl. The others yelped in chorus. Their grip on the prisoner tightened. They rushed him past the furnace and toward the cliff lip. Walt resisted fiercely but he was almost on the edge before his efforts brought forth any results.

There he managed to kick one man's feet from under him. Another stumbled over the prostrate one and the whole group was brought to a milling halt. Walt Bowman cast a glance over the cliff lip and fought with maniacal despair.

He had seen the Shining God!

A SCORE OF feet below was a pool, the surface of which shimmered and coiled and glittered. Sparkling drops falling from the channels grooved in the stone sent dancing ripples over its surface. It was sublimely beautiful, there in the bright sunlight, but with the beauty of terror.

"Quicksilver!" the cowboy panted, as he struggled with all the strength of his lithe body. "A pool of quicksilver!"

Madly he strove against the death of horror that awaited him there at the foot of the cliff. He jerked one hand free and drove an iron-hard fist into the face of one reeking horror. He swept another to the ground before the hand was pinned again. But numbers were telling. They were slowly dragging him back to the cliff lip.

His feet were on the very edge. The sinister pool flashed its blinding beams in his eyes. His captors tensed for the final lunge.

Above the grunt and gabble of the straining Indians sounded a high-pitched voice shouting an angry command. Walt's captors hesitated, holding him helpless but no longer striving to hurl him over the edge. Again the voice sounded—harsh, peremptory. WALT WAS DRAGGED back from the cliff lip and thrown to the ground. His hands were bound again, more firmly than before, and his feet likewise. The group about him dissolved and he gazed up into the face of an ancient Indian.

Fell disease had not struck at this man's life; only great age. He was straight as a lance. His snowy hair was thick and glossy; but his glittering black eyes were the eyes of a fanatical madman. He glared hate at the helpless puncher, then turned and barked a command.

   THE BEST OF THRILLING ADVENTURES

Taloned hands lifted Walt and carried him into one of the dark fissures. There he was dumped upon the damp ground and left alone with his thoughts, which were not pleasant. He was not deluded into believing that any prompting of mercy had caused the old Indian to rescue him from immediate death.

"Jest gonna hold me for a proper stage settin'," he decided. "Well, I found out about the Shinin' God and why Rickey wants Hunter's range, but it ain't likely to do me a lot o' good. Yeah, it's plumb simple now—

"Hunter was right, they ain't no gold in these hills; but there's some-thin' darn near as valu'ble. Quicksilver is wuth plenty o' money. Them red rocks is cinnabar ore an' yuh git quicksilver from cinnabar. The Indians roast it out in that furnace an' run it into the pool. They can't hold it an' they can't pick it up an' they think it's a god an' worship it.

"O' course they git mercury-poisonin' from the smoke an' die. That old high-priest jigger is wise enough to keep away from it an' them pore dumb devils think he's ace-high with the god."

All of which was interesting but hardly comforting. No wonder Huyan and his tribe considered *El Negro Infierno* a place accursed. A man dying in the last stages of mercurial poisoning was bound to look as though he had plenty of devils clawing him.

With a sudden thrill Walt realized that his guns had not been taken from him; but his exultation was short lived. Guns were of little use to a man with his hands and feet securely tied. He strained at the thongs but only succeeded in cutting his wrists. His body ached and the damp cold of the ground ate into his bones. Nearby, water dripped into a pool with maddening monotony.

THAT STEADY DRIP reminded Walt that he was desperately thirsty. He located the pool by sound, rolled and shuffled to it and ducked his face down against the water. He sucked up a mouthful, sputtered, gagged and spewed it forth. It was rankly bitter with minerals, un-drinkable. He swore despairingly and rolled over on his side.

His burning wrists shrieked for atten-tion. He writhed toward the pool again, backward this time.

"If I can't drink it, mebbe I kin cool them cuts down a little in it," he mumbled. "Blast rawhide anyhow, an' blast anybody what'll tie a man with it!"

Suddenly a thought struck him.

"Rawhide—water—rawhide will stretch when it gits wet! Mebbe—"

Immediately he put the thought into action. By straining and squirming, he managed to get his wrists into the pool.

To do so he was forced to lie in the water and the chill of it set his teeth to chattering.

The minutes seemed to grow to hours, and still the stubborn rawhide refused to stretch the fraction of an inch. Walt's body was one agonizing ache, his head was splitting; but with grim determination he endured the torture.

AND THEN SLOWLY the thongs loos-ened, stretching almost imperceptibly as he strained against them. Outside the fissure he could hear voices and shuffling sounds. The Indians were doubtless coming for their victim. The thongs were much looser now, but still be could not free his hands. His heart sank as a shadow darkened the fissure mouth. A sudden yelling arose. Then a sound that Walt least expected to hear—the boom of a gun!

Other reports followed it in quick succession; the rattle of sixes. Voices shrieked in agony and among them Walt recognized the cracked tones of the old high priest. Silence followed, then voices—gruff voices speaking English.

"That settles the scum," said one that seemed vaguely familiar. "Wasn't no use lettin' 'em hang 'round here any longer, now that we 'bout got things in our hands. With old Hunter outa the way, I'll git a grant o' his land from the Gov'ment an' a little later we'll 'diskiver this ore deposit, by accident."

"Yuh said it, Boss," another voice chuckled evilly, "an' by this time t'morrer yuh won't have to worry none about Hunter, nor "bout that smart gun-slingin' puncher from Arizona, neither. He'll wish he'd took notice when I chucked that knife side him there in the *cantina!*"

"Yuh shore yuh got everythin' fixed, Squint?"

"Fixed is right," grunted the evil voice. "I got enough dynamite planted under that ranch house to blow the Mexican border inter next year. They won't be no slip-up this time, 'cause they all sleep in there now. I got the same kind of a alarm clock jigger with matches an' sandpaper to light the fuse as I used

on their bunkhouse—it's right under the front porch an' it's set for midnight t'night."

"You an' me better be in town at midnight, where we got plenty o' witnesses."

"Uh-huh, I done told all the boys to be in Watson's *cantina* then. The whole Tumblin'-D will be present an' 'counted for. We'll all be plenty alibied, Boss."

Inside the dark fissure, Walt Bowman jerked the last wet thongs loose from wrists and ankles. He stood up, flexing his stiffened arms and legs. He loosened his guns in their carefully oiled and worked holsters, closed and unclosed his fingers a few more times and stepped out of the fissure.

ALL ABOUT WERE scattered the bodies of the dead Indians, seven of them, including the old high priest. The furnace fire had died to a faint smolder. At the cliff lip two men stood gazing down at the Shining God.

"Cal Rickey!"

The two men whirled at Walt's shout, alarm on their faces. For a split second they stood petrified with astonishment; then they went for their guns.

With effortless ease Walt Bowman flipped his Colts from their holsters, their muzzles streaming fire as they came. Rickey went down, sprawling on his face. Squint Brenmer, the Tumbling-D's sullen-faced foreman, sent one bullet zipping past Walt's head and kicked up the dirt at his feet with another. Then he slewed sideways and lay in a crumpled heap, a black hole oozing blood between his eyes.

Walt holstered his guns and strode

forward. He glanced at Rickey, turned to Brenmer, and as he did so, Rickey came to his feet in a lightning bound.

"Gotcha, yuh range tramp!" he howled as his huge arms closed about the cowboy.

TAKEN UTTERLY BY surprise by the ruse, Walt was hurled backward to the ground. The force of the fall broke Rickey's grip and they rolled apart, instantly to regain their feet. Toe to toe they stood and slugged with all their strength.

Walt was the faster and more agile, but Rickey outweighed him by many pounds. He was forced to give ground before the rancher's attack. Rickey followed him close, his big fists working like pistons.

Walt weaved and blocked. He dared not go for his guns. Let his guard drop but for an instant and one of those sledge-hammer blows would stretch him senseless at the other's mercy. He leaped back a pace and Rickey rushed.

Walt ducked under the flailing arms, gripped Rickey about the loins and heaved with all his strength. Over his shoulder flew the rancher's big body, arms and legs revolving. He cleared the lip of the cliff and with an awful shriek shot head first into the mercury pool.

The shimmering surface heaved and rippled for an instant, then resumed its sinister, lazy coiling. The Shining God had claimed his sacrifice!

The stars a glowing net above him, Walt Bowman rode across the Rocking-R range. He was anxious and worried, for while he had plenty of time to reach the ranch house before midnight, there was the chance that Brenmer might have miscalculated, or that something might happen to speed up his crazy clockwork device. Walt urged the big mount to greater efforts.

The roan surged forward, and stepped in a badger hole! Down he went, hurling Walt over his head. The cowboy struck the ground violently and lay still. The roan struggled up, whinneying with pain, limped a few steps and stopped.

The horse pawing close beside him finally brought Walt back to consciousness. He sat up, dully wondering what had happened. Memory came back and he staggered to his feet. One glance told him that the horse was useless with a badly sprained shoulder. Walt quickly loosened saddle and bridle and threw them to the ground. Then he set out toward the distant ranch house, running awkwardly in his high-heeled boots.

THE MILES SEEMED to stretch out into an infinity of agony. Walt's feet were a mass of blisters, his head one vast ache. He stumbled on, limping and floundering, straining his ears for the sound he dreaded to hear.

But no rending explosion greeted him as he neared the dark ranch house. He yelled twice, then saved his breath to run the faster. As he reached the porch, a low whirring sounded. There was a bright flash, then a steady hissing like that of an angry snake.

The glow of the burning fuse guided him to the dynamite. He hauled the crude bomb out from under the porch and groped with trembling fingers for his knife. With a thrill of despair he realized it was gone. He jerked at the fuse, but it was firmly secured.

GRIPPING THE FUSE with his teeth, close to the cap, he chewed frantically, ripping through the outer covering. A rain of stinging sparks seared the roof of his mouth. The fire was already lapping against the cap!

He ran to the rear of the ranch-house and hurled the dynamite over a stable roof. It exploded with a terrific roar before it struck the ground, knocking the stable to pieces and shattering every window in the ranch house.

Deafened and half stunned, Walt picked himself up and staggered to the front door. He reached it just as Jeff Hunter burst out, a sawed-off shotgun in his hands.

"Hold it!" Walt yelled as Hunter leveled the gun.

He sat down wearily on the step. Alfredo and Huyan gathered around him.

"What in blazes happened, anyway?" demanded Hunter.

"Plenty," Walt told him, tugging at his tight boots. "Squint Brenmer won't chuck no more knives at people, an' Cal Rickey won't write no more notes or start no more stampedes. An', Boss, yuh're a rich man! Jest lemme git these blamed boots off, an' I'll tell yuh all about it!"

Hell's Oasis

BY **ARTHUR J. BURKS**

Swishing Swords and Smashing Fists at a Forgotten Outpost of the African Desert! A Soldier of Fortune Faces Desperate Enemies in the Land of M'Tab!

CHAPTER I

STRANGE LANDS

FOR FIVE GHASTLY days the little band of Americans, led by Sherman Clive, soldier of fortune, had trekked into the heart of the desert. They had long since left the jungles, streams and game behind them. Even Clive did not know where they were. He believed that they had pushed into the Sahara, but he could not be sure.

The sun was a blazing ball in the sky which burned into their brains. The sand under their feet was a furnace which scorched them through their heavy shoes.

Only Sherman Clive himself, hard as nails, with the brown of many suns burned into his face, seemed human. The rest, to the number of eight, were mere automatons who fought on through the clinging sand as though they had no will of their own, but were merely driven by that first law of mankind—self-preservation.

Here and there were scrubby shrubs which lived by some miracle in the hearts of the awful wastes. They seemed to cast no shadow because the sun was always overhead, always at its hottest. They did not sweat because the sun had absorbed all the moisture out of them.

"Water!"

The one word came in a moan from the rearmost of the marchers. It was a mumbled word of utter agony.

Sherman Clive whirled on the speaker, would have knocked him down. Talk of water, when their canteens had long since been left behind because they had contained not one drop among them, might drive the others mad.

But Clive paused with his hand raised. No need to think of this man driving the others mad. He was mad himself. Clive knew that his death was a matter of hours, almost, perhaps, of minutes. His heart was like stone in his breast, for during the past twenty-four hours six of his men had stumbled a last time in the sand and had risen no more. They had been left, bundles in the sand, that the winds might bury them, or the wind-driven sand rip the flesh from their bones.

Even as Clive looked into the mad eyes of the man who had spoken, the man saw the unspoken answer on the face of his commander.

There was no water. A wild scream, horrible in its meaning, broke through the heat waves which swept like hot miasmas through the shimmering awfulness.

And Nash, the man who had screamed, took the easy way out. He took it before Clive could put forth a hand to prevent.

Nash's automatic leaped to his right hand. He swung the muzzle to his temple. The trigger finger closed convulsively. The explosion of the pistol sounded dead and flat in the heat, as though the very flame of the sun had erased it, smothered it.

And Nash spilled into the sand, rubbed his face in it, and where his blasted temple touched the hot surface of the desert, there was a pool of crimson.

None could have guessed what the effect of the suicide of Nash would have done to the men if at that moment another shout hadn't broken out from one of the others—Silas Mardaunt.

"Look! Trees!" he cried.

Sherman Clive's bleared grey eyes stared into the shimmering haze ahead, where the horizon was the top of a stove blotting out whatever vast world might be beyond the curve of the earth. Was this a mirage? He believed it was. It was difficult to figure depressions here, difficult to figure anything—except that heat blistered them, and thirst drove them mad.

BUT THERE WAS, he felt certain, a marching host of palm trees dead ahead. They had come swimming out of the haze the very moment Nash had blown half the top of his head off.

Had he waited a few seconds more, he might have lived on.

But later Clive was to envy the man who had taken the threads of destiny into his own fingers.

For the trees were real. They were only two miles ahead. And soon Clive understood why he hadn't seen them

   THE BEST OF THRILLING ADVENTURES

before. The little party had topped a rise—level though the snowy waste of sand had seemed a moment before—and were looking down into a valley of sand, to a grim, hot oasis.

The tops of the palms bowed and bent in a breeze they could not feel, as though the winds had hidden in the valley from the heat, as the trees had hidden.

The valley was not a valley, actually, but a big depression in the heart of the sands.

IT WAS TOO good to be true. So clear was the air now, that they moved closer to the oasis. They could see figures moving among the dunes, among the trees.

And there were houses! They were as gaunt and grim as the desert itself. They seemed, as they materialized out of the sand, like hummocks of grey stone wrought from the sand itself. They were like fortresses.

Clive had a qualm of doubt as he thought of them as fortresses. There was something antagonistic about them, even now.

But trees meant water, and houses meant food. And they would die without them!

Each of the eight men carried rifles and knapsacks. The knapsacks were heavy because each one of them was loaded with gold and precious jewels. For four days, the last one waterless and food-less, they had marched into the wastes with enough loot to have lived in comfort for many years, and yet they were dying because they could not feed themselves.

It was a grim, ironic touch.

They had found the gold and jewels buried in lost mines of Ophir far back in the mountains. Now they had been trekking over the desert for five days, and their food and water had gradually diminished until their supply had become completely exhausted.

It was small wonder that some of the men had almost gone mad. Yet the gold and precious stones had saved their lives so far, for it had kept them going with dreams of what it would buy for them once they reached civilization.

NATIVES HAD DRIVEN them out of the mountains, into the desert. A trail of blood stretched away behind them. The knapsacks of those who had fallen had not been emptied, but had been left on their lifeless scorched bodies—as though to buy passage into the Here-after. The others had no need of this surplus wealth and those loaded knap-sacks would only prove to be an added burden.

"We'll buy the place with gold," Clive told himself, as he headed down into the lost oasis, "if they won't feed us, give us water, and show us a place to sleep!"

Out of the waving palms came a strange sound. The little band stopped to listen to it. They panted like spent runners, the tips of their tongues pro-truding from their blackened, cracked lips. The sound they heard was a blaring blast from some strange trumpet. Clive had heard it before, several times in his life, among the lost tribes of Africa's interior.

It was like a trumpet of a ram's horn.

It made one think of long-haired pa-triarchs.

NOW IT WAS a warning. It called a tribe together, to take counsel against the newcomers. It was a blast of menace, for Clive could see men running. There were eyes in the houses which he knew to be doors. And as the trumpet sounded its strange and eerie message across the hot sands, the eyes closed. The doors had been slammed. He knew they had been bolted from inside, that the houses had indeed become fortresses.

And then—utter silence, relieved only by the whispering of a rising wind across the sand, wind which lifted the sand's surface in little scurrying, lacy mantles of silt which stung the nostrils, blurred the eyes, and whispered into the ears of terror to come. In an hour the

Malone's rifle cracked and the tortured man fell to the ground.

desert would be a raging Hell of flying sand in which nothing could live. The little band had beached the oasis just in time.

"Unsling your rifles!" ordered Clive hoarsely. "I don't know what we're running into. They don't seem to like us."

Then he deployed his seven remaining men, eight including himself, and ordered the advance. His men were like figures on some strange mad frieze as they moved down the whispering slope into the oasis.

THE OASIS GREW as they advanced. Its extent was far greater than it had seemed to be at first. Trees seemed to rise out of folds in the depression floor.

Houses materialized out of other houses, as though some had been hiding behind others.

And then, across the waste, came the thin barking of a rifle. But before the sound had reached them, Orra Rubin, the hardiest of Clive's followers, had plunged, rubber—legged, into the sand, burying his face in it as Nash had done.

His skull was a gory mess—and Clive knew that he was dealing with perfect marksmen. What was he to do?

If he retreated, his men would die in the sand. If he went on, they would be sniped off one by one by these people who didn't bother to ask why they came.

He came to a swift decision and spoke tersely:

"Scatter as you advance. Run a zigzag course. Fire from the hip as you go. Maybe it'll make them keep their heads down until we can reach some sort of shelter."

Even as he spoke, Sherman Clive ducked.

He had caught the glint of the sun on a rifle barrel. He ducked just in time.

He heard a bullet crack as it sped past his ears. Had he not moved he would certainly have died as did the others.

Now the little band was running. Men that were half dead on their feet, and nearly insane from lack of water and food, were forcing themselves to make their bodies move because life depended on their running. And the thin crackling of rifles spat across the narrowing waste between the band and the hidden oasis.

Clive looked back. The horizon had

Sherman Clive

crept down close to the sand so that he could not see how deep the depression was by the height of the sand walls they were descending. No wonder this place was hidden from the world. Men might hunt for it, even in airplanes, for days and weeks on end, and never find it.

He had heard of lost oases of the desert such as this. Places inhabited by warlike tribesmen who guarded their secret dwellings from the eyes of the world. To approach within miles was dangerous, for usually the fierce tribes dealt swiftly and ruthlessly with strangers. Yet secretly these people retained their contacts with the outside world. **OFTEN CAMEL CARAVANS** trekked across the Sahara carrying food and supplies

Gloria Drake

teeth, shouted again to his men to zigzag. He refused to look at Jonas, and the spurting crimson which gushed from his throat.

Bullets came thick and fast now. The rifles of the six who still lived to charge, grew hotter under their hands, though they were already like the tops of stoves from the blasting heat of the sun.

They gained the first of the trees, under which rose the stone ramparts of a well. They gathered behind the rampart of stone. Clive lifted his head to peer in. Even as he did so, a slab of stone slid out the side of the well, several fell down, and shut out his view of the life-saving water that he had glimpsed far below. And for a moment he almost went mad.

for an unnamed destination, finally to vanish. Only the tall dark-faced men with such caravans knew that they would eventually reach a lost oasis.

Luck was with Clive and his men that they had found this lost oasis, but whether they could get what they wanted there, namely water, depended entirely upon themselves. It was a mad thing they tried, but it would have been madder not to have dared it.

MARK JONAS WENT down the next moment with a slug in his throat. Clive tried to analyze the make of the enemy rifles by the sound. He decided that they were Mannlichers, savage weapons which would knock a man down at an unbelievable range. He gritted his

CHAPTER II

GRIM M'TAB

HERE WAS WATER, almost within reach, yet it might as well have been as far away as the moon. Clive understood the reason for the slab of stone. At times, often several times weekly, the air became so filled with flying sand, as the wind whipped savagely across the wastes, that oases became mere spots of color through the murk, and wells were filled with sand as though they were containers for the flying sand. This, then, was the answer of the people of this grim town to the sands of the desert.

They closed the top parts of their wells, and after the sandstorms had passed, all they had to do was remove the sand from inside the well tops.

"That means," said Clive to himself, "that there are passageways below ground by which the natives reach the wells during the storms. What fortresses these houses are!"

He stared away to the grim fronts of the houses. A rifle cracked. Stone dust, acrid as gunpowder in his nostrils, splashed in his face from the rock rampart, where the bullet had struck. It went whining off into the desert. Clive sat back. He stared at his men.

A M'Tabite

"Keep down," he said. "I don't see any way just now to reach the houses or the water in the wells, certainly not by daylight. We'll wait for darkness, hope that there is no moon, and make a try for it."

Up spoke one, Michael Strawn.

"I'm dying of thirst," he said, his voice a harsh babble. "I'm going to make a run for it. If I get shot it's better than another day under the burning sun. I'll get close enough, maybe, to beg for mercy for the others, for a drop of water—"

Clive had no chance to dissuade the man, for he was gone even before he had finished speaking. His words had sounded as though his voice had been a busy rasp.

Sherman Clive and his men watched the man go, running, his rifle against his hip. Bullets began to come out of the grim houses, kicking up the sand at his feet, as though the marksmen made sport of the running man. He shouted as he ran:

"Water, for the love of God!"

It was a prayer that was strangely answered. A dozen bullets must have smashed into Strawn's charging body. Clive could feel each one of them as it struck, against his own heart. He had been through much with these men. And the natives behind their fortress-like houses did not finish when they had killed the man. They sent bullets into his body, so that it jumped and jerked with them.

THE BEST OF THRILLING ADVENTURES

Clark Malone

CLIVE CAUGHT THE glint of a rifle barrel, spotted a loophole high up on one of the buildings. He had never aimed faster in his life, but had never been more careful with his aiming. He knew that his bullet sped through that tiny hole, a shot he could not have made in other circumstances.

Two feet of a rifle barrel suddenly shot through the hole. The muzzle of the piece tipped upward, as though the man at its other end had released his grip on the heavy stock, and its weight had pressed the butt downward. A thin cheer rose from the five men left with Clive.

It had been a good shot.

Now there came a sortie. A score of men in white garments which made them look like women, save that their faces were bearded blackly, came out of a thin alley, between two houses, spreading out as they came. Their rifles, at their hips, spoke savagely. Their bullets smashed against the rampart of the well.

"Aim carefully," said Sherman Clive, his grey eyes narrowed intently. "Make each shot count."

The rifles of the beleaguered spoke. Four men crashed whitely into the sand, seemed to mingle with it, and lay still. The others came on. The rifles spoke again. Four more went down. The others yelled savage defiance, turned and ran. Calmly, Clive drove a bullet into one just as he would have turned a corner and vanished.

It was a good shot, too. The man fell backward, hurling his rifle over his head, and his torso showed from around the corner of a building. His black beard moved in the wind which crept over the wastes and howled down into the sandy depression.

"They won't," said Clive, "try that again soon."

"Think not?" said short, stumpy Clark Malone, bravest of those who were left with Clive. "They have plenty, and with each charge, though they lose five men, they kill one of us. In five charges they will have us all."

Clive was thoughtful for a moment.

"I'll ask for a parley," he said at last. He took a dirty handkerchief from his pocket, lifted it above the well. Firing ceased. Someone in authority had seen the signal. There was a long hush, pregnant with suspense. Then a door was opened.

Malone flung up his rifle, cuddling the stock against his cheek. Clive pushed the rifle aside. "Don't," he said. It's the emissary."

The white-garbed man came stalking proudly across the sand, straight for the well. He carried a white cloth on a stick. He was immune to bullets as long as he carried it. Clive watched him come, his eyes alight for treachery, roaming over the faces of the walls. He wouldn't rise to meet the messenger. A bullet would cut him down, of that he was sure. The man circled the rampart, squatted among them. His black eyes took note of their number and condition. Clive addressed him in Arabic.

"What hospitality is this?" he demanded. "We come out of the desert asking for water, and are met with bullets. We can buy what we wish. Sell to us and we shall go on our way."

"You have money?"

CLIVE HESITATED. IF he showed his hand, they might never allow him to buy anything. Why should they, when all they had to do was slay and take what they wished? Then he shrugged. What good was all this wealth if they died?

He opened the top of his own knapsack. It was crammed with implements of pure gold, with precious stones spilling out of the tops of vases. The man licked his lips.

"Where did you get this?" he asked.

"From storehouses of wealth no man has ever, before us, been able to penetrate—from the lost mines of Ophir. It is worth a fabulous amount in the marts of the world. This is what is left of my band, which I gathered together in Cairo for the trek to Ophir. See, we have riches enough to purchase all that you have in—what is the name of this place?"

"Know you not that this is M'Tab?"

"I KNOW OF no such place. I have heard of a lost oasis peopled by the descendants of fanatical thieves of centuries ago, driven into the desert from Alexandria. Perhaps they founded M'Tab? I did not know of it. I did not seek this place, but only water, and food—"

"And you did not come to rescue the daughter of Cory Drake?"

Clive's mouth hung open. The color drained out of his cheeks. His eyes were wide with horror. His hands clenched suddenly, until the nails bit into his palms.

"What did you say? The daughter of Cory Drake? Is her given name Gloria?" Clive felt that it was all part of a mad dream. To even hear the name of Cory Drake here was impossible—and as for the girl—that just couldn't be. And yet he had to know.

"Is her name Gloria?" he croaked again.

The face of the M'Tabite became suddenly a mask of cunning. His red lips writhed into a smile.

"You know of her, then? How can you know of her and not come to her rescue if you be of her race?"

Clive's face hardened.

"I know nothing of her," he said grimly. "But I have seen the name in the papers of my country. I did not know she was here. I come with my men merely for water. Go and tell the one who sent you that we have gold enough to purchase all we need—that we will forget those whom he has slain, and go on about our business, because we have slain enough to balance the account."

The man grinned. His black eyes darted from knapsack to knapsack. As he stared at each one, and saw how tightly filled it was, his eyes grew brighter still, and he licked his lips each time. Then he grasped his flag of truce and went stalking back over the sand to the nearest door, the one by which he had come forth to speak with them.

For many moments after he had vanished there came no sound from the grim houses of M'Tab. The dying men held their breaths, awaiting the decisions of the elders of M'Tab. The answer, when it came, was what Sherman Clive had expected.

The parley had merely helped to pass a little time. Bullets came out of many portholes again, to whang against the stones and go ricocheting off into space. The little band was panting, its tongues still hanging out. Their eyes were red rimmed and bleary.

"For God's sake, Clive," said Malone, "let's charge and get it over with. I can't stand much more. I can't wait until darkness, when we won't have much more chance of reaching the houses. And even if we do, how are we to enter?

If they can close their wells, they can close their houses, too, so that not even a battering ram could get past them." CLIVE'S VOICE WAS hoarse and harsh as he answered. "Wait!"

"I'm going to make a try," Malone persisted.

"Try," whispered Clive, "and I'll shoot you down with my own hand!"

Malone cursed and sat back. The others sprawled on the sand. The wind was not high, but in a few minutes it had covered their reclining bodies with a thin layer of dust. In two days it would bury them from sight, as many people had been buried beneath the desert sands.

The sun crawled into the afternoon sky, and was as brazen and cruel as ever. Clive was thinking. Some of his men had their eyes closed, as though they hoped thus to await the passing of time with greater comfort.

Clive resolved to make another try at the well. Now and again overhead passing bullets served as simple warnings to the suffering ones to keep their heads down. Clive wondered if he could get into the well curb without being hit. ON THE POINT of trying it, he heard a thumping sound, of rock against rock. It came out of the well!

With a leap, regardless of consequences, Clive rose, plunged into the circular cup of rock, landing on the flat slab which was just below the normal level of the land about the well. His feet told him that the rock was several inches thick, would have held many times his weight. He removed his pistol, tapped on the rock with its muzzle.

The thumping of rock against rock, below, ceased at the sound—and a voice that was surprisingly clear came up, around the rock. "Who are you?"

It was a voice he would never forget this side of the grave! It was the voice he loved, the voice of the woman whose father's refusal to accept him had sent him, desperate, on the mission to Ophir—the voice of Gloria Drake!

Gloria's voice—and yet he could not believe it. It was some weird trick of the imagination. Even since he had talked to the messenger from the M'Tabite he had refused to believe that their holding this girl of all girls in the world was actually possible. It just could not be!

Still, he had recognized the voice, that voice that he knew better than all others. But how could Gloria Drake be here in this lost oasis far out in the desert?

"Gloria!" he shouted half-fearfully. "Gloria Drake!"

"Yes—that's my name," came back across the rock. "Who are you?"

"Sherman Clive!" he shouted, his voice cracking because he had been so long without water. "It's Sherman, Gloria!"

"Oh, thank God!" she called.

CHAPTER III

DEVIL AND THE DEEP

IN THAT INSTANT Sherman Clive forgot all that had happened to him since this girl's father, a snobbish, ambitious governor of a great state, had told him he didn't amount to much, certainly not enough to marry his daughter, whose social position must be considered. Clive didn't know that he blamed the governor, for it was whispered in political circles that he was in line for the Presidency of the United States, and men of such importance must take thought for the future of their children.

But why was she here?

He shouted down to her, asking the question.

"I ran away," she replied. "I couldn't stand the man father wanted me to marry, so I booked passage on a world cruise. When the ship reached Algiers I came ashore with some of the party. A guide took us to a lonely spot on the outskirts of the city. They must have learned that I was the daughter of a rich man—for I became separated from the others—then kidnaped and brought here by these M'Tabites, who had been disguised as Tauregs."

So! Thus had Gloria's flight to freedom, ended. But what a strange way to encounter him, here in this land the world had forgotten for centuries— this land which the world fed without knowing that it did.

And here and now he and Gloria were as far apart as the width of a desert— though three inches of stone were all that separated them—as far apart as the distance between the cradle and the grave.

"What have they done to you?" Clive shouted down at her.

"Nothing, I have the run of the houses, because they don't believe I'm strong enough to escape across the desert. But, Sherm—"

"Yes," he called, when she seemed hesitant to continue.

"If my father does not answer immediately, if there is any delay beyond a certain date they have set, I am to be given to the Ouled Nails—"

His heart thudded into his boots. Well he knew the fate of a woman cast among the Ouled Nails, that queer sect of women which lived somewhere outside the gates of M'Tab. If any Ouled Nail pleased any guest of the M'Tabs, that guest might buy her out of M'Tab as a slave—and then she would vanish off the face of the earth.

His heart was suddenly cold in his breast. He sat back against the rocky curb.

BULLETS SMASHED ACROSS the well-top in a steady stream. The M'Tabites had seen him dive into the well, but not soon enough to splatter him with bullets. But when he tried to get out again—!

The thickness of the curb separated him from his men. He didn't know what they would do without his counsel. They were already madmen. With his loss they might all race into the storm of bullets and die.

He could hear them swearing hoarsely. He had a duty to them. He had a duty to the girl whose voice had come out of the pit to him.

He was separated from both, from one by bullets, from the other by the stone lid of the well.

Then he heard a scream come shrilling out of the pit.

"Sherm! Sherm! Get out! They've caught me. You'll be dropped into the well!"

Her voice died away. Brutal laughter, coming from below, almost drove him mad with anxiety. It sounded, as they dragged her away, as though they were raining blows upon her. His teeth grated savagely as he realized his helplessness.

And then—

The stone under him began slowly to move! It slid back into the niche from which it had first slipped out to cover the well, and beneath him, far down, he could see the black surface of the precious water, like a winking eye of ebony. It was far, far down.

The laughter showed him the desperation of his situation. If he remained where he was until the rock slid entirely into its niche, he would fall into the well. The depth was enough to kill him unless he fell straight, without touching the sides. But what then? He would die in the water. He would have enough of water, but it was too much to hope that the M'Tabites would spare him.

HE THOUGHT OF grasping the edge of the stone and swinging himself down under it, into the passage he knew must lead from the houses to the well. But they would be thinking of that—and their bullets would riddle his body as he swung, or he would swing against the myriad blades of their knives.

Bullets crackled over his head with added intensity. The enemy knew, of course, that if he chanced a dive out of the well pit, their bullets would get him; that if he stayed where he was he would die in the well, by bullets, or by the knife.

The rock ledge on which he crouched was narrower now. They were moving it with torturing slowness. They appreciated the situation in which he had placed himself. And how did Gloria feel, since she must surely know that but for her signals to him he would never have considered making himself a prisoner in the well pit?

THE SITUATION WAS grim enough for anyone—to say nothing of a man already half dead from lack of water. The odor of water came up to him now, and his whole soul cried out for it. Why not, he asked himself, drop into the well? At least he would have water. Let death come afterward, and he would meet it happily. And, but for his men, he might have done just that. But he couldn't leave his men—and he couldn't desert Gloria Drake.

What would Governor Drake do? The stern old man would probably contact someone in Cairo or Alexandria, demanding investigations, punitive expeditions. What if he refused to pay ransom, or doubted the authenticity of the demand and delayed too long? Clive knew very well what that would mean—and several times during his sojourn in this land he had heard of the Ouled Nails—for there were Ouled Nails among other tribes which the world knew.

There were other things about them he knew. They were loyal to their masters. Often those masters gave them prisoners to be tortured. They were women who knew how to use the blades of knives under men's fingernails, how to work the greatest agony with fire, how to mutilate men until they cried aloud to their gods for death to relieve them of their suffering.

More and more he thought of the horror of the Ouled Nails—and the stone ledge now was scarcely wide enough for him to stand on, his head bent over so that it wouldn't show above the well curb. Bullets were still clearing the top of the curb, a literal roof of them, each one potent enough to smash off the top of a man's head. Now and again one hit the side of the curb opposite where Clive stood, and ricocheted down into the well, caroming back and forth from side to side. If one of those bullets ever hit him it would rip him apart.

And now the M'Tabites' sense of cruelty gave them a new thought, something else by which to torture him. Bullets came out of the passage, slanting upward at an angle, to strike against the side of the well across from him, up through the aperture between the edge of the slab of stone and the wall of the well.

"They're bound to get me," he told himself, for, their intention was all too plain. "I've got to take a chance. There isn't any chance to go down. I've got, somehow, to go up!"

NOW THE LEDGE of stone was just wide enough for his feet. Soon his toes would project over it, and he would then be a direct target for their bullets. And the ricochets from the opposite side of the well were coming all too close. One splattered piece of lead fell between his feet. He had to spread his toes apart, heels together, to keep them from showing—and becoming targets for bullets. He could no longer lean over to keep his head from showing above the curb, for he would overbalance and go plummeting down to the far water below.

"I'll be hanged if I'll let them have the last laugh," he assured himself.

But there was no cessation in the firing. Something had to be done in the next few seconds. The stone ledge moved again. It moved just a little. The M'Tabites were toying with him as a cat plays with a mouse. They were enjoying his desperation. All the cards were in their hands. Soon there would be so little left of the ledge that he would not be able to leap from it.

But to leap—and be struck by a score of bullets—what would happen to Gloria then?

HE CLOSED HIS eyes. He almost prayed, not for himself, but for his men, and for the woman who was prisoner of the M'Tabites, somewhere among their well tunnels and their houses which were grim and terrible fortresses. Even as he prayed he fancied he could hear, over beyond the houses of M'Tab the brittle laughter of the Ouled Nails. In fancy he could see knives tucked in their gaudy dresses, awaiting their grim tasks of torture for prisoners taken alive.

Sherman Clive stooped as far as he dared. His eyes now were fixed on the opposite side of the rampart. He straightened. He put all his waning strength into the leap. He felt bullets snick through his garments. He felt a bullet strike the heel of one of his heavy boots. It almost numbed his foot. But he was curling over the edge of the well. Bullets seemed to be tearing past him to the left, to the right, and over him. It seemed incredible that some did not strike him—for a dozen at least had gone through his clothing.

But he struck the sand, rolled to a sitting position, and stared stupidly at his men. They were sprawled as he had left them. Their plight, with their black tongues and cracked lips, their heat-crazed eyes, reminded him of his own torture for lack of water.

"Quickly," he said, "all your knapsack straps. Fasten them together. Give me the largest knapsack!"

They worked savagely, with fingers which trembled as with ague. Soon he had a strap a hundred feet long. Unloosed knapsacks spilled some of their treasures in the sand, so that it glistened in the sun Clive hurled the one knapsack over the curb, paid out the strap at top speed. He felt the knapsack strike the water, far below.

He raised and lowered it twice—then all hands grasped the strap, pulled lustily, upwards. Clive held his breath. The knapsack, which wouldn't hold water, would hold enough moisture to wet the lips of them all, give them a new lease on life.

Then he heard the slab of stone slide again into place. The strap had caught. He knew that the slab had closed, imprisoning the life-giving knapsack below it—as inaccessible as the water in the well.

CHAPTER IV

THE OULED NAILS

BUT THERE WAS moisture in some of the strap which had been dragged over the lip of the well. Clive felt pity for his men as they fell upon the strap as though they were starving, dogs, in search of a bone. They licked at it with dry tongues. They moaned over the drops of moisture which clung to it.

And out of the pit came the laughter of the M'Tabties, as though they had been able to see everything. What a place of horror was M'Tab!

Clive was beginning to think that it would have been better for them all had they died without ever seeing the ghastly place—out in the desert. But then, what would have happened to Gloria Drake? Of course, had he died before reaching M'Tab, he would never have known that she had come to Africa, stumbled by chance into M'Tab, to a strange meeting with the one man who, of all the world, wanted most to see her—but never in such ghastly surroundings as this!

THE BLISTERING SUN was now sinking behind the mountain of sand to the west. That mountain's shadow was crawling like some evil black monster out across the lost oasis, as though it moved forward to spring upon the unfortunate ones at the well.

Clive watched it come. When darkness settled finally over M'Tab they must make their bid for safety.

The M'Tabites knew what they were planning. They could not have helped it. They made no more sorties, did not ask for parleys, but they kept bullets humming over and past the position of Clive and his men, bidding them keep their heads down. For five hours, at least, Clive had not answered their shots, nor had he permitted his men to do so.

The shadow came closer. The sun had left a blazing shimmer of light at the crest of the mountainous dune. And then, in a flash, as an electric light is snicked off, day had vanished and night had settled over the desert, had swallowed up M'Tab.

"It will happen soon," said Clive.

The others stirred, answered him, each in his fashion. One swore softly at length, for ten minutes, without repeating himself. One prayed. Another laughed immoderately. Clive clapped his hand over the mouth of this one, to still his laughter. In the clear air his laughter would travel far. They had not shown themselves, or fired their rifles, for there was a bare possibility that the M'Tabites thought them dead.

"They're coming," said Malone. "Look, see their white clothing against the sand. They're crawling out to us."

With their stomachs against the sand Clive's men watched the approach of the scouting party. There were seven in the party, they noticed. They crawled through the sand like so many snakes, blending with it so perfectly that only the keen eyes of Malone had been able to pick them out—and they were halfway to the well before even Malone had seen them.

Clive, with his heart in his mouth, watched them come.

When they were close, he whispered to his men.

"Sprawl out, pretend to be dead. When they look down at us, each of you pick your man and down him!"

It seemed a forlorn hope. They watched their attackers come on. Now and again the M'Tabites paused, listening. They lifted their heads, but kept their faces down to hide their swart cheeks and black beards. Then they came on. No bullets had been fired. So tense were those who waited, they had forgotten, almost, their suffering. On came the M'Tabites.

Now one of them dared greatly—he rose to his feet. His left hand grasped a rifle. With his right hand he beckoned to the others, when, after a proper interval, no shots came from behind the well. The seven rose. Still Clive and his men did not fire. The seven came on.

THE WHITE MEN sprawled out, but Clive could feel them, tense in every muscle as they waited for the storm to break.

"Remember," he whispered, "get their throats first, before they can possibly cry out And you mustn't miss. Use your knives. Stab to the heart with everything you've got. We should get three in the first scrimmage. Then drag the others down and kill them behind the curb. Don't dare miss!"

Clive himself sprawled on his back. The first of the M'Tabites stood and looked down at them. He prodded Malone with the butt of his rifle, then kicked him in the side. And Malone grunted with the pain! Instantly the white men hurled themselves at the knees of the enemy. Knives rose and fell.

Three figures, four, sprawled out in the sand. Then the others were dragged down before even one could cry out—and savage, ruthless hands darted to their throats. It was all over in a moment.

"NOW," SAID CLIVE hoarsely, "their burnooses, or whatever those white clothes are. Wrap 'em around you, even to your heads, but keep your rifles in your hands. They may notice that only six of us come from behind the well, when there were seven who came around it."

Quickly the desperate men complied.

"Now," said Clive, "rise and shine. We'll march straight for the nearest building, understand? They may suspect us, but they won't fire on us for fear they may be wrong. Ready?" The answers, eager, hopeful, were in the affirmative. The six men rose from behind the well.

"Don't stagger," said Clive, "or they'll be sure to know. And those of us who don't speak Arabic will have to keep our mouths shut should they challenge us."

Clive started across the sand toward the nearest building as he spoke. No bullets were fired at them, but the walls of the houses were like frowning faces in the dim moonlight—moonlight which was dim only because a night wind had sprinkled the sky above the oasis with fine sand. The six marched straight across.

They were halfway to the first house, which Clive speculated must surely be the house connecting with the well behind whose curb they had spent the most terrible hours of their lives—when a thin cry, as of a man in mortal terror, rose from somewhere beyond the houses, Clive's men swore, then choked their words short. Malone moved close against Clive.

"It's the Ouled Nails," he whispered, "They're torturing somebody."

Clive stiffened. There had been something familiar in the scream of the unknown. Muffled of voice, as though the man had screamed through clenched teeth, Clive had been almost sure of the one word that had seemed intelligible in the scream:

"God!"

The M'Tabites might believe in God, but they did not call Him by that name. And now came another sound—the strange purling sound of tired camels, and Clive knew that some caravan or other had come into M'Tab from beyond the houses. He spoke softly to Malone.

"We'll circle the building, unless we're fired on," he said. "I want to know what that is—and the Ouled Nails must have food and water. With, food and drink we can go ahead, do anything."

They were not challenged, though they could feel hostile, suspicious eyes probing through them, following their every movement. They reached the building. Clive sighed with relief.

IT WAS DOUBTFUL if the loopholes in the buildings were such that men inside could fire directly down at them.

Without being furtive, they kept close to the grim grey walls, reached the alley out of which, that midday, the sortie had come and been driven back, Into the alley they stepped, marching toward a rectangle of light at the other end.

Then they understood something that had perplexed them before. They had been puzzled over the fact that M'Tab, ordinarily a walled city, had given them no walls to scale. And now the reason became apparent.

The wall on the side by which they had approached M'Tab was imbedded in the sand. The Ouled Nails, Clive reflected as he tried to recall what he knew of them, were kept outside the walls. And now he could hear laughter, cruel, diabolic laughter, beyond the walls ahead.

THE SIX STRODE to that wall, unchallenged. They had a break. For only the men in the house directly opposite the well had stayed awake to keep an eye on them. The rest of M'Tab had retired to its rest. They looked over the wall—and into a tent of pagans!

In one vast tent which faced M'Tab, around a fire, were a dozen women. They wore spangles on their ankles and wrists, strange pieces of cloth about their heads. They were brown of skin—girls who would have been beautiful, perhaps, in other surroundings. But now they were imps of Satan, if ever the imps of Satan were women.

For after the manner of their kind they were entertaining M'Tabites who must have reached the city on the half-dozen camels which purled in the shadows beyond the tent.

And what a mode of entertainment! Bound, with his back to the center pole of the tent, was a gaunt white man, his body bare to the waist. Around him, laughing their brittle laughter, in which a dozen squatting M'Tabites joined, swayed the Ouled Nails. One carried a shining dagger in her hand. One carried a burning brand from the fire.

The one with the dagger stepped in. The man screamed as the point of the weapon touched the left side of his abdomen, slid across to the right. And down from the wound in his stomach, in plain view of Clive and his men, dropped the red of his life blood!

The Ouled Nails laughed. The M'Tabites laughed. Certainly this was a place of horror. M'Tabites in the town did not even lose sleep when some prisoner was tortured, did not even mind his screams! Only these dozen who had come from outside, and sought to forget their fatigue by watching a stranger put to the torture.

And now the girl with the burning brand stepped up to the man. She thrust her hand forward—held the flaming torch close under his eyes. His head went back, cracking audibly against the pole.

And then, right beside Clive, a rifle cracked. He whirled on Malone.

"Malone," he said, "you don't shoot women, even that kind!"

"I know," said Malone quietly. "I merely shot the torch out of her hand. It is lucky for the man being tortured that he was in the line of fire! What man would want to live without eyes, even if he could have lived had we been able to rescue him? And now, I suppose, we are in for it!"

"I suppose," said Clive grimly, "we are!"

Suddenly, with shouts of surprise and anger, the men in the tents, the Ouled Nails, and the M'Tabites in the silent-walled town, came to life in the night—filling the darkness with a bedlam of sound dominated by the strange obscene *burblings* of the evil-tempered camels.

CHAPTER V

EVERY MAN FOR HIMSELF

SHERMAN CLIVE SPOKE quickly to his men.

"It's every man for himself. They'll scatter, hunting us. Their doors will be open. Get into the first houses you can. Keep away from lights. Three hours from now we'll meet behind the tent of the Ouled Nails. Find some way to reach the water in the wells. Get food wherever you can. Kill only to save your lives. Do the best you can for yourselves. Scatter, now!"

His men vanished like white wraiths into the darkness which possessed M'Tab. Clive felt very much alone. He slid easily over the wall. In all this confusion of noise and movement he had no fear that he would be picked out immediately. He carried his rifle under his burnoose, straight up and down against his right leg, so that its shape would not show against the cloth.

HE WAS CURIOUS to see what the Ouled Nails had done to the white man Malone had mercifully slain. He was a little sorry that the Ouled Nails directly responsible had not been killed. But they merely did what they were supposed to do. They could not be blamed for acting as they did.

His men were gone. Their fate now was in the lap of the gods. His feet slogged through the sand. He had selected the garments of a tall man, so that the flowing robe hid his foreign boots. His main task, after making sure of the fate of the white man who had undergone torture, was to find Gloria Drake.

His heart was heavy. The girl was somewhere among the grim houses of M'Tab. And by tomorrow, or the next day at the very latest, news would come from Drake, in answer to the demand for ransom. Clive thought he knew what it would be. Drake, would never be able to realize the plight his daughter was in. He would think it some situation out of a story book.

And the fate of Gloria would be sealed.

White robed figures were gathering about the tent of the Ouled Nails, whose flap had been lowered. But there was light against the cloth of the tent still— and even as he noted this the light went out. Out of the tent came the startled screams of the Ouled Nails. If a man were to be lost among them now his tortures would be ghastly.

Clive hurried away from the tent and ducked into the shadows. It was easy, so far, but he knew that a glimpse of his foreign boots, or a sight of his white face, would betray him to the M'Tabites and the dreadful ministrations of the Ouled Nails.

He strode back toward M'Tab. Many of the strange people passed him. They didn't notice him, though one spoke, asking him a question. But he did not have to answer, for the man's fellows bore him along in their midst so that he could not wait—and to the man the whole thing seemed natural enough.

"Now for the shack where Gloria is," thought Clive.

He traveled down the alley by which they had reached the wall, the alley from which the sortie had come this morning—and stepped out into the open just as the moon shone brightly upon M'Tab. Again luck was with him, for the whole open space was empty of a living soul. Nowhere could he see a figure that looked even remotely like one of his own men.

THE DOOR OF the house in which he knew he had killed one man was open. He made for it. He stepped inside as though the place belonged to him. Far back in the building he saw a light surrounded only by women. He knew what that meant. No M'Tabite man must ever look upon the face of another man's wife. If he were caught watching them now he would be torn limb from limb.

He ducked into the shadows, circling the wall of the room, toward the spot where he knew there must be a way

*Instantly the white men hurled themselves
at the knees of the enemy.*

leading to the well-tunnel. He had not been heard. The M'Tabite women were clucking among themselves like startled chickens. But he knew the power of these women for destruction. They would tear him apart if they discovered him.

Now he came to a door. It was set in the face of the wall at an angle, the top tilted back into the wall. Clive studied it. The tunnel must lead downward at an angle. He fumbled for the lock of the door. It was an iron hasp. He found it, tried to ease it open without making a noise.

HE MANAGED THE lock, but the door squeaked audibly when he swung it back. Startled exclamations came from the women. He could hear them running toward the source of the sound, which must be as familiar to them as the sound of the voices of their own families. He entered quickly, knowing that he jeopardized his life, for when they saw the swinging hasp they would know that someone was in the tunnel.

But inside, in total pitch darkness, he hurled himself forward. He estimated the distance, knowing he might step into the well before he discovered exactly where it was. Then, when he knew he had but a few feet to go, he dropped to his knees and inched forward, feeling his way with his hands. Then he was aware that his rifle was missing.

Behind him sounded the chattering of the women, who appeared to be in mad pursuit. Now his fingers touched the edge of the well. He fumbled around him. He found a bucket, to which a rope was attached. He lowered it swiftly over the side.

"I'll drink with all their fingers at my throat if I have to," he declared to himself grimly. "But drink I will!"

The rope paid out. He glanced upward, to see that the slab of stone had been slid back, that the way out was open. But he didn't know where to find the mechanism which worked it. Perhaps the women would show him that.

The bucket came out of the well with savage, vicious jerks. The women were very close now.

He had the bucket in his hands. He darted deeper into the tunnel, pressed himself hard against its side, hoping that the women would pass him, unnoticed, for the tunnel was wide enough for four men to march along it abreast. He tilted the bucket and drank—and the water was like the nectar of the gods! He spilled it down his neck and cried out, silently, and deep inside him, for the very joy in the water's caress. He poured the remainder into his clothing, knowing that by this time his men must also have found water.

Then he hurled the bucket into the well, so that the women would hear "it clatter against the rocks and think that he was somewhere there, pulling on it.

He had to outguess them if he were not to be captured and submitted to their fury.

Now the women dashed past him, headed for the well. There were four women. They stood close together, peering into the water. A splash had sounded there. He fervently hoped they would think he had fallen in. Then he saw a skinny arm upraised, and knew that the mechanism had been touched which closed the slab of stone.

THEN HE ACTED. He threw himself forward. He grabbed at the women with both hands, pushing them aside to keep from hurling them into the well.

The cover was closing. While the women screamed he leaped outward, over the deep well, his palms turned backward to grasp at the edge of stone. His fingers caught and held, tenaciously. With the same movement he shot his legs upward—happy that water had given him renewed strength—and pulled himself onto the stone just in time. In another instant it would have closed on him, trapped him.

He had made it at exactly the right moment.

He wasted no time. He hurled himself out of the well-pit, onto the sands, where the seven M'Tabites he and his men had killed lay still.

The knapsacks of the white men were scattered on the sand. The M'Tabites had run toward the fray before the tent of the Ouled Nails. They had not yet come up to see what had happened behind the well. Quickly Sherman Clive gathered up the knapsacks, a heavy load for one man, and deliberately started back toward the houses of M'Tab. SOMETHING HAD TO be done about his treasures. It would be maddening to see them lost to the M'Tabites. Clive was determined that this should not happen.

Back into the alley he went, and over the wall, en route to the camels. And there, among the duffel which their owners had not yet had time to store in places of safety, he hid the knapsacks whose weight had almost wrenched his arms from their sockets.

Then someone saw him and screamed. He ran back toward the wall.

Bullets whined over his head, but he gave them no heed.

His eyes were lifted to the roofs of the houses.

He reached the alley untouched. There were windows in the backs and sides of the houses. He leaped into the embrasure of the first, and from that, without pausing, into the second

From this, a mighty leap brought his fingers to the roof. He pulled himself over, panting—and knew that he was in forbidden territory, the roof where only women were permitted in M'Tab.

CHAPTER VI

GLORIA

FROM OUT OF the house below him, as he stood erect on the roof, invisible to anyone below because of the narrow coping which protected the roof, came the chattering of women. They were coming up to see what was happening. The house was like a hive of bees. Clive darted into the shadow of what seemed to be a chimney, fervently hoping that it hid him from possible detection, for if it did not, he would have to take a flying leap off the place to save himself.

A broken leg might result from that—and sure capture in the end. Three women came out of an opening onto the roof, moving directly to the coping to peer down at confused M'Tab. Down there rifles were banging, men were shouting. The women watched everything, and even on the roof, where men could not see them, their faces were covered.

But Clive would have known the form of Gloria Drake, even enrobed in a burnoose. Besides, he could see the hair of the women, and quite plainly now for the moon bathed the whole desert in its soothing lemonish glow. He noted the tilt of the head of each woman, the shape of her headdress, the way she moved her body, her hands. Gloria was not among these, nor had he seen her among the women in the room from where he had escaped into the tunnel.

He wondered for a moment what had happened to his men. He had heard no shouts in English. He was certain that they would have cried out warnings to their fellows if captured or fired upon. He felt he could assume that all were still free, and that they had managed, as he had, to find water. If he could have been munching on anything resembling food now, his happiness would have been complete, for he was free to find the woman who had jeopardized her safety, perhaps even her life, to journey into the wastes.

He must look elsewhere for Gloria. The women seemed to be busy looking down into M'Tab. Clive, never taking his eyes off them, bent and removed his boots. Tomorrow, if he went into the sands, his feet would be burned to a crisp, but tonight footfalls of heavy boots might be fatal.

Now, barefooted, he ran across the roof behind the women—utterly without sound. Adjacent to this house was another roof. All roofs were masked from view by high walls across the fronts of the houses of M'Tab. There was danger of discovery from that direction. Every roof seemed to be filled with women. Clive did a mad, desperate thing. He ran along the top of the next roof. The women did not look back, for centuries their roofs had been inviolate—and they did not even conjecture that men would dare invade their ancient privacy.

CLIVE, AS HE ran, studied the backs of the women, seeking Gloria. The second roof was negotiated without mishap, and the third. Then—standing slightly back from the wall, over which several women were leaning, he saw her.

His lips shaped her name;

"Gloria!"

It was almost as though she had heard his whisper, for she turned as though she listened and he saw the contour of her face against the moon. There was no doubt now. He started toward her, moving like a cat. She turned, saw him. Her eyes widened. He put his finger to his lips. She covered her mouth with her hand to keep from crying out. Then she came swiftly forward to meet him.

They clasped hands. Clive drew her into the black door by which the women had exited to the roof. There, safe for the moment, they stopped and each breathed the name of the other:

"Sherm!"

"Gloria!"

Her arms went around him, his around her.

"I've got to get you out somehow. We could escape with the camels, but

I don't know how to manage them—
and right at the moment I don't know
where Malone is. What do you think
your father will do?"

"Tell me where to get off at! He's like
that, and away off in America, being
captured by M'Tabites will be so unreal
he may not even take it seriously. But
he'll send the money *if he believes the
message.*"

"But if he does not believe the
message?"

"Then, my dear Sherm, I shall die."

Convulsively he clutched her to him.
Almost under his breath he said:
"NEVER, AS LONG as I live, as long as my
men live."

"That won't be long, when they begin
searching," she said. "When morning
comes they'll muster the men of M'Tab
and count noses—and then they'll order
the women to search the houses. You
can guess what that will mean if any
of you are found in the houses. Their
women—well, men die who even see
the faces of other men's women. The
only other alternative is the desert—
afoot, and they'd capture you before
you had gone two miles. We must find
another way."

"Then we're starting now. It has to
be the camels."

They clasped hands, started down
the steps. But they didn't get far, for the
women on the roof had missed their
beautiful prisoner. Their screams went
rocketing over M'Tab, and they raced
to the stairs. Clive and Gloria fled into
the darkness. The women came quickly
behind them.

Men hammered savagely against the
outer door of the place.

But the women reached them first.
Clive had no defense against them. He
tried to push the women back. They
ripped and tore at him. A cry of despair
rose from Gloria:

"GET AWAY, DEAR. I'll try to meet you
among the camels within an hour,
somehow. If I don't, wait for me."

There was nothing else to be done. It
was horrible to find her, only to lose her.
The women wouldn't kill her, not until
M'Tab had had an answer to its demand
for ransom. But they had no scruples
about men who prowled through their
houses. Clive bowled them over right
and left as he raced back for the steps.
Two women clung to him, screaming.
One hastened to the door to admit the
men who sought the white fugitives.

Clive pushed the women from him,
leaped up the stairs. Other women were
coming down. He barged into them at
full speed, brushing them aside, disregarding their wild screams, as he raced
for the roof again.

Someone below was yelling at the
women. He didn't understand, but he
got the idea when the women vanished
as if by magic from the roofs. They were
being ordered to get under cover.

The moment they had done so bullets
began to crash into the walls before
which he sped. Clive dropped to his
stomach, inched his way to the coping
which served as a sort of fort, protecting
himself from the bullets.

Then, the bullets ceased—and he instantly saw the reason. Men were boiling

onto the roof behind him, discharging with violence from the black door which for ages must have allowed admittance only to women. How well he knew the price for his sacrilege. He hurled himself into the thick of the M'Tabites. And, as though they knew exactly what was happening, women came crowding out again onto the other roofs. Two roofs distant he saw Gloria in the midst of the women. She was screaming something. As he fought against vicious, stabbing knives, ducked the savage, murderous blows of curved short swords, he tried to make out what she was saying. A blow struck him on the head, but he had understood her strange shout. It was:

"Jeres is the boss of M'Tab!"

She meant, of course, that he was the man with whom to deal, that he was the patriarch of the elders, the man who issued commands the others must obey. Jeres! How could Clive find him in that big place, which was so much like a catacomb, or like the cave dwellings of troglodytes? Yet find him he must, somehow force him to let them go free—give him all their treasures if need be. But why, the man would ask, accept treasures they could have merely for the taking?

HAVING SEEN SO many of the M'Tabites, it was easy for Clive to visualize old Jeres. He *would* be old, a patriarch of the lost tribe which contacted the world in the guise of other tribes, struck in battle and vanished into the wastes— even contacted the outside world by cable and telegraph, by visiting cities in disguise—cities where Arabic was the *lingua franca* of countless tribes. Clive could see the old man, fierce of eye, hawk-like of mien, with a long grey beard to make him look more the bird of prey.

His word must be the law of M'Tab, which must have a ruler to survive. Jeres must be a man without mercy, a fanatic in what he ordered his people to do to those who violated the isolation of M'Tab. Clive could understand the resentment of M'Tabites to everything from the outside world they appeared to have forsworn.

But Jeres, whatever he was, was a man. He must have a wife and children, know something of human kindness, of mercy and understanding.

BUT ONLY FOR the benefit of his own kind—that was plainly evident! Clive could see old Jeres as surely as though he had faced him and exchanged words of war with the leading elder of M'Tab.

Jeres, then, was the enemy. The rest of M'Tab merely were his retainers.

It seemed hopeless, but that didn't deter Clive from fighting like a fiend, nor from answering Gloria in a wild shout of understanding:

"I'll find him!"

Clive grasped one of the enemy about the waist, lifted him high, hurled him straight into the faces of two who were barging in. The man's body, flying horizontal, struck them on the chest, bearing them back.

The coping of the roof caught them above the ankles. They flung their arms high. A rifle clattered to the roof. The two men went over the roof, screaming as their white-clothed bodies whirled down to the ground. And Clive hoped grimly, as he picked up the rifle, that the ground under the roof would be hard enough to break their skulls—for they had fallen head downward.

Now he clubbed the rifle, hurled himself against the others. They didn't retreat. They were shouting something, and at their shouts other men were pouring onto the roof; there were some twenty of them.

They were determined on catching him, making him a prisoner. The butt of the weapon he held crashed against a cowled skull. He knew by the feel that the skull had cracked like an eggshell. The man went down and his fellows stumbled over him. They didn't seem to mind death in the least.

Death! What was it he remembered about these people? They were exceedingly superstitious. They made charms to ward off sickness, or to cause the sickness and death of enemies, from things they dug up out of their own cemeteries. Their rites in this respect were more grim, gruesome and terrible than the Black Mass of the Middle Ages. Nash had told him this, he now remembered.

How could this be turned to account?

Time would have to tell that.

And the M'Tabites were pushing him back and back. Damn it, would he never have a chance to rest? He couldn't fight on forever, without food or sleep. Something had to give. Where were his men? Now, all at once, he had the answer. It came in a crackling of rifle fire from somewhere to the west.

OUT THERE, UNDER the trees beyond the walls, were the vast burial grounds of the M'Tabites. And out of them were coming the bullets which were smashing into Clive's attackers. Clive shouted with excitement.

His men were doing a strange long-distance rescue.

What had they learned? He must find out; he must take a chance. Suddenly he turned his back on the M'Tabites, whirled to the coping, bent, hooked his palms over it, spun over and down. When his back struck against the wall, he released his hold and dropped. He was running when he hit. He hit the body of one man who, of the three who had gone over, had died in the fall. He was running, with the bullets of the M'Tabites whipping him forward.

He shouted to his men to fire high in order to cover his retreat.

CHAPTER VII

WILDERNESS OR DEATH

SHERMAN CLIVE RAN as he never had before, despising himself because he left Gloria Drake behind him. But he could do nothing for her by staying, and might endanger her life further. If he ran he might come back for her later. He knew, at least, that she was still alive, which was something—something to keep hope alive.

Now, as his men sank bullets into the houses of M'Tab, serving notice on her men to keep their heads down, Clive shouted to his followers:

"Keep it up! I'm cutting in toward you. Show a head or a hand to let me know where to go."

And Malone himself, gaunt in the moonlight under the trees which masked the wilderness of graves—so many graves that it seemed all the generations had been saved in death—stood erect, in plain sight. No bullets struck at him, though he must have been seen by scores of men in M'Tab.

Clive wondered.

And when he cut in toward Malone, and the graves were in line ahead of him with the people of M'Tab, their firing ceased as by a miracle. What did it mean?

Now he was in among the graves, every one of which seemed to be well cared for, and raced for Malone. His men had stopped firing. He flung himself, panting, down among them. Malone chuckled.

"You didn't get the dame?" he asked.

"How did you know anything about her?"

"You forget I've spent plenty of time in this place. I know Arabic. I listened to what they said, before we gathered together and came in here."

"No, I didn't get her," Clive reverted. "I had to run away. Thanks for the help. But I'm afraid of what they'll do to her now."

Malone chuckled again:

"That puts us in a fine spot, Sherman, lad. I'll give you the lowdown now. They won't do anything to this Gloria person unless her dad turns her down, for she insisted on one condition—that her dad's representatives from Cairo, bringing the money, must meet her and representatives of Jeres forty miles from here across the desert, and that she must be turned over to them, absolutely unharmed in any way, before Jeres will get the money.

"They'll protect her, for that money, as they would protect themselves—maybe better!"

"But you say we're in a swell spot—I don't see."

"WELL, TAKE A look around you at all these graves. The M'Tabites are not ancestor worshipers exactly, but they do regard their dead with reverence. It's all mixed up with religion, with charms and with spells. They keep their graves nicely cared for. There are graves here dating back to the time the first M'Tabite settled in M'Tab. There always will be.

"They fear their dead, too. They believe in ghosts, and the vengeance of dead who are disturbed. We did some listening, and pooled our knowledge, which I've just given you. Understand?"

"I confess I don't."

"Well, you note they didn't fire on us? And they quit firing at you as soon as you came into line with the graves?"

"Yes."

"Well, that's to keep from sending bullets into the graves and angering the dead, so that the dead may rise from the graves and fill M'Tab with pestilence or march against the town and slay every soul in it. They would no more shoot into this cemetery than they would try to fly to the moon. Know what that means?"

"No, not yet at least."

"THAT WE CAN stay here until Hell freezes over without being afraid of bullets. That we can pick off M'Tabites as long as we have any bullets left. If they attack us they must come barehanded or with knives—and they won't even dare kill us among the graves!"

"But they wouldn't. It would mean great loss of life on their own part, to attack us without a covering fire from rifles."

"But what glory it would be for the dying to know they had died to punish our irreverence toward their dead!"

"You mean they—we—"

"Exactly. You, we, all of us, have violated their houses by entering the parts reserved for women. For that the punishment is death after torture at the hands of the Ouled Nails. And now we've done the unforgivable, the unbelievably horrible—we've wakened the very dead with sacrilegious rifle fire right, as it were, in their ears. And for that—"

"Don't tell me," said Clive shuddering a little in spite of himself. "The Chinese death of a thousand cuts would be nothing compared to what they'll do with us if they catch us now."

"You've got the idea. Now, if you don't mind graves all around you, have something to eat. I don't know what it is, but it hasn't killed the rest of us, so feed your face, and don't worry about the dame—"

"She isn't a dame, she's a—"

"I know. I've read newspapers in my time. She's a daughter of some United States state governor. You're her heavy heartthrob—oh, forget it, Sherman, isn't it better to laugh over it? We've had little enough to laugh at here lately, and every last one of us is with you to the last ditch. And say, didn't we go through M'Tab after we left you? We've got water enough to last all day tomorrow, and we've got most of the food in the place and say, we've lost Corcoran."

"How?" Clive looked about him, noting with a sinking heart that only four of his men were still alive.

"The Ouled Nails got him. We tried to catch them, tried to get him back. But he fooled the torturers. Maybe you heard the firing? Corcoran shot himself with his pistol. It was a smart stunt, and he doesn't have to worry about getting out of here. Wasn't there plenty of shooting, though? The M'Tabites killed one another right and left, thinking they were pouring the lead at us.

"When I yelled out in English nobody understood me except our own men. I yelled for 'em to make for these graves, and here we are. Now, feed your face!"

A GRIM SILENCE had fallen over M'Tab. Clive stared at the eerie, wild place as he put food to his mouth, chewed slowly, thoughtfully. Hungry as he was he didn't even taste the food, scarcely realized that he ate anything at all. He looked at the houses of M'Tab which hid the woman who had dared so much for him. How would they use her, what would they do to her if old Drake would not listen to reason?

One guess was as good as another.

Clive then thought of all the men he had lost. They would always weigh on his soul, despite the fact that every last one of them had known, when he had joined Clive on the trek to Ophir, what he faced. Each man had laughingly "written himself off the books" when he had taken service with Clive—for all knew that few had ever reached Ophir and returned. They died They had expected to die. Nevertheless it would be a long time before Clive would forget the hardships most of them had suffered, or forget the bundles in the sand which had been men—the men who had fallen before M'Tab had been sighted. It had been a grim, terrible business.

NOW THERE WERE no lights in M'Tab. No sentries had been thrown out to keep the white men from escaping in the night. The M'Tabites knew their land. If the whites raced into the desert they could be run down with ease. Besides, this Elder Jeres was a clever man. He would know that these men never would leave M'Tab without the woman.

The emissary Jeres had sent had hinted that M'Tab believed they were a rescue party sworn to die to get her out of the hands of the M'Tabites. The M'Tabites had lost too many men now to let them go, ever, no matter what might happen.

Clive had the feeling that they were all doomed. They would die as Corcoran had died, as Jonas had, and Nash. But the food which went into his stomach, and the water he drank from the buckets his men had managed somehow to bring with them into the wilderness of graves, revived his courage and his hopes.

Other men before him had fought their way out of tighter places than this. They would do so again. Why could not he and his men?

"By the Lord Harry we will!" exploded Clive suddenly.

"Will what?" asked Malone, startled.

"Get out of this, and take Gloria with us," answered Clive with conviction.

"Of course, but how? We can't do it with rifles, for they've got so many they'll keep us pinned to the ground. There's no other way, unless we take to the desert now—never mind, we aren't even thinking of running out on your Gloria! So what's left? Strategy, that's what. You've got to outsmart not only Jeres, but all of M'Tab. That should give you something to think about until morning.

"Speaking for myself, I'm getting some shuteye. The rest of you guys take turns watching, while Sherm figures out how five men can capture a city, kill everybody in it, save our treasure, rescue the fair lady, and get across half of the Sahara to civilization again. It's beyond me. And if anybody else has any ideas, he'd probably be glad to have them!"

Clive did not answer. One man sat up, keeping his eyes on M'Tab.

Clive spoke to him.

"Sleep, if you don't mind a grave for a pillow. I'll keep watch. Keep your rifles beside you. I hope there is plenty of ammunition."

"About two hundred rounds among us!" said Malone grimly.

IN TEN MINUTES the four men were snoring. Little wonder, for they hadn't slept for what seemed like centuries.

Clive's eyes wandered over the graves, a wilderness of grim headstones which seemed to reach to infinity westward. Overhead the wind whispered through the palm trees, a thin, ghostly whispering. The enemy might well sneak up on them, darting from tree to tree, but not very soon. And he would see them when they left M'Tab.

It was all silent, grim, terrible. It was weird, fantastic, unbelievable. He almost had to pinch himself to make sure he was not dreaming.

And then the darkness of just before dawn began to creep over the depression which hid M'Tab. Clive knew that the shadows might hide advancing men, and his men had slept for three hours. He shook Malone awake, then the others. All watched until the blazing sun came out again.

Then all eyes were turned on M'Tab.

And out of M'Tab came a column of men in single file. They formed in a vast thin line whose members faced the cemetery. They carried no rifles. A command barked out. Knives flashed in the hot sun, like burnished silver.

Wind whipped the white garments of the men of M'Tab.

"Well," said Clive grimly, "I guess here they come! Make each shot count."

CHAPTER VIII

KNIVES IN THE SUN

THERE WAS SOMETHING rather magnificent about the advance of the M'Tabites.

They knew with grim certainty that their opponents were all armed, that they would not stop firing—and hitting their living targets—until the last man of them was dead.

"Don't fire until they are close," said Clive quietly.

Now that the crisis had come there was no trace of fear in the hearts of any of them.

They believed they were going to die. They were ready to die. That was the end of it. They were not hopeful that any compromise could be arrived at, for this was M'Tab, and it belonged to its people. They, Clive and his followers, had violated many of the tenets of M'Tabite faith. For each violation the punishment was death. The M'Tabites started around the vast palm trees in a circling movement.

"If they get in among the trees," said Clive, "they can come quite close to us, and if there are enough of them they can overwhelm us in one stiff charge."

"But we may miss if we fire now," said Malone.

"Right! Make sure of each shot before you let it go."

And so, instead of nailing the men at the far flanks of the line which was curling in upon itself, so that its final formation would encompass the grove and the graves on three sides, they remained quietly and allowed the M'Tabites to make their own dispositions, without molestation.

The M'Tabites directly opposite the position of the whites would have to march straight into the muzzles of their rifles, across an open space of burning sand. They came on without sound, knives in their hands. They all knew that many of them would die. Some had to die to wipe out the anger of the spirits of dead and gone M'Tabites whose resting places had been disturbed by invaders whom the M'Tabites should have kept out of the cemetery.

THE M'TABITES WERE now within a hundred yards of their position. The five men were behind two graves, protected front and rear.

"I hate to fire on men who can't fire back," said Clive.

"Yeah," said Malone, "and I hate to have my insides cut out and my eyes burned white by the Ouled Nails, too. I don't like the look of those knives. And at a quick count I'd say there were two hundred M'Tabites against us. I wouldn't be too squeamish if I were you."

"Right," agreed Clive. "Align your sights, men. Pick out your men. Malone, you take the tall man directly ahead. I'll take the second man to his left. Mitchel, you take the man with the yellow band around his waist. Jameson, you take the second man to his left—"

And so, quietly and calmly, he gave each man his target, so that no bullets would be wasted by more than one man firing at the same enemy. "Let them have it when you're ready," said Clive softly.

MALONE'S RIFLE WAS the first to speak. The man whom Clive had selected for him plunged to his face in the sand.

"He got it through the skull," said Malone, matter-of-factly.

"Shouldn't you aim at the chest? It's a bigger target," said Clive.

"Big or little, and with my stomach filled with water and grub, I can hit anything I can see—and they're deader if it smacks into their brains," retorted Malone.

"My error," said Clive.

Then his own rifle spoke.

But he aimed for the heart. His victim dropped his knife, placed both hands over his heart. His head went back as though he straightened his throat to fight for breath. Then the man fell. The three other rifles barked savagely.

Three more men fell. With their first round of shots, each marksman had unerringly planted his man in the sand. Clive studied the reactions of the others. His heart felt numb, a little cold, when he saw how they took it. As far as he could tell not a M'Tabite hesitated, looked toward the fallen, or faltered the slightest.

But now a sharp command broke from someone in authority. The voice came clearly across to Clive and his men.

"What did he say?" asked Clive. "I couldn't quite hear it."

"He said to advance at a swift walk, to be ready to charge."

"Men," said Clive instantly. "Have your cartridges where you can get them fast. And make sure of every shot."

By this time the flanks of the advancing force, which had come forward on the run, had vanished, and Clive knew that its members were advancing through the trees to the right and left of their position. He took a swift look to right and left. The flanks were not yet visible.

But the trap of the M'Tabites was closing on them with the inexorable finality of sure death.

Clive shook off thoughts of Gloria. His first duty was to fight off this attack, to save his own men and his own life. He would be of no use to her without fulfilling that.

NOW THE RIFLES spoke again. The M'Tabites were coming on, their pace increasing. Now it was a swift trot. The rifles spoke faster. Now Clive could see the faces of the charging men. They were alight with a kind of transfiguration—as though they gloried in this opportunity to fight for the spirits of their honored dead. Fanaticism drove men to the muzzles of cannon, even though they knew they would be blown to bits. Fanatic Moslems believed that they went faster to Heaven when they died in battle against infidels. Clive was familiar with such fanaticism, and knew that not even bullets were proof against it.

The rifles spoke steadily now. The men said nothing. The working of their rifle bolts was a rhythmic, musical sound. Behind the advancing M'Tabites the number of white robed figures which had fallen to rise no more was appalling. Clive had noticed the fallen, in an abstracted sort of way, and not one of them had moved after he had crashed down to the sand. The bullets of the besieged were deadly. They never missed.

Clive fired again, and again—and each time a M'Tabite went down.

"They'll rush us in a minute," said Clive. "When they get close enough to use their knives, we'll stand with our backs toward one another, in a tight semicircle. But we'll drive them back if we can."

The whining of the rifles rose to a high crescendo. It was impossible at this shortened range to miss. They didn't miss. The M'Tabites fell like flies. It was inhuman to withstand such slaughter as calmly as the M'Tabites were taking it.

And the rooftops of M'Tab were dotted thick with women who were watching the advance, watching the slaughter of their husbands, sons and lovers. Now the women themselves helped the beleaguered, for suddenly a long wail of anguish rose from the rooftops behind the charging men. Others picked it up, in a wild eerie ululation. The women were sorrowing for the fallen, and for others yet to fall. They probably could pick out their own among the advancing men, among the fallen.

Clive fired again.

"And there goes someone else's father or husband or lover," he thought. "This is tough on the women, but I don't remember that any of them tried to save my life. If they'd only handed us food and water when we came none of this would have happened."

NOW THE M'TABITES were very close. The beleaguered were reloading and firing as fast as they could work their rifles. Clive's face was streaming with sweat. So were the faces of the others. The strain was taking its toll. The knives were now so close they could see the shapes of the blades.

"We'll have to stand in a second," said Clive. "Give 'em everything you've got. Perhaps we'd each better save a bullet for ourselves."

"I'm not going out that way unless I have to to keep out of the hands of the Ouled Nails," said Malone. "I'm not going to kill myself and then be sorry for it afterward—if dead guys are sorry about anything—because if I'd waited I could have saved my life. Not me!"

Clive chuckled. His eyes searched the women on the rooftop. He saw one whose face was not covered—one with golden hair—and knew that the prayers of Gloria Drake were with him. It gave him new courage. She it was who really bore the brunt of all hardship. If the men died, they died like men, in open battle. But for a woman—he refused to contemplate what it might mean to her if her father didn't fulfill her request. The money was a slight matter to old Drake. But with him it was always "the principle of the thing."

THE RIFLES CRACKED. Bullets sped through muzzles so fast that the men's hands were blistered by the heat. But still the M'Tabites came on, though they wavered a little.

"Stand up," said Clive, "and give them a last volley. Then club your rifles."

The chattering of the rifles sounded as though a score of men were firing instead of only five. The M'Tabites fell in groups. They were now so tightly packed that it was impossible to miss.

But still they came on. They could have thrown their knives, now, and that they didn't was an ominous circumstance. At close quarters they could be surer—and to be surer carried ghastly alternatives, for Malone had said that they would not slay them amidst the graves. That meant mutilation to the point of death to make the five captures.

But the M'Tabites, with the redoubled fire, and seeing the five savage, desperate figures rise in their faces to pour in that murderous fire, could stand it no longer. They turned their backs—and their eyes saw, perhaps for the first time, the bundles of white—a ghastly number of them—on the ground over which they had passed. Perhaps it was thus for the first time that they realized the price they were paying for the honor of their dead.

They broke, and the five whipped them forward with hails of lead.

A thin cheer broke from Clive and his men as the attack became a rout. But they had almost forgotten the men on the flanks. Now Malone yelled a warning. The flanks were closing in, and it became a sort of squirrel-shooting defense, for the M'Tabites were jumping from tree to tree like Indians, closing in.

"Careful with your fire," said Clive. "It's easy to miss, now. They will be all around us in a second."

Malone's rifle cracked. A man who had been showing only the top of his head around a tree plunged out into the open.

"I never miss," said Malone quietly. "Look, Clive, maybe there's news. There comes a fast-stepping mob of camels from the northwest. I'll bet it's news from Gloria's old man!"

CHAPTER IX

GRIM ULTIMATUM

BUT FOR THE moment there was no time to think about the racing caravan, which traveled as though it came on urgent business which could not wait. Clive's heart hammered until it almost suffocated him. He knew that the climax would be reached almost at once—and the desperate hope came to him to want to live until he should know what would occur.

His rifle had never been more true. Let a M'Tabite show so much as his face and his bullets went full and unerringly to their marks. The five now sprawled on their backs, throwing intermittent glances at the forefront of the attackers who were in full retreat. Their eyes searched the palm trees, watching the almost ghostly advance of the men who had cut in from the flanks, and who hadn't so far felt the weight of the white men's fire.

They came on as determinedly as the first rank had—and they died as silently, surely and inevitably.

"Pick your targets," said Clive grimly. Don't let 'em get too close. And be careful you don't shoot one another."

Their rifles were moving in short arcs, to catch their moving, almost elusive targets. It was like shooting clay pigeons from a trap. Now and again a white-robed figure sprang from behind a tree, hands clawing at throat or stomach as knives spilled into the sand—just ahead of the reeling bodies which were dead before they even started to fall.

The defenders were almost nauseated with the slaughter.

But their own lives were precious, and Clive would have destroyed all M'Tab— except its women—to save the life of Gloria.

THE RIFLES KEPT up the: volley. The M'Tabites came on. Then the attack seemed to fade for a moment, and Clive whirled to watch the arrival of the caravan. There were six camels in it.

The camels slid to a stop in the sand behind the tents of the Ouled Nails. They knelt at command of their riders, and several men had dropped to the ground. The first of them raced toward the houses of M'Tab. The attackers came on again at this point, and Clive had to look to their defense.

The rifles cracked incessantly.

Now the dead about the position of the defenders, were piled thick and white. It seemed impossible for them to get beyond a certain point. They charged toward them and could not face the redoubled, frenzied fire of the white men.

"Sherm," said Malone.

"Yes?"

"WE'VE GOT JUST enough cartridges to stall off a few more charges, if they aren't any worse than those we've had already."

"Let 'em come a bit closer," said Clive.

"But we hit with every bullet anyhow," Malone observed.

"Then we'll have to do as we planned—fire until the last bullet is gone and then stand ready to meet their charge."

"That'll be in about a minute," said Malone.

One minute left of life, for the M'Tabites must know now, too, that they had little ammunition left. A determined charge now would bring attackers and defenders together. It couldn't last forever. There were too many of the M'Tabites.

The rifles spoke more slowly—but with no better precision, because they had been firing coolly, deliberately, from the very beginning of the attack.

"Here they come!" said Malone softly. "They'll make it this time."

"Stand then, and let them have it!" ordered Clive.

He was conscious that a grim, strained silence had settled over M'Tab. The howling of the women ceased. They had been quieted, Clive felt, by whatever news had been brought from the northwest. Clive stared at the figure of Gloria, away through the brilliant sunlight—and saw the violent hands of women laid upon her, saw her dragged into one of the houses.

Then the M'Tabites made their last charge. It had to be the last charge whatever happened.

He knew that the news brought by the caravan, then, had been evil news, and his heart welled with bitterness over old Drake. He wondered, if the old man could see M'Tab, whether it would have made any difference in his decision.

Probably not. He was the stubborn sort. Well, so much for that.

"WE'RE DOWN TO about twenty-five rounds among us, five aimed shots each," said Malone quietly.

"Make every one tell," said Clive grimly. "Then use your rifle butts. Get the knives of the men you down. We may need them."

It was a grim, savage business.

The M'Tabites were coming closer.

And then, all at once, a strange thing happened—it was a thin, wild cry from M'Tab, in intelligible words. The charging M'Tabites seemed to change entirely when they heard it. They started falling back through the trees, darting swiftly from boll to boll. Clive lowered his rifle, flicked the sweat from his eyes, and then looked at Malone.

"What's up?" he said. "What does it mean?"

"It means us no good, you can depend on that," said Malone gravely. "That was old Jeres shouting, ordering them to fall back and return to M'Tab. He's got something up his sleeve, you can bet your bottom dollar."

"In the meantime, we rest," said Clive. "I wish to God we had some more bullets."

"They wouldn't do us any good," said Malone with an air of authority. "I think the camel train brought news that changes the whole thing. Your Gloria is mixed up in it somewhere, and we'll be knowing just how in a few moments."

Clive's heart sank into his boots.

If she were to be used as a pawn against him—as she might well be now that she was patently no longer of any use to M'Tab—he didn't know what the result would be.

He didn't have long to wait. They watched the remaining M'Tabites file back into their houses. And then a long silence ensued.

"There comes the bad news!" exclaimed Jameson, at last.

All eyes were turned on M'Tab. A tall, gaunt man had come to the coping of the house nearest them. He cupped his hands about his mouth and shouted in Arabic.

"What does he say?" said Clive to Malone, who spoke the language more fluently.

Malone's face was a pasty white. He licked his cracked lips with a dry tongue. Clive had never seen such horror in his face. Clive's own heart seemed for the moment to stop beating. It was bad news, sure enough. Malone looked at the others as though almost afraid to speak.

"Let her go, Malone," said Jameson. "We know we have to take it in one form or another, so we might as well get it over with."

"I'm with you myself, Sherm," said Malone, "but this is a pretty tough decision for the other boys to make."

"Well," said Clive, impatiently, "spill it!"

"WE'VE PLAYED OUT our string," said Malone sternly. "Anyway, what does it matter? Gloria's father failed to pay the ransom in time. She is no longer of any use to them, save as a pawn to use against us and is to be given to the Ouled Nails for torture. But she may be spared that, and sent out of M'Tab in safety, on one condition—"

The men all looked at one another, as though already they knew what that condition was.

"He said," Malone finally went on, "that quite too many M'Tabites have already died trying to punish us for our desecration of their graves and of the sacred rooftops of M'Tab. They will not attack us again—but they will allow Gloria to go free if all of us will surrender, throw down our arms, and turn ourselves over to the Ouled Nails, to stand the torture in the place of the woman."

When Malone had finished there was a long silence. All eyes were on Sherman Clive.

"Ask him," said Clive, desperately sparring for time in which to think, "whether she has been injured so far."

Malone rose to his feet and shouted in a faltering rendition of Arabic.

"He says no."

"Now ask him if he will take me in her place, together with all our treasure, and let you others go free."

After a second the answer came. It was a terse negative.

"Ask him if he will take me and allow the rest of you to fight it out."

The answer again was no.

"I can't ask any of you to do it," said Sherm hoarsely. "The woman is nothing to you. She herself would not ask it of you. I'll wager she did her best to keep them from sending us that ultimatum. I can't ask you—" his voice broke off.

"**SPEAKING FOR MYSELF,**" said Malone hoarsely, "I think it would be sort of swell to go out like that, for a lady, when we know we have to go anyhow. The torture can't last forever."

Jameson rose, stretched elaborately, and yawned.

"Tell him we'll come in, one at a time," he said. "I'll start first and get it over with faster."

"Same here," said Mitchel.

Clive's throat seemed to be filled with cork or cotton as he gazed into the eyes of his men who had already risked their lives so many times for him, and who were now volunteering so calmly to make the final sacrifice.

Malone did not hesitate, did not ask Clive what next to do. He shouted across to old Jeres, who lifted his hand in acknowledgement, and then retired from the rooftop.

It was in that moment that Clive had his inspiration.

"**MALONE!**" **HE SNAPPED.** "We'll go last. Listen, all of you. Once I knew a professional beggar, the best in the business. He often used to panhandle in a way that he called 'working under wraps.' He covered himself with bandages, smeared red stuff on them to look like blood, and played on the natural pity of his fellows. They always shelled out.

"Look, you bind me like that, with my right arm in a sling. In the bandage I'll carry my pistol. Maybe I'll get a chance to use it. It's our only chance. I got you into this. It will be my bid to get you out. Quickly, now!"

Their underwear, which they had ripped off swiftly, sufficed for bandages. Malone led off in the matter of blood by pricking his arm with the end of an empty cartridge. The bandage was saturated by it. Jameson dared not wait too long. He was already striding across the open space toward the tents of the Ouled Nails. Gloria, in the midst of a group of M'Tabites, was also en route to those tents. Too much delay On the part of the whites would make the M'Tabites suspicious. Mitchel went next. The others didn't even watch to see what happened to them, since all would meet among the female torturers in a matter of minutes.

Finally only Malone and Clive were left—and Clive looked as though he could scarcely stand. Who among the M'Tabites was to say that some of the others had not reached the whites in their last charge, and managed to wound him savagely with their knives?

Clive leaned heavily on Malone as the two started across the open space. Behind them reposed their now useless rifles. Clive wondered if they would ever have need of them again.

"Will they see the pistol?" he asked.

"We have to take a chance," said Malone.

And then, they were among the M'Tabites, roughly seized. They were hustled into the tents of the Ouled Nails, where no other women were allowed. Gloria was already fastened to an upright pole.

M'Tabites were seated in a big circle around the pole. Clive shuddered, closed his eyes when Gloria looked at him, fearless, with her eyes wide.

The M'Tabites were binding the other whites. They said nothing, but their actions required no words. The M'Tabites hated these whites beyond all power, in words, to express their hatred. CLIVE STUMBLED, TO catch Gloria's attention.

His lips shaped a question.

"Which is Jeres?"

She got it. Her eyes shifted—and there was no chance of missing Jeres, for of them all, he held the seat of honor, a sort of dais directly ahead of the Ouled Nails, who were gleefully awaiting the opportunity to try their diabolic arts.

Clive stumbled again. He swayed away from Malone. There was no pity in the faces of any M'Tabites for this wounded white man, whom they could thus torture even more, by hurting his hurts. The Ouled Nails would attend to that.

Jeres spoke sharply in Arabic, and Malone answered him in the same language. Clive listened as Malone explained that Clive was gravely hurt, that he could not walk erectly.

"Now," whispered Clive to Malone, "push me with all your might, right at the old man. Shout something about me betraying you—"

"Listen!" said Malone. "He has something to say!"

As they listened, Jeres told them that now that he had them he saw no reason to let the girl escape." He said she had been too much trouble anyhow, and that her father was a fool.

"Hear that?" said Malone. "I rather expected they would welch on their promise."

"Now I'm sure of what I'm going to do," said Clive. "Push me, and yell out." IT MUST HAVE seemed to the M'Tabites that Malone had gone mad, or had suddenly become furious beyond words with his leader. He caught Clive by the shoulders, spun him around, shouted something at him which sounded like an execration of the vilest order—and shoved him with all his power, back toward old Jeres. Backward, apparently clawing to keep his feet, Clive stumbled toward Jeres. He cursed at Malone.

It was obvious he would fall on his back before ever he reached Jeres. He meant it to be obvious.

But he didn't fall. He started to stumble; then suddenly whirled to face Jeres. He ended his plunge with his body almost in the lap of the chief elder of M'Tab, while his bandaged right hand held the muzzle of his pistol squarely against the old man's heart. Deep silence fell, the silence of horror and dismay.

"You die if anything happens to the girl or my men and myself," snapped Clive to Jeres in Arabic, and then in English to Malone: "Tell them what I have just told their chief."

"Right."

Malone tersely told the M'Tabites what would happen to their leader. "What else do you want?" demanded Jeres, who appeared to realize that he was defeated for the time being at least. "Perhaps it is better that I die now—for the honor of M'Tab—than such shame as this!"

"Never mind that," said Clive. "You

know that your people won't let you die—and you also know that I'll kill you if you don't do as I say"

"It shall be so," Jeres nodded.

"Tell them we want camels and camel drivers," Clive called to Malone. "Tell them we must have everything belonging to Gloria Drake."

A few seconds passed as Malone did as he had been instructed.

"They agree," he said finally. "But we'd better work fast. For they may change their mind about protecting Jeres' life. What else?"

"Get our treasure loaded on fast camels—and have everything ready at once."

Minutes passed again, after several M'Tabites raced out of the tent, while utter disappointment showed on the faces of the Ouled Nails. The men returned shortly.

"The camels are ready," said Malone

"Have Gloria and our men taken out!" ordered Clive. "You stay with me, Malone, for a moment."

"Now, Malone," said Clive grimly. "We're marching this old buzzard. I'm not letting go of him until we're twenty miles from here. And tell them not to follow. The walk back will do the old guy good. Maybe, after he does that, he'll know better next time than to refuse water to men who are dying for lack of it."

"They'll come after him," said Malone, with much concern. "I'm afraid he won't take the walk."

"Maybe not, but he's going to have his lesson. He'll march!"

Malone consulted Jeres for a brief moment. He turned to Clive. "You're right—the old guy will march."

Jeres gave explicit orders to his group, ordering them to remain at a standstill. There was very little the old man could say, for Clive pushed him on. The aged Jeres marched, Clive and Malone following.

And that night the camels of Clive's enforced expedition were far from M'Tab. They had already sent Jeres on his lone march back to M'Tab, to suffer as they had.

Rifles of Clive's men kept the camel drivers in hand. Clive and Gloria rode side by side. The moon rose bright in the sky as the camels raced on. "What," asked Gloria at last, "are you thinking about?"

"Nice things," smiled Clive, "to say to a certain governor who does not answer cablegrams on time!"

"Same here," commented Gloria. "By the way, I wonder how Jeres is getting along?"

"I hope," said Clive, "that he feels like hell. And I hope that he hasn't yet found the way back to M'Tab!"